This novel is dedicated to the thousands of American workers who have lost their jobs to unfair foreign competition.

To Steve and Linda,

Hope you enjoy. Pleasure to meet you at Fonda & John's.

Pat DePaolo

The Beijing Games

by

Pat DePaolo

authorHOUSE®

AuthorHouse™
1663 Liberty Drive, Suite 200
Bloomington, IN 47403
www.authorhouse.com
Phone: 1-800-839-8640

© 2008 Pat DePaolo. All rights reserved.

No part of this book may be reproduced, stored in a retrieval system, or transmitted by any means without the written permission of the author.

First published by AuthorHouse 11/26/2007

ISBN: 978-1-4343-4088-7 (sc)
ISBN: 978-1-4343-4087-0 (hc)

Library of Congress Control Number: 2007907292

Printed in the United States of America
Bloomington, Indiana

This book is printed on acid-free paper.

Acknowledgements

I'd like to express my gratitude to all those who shared in the sometimes solitary journey people call "writing a book," especially my wife Phyllis who has been my rock. I wouldn't have completed *The Beijing Games* without her encouragement and patience.

Special thanks goes to my dear sister, MaryLou, and my brother-in-law Mike, who tolerated my writing quirks during two marvelous shared Florida winter vacations. An avid reader with a brilliant mind, Mary Lou read every word of every chapter and edited the final manuscript. I first realized that the book might have merit when she started referring to Justin Gatt and Lynne Hurricane as if they were real.

I also wish to thank the most famous member of our family, cousin Michael Lopez-Algeria, for his helpful suggestion in the section of the book dealing with a modified military aircraft escaping from a Chinese missile attack. Some know him as the astronaut who appeared on the Emeril TV show from a hook-up with the International Space station. Michael, also a Navy fighter pilot, happens to hold the U.S. record for the most time walking in space.

I'm grateful to several people who read early versions of the manuscript and contributed valuable comments, including: Harvard librarians John and Linda C, banker Andy D, financial experts and friends Bob B, Marty G, Jr, Carol D and Evelyn B.

Special thanks to Lee Blasé for reviewing the final manuscript and cover design with a talented artist's eye. Her enthusiasm for the project is greatly appreciated.

Finally, a heartfelt thanks to literary agent John White, who agreed to read a few of the early chapters, as crude as they were, and liked the basic story message enough to encourage me to complete the novel. The fact that he took on a novice writer and contributed so generously to editing and helping me improve my writing skills, says volumes for the kind of person he is.

Thank you all for being so supportive.

Visit our Web site at *www.beijinggamesbook.com*

> If a man take no thought about what is distant, he will find sorrow near at hand.
> — Confucius

> A prince need trouble little about conspiracies when the people are well disposed but when they are hostile....
> — Machiavelli

PROLOGUE

(March 31, 2008) 2am est
Damascus, Maryland

Five innocuous, black SUVs exited the Washington Beltway fifteen minutes apart, and converged on the hidden mansion at pre-scheduled intervals, four hours before dawn.

The vehicles were rented from five separate, off-airport locations in the northeast, using false identifications. The men in the back seats had arrived earlier on red-eye, private jet flights from Paris, Beijing, Nanjing, Boston and New York. All had landed at different private airports in the region, before climbing into waiting SUVs with darkened windows. The vehicles were driven by armed chauffeurs, trained to protect the occupants at any cost.

Phillipe Cusson, the French banker, was the first to turn off Route 27, onto a side road near the small town of Damascus, Maryland. The driver pulled up to a rusty, iron-plate barricade blocking the dirt road and stopped. Cusson stepped out from the vehicle and inserted a perforated, rod-shaped key into the circular hole of a locked stainless steel mail box, sitting at the side of the road on a thick concrete post.

The French aristocrat punched his personal identification code on the keypad inside the box, followed by the numbers *three* and *six*. The metal gate swung away, eerily silent, on specially fabricated titanium hinges, equipped with graphite-lubricated, teflon bearings; and coated with ferric oxide to appear rusty.

The driver switched off the night lights and eased the vehicle unobtrusively over the winding dirt road, guided only by the faint illumination of yellow fog lamps. The road led in the direction of the Patuxent River State Park, an isolated, densely treed area about twenty miles north of Washington, D.C. The road dead-ended at a brick wall, two yards high, with side thickets of spruce and thorny bushes preventing a detour around the abutment.

Cusson lowered a window and shouted his name, followed by the word "Savoy." He watched in amazement as the false brick wall responded to voice-actuation, and disappeared into the ground. The dirt road continued another hundred yards, then met a paved, circular driveway which fronted the 8,000 square foot, modern mansion chosen for the meeting.

Emerson Bromine, the owner of the property, waited anxiously for Cusson and the others to arrive. It would be their first and only group meeting. The international financier, scion of closely held Bromine Venture Capital Trust, and a member of the BoxMart board of directors, arranged this meeting at the insistence of the Chinese. Bromine was in a unique position. He was the only link between an ultra-confidential group of Washington-based power brokers, called the "Three Sixes," and the equally secretive group meeting here tonight, known to its stratigraphic members as the "Savoy Imperative."

Bromine wasn't sure how the "Three Sixes" name originated. He thought it had something to do with the group's political positioning as 'devil's advocates.' He did know that eighteen members employed unprecedented methods to influence the outcome of state and federal elections, and conceal their identities.

He'd taken on the task of coalescing the common objectives of the two clandestine consortiums. It made his life doubly complicated, and geometrically more dangerous. The last-minute call from the paranoid oilman in Houston was not surprising. His calls on the impenetrable 'Sixes' line always came at odd hours.

"We've decided tonight is a perfect time to penalize the informer," the graveled voice barked---referring to a 'Sixes' insider at the U.S. Department of Energy---who'd sold information about a new oilfield discovery off the coast of California.

"Switch to our private video channel before you're done with tonight's meeting. The free-trade zealots in your group, whoever they are, will be signing the same document we require. They should witness this." He hung up before Bromine could reply.

"Come in, my friend. It's been such a long time," the host warmly greeted Cusson. The French banker noticed that fifty-year-old Bromine had aged dramatically since their last encounter, and was squinting from crimson-streaked almond eyes. His brown hair had thinned, and prematurely-graying sideburns framed a chalky complexion and sunken cheeks. He guessed it was drugs, or too much liquor.

Phillipe Cusson was Managing Director of Creditte Bank de Savoy, the 300 year old private French bank in Lyon, France, which was one of the original European banking institutions to invest in regional Federal Reserve Banks in New York, Philadelphia and Boston, when the U.S. central banking system was established by the Federal Reserve Act of 1913.

He stood tall and wiry, with a large hooked nose that supported rectangular, horn-rimmed glasses and an arrogant demeanor. His Sorbonne education and air of superiority had carried him to the top of European private banking. Dressed in dark casual clothes, like the others, he looked more like a second-story thief of the night.

Cusson extended a firm grip to the much shorter and younger host, whose investment empire extended from high rise buildings in Baltimore and Shanghai, to casinos in Macau and Indonesia. In his typical redundant French and English, Cusson declared pompously, "Mon, ami…. My, friend. Today we make history. For the glory of France; for global commerce. And most importantly…for us believers."

Bromine replied brightly, as he noticed the headlights from an arriving vehicle sweep across the front windows of the mansion, "When your plan is implemented, Phillipe…as our group will guarantee tonight… the unresolved disputes we must settle will be history."

The pretentious Frenchman chirped, "The Savoy Imperative will no doubt stifle the American trade protectionists. Our allies in Washington will not have to tear down and rebuild the entire economy."

Bromine ushered Cusson into a large open entertainment area fed from the entrance atrium, then returned to the front door to greet the next arrival. He informed Cusson, over his shoulder, "I have received confirmation, Phillipe, that a powerful lobbying group in Washington will support our efforts." He added evenly, "They are anxious to observe how the events will unfold."

Cusson was alarmed. Had Bromine revealed the Savoy plan to outsiders? "I don't understand," he shot back. "How can they help, unless they know the plan?"

"Don't be concerned, my friend. Nobody knows our plan, except the people who will be present tonight. I'll explain the relationship to everyone, later."

Cusson watched as Bromine opened the front door and clasped the enormous hand of the giant, bald-headed retailer named Rand ("Jake") Kurancy…mumbling something that caused the Chairman of BoxMart Retail Enterprises to smile. Cusson had recently visited the BoxMart headquarters in Massachusetts to propose his U.S. dollar consolidation scheme to Jake… whose cooperation was critical, if Creditte Bank de Savoy was to acquire control of BoxMart's massive foreign deposits.

Kurancy was one of the few people in the world aware of the cached connection still existing between the ancient Lyonaise private bank and the Federal Reserve regional bank in Boston. Or the controlling interest CBdeS held in a Geneva trust bank, which indirectly owned one of America's largest commercial lenders.

Kurancy nodded to Cusson, remembering their conversation at Cusson's Chambery, France chateaux. Li Chin, the Chinese industrialist, had joined them to speculate on how a cunning redistribution of the enormous dollar holdings in the Savoy bank could smack havoc with U.S. currency values and interest rates. Timed judiciously with other events, the shock to the American economy could make the public forget about import limits and global trade issues. Cusson's inspiration was to sagaciously exchange the massive dollar holdings of its members for other foreign currencies.

The plan would drastically alter the U.S. money supply and upset the monetary balancing act of the Federal Reserve Open Market Committee. Interest rates, government budget deficits and mortgage foreclosures would skyrocket. Cusson had calculated the amount of U.S. dollars needed to be deposited in Lyon and Geneva numbered accounts by the Chinese banks, BoxMart RE, and LCE Industries of Nanjing. His genius was to figure out how to trade the dollars for optimum effect.

Li Chin, chairman of LCE, the largest manufacturing conglomerate in China, and Wang Chao, the Minister of Industry and Trade, soon arrived to confirm the backing of the influential Chinese Communist Party leaders whose support was necessary for the Savoy Imperative to go forward. General Ye Kunshi, Deputy Commander of the People's Liberation Army, who controlled state-owned factories on the mainland, and Yong Ihasa, the Senior Vice Premier in the Chinese State Council, had given their assent, although neither was authorized to officially represent the Chinese government.

They were mid-level members of the twenty-four person Politboro, aspiring to higher position on the nine-member Standing Committee—the most powerful men in China. Ye and Yong viewed the Savoy Imperative as an opportunity to replace Party conservatives who were promoting a long-term, "wearing down" policy against America's dominance in world affairs. They desired a more rapid displacement of Washington's influence.

The last to arrive were the Federal Reserve Bank official and the U.S. Senator. Both were adamant free-traders, although the Senator had recently funded TV ads to revamp his political image. He needed to be perceived more as a 'qualified' free-trader. The veteran Senator was about to join other congressmen challenging Governor Martin Merrand of New York, the right wing anti-free trader, leading the 2008 Presidential polls by a wide margin. His goal was far more ambitious than placing a respectable second to Merrand at their party's national convention; although he realized Merrand had a lock on the Presidential nomination.

The Savoy Imperative was ingeniously designed by Cusson and the others to brace open the gates to the ten trillion dollar U.S. consumer market. But the same powerful people who benefited from the unrestrained imports of Chinese-made goods…perched on the shelves of BoxMart and other U.S. discounters…could catapult the Senator's political career.

As Bromine introduced the newly arrived participants, Cusson fantasized about the opportunity to neuter the Federal Reserve Board Chairman's influence on European Banking decisions. He despised the arrogance of Jon Paul Tangus, who constantly acupunctured the French Finance Minister and other European central bankers, into dittoing his Machiavellian interest rate decisions. The crisis events Cusson was staging would likely result in his replacement by the man who just arrived with the Senator.

For Jake Kurancy, the plan was an opportunity to protect and extend the flow of cheap imported goods revolving through his warehouses and stores -- the fuel for the eye-popping merger he and Li Chin would soon announce to the world.

Bromine ushered the group from the large open foyer into the expansive, glass-walled great room, which overlooked a sprawling, wrap-around deck. Sunsets and sunrises were seldom enjoyed in this building, except by the carefully chosen domestic help. They were only allowed in when the mansion was deserted. Meetings had always been during dark hours.

Bromine seated them in tall, cushioned bar stools surrounding a ten foot diameter granite table placed near the ultra-modern kitchen of stainless steel appliances and birch cabinets. He decided to quell security apprehensions about tonight's meeting before discussions began.

"The interior rooms of this structure are protected against surveillance by the most sophisticated electronic-distortion and signal-interception devices available. NSA's most advanced listening equipment will not penetrate the microwave-filtering walls."

The steel and aluminum framed structure had been constructed for secret meetings of the "Sixes," whose other secure meeting place was similarly protected in the basement of a branch of the oldest bank in the nation's capital.

The U.S. Senator was nervous about security, and had worn a long hair piece and a bulky wind-breaker with a high collar on the back-roads drive from Alexandria. He had no desire to be linked in any way with the others; especially the Chinese Minister of Industry and Trade. He worried that NSA had listening capabilities beyond Bromine's anticipation. But tonight's face-to-face meeting was critical. At least it would be their last. Once the Savoy plan was set in motion, future meetings would be too dangerous.

"Gentlemen, please help yourselves to the nourishment of late night conferences," Bromine urged tonelessly. There was wine and cigars, but no food. Laid out on the granite counters were leather cigar holders containing Macanudo Robustos, Torano Exodus, Belmondo Vintage and La Tradicion Cubana cigars. Silver ice buckets containing bottles of Roederer Cristal Champagne,1990, and Louis LaTour Corton-Charlamange white, 1998, sat next to half a dozen high-stemmed wine glasses. Nearby, on a separate mirror tray, were bottles of Pomeral Chateau Certan deMay red, 1986.

When the wine was poured, the Senator raised his glass and snorted, "Gentlemen, I wish to toast your balls. Not many men of power and means, such as yourselves, would attempt such a foolhardy endeavor." The champagne washed down smoothly, splashing over the pint of Tangueray he'd consumed earlier. He laughed at the blank expressions.

Jake Kurancy glanced at Wang Chao's indignant expression. The Chinese Minister of Industry and Trade didn't understand the joke. Had they gone mad to enlist the Senator's services? To bring him into the group and set him up to receive such unprecedented power?

Cusson grinned sheepishly and said, "The Senator is correct. We are about to depart for financial places unknown." He tilted his glass to the others, and added, "Perhaps I can start with an informal summary."

"Tell us about Creditte Bank de Savoy, and its sister bank in Geneva, the Franco-Medici Union Trust," the Fed insider suggested.

"We're almost unknown, except in high government and financial circles." Cusson began in a firm voice. "As of yesterday, Creditte Bank de Savoy is the third largest private bank in the world, by size of deposits. Hundreds of billions of U.S. dollars, and a small amount of other currencies, resides in Lyon and Geneva accounts---for European-based multinational corporations, as well as BoxMart , LiChin Enterprises and the three largest commercial banks in China…as you all know."

Cusson paused for effect, watching the others ritually chop the tips off their premium cigars and ignite them with the gold-plated Cartier lighters Jake Kurancy provided for the occasion. They sipped wine and puffed heliotrope smoke rings for a few minutes, avoiding small talk, as most powerful people do. It was time to move to the lead-lined media room and start the meeting.

Cusson stood in front of the 60-inch flat screen monitor and addressed the others, who had reclined in deep-cushioned theatre seats which faced the screen, flicking ashes into the melamine cavities built into the chair arms.

"The Savoy Imperative, I am proud to say, will begin today--- if we all approve. And if we all agree to carry out the steps to which we've been assigned." He paused, glanced at his platinum Breitling chronograph, and said, "We have limited time, my friends. I suggest we vote now, and sign the necessary ….the security…. documents later. Do we all agree?"

Wang Chao wanted more discussion, although he and the Chinese leaders he represented were committed to the plan. It was the perfect springboard for their more ambitious schemes.

"We should review the plan and the assignments one more time, to be sure," Wang suggested strongly. "There must be no trails."

The diminutive, septuagenarian veteran of the Cultural Revolution was famous for his rare directness, quick wit and bull headed stubbornness. Also, his passion for Chinese dynastic history. He believed in the ultimate superiority of China in the cadre of powerful nations, and sometimes he spoke in conundrums.

"The ancient lead horse found in the tomb of Leitai, in Gansu Province," he lectured, in a high pitched tone, "is a miniature bronze steed swifter than a flying sacred bird. It is posed in full gallop, with only one hoof touching the ground. That hoof rests on the mythical 'sacred bird.'"

The others looked at him quizzically.

"The tall tree is crushed by the wind." Wang Chao warned ruefully.

Kurancy snuffed out his cigar impatiently and said , "Let's start with the dollar analysis. I understand we don't have enough deposits under control in France and Switzerland at this time. According to Phillipe's calculations, we must be fully funded by mid-July."

"That's correct." Cusson was quick to answer. "It will take a critical mass of American dollars to reach our objectives. At least another hundred billion more than currently deposited in CBdeS European accounts."

He flicked the remote control and several rows of numbers appeared on the screen.

"The plan calls for rapid-fire, multi-billion-dollar trades for other currencies; in strategically timed transactions."

The Federal Reserve insider snorted, "That should weaken the Chairman's grasp on the money supply and interest rates."

"It will," Cusson added in a tone of satisfied derision. "And it will also present you with the opportunity you've been seeking for years."

"Shock the American financial system. Draw attention away from the trade imbalance enjoyed by China," Kurancy chimed in.

"And the lost jobs," added the Senator.

"Our goods will continue to arrive in Long Beach and other ports," Li Chin boasted.

The Senator had feared for years that unresolved trade disputes between developed and developing countries would eventually cripple global commerce. "America's political and economic systems could be destroyed if we allow free trade in the U.S. to be restricted," he pontificated uncharacteristically, like a founding father. "The temporary harm to the economy, which our actions will trigger, and which Cusson predicts will be manageable, is an acceptable trade-off. Restricted trade policies cannot be allowed to take hold."

Kurancy drew them back to the numbers. "Am I correct in assuming that BoxMart, LCE and the Chinese banks will have to transfer another hundred billion into CBdeS banks in France and Geneva?"

"That's correct," Cusson answered instantly. "Franco-Medici's American banking interests should have no problem contributing another ten billion for unexpected contingencies." The Fed insider's eyebrows stretched toward the ceiling.

Li Chin, the chairman of the largest industrial conglomerate in Asia, retorted crisply, "LCE will be able to contribute another 18 $billion more than we now have in European deposits. Transfers can be made electronically, without detection, at the proper time."

The Senator was amazed how casually these men discussed billions, as if it was play money. It reminded him of the meetings he attended as a member of the Senate Appropriations Committee. But this was different. The Senate manipulated other people's money. These people tampered with their own.

"Fifteen billion more is all BoxMart will be able to move into the European banks," Kurancy declared incisively. "The events we're about to initiate will stretch the capabilities of our distribution system. We'll have to increase inventory well in advance of the Christmas shopping season, if we want to take advantage of the weakened competition during the first merchandise shock."

"Huge shipments from China have to be arranged in a short period," reminded Wang Chao. "And must be dispersed throughout your warehouse system without drawing scrutiny from the Treasury and Commerce Departments." He glanced at Li Chin, and said, "It will require careful logistics planning…and plenty of cash."

The Federal Reserve Bank official assured them of his role. "I'll keep the Feds in check, until the first dollar bomb drops. Are we still planning late August?"

"Yes," Cusson answered, "subject to unforeseen events that could require earlier, or later money transfers. But yes…I'll begin the currency deals in late June, at the European Finance Ministers meeting in Stressa, Italy."

He bowed to Wang Chao, and said, "Minister, the ivory tower will soon crumble, after China wins the Olympics." He smiled broadly and exulted, "It will be a catastrophe for the Federal Reserve Chairman…the entire U.S. banking system." His dream would come true. Cusson glanced deferentially at the Federal Reserve Bank insider. "Of course…the impact will be temporary."

"By the middle of the third quarter, there will be a significant non-positive effect on the American economy," predicted the Federal Reserve banker, slipping into the typical worried double-speak of an Alan Greenspan disciple.

"And confusion in the elections," yawned the Senator. "But, how can we be sure that Merrand will win; with all these events shaking the economy?" His real question was: "How can I be sure of my position in the new administration, when the dust settles?"

Bromine decided it was time to discuss the "Three Sixes", without disclosing the group's name.

"I can tell you something about a clandestine group---primarily American citizens---who've agreed to support our objectives. I'm sworn to secrecy regarding their methods and identities, and can only speak in general terms about what they do. You must agree to consider the knowledge of their existence a confidential part of the Savoy Imperative." He paused as the thought fermented, and the slow nods indicated reluctant acceptance of the terms.

"Why do we need them?" Li Chin inquired. He was the least knowledgeable about American politics.

"The group controls cartel money of enormous…almost unlimited… proportions. They see that it goes to the right people, at the most opportune time." Bromine paused again, then disclosed reticently, "They dictate the outcomes of several key elections."

The Senator was pleased. "So," he murmured, "several political action committees will be extremely pleased with large contributions next year."

Bromine explained further, "They've never miscalculated on previous elections, except when Kennedy won." He wanted to add, but didn't, "*and they learned how to deal with that problem, later.*"

Kurancy raised his raspy voice, "Sort of like the silent 'Jay Goulds' of the political industry." Purple cigar smoke veiled his face, giving him the frightening appearance of a carnival-machine laughing man.

"And make no mistake," the Senator intoned, "politics is an industry. Last year political action groups spent over $950 million attempting to influence elections."

"Allow me to summarize the situation…so we can complete our purpose for being here before the sun comes up," Bromine suggested pointedly. "This outside group knows only that someone is on their side, trying to prevent new trade barriers from seriously damaging their import businesses. I know of only one member by name, and he describes the others as brilliant, ruthless and rich. They have high-level links to all major industries and institutions—big oil, pharmaceuticals, investment banking, Wall Street, high tech, and defense. They are the source of funds for several venture capital firms, whose names you would recognize. They actually do much good in the U.S. and other countries."

"It sounds to me as if they're not Jay Goulds," Kurancy quipped. "He was tagged as 'the worst man on earth since the beginning of the Christian era' by his critics. I kind of liked his methods."

Bromine countered, "Don't be fooled, Jake. The members of this group would pluck out your eyes and rip out your heart, if you obstructed their plans. Other than that, I'm told the group is essential to the normal functioning of the American economy."

Cusson broke in, "It's getting late. It's time to review specific details of the Savoy Imperative."

Without waiting for a reply, he pressed a button on the remote and slid a disc into the slot at the bottom of the flat screen. The lights dimmed automatically, and an image of the Wall of China, superimposed over a likeness of the Washington Monument, materialized on the screen.

A vote was taken thirty minutes before dawn, following a careful review of the planned actions, and the follow-up required by individual members. The plan would go forward.

Wang Chao and his Chinese backers had demanded a guarantee against confidentiality breaches. They believed in the doctrine of mutual destruction, if anyone disclosed the group's secrets. Each member of the conspiracy must be vulnerable to all the others. The price for carelessness or a weak conscience had to be dreadfully high to prevent that possibility. Bromine had proposed they use the same perilous document the 'Sixes' employed to assure confidentiality. It called for the timely elimination of any individual who breaches his pledge, and the deaths of his immediate family.

Each member was required to inscribe his signature next to a fingerprint of his right index finger, on a page entitled, "Savoy Imperative Members." Seven signed and finger-printed copies of the ominous document were to be distributed to members. This would assure mutual vulnerability. Each signer was required to initial a warning sentence at the bottom of the page, which read: "I agree to be killed, without resistance, along with all the members of my immediate family, if I breach the confidentiality of this noble endeavor."

Cusson collected the signed and fingerprinted Savoy Imperative sheets, and placed them on a small table at the side of the flat screen. He removed seven unmarked teak boxes, twelve-inches-square and two-inches-thick, from a carton under the table, and aligned them in a row on the surface. Pull-off labels typed with the names of the seven men in the room were adhered to the lids.

Each man came forward, lifted the box with his name, and placed his index finger over a rose-tinted glass eye set in the top-center of the lid. The boxes popped open. Cusson inserted the signed copies and closed the lid.

"As we explained earlier," he said, "the boxes are lined with a silver and titanium alloy, which is attached to a pyro-technic substance. It will explode if the box is opened by any means other than the fingerprint identification."

Sweat rolled from Kurancy's massive forehead as he reached for his box.

"A silicone chip has been imbedded in the silvertanium," Bromine explained. "The boxes contain a miniaturized GPS locating device, similar to the one used to track stolen cars, but several times more powerful."

Cusson wanted no misconceptions. "There are two additional receivers which can detect if any of the seven boxes is opened. They can locate an opened box within a ten foot radius, anywhere in the world. The Senator and I will monitor the two special receivers, which look and function like MP3 music players. We will carry them with us until January 31 of 2009, a few weeks after the new U.S. President takes office. If all goes as planned, the sheets will never be seen by outside eyes. A timer in the boxes will set off a small portion of the pyrotechnic material, and destroy the contents of each box on that date."

Bromine reminded them of another detail. "The special receivers are only a backup, in case any of the boxes is misplaced, or destroyed by accident. Your index finger will provide all the information you need to respond to an event." He noticed the strained expressions, and said, "Let's review it one more time."

Dawn was threatening, so he rushed through the explanation. "An opened, or exploded, box can be identified by all the other box holders, when a flashing red number is emitted from the glass eye. Each of your boxes is assigned a number from one to seven. You have all been given a second number, which only you know. It will be your responsibility to respond accordingly if that number flashes in the glass eye. You must check the box at least once a week. If the light flashes the number 'three', for example, whoever is given the second number 'three' must kill the member holding that box number, as well as his wife and children, if he has any." He waited for the sighs to dissipate, then said morosely, "You can fulfill this obligation either personally, or by hiring an assassin."

Cusson interjected, "The others will know which number sets off an alarm, and which number is required to respond. A round robin will eventually catch up to anyone who fails in his obligation. He will be the next one targeted for elimination."

The gruesome details were presented as if they were assembly instructions for one of Li Chin's vacuum cleaners.

"Remember," Bromine warned, "if you fail this assignment, the person holding your number is obligated to kill you."

Moans of dread emptied into the room from several ashen faces. "Of course, we don't expect this procedure to ever be used."

Jake wondered which member was assigned to kill him. Luckily, he was divorced and had no children. He didn't mind if his ex got axed.

Wang Chao was guessing how anyone could reach him in Beijing. Unless Li Chin or Kurancy had been assigned his number. He said, "We must protect ourselves from any disclosure. The price of failure would be larger than our lives."

One more task required completion before the meeting was concluded; and the Savoy Imperative members allowed to depart, in five minute intervals, to blend in with the early morning traffic clogging Route 27.

"The seriousness of this commitment cannot be overstated," declared Bromine. "The outside group I described has prepared a live broadcast. Unfortunately, they've experienced a security failure, and want to demonstrate how they handle the problem." He tapped a few buttons on the remote-control.

A middle-aged man was blindfolded, gagged and tied tightly with leather straps to a heavy chair bolted to the floor. To his right was a woman of similar age, also blindfolded, gagged and strapped to a chair. They faced a video camera set high on a tripod, which revealed only the back of a young boy's curly-topped head. A timer in the lower left of the video screen indicated the scene was recorded an hour earlier.

A tall, broad-shouldered person, whose face was hidden behind a yashmak veil, removed the man's blindfold. The Federal Reserve insider and the Senator immediately recognized the horrified captive as the Assistant Deputy Secretary of the Department of Energy. He'd been mildly drugged, and did not fight to break free. He looked aghast at the figure of his son, unmoving, and leaning awkwardly against the straps which held him in a chair facing his parents. Only the video viewers could see the deep red indentation on the top of the child's skull.

The expression on the bound man's face must have originated in the torture chambers of hell, the only place which could consign such pain. The gag muffled his manic yelps, as the tall person declared, in a harsh, barely-distinguishable Asian-African woman's voice, "You have defied the pledge of confidentiality, and must now pay the price."

The Deputy Secretary gasped through inflamed nostrils, as he watched the female assailant remove a blood-stained cobbler's hammer, with a sharpened, cone-shaped tip, from her burka, and step behind his terrified wife's chair. The assailant began running callused fingers roughly thru the blindfolded women's hair, as if to massage her scalp and diminish her fright. She was actually feeling for the exact location of the softer bone. The Department of Energy employee's wife sensed a new danger and began to sway her head frantically from side to side; but the tall attacker yanked a fistful of hair and jerked her face forward, in the direction of the video camera. She carefully positioned the hammer tip over a specific spot, and raised the instrument high over her head.

The Assistant Deputy Secretary watched in horror as the instrument slammed down with the precision and impact of a hydraulic punch-press. His wife's arms winged up involuntarily, then fluttered. Her fingers curled like a fan of snakes poised to strike…then fell like a puppet's whose strings were cut.

You never see a Brinks truck in a funeral procession. The money he'd been paid for providing information to the 'Three Sixes', and more recently, to an energy information broker, would remain hidden in a numbered account until the end of the twenty-first century. Then, a Swiss banker would confiscate his abandoned account.

The assassin moved in front of his chair…her back to the camera. She leaned over ominously and removed a small, sharp object from a side pocket. The video feed went dead, but the audio continued. A blood-congealing shriek caused the listeners to turn away. The ones with a religious bent prayed never to defy their contract, as the horrific cries of unbearable pain echoed into their memory.

As they departed, Cusson boasted one last time, "The Savoy Plan is full-proof. Don't worry, my friends. If you follow instructions, nothing can go wrong."

Li Chin watched Jake Kurancy knowingly, as the big man slipped out the front door. Kurancy glanced back at his long-time Chinese friend…sharing a moment of doubt. The scale of damage the financial schemes of the Savoy Imperative would cause to the American economy---although impossible to calculate exactly---was at least predictable. If Cusson's estimates were accurate, the currency crisis in America would last for only a year.

In contrast, the strange organism about to be unleashed on American soil by PLA General Ye Kunshi and Chinese Vice-Premier Yong Ihasa, could have unpredictable after-effects. Kurancy, Wang Chao and Li Chin were the only Savoy members with knowledge of the planned biological attack. None of them had knowledge of the recent human casualty at the Northeast China bio-weapons research facility; where several cannisters containing the harmless- to-humans organism were being packaged for delivery to the United States.

Despite assertions by Chinese biochemists---that the genetically-modified agricultural pathogen could not penetrate a human cell---the virus-like organism had apparently mutated at least once; and acquired the morphology to invade and destroy a young man's vital organs.

CHAPTER 1

(MARCH 31, 2008)
BIOLOGICAL WEAPONS LAB, JILIN PROVINCE, CHINA

The robot operator carefully lowered the last of twelve double-compartment brass canisters into a specially designed overseas transfer container shaped in the exact dimensions of a Chinese mortar round. The cone-tipped, impact-resistant polycarbonate cylinder was lined with semi-conductive rubber to protect the contents from damage during shipment, and from electro-magnetic radiation which could activate the dormant crystallized micro-organisms stored inside.

Two brittle glass vials containing a host-bacteria and a virus-like organism---biologically decribed as a *mycoplasma*---had been delicately placed in separate sealed compartments in the canister by Dr. Otto Ho Hot, lead scientist at the Taiwan Research Institute for Agricultural Diseases. Dr. Ho Hot had been mysteriously missing from the Institute for several months, along with two-dozen vials of the 'experimental pesticide' the genetics expert smuggled into the Chinese mainland; under orders from a People's Liberation Army general.

Originally designed to infect the world's second largest corn crop on the Songliao plain in northern China, the agro-weapon had been developed as a potential retaliatory measure. The Taipei government considered the vegetation-specific pathogen an important part of its defense arsenal, to be employed only if mainland China's Central Military Commission acted out its threat to stage pre-emptive strikes against the Taiwan-administered islands of Matsu and Quemoy---the two strategic Taiwanese strongholds located only a few miles offshore from the important east coast port cities of Xiamen and Fuzhou, in Fujian province.

Dr. Ho Hot had not yet been allowed to see his son. He feared that the boy's arrogant ways diminished his chances of surviving the inevitable prison beatings. He had no choice but to cooperate with General Ye Kunshi until he learned the fate of twenty-year-old Shubo. The PLA general promised Ho Hot he would soon join his son, who was arrested for participating in Falon Gong demonstrations on the Beijing University campus.

The Deputy Commander of the People's Liberation Army watched intently from behind the sealed glass window of the Level 4 biohazards room at the military installation near Changchun, in the northeast province of Jilin. Dr. Ho Hot and two assistants wore biohazard suits with self-contained oxygen generators and special filters to prevent contamination. Any micro-organisms larger than a few nano-strands of DNA, or loose chromosomes that might escape from a ruptured host-bacteria membrane, were captured by the micro-fine strainers.

They completed the final task requiring Dr. Ho Hot's expertise: safely packaging the two crystallized, symbiotic micro-organisms developed by his research team at the Agricultural Diseases Institute. Special shipping containers were used to assure that the bio-agents weren't destroyed or prematurely activated during transport to their final destination.

Technicians inserted the canisters into styro-foam jackets and sealed them in specially selected triple-layer cardboard cartons. RFID and bar-code labels were attached along with four-color illustration stickers identifying the packages as: 'BoxMart Heavy-Duty Water Filters.' The radio-frequency identification and tracking labels indicated the shipment would be delivered to a BoxMart distribution center bordering Mexico on the U.S. side.

The critical events Jake Kurancy and the reprobate Chinese leaders planned depended upon the successful overseas delivery of all twelve canisters. Each container held a quantity of the two organisms enough to contaminate an area of planted corn the size of ten thousand football fields, upon first exposure.

(APRIL 1, 2008) AM
NEW HAVEN, CT.

It happened again! he thought to himself, as Rosa approached.

"What are you mad at today?" she inquired sarcastically, having noticed the scowl on his usually placid face as he read the newspaper.

"I don't know what's falling faster," he replied, "the economy or my sex drive."

Rosa faked a blush, then laughed, "You intellectuals are all dirty old men, Dr. Es. I think your brains are squeezing retired sex hormones into your eyes."

She tilted her head sideways, and peeked under his usual table at Bruegger's, adding with a smirk, "But no lower than that."

The professor gaped in amusement as she pivoted like a hooker escaping a police patrol car; and wiggled the disproportionately large buttocks on her thin frame, as she retreated to serve other customers.

Professor Eric Syzmanski of the Yale School of Management returned his attention to the full page article in the New Haven Register, which described the pending failure of yet another small manufacturing company in Connecticut. There was an epidemic of small business failures in the northeast corridor since the 2006 elections, which marked the beginning of the recession most Americans had feared.

Consumer spending in the United States had dropped dramatically in the past six months. The average American was struggling in the financial quagmire of the 2007 surge in oil prices, the spending fiasco associated with winding down the Iraq war, and…for too many…debilitating job losses.

But the business failure described in the local newspaper article was difficult to understand. The company involved, Gatt Recovery Technologies, had been founded by one of the professor's prized Yale School of Management MBA graduates, Justin Gatt. His company had been a model of success and innovation in the plastics processing and recycling industry for twenty two years. Professor Syzmanski, an internationally recognized authority on business and government organizations, had actually used GRT, Inc. as a case study in his popular Entrepreneurs classes at Yale.

Justin had sparked stimulating classroom discussion during his guest speaker appearance. Many of the MBA candidates, now managing large-cap corporations and government agencies, still remembered his controversial espousal---that small businesses in America were more important to the country's future than the large multi-nationals.

He was also a creative engineer and chemist, who'd invented unique processes to convert plastics waste into a myriad of high quality, everyday items. Materials that had once raised the heights of land-fill mountains were now being used to make disposable cameras, fast-food service trays, fleece sweaters, poinsettia pots, decking lumber and park benches.

The Register reporter noted that the same bank which recently foreclosed on GRT's largest customer, also filed a lawsuit the previous day to force the liquidation of Justin's company; sighting an alleged loan default of nearly a million dollars. The bank was demanding immediate payment.

The hyper-active, seventy-year-old professor, whose academic prestige and popular classes trumped Yale's mandatory retirement-age rule, sipped on the lukewarm tea, then crinkled his forehead as he motioned familiarly with his cane to Rosa.

The middle aged, pencil-thin waitress, who'd served him breakfast at Breugger's Bagels on Grove Street for several years, was handing free coffee to a shivering, rain-soaked Russian immigrant, who recently lost her job cleaning rat and monkey cages in the Yale biology labs. Syzmanski thought he recognized the grey haired woman, who was dressed in a tattered brown overcoat, and leaning unsteadily against the glass counter. He recalled that Yale was now outsourcing mundane biology testing to the All-India Institute of Medical Sciences in New Delhi. The biology department was saving eighty-percent of the labor costs for lab personnel.

"Even the decent-paying university jobs for immigrants are disappearing," he quipped in silent guilt. He was part of the well-paid faculty that allowed it to happen. He watched intently as Rosa reached under the counter, then handed the woman a warm corn muffin. The waitress then strode over to the professor's usual table and poured a hot water topper into his cup, which was cradling two limp Twinings English Breakfast teabags. Syzmansky winked affectionately to his dark-haired morning heart-throb, and was rewarded with her usual sarcastic response.

"You again?" she scolded. But her smile escaped the porous facade. Her pretty face warmed the tea more than the hot water.

Syzmansky pushed aside the New Haven newspaper, uncovering today's New York Times. The sensational front page article written by the newspaper's top Asian investigative reporter, Gabriel Oresco, uncovered proof---in the form of a signed Memorandum of Agreement---that a retired U.S. oil company executive had secretly brokered an astounding deal with China's state run oil giant. The Chinese had purchased the development and extraction rights for a newly discovered oil field, containing in excess of a billion barrels of sweet crude deposits, in the vicinity of international waters bordering Pacific Ocean territory claimed by the U.S., about two hundred and fifty miles directly west of Santa Barbara, California.

Several politicians, including New York Governor Martin Merrand, the leading Presidential candidate, had called for an immediate investigation.

"Why?" Merrand asked, at a hastily called press conference, "was a U.S. oil-exploration company allowed to sell a major oil discovery, so close to the U.S. continental shelf, to trading arch-rival, China, when American's have been forced to import seventy percent of our crude oil requirements." The article noted that the sudden disappearance of the Assistant Deputy Secretary of the Department of Energy, along with his family, had sparked rumors of foul play. The DOE official had apparently emptied his bank accounts and fled.

The professor wasn't sure which bad news upset him more: the national oil disgrace, or the career crisis of a former student and friend he admired.

He'd helped nurture Justin Gatt's success. As he re-read the local story, the sense that it couldn't be true dissipated. GRT's number one customer, Slattery Housewares, Inc, the largest manufacturer of plastics housewares in the Northeast, was being liquidated today by order of the federal bankruptcy court in Boston.

He read that the company lost an enormous order from BoxMart Retail Enterprises, after investing millions in new equipment. The article included a list of Slattery's largest unsecured creditors. GRT was at the top of the list. Justin Gatt's company was owed nine hundred and fifty thousand dollars for materials it supplied for the BoxMart order. The professor realized that Justin's company was likely to sink with the Slattery wreck. The bank would never allow GRT to recover the money owed.

The professor folded the paper slowly, then suddenly slammed it down on the table. *Perhaps Justin's smart enough to save his company,* he thought. *It will depend on the willingness of Residents Bank to give him more time.*

Syzmanski couldn't know that the bank's response would plunge Justin Gatt into the maelstrom of an unimaginable international conspiracy designed to shock the U.S. economy. Or, that he'd be responsible for Gatt becoming the target of a Shanghai death squad, a relentless surface-to-air missile launched from the Indian Ocean, and a sniper's rifle.

CHAPTER 2

(April 1, 2008), 10pm
Washington, D.C.

Ross Trenker realized he'd misjudged the purpose of tonight's meeting when Bob McGill, the president of the G.H. Paladin Consulting Group, pulled over to the curb in front of the Navy Memorial on Pennsylvania Avenue between 9th and 7th Streets. The usual crowd of Washington Mall pedestrians had gone home, or herded to after-hours watering holes for power cocktails after the federal office buildings and banks closed.

There was only one person in sight---a tall, thin man in a bank security uniform, standing in front of the white-marble, two-story former bank branch building set back from Pennsylvania Ave., in a courtyard on 7th Street.

Constructed in 1889 by the 170 year-old prestigious Riggs Bank, which had nourished close links with every U.S. administration since the mid 1800s, as well as the Saudi royal family, several dictators and corrupt foreign regimes, the majestic marble structure seemed appropriately located in the belly of United States Government power. The modern concrete FBI building was a few blocks away; and a non-descript grey-stone structure housing the National Council of Negro Women was around the corner on 633 Pennsylvania Ave.

"About the purpose of your meeting with Blackstone." McGill cautioned the 40-year-old GHP consultant, a former Proctor and Gamble brand manager and Yale SOM grad, who'd been chosen for this special assignment. "You should assume it will be the most important meeting of your life." Trenker's pale-grey left eye began an annoying twitch. McGill noticed that the oversized, tortoise-framed bi-focal eyeglasses magnified the bottoms of his pupils. Trenker raised his arm and succumbed to another nervous habit---scratching the back of his perfectly coiffed, dark-brown wavy hair.

Trenker stared ominously at the bank guard stationed in front of the former Riggs branch entrance. McGill added in a threatening snuffle, "You'd better go along with Blackstone's requests."

"Christ, Bob," Trenker snapped, as he stepped onto the sidewalk. "I've already agreed to take the China trade-mission."

The ten-year-veteran consultant was exhausted from the frenetic pace they'd demanded of him since he'd agreed to handle "super-sensitive" projects for the parent company in Washington. The perpetual commutes between Boston and the nation's capitol had dulled his enthusiasm for the initially-intriguing, clandestine meetings with nameless men and women---rich and powerful enough to buy influence *for* or *against* pending Congressional legislation. Identities had been hidden behind curtains, or murky shadows in after-hours Georgetown shebeens he didn't know existed. He'd decided to look for a less demanding job as soon as he returned from China.

"We know a lot more about you, than you think," McGill gibed, as he stomped on the gas pedal, forcing his underling to jump away from the rolling vehicle. The open passenger door slammed shut from centrifugal force as the SUV swung right and headed across the Mall on 7th Street.

"What the hell..." Trenker shouted, as he watched McGill dart away as if he expected a bomb to explode. Ross cast his eyes warily at the departing vehicle, then glanced back to the bank entrance. A full yellow moon dropped sufficient light from the cloudy sky to reveal the bank guard motioning in his direction.

During the shuttle flight from Logan Airport, McGill said very little about the meeting with Tom Blackstone, Chairman of Financial Flow Foundation, the parent of Boston-based G.H. Paladin. He'd revealed only that the meeting would take place at a different location than the FFF offices near the new Convention Center on L Street. Trenker had expected McGill to attend the meeting...not dart away into the nearly-empty streets.

He shrugged, and walked slowly toward the guard.

"Mr.Trenker, *sir,*" the guard addressed him in the military manner of a soldier greeting a senior officer. "Please come this way." He inserted a plastic card into the thin slot of a polished brass box attached to the white marble arch framing heavy glass entrance doors. The soft click signaled the guard to pull open the door.

Trenker entered the shadowy lobby as the guard held the door. Suddenly, the lobby was illuminated in antique yellow from two 19th century brass-and-pewter chandeliers suspended at each end of the sixty-foot length of the lobby.

Trenker glanced up at the ornate paintings on the high ceiling, then at the six white-marble Greek columns spaced evenly in rows of three on each side of the lobby. The chandeliers were each adorned with six etched-glass fixtures directing light upwards, and six smaller, clear-glass cups directing light to the floor.

Trenker followed the guard to the far end of the richly decorated room. Carved-mahogany walls, elaborately draped stained-glass windows and polished marble stone-work reminded him of the aged opulence of a Newport mansion. They descended a carpeted, circular staircase which fed into a long, dimly-lit corridor ten feet wide. Original portraits of 19th and 20th century U.S. Presidents, bank founders and directors of the Riggs Banking empire hung under brass cylindrical lamps, bathing the masterpieces in soft sallow light.

At the end of the corridor was a ten-foot high by six-foot wide 19th century Mosler nickel-steel vault, retro-fit with an eye-level, electronic iris-identification instrument in the center of the massive door. The guard remained stationary in front of the door until a remote signal initiated the whirl-and-click of the un-lock mechanism. The door cracked open when the hardened-steel gears and complicated interlocks disengaged. A calm male voice intoned from a ceiling speaker, "You may return to your post."

The guard nodded to Trenker, then rushed down the corridor and disappeared up the staircase. The foot-thick steel door opened slowly as Trenker maneuvered to gaze inside. He saw a huge, dark-walnut oval conference table through the polished metal bars of the security gate that blocked the entrance to a surprisingly large room of about 30 by 20 feet. The conference table was surrounded by eighteen high-backed chairs covered in plush, multi-colored, thin-striped fabric.

The same hidden voice said solemnly, "Please come in, Ross. Tom will be here shortly. We'd like you to take seat number fifteen at the end of the room."

The seats weren't numbered; but Trenker noticed that the numbers one-to-eighteen were stamped in gold-leaf lettering on black leather folders set on the table in front of each chair. He found portfolio number fifteen, and took the seat. After several minutes of uninterrupted silence, he began to wonder about the contents of number-fifteen folder. Finally, he succumbed to curiosity and the tension of waiting, and slipped his index finger under the upper-right corner of the cover. He had the eerie feeling that thirty-four eyes were watching through the room-length mirror built into the wall behind him. He glanced over his shoulder self-consciously, and noticed an oak panel slide open on squeaking peg hinges. A tall figure stooped to enter the room.

Tom Blackstone, Chairman of the Financial Flow Foundation, was six foot seven, gangly with frameless tinted-eyeglasses and a giant Adams-apple that protruded like a squashed bow-tie. He wore a pale-blue seersucker suit and a cardinal-red collarless pullover, which accentuated his silver crew-cut. At fifty-seven, he was in excellent physical condition, aided by daily work-outs at the exclusive FFF Athletic Club on the top floor of the FFF Building. He'd retired from military service ten years ago as the tallest Special Forces sniper ever to wear an American military uniform.

Blackstone made his way to seat number ten and opened the leather folder. He acknowledged Trenker's presence with a slight uplift of his chin and crimped lips. Ross had removed his tie and left it in McGill's SUV with his luggage. He was sweating profusely, despite the air-conditioning and cool evening temperature. He watched Blackstone read the notes in portfolio number ten. A few minutes later, Blackstone looked up with an indignant expression and said, "Trenker, you've done a good job on every assignment we've given you in Boston and D.C. But you certainly fucked up before you came to work for us."

Blackstone handed him a large black-and-white photograph showing Trenker holding a knotted horse-whip in one hand, and a pitcher of beer in the other. He was leaning over a frightened young man, apparently being abused in a harsh initiation ritual his splinter-group of *non-club students* had devised to compete with the unspeakable initiation rites of the super-confidential Yale Skull and Bones club.

"Where'd you get this?" Trenker demanded. "Cameras were never allowed at the initiation ceremonies in New Haven."

Blackstone smiled contemptuously and growled, "Enjoyed playing with the boys, did you?" Trenker cringed at the implication in his accusing tone.

"What are you after, Mr. Blackstone? That was years ago. It was only a prank."

"I understand this boy didn't think so. He was bi-polar, and was on strong anti-depression drugs. He left a written account of how an unidentified group of Yale students beat him and took away his man-hood. I'm sure you're aware of the recent suicide. His wealthy parents discovered the note and have initiated inquiries at Yale. They'll pay almost any amount to track down and prosecute the participants they believe caused their son's death."

Ross had been struck with remorse when he read about the gay attorney's bath-tub full of blood. It was the cause of frequent nightmares…impossible to share with his devout-Christian wife. She wouldn't harm a stinging tarantula if she could just flick it away.

Blackstone barked, "Open the folder and read the second page." When Trenker finished reading he replied in an anxiety-stained voice, "This never happened. He only imagined it. We had no idea he was so troubled at the time."

"Read the next page."

Trenker read the confidential report describing the disappearance of the Assistant Deputy Secretary of the Department of Energy, including Blackstone's conclusion that he was the source of a troublesome information leak to a New York Times reporter; who broke the story about China's purchase of invaluable off-shore oil fields from a U.S. oil company.

"This man and his family have disappeared," Trenker recalled. "What has this got to do with me?"

"He never completed the task we assigned him. He was a greedy fool who didn't honor the commitment we're about to ask of you." Trenker took that to mean that Blackstone's clandestine group, whoever they were, was responsible for the man's disappearance. He cringed at the not-so-subtle warning.

"What do you want of me?" Trenker admonished. "I've already agreed to shadow the U.S. Trade Representative in China, and report everything I learn about the status of trade negotiations, and insider thinking."

Blackstone pointed to the glass mirror on the wall behind him. "Ross, you're about to be given the opportunity to enter a realm few people know exists. We're considering you for membership in a very exclusive…shall we say… *political group*. But first I want you to think about taking over an important U.S. Department of Energy position."

"This group you're referring to, Mr. Blackstone? I'm not that interested in politics. Or working for the federal government directly." He turned to the sound coming from the panel-door Blackstone used to enter the room.

As it swung open, Blackstone said in the grim tone of a judge issuing a death sentence, "When you agree to join us, you'll be making a lifetime commitment to our group."

Trenker watched in amazement as one of the most powerful men in the world came into the room wearing a black mask.

"Our leader will explain further. When you're ready, his identity and the identities of other members will be revealed to you."

CHAPTER 3

(April 1, 2008), 6 pm
Leominster, Massachusetts

Joe Slattery, the sixty-year-old, silver-haired founder of Slattery Housewares Corporation sat despondently in the high-backed president's chair at the corporate office in Leominster, Massachusetts…for the second last time.

Officials from Residents Bank of North America were mulling around, gathering files and financial records, but also keeping a watch on Joe and the other Slattery employees who were nervously filling small cardboard boxes with personal items. Joe was saddened at having dragged Justin Gatt's company into near bankruptcy, but his own personal problems overwhelmed his anguished thoughts.

He could hardly breath or speak in the presence of Edwin Tinius, the bank's gawking, abrasive vice-president for asset recovery. The sight of the bank's financial hit-man standing nearby, acidified Joe's entire digestive system. Tinius' ferocious nature belied a bony, one hundred and forty pound, five-foot four-inch frame. His thin, manicured fingers had probably never lifted a rake or a baseball bat; or formed a threatening fist.

Tinius and his assistants were supervising the removal of personal items by Slattery employees, as allowed by the bankruptcy judge. Tinius was giving everyone a hard time. He'd insisted that each employee show proof of ownership for even the smallest items they wished to remove. Several of the Slattery office managers just stormed out, leaving behind everything but family photos.

Residents Bank was the dominant lender to small manufacturers in the northeast, and enjoyed a special relationship with BoxMart RE. The giant retailer promoted the bank as the preferred lender when suppliers required financing to fulfill BoxMart orders.

Tinius gazed with satisfaction at the employees departing the premises carrying small cartons of personal items and final paychecks. He smiled cruelly behind their slumped backs. Another hundred manufacturing jobs would be successfully relocated to China. The bank's vulturine foreclosure had produced the desired result. His year-end bonus would be larger than ever.

Tinius'only regret was---there were fewer close-down targets remaining in the depressed New England manufacturing industry. The grim statistics cited in the *New Haven Register* were accurate. Nearly half the small manufacturing companies in the northeast U.S. had failed, or were in the process of failing, since the 2006 elections.

As Joe absently fingered favorite pens, pencils and now-useless business cards, he began leafing through some papers left on the desk by one of the bank employees. He noticed a letter from Residents Bank requesting a quotation from an equipment auction house. It was dated two weeks before BoxMart cancelled its order. Joe was good at remembering dates.

That's a month before the bank notified me of its intention to foreclose. It can't be, he thought incredulously. Attached to the letter was a property tax bill from the city of Leominster, listing all the assets owned by Slattery Housewares company.

"What the hell are you looking at?" Tinius barked, as he suddenly appeared behind Joe, leering over his shoulder like a serpent ready to strike. He recognized the document immediately. Long fingers snatched forward to extract the paper from Joe's hand. The banker was furious that Joe might have noticed the date.

"I want you out of here…right now!" the diminutive vice president with the closely-cropped, thick blond hair demanded in false indignation. His alarmed expression summoned the two husky young bank employees he'd instructed to lull nearby…in case Joe caused a disturbance.

Slattery was shocked to his feet. He fell away from Tinius' violent outburst. Blood quickened to his temples; adrenaline-spiked nerves fired random fibrillations into his cigarette-diseased heart muscles, forcing them to pump irregular rhythms.

"You little punk," he managed defensively. "Stay away from me or I'll kick you in the balls. If you have any."

Tinius flashed an anxious glance at the two employees and waved them to his sides. Vehemence spat from his twisted mouth. "I want your ass out of here… now, Slattery. And don't ever come back." He pointed an effeminate finger toward the exit door, and rolled it nervously in a circular motion. "Out now!" he screeched wildly.

It was late afternoon on the day the bankruptcy court turned over the assets of Slattery Housewares to Residents Bank. Joe started to protest the bank's slimy actions, then decided to conserve energy. He was exhausted from lack of sleep and didn't think he could penetrate the two-man force protecting this fairy-assed Napoleon knock-off. Still, he'd look for an opening to flatten Tinius.

Suddenly, he felt hopelessly weak. His struggle with unbearable tension was taking its toll on his health. He'd finally accepted the exhausting reality that he'd led his family and employees into an insurmountable financial catastrophe. His arms and legs were filled with lead; he felt wasted…unable to recover…to start over. Joe's eyes hardened. Scornful…violent thoughts flashed through his mind. Tiny lightening bolts of hate exited the neurons twitching his facial muscles. The banker-guards read his expression…his body language. One moved to block his access to Tinius.

"Don't try, Mr. Slattery," the young banker admonished. Tinius noticed the crazed look in his eyes and eased back from the desk. Joe raised a fist.

"Calm down, sir," the banker said forcefully, as he stepped in front of Tinius.

Joe hesitated, then gradually lowered his fist. His eyes glassed over, softened, shuttered, then grudgingly opened to the cruel, cautious grin of the bank vice president. Tinius was thinking that he'd pushed Joe too far.

Joe reached slowly into his pocket, extracted a ring of keys, and jammed them into the nearest banker's lapel pocket. Tinius' surprise was cloaked with satisfaction. He said, in a spiteful, condescending tone, "You have five more minutes. Then I never want to see your pathetic face in this building again."

Joe's face blanched. He pressed against the wall, his body wavering. The man with the keys reached forward and gripped his arm to steady him; Tinius caught his pleading glance.

"Drag his ass to the car," Tinius ordered. He turned to the other bank examiner. "You---carry his stuff." As if to poison any hope Joe might have of recovering from this disaster, Tinius spat venomously, "You're too old and tired, Slattery…and too stupid."

A completely defeated person can easily snap. "Fuck you," Joe blared, his eyes ablaze, crazed and bulging with hatred. He reached down to his crotch. "But not too tired for this." The childish urge to defy was too powerful to resist.

They were on him just as the spray from his open zipper splashed over the papers. "Too stupid, huh?" he shouted. "You bastards set me up."

Tinius' body-guards clasped Joe's arms, forcing him to face in the opposite direction.

"I saw the evidence," he cried out as they began dragging him to the front entrance.

The stunned bank vice-president grimaced at the yellow-stained documents.

"Get him out of here."

They escorted him forcefully to the rented Honda Civic in the parking lot and loaded him into the front seat. "Come on, Slattery...zipper up. You'll catch your pecker in the teeth."

The man with the keys patted Joe on the shoulder, laughing in pitiful admiration. He wagged his head and turned back to the office. Joe glanced over his shoulder. Tinius was standing at the entrance, waving torn pieces of the auction letter, and triumphantly mouthing the words, "Good riddance to evidence and you."

Joe's head bounced off the steering wheel so hard it nearly activated the airbag. The next crack of his forehead against the hard vinyl circle succeeded only in activating a painful reminder. *"How can I face them?"*

His mind visualized the tears rolling down the cheeks of his beloved thirteen-year-old daughter, Marsha, when she was informed that she wouldn't be attending the private school which practically guaranteed acceptance into an Ivy League college.

The key was jammed into the ignition slot and turned. Joe was mindless, except for one thought, as the car pulled away from the company parking lot. *"I can't go home...not yet."* He drove past a tavern near the factory that he'd passed a thousand times...but never entered. The lot was empty except for a late model pick-up. He was desperate to escape the crush of guilt, even for a few minutes.

"Bourbon on the rocks," he decided. It was his first alcoholic beverage in seven months.

"The bar's never been this empty," complained the husky, pot-bellied bartender, as he dusted off the bar surface in front of his only customer with the edge of a cardboard coaster. "Especially when the houseware company's first shift gets out." He wiped his hands on the triple-X red flannel shirt draped loosely over wrinkled denims, and poured a tall drink for the man he didn't know was most responsible for his problems.

Joe stirred the chilled alcohol for several minutes, gazing dreamily as the sharp edges of the ice cubes rounding away in the swirl of a thin plastic straw. He finally lifted the glass and mumbled in the dim light of the tavern, "Cheers," to the face in the mirror behind the bar...which blandly toasted its twin.

"Did you lose your job over there?" the curious bartender asked. Joe appeared to be the most depressed customer he'd ever seen. Joe didn't answer. He was fixating on the likeness in the mirror. It was now judging him, unmercifully. He said something under his breath that sounded like, "You're too tired…too stupid."

The bartender turned away from Joe's unpleasant grimace and focused on the creaking sound coming in from the front entrance. He shaded his eyes as the last brilliant rays from the late afternoon sun beamed blindingly in from the street. He was relieved to have another customer, and decided to turn up the brightness of the indirect lamps above the hand crafted mahogany bar. It gave a better view of the initials jackknifed into the surface during the first world war. He almost turned the lights down again, when he saw disgruntled Ernie waddle in.

The chain-smoking, overweight former fork truck operator for Slattery Houswares Company recognized Joe immediately.

"Mr. Slattery, you old fucker," he blurted out aggressively. "How's it going?" His tone was sarcastic. He knew the company had just been shut down. Joe didn't appreciate the arrogant interruption to his solitude…his only comfort. Its sudden departure caused him to think about his wife's paranoic depression. To her, the family's financial problems were not just about money. She believed their social identity had also been taken away.

"Fine, Ernie," he answered reluctantly. "Can I buy you a drink?"

It took only a few Schaeffers before the ungrateful, middle-aged fork truck operator became loud and aggressive. "This here's the owner who had me fired," he crowed to the barman, slamming his fist on the bar and flexing his flabby, dagger-tattooed biceps in a threatening manner.

"Joe, you fucker…you screwed my family. We have no medical coverage because of you." The overweight alcoholic emptied the beer bottle, and continued his whining. "I can't afford the COBRA premiums, or get prescriptions for my kids." He turned the empty beer bottle upside down and watched the last drop spill on the bar.

"I got plugged arteries from moving your plastic shit around the plant," he spit out, "and my bitchy wife is running around with a young stud; because your foreman-whore fired me for squeezing her ass…accidentally."

Joe shrugged helplessly. The strung out boozer was insane.

"Have another, Ernie. It might help," he said, thinking more of himself than Ernie. He snatched the man's empty bottle and gestured for two refills. Ernie's mood morphed from aggressive to passive in an instant. The bartender attempted to defuse the antagonism between his only two customers. "These are on the house."

"How about a shot of Jamisons…all around?" Ernie didn't miss a beat.

"Why not?" Joe and the barman shouted simultaneously. Long forgotten were Joe's medical problems.

Four refills later, darkness arrived with the saturated clouds that had blown east from the Great Lakes over the Berkshire Mountains, as Ernie strode from the bar---completely mellowed. His biggest problem had been solved, at least temporarily. The complimentary ethanol surging pleasantly thru his circulatory system , had instructed his fogged brain that he was happy.

"I think I'm ready to go home, now," Joe announced to his new buddy behind the bar. "My wife will probably be pilled up and floating like a duck by now."

Joe slid from the bar-stool, nearly lost his balance, recovered, and pranced toward the exit door like a step-over-step fashion model on a Milan runway. He made it out into the poorly lit parking lot, and fumbled for car keys. In the sparse mercury lumen, he realized that a spare key to the Slattery Housewares office was still on his chain. The early evening sky seemed to be spinning in slow motion, as he struggled to regain his focus. He looked up and saw no stars. A sliver of the full orange moon peaked out between heavy rain clouds, hurrying seductively in the shadows of orange and yellow lunar reflections; large droplets began to plummet from the unnerving sky. Joe barely noticed the flash-shower soaking his body. Not much registered, or mattered to Joe, at this moment.

Finally, he shivered away enough alcohol to revive a residue of common sense, and climbed into the front seat of the compact car. Small marbles of rain strafed the windshield and slapped at his face through a partially lowered side window. He remained still for several minutes…broken in spirit. Salty moisture soon joined the cold clear rain rolling down his left cheek.

Thirty-minutes later, he was sitting in the comfortable SHC president's chair…for the last time. Oblique, shimmering shadows, distorted by the driving rain, jutted from the parking lot lamps through shear-draped windows…partially illuminating the office. Papers left there by someone from the banker's group lay scattered over the desk surface. Joe's damp forearms rested on the desk, cupping his forehead.

He sat up and rested on his elbows. Two computer printouts were stuck to his arms. Joe peeled one and examined it in the catches of light. His weakly focused eyes recognized the list. Gatt Recovery Technologies was at the top of the page.

Suddenly, his uncooperative pupils rolled out of focus. An uneasy weakness seemed to release the muscle tension above his knees; his hands began to tremble. His instinctive diabetic thought was: "I'm low on sugar."

Joe reached for the telephone...then remembered...*She can't help me anymore.*

His college-age sons would have to transfer to less expensive community colleges; and apply for student loans. Marsha's enrollment at the Groton School would become a sad memory which never occurred. His wife's beloved four-bedroom colonial was already second-mortgaged for more than it was worth in the depressed Massachusetts real estate market. Credit cards were maxed. Residents Bank had coldly attached their savings accounts and stock certificates; a result of Joe's ill-advised unconditional personal guarantee of the bank's two-million dollar loan to the business. All that was left in the Slattery family estate was a one hundred and fifty thousand dollar life insurance policy on Joe, and a few thousand in cash.

The shadows seemed to step back, clearing a path to the corner credenza still piled high with the trade magazines left behind. He glanced at the bottom drawer and rose unsteadily from the desk. The drawer slid open easily. He pushed aside two rolls of paper towels and reached back for the hidden bottle of 150-proof liquor the bankers hadn't yet discovered.

Bent over...the pressure in his temples fought to expand like a helium balloon entrapped in a boiling pressure-cooker. His legs weakened and gave; he tumbled awkwardly to the floor. When he finally managed to sit up, he was leaning against the sharp corner of the credenza. Next to his outstretched legs sat a white plastic bottle which had tumbled from his pocket. It contained thirty thumbnail-sized tablets of the strongest prescription available for a combination narcotic pain killer and amphetamine anti-depressant. The cotton-less bottle click-clicked as it dropped to his lap. He reached frantically in silent shadows for the liquor bottle, which had fallen to the carpet. He tore open the cap.

A short sip wet his tongue and lips. Then a five-second gulp ignited the nerves in his throat and stomach, causing his head to rocket back involuntarily against the sharp corner of the hard-wood credenza. The nauseating pain eventually dulled; replaced by a vivid, yet indescribable revelation that warmed the large blood-ball forming in the back of his head. Stars burst wildly behind Joe's closed lids...like a fireworks display celebrating the passionate conflict between the sharp pain ...from the impact...and a dull headache brought on by alcohol intemperance.

Joe reached out desperately in the darkness...for something...anything, to record this astounding revelation. This marvelous, crystal-clear image of the truth. He could finally understand... but not accept.

His outstretched fingers found only the pill bottle, with its easy-off cap.

Minutes later, the crystal truth drifted away forever with his ebbing consciousness: Joe Slattery would be remembered as a pitiful failure...because BoxMart's Chinese supplier paid its peasant workers two-dollars a day.

CHAPTER 4

(April 2, 2008)pm
Emei Shan, Sichuan Province, China

Lili Qi arrived at Emei Station in Baoguosi, the region's tourist center, at the base of Emei Shan, via the Kunming Express, as the sun disappeared behind misty caps. It was too late to prevent her uncle, Zhang, from chopping up her forty-six year old mother's body, and feeding it to the vultures nesting near the Yuxiansi…the Temple of Meeting Immortals, on the southern route to the 10,164 foot summit of Emei Shan.

Lili Qi's job as an English-speaking tour guide for the Beijing Tourist Bureau did not give her special traveling privileges. The government's relaxation of tourist policies only benefited a select twelve percent of the Chinese population, from thirty-two mainland cities, who'd been issued permanent travel papers. Despite her mother's critical condition, an unmarried middle-aged Beijing bureaucrat had delayed Lili's permit for travel to Sichuan Province. The sour-tempered woman resented the stunningly attractive tour-guide's popularity with the young men working at the travel bureau.

The twelve hundred mile trip southwest from Beijing, across the Provinces of Hebei, Shanxi, Henan, Hubei and Sichuan, by train and bus, was agonizingly slow. It was made more stressful when her uncle Zhang did not return her calls. He'd lost patience, and ignored her plea to wait until she returned.

Mount Emei, as it is called by foreign visitors to Sichuan Province, is famous for its snow capped peaks, lush forests, waterfalls and underground caves and rivers. It is also one of China's four "Buddhist Mountains," and has been considered a sacred place for pilgrims since the arrival of Buddhism in China at the end of the first century AD.

Located one-hundred and five miles southwest of Chengdu, the capital of Sichuan Province, Emei Shan is home to several Buddhist and Taoist temples, built between one and two thousand years ago. Visitors to the temples share the breathtaking views on the trails that lead to the top, with spring multi-colored rhododendrons, pillowed clouds, mystical suspended shadow-fog and the famous waist-high Emei monkeys, which roam the hills.

It had recently become well known in the thriving Chinese clothing industry, as the location of the most efficient tee-shirt factory in the manufacturing conglomerate controlled by generals of the People's Liberation Army. The government had relocated an east coast garment factory from the Shenzen industrial area to this remote region, in order to provide jobs for the unemployed peasants and farm-workers refusing to relocate to the big industrial cities.

Lili waited outside the train station as climbers and pilgrims dispersed from the train into the crowd of poets, artists and peasants jamming the area. Finally, her mother's best friend, Nin, appeared. The tall, starkly beautiful girl in her late teens had jet-black hair, triple-braided to shoulder length, and perfect features. Nin recognized the daughter from a photo Lili's mother, Buwei Qi, kept in the sparsely furnished factory dorm room they'd shared.

"You're more beautiful than my mother described," Lili exclaimed brightly, as Nin introduced herself, bowed, then suddenly wrapped her long thin arms around Lili, sobbing as her grip tightened with emotion. Lili held her gently. It seemed as if their hearts had instantly tethered a bond. Nin eased away, wiping tears, and studying Lili more carefully. She noticed the familiar warm, brown eyes and the high cheekbones. "Buwei was like a mother to me," she said sweetly. "My heart is broken."

Nin had been at Buwie's side when she died in the filthy infirmary room provided at the tee-shirt factory. She'd also witnessed the accident which had guillotined Buwei's right hand at the wrist. Nin was still wearing the unwashed, white cotton work shirt she'd worn that day. It was still spotted with the last drops of her friend's blood.

Frugal uncle Zhang peered out at his niece from a hidden corner of the train station, still too embarrassed to show his face. He was the only family member who could afford to pay for a proper cremation…the only method of burial the Communist government allowed for the majority of its citizens. But, Zhang did not want to spend his hard-earned savings that way. Instead, he'd purchased a large burlap sack and small containers of ginger and coriander-spiced incense; and followed the "sky burial" tradition, practiced for centuries by the mountain peasants in his family. Lili's offer to pay for her mother's cremation, if only he waited, went unheeded.

"Your uncle told me he brought Buwei to a summit," Nin explained, knowing Lili needed an explanation for her uncle's actions. "Mr. Zhang waited a week, but then became frightened of his ancestor's wrath. He said: 'Once the spirit has departed, a lifeless body is not important to Emei Shan believers, and should be disposed of quickly.'"

Lili remembered reading that Tibetans and native American Indian tribes had also used sky burials in the mountains of China, and in the high mesas of the southwest United States. They disposed of the dead by allowing vultures to consume all the fleshy parts, leaving only the bones.

A cool mountain breeze swept into the town, and convinced the two young women it would be pleasant to walk to the nearby Hongzhushan Hotel, the region's largest, where Lili had reserved a single room for three days. Nin joined Lili for dinner at the hotel, where they talked about childhood experiences, and ate steamed dumplings garnished with Sichuan hot peppers, seaweed soup and boiled rice. They drank warm rice wine in double-bottom cups, and sipped faintly sweet Litchi tea, as they marveled that they hadn't met before. Perhaps they passed by each other during family visits to the mountain temples; or on a sight-seeing trip to the colossal 12th century *Sitting Buddha of Jiading*, the 394-foot figure cut from rock overlooking the Min River, near Emei Shan. It was one of the famous Buddhist statues of China.

"My manager at the tourist office in Beijing offered to issue me a special travel permit to Emei Shan if I would accompany a group of European historians to the famous Buddhist statues of our country." She added mournfully, "It would have added weeks to my trip home. But I was still too late for uncle Zhang's conscience."

Lili told Nin about her training with the grand master of Juko-kai at the mountain monastery near Wanniansi, the Temple of Myriad Ages, when she was fifteen. By eighteen, she'd become only the second woman ever to attempt the Combat Ki Masters Test. She explained to Nin, "Vital internal energy and relaxation is summoned and used to prevent fatal damage to organs, when someone or something attacks you."

Lili explained that the Master and his ancestors at the temple had created a secret method to magnify the powers of Ki--vital energy; Jigo-Tai--defensive posture; and T'ai Chi--balance and graceful movement.

Nin winced at the story, so Lili did not explain how she'd been blindfolded, then kicked and punched by eight stations of attackers, some applying two thousand pound impacts with their feet and hands, all over her body. Sometimes an arm smashed at her throat and she faltered. But she had passed the Masters test---no internal injuries, no visible bruises, no broken bones.

"The grand master of Juko-kai, Zong Keba, had taken the name of the founder of the Yellow Hat sect of Tibetan Buddhism," Lili said proudly. "He adored me and taught me how to endure and prevail against surprise attacks."

Nin whispered, in amazement, "Life is full of surprise attacks."

Before the evening ended Lili and Nin were like sisters. Nin returned to the dorm room at the factory, and tucked her new twelve-year-old roommate and co-worker, Lihua, into bed for the night. Lihua would be busy tomorrow, packing tee-shirts for delivery to BoxMart distribution centers.

Lili showered for the first time in four days then collapsed on the small mattress. She couldn't stop thinking about Nin's recounting of her mother's accident, and how Buwei had quietly endured the pain and blood loss from the severed hand for three days, before her spirit was freed. Lili wept with pride at the thought of her mother's enormous internal courage. She also wept in anger at her needless accidental death. The factory manager had been too cheap to replace the worn spring on the fabric cutting machine Buwei operated; and too lazy to install safety stops. When the rusted steel spring broke, the heavy, razor-sharp cutting die plummeted.

The factory manager had been refused permission by the government officials ministering the factory, to pay for transferring Buwei to the surgical hospital in Chengdu, the capital city. Neither would they allow the doctor in the region to alter his medical rounds to treat Buwei before his regular Emei visit in a few days. After all, they reasoned, many of the workers had serious accidents. And an older woman, like Buwei, was not as productive as the younger girls, anyway.

The next morning was shrouded in mist as Lili set off to find her mother's bones. She packed bottled water, a hand towel from the room, and the red silk scarf her mother had given her last year for her twenty-fifth birthday. Her uncle, Zhang, finally emerged from his hiding place in the rice fields, just before Lili started searching for him. He shamelessly described the location, and the directions to the southern route, leading to the high cliff where he had placed Buwei's worthless remains.

It was mid-afternoon when Lili arrived at the cliff. She knelt at the overhang of the pine-adorned terrace near Yuxiansi, and peered down into the cloudy abyss. The area hid an ancient Taoist temple built by the Eastern Han Dynasty in the second century , and a troop of wandering Emie Shan monkeys. She squatted on the damp earth and rested. A strange serenity sifted in with the light fog, and engulfed her in cool mist.

She could sense the presence of ancestral ghosts, hiding somewhere in the area. She hoped one of them was her mother. Then she glanced around and saw the bones---lying randomly on the large burlap rice sack uncle Zang had used to carry Buwei to the summit. She covered her eyes with both hands, fell to her knees, and vomited.

    A minute later, loud flaps from a heavily winged menace grew louder. She looked up and saw a large vulture with a seven foot wing-span suddenly emerge from the fog, like a flying ghost ship, and land heavily on the burlap sack. Startled, Lili hurled her water bottle at the giant bird-of-prey. Its wings opened and closed in defiance, separating the damp air into deep, frightening vibrations. The preditor seemed to be protecting the bones by pecking violently at the rock ledge supporting the sack.

    Lili screamed as the giant bird suddenly sprung up and winged in her direction. With talons outstretched, the defiant vulture went for her hair, but veered skyward and disappeared into the fog when Lili dropped to the ground and covered her head with her arms.

    Lili remained motionless until she could no longer hear the bird in flight; then grasped the heavy walking stick her uncle had provided, and approached the bones. She knelt slowly…reluctantly…releasing the hardwood staff from her Juko-kai death grip. She slid the red silk scarf from her small knapsack and tied it tightly over her eyes.

    Following the grand-master's instructions, she commanded her neck, shoulder, thigh and calf muscles to relax; then inhaled rapidly and trapped moist air in her lungs, until the twenty-percent oxygen content in air was absorbed into her blood stream. Each time, nearly pure nitrogen gas exploded from her nose. This she repeated several times, before summoning the secret techniques taught to her by the grand master---which unleased the enormous reservoir of internal energy stored in her heart, mind and soul. Lili's chest pounded violently; veins swelled; relaxed muscles sprung to high tension. Attenuated brain waves interfered with satellite transmissions bouncing off Emei Shan. She felt the enormous surge of energy …a swirling gusto from the past engulfing her soul. Buwei suddenly appeared.

    Mother was wearing a bright violet silk gown and smiling lovingly. The vision of Buwei was so intense…so real. Lili tore off the red scarf…expecting to see her mother…expecting to take her in her arms.

    Instead, she watched helplessly. The bones and the burlap sack rolled over the side of the cliff and disappeared below, as an intense blast of cool air jetting down from above. Lili dropped the red scarf, and trembled. A troop of monkeys somewhere below howled in unison, as if each had been bitten by a devilish predator. She gazed in horror, as the precious gift from her mother was caught by a tail-gust from the same wind, and followed Buwei's bones over the edge.

The coal powered train pulled away from Emei Shan station, packed with pilgrims and tourists. Lili waved good-bye to Nin through the dusty window. The eastern sun projected etchings of greasy fingerprints and oily foreheads on the glass. Still, Nin had the appearance of an angelic nurse, not a stitcher of tee-shirts. She tearfully waved back, wearing the white cotton workshirt, now washed and starched, and void of Buwei's precious blood. She wondered if Lili would ever return.

The arduous trip back to Beijing required frequent stops, and changes in mode of transportation---from rail to bus, bus to rail and bus again. Finally, she was in a taxi heading for her small, two-room apartment near the new Silk Alley Mall building which abutted the U.S. embassy in Beijing's diplomatic district---one of the city's most popular tourist destinations.

The high rise mall had replaced the 150 open-air, make-shift stalls that once sold cheap counterfeit and pirated goods in the original Silk Alley marketplace, a few yards way. Despite endless rhetoric to the contrary, the local subdivision of the city government continued to look away from the obvious abuses of intellectual property rights, openly perpetrated by the merchants. Too much money was flowing into their Bank of China accounts.

Lili liked the location of her tiny apartment because she could walk to the tourist office on the ground floor of the mall building, where she reported each morning. Assignments consisted mainly in guiding English speaking tourists around city sites, such as: the Palaces of the Forbidden City, the Temple of Heaven, the Beijing Zoo, Ming Tombs and the Badaling Great Wall. Occasionally, she'd be assigned to assist other tour guides on sight-seeing trips to the ancient dynasty treasures in faraway provinces.

The U.S. Embassy frequently requested her services because she spoke perfect English. She was always warmly received by the constant influx of American and U.K. businessmen, who trawled China in search of the "callouses of gold," as her friend at the U.S. Embassy, Anthony J. Hau Luing, had tagged China's notorious low-cost skilled laborers.

Lili would be meeting with AJ soon, but not to discuss arrangements for pleasure trips. AJ had somehow discovered that part of Lili's job with the Beijing Tourist Bureau was to extract sensitive business information from American and European businessmen. Foreign operating plans for China-based facilities could be useful to her superiors at the Bureau; and to the Bureau Chief's superiors on the Standing Committee of the National People's Congress.

Lili entered her apartment after midnight, just as AJ Hau Luing was dialing her number…as if he knew the exact time of her arrival.

"Hi, Lili. I hope I didn't wake you," he said softly, knowing that he didn't. "How was your trip?"

Lili dropped her soft-fabric carrycase, and hesitated, before replying, "Our ancestors would probably be pleased that I went. But...I was too late." She caught herself beginning to tear. AJ sensed anguish in her reply and remained silent for nearly a minute, as she gathered her emotions. The barely audible *ting* in his phone indicated the conversation was still scrambled.

Finally, she answered, "AJ...I understand what you were asking. I accept your offer. When can we meet?"

He hadn't expected such a blunt and direct response to his "unofficial" inquiry. Something had occurred during the trip to Sichuan prompting her apparent willingness to switch allegiances. Perhaps a government action. Or, more likely, *Wu-Wei*...as the Chinese say...*action through in-action*. He felt it somehow related to her mother's death. Still, he had to be cautious. Lili was a low-level information gatherer, not a trained spy. But she could be very useful to the intelligence people housed in the embassy and scattered throughout the country. She spoke flawless English, perfect Putonghua---the national language commonly referred to as Mandarin---in all four tones; as well as the ten major Chinese dialects.

She'd mastered the world's oldest continuously used language, with its un-phonetic alphabet of *ideographs*, denoting objects, actions and abstract ideas in 5,000 different artsy squiggles, when her Juko-kai master arranged... through a benefactor...to send her to Beijing University to study language history. Her unknown benefactor was the Minister of State Security in Hubei Province. He was paying a debt to the grand master for training his best officers in the art of Juko-kai.

AJ thought quickly. "How about Beihai Park, in front of the Nine-Dragon Screen? I heard it deflects evil spirits that fly only in a straight line." He added ruefully, "Like bullets." Lili was familiar with the proposed meeting place. They could easily be spotted if anyone was interested in their relationship. The Dragon screen was sixteen feet high and ninety feet long. Something told her to meet elsewhere, and to end the call.

"I'll be at the West Chang'an Avenue McDonalds at twelve fifteen tomorrow." It was nestled among other garish, neon facades in one of Beijing's busiest shopping streets. "See you then." She pressed the red button before he could reply.

AJ smiled at the thought of conspiring with Lili. Good agents could come from the strangest places.

CHAPTER 5

(April 2, 2008) 3 pm
North Haven, Connecticut

Justin Gatt, the founder and CEO of Gatt Recovery Technologies, Inc., rushed into the spacious interior conference room of the GRT headquarters in North Haven to join the other managers. The emergency meeting had been precipitated by a "Notice of Loan Default" hand-delivered the previous day by a courier from the Residents Bank of North America. His pained expression was void of color. Normally bright blue eyes were buoys of dark sea water.

Gatt stood at the head of the long conference table for a moment, then settled clumsily into the chair without speaking. His best friend, Bob Somersall, the company attorney called in for the emergency meeting, was alarmed.

"Hey, friend, it's only a financial hit. Nobody died."

Justin glanced up at Sumersall with a blank expression, and said sadly, "I just got a call from Slattery's plant manager, Tim Corran. Tim was kept on by the bank after the bankruptcy, to help liquidate equipment." He faced across the table. Joanna Yates, the chief financial officer looked up. "Joe Slattery is dead, Joanna." She'd worked closely with the Slattery people when they got into financial trouble, and Justin knew she'd be shaken the most.

"Oh, my God," she bellowed, straining to gather her emotions. She was first to ask everyone's irrelevant question, "How?"

"Tim says he came in early and found Joe on the floor in his old Leominster office. He must have used a spare key, and returned at night when nobody was around."

"He had a bad heart, and diabetes." Joanna remembered sadly.

"Tim says the paramedics on the scene think he died of respiratory failure, and subsequent cardiac arrest. I guess he was drinking again."

Justin didn't need to reveal more than the partial truth. Tim had informed him, in confidence, that there was an empty pill bottle and a few pills on the floor next to the body. Tim was a good friend of the Slattery family, and knew they'd been wiped out financially. He'd risked a police charge of evidence-tampering, when he removed the empty pill bottle. Joe had mentioned the insurance policy a few days earlier.

The collective silence in the conference room suggested that the GRT managers were no longer furious at the man who'd brought their company to the brink of disaster. Justin's mind was in neutral. He listened through the adjoining wall to the comforting whirling and clanging of twenty-five plastic injection molding machines, still stamping out GRT's proprietary plastic containers. Unfortunately, the company's main processing equipment—the large compounding machines which produced most of the company's profit---sat idle in the back room of the factory.

Justin was deeply troubled, trying to rationalize what happened to Joe. They hadn't been close friends, but Joe gained his respect for many years of hard work and dedication, building SHC into the largest privately owned housewares manufacturer in New England. Last year SHC had earned a plum, at least they thought. BoxMart Retail Enterprises had approved Slattery's new line of household products, and had placed the largest order in company history. An unexpected breakthrough!

Joe'd invested heavily in new molding and packaging equipment, supposedly to meet the quantity requirements. BoxMart had become the fastest growing, most profitable discount chain in the world; second in total revenues to WalMart.

Joanna returned from the ladies room bleary-eyed, and announced stoically, "We have to deal with today's problems, gentlemen. We can't let what happened to Slattery happen to us."

"You're right," the sales manager responded. "It's just hard to understand why BoxMart suddenly cancelled the order. Those hard-asses had no quality problems or pricing issues that I'm aware of."

"We supplied Slattery with more than a million and a half pounds of plastic materials for the BoxMart order," the production manager boasted.

"And haven't received a penny in payment," Joanna replied painfully.

Bob Somersall didn't have to remind them, but did anyway, "Residents Bank is now coming after us. As soon as Slattery folded, the $1.3 million receivable on our books from SHC became worthless. Christ, they didn't waste a second to inform us that we're in default on a loan covenant. In the bank's eyes, the asset is already deducted from our balance sheet. That causes our asset–to–liabilities ratio to drop below the minimum requirement of 1.2 to 1.0."

Joanna did the calculations, and corrected him gently. "That causes a default on two of the loan covenants, Bob. The acid ratio you mentioned, and the quarterly profit requirement." Justin remembered the wording in the loan documents. "We can't have two consecutive quarters with losses. Tinius is sure to book half the $1.3 million loss in each of the last two quarters. Their auditors will overlay $650,000 in quarterly losses on each bottom line."

"It more than wipes out our regular quarterly profits," Joanna frowned.

The sales manager was still puzzled by the unexpected and unexplained order cancellation by BoxMart. "I remember reading in the Wall Street Journal that BoxMart is now second to Wal-Mart, and gaining rapidly, in U.S. retail sales. They've become the largest importer of consumer items from China. Somehow, they've figured a way to offer lower prices than any other competitor."

Justin angrily conjectured a reason, "They've struck the mother-load in cash flow management and risk avoidance. The financial burden of stocking product on their shelves has been deftly shifted to suppliers and sub-suppliers---like Slattery and us. It's a win-win arrangement, with both wins going to the retailer."

The production manager shifted in his seat uncomfortably, and said, "I have to go supervise the shift change, even though we're only running the molding lines." His mocking tone reminded everyone that he hadn't agreed with the decision to give Slattery such long payment terms.

Justin countered, "Let it go for a few minutes, Hank. We need to decide, as a team, how to respond to the bank's default letter."

The intercom interrupted Gatt's anticipated plea for a team-inspired solution to the loan problem.

"Mr. Gatt, I'm sorry to interrupt your meeting," the receptionist apologized. "There's another delivery from a Residents Bank courier. Someone needs to sign proof of receipt."

Joanna rushed out as the others began to discuss options. She returned a few minutes later. Her pace and complexion could have been that of a drugged anemic. "Another notice from Tinius," is all she could muster. She handed the registered letter to the nearest manager.

"Ouch!" he blurted after reading the first two-paragraphs. He handed the document to Justin.

The others watched their leader as he read. They were surprised at his lack of body movement. "It's about what I expected." He calmly handed the letter to the attorney. Joanna couldn't hold back. "We all got into trouble with the same bank. They must be hard-wired to every BoxMart supplier who loses an order." The statement---almost a question---required a few moments of reflection.

Justin studied Somersall's reaction to the letter: the clamped mouth, deep breathing and professional frown. He recalled how the BoxMart buyer had practically forced him to deal with Tinius' bank.

"I remember the BoxMart buyer's exact words during his supplier-qualification tour of our facilities:'Residents Bank understands our needs for expeditious transactions. We strongly recommend you call Edwin Tinius for your working capital requirements.'"

Somersall finished reading the notice, then turned to Gatt and said, "April seventh. That's less than a week away." He paused, then passed the letter to the others.

The spigot of emotional responses opened wide.

"This can't be happening."

"Are they serious? It can't be done."

"They know that."

"That only gives us five days."

"They know that."

"We need more time. The back-to-school season could pull us out of this mess."

"I think they know that, too."

"What should we do?"

"What *can* we do?"

Somersall shouted above the clamor. "There's only one option, people."

The others quieted, as he nodded to Justin, and confirmed a discussion they'd had when the first notice arrived. "We're screwed, unless the bank gives us more time; which I doubt, based on the second notice they've dumped on us today."

"Okay, the meeting is adjourned." Justin stood, signaling it was time for the others to leave. "Bob and I will take it from here."

He and Somersall remained in the conference room, as the others dutifully wandered off to contemplate the likelihood of a distressing lifestyle adjustment in the near future.

Somersall dialed a cell number and waited for the attorney at the other end to pick up. He said to Justin, as they waited, "Ken Levine is the most competent bankruptcy attorney around. He knows the bankruptcy laws and negotiating tactics better than the judges."

Levine felt the vibration in his chest, and pressed the off-button through his cotton shirt pocket. He didn't want the ring to interrupt the negotiating session he was just completing in a side room of the Federal Bankruptcy Courtroom, located in the Connecticut Financial Center building, across from the green in downtown New Haven.

As they waited for the return call from Levine, the two friends talked about old times and young girlfriends. But the subject inevitably drifted back to the present. Justin recalled a discussion with professor Syzmansky at Yale about some of the key players in the retailing industry.

"A guy named Rand Kurancy built BoxMart from a regional peanut and dry goods distributor, into this massive chain of discount super stores. He visited Yale School of Management for a Chief Executives'conference hosted by Professor Syzmansky, last year." Justin recalled. "Kurancy boasted how the most successful 'big box' discount chains will eventually dominate retail sales in every corner of the globe, sooner than later."

Somersall had read a recent article on BoxMart in the Wall Street Journal. "They're now, supposedly, the largest private importer in this country. They buy and sell more Chinese-made goods than any other retailer. What purchasing power!"

"Yeah, but their draconian methods are causing an avalanche of exterminated American businesses," Justin said bitterly. "The government does nothing to help. The message small manufactures are receiving is: *You're not important enough to bother with. Either adjust to global conditions, without our help, or go out of the business.* Someone should investigate."

Somersall's cellphone chimed. "Hello, Ken. Fine…They are too. How's your wife and daughter?" Small talk between busy lawyers is never more than two sentences. "It's about my client, Gatt Recovery Technologies. You may have heard about them. Yes, the high-tech recycling company run by Justin Gatt." Bob explained the situation then handed the phone to Justin.

"Hi, Mr.Gatt. Bob said you received two notifications from Residents Bank. Could you read them to me, please?"

As soon as Justin mentioned Edwin Tinius, and the April seventh deadline, Ken was speeding north on Route 91 in his gas guzzling SUV, with the "for sale" sign taped to the back window.

CHAPTER 6

(April 2, 2008) noon,
Beijing

AJ Hau Luing arrived at the crowded West Chang'an Avenue restaurant one minute before his shadow.

By twelve fifteen, the crowd waiting to be served had packed the restaurant. They chatted food orders, sports results and weather predictions loud enough to drown out any form of eavesdropping. Lili had chosen a good place to meet.

He sat at a table far from the entrance and glanced casually through the crowd at the low-level security agent who'd been following him for a month. The man was wearing the same padded brown jacket with the high mandarin collar, and had his hands tucked up inside the long sleeves, as usual. His wrap-around sunglasses hid the satisfied expression of Chinese Communist Party eyes. They were selfless, and committed to the cause.

The middle-aged man of undistinguishable appearance and manner peered in from the garish facade of McDonald's busiest unit on Beijing's busiest shopping street, and decided to observe his target from street-side. His job was to follow the U.S. Embassy employee, and report any suspicious movements or meetings which suggested the employee was engaging in espionage. It was standard practice. The Beijing Security Ministry kept track of all foreign embassy personnel this way. So far, AJ had displayed no suspicious actions, so the shadow was not equipped with the surveillance device needed to hear his conversations from a distance.

By twelve twenty-five, AJ had eaten his spring roll, tofu burger and french fries. He wondered if Lili would show. It was a dangerous situation for both of them, and he wouldn't be surprised if she'd decided against the meeting at the last moment. The shadow wouldn't be surprised to see her, because he'd already witnessed their conversations at the Tourist Bureau's receptions for customers from the U.S. Embassy. He would report that their meeting and conversation were "suspicious."

At twelve thirty, a soft-spoken factory worker sitting at the next table asked AJ to pass the *shi-yau*. The elderly woman with the weathered face asked again, but instead of repeating the Cantonese term for regular soy sauce, she said *sheng-ch'ou*, the Mandarin term for first quality soy sauce. AJ noticed that the woman was bundled in a black overcoat, with a grey scarf covering her head and a cotton surgical mask partially lowered to her chin. He recognized the eyes.

"Here, madam." He answered in Cantonese, using the high pitched tone, which signified that 'Madam' was important. Then he looked away casually.

The elderly woman took the bottle and splashed the dark sauce over Shanghai noodles and a chunky, full bodied soup. She dipped a few of the famous french fries into the soup, then whispered in Cantonese, "You remind me of my grandson. He speaks Hunan dialect."

Hau Ling understood. He'd also studied Chinese dialects at the Institute of Asian Languages. It was unlikely that anyone in the vicinity of their conversation would understand their muffled exchange.

"And you remind me of my grandmother, from Emei Shan." He answered in quiet Hunan dialect.

Lili slurped loudly, the traditional signal of respect from Chinese diners that the soup is hot and tasty. Then she said in a low voice, "I believe you're being followed."

"I know. He's seen us together in the past---he's just a third-class trailer. We can talk."

Lili slurped again. "If I do this, we cannot be seen together in the future."

AJ was impressed with her covert instincts. If she was suspected of aiding a U.S. Embassy official, she'd suddenly disappear, and likely be executed without hesitation or trial.

"Agreed. But I reserve the right to marry you in another country."

Lili choked on the soup. Cadres and students at the neighboring tables began to laugh as she covered her mouth with the large white plastic soup spoon. The shadow was now positioned just inside the entrance to the restaurant, sipping oolong tea and looking directly at AJ---the only person not laughing at the choking old lady.

"There's a note and a secure communications unit in this bag. I'll drop it on the floor as I leave. Wait a few minutes to pick it up. The note gives the location of a contact point, and the method to use for dropping off information for our analysts. The secure communications unit will page me whenever you call in. I will be your only contact. If I'm not available, for any reason, you are to pass along information only to a visiting American businessman, who will be identified to you later. Just so you know---Forrest Balzerini, the U.S. Ambassador to China, is my direct supervisor. He is the only other Embassy official you should trust, if you run into danger."

He hesitated, then said in a barely audible tone, "We've uncovered evidence that certain Chinese Communist leaders may be plotting to damage the U.S. economy. Worse…we believe several American businessmen are involved."

He looked away to the next table, smiled and circled his hand over his belly. The students smiled in return, as they set down full trays of the new ethnic delicacies the fast-food chain now offered to the Chinese masses.

"Some of the suspect businessmen, mostly executives or retired executives from large corporations, will be visiting China as part of a U.S. trade mission now being planned for early August. We want to make certain you are part of the tour guide program."

He then alluded to unknown events. "We don't know what, how, or when…something bad may happen…exactly. The intelligence people are deep diving for additional leads. They suspect the timing may be right after the Beijing Olympics, or just before the American presidential elections. A prominent candidate may be in danger."

The shadow moved toward AJ's table in a blatant effort to determine why AJ's lips were moving as he stared at the food. When AJ looked up, he retreated to his former observation post near the street entrance.

"I'll tell you more later. Be careful. This information was obtained from assets in the field, who, unfortunately, have recently disappeared."

The weathered old woman nodded, as if saluting the noodles dangling above a styrofoam bowl from the ends of her plastic chopsticks.

"What do you want me to do?"she whispered apprehensively.

AJ spoke rapidly, having noticed the shadow staring at the woman. "It's all in the note…in the bag…written in an ancient Mongol language you will understand. Memorize the information and destroy the note. The SCU looks and functions exactly like a regular cell phone made in China, except a code will connect it to the embassy's encrypted communications system."

Lili wanted to assure him of her sincerity. "I love my country, AJ. That's why I'm here. The greed and corruption of our high ranking, privileged Communist leaders is destroying the peasant people's will to better themselves."

The noodles slid from her suddenly placid grip on the plastic chopsticks, and dropped into the bowl. The shadow noted the strange occurrence, but could not connect it as a significant incident involving his target, who was sitting close to the old women's table, but looking away, and sometimes joking with the students.

"They must be stopped," Lili whispered, "or they'll climb the backs, and chop off the hands of the peasants….and poor women…. and helpless young girls."

AJ could feel her sudden anguish, and sensed it was more than the loss of her mother. A surge of sadness reminded him how difficult it was going to be to suspend all physical contact with Lili, until her assignment was completed. If it was successful, he realized, she might have to leave the country. He began to wonder, for the first time, if he was in love with this sweet girl from Emai Shan; who had mastered a dozen languages… and the mysterious and deadly martial art of Juko-kai.

He smiled at the students sitting at the next table, and commented on their hearty appetites. As he stood to leave…the bag fell to the floor.

(April 2, 2008) 7:30am
BoxMart Headquarters, Massachusetts

Heironymus Cashman, the BoxMart CFO who controlled millions in daily cash flow transactions, pushed the food cart containing two dozen baked oysters, scalli toast and an assortment of fresh fruit, surrounding a silver and gold pot of steaming Turkish coffee. He was eager to report the good news to the Chairman.

He tapped the brass dollar sign on the nine-foot, hand carved oak door, and waited to deliver the Chairman's usual breakfast, which he'd just commandeered from Jake Kurancy's personal assistant.

Rand "Jake" Kurancy, the founder and Chairman of BoxMart RE discount stores, clicked off the buzzer then pressed the 'OP DR' button on his communications and access control console. The front door swung open.

He sat up groggily on the $7,000 Marrakesh influenced, Italian handcrafted maple and cherry veneer, king poster bed. His private five room suite at the company-owned guest house, attached to the headquarters building by an underground tunnel, was replete with similarly hand-crafted furniture. Definitely not discount priced.

He was still bone-weary from a hectic schedule of private jet visits to several western retail outlets, and the late night arrival at BoxMart's campus, 30 miles northwest of Boston. Store managers in Spokane, Seattle, Portland, Boise, Fresno, Bakersfield, Yuma, Los Cruces and Odessa, Texas had elated him with sales and profits well above budget. The competition from small retailers in the west was disappearing as fast as Cashman had predicted.

Same-store sales in the Riverside, California to Medford, Oregon region had increased eight to ten percent, as well. If they could sustain this performance, BoxMart Retail Enterprises would soon be the sales leader in the Western States retail market.

"The temporary dockworkers slowdown in Long Beach is ended, at least for us,"Cashman informed his boss enthusiastically, as he rolled the food cart to the glass dining table, set in front of 14 foot, shatter-proof double French doors, which overlooked the expansive manicured lawn of the BoxMart campus. The historic Massachusetts towns of Essex and Gloucester were lively with early spring tourists, about twenty miles east.

Kurancy was dressed in cuffed, black cotton pants, an emerald-green satin shirt with a *BM* embroided above the company's unusual *Liger* emblem, and size fourteen, perforated Gucci leather and suede loafers.

"I thought the strike was still on," the huge man with the threatening disposition snickered. "It's costing us a fortune to sit on those containers for an extra week."

Cashman poured coffee and rotated the food plate so that the fresh oysters were closest to Kurancy. He'd settle for the toast and fruit. Jake flashed steel grey eyes, shaded by dark, bushy eyebrows, and lowered his perfectly round, bald head an inch above the raw seafood, before slurping down several of the pearl-less nutrients. His massive head nested on enormous neck-less shoulders, and was humorously accentuated by un-naturally small ears. Curly tufts of fine, red-tinged hair peeked from his collar.

At six-foot five and nearly three hundred pounds, Kurancy reminded his oriental partners of Buddha, except for the tiny ears. In Buddhist iconography, large ears were symbolic of wisdom. During the early stages of the Vietnam War, LBJ had been unaware that he was the brief beneficiary of that cultural concept; until many Americans and Asians alike soon viewed his large ears as plugged receptacles.

"Our containers have been moved to the front unloading yards, and are now leaving the port for our distribution centers every five minutes," Cashman bragged.

"Cost?" Kurancy inquired indifferently, as he bit into a huge slice of melon.

"The California dockworker's benevolent fund is two hundred thousand dollars richer."

"Cheap enough," replied Kurancy.

"That's not all." The handsome Greek with the dark, sharply honed features, and a 1990 graduate degree from London School of Business, added proudly, "Several truckloads of our competitor's Asian merchandise will be delayed in port for an additional week."

Jake looked up from the small demitasse tilted below his bulbous nose. "How'd you pull that one off?"

"We gave several truck drivers from Atlanta, Plano and Chicago a thousand in cash, to call in sick."

At eight am---the computer screen in Kurancy's private office logged on automatically. Sales and profit reports from all the BoxMart stores spewed from the high speed laser printer, and were automatically collated by geographical district. Kurancy scanned the bottom lines of several district summary reports. He spot-checked the sales figures from a few of the three thousand and eighty individual store locations in the BoxMart chain, to determine if the bad weather predicted for those locations had resulted in the expected sales increases of weather-related goods.

Cashman looked up from his copy of the report, and said, "We've surpassed all other retailers in sales of umbrellas, raincoats, and suntan lotion, not to mention last winter, when our northeast and mid-west stores took first in snow-blowers, shovels, boots and winter clothing."

At nine am---the printer began delivering financial reports, including cash balances in various bank accounts throughout the world. Legal tender exchange-reports converted the company's yuan, euro, yen, pound and peso balances in various foreign accounts, into U.S. dollar equivalents. Cashman would be exchanging between ten and twenty percent of these foreign denominations for dollars, which would be wired to various bank accounts in the States by the end of the day. The balance would remain in local currencies for use at the retailing and distribution centers in the countries of origin.

The new supercomputer and proprietary software installed below the headquarters building a few hundred feet away, also calculated daily profit and loss statements for each store and region, as well as real-time balance sheets, with year-to-date, month-to-date and day-to-date comparisons with last year's results.

At ten am--- The president of Li Chin Industries, the largest manufacturing conglomerate in mainland China, called from the LCE management center in Nanjing, China to confirm that Li Chin, the CEO of LCE, and his assistant would be arriving at Logan International Airport at 3pm the next day. She appreciated Mr. Kurancy's assurance that Mr. Li and his assistant would receive the honor of being met at the airport by the Chairman himself, and transported comfortably to the BoxMart offices for scheduled meetings.

"I always look forward to Chairman Li's visits." Kurancy assured the formidable lady executive. Cashman, who was about to leave for a staff meeting in his office across the tunnel remarked, "Mr. Li and the People's Liberation Army generals now control more than five hundred mainland Chinese factories."

Jake spooned fresh horseradish over the last three oysters, and swallowed them as smoothly as a pit viper devours a rat. "Twenty two years ago, I helped

Li Chin build his export business," he recalled fondly. "At the time, LCE owned a small shoe factory in Fujian, and a metal casting and chrome-plating facility in the rust belt region north of Beijing, in Hebei Province."

Cashman was well aware of the history. Kurancy and Li Chin had supported each other's unprecedented growth for many years. He also knew that previous deals paled in comparison to the business transaction they were about to complete.

"LCE is now the world's dominant manufacturer of footwear," Jake noted with the satisfied tone of a proud parent. "Something like seven billion pairs of shoes, sneakers and boots last year. They own ninety two point six percent of the American market."

Jake had a photographic memory for sales numbers. He knew the sales and gross profit figures for thousands of products sold at BoxMart stores, including locally sourced and ethnically targeted items.

"LCE and its subsidiaries produce the most of almost everything they make." He marveled. "Sporting goods, small appliances, HD TVs, electronic games…toys. Almost anything made from plastic and rubber. We sell their tires, garden hose, printers and PCs. They're even taking over the housewares business in the States, which has traditionally been locally sourced because of the bulkiness and low profitability of most items."

Cashman said enthusiastically, "If there's a market, LCE will make the product…even if they have to steal the designs."

Jake smiled. He'd helped Li Chin's industrial spies do that many times.

"A division of LCE," he continued, "has recently become the first China-based Tier One supplier for instruments and other electronic components used in foreign car and truck factories operating in China. They're rapidly acquiring the advanced manufacturing techniques of the big U.S., Japanese, German and Korean automakers. Otherwise, it would take them a decade to duplicate this technology on their own."

Kurancy's enthusiasm bubbled over, as he added, knowingly, "Next will be an amazing micro-car we're going to sell for them in the United States." Then he regretted the comment, even to this high ranking executive. "That's highly speculative, of course, and confidential, Cashman. Forget I mentioned it." It was not a casual suggestion.

Kurancy's earlier commitment to purchase as many consumer items as possible from his Chinese friends had caught the eye of high level Communist leaders in the Politboro, who benefitted financially from ties with LCE. They granted the burgeoning BoxMart discount chain special price concessions; a strategy still supported by General Ye Kunshi, and the other military and civilian officials controlling the majority of state-run businesses.

The Chinese desperately needed the merchandising foothold BoxMart provided in the ten trillion dollar American consumer market. Their massive trade surplus with the U.S. was filling the coffers of the four central banks in China, and the French bank in Lyon, with American dollars.

Kurancy had expertly leveraged these price advantages into record-breaking sales events. BoxMart consistently offered the lowest advertised prices, as if the merchandise managers were aware of competitive loss-leader prices ahead of weekly newspaper inserts. Only Wal-Mart, Kurancy's former employer, was not muscled aside in the fierce battle for market share. The two retailing giants seemed to coexist in an uneasy, unspoken, semi-competitive relationship. Retail analysts at the big brokerage houses speculated that a secret edict had been issued by Kurancy's former boss: he wouldn't crush BoxMart if Kurancy avoided the prime locations chosen for future superstores. The analysts suspected that Kurancy had helped formulate his former employer's growth strategy, and was cognizant of which locations to skirt. BoxMart vehemently denied that such a relationship existed.

"Are we on schedule for the new Super-Boxes in China, India and Australia?" Kurancy shouted vociferously as Cashman eased toward the front door.

"Yes, except construction in India has slowed," Cashman answered. "International expansion is still the key, if we want to remain the fastest growing discount chain."

"We're still only the second largest retailer in the world." Kurancy scowled.

"But gaining fast," Cashman spouted over his shoulder. "Number one doesn't seem to be concerned, for some reason. Maybe its arrogance, or overconfidence." He alluded to the rumors: "You'd know better than anyone."

"Combined," Jake declared bombastically, "we account for more than 25 percent of total consumer purchases of non-durable goods in the U.S."

Jake detected the humming of the printer, as it collected and memorized additional data before tonguing out new reports. "We also share almost ten percent of consumer purchases in the developed and emerging countries." He smiled pompously. "Every competitor within ten miles of our stores is in trouble."

"Destroying competition is the name of the game," replied Cashman. "Every general merchandise store, home improvement center, drug store and supermarket is fair game."

"Fortunately for us," Kurancy spewed with enthusiasm, "the consumer markets in the U.S., and in other developed countries, are so huge and diversified that even the spectacular growth of BoxMart has been a third page story in the financial and business publications."

Cashman's last words as he headed for the tunnel were, "If the Journal knew the purpose of your meeting today with Li Chin, and the planned outcome, Wall Street would spotlight our new venture for weeks."

Li Chin and Kurancy had agreed, in principle, to an astoundingly aggressive plan. But a few details still had to be decided. The venture was so large, it could change the monetary dynamics between the world's two most influential trading countries. So important to China's trade policy, that it would require the approval of the Standing Committee of the Chinese Communist Party.

Kurancy dreamed of dominating global retail trade. If the venture went as planned, BoxMart and its Chinese partners would be creating the largest business enterprise ever tolerated by the international community. One that could never be surpassed.

At 11:30 am---Kurancy received a call on his secure phone line from Owlin Pickett, the Government Affairs Officer for BoxMart, recently hired away from a large defense contractor. Pickett reported that his morning meeting in Washington with the U.S. Trade Representative, Butler Humphreys, and the U.S. Ambassador to China, Forrest Balzerini, did not go well. They'd pushed hard for voluntary cutbacks in the relentless stream of consumer goods BoxMart was importing from China.

"I suggest we seriously consider their proposal, Mr. Kurancy," the black executive with eloquent manners and a Mr. America build cautioned his new boss. Pickett was seasoned in the art of government relations, and had nurtured valuable political and military contacts in Washington, DC. Kurancy despised and avoided politicians and government officials, the reason he hired Pickett to fill the gap in high-level government relations at BoxMart.

"There are some in Washington, Mr Kurancy, who are overly sensitive to the spiraling job losses in the manufacturing sector, and the massive balance of trade deficits burdening the country."

"We'll certainly consider your suggestion, Owlin. Why don't you remain in D.C. for a few more days? Contact some of your friends at the Pentagon. Ask them to help relieve the pressure. We save them lots of money in clothing costs for military personnel. Good thing there aren't any viable domestic suppliers, anymore, or the armed services would be forced to pay twice as much for military garments."

Pickett agreed to pursue the D.C. contacts, but didn't believe it would do much good. Neither did Jake. As the conversation ended, Jake didn't bother mentioning to Pickett that his suggestion could have been acted upon last month, but it was now too late.

Powerful people were committed to a plan that would have the opposite result. BoxMart would be more, not less, closely linked to its low-cost Chinese suppliers. The free flow of Chinese goods into the United States would continue unabated.

If all went as planned, the palliative measures about to be activated by members of the Savoy Imperative…designed to temporarily disrupt the American economy in a controlled fashion… would end the incessant cries for limits on Chinese imports….at minimum human distress for most Americans.

CHAPTER 7

(April 2, 2008) pm
North Haven, Ct.

"Most banks wouldn't move so quickly to shutter a successful business like yours," Ken explained, as he placed his polished aluminum briefcase gently on the conference table and settled into the chair next the Justin. He gestured with open hands for Justin to respond.

"GRT has a long-standing history of financial stability," Justin began. "That lousy bastard Tinius moved on us for no good reason." He sipped the twenty ounce black coffee Ken had thoughtfully brought, and continued. "We're in default primarily because of the *current ratio* covenant in the loan agreement. Consecutive quarterly losses may also be a factor, depending upon how the bank treats the Slattery receivable of about $1.3 million. When they deduct this amount from our current assets, we dip below the minimum 1.2 to 1.0 loan requirement."

He shifted some papers to find the list of sales projections, and proclaimed sourly, "Last week, when the bank examiners reviewed our projections for the next two quarters, they acknowledged that we would likely correct the loan default within a few months. That's when our most profitable, back-to-school season for molded products kicks in."

Ken unlatched the lid of his briefcase and lifted it slowly, as if to reveal a stash of valuables. He pulled out a standard bankruptcy filing form.

"Don't you still owe them almost a million?" He'd already contacted Hyman First, the bank's New Haven attorney, on the way to the meeting. Ken and Hyman were members of a small band of legal protagonists and antagonists, which made up central Connecticut's bankruptcy attorney forum. They always returned the other guy's call immediately.

Justin hesitated, then answered unconvincingly, "I can raise that much pretty fast, if I have to."

Ken looked directly into Justin's deep blue, worried eyes. He thought to himself, *Here's a guy who deserves a chance to save his business. He's probably busted his ass and committed everything he owns to making the business a success.*

The bankruptcy attorney repeated an earlier thought, "Most banks would cooperate, if the seasonal business you talk about is historically consistent. Forcing a company into bankruptcy," he emphasized with a brush of his hand, "is usually the least desirable method for recouping a bank's loan losses. That is…if the company is reasonably viable."

The burly, 39 year old former college lacrosse star said confidently, "But I've seen this bank operate lately. Ever since they bought out most of the small, state-chartered commercial banks in the northeast, they've been on a vendetta to jettison struggling manufacturing businesses. Hyman First, who I've dealt with before, claims the parent bank in Europe has demanded that Residents reduce its troubled-loans portfolio by fifty percent. I just can't figure their strategy."

He reached for his own black decaf and one of the sugar-free jelly donuts just introduced by a large coffee and donut chain. "I wasn't aware that Residents Bank has a European parent."

Ken then placed the Chapter Eleven filing papers in front of Justin, along with a copy of *Collier's Bankruptcy Terms and Filing Procedures*, and a CD disc of the standard Collier computer program used by most bankruptcy attorneys.

"I don't think Tinius will back off his demand for immediate and full payment of the million." He conjectured, "You'd better review this information before we decide how best to respond to his demand letter. You'll need the program disc if we have to file."

He paused reflectively. "There's still a chance the bank will give you more time, according to Hyman, who expects to be assigned your case. He's next in line at Wilton, Stash and Hilton, the firm that handles lawsuits for Residents Bank."

Justin stared ominously at the forms. "We've already presented seasonal projections to their financial people." He sighed. "Any accountant half-wit would conclude that GRT could fix the ratio default within six months."

He was more angry than frustrated. Twenty-two years of consistent growth and profitability meant nothing to Residents Bank, or to any large bank, in today's cut-throat business environment. "The young studs running banks today could care less about how their decisions impact small businesses," he complained. "It's all about large multi-nationals…mergers and acquisitions…and big depositors."

It hadn't always been that way. A few years ago, a small local bank, now absorbed by Residents Bank, had treated GRT like a partner in the community. Today, Tinius and his cohorts made small business borrowers feel puny, like distant relatives begging for a handout from a lottery winner.

Ken stared lasciviously into the open briefcase at the new pack of Newports nesting in a business card compartment. He closed the case and rejected the temptation once again.

"It sounds like a reasonable argument, Mr. Gatt, but Tinius is not a reasonable banker. They've filed so many foreclosure actions against small manufacturers, based mostly on technical defaults in loan agreements, that Judge Rooter has quietly asked the attorney general of Connecticut to investigate. Tinius was warned of the judge's concern, but didn't seem to care." Ken stood and started circling the room, deep in thought.

"As I said earlier," he interjected, "Residents Bank is not acting like a reasonable bank. Here's what I suggest we do to protect GRT's interests."

When Ken left the office two hours later, Justin decided to walk out to the factory for his usual brief meeting with Roberto, the second shift molding department foreman. He couldn't resist wandering into the back room, to agonize over the idle compounding equipment which produced GRT's remarkably high-quality recycled compounds. Roberto followed at a distance. He appreciated the boss's frequent appearances in the factory during off-hours. It demonstrated management's interest in his work.

Justin's thoughts drifted to Joe Slattery's wife and three children… and his dreaded wake, as he stood motionless among the big machines that had churned new life into cast-off materials. Joe's family lost everything when he gambled so much on one customer; and agreed to the adamant, yet unjustified, demand of an inexperienced BoxMart purchasing manager, that he immediately modernize Slattery's manufacturing facilities. The young pock-faced buyer in his late twenties, had no manufacturing experience and no knowledge of the output rate of Slattery's current machinery. He simply wanted to see gleeming new processing and packaging equipment at his suppliers' facilities. Following home-office instructions, he'd also demanded that Residents Bank be used to finance the expansion. Slattery had been so excited by the enormous BoxMart order that he hadn't bothered to check with other local manufacturers, who'd also received unexpectedly large orders from BoxMart. Most had also received shocking cancellations.

Justin returned to the dim lights of the conference room, following a brief exchange with Roberto in broken-Portuguese. He leaned back in the worn, incredibly-comfortable maroon leather executive chair he'd purchased fifteen years ago, and wistfully admired the gigantic world map his employees had given him last Christmas.

Pasted in congruent sections on an entire wall of the conference room, the torso sized continents in bright primary colors seemed raised from the surface. The entire world was before his wary eyes. Just looking at the deep green and lightened blue-green shades of the oceans surrounding the land masses, calmed his frazzled nerves. The world seemed to be shrinking each time he studied the map.

His eyes drifted ruefully back and forth between the United States and China; trying to picture more than two thousand cargo container ships dotting the Pacific. He wondered how many would be loaded with plastic housewares and other consumer products formerly produced at American factories. They were probably made at the famous Suzhou Industrial Complex, fifty miles west of Shanghai, China.

Late-model processing machines were being torn from American foundations and installed on factory floors made from Chinese cement. Machine operators were mostly Han peasants, happy to earn the equivalent of two U.S. dollars a day.

(APRIL 3, 2008) 2:45 PM
LOGAN AIRPORT, BOSTON

Kurancy sensed the chauffeur's weight lift from the fender, and heard movement from behind. He slid aside the brown curtain shielding him from public scrutiny, and saw Alicia Wang direct a luggage steward toward the limo.

"Hong Qi." She shouted impatiently, then repeated in English, "The Red Flag Limo."

Alicia was forty, but looked twenty. Her long, glossy black hair swept across her face, inches above bright olive eyes, then dropped to the front and back of her shoulders, partly covering still-perky breasts. She wore a tailored bi-stretch charcoal jacket with a band collar and multi-sized black buttons, a cerise crepe shirt, black flared stretch pants and an eggshell shimmer scarf. She was almost as tall as the chauffeur, and almost as stocky.

The Red Flag limousine, one of only two hundred hand-assembled in 1982 at the state owned truck factory in Changchun, in northeast China, waited at the curb near the private jet arrival gate at Logan International Airport in Boston. The classic vehicle, which Li Chin had given to Kurancy several years ago to commemorate their first one-hundred million dollars in export business, had been modified to meet U.S. safety and environmental standards. It was only driven when Li Chin visited Boston; as a sign of respect for the most powerful industrialist in Asia.

The stretch limo was almost terrorist-proof, with one-inch plexiglass windows and enough anti-explosion, ceramic undercoat-plates to keep it from burning up, if it ever had the occasion to re-enter the earth's atmosphere. A red silk flag, hung officially from a three foot antenna extending from the front fender, indicated the occupants were probably high officials. Although, that didn't mean much in Boston.

Jake sat in the deeply cushioned, red-calfskin rear seat of the spit-polished, black Chinese classic, holding a folded Investor's Daily issue, and waiting for his most important supplier to arrive from Little Rock. He was physically aroused from seeing the "BMRE" symbol of BoxMart Retail Enterprises listed in the Large Cap stock report. Especially today.

BoxMart stock had risen five and a half points on yesterday's press release of the company's latest quarterly profits. The discount retailing industry's second largest business showed a nineteen-percent profit increase from the same period last year, to nearly one billion nine hundred million dollars. Not bad for a former Asian shoe buyer, he mused.

The stocky chauffeur of average height, in his early 30's, waited on the sidewalk, ready to hold the door open for the arriving guests. He was a former Department of Homeland Security agent, who'd been booted from the security force for picking off allegedly armed Mexican aliens trying to cross a remote section of the Arizona border. He also served as Kurancy's body guard. Only half the size of the man he was hired to protect, the bulge under his green woolen blazer suggested he was licensed to carry serious hardware.

When Alicia noticed Kurancy peering from the vehicle, she quickly moved to his window, which hummed down as she approached. She greeted him with a warm smile and a bow. Kurancy gleefully anticipated her visits, remembering the soft, smooth oriental skin, and the authoritative body that could inflame his ileum.

"Mr. Kurancy, so happy to see you." She bowed again and explained, "Mr. Li has been detained for a few minutes. Please accept our apology."

Kurancy glanced back through the glass exit doors of the private gate and noticed Li Chin in heated conversation on his cell phone. The small man, supposedly in his late sixties, soon finished the conversation, slammed the clam-shell closed and darted out to the limo, looking left and right briefly, as if he expected someone else to be there. The Chinese pair jumped into the back seat and Li Chin bowed to his old friend; then held out both hands. Jake took them cordially, in a double greeting, and bowed in return.

"At last, the time has come!" Li exclaimed with a knowing smile. He glanced furtively to Alicia, who hadn't been informed about important details of their merger plan. Li then sat back and closed his eyes. As if savoring whatever was to come.

Kurancy tapped a button on the door console, and the limousine pulled away for the thirty mile trip to the BoxMart campus, which had been constructed in the midst of a forty acre triangle of open fields and majestic hills, between North Andover, Boxford and Georgetown, Massachusetts. The high-tech headquarters building was set behind thickets of tall, rolling pines and majestic elms, and an immense, green macadam parking lot for seven hundred employees. The twelve-story building consisted of seven cylindrical and box-shaped segments, strung together in an eclectic assembly of glass and bronze. Its design was inspired by the Lloyd's of London office building in the financial district of London…the masterpiece of British architect Richard Rogers. The mouth of the Ipswich River and the famous tourist destination of Rockport met the Atlantic Ocean about ten miles east.

Alicia smiled softly as she and Kurancy watched Li Chin nod off for one of his famous instant power naps. They drove the rest of the way in silence. Once, during the drive north on crowded Route 1-A, Kurancy reached across and caressed Alicia's knee. He began to whisper something, but she quickly raised her index finger to her lips. Kurancy had nearly forgotten.

Li Chin slept like a dolphin. Half his brain was asleep, but the other half was always awake. A brain wave exam would have suggested that the energetic Asian industrialist was really a fish mammal.

The Oriental Suite in the forty-thousand square foot, private BoxMart guest house, was designed and decorated specifically for Li Chin's environmental preference. The ancient Feng Shui tradition of design and object placement, created harmony and balance in the five spacious rooms reserved for BoxMart's important Asian guests.

Placed thoughtfully on carved tables, hand-crafted metal wall brackets, and in corners around the suite, were cast-bronze vessels, carved jade bells, rare oracle-bone inscriptions from the Shang Dynasty of 1045 BC, and 14th century Ming paintings of birds and flowers of great delicacy and detail. Two hollow lacquered fat Buddhas, handmade by Fuzhou artists in the early eighteenth century, squatted behind pink-tinted glass in curio cabinets, alongside sandalwood fans, an acupuncture doll and woodcuts of traditional Chinese landscapes.

To the side of the nine-foot entrance door to the Oriental Suite, hung a sixteenth-century patterned silk embroidery, a yard square, displaying lines of classic Ming poetry---a gift from the vice-premier of China. The only sharp object in view was a tarnished bronze *yue*, a blade used to behead human sacrifices. Kurancy had purchased the ancient artifact from a corrupt government official in charge of excavating an ancient Shang Dynasty tomb in Anyang, believed to be the resting place of the last Shang Dynasty ruler in 1066 BC.

The understated white cement exterior of the guest house, with large black clapboards framing custom-made, nickel-tinted oval windows, contrasted with the oriental and Danish-modern thematic interiors of the five and six-room suites, which were available only to important customers and suppliers.

Kurancy was the only BoxMart executive maintaining a residence at the quarters, which was attached underground to the headquarters building a hundred yards away, by a white-tiled tunnel with an airport-style walking conveyor.

Alicia unpacked their travel bags and flopped on the king sized bed in the only bedroom of the suite. Her attention was immediately captured by the ocean-blue panes of floor-to-ceiling, ultraviolet-filtering glass, set in a circular observation turret. The view faced west from bedside. A groggy sun overlooked an authentic Chinese garden modeled after the Wangshi Garden in Suzhou, built by the Song dynasty rulers of 960-1279 AD.

The garden emitted waves of contemplative relaxation, marrying the traditional elements of ponds, rock grottoes, zigzag bridges and a miniature five-story pagoda---with the lush garden of Peony bushes in brilliant violet, red and white. Koi ponds were spotted near graceful willow trees, which rose above high brick walls facing the sun-drenched lawn and rolling hills on the north side of the building. The awesome view reminded Alicia of the sunny days of her childhood in Suzhou, visiting the most beautiful gardens in China with her parents, who were spiritually elated by their ancestor's artful manipulation of nature's beauty.

The thatched roof of a doll-house-sized pavilion placed in the garden on an island surrounded by a lilly-pond moat inhabited by red, gold and white ornamental carp, gave the scene a rustic air, and pleasantly accentuated the Feng Shui decor of the guest suite.

The only disruption to the wind and water sense of the garden and Oriental Suite was an electronic eavesdropping device, which was detected by a quick room scan of Alicia's gold bracelet. She was not surprised. Kurancy was either overly cautious, or perversely curious.

A tiny video camera was cleverly hidden in the corner wall, above a view-dominating tropical fish tank, set inside a hanging bamboo bird cage. Eight multi-colored, striped and spotted exotic flat fish drifted by. Infinity and unlimited happiness, she knew, were associated with the number eight. She decided not to disable the camera. General Ye had instructed her to drop tidbits of disinformation.

It would be another hour before Li Chin and Kurancy completed their planning session for the new joint venture. She was exhausted from the Arkansas, Illinois and NewYork negotiating sessions they'd just completed with several of the large LCE retail customers. The new wave of young MBA-educated buyers that dominated the meetings, were not much different from the older high school graduates, who'd worked their way up to senior buyer positions. They never stopped asking for more concessions.

They used the political rhetoric from Washington, D.C., which increasingly called for limits on imports, as a negotiating lever for lower prices and longer payment terms. They claimed it was becoming more expensive for their lobbyists to influence Congressmen and federal regulators. "Keeping the flood gates opened for Chinese goods is costing too many American jobs," a merchandise manager had complained, as if he cared. "Everyone's calling for higher import tariffs and new quotas. Such hardships for our hard working countrymen …blah, blah, blah."

Retail buyers didn't really care, as long as their pricing demands were met. But this was old news. The latest news was that Alicia had firmly rejected their requests for concessions; as Li Chin and General Ye had ordered.

Alicia hadn't expected to play a pivotal role in the negotiations. She'd been appointed Assistant President by LCE's Communist-dominated board of directors, just prior to departing from Beijing for the meetings with the big U.S. retailers. It was thought to be a symbolic title by some who knew that her expertise was more physical than intellectual.

But, she would no longer just tag after Li Chin, to make certain his actions coincided with the General's desires; or ply Kurancy for assurances that the massive dollar deposits scattered around the world in BoxMart bank accounts would be available at the exact time required. She had no idea when, or why!

Ms. Wang appeared to have successfully transgressed into a dominating Chinese executive, who could artfully and coldly reject the demands of predominantly male buyers. Strangely, she was comfortable with her new role. It gave her the same satisfaction she experienced when Li Chin and Jake Kurancy begged for more of the oriental procedures which brought them such exhilaration.

She'd followed Mr. Li's careful instructions prior to the negotiating sessions, and played the "bad-guy" role to perfection. She'd insisted, stone-faced across the negotiating table, "LCE must receive higher prices and shorter payment terms from all our retailer customers. As newly appointed Assistant President, I carry the backing of the Standing Committee of the Communist Party. Since I am now in charge of international marketing, all pricing decisions are my responsibility." Her soliloquy left no room for discussion.

Li Chin had positioned himself as the "good guy", to offset Alicia's iron-lady facade. He always kept bridges open with business associates. You never could tell how they'd react when LCE and BoxMart announced their new venture.

Alicia was not sure why BoxMart was the only customer given such low prices and other concessions not offered to the other giant retailers. She supposed there was a strategic reason to set BoxMart apart. It probably had to do with General Ye's obvious interest in BoxMart's massive dollar and yuan deposits in Chinese bank accounts.

Following his brief meeting with Kurancy, Li Chin entered the Feng Shui suite and immediately sniffed the jasmine and pepper scented pillar candles, which were suspended over the bed on cups sculpted onto a bronze sconce, adorned with brass berrys and fig leafs. Alicia was lying on the bed wearing a short, diaphanous white nightgown, reading an American women's magazine which promised to instruct the reader, in huge lettering on the front page, how to lose thirty pounds in two weeks , bring your boyfriend to heated frenzy in two minutes, and have multiple orgasms twice daily, while watching the weather channel.

She heard a grunt as the lecherous juices flowed from the spry old man, who was shedding his clothes along the path to the bed. She cast an indifferent glance at his well-maintained, reedy physique, and was amazed, considering his real age. Li Chin once claimed that his older sister, ten years his senior, was born in the year of the last imperial ceremony in Qianging Gong, the Palace of Heavenly Purity in Beijing. She'd checked to discover that Pu Yi, the disposed, hapless last Qing Emperor, was married at this ceremony in 1922.

Mr. Li knelt at the foot of the bed, and readied his advance on the inviting dark sheen triangle which resided at the top of Alicia's slightly parted, plump thighs. Alicia continued reading the magazine, ignoring him, until he started tickling the baby-soft skin of her delicate toes and licking in circles. He was getting firmer with each circumvention. She peered down at the top of his head and remembered a famous Confucian proverb.

"It does not matter how slowly you go, so long as you do not stop."

Soon, she lost patience and flung the magazine across the room. Her legs shot up and clamped forcefully around his bowed shoulders, drawing him up to her mid-section. The former peasant smiled, as he ripped away the sheer panties and acquiesced to Alicia's prodding for him to partake in oral pleasures that stimulated all five human senses of both participants.

As the climactic moment approached, she arched her back and moaned loudly, then reached between his legs with velvety digits and gripped tightly, flicking new life into a tired warrior. At the appropriate degree of stiffness, she rolled over with the athleticism of a professional wrestler, surrounded him, and giggled like a silly child as she climbed aboard.

As Li Chin gyrated vigorously, searching for a small explosion, Alicia worried about his heart. She knew, by now, that there was a dangerous cardiac-rate which her seasoned lover should not surpass. She forced his arms against the mattress, and pressed her sensitive fingers onto the veins of his wrists. As the instant of severe pleasure arrived in jerked thrusts, and lasted the usual ten seconds, she counted the number of beats. *Multiply the number by six*, she recalled, as her mind did the calculation. *Good. His heart rate is only up to 90. He'll live.*

CHAPTER 8

(April 4, 2008) 6pm
Fitchburg funeral Home

The ninety-four year old woman went berserk. She shrieked at the top of her lungs and began beating her breasts. Justin practically fainted as the outburst shattered the silence of solitude prayers. The other family members managed to remain calm, until the woman jumped up and started yelling, "Why...Why....My God. He was so young." Then fainted into the arms of the deceased man's seventy year-old baby sister.

Justin feared wakes and funerals ever since that night, as an eight year-old altar boy, when he'd accompanied a young priest from the archdiocese of Worcester, Mass to a private home, where a mother was mourning her son. The priest must have believed that holy water was the key to heaven, because he drenched the casket, then wristed a silver ball of the holy water directly into the face of the grieving mother. She freaked.

Every visitor in the room panicked, and joined her cacophonous shrieks as they rushed to her side. Arthritic bodies in black toppled over each other, landing in a pile of arms, legs and damp handkerchiefs. The young priest couldn't think of anything else to do, so he doused the family pile with more holy water.

Justin remembered running out the door and racing home through dark alleyways littered with trash and squeeling black objects with thin tails; and nothing more about that night. His last as an altar boy.

He signed the visitors book placed on a dark walnut pedestal near the entrance to the Fitchburg Funeral Home, then joined the crowd of family and well wishers. Many were from the local plastics industry, of which Joe Slattery was a prominent member. It was exactly six pm...half way into the four hour waking period. Justin had discovered over the years, that arriving in the middle of the mourning period, to pay respects to a deceased person's family, was the least traumatic experience…for him.

He circled to the opposite side of the room, away from where Mrs. Slattery and her three children were seated, greeting relatives. He eased into the waiting line, then approached the open casket as inconspicuously as possible. He didn't know many people in the room, and had met Joe's wife briefly at a local trade show. He knelt and offered a prayer for Joe's soul. This man had worked hard all his life and had not deserved to die so young. He'd earned a better legacy---than to leave his family in poverty.

Justin glanced into the casket at the puffy face. He wished he'd known Joe better. Inserted into an oversized black suit, the dead man's bluish hands barely protruded from long cuffs. They were entangled with white plastic rosary beads. Justin lingered for a respectful time, curious about the small personal items Joe's family had placed on the white velvet pillowing the body. He presumed the items would remain when the casket was closed.

Then unexpectedly, he began to tear. The aromatic fumes from the semi-circle of large flower arrangements surrounding the raised coffin, blended with traces of embalming fluid from somewhere, and set off his allergies. He sneezed, then rose and touched the casket tenderly, as he grabbed a handful of the Kleenex tissues which the funeral home had thoughtfully placed in front of the framed photos of Joe and his family. The relatives sitting on cushioned chairs in the front, facing the deceased, nodded approval as he wiped away the tears.

When he turned to face Mrs. Slattery and her children, his heart sank. He paused in anguish and retrospective guilt. Joe's wife had collapsed into a chair, sobbing uncontrollably. Her face was buried in her lap. Marsha, their thirteen year old daughter, was kneeling before Mrs. Slattery, holding one of her mother's hands in each of her own, trying to absorb more of the heartbreak than she already had. It was too much for a child Marsha's age. The young girl's saddened eyes and chewed lips said enough. She was inspiring everyone in the room.

Joe's two sons, who missed final exams because of their father's funeral, stood bracketing their mother from behind. As Justin approached, the boys lifted hands from their mother's shoulder, and offered a thank you for coming. He said softly, "God bless you…Joe is in my prayers."

He then told the boys, who had no idea who he was, how special Joe had been: a pioneer in the plastics industry, a management genius, even a mentor to him early in his career. The boys knew he was just being kind. Nobody that good could leave such a mess for their family. But there was truth in Justin's claims.

If BoxMart hadn't cancelled the orders; and if Residents Bank hadn't shut him down so harshly---Joe and his business would probably have survived.

Justin moved aside for others to greet the family, then angled through the crowd to a seat in the back of the room. Brad Stalker, the general manager of Leominster Plastics, was talking with Tim Corran. Brad's company had inherited the position as GRT's largest customer, because of the Slattery business collapse.

"Hi, Brad...Tim. What a shame," Justin whispered, his emotions leveled.

Tim replied, "We were just talking about trying to help the family."

Brad looked worried and impatient. "We're thinking about a fund raiser for the kids'education." He studied Justin's mood, then surprised him, "We need to talk...in private. Are you available for dinner?"

They moved smoothly toward the exit, just as a middle-aged Nigerian priest and an altar girl entered to pronounce final blessings on the open casket. And...probably, to sprinkle incantations of holy water.

In the parking lot, Justin lit up the cigarette Ken Levine had given him after last week's meeting. He glanced back at the entrance to the building, and said to Brad, "I'm not sure how much Tim told you. I know you and Joe were close friends. We can't let them get away with this."

Brad replied, "Did you know the casket was made in China? Tim says he bought it from Costco. They sell fifteen thousand each year." His mind seemed distracted and drifting. "I'll meet you at the Cornerstone restaurant in Leominster. Half an hour okay?"

"Sure. That's only a few blocks from the LPI plant, isn't it?"

"Yeah," Brad answered with more conviction, then turned back and said sadly, "Justin, I'm afraid we have to discuss more bad news."

Dinner was a disaster. They did agree on one thing: U.S. multinationals were sucking their own country dry.

"I'm sorry, Justin, we just won't need your materials for the foreseeable future."

Stalker had recently been hired as general manager of Leominster Plastics Company, a large custom molder producing mostly seasonal items for New England mass merchants, drugstore chains, and office supply houses.

"This is a shocker, on top of everything else," Gatt uttered grimly.

Brad finished his third cup of coffee, then pushed aside the half-eaten Rueben. He explained apologetically, "Not only did BoxMart retract their orders for our kits and supplies, but they undercut the prices our other customers are charging for LP products."

"I can guess how they did that."

"Yeah! They sourced Chinese-made knock-offs for our entire line, then blasted the prices. I believe they're responsible for the drastic reduction in re-stocking orders we have on the books from Staples, Walgreen's and Sears."

"So, you're in trouble, too." Justin waived the empty bottle of Amstel light at the voluptuous teenage waitress, who was engrossed in eye-locking conversation with a smooth-talking bartender twice her age.

Brad was a vibrant, thirty-four year old MBA graduate from the University of Maine, with light brown hair and eyes, and an honest answer for every question. Justin liked him immensely. Brad's family still lived in the blue-collar, southern Maine town of Sanford, where he was raised. His father and mother had both worked at a mill factory, making components for the shoe industry, until Maine's few remaining footwear factories succumbed to off-shore competition during the Clinton administration.

"Tell me more about your career, Brad. I wondered how you got involved in the plastics industry."

The waitress finally noticed the roomful of waving arms, and decided---like---uh…there were actually customers who needed her attention. Justin was frantic for another cold beer.

"My first job was with Portland Advisors, a group of business consultants. Actually, they were former business executives who'd lost their jobs. The Maine Department of Economic Development hired our firm to develop an incentive package for manufacturing businesses planning to move out of state. Particularly those in the footwear industry."

He snatched the last cold french-fry tucked under the Reuben. "It didn't work!"

Gatt knew part of the story. "Then you were hired by the Orcutt family to salvage Leominster Plastics."

"I'd written a new business plan for them, and old Mr. Orcutt apparently was impressed." Brad replied somberly. He shook his head side to side, and added, "I talked him into investing a good chunk of his retirement nest-egg in modern, high-speed processing equipment: robots, computerized controls, automated handling and stacking machines---the works. It's been a successful program….up until now."

"It sounds like you did all the right things, Brad. You cut labor costs, increased output rates and upgraded quality."

"We did that," Brad noted, "and also cut raw material costs by using your compounds." It reminded him of the purpose of this meeting. "I feel awful about whacking you right now, Justin; especially since I've learned the bank's dangling you over a flame. Hopefully, we'll get some of the business back, and can begin ordering materials again. We love your technology, and the processing consistency of GRT's recycled compounds."

"What about pricing?" Gatt inquired, knowing it was the bottom line determinant for most business deals. "Did BoxMart throw that in your face?"

Brad's face distorted and crimped out a weak sigh. "Do taxes come due on April fifteenth?" His features hardened. He said, "Since I've been general manager, we've cut prices to the bone. Mr. Orcutt agreed with my suggestion that we build volume, by limiting operating profits to the level needed to amortize the new equipment. Even that wasn't good enough for BoxMart. They flatly refused to accept pass-along price increases."

Brad paused, then asked, "Do you remember Rubbermaid?" He held up the empty ceramic coffee mug and was ecstatic to catch the attention of the waitress. "They were once a brilliant corporate star with strong brand recognition and a fantastic reputation for skilled management. Some years ago, new management thought they could dictate higher prices to you-know-who. It didn't take long for the company to shrink, from one of America's most admired corporate citizens, to a mere competitor in the house-wares market. Many of their largest U.S. production facilities are now closed."

Gatt added somberly, "Today's eighty-dollars-a-barrel price for OPEC and Russian crude doesn't help the profit picture. It's ludicrous. The average raw material cost for our molded products is over sixty percent of total manufacturing expenses. It used to be about forty."

The young waitress in the tight, white leather mini-skirt caused him to alter his train of thought. She bent over to pick up a fork from a table across the aisle. Brad also caught a side glance at the two fleshy, round parts connecting her bare legs to the sides of generous hips. Justin barely won the battle to regain his concentration.

"The Chinese also have to pay high market prices for materials. In the molding business, labor costs are almost insignificant compared with raw materials, or the capital investment load."

Brad also returned from a moment of fantasy. "I still don't understand why America is rapidly losing so many plastics processing businesses to foreign competition."

Justin pyramided his hands under his nose, as if petitioning an answer from above, and replied, "Perhaps, it's the other costs that we have… that they never will. Or, at least not in the foreseeable future. A U.S. factory has to pay high premiums for medical insurance, unemployment benefits, and workman's compensation… not to mention vacation and sick pay. Here, the perks are higher than China's total labor costs."

"You guys want anything else?" the young waitress asked, leaning over the table for the benefit of patrons across the room.

"Coffee refills, if you don't mind." Gatt decided he needed more caffeine for the drive home to Connecticut. The waitress glanced curiously at the empty beer bottle in his hand.

He smiled at the analysis of his young friend, and offered a more detailed explanation.

"We left out freight, water, power, maintenance, repairs and tooling costs. They're all subsidized by the Chinese state."

He recalled a provocative discussion he'd had with Professor Syzmansky. "You also have to factor in the corruption costs."

Brad asked, "How's that tracked? I've heard that Beijing is cracking down."

"It's as low as three percent, and as high as twenty-five percent, according to my friend at the Connecticut branch of the Import-Export Bank. The Communist leaders don't seem to be alarmed, or doing much. Obviously, they're part of it."

"What would happen?" Brad asked his more experienced business associate, "if the Chinese factories were forced to compete fairly…on a 'level playing field?'"

"My guess? They'd still do pretty well." Justin answered honestly. "The average Asian has an amazing work ethic, especially the young women. They're just starting to reap the benefits of their hard work. We should worry more about the blatant greed of their domestic and foreign bosses."

"I know what you mean. Our own cold-hearted multi-nationals have jump-started thousands of mainland factories…at the expense of our own small businesses. It really pisses me off."

Justin added to the knock, "It seems as if this country is collectively gifting the Chinese the technologies it took American ingenuity and risky investments years to achieve." He was visibly upset.

"Doesn't our government care?" Brad asked emotionally.

"Absolutely, not." Justin slightly overstated.

The waitress returned with a beer in one hand and a pot of hot coffee in the other. She placed the beer on the table in front of Justin, then extracted the lipstick-stained bill from her bulbous lips and handed it to Brad. As she started to pour Brad's fourth cup of coffee, he grumbled, "Someone should light a fire under those bastard's sex organs, to get the pricks to respond."

The hot coffee missed the cup, and splashed down from the table's edge.

CHAPTER 9

(April 4, 2008)
BoxMart Headquarters

Kurancy and Li Chin descended to the surveillance-secure conference room, a thirty-second elevator drop below the BoxMart headquarters building, not far from the 3P-BIO supercomputer. Jake wanted his new partner to see the world's first three petaflop number cruncher, which was housed in a room the size of a basketball court, on the same sublevel, adjacent to an utility room containing forty-thousand square feet of cooling equipment.

Engineers from India were teaching BoxMart's American programmers how the amazing machine, with the theoretical capability to process three thousand trillion mathematical computations per second, stored and accessed new programs. It was break-through technology that only a handful of people even knew existed. Li Chin was impressed.

"Next year, this machine will automatically place the largest orders your five hundred factories have ever seen," Jake boasted to his friend and soon to be partner. "Several other LCE facilities in Vietnam, Indonesia and Thailand will also receive orders."

"Your marketing strategy is working better than I expected," Li marveled. "You're a merchandising genius, my friend." His widened eyes focused on the long rows of parallel-linked processing servers; while his sensitive Han ears acquired the subdued waves of digital melodies, as ones and zeros tap-danced across silicone microprocessor boards. Faint air vibrations escaping from the rotary compressors in the cooling room intermixed with the strange resonance of a trillion calculations, and created a muted, out-of-world sound sensation.

Kurancy led Li Chin to the main control room to meet the machine's creator, Kapeed Pandlidesh, the Managing Scientist of Gujarat Supercomputer and Supersoftware Company, a subsidiary of BoxMart recently purchased in India. Kapeed and three other genius-level computer engineering graduates from Cal Tech, now working for GSSSC, had partially developed the machine technology at the Lawrence Livermore National Laboratory in California, where three of the ten fastest supercomputers in the world are located. Their technology far surpassed the famous modified IBM Blue Gene/L---the world's previous fastest supercomputer, which was capable of two hundred trillion mathematical calculations per second.

"Kapeed and the other vegetarian nerds were hired by Livermore to speed up the development of complicated software for the multiple-processor architecture of a one petaflop machine being developed for the Pentagon," Kurancy explained, as they approached Kapeed.

The Gujurat engineer was leaning over an operator at the main control panel, wearing a badly wrinkled oxblood long-sleeved shirt with rolled up sleeves and tails protruding over the back pockets of similarly wrinkled khakis. He was lanky, with glossy black hair that badly needed washing, and eyes of coal. Behind those eyes was an intellectual brilliance that dwarfed the hardest jewels. Li noticed his badly blemished complexion and the worn sandal he was rotating to relieve the stiffness in his right ankle. Kapeed had been standing at the console for hours.

"Mr. Kurancy, I'm so glad to have your presence, sir." Kapeed smiled enthusiastically, revealing large, egg-shell teeth. "We have some very good reports, I might say."

Jake took Kapeed's limp hand and tried not to crush bones as he shook it. He moved behind his oriental guest and said, "Mr. Pandlidesh…meet Mr. Li."

"My pleasure, sir," Kapeed replied, assuming Li was a very important person, because Kurancy gave few people a tour of this facility.

"I understand you have developed a fast machine," Li understated, to the engineer's dismay. "Which can do a lot of calculations."

Li Chin had very little background in computers, and could not appreciate the incredible calculating power Kapeed and his team had created. China's most successful entrepreneur had started as a peasant laborer, assembling canvas sneakers. He'd learned the footwear trade, and eventually opened a small athletic shoe manufacturing company. His first customer for low-end sneakers was Jake Kurancy, who at the time was a buyer of Asian merchandise for a distributor to Wal-Mart and other mass merchants. His drive and willingness to grant financial favors to high level Communist leaders eventually led to his appointment as chairman of the conglomerate of state-run businesses, which General Ye had positioned as the preferred manufacturer to replace bankrupt U.S. suppliers.

Jake attempted to embellish the supercomputer's features for the benefit of Kapeed's delicate ego. "This is the only computer in the world which can supercharge muon-emitting ...what is it, Kapeed bio-diodes or something?"The thirty-five year old computer designer had mastered the technology of microprocessors twenty years ago. He was at a loss to explain, in simple terms, how a parallel array of powerful micro-processors, stacked in three separate machines, could be connected and supercharged by his own nano-biochemical chip(NBCC) design, to ten thousand times their original data processing speed. Or how his radical design to combine three computers in one by-passed previous supercomputer design logic. The first machine processed rough calculations, with raw computing power. The second provided more precise computing. And the third used intelligent software and the NBCC processors to create "learning algorithms."

"The 3P-BIO," Kapeed answered simply, "fills Mr. Kurancy's needs… and more. It learns how to convert basic data into accurate prediction equations."

Jake accepted this explanation, then added, "I learned from my early days in the retailing business, that investment in high technology pays enormous dividends if it allows a company to pull away from competition."

Kapeed reassured his boss, "We just proved about that, sir. The 3P-BIO produces incredible accurate models. She can predict some secrets of the marketing things of our competitors."

Li Chin asked, "Will it predict how they price each product line?"

Jake boasted heartily, "We'll be able to predict how they price individual SKUs*within* a product line… prior to their printing newspaper inserts and other price promotions. BoxMart will have the ability to undercut our competitor's loss-leader promotions, and kill the effectiveness of their ads." He swept an enormous arm across the horizon of the computer room, and exulted, "Every retailer who does a Sunday paper insert in the U.S., or a web page promotion, will be vulnerable."

Li Chin pictured General Ye, China's top military strategist, and Yong Ihasa, the Vice Premier, salivating over the potential military benefits of controlling the 3P-BIO supercomputer. It was possible that sometime in the future, the People's Liberation Army Generals could gain control of this amazing data-processing power through its Bomali joint venture with BoxMart.

He wondered if Kurancy could continue to conceal its existence from the U.S. Military. So far, he'd skirted government scrutiny by having the engineers construct the machine in-place, using processors and other components secretly shipped to BoxMart from as far away as a Taiwan medical research lab, and as close as Route 128, the original "information super highway," a few miles away.

Li Chin accepted the crystal glass of Opus One Mondavi/Rothschild 2000, considered by Jake to be the best American red ever produced in Napa, and reclined in the sweeping curves of a cushioned plantation-style Malabar chair, which was placed in pairs around the periphery of the conference room. Kurancy filled his own glass and sat in an identical chair next to his close friend and business associate.

The cherry paneled walls of the subterranean conference room were embellished with a diverse combination of original Miros; what appeared to be a master reproduction of Rembrandt's only known seascape, *'The Storm on the Sea of Galilee'*; and five drawings by Degas. They were identical to the art stolen in 1990 from the Isabella Stewart Gardner Museum in Boston, which had never been recovered. The room emitted a subtle luster from the indirect lighting and the inlaid New Zealand wool rug, decorated with hand-knotted, silver and tan geometric motifs, layered over a vibrant maroon palette. In the center of the large room was a twenty-by eight foot rectangular teak-block table, surrounded by armless, aniline-dyed, tan leather Trevor chairs.

"If we complete this deal, Li, you and I will someday be richer than the Sheiks."

"General Ye and Vice Premier Ihasa have assured me that the new Macau laws will be approved by the Standing Committee at the next meeting of the Politboro. They will be pleased when we present the final draft of our merger agreement."

Not many words had been wasted between the two intensely competitive businessmen over the years. Both wanted a concise draft agreement, with the major terms of the planned merger of BoxMart Retail Enterprises and LCE spelled out in as few words as possible. The international-mergers attorneys could later work out the governance and profit-distribution details with Emerson Bromine, who would serve as the joint venture's first chief executive. It would be a fifty-fifty partnership, with operating responsibilities for the retailing and manufacturing businesses remaining under current leadership, for the time being.

"The surviving entity will be based in Macau, and named 'Bomali Corporation,' as previously agreed," Kurancy summarized. "Subject, of course, to Politboro approval of the new Macau tax-free and merger laws."

Within an hour, they reviewed and agreed upon every major term and condition of the proposed agreement, then signed the "Letter of Intent." Li Chin was more animated than Jake could remembered.

"Bomali Corporation," he raised his voice in triumph, "will be the largest joint venture ever conceived. Bigger than Exxon-Mobil."

Kurancy added wryly, "It will be the biggest trading, retailing and manufacturing conglomerate the business world has ever known. I can just hear the other big retailers screaming for quotas on our imports. The turncoats will reverse their pro-free-trade positions and publicity releases. They may even join Martin Merrand's call for 'selective-protectionism', and support his presidential campaign."

"We'll fax the draft agreement and the signed letter of intent to Langreen in Macau, tomorrow," Li Chin suggested. He was referring to Vargos Langreen, the managing director of Smith and Week, Asia's largest international mergers and acquisitions firm. Emerson Bromine, who owned vast real estate and gambling operations in Macau, was chosen to run the Macau headquarters office of Bomali, once the joint venture was formed.

"Macau is on Beijing time, so they wouldn't see it tonight, anyway," Kurancy responded flippantly. He was savoring the fine wine with a rolling tongue; and the deal with sealed eyes.

Li Chin raised his glass of Opus One to his friend, and boasted, "What we have done tonight, my friend, will forever be acknowledged in business history."

"Bomali will trample everyone in its path," Kurancy prophesied. His huge physical presence reminded Li of his partner's fierce competitiveness.

"We'll win every contest," Li countered. "The future may be pocked with some uncertainties, but one thing is certain: our four hundred billion dollar enterprise will dominate consumer product manufacturing and retailing for years to come." His small frame radiated a competitive nature rivaling that of Jake, who now expected to achieve his long awaited dream.

"It *can* be done!" he said, in a tone that hinted doubt. Li Chin didn't quite grasp his meaning when he added, "It's worth the risk."

Jake was recalling the unnerving requirement of the Savoy Imperative: linked to the merger's success was the requirement that BoxMart temporarily hand over billions of dollars---nearly half its working capital---to the French banker.

Li Chin's concerns were on a different plane. The Chinese Central Bank and the four big Commercial banks in China already controlled LCE'S billions. They also controlled hundreds of billions of U.S. dollars in government reserves---resulting from the massive trade surplus with America and other countries. As long as China's trade surplus with the developed nations remained high, Beijing's trading strategy could function as if the Bank of China printed yuans without limits.

The risk of transferring China's massive reserves to the French bank was a shared decision of Yong Ihasa and General Ye Kunshi, who were also in a position to catch the biggest prize. They were gambling for higher position in the Politboro, and control of the Chinese Communist Party.

Li Chin wasn't seeking higher position or more riches. He wanted China to reach its rightful destiny as the world's dominant trading partner. The formation of Bomali Corp, as a Macau special tax benefits corporation, could make that happen. Yong Ihasa, the Vice Premier, was doing his part to convince the Politboro to approve the new laws. Soon, Macau-based foreign corporations would be allowed to merge with state-owned businesses on the mainland; provided that the mainland company owned at least fifty percent of the joint venture.

No income taxes would be collected for ten years. Current BoxMart and LCE stockholders would each own fifty percent of the most profitable company in the world.

"We've got a busy day tomorrow, my friend." Li Chin grinned sheepishly. "Please excuse me if I bid goodnight." He and Alicia had met all day with Jake and BoxMart's merchandise planning staff to schedule shipments for the Christmas season. They'd also spent time with Cashman, reviewing the products currently being made by the small American manufacturers targeted for foreclosure by Residents Bank within the next few months. LCE factories could get a head start on making replacement items.

"Owlin Pickett will be returning tomorrow from political meetings in DC," Kurancy informed Li. "He strongly suggests we pull the political contributions lever one more time. When I'm finished meeting with him and Cashman, I'll approve the list of products LCE will have to produce as we drop U.S.suppliers. I'd like to move that program forward as fast as possible. The stores have to prepare for the holiday season, and I want as few American-made gifts on our shelves as possible."

Tonight, Kurancy smiled to himself, *Alicia will come to my suite and deliver an early gift.*

(APRIL 7, 2008) 10AM,
LILI'S APARTMENT, BEIJING

A digitized voice prompted her to answer: "Yes," "No," and "Maybe," to a series of mundane questions pertaining to Olympic diving events. The secure communications unit, which doubled as a normal cell phone, was learning to recognize her voice.

At exactly ten a.m. on Monday, she tapped six numbers, twice each, into the cellular communications device her friend at the U.S. Embassy had left in a paper bag on the floor at the Chang'an Ave restaurant. Following directions exactly as written in the ancient Mongol language, Lili listened for three chimes, followed five seconds later by the clang of three bells and a drum roll. She then tapped in the original six numbers in reverse order, and destroyed the note.

The final prompt asked Lili to spell the name of a close friend. She answered, "N.I.N." Micro-seconds later, the scrambled microwave transmission from her handset was converted into a top secret, mixed-frequency, mixed-wavelength signal, which bounced off a satellite positioned over Ulan Bator, the capital of Mongolia, several hundred miles north of Beijing. The transmission was then relayed to an Observation and Communications satellite positioned over the northern most border between India and China, directly above Godwin Austen mountain…better known as 'K2', the second-highest mountain in the world. The signal was then relayed to the National Security Agency receiving station outside Washington, D.C., and finally transported via NSA's shielded global communications network, to the false top-floor of the U.S. Embassy in Beijing, a few blocks from Lili's apartment.

A familiar voice at the other end of the line asked, "Are you alone?"

Lili was sitting cross-legged on the undersized twin-bed in her small two room apartment. The bedroom door and the one window in the apartment were closed. She'd called her supervisor at the travel bureau, and was not expected in the office until noon.

"Yes…in my apartment."

"Do you understand the instructions?"

"I do, except I don't understand how to make contact with the American…. businessmen." She almost said 'targets.'

"You'll receive that information at the proper time. Are you clear on the location?"

Lili had memorized the number of the flagstone in Tianan'men Square, were she was to drop messages into a green metal trash container, set at the northern edge of one of the thousands of numbered, rectangular stone tiles placed in the square to position military honor units during state celebrations. She'd receive further instructions when "Nin" called her SCU at the specified time. Or, by sitting at a specific bench near a different numbered flagstone in the one-hundred acre square---a back-up procedure in case phone communication had to be aborted.

"Someone with a language problem will approach the bench and ask for directions to the lovely gardens of Zhongshan Park, on the western side of the Imperial Palace." AJ explained further, "You are to point north west, then, in frustration, write the directions on a slip of paper, and hand it to the visitor. This action is too open and obvious to be suspected as an espionage exchange, if anyone happens to be watching." No trained agent would be dumb enough to pass information this way, he postulated somberly.

"I've been there a thousand times," she answered.

"Good. And you understand what to do if there is a problem?"

Her instructions addressed the possibility that nobody would appear at the designated bench within the fifteen-minute window. She was to go directly to the U.S. Embassy gate on Ritan Road, and ask to see the tour manager. The guard at the gate would know what to do by then.

"I can take care of myself," she answered, more to assure AJ than herself. "A Juko-kai disciple never forgets how."

AJ smiled, and replied in a rhapsodized voice, "Someday, I would like to learn your attack techniques."

She retorted coyly, without hesitation, "My attack is not as ferocious as my defense. Perhaps you can arrange to test my defensive methods….some day."

If he were slurping hot soup, he would have choked.

AJ realized that the balance between their budding friendship, and a dangerous professional relationship, was about to shift. A potential major conflict between the U.S. and China could emerge if the recent intelligence intercepts proved accurate. Lili could play a key role in the discovery and containment of planned events.

"Lili, we'll arrange for you to receive information pertaining to certain visiting American executives, and their businesses. This will consist of confidential financial operating data and proprietary processing designs, which would be of particular interest to the Minister of Competitive International Commerce. You'll pass it along to your superior…the Deputy Minister at the Beijing Tourist Bureau.

Lili didn't understand…this was the opposite of what she expected.

"Why will I receive such information?" she inquired hesitantly.

AJ paused before answering. "It's a bit tricky. We want to enhance your credibility as an information gatherer for the Party. This should assure you an assignment as a tour guide for the upcoming U.S. Trade mission delegation. Remember, we're trying to determine if certain American executives, who'll be part of the delegation, are selling their country down the Yankze River gorge."

"So, I must extract this information?" she quipped. "Just how friendly am I supposed to be?"

AJ winced at the implication that he would expect her to be overly "friendly."

"Lili, I don't know what your Tourist Bureau bosses expect from you, but I would personally shoot the one who asked you to compromise….your… friendliness."

Lili was embarrassed. "They never considered me worthy of such a high sacrifice." Her reply was awkward. "I'm still considered…a mere information gatherer." She wondered: *If I became more important, will they ask for more?*

"You won't have to do anything out of the ordinary," AJ assured her. "We'll supply the information for you to pass along; as if you extracted it yourself. The information will seem quite genuine and useful to the party, but it's disclosure will be harmless."

"Harmless!" she intoned in a fierce whisper. "That's not the word I'd associate with government lackeys and corrupt officials. They've evicted some of my friends from Silk Alley stalls, and are now selling counterfeit American and European branded products from a modern, high-rise building next door."

"The Chinese Communist Party still holds an iron grip on the big money sources in this country, Lili. It allows them to harness the energy of the people. We Americans worry that the enormous U.S. dollar holdings they control in the Bank of China, and the increasing dependence of our citizens on Chinese imports, could eventually give the Politboro a strong grip on our people, as well."

"My mother slaved over an antique fabric cutting machine," Lili said bitterly, "so a Chinese business mandarin could sell cheap tee-shirts to one of your department stores. Don't you believe that your people benefit from the low prices?"

"Yes, of course, Lili. But don't you think the Chinese people are benefiting at least as much---by acquiring most of the manufacturing jobs once held by American workers? The blue-collar workforce in the U.S. is being obliterated." He realized the discussion had drifted away from the main topic. "A genius will figure it out…someday. For now, we have to do our best."

His final comment before aborting the scrambled communication was: "Be careful, Lili. There are very smart, very bad people out there. We'll contact you soon." The line died.

AJ mulled over the conversation before drafting his report on Lili's progress to Forrest Balzerini. He was born in Santa Ana, and attended the University of California at Berkeley. A college education in California was a bargain, but he recalled how other living expenses in the state were among the highest in the country. Lili's comment about tee-shirts had sparked a flicker of guilt.

Sure, he'd purchased bargain-priced imported tee-shirts at BoxMart superstores. But he hadn't thought twice about spending a hundred dollars for a decent dinner; or a ticket to a rock concert. Admittedly, he probably wouldn't spend an extra buck or two to purchase an American-made tee-shirt, if it was displayed next to a cheaper Chinese knock-off. Why wasn't he embarrassed to admit it? Was it a warped sense of value? Or was it something more deeply rooted in his American psyche? Nurtured by the constant bombardment of suggestive advertising messages? He decided it was all about how perceptions influence buying decisions. Ten trillion dollars a year worth. American consumer decisions constituted two-thirds of the largest economy in the world.

CHAPTER 10

(April 7, 2008) 3:15pm
North Haven, Ct.

"**W**e've lost the one chance we had to pay off the loan by today's deadline," Gatt barked into the speakerphone on his desk. "The factoring house in New Jersey backed out this morning, Ken."

"They were the ones willing to factor your receivables and inventory at mafia rates?"

Joanna leaned over the speaker-phone and replied in a firm voice, "Their due-diligence people apparently made an inquiry at Residents Bank. Tinius must have deduced we might be able to refinance the loan. That mean son-of-a-bitch just obtained a court order from a Waterbury judge, and locked up all our working capital."

Ken replied into the dashboard of his new micro-car, "Then, we're out of time. Now I understand why that legal lizard, Hyman First, wouldn't return my calls. We'll have to file."

Justin wasn't surprised. He'd expected the bank to stall until the last moment, but had still hoped Tinius would be more reasonable.

Ken accelerated in the middle lane of Route 84, passing a Connecticut State trooper in the left lane who was cruising west in a good mood. The officer in the unmarked Ford Mustang pulled alongside, whirled his siren for a few seconds and shook his head in admonishment. Ken whispered into the dashboard, "I'm clicking off for a minute."

He slowed immediately, then waved an apology to the familiar face he'd seen at the court building several times. The officer waved back, indicating for him to slow down, as he admired the first micro-car he'd ever seen on the busy highway between Hartford and Waterbury. The Mustang accelerated ahead as Ken punched the auto-redial.

"The Chapter 11 filing papers are ready, Mr. Gatt; I'll be in your office in thirty minutes."

Justin stared blankly into the concerned eyes of Joanna Yates, who was sitting stone-faced across the small cherry desk his grandfather, Cosimo Gaettano, had made as a college graduation gift. She leaned into the speaker and informed Ken, "Residents Bank has apparently invoked a little-known Connecticut law."

"One of the state's worst," Ken confirmed, as if admitting to a felony by not having warned them ahead of time. "The law allows current creditors to petition state courts for a 'set aside' amount equal to a 'reasonably collectable claim.'" He paused like a hung jury, then said, "The problem is---very scant proof is required to justify the size of the claim."

Joanna replied, "The Superior Court judge in Waterbury has sequestered the entire $260,000 in our working capital account at North Haven Bank and Trust. Fortunately, our payroll account wasn't tapped." She'd wisely set up an automatic transfer from the regular depository account to the payroll account each Monday morning. This week's payroll would be covered.

"It looks as if we're void of options." Justin frowned. "I'll sign the papers as soon as you get here. You can rush them to the Church Street courthouse. I assume we still have time to file?"

"Just about!" Ken conceded. "But I'm afraid the bank was on the move before we were."

Joanna spat into the speaker, "Tell me about it!"

Ken started to click off, then asked, "How many GRT executives and managers are in the building?" He reconsidered the question. "Never mind, it doesn't matter. Just get them all out of the building before four pm. A Sheriff, or U.S. Marshal, will be arriving at exactly one-minute past four to serve papers. I don't want anyone there who can legally represent the company; or acknowledge that legal notification has been served. The official will attempt to convince whoever is left behind, that he's authorized to take possession of the premises, and all the company's assets. He may even display a box of padlocks, for effect." Ken could picture the uncertain expressions at the other end.

"Here's the only response your employees should be told to make," he added: "'*I don't know what you're talking about!*' Find a big body to firmly escort the official to the front door. Then have him lock all the access doors to the building."

Fifteen minutes later, Levine sped into the parking lot in North Haven, landing almost sideways in the handicapped space next to Gatt's restored 1987 canary-yellow Corvette convertible, with the license plate insignia, COSIMO. He snatched the silver briefcase from the passenger seat of his 2007 Brazilian-made Obvio 828/2 microcar, and bolted through the front door, past the wide-eyed receptionist, and into Gatt's office.

Employees leaving for the day marveled at the porcelain-blue microvehicle. Ken wished he had time to show them the BMW 4-cylinder, 170 horsepower power train, the same engine in the Mini Cooper S, which sipped one gallon of regular gasoline every sixty miles, and could propel the endearing vehicle at 137 miles per hour. They'd also be impressed with the Apple nano iPod built into the stereo system; and the wireless module that enabled internet access and voice activated phone calls. Ken's wife was most impressed with the Obvio's fourteen thousand dollar base price tag.

Justin held the phone in one hand, and raised the other, politely quieting Levine, as he spoke with one of his loyal suppliers. "I suggest you recall shipments en route, Tony, and send in trucks tonight to remove recent deliveries." Ken looked away as if his eyes were his ears. "Destroy the related invoices when your merchandise is removed from the warehouse. Otherwise..." Gatt looked up...suddenly realizing that an officer of the court was standing before him. Ken finished the sentence for him, "The goods become the collateral property of the secured creditor, and payment could be held up for months...or years. You may never be paid."

Lawyers must sometimes make decisions that aren't purely jurisprudent. Ken was one who occasionally disregarded the Letter, and focused on the Spirit of the law.

Joanna arose from the lone chair in front of the small desk, and offered it to Levine, who declined, as he caught the end of Justin's telephone conversation. He remained standing, and glanced at his watch. Gatt snapped his fingers and dialed the number of another supplier friend. Ken didn't have to inquire as to the nature of the exchange. He looked around Justin Gatt's office.

It was small, by any CEO's standard. Ken guessed about twelve by fourteen feet. The walls and shelves were cluttered with photographs, ziplock bags of colorful plastic pellets, and memorabilia. On the top shelf of a large oak bookcase rested a framed ten-inch black and white photograph of Justin's deceased parents. They were arm in arm, dressed in black satin cap and gown, smiling playfully into the camera. The inscription written in long-hand at the bottom of the photograph read: *Holy Cross College graduation day—OUR WEDDING, June 15, 1958.*' Ken looked closer at the photograph, and noticed that Justin's mother was holding a bouquet of roses in the hand resting on her husband's chest.

On a lower shelf was a larger color photo of an old man wearing a welding mask, swiveled up to reveal deeply creviced cheeks and dark blue eyes. He held an acetylene torch in one calloused hand and a bricklayer's trowel in the other. Set proudly on the floor before him was a collection of toys he'd made for Justin: a set of miniature rifled-soldiers, in aggressive kneeling and standing positions, shaped expertly from welding rods; and a complex, yard long machine…geared and pulley-winched like a high school science project. It lifted a small metal bucket of sand from one end of the machine to the other, without spilling a grain. Made from discarded bicycle pedals and gears, it was hand driven by the same mechanism young Justin had used to deliver newspapers on his early morning route.

Next to Cosimo in the photograph, sitting majestically, almost out of place, on a chest-high, wrought iron display table, was a gleaming cut-glass vase shaped like an open-top pineapple. Even the display table seemed to be a work of art; with side reinforcements cut in figurine shapes and painted in rainbow colors. Ken saw the vase in the picture, resting on a window sill behind Justin's desk. It seemed to emit iridescent hues of opal, pearl and peridot.

Ken studied the contents on the wall next to the bookcase, as Gatt completed his call to a wood pallet supplier whose shipment was en route. Front page reprints of several U.S. and foreign patents were framed in coral enamel. Each had been issued to Gatt Recovery Technologies, Inc., and listed Justin Gatt as the discoverer of the technology.

Most of the patents were for new compositions of matter…unique combinations of ingredients with unexpected uses. All were produced from previously discarded plastic scrap. These new materials could be shaped by heat and pressure into a myriad of impact and weather resistant parts and common consumer items.

"My grandfather made the vase, and several others like it," Justin said proudly, having noticed Ken's interest in the magical, light emitting object. "He gave them as coveted gifts to relatives and friends. But, I'm the only one he revealed the formulation and process to." Justin thought of the superheated mixture of tinted coke and wine bottles, hammered into shards in a kettle of crushed ice; the base mixture of Portland cement and finely filtered white sand from Old Silver Beach on Cape Cod; and a secret fluid which seeped from deep marble quarries outside Rome, only during the spring months. Cosimo had imported a wine keg of the fluid from a friend who worked in the quarries.

Justin had analyzed the fluid, and was amazed to discover that it captured free gamma rays from the frequent solar flares bombarding the atmosphere, and emitted fluorescent rainbows when heated to glass-melting temperatures. Somehow, his grandfather had discovered a process to crystallize the mixture into a color-emitting glassy solid, which could be formed into vases and other open-top vessels.

"Please, sit, Ken," Justin suggested, as the mesmerized attorney closed his mouth. "Joanna will be rounding up the other managers and departing in a few minutes."

Joanna was an attractive, widowed mother of twin teenage girls, with sparkling brown eyes and short auburn hair. She'd thrived under Justin's tutelage during the last twelve years, rising from assistant bookkeeper to financial manager of the fifteen-million-dollar business. She was the glue which held the company together during hard times.

Her dedication and bull-headed drive kept every GRT penny in place. Cash was managed as if it were her own, and accounts payable and receivable were kept under incarceration-like control. Finances at GRT had been well managed… until Slattery Housewares and Residents Bank blind-sided the company.

It was nearly as traumatic for Joanna as the financial and emotional crisis Justin had helped her through, when her husband died of a malignant brain tumor. She was more than loyal---she'd do anything for Justin. Knowing his request would always be honorable, as well as logical.

Ken took the seat as Joanna departed to round up the other managers. He placed the Chapter 11 filing papers on the desk, and said, "We'll need to get these to the Clerk of Courts before five. He's a friend, and will make sure they're properly filed and recorded with today's date."

Justin quickly signed four different forms and handed them back to Ken. "What exactly does this do for us, besides setting up hurdles for the bank?" he asked ruefully.

Ken peered into the intensely penetrating, yet unthreatening blue eyes of the six foot executive-scientist. Or was it scientist-executive? He marveled at the apparent emotional control Justin displayed.

"I have to be honest, Mr. Gatt. The bankruptcy law enacted by Congress in April, 2005, has doomed many previously viable companies trying to recover from Chapter 11. The new restrictions were designed to protect creditors and shareholders from the managers of large corporations, who treated the old bankruptcy law as just another financial instrument to cook the books."

He checked his watch again, as he began to stand. "You'll initially be able to continue operating the company, as debtor-in-possession. But, only as long as you don't reduce the value of the assets pledged as collateral against the bank loan. Which is just about everything you own. GRT will be required to submit detailed financial status reports to the court every few weeks. It's a real pain, but you have no choice. Joanna will be extremely busy." He heard the commotion in the hallway as Joanna shuffled bodies toward the exit.

"The bank's attorneys love it. They collect fees for every court review session; then attempt to force you into Chapter 7 liquidation. That's when they make the real money."

Gatt asked the obvious question, "What happens if the collateral value falls below the beginning amount?"

Levine answered patiently, "If the collateral value falls below the beginning level, which the judge will establish at the initial court session for your case, the bank will force the issue. Debtor-in-possession status will end, and you'll lose control." He glanced at his watch again…seconds since he last checked…and turned as he headed for the door. "You also have an exclusive right, for 18 months, to present a Plan of Reorganization to the bankruptcy judge; if you're able to maintain d.o.p. control."

Justin came around the desk and clasped Levine's hand. "You'd better go, Ken. Thanks for giving us a fighting chance. I appreciate the prep work you did over the weekend. And, please call me Justin. I'm feeling too old as it is."

Levine responded warmly, "As I understand it, Justin, your toughest challenge will be to raise outside money to enable GRT to operate until the back-to-school season kicks in. With some luck, profits will be high enough to settle with the bank and the other creditors caught in the middle." Trying to be more positive, he added, "At least you're the only stockholder."

Ken allowed himself a smirk, if not a smile, as Justin's brow wrinkled. "We don't have to worry about stockholder lawsuits," he explained. "Unless you decide to sue yourself."

In a more serious tone, he asked, "How will the company be able to operate without the bank's line-of-credit, Justin? How can you buy raw materials?"

Without hesitation, Justin replied, "I have some personal reserves I can loan the company. Also, some suppliers have agreed to ship materials in on consignment."

"How will you pay them?"

"They'll bill us weekly, as the materials are consumed. I gave my word to accurately report any use of the consigned materials. There'll be a 24 hour open door policy at the factory. Their people will be free to inspect the inventory at any time. That's all they required."

Levine was impressed; but had other concerns. "How about the big security deposit the new bankruptcy law allows the utility companies to demand? What about your key people? Do they realize the company can't pay bonuses during the court battle?"

"I don't think that will be a problem."

"Justin, you have to be very…very…very careful how you put more money into the company. Already, any loans you've provided in the past are worthless. The bankruptcy judge must approve any new loans. Tinius and Hyman First will pressure him to subordinate the loan paybacks to their current claims. We can't let that happen."

Justin nodded emphatically, and started packing his briefcase as Levine hurried to the front entrance. GRT had never given bonuses to keep top managers. Just very good salaries, flexible hours and the most expensive, company-paid medical coverage available for their families. Yes, there had been occasional loans and handouts to needy employees; but that was a personal issue, not company policy. The money came from his personal account, and he'd been paid back one-hundred-percent by the people he'd helped. He recalled his grandfather's advise when he lost a key manager to a higher-paying major corporation: "Encourage him. Give him a good recommendation. A person should be admired for trying to better himself."

In his heart, Justin believed that key GRT employees remained more loyal to the challenges the company offered, than to him as an individual. Many had improved their inherent abilities, and took pride in participating in the noble process of making useful products from waste. He was convinced that there is a special gene in the DNA of creative people, which exudes satisfaction-enzymes, when something new and tangible evolves from their efforts.

At GRT, the employees created new materials, and learned new processes. They converted baled, chopped and crushed plastic bottles, carpet fibers, spent agricultural film and mixed plastic from diaper factories, into more than thirty million pounds of high quality plastics, used by processors like Slattery Housewares and Leominster Plastics Company. GRT employees were encouraged to walk into Sears, BoxMart, JC Penney's and Home Depot stores to look, touch…and purchase…the products they produced at GRT from recycled materials.

At 3:45 pm, Justin waved at Roberto as he arrived in the parking lot to supervise the first and second shift personnel exchange. He eased into his dream car and pulled out slowly When he reached the main road of the industrial park; he sank low in the driver's seat. The Sheriff's Lincoln Mark LT luxury pickup truck slid to the side of the road, and parked at the driveway entrance….waiting until 4:01 pm

CHAPTER 11

(JUNE 6, 2008) AM,
BEIJING, HEADQUARTERS OF THE CHINESE COMMUNIST PARTY

"The United States is fulfilling Lenin's doctrine, just as we predicted." General Ye Kunshi said over the secure military-issue cellphone connecting him with his subordinate at Yale University. "Your mission at the American universities is complete, Colonel Wen. I expect you to return to Macau immediately."

"As you command, General. I can assure you---from what I have learned---the American public will not stop purchasing the rope with which we plan to hang them."

General Ye, Deputy Commander of the People's Liberation Army, was also the top business executive of the PLA's state-run businesses. He clicked off and returned to his seat in the waiting area outside the most private meeting room in all of China.

He lost patience after sitting for ten seconds in a deep-cushioned red velvet armchair facing the twelve-foot, hand-carved teak doors leading into the Chinese Communist Party Conference Hall. He jumped up and began pacing like an expectant father in the antique-decorated reception area that few foreigners had ever viewed.

The inner sanctum of Chinese leadership, located near the Forbidden City complex, was furnished with treasures from the Ming and Qing dynasties, as well as other ancient Chinese artifacts that had been taken by the Kuomintang Nationalists on their retreat to Taiwan, but had been returned to the mainland.

His scowl and stomping military-gait unnerved the attractive receptionist, a grand-daughter of Wang Chao, the Minister of Industry and Trade, and Ye's close ally on the Standing Committee of the Chinese Communist Party.

She knew to look away and remain silent when the mercurial General Ye was made to wait for the nine most powerful men in China, assembled inside the Conference Hall, to reach consensus on the critical issues influencing Party control of the country.

Dressed in an impeccably starched tan uniform, with his rank indicated only by small shoulder emblems, General Ye's erect six-foot frame and authoritative demeanor marked him as a high-ranking military officer even when he was dressed in casual attire.

The Chinese government's global communications center was located in a room adjacent to the large conference hall. Jammed with technicians manning Russian-designed, state-of-the-art satellite-linked telecommunications equipment, the Chinese leaders could communicate within seconds with embassies, consulates and one hundred and sixteen foreign heads of state.

General Ye was interested in only one decision the Standing Committee would make today: to accept or reject the Macau Tax-Free Foreign Joint Ventures Act. The new law was already approved by the National People's Congress, China's version of a democratic parliamentary body, made up of elected representatives from the provinces, autonomous regions and the military.

The agenda for today's Standing Committee meeting included: the recent calls by American politicians to establish new trade barriers; LCE's request to secure more foreign sources of petroleum for Li Chin's booming factories; and a proposed investment in new mining technology offered by Estonia, the only country other than China producing shale oil at the beginning of the twenty-first century.

The Macau Act would allow large state-run manufacturing enterprises controlled by the PLA to merge with more financially-stable foreign firms. The joint-venture he had in mind would provide needed relief from the billions in bank loans forced on LCE, the PLA's largest manufacturing conglomerate, by the recently replaced President and General Secretary of the Party. A financially-healthy LCE was needed to underpin the Chinese government's aggressive export policy. Li Chin's conglomeration of factories was China's largest exporter of low-cost consumer goods.

Although only marginally profitable, the 500 mainland factories Li Chin amalgamated into a two-hundred $billion manufacturing enterprise, generated massive U.S. dollar reserves for the Central Bank of China. The Macau law would stabilize LCE's financial condition, and allow the company to continue shipping low-cost goods to BoxMart and other retailers around the globe. The new law provided for a ten-year reprieve from income taxes and export duties, for any joint venture between a state-controlled manufacturing business and a 'qualified' foreign company.

Chang Hui Chen, a member of the Standing Committee and Chairman of the National People's Congress, was already authorized under the Chinese constitution to implement the law passed by the NPC. But he knew it was political suicide to do so without the stamp of approval from President Mu Jianting and the other seven Standing Committee members. He could not afford to jeopardize his position as leader of the NPC. It gave him the leverage to forge Committee decisions favorable to the aims of his secret alliance with Yong Ihasa's secret society.

As the chief representative of NPC deputies…elected from China's provinces, autonomous zones, the five municipalities administered by the central government, and the armed services, NPC Chairman Chang enjoyed support across a broad spectrum of the population. He and the three expansionist members on the Standing Committee needed all the political power they could muster to contest President Mu and the five other conservative members, who were not about to share power voluntarily. The balance of power and the future direction of China in world affairs was at stake.

General Ye was furious at the indignity of being forced to wait outside the meeting chamber at Zhangnanhai, the headquarters complex of the Chinese Communist Party, located on the western fringes of the Forbidden City, in the heart of the nation's political and cultural capital.

One of the few PLA generals who had survived Deng Xiopeng's purge of army officers following the end of the Cultural Revolution in the early eighties, Ye Kunshi benefited from China's esteem for military heritage and its proclivity for ancestral worship.

His late uncle, Lin Biao, an influential figure in the military, had been named successor to Mao in 1969, until he fell out of favor for disagreeing with Mao's plans to overcome bureaucratic entrenchment by reforming all areas of Chinese life during the Cultural Revolution. General Ye's greatest military ancestor was Qi Jiguang, a Ming General who led many victorious battles in the south, and designed the twenty-two towers of the Great Wall section at Mutianyu, seventy miles northeast of Beijing.

Despite being passed over for a position on the Standing Committee, General Ye was the most influential of the 'fourth generation' Chinese leaders, which surfaced in 2002 after Jiang Zemin was replaced as General Secretary and President. A junior-member of the 24-man Central Committee of the Politboro, and Second Vice-Chairman of the Military Commission, answering only to President Mu Jianting and PLA Commander, Marshall Tong Shu, General Ye wielded unusual influence in political, military and business circles. His power had been enhanced when he was appointed chief executive officer of the state-run industries controlled by the People's Liberation Army.

Ye believed he was more deserving of a Standing Committee leadership position than several of the men now bickering in the Inner Hall…wasting his precious time with yin and yang exchanges to reach consensus on every issue. He was more feared than respected by President Mu and the other leaders, for his tendency to crush opponents. They saw that he lacked characteristic Chinese-patience, and the negotiating skills to resolve domestic and foreign conflicts in a non-confrontational manner.

President Mu and the five members following a conservative inclination for China's future, were determined to limit the leadership roles of General Ye and the three 'expansionist' members of the Standing Committee aligned with the General---Yong Ihasa, the Vice-Premier and Minister of State Security and Monetary Policy; Wang Chao, the Minister of Industry and Trade; and Chang Hui Chen, the NPC Chairman. Mu had no knowledge of the secret alliance the three Committee members had formed with General Ye.

The doors to the inner hall suddenly opened and Yong Ihasa, the lanky, sharp-nosed Vice-Premier of the State Council, strode over purposefully and greeted 69-year-old General Ye with a respectable bow.

"Lao pengyou. Old friend." He addressed the general.

"Tongzhi, Comrade Vice-Premier Yong," he nodded, unable to mask the expression of displeasure pasted on his face. "Are the committee members now disposed to discuss the new Macau law?"

The seventy year-old poker-faced vice premier, with the pure-white tonsured hair line, answered charismatically, "Please do not appear impatient, General Ye. President Mu and the others are rightfully concerned with the street demonstrations and the reappearance of the giant posters outlawed in public areas of our largest municipalities. They are also very troubled by the recent migrant worker outcries and violence in Shanghai and Chongqing."

Ye Kunshi said contemptuously, "That low-life is claiming that the government is exploiting their rights. Migrant people *have* no rights in the central municipalities. The harsh treatment they received was justified." He was referring to his own order to pepper the demonstrators outside the Summer Palace and in the business and diplomatic districts near Tianan'men Sqaure, with hard rubber bullets.

Ihasa added vehemently, "The common people just do not appreciate our efforts to catapult China to the forefront of world affairs. They even complain about the smog and green dust settling on the billboards promoting the upcoming Olympics." He emitted a cautious smile as the intense dark eyes of the wiry-built general projected a sense of distrust…straining to discern a hidden meaning in his words.

"President Mu has requested your analysis of the consequences the Macau law will inflict on China's booming economy. He's overly cautious these days about allowing the Committee to approve new initiatives."

"It's true that the new Act could alter the way China conducts business with foreign multi-nationals," Ye admitted. "But that's exactly the result we desire." He leaned closer to Ihasa and whispered, "With a properly-structured joint venture between BoxMart and LCE, the PLA can gain the upper hand. It will guarantee the long-term stability of China's U.S. marketing base. Command over the purchasing decisions of LCE's largest American customers will be ours."

Yong leaned close to the General's ear, and whispered, "In that case, lao pengyou, we must be extremely cautious with Mu and the other members who are not aware of the Savoy Imperative, or the other events we have planned." He glanced over his shoulder to an aide waving frantically for them to join the others.

"I suggest you emphasize the importance of the new Macau law on the financial success of LCE," Yong said softly...almost inaudibly. "The Governor of the Central Bank, Yew Bai Tsin, is the only comrade with sufficient financial acumen to question the details of a proposed merger between LCE and BoxMart."

Yong turned as the aide poked his head out from the conference room again and signaled with his watch that the fifteen minute break had ended. The vice-premier added somberly, "I suggest you bring it up only as a possibility. Let the numbers do the convincing."

General Secretary Mu Jianting stood and greeted General Ye as he entered the room. The others remained seated at the large conference table, sipping tea and exchanging hushed comments. Only Wang Chao, the Minister of Industry and Trade, and Chang Hui Chen, Chairman of the National People's Congress, followed Ye's movements as he took a seat next to Yong Ihasa near the podium in the front of the room. The others simply ignored him.

"So kind of you to join us, comrade General," President Mu exclaimed loudly. "The Committee appreciates your recent success in responding to the Beijing street riots. We cannot tolerate public challenges to the Party's absolute control of the country, especially from the misinformed environmental groups and the illegal assemblies of cranky citizens."

The others grunted approval, but several had still not looked at the general or acknowledged his presence. They disagreed with his harsh methods of quelling riots; but not the results. General Ye recorded the snubs in his memory. It was an unacceptable sign of disrespect. A mistake he hoped to correct later.

Chang Hui Chen opened the discussion of the new Macau law. "It is appropriate that the executive in charge of China's largest business enterprise join us today. We will not waste General Ye's time with petty discussions."

He then turned to Ye and said, "You should be aware that the Standing Committee is split in its deliberation regarding the Macau Tax-free and Foreign Joint Ventures Act." He scanned the doubtful expressions of those opposed to the new law, then added tersely, "Despite the Act being approved by the National People's Congress…of which I am chairman."

President Mu responded sharply, "Some committee members are concerned that the law is poorly designed. What is your response, General Ye? There are allegations that the new law is a dangerous business experiment, which could backfire to a loss of control of our large domestic enterprises?"

General Ye rose deliberately from his chair and strode in a stiff military canter to the podium. An aide placed a stack of multi-colored cardboard charts on a display frame near the podium and handed Ye a small laser pointer.

"I will explain why the new law is important to China's growing economy…and critical to the continued financial health of LCE and its 500 factories. But first allow me to comment that the bad-loan problems at the China Edifice Construction Bank and the other central Chinese commercial banks that underwrite exports, are directly impacted by the financial health of state-run manufacturing conglomerates, such as LCE."

The governor of the Central Bank of China uttered a guttural laugh, then declared in a derisive tone, "We are well aware of the problems your manufacturing arms have dumped on the central banks, General. However, I will acknowledge that LCE has contributed mightily to China's economic growth and employment opportunities for peasant workers." The central banker, Yew Bai Tsin, shifted uncomfortably in his seat as the dangerous general's pained dark eyes registered unforgettable resentment for the verbal attack.

"General Ye, please explain how you will maintain control of our domestic businesses when they are locked in fifty-fifty joint ventures with powerful foreign companies?"

"An astute question, Governor Yew Bai. The answer, in one word, is: *Macau*."

NPC Chairman Chang interjected. "The National People's Congress has studied the potential effects of the Macau Act on the delinquent loans of state industries. We believe that any further consolidation of Chinese domestic businesses could heighten the chance that China's central bank will experience a catastrophic default. Without foreign financing, many factories could be forced to close."

"Could this not occur in mergers with foreign companies as well?"

General Ye ignored Yew Bai's question. He pointed the red laser at the first chart, and replied, "My primary concern is to prevent the tax-free Macau zone from becoming a magnet for well-established mainland businesses. We've spent enormous sums on infrastructure and work-force training at the business centers, such as the Suzhou manufacturing complex west of Shanghai. We do not want to relocate these factories."

Chang said enthusiastically, "The advantages of the new law for our largest state-owned companies are noteworthy…if not enormous. Tax-free, equal-ownership joint ventures between our … moderately efficient state-controlled businesses, and the super-efficient foreign multinationals…will upgrade China's factories to state-of-the-art practices."

General Ye added unabashedly, "With minimum investment by the PLA."

Vice-president Sun Linglong, a Princeton-trained economist, joined the discussion. "Large joint-ventures based in Macau should revitalize the gambling industry we've carefully protected since China repatriated the Portuguese colony in 1999."

General Ye broke in, "To answer comrade governor Yew Bai Tsin's concern---the recent governance changes forced on Macau by this body should give the PLA effective control of any joint ventures, even with a balanced board of directors."

Ye displayed another chart showing projected profits of a theoretical joint venture, which utilized data generated by BoxMart's supercomputer. "If structured properly, the new ventures will become *cash cows*…as the Americans say. The bad-loan portfolios burdening our large commercial banks in Shanghai and Beijing will dissipate rapidly."

President Mu, who also controlled the armed forces of China as Chairman of the Central Military Commission, had made a critical error several months ago. By loosening restrictions on China's four largest commercial banks, he'd allowed speculative loans to struggling state-run factories to balloon. The disturbing consequence was a sharp reduction in the investments Citigroup, Solomon and other international investment banks were willing to make in the public shares of China's lending institutions.

Mu's rivals had begun questioning his wisdom and stranglehold on power. He became gun-shy and declared that the decision-making pace of the Communist Party must be slowed. His solid base of domestic and military supporters on the Standing Committee was now split between Mu's conservative majority---which desired to slow China's unbridled economic expansion, and three influential members of the ruling body, who believed

China should accelerate its frenetic pace to overtake the United States in global trade and diplomatic influence.

General Ye had joined forces with the three liberal members: Yong Ihasa, Chang Hui Chen and Wang Chao. They believed the time had come for China to break out of its *less- than- superpower* status and take its rightful place as the world's dominant society. The strong support of Jake Kurancy and the *Savoy Imperative* gave them the opportunity to usurp power from Mu and the other Party conservatives on the Committee.

The Prime Minister, Zhoa Zhoa-gang, a dumpy man in his late seventies with large hands and deep frown-lines on his stern face, murmured in a raspy voice, "Do you have any deals pending which could utilize the provisions of the Macau law?"

"Yes!" Wang Chao, answered quickly. "There could be a very large merger in the near future." He turned to General Ye and said, "Please explain."

The general gripped the edges of the podium tightly and stiffened his arms, as if bracing for a frontal attack. His head tilted backward, to emphasize the gravity of his response. "We have explored the possibility of combining LCE---our largest state-run manufacturing conglomerate---with several of the world's largest retailers. The strategy is to cement closer relations with China's prime export customers, and protect our position in key export markets."

Wang Chao chirped, "There is no closer business relationship than a fifty-fifty partnership, on which both partners rely for success."

"Which retailers have you contacted?" asked Yong Ihasa, feigning ignorance.

All eyes centered on Ye as he slowly shuffled the exhibits and placed a new one on top. The heading: *Potential Partners*, was followed by a list of ten of the world's most famous retailers. He spoke with a forced enthusiasm about two European companies listed at the top of the chart.

"Li Chin, the able chairman of LCE…. most of you have known him for many years…recently met with retailers in Germany, France and the United States." The chart listed the world's largest merchants of consumer products.

"Is there any interest?" Vice-Premier Yong asked, again pretending to be uninformed about the negotiations.

General Ye had no patience for such games. He blurted out, "A Wal-Mart executive laughed in our faces, then was rude to Li Chin. Mr. Li does not care to partner with such an arrogant manager, and neither do I."

"Perhaps a higher level contact should be pursued," President Mu suggested. "The discount behemoth is well aware of its considerable dependence on this committee's decisions; despite the fact that we need their new super-stores to help promote peasant tranquility."

Central bank governor Yew Bai snickered, "There would be an ugly uprising from the middle-class cadre in the rural provinces and autonomous zones if these stores were forced out of business."

"It is the same with the other foreign retailers we've allowed in the front door…at the expense of our *back-door* enterprises." The Commander of the People's Liberation Army, Marshall Tong Shu, broke his silence. The oldest man in the room lacked common sense and was impulsive, but his cruel and greedy tendencies made him fearsome and enormously wealthy. He was a Politboro member not to be underestimated.

"The Chinese people have embraced the gigantic discount stores as if they are revelations from Confusious or Mencius," replied Prime Minister Zhoa Zhoa-gang, a short, thin man in his late seventies, with furtive eyes framed by a waxen complexion, and thick grey hair brushed straight back. "Their popularity borders on fanaticism. I wish the Communist Party could capture their magic. Perhaps there is a lesson to be learned from the BoxMarts and Wal-Marts, which could help the Party regain its esteem in the eyes of the younger generation."

Sun Linglong, the Vice President of China known for his introspective manner, seemed lost in thought as the other committee members exchanged views regarding the new law. Impeccably attired in a dark blue suit and China-red tie ornamented with a full-length snake of gold stars, his narrow eyes studied the expressions of General Ye and Yong Ihasa. He sensed a tension in their frequent exchange of side glances.

"How do you propose we respond to the giant retailer's rebuttal?" Sun Linglong asked.

General Ye snapped, "Wu-wei. Do nothing. There are other, more appropriate partners."

Wang Chao raised his voice. "This thousand kilogram Godzilla will soon recognize the negative implications of competing against a retailer with strong ties to the Chinese Communist Party."

President Mu shrugged at Wang's peculiar warning. "Who else has Li Chin approached?"

General Ye pointed to the list of retail companies on the chart and replied, "Mr. Li has compiled the report contained in your daily agenda file. It is my understanding that he approached the French retailer, **PPR**, who owns the Gucci luxury group and the **Fnac** retail store chain. Also, in Germany---the Otto family. They generate revenues of about twenty billion dollars annually from the Eddy Bauer and Crate & Barrel stores in the United States. They also publish two thousand retail catalogs in twenty one countries, including the century-old Spiegel catalog in Chicago."

The General reached for another display board and placed it over the previous one. He turned gradually to face President Mu. "Unfortunately, both of the European retailing giants have serious financial shortcomings."

Mu Jianting repeated his earlier question, "Who else have we approached?"

Sun Linglong caught the quick eye contact between Ye and Yong.

"There is one multinational consumer-products retailer committed to a fifty-fifty venture with LCE," General Ye answered, slowly lifting a water glass and succumbing to an irresistible impulse to adrenalize their curiosity with a delayed answer. "Sears-Kmart, JC Penney's and Target have been overly cautious in responding to Li Chin's overtures." The sparkle in General Ye's eyes suggested the next information was prepared well in advance.

He lifted the last chart from the bottom. Everyone stared anxiously at the large red letters: **BoxMart Retail Enterprises**.

"The Chairman of BoxMart, Jake Kurancy, has signed a letter of intent to merge his company with LCE; pending the approval and implementation of the Macau Business Act being deliberated by this Committee," exulted Ye.

Wang Chao removed a stack of printed reports from a small box beneath his chair and handed them out, saying, "These are pro-forma sales and profit projections for the proposed merger of LCE and BoxMart. Please note the balance sheet projections as well. Also, the resulting decline of bank debt for the LCE subsidiary after the first year."

General Ye was too aroused to let the numbers do all the selling. He announced, "We have tentatively named the joint venture ***Bomali Corporation***. It will be the largest, most profitable business enterprise ever formed."

The Governor of the Central Bank read the Executive Summary, then focused on the financial projections. Ye, Yong and Chang smiled as President Mu and Yew Bai Tsin gaped at the astonishing figures. Finally, the central bank minister gingerly placed the report on the table and admitted grudgingly, "These numbers are fantastic. How can we not approve the new law?"

CHAPTER 12

(June 11, 2008) 2pm
North Haven

It was called *Casual Wednesday,* Joanna's creation, but there was nothing casual about the disastrous financial reports she dropped on his desk before rushing out.

"Lots of businesses allow a *Casual Friday* for their employees." She'd argued. "It's just early preparation for casual weekends. But a Wednesday dress-down will invigorate people---make them more productive and creative." At least that was her theory.

She returned to Justin's office a few minutes later, carrying a fresh pot of coffee, two styrofoam cups and a fistful of dry cream and sugar-substitute packets—her props for long and difficult financial reviews. She was dressed in loose-fitting blue-jeans, folded to her knees, white bobby-socks crumpled above pink Nike walking sneakers, and a white cotton Relay-for-Life tee shirt with the sleeves rolled up. Of medium height, with her auburn hair combed to an upsweep, the middle-aged financial manager, with the light brown moon eyes and glowing skin, looked beguiling. A heart-shaped gold locket containing a miniaturized photo of her twin teenaged daughters, dangled from her ivory neck on a serpentine gold chain.

Justin smiled at the engaging woman who stood by his side during many crises. He cleared a spot on his small desk by brushing some of the discouraging financial reports she'd given him, over the edge into a wastebasket. He was dressed in the pale blue dress shirt, pressed cotton cords and soft wool Navy blazer he'd worn earlier in the day to a meeting with a vulture-capital firm in Greenwich. The tie had been tossed in the trash.

Joanna leaned over and released her armful. Before she descended to the lone chair facing the desk, he said awkwardly, "Please close the door." It was a seldom-made request. The founder of Gatt Recovery Technologies believed in sharing information with his employees; at being accessible to their ideas and problems. His policy was: "My door is always open …call first, if you can. Or, just come in if you have to."

"Do you see what I see in the figures?" he asked grimly.

"Sales are down," she understated, then admitted bravely, "and probably not coming back. It'll be impossible to replace the business we lost from Slattery and Leominster Plastics." She shifted in her seat as he whispered hoarsely, "We've burned through all our cash."

Joanna didn't have to remind him that the two-hundred-thousand he'd recently loaned to the company had gone up the same smoke stack. Justin's decision to keep all employees on the payroll during the first few months of the debtor-in-possession operating period, hadn't helped conserve working capital. The factory manager had been instructed to continue running back-to-school items, although the expected orders had yet to materialize. Joanna suspected he just wanted to keep the machines running so employees could weather the downturn, while he attempted to save the business.

"The venture capital firm I met with this morning, in Greenwich," he said morosely,"was enthusiastic about the new technology and pending patents." Wagging his head side to side, he added, "They recoiled like heated shrink-wrap, and quickly escorted me to the exit door when I informed them that Residents Bank held a first lien on all our assets."

He tore the edges off four pink packets and emptied the powdery sweetener into the plastic cup, without thinking. He usually drank his coffee black. Joanna watched in horror and quickly drowned the equivalent of eight spoons of sugar in his cup with steaming coffee. "There hasn't been any other investor interest. Even the bottom feeders have disappeared."

The upside of GRT's new material separation technology wasn't easily understood, even by the technically proficient venture capitalists. It required a visionary with an imagination- stretch that was probably reserved for biotech and gene-splicing start-ups. The recycling industry had long since vanished from the target lists of technology venture funds, although an extrapolation of GRT's new recycling and separation technology into the oil industry had startling implications.

GRT had recently tested the new separation process on samples of oil shale from the Green River Formation deposits in Utah, Wyoming and Colorado. Geologists estimated that the area contained 500 to 800 billion barrels of *kerogen*, the waxy organic material which was costly to separate using current extraction methods, but could be processed and refined into gasoline, diesel fuel and jet fuel. At world oil prices, the current extraction process was not economically feasible. However, the lab tests of GRT's process indicated the *kerogen* could be separated at a fraction of this cost using the new technology.

Justin planned to test the separation technology on tar-sand deposits just received from the Fort McMurray Bitumen Plant in the lower Athabasca River of Alberta, Canada. The loose, grainy tar sands there contained more than 900 billion barrels of *bitumen*, a mixture of hydrocarbons with glue-like consistency, which could also be extracted and refined for use as a fuel, heating oil or raw material for the chemical industry. The Alberta tar sands area was the largest known deposit of crude oil in the world; although still more expensive to extricate than the proven reserves of oil, natural gas and coal being tapped today.

*If the new GRT material separation process could be proven on a commercial scale, and the cost of recovering bitumen and kerogen greatly reduced....*Justin was having trouble processing the implications. An inexpensive *bitumen* and *kerogen* recovery process was a concept too immense to contrast with his immediate problem---trying to rescue his small business.

He folded his arms and recalled, sourly, "We presented a conservative business plan to the Naugatuck valley bank which supposedly was committed to helping finance small businesses in central Connecticut. Then, an optimistic, five-year plan to the commercial lending officer at the Bank of Columbia, which was authorized to issue SBA loans. And...."

Joanna noticed the pursed lips and sudden ashen expression, as he stopped in mid-sentence. "It's been a waste of time," he croaked. "All the lenders we approached were aware that any new loans would first be applied to pay off Residents Bank. They weren't that concerned. Our projections showed GRT would generate enough working capital to operate the business and make the required payments on the loans."

Joanna nodded knowingly, "They got jittery when Tinius refused to subordinate the bank's first claim on the new money, during the bridge-financing period."

"They're afraid of getting screwed by Tinius," Justin snapped, "if there's a delay in closing the loan while the documents are being prepared."

"His own peers don't trust him," she replied. "We probably should have realized that a new loan, under the circumstances, was too risky for a traditional lender."

Justin shook his head. "There's been too many small business failures in the northeast, lately. It's spawned super-conservative loan policies."

Joanna thought about her favorite description of a conservative bank policy: "If you don't need a loan, and have plenty of cash or credit, we'll gladly loan you any amount. Otherwise…don't call us. Unless, of course, you're willing to guarantee the loan, unconditionally, and hand over stock and savings certificates and real estate deeds worth more than the loan balance. The bank will, of course, volunteer to hold this collateral in a non-interest bearing escrow account until the entire balance is paid."

"Ken Levine claims the market for refinancing salvageable Chapter 11 businesses has dried up," Justin replied stiffly. "It used to be that some companies with a history of profitability--- the ones decently managed, but which stumbled on market changes that came too fast---could be good investments."

Joanna recognized the transformation in his tone. Justin's 'state-of-the-world' lecturing voice had emerged.

"I believe globalization and the new bankruptcy laws are destroying the opportunities for companies like GRT to recover." Justin rose and sauntered to the window, pausing to stare wanly at the cars in the employee parking lot. "The federal government doesn't seem to think the phenomenon of small business failures is much of a problem in the big picture."

He's right, she thought. Several Congressional leaders had publicly stated that the globalization movement *required* a downsizing in the U.S. manufacturing sector. Many had confused their constituents after the November, 2006 elections, by e-mailing promises to introduce legislation that would "assure the continued health of small businesses, which are the primary job creators in this country." While the rhetoric was impressive, the follow-up action was non-existent.

Proposed bills to aid small manufacturers had been pummeled to death by special interest groups in committee wrangles. Not one assistance bill reached the floor of the House or Senate for a vote. Deterioration of the U.S. manufacturing industry continued unabated, as only a few politicians even admitted the country had a problem.

Martin Merrand, the Governor of New York, was one who did. An anti free-trader with strong convictions, the Governor didn't believe that job losses in the U.S. manufacturing sector were inevitable, unavoidable or harmless to the country. He was championing the idea that well-conceived trade restraints were an acceptable substitute for the job losses which he claimed had become "the sacrifice of choice for the free-trade worshipers."

"Merrand's ideas frighten a lot of business leaders who are stampeding their U.S. operations to China." Justin could go on for hours. "Merrand recently made a good point on *Ask the Media*, reminding the TV audience that discount-retailers have replaced most of the lost manufacturing jobs with much-lower-paying jobs offering less benefits. Merrand claimed that most of the good-paying skilled jobs are on a one-way trip to the dirt beneath our feet, like sudden death. Except six feet has become the diameter of the planet, and leads to the home of 1.3 billion people."

Joanna shot back. "I read that BoxMart hired a hundred and ten thousand people in the past two years, and most of those jobs are low-paying positions at the new superstores."

"Yeah…The starting pay for a BoxMart 'super service rep' is a few cents above minimum wage. Full-time workers can earn ten percent more for perfect weekly attendance. Some deal! Miss and hour…it costs you ten percent."

The remaining inch of coffee-syrup in his cup was now cold. Joanna leaned forward and flooded it over without asking. He was on a roll.

"Sure, there are other benefits," he continued ruefully. "BoxMart offers paid major- medical insurance which covers most health related expenses; except there's a twelve-thousand dollar annual family deductible. That's about half of what the average employee makes in a year."

Joanna nervously fingered her copy of the latest financial-condition report with its horror-provoking numbers. She wanted to derail Justin from this train of thought, and address the issue of: *What do we do now?*

"Maybe we should discuss our next move."

"They have a liberal vacation policy," he snorted, oblivious to her comment. "Forty hours vacation pay for every three thousand hours worked. Do the math! And, career advancement opportunities…if you're willing to attend Saturday morning training sessions for a year...without pay."

Joanna gave up. She joined the complaining. "If financing for companies in Chapter 11 was available from the SBA, or the State's Economic Development Agency, we'd have a good chance to recover. Connecticut's politicians claim to be concerned about saving jobs, but they're more concerned with collecting exorbitant business taxes, than helping companies having financial difficulties because of foreign competition."

Justin finally noticed Joanna nervously opening and closing the gold locket. He realized they'd drifted to improbable scenarios, and it was time to address reality. He concluded his tirade with, "Our industry is in deep muck."

The phone rang as Justin bent down into the wastebasket to retrieve the discarded financial reports. His free hand stretched across the desk and lifted the receiver. "Gatt here!"

Ken Levine barked into the phone, "I just found out why the anticipated back-to-school orders never came. Edwin Tinius made sure they didn't."

"What?" Justin was stunned. He hammered the speaker button so Joanna could listen and allowed the financial reports to slip back into the trash bucket. "You're saying he had something to do with it?"

"The sleaze-bag mailed registered scare letters to all your customers. He listed the specific inventory items they might purchase, and the bank's intention to prevent the sale, claiming first priority on all GRT's assets." They could hear him inhale deeply. Ken was having trouble breathing."The letter also claimed the bank would shut down the business at the conclusion of the bankruptcy case, which they suggested would be in the near future."

Justin dropped the receiver on the desk. "Ken...how could the judge let that happen?"

Ken's exhale sounded like a last breath. "The letter was pre-approved by Judge Rooter! Without notification to me, the U.S. Trustee or the lawyer for the unsecured creditors. The Clerk of Courts claims it was because the interests of GRT's customers had to be considered a high priority. What bullshit! I went ballistic. I told Rooter his letter bordered on intimidation and disregard for the debtor-in-possession rules."

"This is unbelievable. What can we do about it? I'll sue....." Justin's rage fogged his thinking. "I'll kill the bastard!" Joanna's startled expression precipitated a more logically response. "Who can we sue?"he pleaded to Ken.

"I know this won't help, Justin, but Rooter took pains to explain his position."

Ken then recounted Rooter's confidential disclosure. "He's initiated an investigation of Residents Bank, and can't be perceived as overly antagonistic. They're a powerful institution, with strong allies in Congress and the state legislature. Rooter needs his backside covered, if the investigation is to have any teeth."

"So, we have to be the sacrificial lamb?"

"It's a shame," acknowledged the lawyer.

Joanna's voice cracked, "No wonder our customers placed rush orders with the 'majors.' They all ran for high ground after receiving the letter." The giant chemical companies, which sold almost one-hundred-billion pounds of prime plastics in the U.S. each year, offered virgin polymers which substituted for GRT's recycled compounds. Availability was guaranteed, although at significantly higher prices.

Justin glanced down at the financial reports he'd dropped into the trash. "The bank can't fail to notice that the book value of their collateral has deteriorated." He inhaled deeply, and without releasing the warm air in his inflated lungs, whispered, "We're going to lose control to Tinius next week."

Joanna had seen it coming. "We can't make it." She leaned over the speakerphone, almost brushing it with her lips, and said, "What do you suggest, Ken?"

"That we file a Plan of Reorganization before the bank receives the next collateral status report." Ken's tone was reticent, failing his attempt to hide the embarrassment of being out-maneuvered by Hyman First.

Justin was slow to reply. "The problem is---we won't have much to save after the bank sells our hard assets at auction prices. The net value of GRT will probably be---worthless."

Ken was late for another bankruptcy court session. "Call me if you need help with the plan." The speaker went dead. Ken had reacted unprofessionally for the first time; leaving them in a void of uncertainty.

Their eyes locked in a silent, mutual acceptance of defeat. Large tears squeezed from Joanna's pretty brown eyes and smudged her light mascara. She unrolled a tee-shirt sleeve and wiped them away, as Justin glanced at the photograph of Cosimo standing in front of the beloved gadgets he'd made for his grandson. His mind drifted for a few seconds. Unconsciously, it settled on the single entity that almost always provided Justin with answers to complex business problems: *numbers*.

Random numbers: for some reason, they always popped into his mind during moments of severe frustration. They were flashing now.

Twenty two: he guessed it meant the years he'd spent building the business, now wasted.

Ninety two: it was probably the number of good-paying GRT careers about to disappear.

Two hundred thousand: easy, his personal savings, used up trying to keep GRT afloat.

One: the number of unprofitable years for the company; too bad it was this year.

Thirteen: no connection yet? Was it the number of patents he'd been awarded?

It reminded him of the technical discoveries GRT had produced over the years: the proprietary formulations and unique processes; the twelve patents. Ah…now he remembered. There were twelve patents, so far. The *next* one would be thirteen---the technology they'd developed to recover difficult-to-separate composites, like shale oil. All their experimental technology could soon end up in a dusty file cabinet, to be thrown into a dumpster by an auctioner's clean-up crew.

His logic circuits had escaped into his subconscious, and were running free…unencumbered by purposeful thought. Perhaps they could salvage the new technology; breath life into the material separation process; *prevent it from being buried before birth.*

"Worthless," he suddenly cried out in frustration, almost violently. Joanna jumped back from the desk. "Worthless…and dumb shit out of luck." He growled the number, "*thirteen,*" which flashed across his mind like a rolling neon sign. *Thirteen wasn't always an unlucky number*! He couldn't remember a single bad thing that happened on Friday the thirteenth.

"Wait!....!" In sudden exultation, the idea exploded from his memory cells and splattered over the soft, association-tissue of his cortex brain.

Joanna leaned forward, her head tilted cautiously. "Are you alright?"

"Joanna. It's not worthless at all!" he said in a hoarse whisper.

"I know…I know…Justin," she answered tenderly. "It's been a good twenty two years. But we have to move on." The sudden sparkle in his eyes….his lips mouthing the words: "new patents." She remembered.

"Our accountant estimated that the potential value of the new technology could be several million dollars, if it could be scaled up to commercial size."

Justin spoke trance-like, "Not worthless at all. Damn it. Not worthless at all."

Joanna's mood spiked, then sank just as fast. "We'll need lots of money to do it." She saw new hope in Justin's sparkling blue eyes. The semi-smirk she secretly adored returned to the handsome face. She realized Justin was formulating a new plan. He spun to the window overlooking the employee parking lot.

It was now clear: continuing the battle to save the business---under the choking restraints of debtor-in-possession rules…with Tinius determined to block his way….was ludicrous. But, if he could salvage the technology…start over; re-hire the laid-off employees. His mind was speeding too fast and too far into the future.

But, he could abdicate the meager operating control he still maintained, and give the bank what it wanted most: the hard assets and a quick resolution to the bankruptcy case. He'd leverage the $50,000 back-pay issue; disdain and minimize the potential value of the pending patents…yet outmaneuver Tinius to keep the patent rights.

Cosimo's light-emitting vase on the window shelf refracted a kaleidoscope of colors from the afternoon sun onto the financial report in Justin's hand. He moved away from the window and paced the room; focusing on a new idea…a new hope. Sadness dampened his exhilaration as he realized the ninety-two GRT jobs could not be saved.

"We'll agree to pay the application fees for the U.S., European and Japanese patent applications." Tinius was unaware that the company had received a notice of tentative approval for the new patents. "Twenty-five thousand dollars should do it," he bellowed confidently. "It shouldn't be difficult to convince Tinius to leave us some crumbs. My back-pay of $50,000 is a priority claim, and the court has to settle back-salary issues before dispensing estate funds to creditors, including the secured creditor." He hesitated, then added, "I'm willing to forfeit half, or all of it, if necessary."

"Are you insane, Justin? You've already dumped in most of your savings. Even if you get the patent rights, how will you pay the registration fees?"

"I don't expect to collect the $50,000 anyway, Jo. Most of Ken's legal fees were covered up front, but the city will be coming after GRT, and me personally, for property taxes, which were postponed until the case is settled. Then, there's the U.S. Trustee's quarterly fees the company must pay until the case is officially closed."

"Justin, are you sure Tinius won't pay the patent registration fees and claim the rights to the technology?"

"I'm guessing he doesn't have the guts to expose the bank to an additional twenty-five- thousand-dollar loss. The patents might not be validated. The technology is unproven, and could be useless. Yada…yada."

"He could still demand a share in future profits." Joanna's instincts to protect Justin had become stronger. Without realizing it, she'd crossed the emotional barrier she erected when her husband died. She could no longer deny that she'd fallen in love with Justin. Now was not the time to reveal her feelings.

"I'll stand firm. Somehow, I don't think the bank's main objective in foreclosing on GRT is to maximize payback on the loan balance. Otherwise they'd be acting differently." He imagined telling Tinius: *Hey, the technology really is a gamble. Either we get the full rights, unencumbered, or I take my fifty-thousand and go home. Your call, buster*!

Justin glanced at his gold Seiko, a gift from employees, and said with renewed conviction, "Joanna, I'd like you to call Ken back. Tell him I'll have a plan-of-reorganization completed by Monday morning. I have the report template on the Collier disk he gave me months ago. Tell him I want to submit it to the court immediately, without discussion or review. Have him notify Judge Rooter, and whoever else needs to know."

He started for the door, then remembered what he'd forgotten. He circled behind his desk and lifted a gift-wrapped box, then began stuffing files into a boxy, black fabric bag.

"I have to go. It's Cosimo's eighty-ninth birthday."

Joanna's broad grin revealed the affection she held for Justin's remarkable grandfather. "Give…Cosimo my love." She smiled, silently overwhelmed by the submerged emotions she'd bottled, but would soon have to release. She was frightened by the thought that Justin probably didn't feel the same way about her. She watched him zip the fabric bag he'd purchased several years ago, when it carried his first portable computer---a twenty-three pound 64K Osborne lead brick.

Elim Park Assisted Living, Cheshire, Ct.

Cosimo Gaettano was surrounded by five attractive ladies in their eighties, as Justin removed his Navy blazer and hung it in the visitor's closet near the entrance to the eloquently decorated dining room at the Elim Park assisted living residences in Cheshire, a few miles from his modest two bedroom home in Wallingford.

Cosimo, a short man with broad shoulders, thin grey hair and a bushy, silver handlebar mustache turned up at the edges, was seated at a round, linen-covered table set for seven. Mary, Rosie, Gertrude, Spicy and Eleanor, who he called the "marogespel" girls, were seated with him, waiting for Justin and Cosimo's favorite dinner to arrive. A battery-powered wheelchair was parked behind the empty upholstered seat next to him, which was reserved for Justin.

Cosimo was dressed in a shirt and tie, and was cradling a clay turkey, the size of a ten pounder, which he'd sculptured and kilned earlier in the week. The ladies were enthralled. He'd touched it up with brown and black latex paint, and primary acrylic pigments. The damn thing looked real.

A young attendant hurried from the kitchen and placed a warm pumpkin pie next to the clear cups of strawberry jello laid out for the seniors having regular dinners. Soon the cranberry-marmalade sauce Cosimo loved was placed on the dinner table, signifying the start of his birthday celebration. The diabetic diets would go out the window today. Same with the low-carbs. Cheating was the theme. A glass of cider, or merlot, or chardonnay would accompany the meal. After-dinner-medications would be dispensed an hour later than usual.

Seated next to Cosimo was Spicey, the silver-haired exercise instructor with the giant bosom and cherry-red lipstick She was dressed to look ten years younger than her actual age, in an aqua, knee length satin evening dress adorned with a cultured pearl necklace and matching earrings. Oyster pumps had replaced black jogging shoes. The other women wore almost identical black pull-on polyester pants with elastic waists , and solid pink or yellow sleeveless tops trimmed with ruffles or Italian lace. Cosimo's attractive and relatively trim harem contrasted with the enormous woman sitting at the next table.

With fork and knife flashing upwards in each hand, ready to attack the meatloaf dinner, the spherical woman's anxious eyes gleamed beneath unruly silver curls, staring expectantly at the swinging door to the kitchen. Her size twenty-four pink flannel kitchen smock tented over the tops of food stained sneakers.

Cosimo had sculptured amazingly life-like clay busts of each of the girls, but had refused to give them these personalized works of art. He'd only allow the "marogespel" girls to come to his apartment for private viewings. Justin once asked his still handsome grandfather how the ladies responded to his private viewings. The winking old artist claimed he didn't remember.

Justin was still amazed at Cosimo the artist, whose metal sculptures had been placed on the lawns and near entrances to the Elim Park complex of buildings ten years ago. His favorite metal rendition was made with stainless steel welding rods, which Gramps had spot-welded into a dish-shaped cobweb, six feet in diameter. At its center was a twenty-inch diameter globe of the world, with an arthritic hand reaching up through the North Pole, as if it was pleading for someone to straiten the distorted fingers.

Justin respected Cosimo, the grandfather, who'd provided a good life for both of them, by shear force of will and the skills and rare work-ethic that many immigrants brought to this country in the early twentieth century. He'd never forget the day of his last Little League baseball game. Justin was pitching a perfect game no-hitter after the fifth inning, and noticed Gramps whispering tearfully to the coach, holding a yellow telegram in his trembling hand. He'd asked the coach to allow the young boy to finish the game. Justin struck out the first two batters he faced in the sixth and final inning, then dropped his glove and ran off the field, when he saw Cosimo collapse along the sidelines.

The local newspaper wrote an article about how a twelve year old Little Leaguer had pitched 17/18ths of a perfect game no-hitter for his deceased parents and grandmother, who'd been traveling the Amalfi coast in Italy to visit relatives, when the bus driver misjudged a treacherous curve and plunged himself and the passengers three hundred feet onto the rocks.

Cosimo had worn out his knees and hips working as a stone mason to pay for Justin's chemical engineering education at Worcester Polytech, and had insisted on helping pay for his MBA from the Yale School of Management. He'd built brick and stone walls, cobblestone driveways, flagstone patios and marble fireplaces until he was seventy five.

He entered Elim Park at Justin's urging, because his knees and hips had deteriorated to the extent that he couldn't continue living alone in the small, two-story stucco house in Worcester, with the bathroom on the second floor. It took Cosimo only two days to convince the maintenance supervisor at Elim Park to grant him access to the welding and metal working equipment in the machine shop. He immediately started producing the items most people called "works of art," but he referred to as "hobby items."

Cosimo noticed the worried smile as his only grandson approached the dinner table. He gently passed the clay turkey to Spicy.

"Good evening, ladies." Justin bowed. "Is he behaving himself?" Then he surprised the ladies by pulling a handful of large, yellow chrysanthemums from behind his back. He gave each of them a flower, and a kiss on the cheek.

Spicy replied mischievously, "He never behaves himself. He says he got that from you."

"That's no exaggeration," Rosey snickered. The others nodded in mock agreement.

"Well, I admit nothing," Justin laughed. "It's tough bringing up your grandfather." Then he turned to Spicy, in a pseudo-sarcastic grin, "Just what did he get from me?" Spicy's pretty face morphed to the color of her lipstick.

Cosimo broke in, faking exasperation and the colorful Italian immigrant dialect he'd shed years ago, "Neva minda....neva minda." Hoping to lighten his grandson's mood, he added, "Tella me, what'sa goin on ata tha shopa?" He'd already noticed the strain on Justin's face, despite his jovial entrance. Cosimo knew Justin was fighting to save his company. His grandson had always confided in him about the important things in his life.

Justin wanted to talk about it, but not now. "Let's eat. I'll explain later."

The waitresses started serving mashed potatoes, creamed corn, butternut squash dusted with cinnamon and thick slices of white turkey. Small wine glasses were half filled. Warm flakey rolls were delicately topped with small dabs of smart spread….because big dabs tended to slip off the tips of their wide butter knives, and puddle the linen. After the main meal, the home-made pumkin pie was heated and swamped with low-fat whipped cream, or vanilla yogurt. Justin noticed that Cosimo swished the food around on his plate, but ate very little. The ladies gorged themselves.

Gertrude told a dirty joke about the wife who pleaded with her retired husband to go golfing every day. The staff and a few other seniors joined them in singing happy birthday to Cosimo--- simultaneously in multiple keys and with different lyrics.

When the meal and partying were over, a nurse reminded the seniors to prepare for medications. Justin helped his grandfather into his electric wheelchair, and followed him to a quiet spot in the community library down the hall. Justin sat in a comfortable armchair next to a large bookcase housing classic literature donated by the residents and their families. Cosimo parked the electric close enough to reach up for his favorite book.

"Niccolo once told me, in a dream," he said, with inquisitive eyes reading Justin's mood over the rims of his granny wire frames, "that life is always plan

B." He fingered *The Prince*, Machiavelli's classic treatise of statesmanship and power.

How could Justin refute that? He'd read the book, and was almost certain Machiavelli never wrote those words. He did recall another passage:

"Princes who had held their possessions for many years,
Must not accuse fortune for having lost them,
But rather their own remissivness
Having never in quiet times considered that things might change."

The middle-aged nurse with the identity tag: "Fanny, RN, VNA" in large black type, and in larger red hand-marker---"Very VIP," stood nearby and started dispensing plastic ketchup cups containing pills with at least five different shapes and colors. The line of well-fed diners was jabbering away louder than usual.

Fanny had recently informed Justin that his grandfather was experiencing occasional dementia, and would sometimes wander off in thought. "But he's lucid, and a fresh guy, most of the time," she laughed. "Sometimes, he startles me with his clarity of thought, when we're in a normal conversation. When he's around the 'marogespel girls' his mind is usually as sharp as the wonderous hands that still create those amateur masterpieces." Fanny was aware of Justin's chemical training, and felt obliged to explain in technical terms. "It's just natural aging. It causes neurons and serotonin uptake nerve endings to malfunction more often." She admitted that her own nerve endings malfunctioned quite often lately. Particularly when her high school freshman daughter dressed for a date at a girlfriend's house, and uncovered portions of her belly, hips and small breasts that had not previously been revealed in public.

Justin spoke frankly to Cosimo, as always, but didn't reveal the details. "I may be looking for a new career." Trying to sound positive, he added, "It looks like GRT is coming to an end."

Cosimo was not surprised. He replaced the book on the shelf, loosened his blue and purple checkered tie, and unbuttoned the top of his starched white dress shirt. He murmured sadly, "After so many years…so much hard work." He seemed to drift off to a different place. A moment later he returned, and whispered hoarsely, "If it's time to let go---let go. You'll be better off if you don't fight it so hard. Nana tells me that all the time—*don't be afraid to let go.*"

A lump in the grandson's throat prevented him from replying. Cosimo had a weak heart, failing kidneys and a cancerous thyroid gland. He wasn't expected to live much longer.

Cosimo murmured in a troubled voice, "I always wanted ….to do a bust….of your beautiful mother…when she was….alive." He gravitated to that different place. "When Nana and me changed you're father's name… to be more American…..we thought …."

A painful expression deepened the wrinkles on his face. "I was wrong." Cosimo's eyes blinked noticably, as he said, "Did he sell sunshine insurance?"

"Gramps, we've got lots of good days ahead. Let's get you to your room, you're exhausted."

The wheelchair turned and Cosimo suddenly bolted upright. He blurted out, as clear as a Greek philosopher in his prime, "You studied great men of science, Justin--- Edison, Einstein, Tesla…..Newton and Leonardo deVinci—the visionaries. You read about the good Popes; and America's best Presidents." His piercing glower inflated Justin's heart and confidence, as it had many times before.

"You know body chemistry as good as most doctors. You're one of the few people who still cares about recycling and reducing the world's waste." He paused for a breath; then regressed to stilted words. "The world's …crazy. There's…too many people. Nobody's in charge."

Cosimo jerked his head upwards and administered the final kick in the butt: "Use what you learned at Yale and Polytech, Justin. What you already know…to change things. That's your purpose. Not to look after an old grape-crusher like me."

Justin gaped in wonder, as Cosimo then presaged his final concern: "Your employees will find other work."

Justin was convinced that Cosimo could read his mind.

CHAPTER 13

(June 16, 2008), am
Over the Atlantic Ocean

The Bombardier Challenger 604 banked southeast, as it passed over the mid-Atlantic Ridge, about eight hundred miles north of the Azores, and headed for the Bay of Biscay bordering northern Spain and the southwestern coast of France. A strong tailwind added seventeen percent to the speed of the large company jet; the BoxMart executives expected to land in the capital city of Andorra in less than three hours.

The Chairman and the CFO of BoxMart Retail Enterprises had ten million dollars in untraceable one-hundred dollar bills stowed in an overhead compartment of the private jet. They were en route to a clandestine delivery in Andorra, the smallest land-bound country in Europe.

Bordering northeast Spain and southeast France, this 181 square-mile co-principality dating back to the thirteenth century was the preferred venue for the frequent exchanges of favors between Phillipe Cusson and Jake Kurancy. The well paid immigration official awaiting their arrival at the private landing field tucked into a narrow valley of the eastern Pyreness mountains, south of the capital city of Andorra la Vella, would not bother to inspect their six bags of baggage.

The tiny duty-free resort country, officially named the *Principality of Andorra*, boasted the highest average life expectancy of any European country, at 83.5 years. The population of sixty-six thousand in this nearly unknown sovereign nation was governed jointly by the Bishop of Urgel in Spain and the President of France…both important clients of Phillipe Cusson's private bank in Lyons, France.

Kurancy and Cusson met in this mountainous region on prior occasions to conclude business deals which usually involved exchanging cash for negotiable securities. But today, Kurancy would exchange cash for only discreet promises, which Cusson had extracted from several European finance ministers. They would "assist" the French banker in currency trades between Creditte Bank de Savoy and the central banks they regulated. For an inconsequential stipend of a million dollars each, eight men and two women would arrange silent trades of billions of euros and other denominations held in their central banks, for Bank de Savoy's U.S. dollar deposits.

The swaps would be at prevailing market valuations---timed according to Cusson's master plan. The minimum transaction would be a billion dollars. The trades would begin at the World Finance Ministers Conference in Stressa, Italy in a few months. Cusson had explained to the suspicious money traders that his 300 year old private bank accumulated excess dollars as a result of its special relationship with the Central Bank of China. The Minister of Monetary Regulation in Beijing, Yong Ihasa, had chosen his institution as the European depository and transfer agent for the massive trade-surplus dollars pouring into China from the United States.

The finance ministers were surprised to learn that the bank's relationship with China dated back to 1805, under the late Manchu rule of the Qing dynasty. Creditte Bank de Savoy, originally known as the Napolean Truste de Lyonnais, had maintained branches in Shanghai, Hong Kong and Tianjin on the east coast, and had survived many Chinese political upheavals during the land reforms of the early 1950s, the Hundred Flowers campaign of 1957, the Great Leap forward—with its resulting food shortages in 1958, the Cultural Revolution of the late Sixties, and the factional battles in the Seventies.

The bank's relationship with Mao Zedong, the leader of the Chinese Communist Party who defeated Chiang Kai-shek's Kuomintang Nationalist Party in 1949, and drove them to the island of Taiwan, was cemented many years ago. Cusson's predecessors at the Shanghai branch of Napolean Trust helped finance the first Communist-led uprising at Nanchang City in Jiangxi Province in 1927. The bank changed its name to Oriental Bank de Savoy in 1949, when it reluctantly handed over deposits left behind by the Kuomintang to Mao's Communist revolutionaries.

Cusson himself had enhanced the banks' standing with Chinese leaders when he helped Deng Xiaoping, the Chairman of the Communist Party, reorganize China's central banking system in the eighties, to support Deng's economic reforms. Chinese leadership for the first time praised people who got rich. According to Deng's teachings, capitalism was no longer a crime against socialism.

Cusson further impressed the European finance ministers with his knowledge of other important historical events in China's history: Jimmy Carter's normalization of U.S. relations with China in 1978; opening of the first media bureaus of the New York Times and Washington Post in Beijing; and China's first currency manipulation---as far back as the early 1980s…when the government allowed Chinese producers to modify the official exchange rate, from 1.5 yuan per dollar to 3.0 yuan per dollar, to meet prices on the world market.

It was essential for Cusson to convince the European finance ministers that his bank's special relationship with the Chinese gave it extraordinary financial strength and stability. Otherwise, they might suspect that Cusson was dumping dollars out of fear. He knew that money traders avoided transactions if they suspected uncertainty could precipitate a downward trend in valuations.

Cusson explained that huge dollar deposits were flowing too rapidly into Bank de Savoy. The Chinese were accepting negligible interest payments to compensate for the bank's willingness to ignore transparency rules for money flows, and discreetly transfer funds to its Franco-Medici Bank and Trust subsidiary in Geneva---a portion of which was repositioned into numbered accounts in Barbados and Grand Cayman in the names of layered shell corporations operating Beijing-owned businesses in California. Deposits and withdrawals at the Geneva subsidiary were reverently buried under the headstone of Swiss confidentiality law.

Hieronimus Cashman, the Chief Financial Officer of BoxMart, was reviewing the latest operating results beamed to the aircraft from BoxMart retail outlets around the globe, when the urgent e-mail message from Emerson Bromine in Macau was received via data relay satellite. Cashman's laptop screen was programmed to overide current applications and immediately display incoming e-messages tagged with a priority code. The message read:

China: Macau JV Tax Act approved by Politboro. Continue on to Vargos Langreen law offices in Macau. Papers and partners will be present to review formal Bomali Corp agreements in a few days. I have informed only need-to-know others. SAVOY IMP is a go.

Em. Brom.

The cloudless purple sky and the magnificent sunrise emerging in the eastern horizon forced the pilot and co-pilot to clip on their double-strength, UV-absorbant mirrored sunglasses. The low whining from the new, super efficient jet engines recently retrofit on the Challenger provided pleasant background noise for contemplating the good news.

Kurancy was smiling broadly across the aisle after receiving the same message on his own laptop. He grinned at his CFO and said enthusiastically, "The Bomali joint-venture is going to catapult BoxMart beyond every competitor, before this decade ends, Hiero."

The handsome, dark-haired accountant in his early forties responded brightly, "Sometimes I can't believe our company has gathered so much momentum."

"It's too early to celebrate," Kurancy said as he tapped the intercom. "But, let's have a nightcap and doze off. I get very tired when I'm about to give away money."

The Dom Benedictine-and-Brandy settled in nicely, relaxing Cashman's throat and belly and stroking his desire to discuss other good news. "Operating results are ten percent higher than last month, Jake. I believe your employee-eavesdropping program has been a big factor. I'm glad we're the only ones who hear the gripes from the employee locker rooms."

Kurancy's wide grin ballooned his pink fleshy cheeks. "It *was* one of my better ideas," he chirped.

"It's also allowed the company to weed out potential trouble-makers," the CFO retorted. "I'm still amazed at how efficient a retail operation can function if you hire only passive, low-intelligent-level people who are the most income-dependent workers available. Nobody would believe the extremes we go to trying to hire the least disruptive people we can find."

BoxMart hired only part-time floor workers when the company opened a new store. The employees unloaded merchandise deliveries, stacked and re-stacked shelves, and did just about everything required to physically position merchandise for sale. Brainwashed store managers and well trained cashiers handled the money. If a part-time employee had perfect attendance for the requisite six-month trial period, he or she would receive twenty-five percent of a full-time employee's health insurance and holiday benefits. Vacation pay was given only to full time workers.

"Our average employee cost is sixty eight percent of the industry average for a large retail business," Kurancy boasted proudly. "Only the big guy comes close."

Cashman flipped through a few pages of data, then settled his eyes on a chart generated by the new three-petaflop supercomputer. Data acquired from the industrial spies he'd recruited at Home Depot, Target and Costco had been fed into Kapeed's programs. The chart compared the prices being charged by BoxMart and its major competitors for high-volume, high-ticket merchandise. In all cases, BoxMart's price was exactly ten percent lower than competition…just as the 3P-BIO supercomputer had predicted. A different bar-chart compared the prices paid by each retailer for identical products.

Cashman swiveled his head in amazement as Kurancy began to nod off in the semi-darkness of the otherwise deserted fifty-seat jetliner. "Li Chin and General Ye have made good on their promise to charge BoxMart the lowest prices for every item we purchase from LCE. Our net profit for the fiscal year ending in September will come in about twenty-two percent higher than last year."

"BoxMart's share price could double," the big man exclaimed crisply. "I can't wait for the books to close and the accountants to sign off." He yawned happily, as the plane leveled to ten thousand feet below its previous flight path.

Cashman said, "We'll start the process with the usual press releases and conference calls to the Wall Street analysts. The preliminary year-end figures should cause the brokers to salivate."

Kurancy mused, "Kapeed and his Indian geniuses don't yet know the history they're making. I asked him to develop a program which could predict the cost-price-profit numbers of our damn enemies. Fortunately, his unscrupulous, oversized brain went to work, and he integrated some actual competitive data into self-learning algorithyms."

"Presto info!" Cashman joked. "But he won't admit he stole the basic algorithym formulas from Livermore National Laboratory programmers before he quit there."

Jake leaned his head back to snap a few vertibae into place, and said with fervor, "The baffling result is an almost perfect prediction tool. We've tested his program against operating data stolen from competitive stores in both the west and east coasts. The accuracy is uncanny. This will allow our merchandise managers to price every UCC-coded product just slightly below the other big boxes. It's almost as effective as having copies of their performance printouts. Our profit margins will be comparable, but our volumes will skyrocket."

The attendant buzzed and asked if they would like to be served breakfast. It would be a few more hours before landing at the thin strip of flatland they'd purchased and covered with concrete to provide a runway in a narrow valley of the central mountain region. The pilot would have to call ahead to make sure the runway was cleared of the wild sheep and goats that grazed the low-lying areas. Andorra was probably the only nation in the world without a public airport.

The welcomed aroma of freshly brewed Kenyan coffee stirred Kurancy's digestive fluids. He was undecided whether to eat, swill strong coffee and wake up; or nap on an empty stomach. His meetings with Phillipe Cusson were usually a test of his nerves. The proud Frenchman had a habit of speaking half in English and half in French, when he conversed with an English-speaking person.

Kurancy decided to compromise. "I'll have decaf and toasted Portugese sweetbread with peanut butter."

Cashman was starving. Unlike Kurancy, he'd managed to sleep a few hours during the first leg of the trans-Atlantic flight from Logan. "Regular coffee, black… and two pieces of baklava." He dropped some files into his alligator-skin briefcase, then reconsidered the food order. Remembering the hectic travel schedule they'd set for the next few days…he pressed the intercom and said to the attendant, "Please add fresh-squeezed prune juice."

The attendant released the intercom button and laughed. *So that's what the tiny hand-press is for.*

Kurancy shuffled papers into a folio and slid them into the side compartment of his black leather carry-all. He glanced across the tenth-row aisle and watched Cashman staring out the window at the swept wings slicing smoothly through thick clouds. He caught a first-light glimpse of the cold Atlantic from his own window, and dreamily imagined floating on the surface, kicking away attacking sharks. He lowered the tray and his eyelids; and waited for the food in the stillness of the faintly-lit cabin.

"We should probably discuss the 'Made in America' campaign," Cashman interrupted Jake's solitude, without looking up from the inventory report resting on his tray. The data indicated that several BoxMart distribution centers in the U.S. were filled with gift merchandise for the Christmas holiday season….several months earlier than usual. He was a bit puzzled.

Kurancy impatiently shifted his massive body in the specially fabricated double-width seat, and yanked down his food tray. Cashman knew the *Made in America* campaign was not Jake's favorite subject. The attractive forty-year-old former airline stewardess arrived with refreshments just in time to quell his anger. Jake leered at the tall, full-bodied redhead as she casually patted his giant hand and lowered the breakfast to his tray. Cashman suspected that this flirtatious, well-maintained cabin attendant had probably lowered more than food to Kurancy's enormous lap.

"Let's talk about cash flow and inventory," Kurancy suggested, as he sipped the steaming decaf and fisted a large slice of the toasted sweetbread. "Have we been as successful as you-know-who, in shifting costs and cash-flow requirements to suppliers? That's the key to our profitability."

"In general, yes. But there are a few hold-outs. Mostly the local nurseries who supply seasonal plants for our garden centers," the CFO answered. "Also, a few of the domestic brand-managers are complaining. They don't like the shelf positions of their products in our new plan-o-grams. Everyone thinks their products should dominate end-of-aisle and check-out counter displays."

Kurancy remembered the instructions he'd stamped on the foreheads of the BoxMart's buyers and merchandise managers: *beat on these suits whenever possible.* "How many of them are suppliers we've decided to replace with BM-brand items from other sources?"

"About half, Jake. Alternate suppliers have been identified, but we're still negotiating payment terms. I expect all of them will buckle under once our price demands are submitted with gigantic take-it-or-leave-it purchase orders. We still have to redesign some packaging, and sell off non-returnable national brand inventory." He then conjectured a wry warning, "Your door will have to be reinforced with radioactive materials to stave off distraught name-brand managers and their lawyers from a frontal attack."

"We've fought that battle before," Jake replied arrogantly. "They can't win."

"They'll try. Some are already claiming that BoxMart is nothing more than a giant consignment shop." Cashman dunked the Baklava in the prune juice and bit off a corner. Half-seriously, he added, "I think there are separate laws that govern consignment and bartering transactions."

Kunrancy couldn't be bothered with the details. "We have reams of lawyers stalling on more pressing lawsuits. They'd stall this one to death with their Medusa eyes."

"In any case," Cashman continued, "we've succeeded in re-allocating most of the sales risk." This time he dunked the baklava in black coffee.

"The total cost to replenish stock and remove unsold goods from BoxMart shelves *should* be on the seller," Jake said authoritatively. "It's a priviledge to be in our stores."

"Our buyers agree; they're now sleeping better. But the brand managers and their service crews have started to contract wide-awake apnea." Cashman dipped the last piece of Greek desert into the prune juice and swallowed.

Jake wondered if *wide-awake apnia* was a real disease, or an oxymoron.

"Most of the small and mid-sized American manufacturers will be replaced by LCE's mainland factories very soon," he reminded Jake. "Edwin Tinius is leading the way. But I'm a bit concerned that Residents Bank is moving too quickly."

Jake knew the plan. He'd approved it. But he didn't remember many details.

"Heiro, as I recall, Tinius receives a bonus for every small business failure that ends up shifting production from a closed U.S. factory to Li Chin's plants in China."

"Yes. He's targeted the plastics processing industry in the northeast and mid-west because they're easy prey. Most of these small operations rely on sub-contracts from the large multinationals, who have recently set up manufacturing subsidiaries in China's modern industrial parks. Any manufacturing that shifts to the mainland will never return to America."

Jake leaned into the aisle toward Cashman and yawned liked a beluga whale trying to swallow a school of giant squid. "Li Chin and General Ye have made it clear---they want those skilled and semi-skilled plastics jobs relocated to LCE factories on the mainland as soon as possible."

Cashman expressed his concern in a mildly-plaintive tone, "Someone has to defuse the unwanted attention the plethora of small-company bankruptcies has created, Jake. Both locally and in Washington. That's why I agreed to fund Blackstone's FFF firm in D.C., and his Boston affiliate, GH Paladin."

"Fund them for what?" the surprised chairman muttered, groggily. He was beginning to drift into dreamland.

"To create a diversion." Cashman downed the last of the black coffee. His grandfather from the island of Sifnos had invented the sweet laxative combination of prune juice and baklava. It reminded him of a true story his grandfather told about a Greek island man who wandered home drunk and fell asleep in the out-house.

The CFO continued his explanation. "Tom Blackstone at FFF in D.C., and his partner, Bob McGill at the GH Paladin consulting group in Boston, have come up with a plan we can well afford."

Jake was half-listening as his heavy eyelids slid down over bloodshot eyes to shield out the cabin lights and slivers of sunrise sneaking in from the edges of the drawn window shades. Cashman persisted with his explanation, until he heard the snoring. He hadn't yet informed Jake that the 'Made in America' project was cancelled. The hopeful American manufacturers of Vermont maple-wood building blocks, New Jersey pet supplies, South Carolina cotton briefs and Georgia throw rugs, would all be disappointed. Anticipated orders from BoxMart would never materialize.

Jake will be pleased, Cashman thought to himself. *He despises giving business to U.S. manufacturers; he's convinced that American workers are underworked and over-paid. The big man actually agonizes if BoxMart is forced to purchase American-made products because Asian alternatives are not available.*

Kurancy usually ignored the political fall-out created by BoxMart's emphasis on selling imported merchandise. Cashman was more alarmed by the warning signals. Influential politicians throughout the country were beginning to acknowledge that the free-trade myth was undermining America's future. Some claimed that international trade was being manipulated by mega-retailers and importers like BoxMart; and that America's open-borders policy had allowed cheap imports to create the equivalent of a hallucinogenic drug---compelling consumers to shop primarily at discount stores.

Cashman was heartened by the realization that the apparent deterioration in the standard of living for many Americans actually benefitted BoxMart. By necessity, rather than choice, millions flocked to stores selling low-cost goods. A majority of struggling middle-class and low-income American workers could no longer visualize shopping elsewhere. Except for special occasions…they were captured by the lure of inexpensive staples.

Cashman leaned across the aisle and flipped off Jake's reading light; then relaxed in the calmness of the muted sounds and lazy shadows accompanying them on the pre-dawn flight. He closed his eyes and attempted to snatch a few hours sleep.

The runaway locomotive snoring across the aisle made it impossible. *The giant man must be dreaming again.*

* * *

"You're a manic depressive, with a psychiatric disorder," the bruised red-head shouted analytically, as she gathered her clothes and ran from the room. Kurancy loved when she was pissed.

A bulky, foul-smelling figure leered in from the bedroom closet and snorted in derision, "With effusive highs and lows of paralyzing despair." The oriental voice sounded familiar. But its shape was not human; the creature projected a serpent-like shadow as it watched Buddha-Jake bouncing upright on the bed.

"A friend can lend his concubine…even his wife…to a conqueror," the creature growled, sage-like, from its grey silken snout.

The giant lizard's tail lashed out at Jake's massive body, clad only in white boxer-shorts large enough to conceal a metric barrel of oil. Kurancy fell from the bed to the floor, and landed on a stack of collapsed cardboard boxes labeled in fine red print: *Savannah Box Company.* In larger black print, on the flattened sides, were the words: *Fresh Peanuts, 12 lbs, The Boxed Product Outlet, Hardeeville, S.C.*

The grotesque figure in the closet leaped onto the bed, revealing three clawed feet and a reptilian tail as thick as a lamppost…tipped with a sizzling red-hot pointer. The bed caught fire and the creature was suddenly bathing in acrid, lapping flames. It let out a deep reverberating croak, "Fat man…counterfeit Buddha…prepare for your just reward!" Scorched by the flames, Kurancy backed away from the bed in horror and stumbled to his feet. His flabby arms shielded the hairless skin on his face and head…reaching up wildly. His hands touched something above his head…and gripped forcefully.

Suspended in the hot air above was a small teak box, overflowing with hundred-dollar bills. He held onto the box until the creature's smoldering tail lashed out again and knocked the box away. Bills became airborne, burst into flames and floated down to Kurancy's bare feet. The giant chairman stomped on the burning cash, like an intoxicated fire-walker.

Suddenly, the voluptuous red-haired woman reappeared, and was drawn to his immense body like dust to a vacuum. Now fully clothed, in her dark blue uniform, she pressed against his involuntary erection in rhapsodized awe. Kurancy struggled to breath. His middle ears popped and he sensed a change in the cool, pressurized air around him. Gradually his eyes slid open and he glanced up groggily at the woman shaking his shoulders.

"Mr Kurancy," she whispered gently, "Mr. Kurancy. The sun is rising in Andorra. We're descending and almost there." She reached across the double-width seat to secure the safety belt around his massive girth and noticed the bulge in his pants. A glance across the aisle revealed that the CFO was still asleep. The playful attendant lightly brushed the back of her hand over the familiar swell several times. Kurancy's eyes registered surprised pleasure. She whispered sweetly, "The bird will be landing at dawn."

Jake's instant thought was, *It's the stroke of midnight in Boston.*

CHAPTER 14

(JUNE 30, 2008), 9:50AM
NEW HAVEN FEDERAL BANKRUPTCY COURTROOM, CONNECTICUT

Justin Gatt knew the outcome would change his life forever. He stood motionless in the back row of the modern oak-paneled courtroom on the ninth floor of the Connecticut Financial Center, waiting for the bankruptcy proceedings to begin. His grandfather, Cosimo, had failed to convince him that it wasn't so much a case of his failing, as it was bad luck.

Joanna Yates, GRT's financial manager, stood next to him, dressed in a plain black sleeveless dress, with no discernable make-up or jewelry. They huddled in quiet conversation, interrupted only by the muffled sounds which drifted faintly from brief staccato-exchanges between the lawyers gathered in the front rows. They were waited for the presiding judge to enter the courtroom at 10 am.

All heads turned to the entrance door in the back when the subdued conversations were interrupted by the deliberate hammering of Edwin Tinius' hard leather Bostonian heals on the marble floor. Followed closely by the bank's attorney, Hyman First, and the local branch manager of Residents Bank, the diminutive VP of Asset Recovery for Residents Bank stormed down the center aisle of the courtroom as purposefully as Caesar entering Egyptian territory. He slipped into the second row of benches directly behind the three lawyers. Ken Levine, the U.S. Trustee and the attorney for the unsecured creditors committee turned to observe the arrogant banker, standing erect like a proud conqueror.

This was his day of triumph. The final day in court. Assets would be recovered. Another bothersome small manufacturing business would be eliminated. His additional bonus was assured.

Ken Levine and the lawyer representing the unsecured creditors in the GRT case were re-counting the votes received by yesterday's deadline. GRT's Plan of Reorganization, as modified by the judge to eliminate the back-salary of $50,000 due to Justin Gatt, had been approved by 92 percent of all eligible *parties-of-interest*.

Tinius glanced arrogantly over his shoulder at Gatt and Yates. His sicko expression suggested that he'd just envisioned Justin Gatt as a wraith. He was pleased that his dramatic entrance had been duly noted. Tinius was less than medium height and build, and his short blond hair was spiked and greased like a rock star's, making him appear even younger than his mid-thirties age. He wore a custom tailored, dark-blue Armani pin-striped suit, a white shirt with a pink, button-down collar, and a solid black silk tie. His attire was accentuated by a blue and white striped handkerchief dangling in multi-points from his pectoral suit pocket. He was not your typical banker, and he dressed to make sure everyone knew.

Gatt waited for the purveyor of financial cataclysms to march to the front of the courtroom. He then turned on his heels and started forward. Joanna reached for his arm and tugged strongly. She shook her head adamantly and whispered, "Don't bother."

Justin calmly signaled for her to relax and remain seated. He then walked deliberately to the second row and slid in beside Tinius, brushing against his shoulder. He stared straight ahead for a tense minute that seemed like an hour, focusing on the rotund Clerk of the Court readying papers for the judge at a small desk set in front of the judge's raised bench. Tinius edged away in alarmed curiosity.

Then Gatt said evenly, with no intent to mask his anger, "I understand you've threatened to put my CFO in jail for financial fraud." He continued to focus his eyes on the clerk, sensing the smug expression on Tinius's face without looking his way.

The bank's asset recovery guru remained silent, until his aggressive nature took over; and he blurted out an offensive rebuttal. "She manipulated the payroll account, so you could rip-off the bank and pay your buddies."

Justin's fists tightened. He knew it was just a scare tactic…a mean ploy that the bastard didn't need to use. Joanna already had enough problems to deal with—two hyper-emotional teenage daughters, and now, no job. Tinius was perfectly aware that payroll is a higher priority settlement payment in bankruptcy cases than a bank's claim as a secured creditor. Joanna's transfer of funds to the GRT payroll account was perfectly legal, and had been upheld by the judge.

"You're a son of a bitch, Tinius," he spat. "Someday…someone's going to make you sorry."

Tinius flinched as Justin's fist was suddenly suspended in front of his thin bony nose. He turned away instinctively, clasped his hands on the shoulders of the branch manager standing next to him, and spun the man between him and Gatt… creating a human shield of lower rank.

"How dare you threaten me, you miserable failure," he shouted…loud enough for everyone in the crowded courtroom to hear. That was over-the-edge for Gatt. He brushed aside the branch manager with his left arm…like a discarded paper bag in a gusty wind…and exploded his right fist toward the cowling banker's frightened eyes. Just before it landed, an honorable-mention All-American lacrosse player's vise-grip stopped the angry thrust in mid-air, preventing a shattered nose, and an assault-and-battery charge that Justin didn't need. Ken Levine's legal mind had kicked in; almost before his instinctive, lightning-quick motion.

There'd be severe penalties for committing felonious assault in a federal courtroom in front of a judge. Samuel Rooter had just entered the courtroom from a side door.

The confused Clerk of the Court witnessed the confrontation in the second row, then turned an alarmed eye to the Judge entering from the side door. She dropped her papers on the small desk and leaped up, shouting commands in an unusual, tentative tone, "All relax…all relax. I mean---All Rise!"

Judge Samuel Rooter strode in buttoning the top of his black silk robe, wondering what the commotion was in the normally subdued front rows of a final bankruptcy session.

The case was declared settled ten minutes before noon. Order had been restored in the courtroom by separating Tinius and Gatt to opposite ends of the second row and stationing a security officer to guard Gatt's movements. Joanna nestled in next to him, and insisted that he swallow a proton-pump-inhibitor to offset the presence of the nauseating banker.

The legal people soon completed their professionally choreographed ritual of dissecting the failed business, and applying the rules of the recently updated federal bankruptcy law to the case. The new law, which Congress and the President dared call the '*Consumer Protection Act*', had been modified in 2005 to add new restrictions and penalties for *deadbeats.*

The term apparently referred to the ninety-one percent of the people filing for bankruptcy protection because they couldn't pay tens-of-thousands in uninsured medical bills, or lost their jobs; or were experiencing debilitating emotional problems. These were the *deadbeat poor.*

The *deadbeat rich,* who the law was supposedly designed to penalize, still managed to shelter their mansions and jewelry in asset-protection trusts and homestead exemptions. The companies collapsing because of a sudden loss of business to foreign competition---not because of human folly or mismanagement---were also treated brutally by the law.

Slattery Housewares, GRT and several other bankrupt companies in the northeast had something else in common: the actions which caused their downfall were initiated by the same financial institution and the same retail customer.

In each case, BoxMart had issued an unexpected order cancellation; and Residents Bank of North America had moved at warp speed to foreclose. Company loans taken to finance production for large BoxMart orders were called for immediate payment. In several instances, the bank's foreclosure actions were based on minor breaches of the financial-ratio stipulations in the loan documents.

Judge Rooter glanced at the spring-wound Big Ben clock on his bench and decided it was time to finalize the case and break for lunch. His backlog of bankruptcy cases extended well into the next year. He needed nourishment to handle the load.

"Since the Plan of Reorganization submitted by attorney Levine has been approved by ninety-two percent of the eligible voters, Residents Bank will hereby be awarded all the hard assets of GRT. Mr. Gatt will retain the rights to the pending patents for a new recycling process developed in company laboratories."

Minutes after completing the mandatory declarations regarding dispersal of assets and settlement of various priority claims, Judge Rooter directed his attention to the far side of the room.

"Mr. Gatt, you will have to pay the twenty-five-thousand dollar patent registration fees, which I understand will be due in a few months." Maintaining a fixed gaze into the resigned blue eyes, Rooter said compassionately, "Mr. Gatt has also agreed to forfeit fifty-thousand dollars in back salary that is legally due to him from the bankruptcy estate. This court stipulates that the money will be used to pay unsecured creditors."

Tinius' sigh could be heard at street level through the open windows nine-stories above. Rooter added, "The funds remaining in GRT's operating account will be transferred from Residents Bank to the unsecured creditor's settlement account at Bank of America." The judge then nodded to the bank's attorney, Hyman First, who had requested an opportunity to argue for a lower settlement payment to the unsecured creditors than the Judge intended to allocate from the bankryptcy estate, once the assets were sold.

"Unsecured creditors should receive only a small portion of the proceeds recovered from the sale of company assets," First began. He then spiraled into his most effective boilerplate presentation. *Here's were I earn my fees.*

He'd done this enough to know how to prod the judge into slicing off and allocating most of GRT's assets to his client. In a legal ritual akin to a cannibal's dance before the big soup, the bank's attorney piously cited the Christian principles of the new bankruptcy law.

"Lenders should not be penalized by the deadbeats who take money out of the pockets of the poor bank depositors and stockholders, and fail to repay." He did not bother to mention how the banks bombard common-senseless college students, people over their heads in debt, and a family pet named Carl, with pre-approved credit card applications. Or how they increased interest rates to twenty-five percent or more, when people can't make the minimum payments.

Hyman First made sure that the guts of GRT's assets went to Residents Bank. Processing equipment, molds, accounts receivable, inventory and most of the cash in bank accounts were all turned over to the bank, effective immediately. He concluded his presentation with the declaration that, "The bank has no problem with allowing Mr. Gatt and his employees one day to remove their personal items...under the supervision of bank officials."

The lease on the 70,000 square-foot modern industrial building in North Haven was cancelled, subject to a three month extension needed to conduct an equipment auction. Justin guessed the income from the forced auction would not be as high as the bank expected. So many plastics processors had been put out of business recently, that there was a surplus of late-model used equipment on the market for cheap money.

As Justin listened to the judge and the attorneys agree on the final paperwork and court filings, he suddenly felt an unexpected sense of relief. His painful anticipation of failure was finally over, along with his career as a small manufacturer. But so were the sixty-hour work-weeks. He'd risked his life savings for twenty-two years and finally saw it sponged away by circumstances beyond his control...along with the business assets he'd worked so hard to build. The company which once thrived against incessant competition from the major plastic producers, and consistently matched customer demands for better products at lower prices, had finally reached the end of its business cycle.

The gut wrenching, bi-weekly court battles he'd fought to maintain debtor-in-possession control of GRT had taken a toll on his nerves. Several months on Prozac had helped. But, the loss of management control he'd feared..the hollowness of a career prematurely aborted...the anticipated void in his daily routines... now seemed more of a revelation than the nightmare he'd anticipated.

Joanna gripped his arm with both hands and gritted her teeth to hold back sobs. As her head leaned against his shoulder, Justin lifted her chin gently and peered into the lovable brown eyes suddenly moistened. A guilty feeling landed like a anvil dropped on his chest from a roof.

Ninety-two of his best friends were out of work; with no prospects for decent-paying jobs in the depressed Connecticut economy. They'd involuntarily joined thousands of other unemployed manufacturing workers recently forced into catatonic insecurity. The careers of GRT's former employees were now dissolved in the weakly-defined amalgam called *globalization*.

We're all free trade pawns, he thought, *political unmentionables*.

His mind slipped briefly from its rational zone to abstract territory. *No wonder the divorce rate is so high in this country---there's a business template. The import-dominated American economic system is incompatible with the entrepreneurial spirit, which creates most of the new jobs in this country.*

Justin had always made his living making things…inspired by Cosimo's creativeness. He wondered if he'd ever again experience the exhilaration of developing a new product beneficial to the human race; or the exciting challenges one faces in attempting to bring a product to market. Cosimo had convinced him that people exuded a happiness-substance when they created something new with their hands.

A gavel hammered the thought from his mind.

"All rise!" the clerk shouted. This time her tone was more a demand than a plea.

Judge Rooter stood, gathered his papers and nodded to the three smiling lawyers. They'd just been awarded huge legal fees. Only Ken Levine was glum. *At least Justin got the patent rights.*

"This case is hereby declared settled."

Rooter glared at Tinius and declared in an obviously frustrated tone, "I wish this matter could have been resolved outside my jurisdiction."

He squinted clear displeasure at Tinius, turned and disappeared through the side door.

CHAPTER 15

(July 1, 2008) p.m.
North Haven

Roberto could balance the cherry desk on the tail end of the van for at least that long.

Gatt trudged from the back of the van to the shaded side, climbed into the front seat and closed his eyes. Biofeedback would hopefully take only a few minutes to relieve the vise-like tension gripping his forehead, which had started as he was handing out pink slips to GRT's employees.

He pictured his hands, arms, legs and feet suspended in warm black clouds. Gradually, he willed a portion of the blood oozing into his brain through carotid arteries, to be redirected.Slowly…steadily…the blue fluid eased down into the wide arteries feeding his arms and legs, and eventually pulsed into the tributaries of his fingers and toes. The slight tingling sensation in his digits indicated the process was beginning to work. He could still feel the activated cell phone in his hand; and imagine the familiar face of the man waiting patiently on the open line.

He then willed the obstreperous gurgle, which only a stethoscope can detect, to trickle back into relaxed veins. His blood pressure soon dropped from 175 to 110. His head became lighter…his arms and legs heavier. In a few seconds the blind spot from the nerve-fired, cramped focal-muscles behind his eyes diminished. The blinding oval aura became a few tiny sparks. Slowly, the throbbing ache disappeared. He was exhausted, could hardly speak, but didn't wish to offend his friend.

As Justin and Roberto were lifting the heavy wood desk they'd carried across the parking lot from his nearly-empty office, his cell phone had sounded the familiar chrome wave. Roberto had nodded for him to take the call, as he balanced the desk on the edge of the truck bed with his shoulder. Justin was expecting a call from Ken Levine, who'd been instructed by Judge Rooter to prepare the legal documents granting Justin exclusive rights to the patents for his new recycling technology.

"Hello?"

"Justin, this is Eric Syzmansky. Did I catch you at a bad time?" The Professor's familiar voice brought the day's first faint smile. His classes at the Yale School of Management had always been Gatt's favorites.

"No, not really, Eric. Just a minor change in venue."

"Some minor change, my boy. I'm aware of your unfortunate circumstances." He paused to find the appropriate words. "I've been following GRT's progress."

Justin thought he meant to say *regress*.

"How's your grandfather doing? Still chasing away the ladies?"

Justin's faint smile transmuted into a broad grin. "He's still making art pieces, and I'm not sure what other kinds of pieces. But, thanks for asking, Eric." He added reticently, "He's in failing health, as you'd expect at his age."

The Professor hesitated, then attempted an appropriate philosophical reply. "Well, the Lord adds and subtracts. There's a time to come and a time to ship out." He didn't remember the exact scripture of Ecclesiastes, Chapter 3. His expertise was business and finance.

Justin was reminded of the metal plaque Cosimo fabricated for his night table: *Man should eat and drink, and enjoy the good of all his labor; it IS the gift of God.*

Roberto was still balancing the desk on the edge of the van with his shoulder, as he watched the employees leave the office carrying boxes of personal items. Their blank expressions were pale profiles of pure dejection. Suddenly he shoved the edge of the desk past the drop gate. It settled in without a scratch. He circled to the front of the van and waved to Mr. Gatt. Then he walked wearily past the front of the GRT headquarters building for a last look, before heading to the employee parking lot.

"That's a quotation I didn't learn at Yale School of Management," Justin quipped. He returned Roberto's wave by wedging a grateful right hand to his forehead. Roberto had asked the same question as the other jobless employees did: "Will we ever get our jobs back?"

Justin couldn't lie. "Not likely," he'd answered.

Professor Syzmansky knew Gatt to be self-deprecating. He was also the brightest student he ever taught. Justin had returned to Yale several times as a guest speaker, to participate in the School of Management's Entrepreneurial Business Planning seminars. The professor remembered how Justin dazzled the business school graduate students with his presentation on the realities of entrepreneurship. His ideas on how to successfully nurture an under-funded small business through the start-up phase were astoundingly insightful.

He'd also startled a *Small Business Marketing Concepts* class, during one of Syzmanski's famous "What If?" sessions, by telling them that most consumers are unaware of the forces that influence their spending decisions. Furthermore, he'd postulated quite controversially---that big companies were much like typical consumers. Executives in charge of buying decisions at multinational corporations were probably not making investment decisions in the controlled, objective manner most stockholders expected.

The flaky students who became advertising executives, and created subliminal commercials for the media, were probably the only ones who understood Gatt's borderline-abstract message. Their agencies convinced sponsors that rapid-clip TV messages could dictate people's purchasing preferences, using blindingly-fast imagery which only the sub-conscious mind could assimilate.

"Justin, I'm sorry it turned out this way for your company," Syzmansky said wanly. "You didn't have a suicide bomber's chance for a long term solution. I've been studying the records of business failures in the Northeast states. I believe there is a vendetta against small manufacturing businesses… some kind of poisonous fishnet."

"Well, it's too late for GRT to do anything about it. I guess we were snagged," Justin replied, as he climbed out from the driver's compartment to the parking lot.

Syzmansky lowered his voice, "Sam Rooter has asked me to help investigate."

Justin leaned against the van and watched as one of the hard-assed guardians of the bank's collateral emerged from the front office carrying boxes for Joanna. She was motioning authoritatively with her finger in the direction of a fire-engine red 1999 F-150 pick-up. *There must be good in all people*, he conjectured. Joanna just finished doling out the last paychecks and encouraging embraces. A few of every GRT employee's tears splashed on the sealed envelopes.

The auctioneers prepared an inventory of equipment; listing the make, model and serial number of each item, from a 500-horsepower compounding extruder, to a ½- hp desk fan. Photos were taken of the late-model machines. They'd be used on the front and back covers of the auction brochure, which would be mailed to every plastics compounding and injection molding dealer and manufacturer east of the Mississippi; and posted on the internet within two weeks.

"But I'm not a private eye. Anyway, that's not why I called," the Professor continued, trying to break past the brain-wave barrier he suspected Justin had erected to block out any notions of assuming new responsibilities. Especially if consequences for other people were involved.

"I know it's early, my boy, but there's an opportunity you might be interested in."

"I appreciate the thought, Eric. But I really need time to think. You know---unpack my stuff---unbridle my mind." He noticed that the stream of people leaving the office had vanished. "Can I call you back, Eric? I still have a few things to pick up from my office."

The fourteen-foot leased van was filled with mementos and cartons containing personal items and technical reference materials he'd accumulated over the years. The most valuable item was gently placed on the front seat in an open cardboard box. Cosimo's vase sparkled with gold, ruby and sapphire-blue reflections from the descending afternoon sun. A few college textbooks and the patent certificates hanging on his office wall were all that needed to be retrieved.

Tinius's young lieutenant wanted proof that the books hadn't become the property of Residents Bank. Justin opened one of the old college textbooks and pulled out a 1981 receipt from the Yale Coop. He remembered using it as a page marker for Professor Syzmanski's definitive publication: *International Trade Cartels*.

The dutiful guardian of the bank's property loosened his tie, then stomped from the office. He told Gatt to remove anything he wanted. Anyone who kept receipts that long, he surmised, would eventually produce ownership documents for the other junk.

Syzmansky was aware that Justin lost a small fortune attempting to salvage GRT. He imagined, correctly, that his prized pupil had few financial resources remaining. Perhaps his small Wallingford colonial, some mutual funds or IRAs. Certainly not enough cash to live comfortably for an extended period, or pay the upcoming patent-registration fees. He persisted.

"The opportunity pays well, I understand, and has flexible timing. Rather than go into details now, except to tell you it involves helping other small companies---and seems a perfect fit for your qualifications--- how about joining me for lunch tomorrow at the Donaldson Commons?"

The last thing on Justin's mind was to try saving another company from financial disaster. He wanted to emulate the timid *royal python*, which he'd learned about on a trip to equatorial West Africa. It was the most beautifully marked snake in the *boidae* family of cobras and pythons...which kill prey by constriction. This animal had large, elongated clear markings against a deep brown skin, and was often referred to as the 'ball' python. Less than six feet in length---when confronted, it rolls itself into a ball, with its head tucked inside. Coiled so tightly, it takes great force to open.

"Maybe, in a few weeks, Eric."

Justin tried to visualize what he'd do in that period: unpack boxes, shop for groceries, mow the lawn. Maybe finish reading Bishop and Waldholz's book, **Genome, The story about man's attempt to map all the genes in the human body**. Or other light reading. He would probably read the obituaries and job-wanted ads. Ugly thought. Not much to look forward to, except visiting with Cosimo. He hoped his grandfather would hang on to his harem for a few more years; but at his age, many people seemed to pass away during the hot summer. He wondered if the Census Bureau kept statistics on this phenomenon. Or was it just his imagination?

Gatt's biggest fear had always been boredom. It was probably one of the reasons he never married. He'd never found the woman who could hold his interest long enough to commit a lifetime to. At the age of 48, he realized compromises were in order. Now that he'd lost his sense of purpose…there was nothing left of real interest to expend his energies on.

He stared at the empty GRT parking lot, balancing his fear of boredom against his reluctance to re-engage battle with the demising forces surrounding a troubled business. Somehow, *fear* overcame *reluctance*.

"Perhaps I could join you for lunch, Professor. Tell me a bit more."

Syzmansky spoke rapidly, sensing Justin's need for a concise answer at this particular moment. "Here's the kicker, my boy. The firm involved, G.H. Paladin, has lined up significant capital to re-finance troubled small businesses. They need someone to tell them how to spend the money most effectively."

Gatt thought about this. "You mean a company emulating GRT's situation could be saved?"

"That's what Ross Trenker at Paladin indicated. He's in charge of hiring the initial staff. I took the liberty, based on our years of friendship, to give him a 'grab this guy fast' resume of your background."

"Thanks…I think. What's the timing?"

"He's already interviewed several experienced executives from around Route 128." That road in Massachusetts was America's technology super-highway. "But most of the candidates are not familiar with the challenges of small manufacturing businesses. They can explain how empirical management techniques are used for loss aversion; but they couldn't tell you how to transfer plastic pellets from a supersack to the hopper of a molding machine."

Syzmansky stopped for a breath. Justin was quiet. *He must be interested.*

"Tell me more about Ross Trenker."

"Ross graduated from Yale School of Management several years after you. He'd like to hire an Eli."

WASHINGTON, D.C.

Ross Trenker watched in amazement as several of the most powerful men in the world filed into the vault room from behind the walnut panel. He recognized a few from *Fortune Magazine* executive photos in the annual issue ranking the 500 largest companies and financial institutions in the country. Some were current CEOs...most had retired. They were all dressed in formal black tuxedos except for Blackstone. Jeffrey Richards, a Houston oilman took the seat at folio number one.

When the others were all seated, Richards spoke in a silky drawl, "Thank you foraccepting our invitation, Ross. Now, let me explain why you're here, and what we want from you. We sincerely hope that this unique opportunity will advance your career."

The retired executive seated next to Richards interjected boisterously, "But you must first sign the commitment and confidentiality document that the Three-Sixes require."

The U.S. Senator watched from behind the one-way mirror for nearly an hour as the Three-Sixes membership committee grilled Trenker. The evidence they'd compiled on Trenker's corrupt activities in Asia was convincing. There was no doubt he'd cooperate and join the group, although he hesitated before reluctantly signing the frightful confidentiality agreement.

Trenker cowered at the hateful expression on the blotched face of the sclerotic retired executive seated at position number-two at the conference table. Trenker had extorted more than a million dollars in kick-backs from local Chinese businessmen in Shanghai, Tianjin and Chongqing, by arranging exclusive distribution deals for the popular consumer toiletries his former employer marketed in China. Executive number-two was once the chief executive of the personal-care products division of the company. He was riled to learn that Trenker sold the proprietary formulas for several shampoo products designed specifically for China's raven-haired consumers.

"You've proven to be sufficiently corruptible to take on the assignment, Trenker. Welcome to the group," spewed the man of seventy with the hard, dark hollow eyes. "As long as you understand the severe consequences...if the assignment fails."

Jeffrey Richards added stiffly, from position number one, "The Department of Energy is the primary source of data our cartel utilizes in influencing worldwide gasoline and heating-fuel prices. If you're appointed as the new Deputy Secretary, the information you provide to our group will have global impact. It must be accurate and timely."

The Senator behind the mirror mused, *I'll see that he receives fast-track approval from the Senate Sub-Committee.*

Trenker was sweating profusely when he departed the bank..the last man to leave. The others filtered out individually every few minutes through a secret underground passageway built decades earlier to hide slaves migrating from Baltimore to Pennsylvania and New York. The tunnel ran north---parallel to the Yellow Line of the Metro Rail Subway---and led to the parking garage under the Shakespeare Theatre on 7th and E Street. Several of the Three-Sixes on the member-committee joined a post-performance reception for dignitaries, which followed the final enactment of *A Midsummer Night's Dream*.

Trenker greeted the night guard and exited the front door of the bank building, as instructed. McGill was parked in front of the Navy Memorial a few yards away.

"I assume the meeting went well?" McGill inquired absently, as Ross climbed into the front seat. A blank countenance painted his face pallid. McGill had been briefed by Blackstone.

"I'm not sure what I can tell you," Trenker replied hesitantly. "I assume you're in the loop, but my instructions were very specific."

Blackstone smiled as he listened to the conversation from a stretch-limo parked outside the Shakespeare Theatre. The electronic bug in the communications unit Trenker was now required to carry wherever he traveled, functioned perfectly. Trenker passed the first test.

"You're correct, Ross. Tom only informs me of certain things, on a need-to-know basis. I do know that FFF must quickly replace you on the U.S. trade mission leaving for China in a few weeks."

Trenker's mind was casting off fragments of angst at an intense tempo. The unsettling confrontation with Blackstone and the others left no doubt that his life had just changed forever. He'd been drawn into a conspiracy with mind-numbing implications---not necessarily good for his health.

The people who revealed themselves to him tonight were more dangerous and powerful than the *Terrible Tong* secret societies in Southeast Asia, and the *tu-fei* thugs he'd paid to cover his tracks in the illicit deals with the *cai gou yuan*...the fixers and buyers in the major Chinese cities who routinely traded items and favors which the official government did not provide directly.

"I can't think of anyone right now," Trenker said, subconsciously anticipating McGill's next question. "Someone in Boston?"

McGill drove to the Hotel Hamilton Crest on 14th and F Street near the historic tariff building between Capitol Hill and the business district, where FFF maintained several year-round suites for visiting GH Paladin employees and important out-of-town customers. Blackstone and the FFF staff solicited most of the firm's government consulting contracts from this hotel...usually with the assistance of dowdy female *associates* wearing black-rimmed eyeglasses and unfashionable frumpy dresses. The instant snap-off clothing masked their voluptuous and readily available torsos.

McGill had scheduled an early breakfast meeting with Richard deLeone, the Assistant U.S. Trade Representative, to review the mission agenda for the FFF representative traveling with his group to China. DeLeone reported directly to Butler Humphreys, the USTR, and was responsible for scheduling negotiating sessions with the Chinese trade officials, as well as guided tours for the American delegation; typically to factories, universities and ministry offices pre-approved by Mu Jianting's repressive government.

"We'll have to inform deLeone that you won't be making the trip to China."

"I'm sure he'll be delighted," Trenker replied sarcastically. "He's made it clear that my presence is not appreciated."

"You may as well know," McGill said as they drove into the 14th Street parking lot. "That ass-hole is on Blackstone's payroll. The greedy bastard has been demanding more money, and less interference from others in our group. He accompanies Humphreys on all trade missions, and wants to control the flow of information. That's part of the reason we wanted you to make the trip. I think he's lost Blackstone's trust---a very dangerous situation to find yourself in." McGill's fiery sideways glance scorched the message into Trenker's permanent memory.

(July 2, 2008) noon
Yale University School of Management, New Haven

Donaldson Commons, also known as the School of Management Dining Hall, was a popular gathering place for meals and informal student-faculty conferences. Located on Mansfield Street, near the four historic mansions in the Hillhouse area that housed the Yale School of Management, the former carriage house and chapel of the Berkeley Divinity School had been named in honor of William H. Donaldson, a Yale graduate.

Donaldson was the founder and first dean of the School of Management. A former Chairman of the Securities and Exchange Commission, and CEO of Aetna Corp, he was most famous as co-founder of the prestigious Wall Street brokerage firm of Donaldson, Lufkin & Jenrette.

Professor Syzmansky's office was located nearby in Horchow Hall, a nineteenth century mansion which was once the residence of the New Haven Mayor…also a Yale graduate. Horchow was now used for class rooms, faculty offices and study halls.

Gatt grabbed a tray and revisited the familiar food line he hadn't seen in years. He then joined the professor in a quiet area in the back of the dining room, unofficially reserved for faculty members. It was far enough away from the plate rattling and incessant chatter of the MBA students, who were discussing final exams, and the lack of job interviews being scheduled this year by the multinational corporations. A photo portrait of President Hu Jintao of China hung on the wall, commemorating his 2006 highly publicized visit to Yale.

Only the foreign students from India and China were assured of gainful employment after graduation. Many of the Asian M.B.A candidates already held positions in government agencies, and had been sent to New Haven to pick the brains of Yale's elite international government scholars.

Gatt noticed the large contingent of Chinese students gathered at a table not far from the faculty section. They were mostly men in their thirties and early forties. A few younger female and male students, brilliant beyond their years, shared the animated conversation, but seldom interrupted.

Syzmansky recognized the very tall, sharp featured man in his mid forties, who seemed to dominate the conversation. Colonel Wen Ma Ming was wearing finely-tailored clothes and expensive shoes. His chest was pushed out as if he was displaying a monogrammed message from Chinese Communist Party Chairman, Mu Jianting. Syzmansky guessed the Chinese students were not discussing morning classes in Public Policy Concepts, or The Role of Private Foundations in Helping the Poor and Unemployed.

Many of the Chinese students were mid-level ministry and provincial government officials, sent by Beijing to study advanced financial concepts, international governance and management of large-scale programs. They'd likely return to China before completing the MBA curriculum.

Wen Ma was the highest Chinese official ever to attend Yale. A full Colonel in the People's Liberation Army, he was also second in command to General Ye Kunshi, the influential Politboro member who controlled China's massive, state-run businesses. Wen Ma had been dispatched to Yale for a Management Leaders Forum, and also attended workshops at the Chief Executive Leadership Institute in Atlanta, which was affiliated with the Yale School of Management. The professor believed he was being prepared to manage a large enterprise on the mainland.

The arrogant and boisterous oriental boasted of his high rank and influence in Beijing leadership circles to faculty and students alike. His uncle, Yong Ihasa, a Vice-Premier of China, had directed him and hundreds of other Chinese cadre to American universities, for the sole purpose of collecting information useful to the Party. Some of their specific information-gathering activities were clandestine in nature.

The Chinese students had been welcomed with open arms---and open palms--- by Yale and the other preservers of America's most advanced technology and management methods. Top private and state universities in the United States gladly accepted the fists full of money the Communist government provided. Prestigious consulting firms and Congressional lobbyists based in Washington, D.C. similarly detected no conflicts. They openly exchanged prized information and political influence for the large sums the oppressive Chinese Communist Party provided. The Chinese were paying with dollars Beijing had accumulated from the country's massive trade surplus with the United States.

China's more progressive leaders apparently believed that economic growth alone was not sufficient to solve all the county's problems. China needed to draw experience from the successes and failures of other ruling parties in the world. Beijing would have to improve the governance capabilities and efficiencies of local, provincial and central leaders and committees. The Party needed to convince 1.3 billion people, and the free-trade world, that the iron grip of the Chinese Communist Party was still the crucial political contributor to China's unprecedented economic advancement.

Professor Syzmansky nodded toward the Chinese group and said to Justin, "I hope that many of the Asian students participating in Yale's organization-management programs will eventually become vice-ministers and deputy provincial governors. Along with the Chinese attending Harvard's Kennedy School, Syracuse University and the University of Maryland Asian teaching programs, these students could become candidates for higher ranking national posts."

"Why are so many here?" Gatt inquired, as he placed the food tray on the table.

"Mostly to learn how America manages large institutions and enormous social and technology programs. I believe they could teach us a thing or two about how to apply technology to small commercial ventures."

Gatt was pleased to hear the spritzy tone in Syzmansky's voice.

"You look well, Eric. Semi-retirement must favor your health." He extended a warm handshake, and noticed the cane hanging on the chair. He remembered that Syzmansky had a hip replaced last year.

"How's your ceramic and titanium joint doing?"

"Fine. I don't really need the cane; I carry it to extract sympathy from my students." He glanced back at the cluster of Chinese students.

"The latest crop is hard as nails. Especially the Asians. They want black and white answers for every conceivable socio-economic situation." He noticed the items on Justin's food tray and said, "You took the mild chili and crackers. You won't need to add pepper." In a peculiarly suggestive tone he added, "The tuna salad isn't bad, either. They still have some left."

"How long has it been, Eric? Two...Three years?"

"Much too long, my boy. I wish you had more time to spend at Yale. Perhaps in the future." Syzmansky looked closely at his tired eyes. "Not much sleep lately, eh?"

"Like when I had to study for your exams on organizational behavior." Justin scooped a large spoonful of the mild chili, swallowed it rapidly, and immediately began choking. He grabbed for his diet root beer as the professor laughed.

"Some kind of mild, huh?" he chuckled. "The cook does that to us at least once a week. He throws a mysterious species of South African pepper-dews into a surprise dish. Usually it's chili. Even the giant fire-ants of Africa spit it out."

When Justin finished the twenty ounce soda, he wiped his tear-soaked eyes with a napkin, and managed to mutter, "Tell me more about Ross Trenker."

Syzmansky was grateful for his directness. It showed the interest he'd hoped for.

"As I said earlier, Ross is an SOM grad, about eight years after you. He worked for Proctor and Gamble for several years after graduation, and eventually became a brand manager for Asian markets . He was always fascinated with the multinationals, and wanted to be a part of big-enterprise excitement. I think the feeling of invulnerability and power attracted him. He took a different path than you."

Justin was still recovering from the fire in his mouth, but managed to ask, "Why did he decide to join a smaller company, as I imagine G.H. Paladin must be? Everyone is smaller than P&G."

"I guess it was more his style. Paladin is a Boston-based business consulting firm, with ties to Washington. Ross maintains his links with big enterprises, but without the pressure to perform quarterly sales miracles. The consumer-product businesses of the big multinationals are worse than cockfights. Especially if you rely too much on sales to the giant discounters, like Wal-Mart and BoxMart."

"What about G.H.Paladin?"

"Ross told me he joined them in 2002, not long after 9/11. I think a lot of bright young people changed careers at that time."

Justin was sure his tongue was starting to bleed. He stuffed crackers into his mouth and gulped the professor's ice water without asking.

"Whaff does Paladin speffialize in?" Justin inquired, as he chewed on wet crackers to deflame the roof of his mouth.

The professor curled his lips inward to avoid laughing; then pushed away his tray and leaned on the table. "For some reason, I'm having trouble acquiring their business profile on the web, or through Sterling Memorial's data retrieval capabilities. As good as the Yale library system is, I may still have to access Harvard's business school library to get more information."

"You said earlier that Paladin was associated with a D.C. think-tank called the Financial Flow Foundation. What can you tell me about them?"

"Their funding sources are apparently confidential, as well as the projects they're managing. Ross could only say that FFF is loosely linked to a federal agency in Washington. Apparently there's a high level of security involved in their projects." He paused, then added in an uncertain tone, "I think it's the Commerce Department; or possibly the Small Business Administration."

Justin wanted to know where the promised financial aid was coming from. His request for an SBA loan during the GRT debtor-in-possession period had been flatly refused by the banks administering SBA loans in the region. They claimed a company in Chapter 11 was not eligible. Had the Small Business Administration suddenly changed its loan policy? He knew it wouldn't be the first time a federal agency altered its appointed task for political expediency.

The Professor wished to assure Gatt that the program was well-funded. "Ross says Paladin has just received a huge contract from FFF in D.C. They've been commissioned to design an aid program, specifically designed to help small manufacturing businesses which are struggling against foreign competition."

That sounded familiar. "That's just about every small business in the country."

"They've targeted a specific industry, which is why I thought you'd be particularly interested."

Justin pondered the comment, then guessed, "The plastics processing industry?"

"Ross will tell you more. He's about to call at one p.m."

Eric Syzmansky's cell phone chanted the aggravating *'happy cricket'* melody his twelve year old granddaughter had programmed in. He vowed to change the ring-setting to the more pleasing *slotmachine* tone, as soon as he could figure out how. He pressed the green button instantly.

"Hello, Ross. How's the weather in Boston? That nice? Yes, he's here. Yes, we talked. Just a second." Eric passed the phone to Justin.

"You probably don't remember me," Trenker began, "but I sat in on your guest speaker presentation a few years back. You told the Yale MBAs that big companies are irrational buyers of goods, or something like that."

"Hi, Ross. Yes… I mean…no. I didn't have a chance to meet many of the students that day. I felt it was better for my health if I didn't come too close to the boisterous scholars in the audience who insisted multinationals could do no wrong."

Ross laughed. "Their fathers were probably the CEOs." He remembered the dismal success rate for new consumer-product roll-outs. The expensive ad campaigns were mostly wasted money.

"Justin, I won't spoil your lunch with a long narrative. As I explained to Eric, G.H.Paladin has just initiated a program to help small companies in financial trouble due to foreign competition. The initial funding is in place to hire staff. From the information Eric has provided, I'm very interested in your qualifications. We need an experienced executive who can analyze small business problems and come up with creative solutions that can save the day."

Trenker was aware of GRT's bankruptcy from the professor's dossier on Gatt. He added, "We can prevent a lot of people from losing their jobs if the program is successful."

Justin had to ask the question, knowing the answer could immediately end the discussion. "Are you aware of my company's recent....closing?"

"Sure. And I'm sorry it's too late for GRT. But that's just the type of situation we're trying to prevent. From what I understand about your business---the years of success, the innovative technology you commercialized....without a doubt you could have received benefits from this program!"

Justin looked incredulously at the professor. Over his shoulder he saw the students departing for their next lecture or study period. Only the tall Chinaman and a few young female students remained at the Asian table.

They're the financial future of this world, he thought.

"Listen," Ross broke in, "I have a tight schedule. Can you come to Boston next Tuesday and meet with Bennett McGill, the president of GHP, and some other people---me included?"

Syzmansky somehow heard the question, and began nodding his head vigorously. Justin answered tentatively, "I guess I can make it, Ross."

"Good! Why don't you come in Monday night? We can have a pre-interview dinner. I'll make arrangements for you to stay at the Sheraton-Boston hotel next door. Our offices are on the twentieth floor of the Prudential Center building. We took over some of the old Gillette space when P&G relocated many of the Gillette executives to Cincinnati following the merger."

"Where shall we meet?"

"The front desk in the lobby will be okay. I need your cell number; here's mine."

Syzmansky caught the eye of the tall Chinaman by waving his cane above his head. He said to Justin, "I'd like you to meet someone before you leave."

Wen Ma Ming waved back to the eccentric teacher without smiling. Syzmanski's lecture explaining the influence yielded by the Business

Roundtable's D.C. lobbying groups on Presidential decisions, had been the most provocative during his brief, state-sponsored exposure to U.S. academic experts.

He'd learned about the cozy relationship between America's big business and the Executive branch of the federal government, at Harvard's Kennedy School of Government. But not as much about effective governance policy at local, state and federal government levels as he acquired from the Yale SOM.

"He prefers to be addressed by his military rank." Syzmansky watched Wen Ma sweep away the young students with a backhand toward the exit door.

"Colonel Wen Ma Ming…it's good to see you again. How was the morning seminar by Dean Ingerstein on international trade?"

At six foot two, Colonel Wen was taller than most Chinese, and was as thin and fit as an astronaut. He was dressed in his usual casual elegance---an eight hundred dollar Michael Kors tan suede sports jacket, Cole Haan shoes, and a three hundred dollar espresso-colored Hilfiger shirt with Chinese characters embroidered in small white print on the pocket. The translation in English was: *Deputy President of State Industries.*

The forty-two year old military-industrialist, with dark, close-cropped hair and an air of superiority, looked more like a movie star, or a Bolivian drug lord, than a Communist Party comrade with vast business interests and high contacts.

"The SOM seminars are always disappointing, except for yours, which I find mildly instructive." He sat without asking and ignored Gatt, who he assumed was a junior faculty member not worthy of acknowledgement.

"Who's this?" the Colonel inquired, turning briefly to Justin, then rudely back to face Syzmansky.

The professor answered without hesitation, in irritated staccato fashion, "This is Justin Gatt. A prominent guest speaker…my best former MBA student… a successful businessman …and a dear friend." He was embarrassed for Justin, who picked up on the Professor's tone.

"And what are you here to learn from our prestigious universities, Mr. Ming, that you can't learn from Fudan, Quing Hau or Beijing Universities in China?" Justin purposely used the improper given name 'Ming', instead of 'Colonel Wen.'

Kung-fu daggers flew from Wen's eyes. "Nothing of importance, Mr. guest speaker," he answered venomously. "China has forgotten in a few thousand years more than America will ever learn. We're going to lead in every measure of global success before your next promotion."

Syzmansky thought it was time to deflate the abrasive exchange. He was sorry he'd waved the arrogant Colonel over to meet his friend.

"The Colonel is one of the military ministers of China's state-run industrial empire. We hope that his career flourishes, and that someday he and other Chinese leaders will express mild appreciation for the academic open-door policy of United States universities. It has helped nearly two-hundred thousand Chinese mid-level cadre, and many bright young students attend the most prestigious business and management teaching institutions on the planet." He reached for his cane and began to stand.

"Professor…professor….don't be offended. Chinese academicians are not as sensitive as you Americans. We Communists frequently downplay the role of university scholars in the enormous economic success of our country. But I can assure you, there are those of us who appreciate their patriotic guidance." He tilted his head toward Justin, almost imperceptibly, and added, "We sometimes say things from habit, not from the mind."

Gatt took that as a form of face-saving oriental apology. As he stood to leave with Syzmansky, he extended a hand and exclaimed morosely, "Colonel Wen, we have tremendous respect for the accomplishments of the Chinese people. Even if it costs us thousands of jobs and numerous bankruptcies in our businesses. At some time in the future, I hope the U.S. can catch up with China, and compete on equal footing. We have as much to learn from your methods as you do from ours."

Wen Ma reluctantly shook his hand, but had nothing more to say. He'd remember this arrogant junior teacher. He may someday have the opportunity to repay his disrespect for Chinese authority. Just as he had done to the rioting peasants he'd ordered massacred in Hebei Province earlier in the year.

When they arrived at Syzmansky's office in Horchow Hall, a hot pot of Earl Grey tea was waiting on a side table near his desk.

"Not all Chinese leaders are like him, my boy. I've met the most wonderful Asians at Yale, including some of our own professors, who migrated from the Chinese mainland to Taiwan during the purges. They escaped Mao's youthful Red Guards, who tortured and murdered nearly every professional they could locate." Syzmansky hung his cane on a door-hook and beamed at the pot of tea. He peered into the hallway for the person who prepared the tea.

Justin noticed the impressive book collection in Syzmansky's large office. The shelves held at least a thousand books and periodicals on mahogany bookcases built into the walls. Several of the books addressed the subject of Asian history. Others from his private collection of leather-bound eighteenth-century first-editions, including British economist Adam Smith's 1776 *Wealth of Nations* and 1759 *Theory of Moral Sentiment*, were worthy of inclusion in Yale's world-famous Beinecke Rare Book and Manuscript library.

Syzmansky smiled as a short, dark-eyed Asian man with black-hair peeked into the room. "Did my countryman give you a hard time?"

The professor beamed. He was obviously glad to see the thirty-two year old Taiwanese student. "Justin, I can finally introduce you to a fine Asian gentleman. Meet Robert Changhui; our best tea-maker, and an accomplished Chinese historian."

The diminutive man exhibited a smile so wide his back teeth showed. He grasped Justin's hand and practically crushed it with enthusiasm.

"So glad to meet you, Mr. Gatt. The professor tells me you have accomplished much. May I congratulate you?"

Justin wondered which fantasy drug the professor was using, lately. "You're too kind, Robert. You must know, if you're a friend of Professor Syzmansky, that he tends to embellish at times."

"Robert just completed his MBA curriculum in June. We're trying to talk him into remaining in the U.S. He has a job offer in Washington." Robert frowned, and pivoted his head side to side. "My family wants me back in Taipei, to coordinate the move of our electronics business to Shenzen. But I prefer to acquire experience in the States first."

Syzmansky reached for the tea pot and poured three cups into the exquisite seventeenth century Ming tableware he'd received as a gift from the current Ambassador to China, Forrest Balzerini. His old Yale roommate had offered Robert a job in Washington as an Ambassador's aide.

"Let's talk a bit about China," Syzmansky suggested. "Robert, you know more about China's current situation and glorious history than anyone at Yale. Can you give us some insight into why a creep like Wen Ma could reach such a high position?"

Robert lifted his cup gently from his lips and replied, "Wen Ma Ming is the nephew of Yong Ihasa, the Vice-Premier of China. Yong also happens to be a Communist Party hard-liner." He sipped again. "Some consider Yong to be the most ruthless and aggressive member of the Standing Committee."

"What else can you tell us about Wen's involvement in Chinese industries?" Justin inquired. He wondered if Colonel Wen's empire extended to the plastics molding businesses in China which displaced Slattery and others at BoxMart stores. Robert stepped to a bookshelf and pulled down a 2007 periodical listing China's national statistics.

"Page 134--Agriculture. China has now approached the U.S. as the largest producer of corn in the world. In 2007 the corn production was 300 million bushels.

"Page 215--Steel Production and Consumption. China is now the world's largest producer and consumer of iron. In 2007 the country consumed a billion iron ingots to produce re-bar for construction projects, compared with only 550 million ingots used in the U.S.

"Page 256--Population Growth. Slowed, but estimated at twenty million per year. Over seventy-five-percent of China's 1.3 billion population is of job-holding age.

He cited other Chinese mainland statistics: "the most concrete produced and used....the world's second highest consumer of oil....the top twenty most polluted cities in the world....300 skyscrapers in Shanghai....the largest buyer of U.S. Treasury bonds." One statistic stood out from the others: "*The Chinese government holds the largest reserves of U.S. dollars in the world.*"

"He's involved in all of it, through the tentacles of the People's Liberation Army."

CHAPTER 16

(JULY 7, 2008) 6 P.M.
BOSTON

Justin slipped the Northeastern University criminal-justice co-op student a ten, then watched apprehensively as the part-time valet smiled roguishly and dropped behind the steering wheel. The six sparkling zirconium stubs piercing each of his ears reflected tiny gold blasts off the body of his canary-yellow 1987 Corvette convertible, as the student eased the prized restoration around the corner of the underground parking garage.

Two seconds later, Gatt cringed at the sound of spinning tires. Ten seconds later, the screeching of locked disc-brakes drifted down to ground level, along with the pungent odor of burnt rubber. At least his insurance was paid until September.

He pushed through the rotating glass door of the street-level entrance to the Sheraton-Boston Hotel, and rode the escalator to the lobby floor above. Several young and middle-aged women wearing white rubber-soled shoes crammed the lobby and the check-in lines. Gatt guessed there was a nurse's convention, or some other medical conference. Boston was renowned for its world-class hospitals, medical schools and state-of-the-art medical technology. Few weeks passed when there *wasn't* a medical conference staged.

Ross Trenker had arranged for rapid-check-in, and Gatt decided to drop his overnight bag in the room. Ross wasn't expected for another hour. As he waited for the elevator, an attractive women in her late twenties approached with a quizzical expression on her face. She reached him just as the elevator door slid open.

"Are you by any chance Mr. Gatt from Connecticut?" she asked, in a melodic, slightly raised voice that reminded him of a sexy Italian tour guide he'd met in Venice. Her five-foot four-inch frame was busty, and well proportioned, and her adorable face was bordered with auburn and blonde-streaked curls. A few straitened blonde strands poked loosely over radiant green eyes, which peeked out in a sensual squint. Her smile was infectious; and was framed by sculptured, seductive full lips, moistened with glossy red covering and pursed cutely.

He was smitten. Justin's first impression was: male or female…one could easily develop a crush on such an attractive young woman.

"Yes, I'm Justin Gatt. Are you with G.H. Paladin? Ms…?"

"Lynne Hurricane," she answered with a broad grin and a silly expression. "Friends call me Lynne; or Lynney; or L.H. But, ya doesn't has to call me Ms. Hurricane." She mimicked the old "Mr. Johnson…you can call me Jay," joke that was way before her time.

Justin began sweating, as he experienced a rush of focused energy he hadn't felt in years. Lynne was startlingly attractive in a cocoa Spanish leather jacket, crimson retro cardigan sweater over a crisp white cotton blouse, and a grey cotton-tweed skirt to her knees.

"Yes, yes," she murmured dramatically, as if she was in the final scene of a Broadway drama. "I am a business analyst and research associate at GHP."

She held out her hand like a Diva, and Justin felt its warmth. He held on a bit too long. She didn't seem to mind.

How absurd, he thought to himself. *She's maybe twenty years younger than me…but I think I just experiencing the 'vital force of natural attraction' for the first time.*

He'd read that homeopathy doctors considered the 'vital force' the basis for all health and disease. Maybe just being in the presence of certain people could make you healthier. Or sicker? Edwin Tinius came to mind. Or, perhaps his strong attraction to this strange young girl was because he'd always wanted a daughter. As usual, he became more philosophical about life's mysteries when he traveled and met new people.

"Ross asked me to welcome you," she explained. "He'll be a few hours late. Bennett McGill, our President, called him about some situation in Washington, D.C. that they have to resolve right away. Ross has been traveling between D.C. and Boston frequently."

Lynne noticed his overnight bag. "Why don't you relax in your room for a few minutes. I'm early, and you must be tired from fighting the traffic. The new ramps and tunnels of the Big-Dig have helped, but Boston still has the most confusing traffic patterns of any major city."

Justin glanced at the cocktail lounge across the lobby. "Why don't we meet in the bar, in about thirty minutes…if you don't mind."

"I'll order drinks in twenty five minutes. What's your poison?"

"I jump around---depending on the weather, and if the Red Sox are winning or losing. I like beer, wine or bourbon. Since they've been winning lately, I'll have a bourbon Manhattan, up, without the cherry."

Ross Trenker dialed Lynne's cell number an hour later, and apologized for not being able to join them. He instructed Lynne to play host for dinner, and to describe for Justin the basic details of the new business aid program. He then asked to speak with him.

"Justin, Lynne has been assigned to the new business aid program. She'll fill you in. I'm terribly sorry I can't join you, but something has come up which I didn't anticipate." The frustration in his voice was intense. "We're still on for tomorrow, but could you sleep a bit late and come to the office around ten?"

"Sure, Ross. No problem." He hesitated, then said awkwardly, "I don't often get to spend business time with such an attractive…research associate." He winked at Lynne, who was finishing her third glass of Merlot and staring intently over the rim into his deep blue eyes. He noticed the sudden rush of pink in her cheeks, as she reached to lift the cherry from his third cocktail and gulped it down.

When he handed the phone back, she cooed, "I know a great little place to dine, if you feel like noodles."

It wasn't a bad approximation of the sensation he was experiencing in the interior lining of his stomach ; or his emotional state. "We're probably both starving," he replied with a slight slur.

"It's only a few blocks up Huntington Ave. They have quick service."

Betty's Wok and Noodle Diner was a ten minute walk from the hotel. A balmy summer breeze was at their backs as they crossed over the T-tracks imbedded generations ago in the middle of Huntington Ave. Justin grabbed Lynne's hand firmly and guided her across the street, just as the over-head-powered electric tram rushed by with no intent of stopping for jaywalkers or confused tourists. Passengers would be exiting at Northeastern University, the Christian Science Mother Church and the Museum of Fine Arts.

"These Shanghai noodles are delicious," Justin said, as he rotated a thick round noodle between the tines of his fork, then stabbed for pieces of stir-fried shrimp, beef and chicken.

Lynne stung him with an infectious Meg Ryan smile, and watched with more than casual interest as Justin removed his tie and suit jacket, and unbuttoned the top of his white shirt. She noticed the thick tufts of dark chest-hair, and wondered if it propagated curls like that on other parts of his body.

"I like the grilled vegetables best," she baited him. "The chef uses special sauces, and I've never been able to identify the tastes."

Justin chewed slowly on some broccoli, pea pods, bean sprouts and bok choy. "You're right. The taste is eclectic." He rolled his tongue to wipe the residual ingredients from inside his mouth, and guessed. "I think saffron and dill weed." Then he added, "Is there such a thing as oriental oregano?"

Lynne's turn to guess, "Coriander and curry." She laughed, "Is there such a thing as Asian balsamic vinegar?"

Large white ceramic mugs of jasmine tea completed the meal. Lynne held hers in two hands, despite the single stem, and leered precosciously at Justin as she took tiny sips. Justin began to have lascivious thoughts. He decided the safest response was to return to a discussion begun earlier, when they discovered that their alma maters were the ultimate Ivy League competitors.

Lynne was a "Cliffie," and a 2007 MBA graduate of Harvard Business School. Her undergraduate major at Radcliffe College was economics, with a minor in library sciences. She teased Justin that she liked books better than people. Either way, she claimed, you could learn a lot more about life from the well thought out words in a book, than from the mostly inane, mostly spontaneous utterings of rushed people. Justin became a bit self-conscious about their conversation.

"I never thought of Harvard as a major rival to Yale, except in football and crew," Lynne said, as she grabbed the bill from the waitress before it hit the table.

Justin replied in an enthusiastic tone, "Both MBA programs are highly rated. Yale more so for international finance and policy-management of large government institutions. Harvard excels in big organizational behavior and management of multinational businesses."

Lynne thought a moment, then replied, "I studied the history of Ivy League schools for my library research thesis. You'd be surprised how many graduates from one school attended or taught at the other. It's almost an intellectual exchange program."

"The same could be said for some of the other Ivy League schools," he answered. "Dartmouth and Columbia were started by our grads." She liked the way Justin paired up their schools.

"Did you know that a donation from Edward Harkness, a Yale grad and Standard Oil heir, paid for Harvard's red brick residents houses on the Charles River?"

"No, but I do know that at least one-quarter of the Yale School of Management faculty once taught at Harvard, including Professor Eric Syzmansky… probably the most brilliant organizational academic in the world." He didn't bother to boast that Syzmansky was also a dear friend, and his reason for being here.

Lynne summoned her memory and said, "One of our business school professors matriculated to Yale, after ten years at Harvard, to become Associate Dean for Executive Programs at Yale SOM."

Justin thought it was fun to make other comparisons. "Do you know which university produced the most U.S. Presidents?"

"I would guess Harvard," Lynne ventured. "Five or six, I think?" She continued the quiz, "How about Senators and Supreme Court Justices?"

"I think Yale leads in recent Presidents, and probably Presidential candidates. Think of Clinton, George W.H. and George W....and John Kerry."

"No cheating," she replied. "George W. counts for Harvard. An MBA takes precedence over a Yale B.A."

"The number of leaders from both Universities, who've controlled the U.S. Government is astounding," Justin continued. "Did you know that Bill Clinton was not the first Clinton to occupy an Executive Branch residence?"

She folded four twenties around the dinner tab, and anchoring it on the edge of the table with a salt shaker. "I'm having this troublesome thought," she interjected, "that this political domination may have been planned long ago."

"Maybe by some secret Ivy League society hiding in the background," he encouraged the thought.

Lynne replied in a perplexed tone, "The demographic statistics just don't coincide with the frequency. Four of the sitting Supreme Court Justices are Harvard grads. So are twenty percent of all the Supreme Court Justices in U.S. history. Perhaps it was set in place many years ago, by the Ivy League off-spring who became Wall Street barons."

Justin was delighted listening to Lynne's inquisitive mind gallop along the conspiracy path. "Or CEOs of multinationals?"

They were hot on the trail. Lynne's fourth merlot and his first Sam Adams-dark fueled their suspicions even further.

"There must be written proof, somewhere in the archives of Houghton or Beinecke,"she concluded, referring to the famous rare book and manuscript libraries at Harvard and Yale.

"Or somewhere else in these vast libraries. My God, Yale has more than 11 million volumes in its library system. I think Sterling Memorial alone has about 4 million."

Lynne said, "Harvard's library system is even larger. If we combined them, we'd have a collection that would rival the Library of Congress---the largest library in the world. There's twenty eight million books and manuscripts stored somewhere on the 500 miles of shelves at the Jefferson, Adams and Madison buildings of the LOC system in our nations capitol."

"You're the library expert, Lynne. Let me know, in ten years, how you make out in the search for printed evidence of a conspiracy."

They locked eyes and parried jovial smirks. It seemed time to move to other subjects. Lynne had one more trivia item she just had to disclose: "All forty-three U.S. Presidents were born of Dutch, English, Irish, Scottish, Welsh, Swiss or German ancestry."

Justine wagged his head in amazement. He had one not-so-trivial question to ask, as they reached for their jackets. "Could you use the information retrieval system at the Harvard library to acquire information about banks and discount retailers?"

"Sure…down to the level a stockholder would receive, at least. Probably all the public subsidiaries and off-shore related entities they control; and the financial data the law now requires both the CEO and CFO to certify. The bad news is usually hidden deeply in the bla-bla narrative of the 'Financial Notes' attached to back pages in the annual reports. Our finance professor used to call this information *coded ambivalence data*. He complained that it was imbedded and disguised, in tiny print. Only the public auditors could find and understand the information, although they usually chose to ignore it."

As they arose to leave, Lynne added, "There are search capabilities on Harvard's data retrieval programs so powerful that the Treasury Department occasionally uses the system for top-secret projects. Why do you ask?"

He wasn't sure if she was serious. "I'm curious about the relationship between Boxmart Retail Enterprises and the Residents Bank of North America."

A chilled northeast wind nipped at their faces as they walked shoulder-to-shouldeer back to the hotel. Before Lynne climbed into the cab in front of the hotel, for the short ride to her one-bedroom apartment in Cambridge, she whispered sweetly, "I didn't tell you much about G.H. Paladin because I don't actually know much." She turned up the small collar of her thin leather jacket, and Justin moved to dampen the chill by shielding her from the sudden gusts, blowing southwest across Boston Harbor. It began to sprinkle.

"We could have taken a taxi back," he said, noticing her start to shiver. "Would you like to go into the hotel to warm up?"

Lynne glanced longingly into the warm, dry entryway. Her mind drifted to an image of long, soft pillows on Justin's king-sized bed. The night had gone so well…so well. She didn't want to spoil it with an awkward ending. Escaping into the harsh night---in a sudden rush---would be more romantic; more Bogie and Becall.

She stood bravely in the chilly nor'easter, curls nearly damp enough to drip. Oblivious to the harsh conditions, she continued her revelations about GHP. "When I accepted the job offer from Paladin, I assumed they'd give me a fancy brochure listing staff officers and the consulting services the company offered. But Bennett McGill called me into his office the first week and explained that GHP was one of the few business consulting firms in the country with *Level Three security clearance* from the State Department. I'd never heard of clearance levels for consulting firms, but guessed it was a confidentiality he couldn't discuss."

She folded her arms across her chest and leaned in toward Justin. His hands reached out instinctively, and drew her closer, as Lynne's velvety palms turned and pressed hesitantly against the warmth of his chest. He cautiously drew her into a protective, relaxed embrace. The musky scent from Lynne's damp hair brushing against his face must have matched the smell that drove cavemen into a frenzy over damp cavewomen. He inhaled deeply. He could only manage a stilted reply.

"Probably meaning…that funding sources…and project descriptions…are ..ahh…confidential."

She nodded mischievously, and said, "I haven't looked deeper.…yet."

The irritated cabby waiting to drive Lynne to her apartment suddenly shouted in an island accent, "Hey, lady, I can't wait forever. The meter's a-jerkin and a-heatin down, woman."

"It's been a very remarkable evening," Justin said hoarsely, as he opened the rear door. "I guess I'll see you again, soon."

"Yes…yes," she sighed courageously. "Goodbye, Justin." Then she slid sadly…dramatically…into the back seat; flipping her hair to the side boldly. As the taxi drew away, she peered back through the driving torrent. The strange man was waving back; oblivious to the trickling mist and two mile-per-hour summer squall. Probably overcome with the emotion of their inevitable separation.

Did he really care? Would she ever see him again? Perhaps…in about twelve hours.

CHAPTER 17

(JULY 8, 2008) 10AM
BOSTON

The President of G.H. Paladin, Bob McGill, slammed down the phone, then picked it up just as fast and stabbed three numbers into the intercom with his Dunhill Torpedo pen. Another futile argument with the inside man at the U.S. Trade Representative's office left him furious.

"Ross, are you there?" he growled into the speaker.

"Just finishing with Justin Gatt's interview," Trenker answered hesitantly. "It's going very well."

McGill's tone changed to slight irritation. "Could you please pick up the handset?"

"What's up, Bob?" Trenker asked, as pleasantly as possible…realizing McGill was upset. He didn't want to spook his prospective replacement.

McGill whispered into the receiver, "When you're finished, bring him up. We may have to move faster than originally planned. If he's qualified to fill the gap, let's hire him… now. That shit-head deLeone wants you in Washington as soon as possible. He's organizing a high level pre-mission conference for his boss, Butler Humphreys. We've won a new consulting contract with the USTR through Blackstone's FFF group in D.C.. There's big money for all of us, if we can help Humphreys pull some plums during his negotiating sessions with our Chinese friends." He didn't bother to reveal that deLeone was still resisting Trenker's assignment to the mission. He knew that Trenker would be replaced on the China assignment, now that he'd signed on with the Three Sixes.

"deLeone is insisting on a larger cut of the contract money."

"We'll be up, shortly." Trenker smiled at Justin, as if the call was good news. In reality, he was not thrilled.

McGill added tersely, "Blackstone will guide your replacement through the process. He thinks we should find someone with merchandising experience."

Trenker returned to the interview, and glanced down at Gatt's dossier… which Eric Syzmansky had thoughtfully e-mailed. The professor was correct. Gatt was undoubtedly qualified to analyze troubled plastics businesses. Whether he could develop feasible restructuring plans was a different question; although it hardly mattered.

"A very impressive track record," Trenker concluded, as Justin shifted uncomfortably from a side of the job-interview desk he was not accustomed to. "If not for the recent loss in business---which was caused by forces beyond the firm's control---GRT would be considered a decidedly successful small business. You earned a decent profit every year, except the start-up year of 1985."

Syzmansky's summary indicated that Justin's reputation as a business manager and materials scientist was almost legendary in the close-knit plastics processing industry. No other company in the Northeast had succeeded in producing the high-quality recycled compounds which GRT had commercialized.

"Justin, I'm curious. What really happened to cause so many plastics recycling companies to fail in the late nineties?" He paused, then acknowledged, "GRT did better than most."

Gatt raised an eyebrow and reached for the pitcher of ice-water placed on the edge of Trenker's desk. "Have you got a few hours?" He wet his throat and answered the question in an weary timbre, "Competition from the billion-pound-per-year polymerization plants at Dow, Dupont, BASF and Exxon-Mobil, among others. The recycling industry was decimated by the majors. Most of the 110 recycling companies which flourished in the late '90s couldn't match the oil and chemical giants' predatory price reductions." His chest tightened as painful memories returned. Ross recognized the sudden tension in his expression and said, "Let's talk about the future, instead."

"That's okay, Ross. It's just reality. I think the crisis point came in 1998, when the price for a barrel of crude oil fell to less than twelve dollars; and virgin plastics prices went down the tube."

"Those were the good old days," Trenker joked to lighten the mood. He recalled how his former employer reluctantly used a small amount of recycled materials for store-brand product packaging. Production efficiencies had decreased slightly, until process conditions were adjusted. But most of the large consumer-product manufacturers didn't want to bother making the small processing adjustments. They just crowed "green" in publicity releases, and budgeted less-than-adequate funds for go-nowhere, pilot recycling projects designed only to placate environmentally-friendly stockholders and public opinion.

Gatt said, "More was written and spoken, yet less done, about recycling plastics and rubber in the '90s than almost any other environmental issue."

"How did GRT survive?"

"We developed processes which converted a potpourri of polymer by-products and scrap materials into niche applications. Instead of selling on price alone, we offered compounds with unique properties. Some of our customers actually had 'green' consciences, and wanted a good source of recycled materials."

Trenker said, "Let me guess: the others continued to use slightly less expensive virgin resins, and opted for the type of 'green' having a crispy paper texture."

Gatt added wistfully, "Only a dozen recycling businesses survived into the new millennium. But, even with the price of oil and plastics recovering....or should I say skyrocketing...there is no longer enough scrap polymer available to support plastics recycling as an industry."

"Let me guess again," Trenker mused, "The Chinese are buying up the bulk of America's scrap materials."

"That's exactly true. The Chinese have been stuffing baled, boxed and chopped plastics scrap into those twenty-foot lead-red overseas vans; and loading them onto the same container ships which deliver Chinese-made goods to our ports. Otherwise, the giant cargo ships would be returning to Asia nearly empty. Boeing still hasn't figured out how to jam planes into a twenty-foot container."

Justin welcomed the opportunity to discuss those traumatic days with someone who was involved at the opposite end of the marketing spectrum. "The prime plastics suppliers no longer view the recycling industry as a threat to their market share," he continued. "A dozen or so scrap re-processors are now scattered in Canada and the U.S., working like junk-yard dogs to keep operating costs manageable."

Justin shrugged, then leaned forward on the ergonomically designed metal and leather chair, placing his hands on his hips. He strained to coax good memories from the stored experiences of his recycling days---but none surfaced.

"I'm still longing for the day when people might actually care again about recycling. Our throw-away society is a menace to future generations. It's criminal the way we waste resources in this country, and in other developed nations."

Trenker was impressed with his sincerity. "The laws of supply and demand can be a bit distorted, especially by the consumer products companies and their retailing customers. The BoxMarts of the world could care less about designing packaging for easy recycling of the materials used. It's an afterthought…at best. It's all about point-of-purchase displays and visuals---impulses, attractive colors and suggestive shapes and feel."

"A lot of today's packaging is very creative," Gatt replied. "The designs are usually efficient, except for the anti-theft ones. You need two hands to carry a two-inch memory chip used in your digital camera, computer or printer. The five-gram chip is postage-stamp size, yet is heat-sealed in two-foot square enclosures made of flexible, superstong polyester thin-sheet. You need a hacksaw to open the package."

"It still comes down to price, when a material is chosen," Trenker recalled from the budget meetings he attended during his merchandising years.

"Packaging is the largest market for plastics," Gatt summarized.

Ross knew, from his days at P&G, that Gatt's next statement was correct.

"The commodity plastics suppliers won't give up a spec of market share without a bloody fight. The recycling industry was really no threat back then. The combined production capacity of the entire industry peaked at less than one-half percent of the 80 billion pounds per year used by the U.S. plastics processing industry. We thought there was plenty of room for peaceful coexistence. I believe that was the reason the recyclers allowed the 'majors' to dominate recycling trade groups. The big chemical companies were willing to pay hefty membership fees, based on the size of the company, as long as they could control the agendas; which stalled and eventually killed the industry."

Ross stretched his memory, "What happened to the 'minimum content' recycling laws on the books at the time? There were several mandatory-recycling bills being promoted in Congress and in state legislatures."

"They were scoffed at by the major plastics producers and the end-users who refused to buy less-than-prime materials. Some people believe the oil and chemical companies used their extensive lobbying resources to kill all the mandated-recycle-content laws and proposed bills. Some industry heavy-weights even derailed a federal law already on the books, which required the addition of up to seven percent ground recycled tires in new asphalt highways. The technology was proven in several test-road installations, and could have greatly diminished the tire-piles that have grown at a rate of about 150 million bald-tire carcasses each year."

Trenker shook his head, as Gatt continued his tirade. "Joe Slattery claimed we should thank someone in the Clinton-Gore administration for that fiasco. Joe said Gore's image as the great ecological champion is distorted, if you look at the results when he was VP."

Trenker was not about to argue with a dead man. The conversation ended a few minutes later, with Trenker convinced that Gatt was the best candidate for the new position.

"Justin, I think we're ready to have you meet Bob McGill. He makes final decisions on key employees. But first I have to ask…are you really interested in the position? You seem a bit tentative."

Justin placed his hands in the side pockets of his suit jacket, removed them, crossed his arms, then cupped his hands behind his neck. He then unscrewed the cap of a large water bottle set on a tray, poured some water into the iced pitcher, and re-screwed the cap. He was obviously stalling for time.

This was the moment of decision he'd dreaded. *Was it too soon?*

"Ross, I'm sure you know of my recent….experience, with the bank." He still couldn't say, 'my company's bankruptcy.'

"We know enough…from Syzmansky's report," Trenker answered quickly. He was anxious to bring the conversation to a conclusion. "Yes, he was kind enough to give us a very strong recommendation on your behalf."

"Well, I'm very interested in the position; it's just that I'm still not totally settled from the….bank situation."

Trenker was becoming impatient. "Look, Justin, I think these troubled companies…" he thwacked an open palm on the pile of manila folders stacked on his desk, "these companies are in a position similar to where you were six months ago. But they have a chance to survive. From what we know about your situation…you didn't."

He rose from the leather executive chair, indicating the meeting was over. "There's no doubt in my mind that you have the knowledge and experience to help them; and we have the money. The new federal program will finance any viable restructuring plans you and Lynne can develop."

Justin thought, *Me and Lynne… can develop.*

He stood with Trenker and reached out a hand, hesitantly. *Oh, what the hell*, his subconscious relented.

Trenker sealed his decision before their hands met. "I haven't mentioned the salary yet. It's a quarter million per year."

While Lynne escorted Justin to the Managing Director's office ten stories above, Trenker informed McGill that Gatt had accepted the job offer. The Human Resources manager thought Gatt fit the job requirements perfectly. Ms. Hurricane seemed more than enthusiastic about working with him on the new business aid program. Also, Gatt had agreed to start work next Monday Subject of course…to McGill's final approval.

"Good luck in there," Lynne said, as they entered the sanctum of GHP's executive suite. "He's tough, but deep down, he seems like a nice guy. I heard he supports several underprivileged children in Guatemala, and visits the villages every year with his wife."

Lynne turned to leave, then froze. She believed Justin was approaching a turning point in his life, and somehow wanted to be a part of it. She spun back to face him. "I really, really hope you get the job, Justin." Her sparkling eyes bore into his with the intensity of emerald lasers. She did the hair flipping thing; then rushed to the elevator. Justin was speechless. The emotional draft from her departure almost sucked him into her wake.

"You may go right in, Mr.Gatt." McGill's fashion-model secretary, Holly, announced. "He's expecting," she added in secretarial short-mouth.

"Hello, Mr. McGill?" Gatt called out ardently, as he held the door open but didn't enter. He noticed McGill on the phone at his desk. McGill waved Gatt to a seat at a round conference table set off to the side of his wrap-around-window corner office. Justin couldn't resist peering down from the tinted-glass interior walls. The view of Boston was fantastic.

To the east and north were the downtown shopping areas on Washington Street; the harbor piers and the New England Aquarium along Atlantic Avenue. He could see the shipyards bordering Logan Airport across the harbor in East Boston. Fenway Park near Kenmore Square, the Parker House Hotel and Boston Public Library at Copley Square were easily recognizable. The 18th century stone residences in the Back Bay, and the Boston Public Garden---the oldest public garden in the U.S.---were exploding with blossoming summer annuals. The famous gold-domed State House sat majestically on Beacon Hill.

Justin remained standing at the window until he heard McGill whisper, "I'll call you back."

"Please sit, Justin. Can I offer you a soda…coffee…water?" McGill joined him at the table.

"I'm fine, sir. Nice to meet you." McGill's handshake was firm, but he seemed anxious and rushed.

McGill's full crop of silver hair was partially streaked with thick bands of black, reaching from his forehead to his neckline. His coif looked like it was indigo-inked with an artist's broad-brush. The hairdressers in Boston called the style *zebra-ass*. Several indigenous Boston executives wore the style to distinguish themselves from visiting businessmen. McGill's protruding forehead shaded deep brown eyes which emitted a menacing glare, even when he was smiling. He was on the downside of fifty-nine, with an average build, exquisitely attired in a gray Etro suit with purple pinlines, a striped cotton Prince-of-Wales shirt and a $200 Richard James mini-checkered silk tie.

"Ross tells me you're interested in taking on the business-aid management position, and can start next week." *No small talk here*, Justin thought.

"That's right, Mr. McGill. I'm anxious to join the team." *Which currently consists of Lynne Hurricane.*

McGill said, "We're very excited about this new project. It's groundbreaking for the Washington group providing the financing. They believe the plastics industry is a key job-producer in the small business sector. I believe that this country cannot afford to lose such a vital industry to the dismantling forces of unfair foreign competition."

Wow, Justin thought, *he's really wired in to our problems.*

McGill was pleased that he'd guessed right about Gatt's hot-button. His deep voice resonated with the confidence of a TV evangelist, and the impeccably tailored five thousand dollar suit made him look almost as natty.

"You know, Justin…may I call you by your given name? Most people don't realize that small businesses have been crucial to our country's quests to win wars, upgrade our standard of living and provide life-saving medical products. I've seen it first hand, over the past two generations. We can't allow our small business sector to be chewed up and spit out; especially the plastics industry, which is crucial to our single-use, disposal-oriented society."

Justin was surprised by McGill's enthusiastic diatribe. "They're in dire need of help," he responded evenly, as if *he* wasn't a member of *they*.

"Ross was going to take on the job of managing the program," McGill said in a wistful tone, as he glanced down at Fenway Park from his corner office view. "But he's needed in Washington for a different assignment." He spun around to face Gatt.

"That's what I understand," Gatt replied, slightly disoriented by McGill's power-drill stare.

"Well, there's no sense circling the issue, Justin. We'd like you to join G.H.Paladin and manage the new business-aid program. Lynne Hurricane will be your assistant. You'll report directly to Trenker, and indirectly to me, until Ross leaves for D.C." McGill left unresolved how the chain of command would later unfold.

"I appreciate the opportunity, Mr. McGill."

"Call me Bob."

"Okay, Bob." Justin was hesitant to ask the no-nonsense executive a trivial question. "Would it be possible for me to study the troubled-company files during the weekend? I'd like to hit the ground running when I start next Monday."

"I like that idea," McGill lied. "See Trenker on the way out. He'll give you the files, and show you around. Holly will provide you with an employee information packet—insurance, benefits and all that. Before you leave the building you'll also have to sign a standard GHP Confidential Disclosure agreement. The government projects we're working on require it."

"I understand. And thank's again for the opportunity, Bob. You won't be disappointed in my effort." Justin felt like a recent GED recipient---starting his first job as an assistant copy machine operator, in the lost-and-found department of a Goodwill store.

McGill escorted Gatt to the double doors, shook his hand vigorously and said, "Holly is my eyes and ears. She can reach me anywhere, anytime. As we get more into the project, you may need to contact me when I'm away from the office, which is frequently. She'll track me down.."

"Where will my office be?"

"Same floor as Trenker and Hurricane…a corner view, I believe."

Justin waved the company-benefits information file at Holly as he headed for Trenker's office. The Cindy Crawford look-alike smiled and jumped up from her U-shaped enclosure to escorted him to the elevator.

"Welcome aboard, Mr. Gatt. I'm sure we'll be speaking regularly in the future. Mr. McGill wants me to pay particular attention to your needs."

When the door closed, Justin collapsed against the railing in a gleeful relaxation of taut muscles. *I can't believe it. A corner office…a quarter million dollar salary…an intelligent and attractive assistant. Maybe I should have done this earlier.*

As the high-speed elevator descended rapidly, his subconscious was suspicious. *What's wrong with this?*

Then he remembered.

Joanna and the rest of his GRT friends were still unemployed.

When Gatt left the executive suite, McGill returned to his desk and instructed Holly to hold all calls and interruptions for the next hour. He punched a button on the communications console and the phone redialed the number of the last call.

"Sorry I had to cut you short, Thomas. We just found the perfect guy to replace Trenker, and neither of them has a clue as to what's actually transpiring."

Tom Blackstone was chairman of FFF, better known in D.C. as the Financial Flow Foundation. A think tank specializing in global finance and foreign currency analysis, the partners at FFF also controlled a private insurance company in Grand Cayman which discreetely gave large sums to lobbyists and malleable politicians working to promote the Three Sixes' agenda. FFF's aggressive growth strategy had positioned the firm as a favored independent consultant to various Cabinet members, as well. Particularly the Treasury and Commerce Secretaries. Blackstone's staff could always be counted on to publish "white papers," which reflected the positions of their hierarchy Administration clents.

FFF's latest confidential report expounded the advantages of relocating U.S.manufacturing facilities to other countries. *Shifting the financial burden of maintaining these enormously expensive facilities will reduce the investment risks of U.S. lending institutions, and benefit the country as a whole.*

There were no references in the report of lost manufacturing profits, displacement of workers, or the depletion of corporate and individual income taxes at federal and state levels. The FFF report argued that: *an acceptable loss of a few million manufacturing jobs was a small price to pay for protecting this country's banks against risky investments, such as new refineries, textile factories and automobile assembly lines.*

Blackstone hunched over and lowered his voice as a group of familiar government officials emerged in the main concourse of the train station from a sub-level track platform. "I'm at Union Station…about to leave for New York on Amtrak. Call the Senator and the man in Paris. Also, send a secure e-mail to Bromine in Macau. Tell them of your progress."

McGill wanted to make sure they were talking about the same information. "Should I inform them that a more viable front man than Trenker has been hired to draw attention away from BoxMart's business-extermination deal with the bank?"

"That…and our repositioning of Trenker in the scheme of things. But don't inform them of the true purpose of his relocation to D.C. He's made his decision. Now he either performs, or…" Blackstone didn't have to spell it out.

McGill recalled Trenker's dossier. The information they'd uncovered during a routine pre-employment background investigation had been used to coerce him into joining their group.

"He wasn't an easy recruit," McGill reminded Blackstone. "Trenker once turned down an invitation to join the super-secret Scull and Bones Society at Yale. Even George W., Clinton and Kerry didn't have the guts to do that." Then he added, "We never found out why."

"I understand you and deLeone had a heated conversation," Blackstone lowered his voice as more familiar faces walked by. "He called to complain."

"What a dumb shit. He was all hot and bothered about Trenker's relocation to D.C. He doesn't trust Trenker, and insisted on excluding him from the upcoming trade mission. I hung up on him when he got abusive."

"Bob, you've got to be more tolerant with the trade people. Remember, deLeone is on our side. He says you called him a greedy sleeze-bag. The

Three-Sixes rely tremendously on the information he provides. Call him… and apologize."

McGill's blood pressure spiked. "Did you approve an increase in his cut of the consulting contract?"

Blackstone glanced up at the wall clock and the digital track schedule showing his train was due to leave in five minutes. "I had no choice. It's a small issue." He darted for the track to New York and barked impatiently, "Back to Trenker. I think he'll acquiesce to our demands once his optionsor should I say, lack of options…are clearly explained. If he refuses the DOE job, the Three Sixes will arrange a long tenure in a cold dark place."

"My guess is…he'll go along," McGill remarked confidently. "He won't want the evidence of his past departures from acceptable moral code being exposed."

"Only his sinless wife would care," Blackstone replied. "It's too bad he doesn't have a larger family to worry about. Look, Bob, I have to run. It might be a good idea to have your investigator check deeper into Trenker's past. Also, we should not assume the new recruit will be a puppet. Acquire whatever information you can on him. It could be useful later. What's his name?"

"Justin Gatt. He's from Connecticut. A Yale MBA, like Trenker."

"Good grief. Doesn't Harvard compete for our jobs, anymore?"

"Sure. Gatt's assistant, Lynne Hurricane, was recently recruited from Cambridge."

"That should make for an interesting combination. Keep me posted."

CHAPTER 18

(JULY 14, 2008) 9 AM
PRUDENTIAL CENTER, BOSTON

Justin entered his new corner office on the tenth floor of the Prudential Center Office Tower carrying the tannic anaconda-skin briefcase he'd acquired on a business trip to Brazil, and a large Starbucks coffee. His new secretary, Madelaine, had introduced herself, and was parked at a small cubicle a few yards out of view from his opened door. He liked that.

His favorite method of communication was to shout through an open door…or through a thin wall…to someone on the other side. There was something puckish about a live, non-electronic conversation with a person you couldn't see. You didn't have to look into their eyes or interpret their body movements. Sort of like lying in the dark after sex. He'd frequently barked outrageous instructions to unlucky assistants passing by his GRT office…just to guess at their expressions.

Justin placed the five folders Trenker had given him on the large executive desk flush with modern accessories, and rotated the expensive black leather ergonomic chair to face the window overlooking the fashionable Prudential Center shops. From a different angle he peered down at the enclosed pedestrian bridge linking the Prudential Center with the Copley Marriot across Huntington Avenue. The view wasn't quite as impressive as from McGill's window, but the office was twice the size of his former quarters at GRT, and was furnished with a coordinated walnut ensemble worthy of a front page spread in *Modern Offices Magazine*. Hardwood credenzas, bookcases and file cabinets were perfectly placed for convenience and aesthetics.

As he settled into the high-backed chair and adjusted the height with the air-actuated valve, he was already concerned about crossing some invisible protocol line. The company files he'd been given did not contain enough information to accurately assess the chances of restoring the struggling businesses to financial health. He'd have to ask Trenker or McGill for more company data.

He was convinced that the five bankrupt companies they were trying to save had been impacted by the same problems which forced GRT and Slattery out of business. The sparse information in the files Trenker handed him did not reveal a specific link, but all five of the small plastics processing companies had experienced a sudden drop in sales and revenues... followed by a defaulted bank loan. The pattern of failure was painfully familiar.

Strangely, the banks involved in the loan defaults were not identified; nor were the customers who suddenly stopped buying. Perhaps it was a policy of GHP to exclude this information in reports submitted to the confidential funding agency in Washington. Government bureaucrats were quirky about the dissemination of sensitive information. Probably more-so...if the source had *level-three* security clearance.

Hopefully, Lynne had already examined the balance sheets and the net cash flows---which he considered crucial to any recovery effort. The only useful financial information in the files was a tabulation of the defaulted-loan balances, and the magnitude of the recent sales declines. In each case, bank examiners had requested sales projections about six months earlier, and had subsequently issued reports criticizing management. They'd charted and compared actual sales figures for the final months of operation, with management's projections. The reports were titled: *Inaccurate Executive Projections.*

Justin was revisited by a haunting sense of futility when he reviewed the files. Each company had been forced to file Chapter 11 petitions in federal court.

"Madelaine," he blurted into the intercom. "Could you please come in when you have a chance? No rush...finish what you're doing."

Madelaine was seated at the chair opposite his desk within fifteen seconds.

"What can I do to help you, Mr. Gatt?" She was in her early thirties, attractively plump and genuinely blond. Thin reading glasses rested on the tip of her pug nose, revealing kindly hazel eyes which projected a desire to please. Her closely cropped flaxen hair was dramatically accentuated by enormous, triple loop gold earrings nearly touchinf her shoulders. She wore a belted, black knee-length dress with a high neckline and half sleeves trimmed in gold lace.

"I was wondering if you could orient me, Madelaine, as to how work flows around here? I was always considered a pain to the office people at my own company for circumventing my own rules. I don't want to continue that tradition at G.H. Paladin."

Madelaine smiled prudently, revealing perfect teeth and an amused expression.

"It's not a high pressure environment around here except at bonus time. On the last day of each quarter, the partners in the bonus pool are usually tense about receiving the money they've already spent." *Good. Madelaine has a sense of humor.*

"How about your own work load and schedule?" he asked.

"I'll be allocating my time between you, Mr. Trenker and Lynne---that is, Ms. Hurricane. I assume you've met them both?"

"Yes. Ross is primarily responsible for my being here; and Lynne treated me to an orientation dinner last week. They both seem very pleasant—and sharp." Then he said, "I'm curious---have you received any information regarding my background? It's usually easier working with someone you know something about."

Madelaine hesitated, and then structured a careful response. "Both Mr. Trenker and Ms.Hurricane seem anxious for you to join the team. I don't normally know much about the people I work for. Not because I'm not interested---but because there is very little spoken regarding personal backgrounds. I think it may be part of the security requirements."

"How about my daily itinerary? Any regular staff meetings...that sort of thing?" Justin felt silly asking these entry-level questions.

"I was told you will be reporting directly to Mr. Trenker until he transfers to our Washington affiliate in a few weeks. Ms.Hurricane will report to you."

"Does Mr. McGill call regular staff meetings?"

"Yes, Mr. Gatt. Mr. McGill calls meetings all the time. But they're hardly ever pre-scheduled."

That sounded familiar. Joanna once accused him of being a terrorist, for sneaking up on GRT managers with drop-of-the-hat inquisitions regarding some long-term strategic issue, which he decided had to be addressed immediately. She'd tagged it the *owner's excessive-compulsive fear of the future.*

Madelaine shifted in her seat, then said, "I guess you'll be setting the schedule as you prefer, Mr. Gatt. Mr. Trenker and Mr. McGill made it plain that you will be running the show for the new business-aid program. Mr. Trenker will return from Washington later in the week following his meeting with Mr. Blackstone and Mr. deLeone at the U.S. Trade Representative's office." She suddenly noticed his expression of mild anxiety.

Justin looked intently into her kindly eyes, then said in a stern but friendly tone, "Look, Madelaine…the first thing I'd like you to do is drop the 'Mr.' My first name is Justin." He paused for effect, as she struggled to reconfigure her first impression of this interesting and attractive man.

"Or," he suggested pointedly, "you may refer to me as…*Your Highness*.'"

A curly, auburn tressed assistant suddenly stood in the doorway. "May I enter…*Your Highness?*"

Gatt continued to stare at Madelaine, until she finally broke down and began laughing hysterically. Lynne joined in. The false scowl left his face.

"I take it you want me to refer to you by your first name, Mr. Gatt?" Madelaine giggled, tentatively. She wasn't there yet.

"Please!" he said.

She stood and offered her chair to Lynne, who was carrying an armful of computer-generated reports. Madelaine's instincts for office etiquette were perfect, as she headed out the door.

"Call if you need anything, Mr. Justin." She was getting there.

Lynne had lingered for several hours at a limited-access computer terminal at the Baker Library, extracting bits of relevant information from the massive data base accessible only from Harvard's School of Business departmental library. She was anxious to discuss her findings with Justin.

"Have you read the files of the five companies Ross targeted for business aid?" she asked, in a serious business voice.

"Yes, I read what little info is provided. It's not very helpful." Justin had studied the files, searching unsuccessfully for clues as to how each company could be un-dangled from the gallow-ropes of Chapter Eleven. The hollow in his chest echoed bad memories of his own failure.

During the weekend, he'd succumbed to an irrational masochistic impulse and drove to the GRT building in North Haven. He'd parked in the empty employee lot and allowed his mind to drift into the past. For a few minutes it searched for a potential self-healing explanation for the recent chaos…his failure. Then the Corvette crept around the building to the shipping docks in the rear…seemingly on its own.

His heart chilled like a frozen transplant organ when he saw GRT's super-efficient recycling extruder being loaded onto a flat-bed with New Jersey plates. The driver was standing several feet away, smoking a cigarette and watching a ten-story crane precariously tilt the heavy end of the 50,000 pound machine onto the edge of the truck. For a moment, the extruder barrel resembled a cannon from the German destroyer, Bismarck, aiming toward a distant target at forty-five degrees. Justin learned that the machine was being delivered to the Port of Elizabeth in New Jersey; for loading onto a ship destined for Asia.

"Well, I came to the same conclusion a few weeks ago, so I dug a bit deeper," Lynne said proudly. She then placed the computer printouts on the edge of his spacious desk and separated them into two piles that had been stacked perpendicular.

"Let me guess," Justin offered. "One is bank records…the other is a list of recent customer activity."

Lynne looked at him in amazement. "How did you know?"

"They teach Harvard and Yale MBAs to think along the same lines."

She recited the most basic of business tenets: "Find the necessary information before drawing conclusions; then prepare a plan of action."

"Exactly!" he said. "So, what have you discovered?"

She tapped a fist on the left hand pile, and said, "I don't think you'd be surprised to learn that these bank documents pinpoint Residents Bank of North America, or one of its U.S. subsidiaries, as the primary loan providers in all five bankruptcy cases."

"My friend Edwin Tinius has a broader reach than I suspected….the bastard."

"It gets better," she retorted. "Residents Bank is also the primary destination for massive daily deposits from BoxMart stores all around the country. They centrifuge the money in and out of the U.S. as steadily as the click of an atomic clock. Most of the spin-out goes into numbered accounts in European banks. That's as far as I got."

Then she added. "My friend at Harvard runs the research and retrieval departments at Widener and Baker. He can access an unbelievable data base of international business activities." Justin was impressed. He asked Lynne if the Yale library system was linked to Harvard's.

"One way or another, Harvard's system is linked to nearly every library in the world, including: The Library of Congress, New York and Boston Publics, Beijing National Library, and the great European book collections in the British Library and Bibliotheque National de France in Paris. The system also accumulates information from every public stock exchange in the world, in real time. Mergers… acquisitions…new business and tax laws in any country that reports them. It's all accessible, if you know how to use the new Google search tools recently added to the system.

"How about the various sectors of the economy? Can the system compartmentalize?"

Lynne nodded, then tapped the pile of reports under her right thumb. "This is private information supplied by the owners of the five companies we're attempting to rescue. I called them a few weeks ago and described the new aid program. They were very cooperative." She lifted the top sheet and said, "This page shows the customers for each business." She then extracted another tabulation from the pile and snorted. "These are cancelled orders, just prior to, or just after, the loan defaults." She slid the paper across his desk.

Ten of the best-known mass retailers were named on the list. Justin read from the bottom up, inhaled deeply, then blew out a birthday candle. "Why is the list in this order? It's not alphabetical."

Lynne anticipated the question. "I queried the system to record and rate the retailers by the highest number of days between the Chapter Eleven filing date for each company, and the first date a major retail chain cancelled a large order."

"I see all the big retailers on this list. What does it tell you?"

"I'm not sure," she answered honestly.

"Do you believe that all the big-box chains and department stores in the country are implicated in the failure of five small Northeast manufacturing companies?"

"Yes, I guess I do. But not in the way you might expect." She paused to crystallize her thoughts, then said, "Some just followed the leader, and pulled orders after they found out about the supplier's financial problems. But some of these mammoths may have initiated the problems."

Justin studied the list one more time, then said, "The company on the top of the list, and the company on the bottom….what about them?"

She'd memorized the sequence. "A few of the cancelled orders were small seasonal adjustments, made several weeks before the bankruptcy filings. I believe they are typical practices of the better department store chains. Sometimes a buyer will over-schedule deliveries of seasonal merchandise because he doesn't want to be caught short during a major selling season. They react by canceling deliveries and purchase orders if the merchandise isn't hopping off the shelves at a computer-generated target rate. You could consider this a normal market condition since their sales volumes are lower than the big discounters."

"What about the others? Are there any trends?" He'd already spotted the answer.

"Check out the retailers in the middle of the list. They cancelled large orders only a few weeks prior to the loan defaults."

Justin looked at the fifth and sixth company names on the list, and said, "I'm not surprised. These are both ruthless competitors who treat their suppliers badly. But I still find it difficult to believe they would conspire together to put small companies out of business." Then he realized how ostrich-like he'd become in such a short time, recalling his own experience.

"I must be getting senile," he smiled wryly. "BoxMart did this exact thing to my big customers. As I recall, several other discount chains cancelled orders with Slattery Housewares shortly after BoxMart pulled out."

"There may or may not be a connection. It's not uncommon for one retailer to trail another out the door of a struggling supplier. Everyone thinks his competitor knows something he doesn't. Especially if Chinese importers are camped on the front stairs with lower-priced offerings."

Justin was already framing a plan of action. Lynne lifted another typed sheet from the stack of reports on the left and handed it to him. "Here's something you may be interested in."

The title on the top of the page read: *Residents Bank of North America: Mergers, Acquisitions and Offshore Subsidiaries.*

An hour later, Madelaine was asked to schedule immediate appointments with the owners of the five plastics processing companies on Trenker's list. They'd have to move rapidly to stave off the transfer of idle equipment to a flat-bed headed for New Jersey…and eventually to an overseas transport bound for China.

CHAPTER 19

(JULY 15, 2008) AM
BIOLOGICAL WEAPONS LAB, JILIN, CHINA

Dr. Ho Hot was convinced that the PLA bio-weapons experts had underestimated the potential damage the spore-like eruptions could create once the twelve canisters were exploded over the targeted Iowa cornfields. He'd calculated that the contamination could infect as much as a third of Iowa's twelve-million acres of planted corn; not the few hundred-thousand acres they predicted.

Dr. Ho Hot's argument fell on deaf ears. The actual efficiency of the application would depend on the prevailing wind conditions when the organisms were dispersed over the fields. The explosion was actually a mortar-fired *implosion*, which would fuse the host-bacteria *Escherichia Coli (E. coli)* and the *parasite mycoplasma*---technically described as a 'slow' or 'incomplete' virus because it lacked a cell wall. The toxic combination was deadly to cellulose materials, especially the stems, husks and leaves of a corn plant.

The most amazing pathogenic activity occurred when the host-bacteria *E. coli* became lysogenic, and produced a virus that destroys the host-bacteria (a bacteriophage). Instead of eventually dying off in the absence of a living (bacterial) host to sustain it, the strange viral *mycoplasma* mutated to a form capable of surviving *outside a living host*, by feeding on cellulose molecules.

Like no virus yet discovered, the *incomplete mycoplasma*, dubbed the **corn-virus** by its inventors, miraculously adapted its internal chemistry and remained alive outside a living host for weeks. It produced an enzyme similar to the saliva of a termite or snail, allowing it to feed on cellulose materials... not normally ingested by carnivorous animals or humans due to a lack of the enzyme required for hydrolysis. In effect, the *corn-virus* organism acted more like a microscopic termite than a virus.

This new species was a self-recombinant nucleic acid derived from the modified *Brucella abortus* RNA retrovirus stolen by Dr. Ho Hot from the Taiwan BioGenetics research facility near Taichung.

Dr. Ho Hot had decided to withhold information from his Chinese captors, that the crystallized form of the organism was not as harmless to humans as originally claimed. There was recent evidence suggesting that, under certain conditions, the agricultural pathogen *could mutate into a human pathogen* similar to the frightening organism from which it derived---the unmodified *Brucella abortus* virus---which was more deadly than Ebola, avian flu H5N1 or the AIDS virus which kills 8,000 people daily.

However, Dr. Ho Hot had calculated---as infinitesimal---the odds for an *in-situ* molecular alteration of the dormant crystalized form of the mycoplasma RNA segments...into a form that could penetrate a living human cell. Although his research proved beyond a doubt that the *corn-virus* only reacted with cellulosic substances, he was concerned that it multiplied exponentially when fed by the *lambda E.coli* bacteriophage, which itself had a genetic 'switch' and could mutate if stressed by trauma. He worried that the cellulose molecules the micro-organisms broke down and devoured, could produce fragments almost identical to human-digestible sugars like fructose and sucrose.

A young lab technician who handled boxes containing corn kernals infected with the corn virus, was now writhing in agony in a local hospital, with acute flu-like symptoms and signs of cardiac congestion. General Ye and the PLA scientists attributed the unfortunate boy's illness to inadvertent exposer to aflatoxin, a poisonous by-product of fungus growing in minute quantities on the Iowa corn samples used for testing. Dr. Ho Hot hadn't bothered to inform his captors, or the Chinese hospital officials attending to the technician, that his symptoms were similar to those observed when test patients were exposed to the co-plasma *brucellosis* variety, developed by the U.S. in 1991. The U.S. inventor, Shyh Ching Lo, had patented the biological substance as a death and disease weapon of mass destruction. There was no antidote, vaccine or cure. The patients all died within fourteen days.

Shyh Ching had assigned the patent rights to the American Registry of Pathology in Washington, D.C.---a federal government agency.

General Ye had forced Dr. Ho Hot to smuggle the micro-organisms from Taiwan to Hong Kong, and then across the border into Shenzen on the mainland. Otherwise he'd never see his only son, Shubo, alive. The loud-mouth exchange-student attending Fudan University in Shanghai had foolishly joined a group of regular students practicing Falun Gong exercises in front of the People's Liberation Army barracks located on the campus. He'd been arrested along with hundreds of other disrespectful students several months ago. General Ye threatened to torture the boy if Ho Hot didn't cooperate.

The genetic biologist was world-renowned for scholarly work splicing cancer-causing Simian-viruses, such as SV40, onto human embryo cells. The cancer-causing serum had immortalized the growth in a glass dish of first-generation cell divisions from a young boy's foreskin. Normally, the young cells would die after a short period in the dish; but the treated cells continued to reproduce.

General Ye had promised Ho Hot he'd be allowed to join Shubo as soon as the bio-project was completed. He was about to honor his promise.

General Ye whispered instructions to a PLA security agent in plain dark clothes watching Dr. Ho Hot complete the final packaging of retained samples of the deadly form of the organism.

"When he's finished, you are to proceed with the final interrogation." He turned away and departed for an important meeting at Yong Ihasa's estate in Baideihe, a thirty-minute flight to the Hebei Province seacoast.

Dr. Ho Hot noticed the conversation as he exited the level-four security area. Shortly after, he completed the decontamination procedure and dressed in the white coveralls they insisted he wear. *Perhaps the constant surveillance will now be relaxed. Perhaps I will now be allowed to see Shubo.*

The PLA security agent waited outside the dressing room until he exited. "You will follow me," the burly man in his forties barked as he turned and led the doctor to an elevator which descended several levels to a dark hallway in the basement of the facility. Splashed with urine and blood, the stench was unbearable when Ho Hot was shoved beyond a rusted steel door into a large, brightly-lit cell at the end of the corridor. He immediately saw his nude son and stiffened. Seconds later, his knees buckled from sorrow and he collapsed in a puddle of his son's involuntary body fluids.

Shubo was kneeling doggy-style on a steel table, with dark-blue welts all over his bare body. He was blindfolded, with hands strapped to the table surface and feet dangling over the edges of a sharp metal-plate extending several inches beyond the frame of the table. His feet were clamped to the cold steel plate by cruel pincer-shaped alligator clips twice the size of jumper cables...which cut deeply into the skin behind his toes. Thick copper wires extended from the blood-stained scorpion-clasps biting into his flesh, to a boxy electrical apparatus placed under the table. Other wires from the high-voltage generator extended to the four table legs and a twenty-inch, jagged-edge iron rebar leaning against a leg.

The security agent shoved Dr. Ho Hot in the direction of a plain wooden desk positioned next to a top-load chest freezer set against the far wall. The bio-scientist limped to the desk, experiencing severe sympathetic pain in his feet, as he turned to see his son thankfully passed out. He stared in horror at the bleeding feet. Shubo's chest was heaving over the inverted metal ammunition case supporting his body. He looked like a rag doll collapsed on a toy block.

The Chinese agent pushed Ho Hot into a hardwood chair gouged with impacts and cut-marks from the missed thrusts of an interrogator's 'tools.' He commanded gruffly, "Take up the pen and paper. You will write down the words from the scroll on the desk and sign the letter. Also, you will speak these words into the voice recorder." His tone left no doubt that there'd be unpleasant consequences if Ho Hot didn't comply.

Dr. Ho Hot read the instructions slowly, and replied meekly, "I cannot sign this. I have not plotted with the Kuomintang Party in Taiwan against the People's Republic of China. I have not come here to destroy the animal-feed maize and starve the Chinese people of their hogs, chickens and cattle." His eyes teared with frustration and anger. "My son has done nothing to justify my admitting he engaged in treason and espionage."

The agent's large square chin jutted up as if stung by an uppercut. He was a repulsive man, with defiant grey eyes projecting the warmth of a striking cobra. The burly agent in black clothes pulled open the freezer door and extracted a cube of ice the size of the ammunition box. He walked to the steel table and shoved the ice block under Shubo's chest, knocking the ammo container to the floor in a loud clang that startled the boy back to consciousness. In his delirium of pain, the cold ice on Shubo's skin temporarily relieved the terror of being tortured.

The torturer turned to the scientist, a feeble man with pleading brown eyes and a full crop of black hair. He snorted, "I'll give you one last chance. Speak into the microphone the words on the scroll. Now!" His expression hardened when the prisoner shook his head.

Dr. Ho Hot watched fearfully as his son began to shiver and cry. "Father, is that you? Please…help me." He noticed the ice beginning to melt, along with his heart. General Ye could not let them live---even if he signed the false confession, or spoke PLA lies into the voice recorder. The PLA was sure to use his confession to justify a terrible action against his beloved Taiwan island. But he could not just stand by and witness the unmerciful suffering of his only son.

Suddenly, Shubo began screaming in unfathomable agony, as blood gushed loosely from his rectum. The pitiless agent had jammed the one-inch thick rusted-steel rebar past his tightened sphincter. The scientist sprang toward the steel table and knocked the agent to the floor…in a surge of energy only a parent protecting his only child could muster. Unfortunately, the agent was as strong as a bear and easily pushed away Ho's hands, which had wrapped a manic grip around his neck.

The agent jumped up and pulled out his QSZ-92 handgun chambered with proprietary 5.8 mm pointed bullets. He lashed the butt across the uncertain expression on the scientists face... knocking him to the floor. Blood oozed from an ugly gash forming in the center of his forehead, then spouted into a thin line of red.

"You foolish *wang-ba-dan*. Now your family ancestry will end."

The agent reached under the table, flipped a switch and turned the control knob of the voltage regulator to maximum. The blood pulsing from the wound in Dr. Ho Hot's forehead blinded his eyes; but he could hear Shubo's excruciating high-pitched shrills and the sickening crackle of surging sparks. Shubo's chest was a mass of confused pain. White-hot voltage surged through the steel table, the invasive iron rod and the conductive block of ice in a blue maze of sparks...charring and biting at his insides and smoking the skin of his jerking body. The nerve-generated electrical impulses which normally controlled the pace of Shubo's heartbeats from his right ventricle, raced into a frenzied circumvention of violent overvoltage. His heart literally started to burned up; then was shorted-out. His lungs rasped one final complaint, then collapsed.

It was over in thirty seconds. When the father finally recovered full consciousness, he could smell his dead son's burning flesh. The haunting echos of his Shubo's pathethic screams still reverberated in his ears.

Suddenly, he was lifted from the floor and slammed down in a sitting position onto the hard chair. "You're worthless to us if you don't sign the confession," the agent hissed. "General Ye will allow you to live if you do. He wishes for you to continue the important medical studies which benefit the Chinese people."

Ho Hot stared down at the scroll. His eyes were blank---devoid of emotion. Feelings had departerd his consciousness in a self-defensive retreat. The hollow in his chest floated up and took residence in his brain. Visions of his son's vicious murder were blotted out. He was in a stupor...no longer in the cell.

The security devil lost patience and slapped him viciously across his blood-caked face. Ho Hot was shocked into lifting the voice-recorder from the desk. He began to speak in a manic tone. The sounds of his voice distant...barely recognizable.

"*The universe is made up of harmonious balances,*" he mumbled etherically, from an ancient memory of Confucius philosophy. His eyes widened as his mind acted on its own. Slowly...he mumbled, "*Educated men know the laws of the universe...men of knowledge command political authority. Small men, like me and Shubo, can become professional gentleman only through study and hard labor."*

The agent moved behind him…his expression puzzled. He fingered his weapon, as Ho Hot garbled faintly, *"There is no reason to believe everything can be in harmony."* Ho's eyes locked on the freezer. The security agent grinned. The prisoner had gone mad. He'd be of no further use. They could synthesize the words he'd already spoken, and forge his signature. General Ye would have his oral and signed confessions.

As Dr. Ho Hot continued his surreal valediction,---*"General Ye carries out benevolent rule over small men such as me. Like an emperor over a subject; a magistrate over a peasant; a husband over wife and child."*---he began to sob uncontrollably.

"If only men could follow the wisdom of Tao…the 'way'…then…" His voice was drowned out by the blast.

Dr. Ho Hot would not have been able to explain this meaning to the guard holding a smoking pistol. Not all men had the capacity for enlightenment. Including the heartless torturer loosening his grip on the QSZ-92 trigger.

CHAPTER 20

(July 16, 2008)
Beidaihe, Hebei Province, China

The Gazelle SA 342L helicopter descended onto the concrete helipad a hundred meters from Yong Ihasa's summer villa in Beidaihe, a favorite vacation spot on the Bohai Gulf enjoyed by China's top leaders. General Ye was seated next to the pilot, shouting instructions from the aircraft to the Jakartan leader of the *White Lotus Jemaah*, a terrorist splinter sect associated with China's Triad Secret Society.

"Move ahead with the next phase of the de-stabilizing strategy," he barked into the military communications unit. "The White Lotus of Java is now authorized to relocate the Bandung operatives to Belize City." His voice cracked as he strained to hear the response above the thumping and whining of the European-built aircraft. "Get them on the move as quickly as possible. The sum we agreed upon will be wired to the Commercial Bank of Syria immediately."

General Ye and the three men waiting for him inside the villa were the current sovereigns of the 900 year-old Triad Society of China---which included five secret sects operating unabated throughout southeast Asia. The Triads were the most corrupt and secret Chinese organization in the world---an economic rival to the Chinese Communist Party. Several honest and patriotic leaders of the National People's Congress had failed several times to identify and purge Triad members said to have infiltrated the highest ranks of government.

Genral Ye and the other Triad insiders on the Standing Committee of the Chinese Communist Party were meeting here today to initiate an action with global implications, which was *not* authorized by the official Beijing government. If conditions were favorable, they'd also initiate a coup against Party strongman, Chairman Mu Jianting, and the other conservatives on the Standing Committee, who controlled the Party...thus the Chinese government.

Their conflicts with the ideologies and global priorities of Mu's Beijing majority aside, Mu was leaned dangerously toward reducing conflicts with Washington. Mu was quietly pursuing policies detrimental to the economic interests of Triad members in China, Singapore, Malaysia and the Philippines.

"The papers are prepared," the thirty-four year old Indonesian businessman replied in a heavy voice at the other end of Ye's scrambled line. "The operatives learned to speak sufficient Spanish at the Yemen school to pass as migrant workers. The authorities in Belize City will never suspect the men are other than cabin-stewards replacing flu-stricken Indonesians on a cruise ship anchored off St. George's Caye."

"But they'll never board the ship?" Ye raised his voice, as the copter touched down.

"The regular cabin stewards will experience miraculous recoveries at the last minute," the terrorist planner replied confidently. "Other than the disappearance of the replacement crew in Belize---there'll be no loose ends."

The General was satisfied. "Triads dominate the large Chinese population in Belize City, thanks to our far-thinking predecesors. It's the most established Chinese foothold in Central America. When the ghosts of the disappearing cruise-ship replacements receive temporary visas, they will be hired temporarily by the benevolent owners of Sing's or Archie's Club restaurants."

The communication ended as the Jakartan blurted out loudly, "Nobody will miss them when they cross both Mexican borders."

Beidaihe is one of China's best-known resort areas. Located about 200 miles northeast of Beijing, on the Bo Hai coast above the Yellow Sea, this peaceful town of less than 30,000 full-time inhabitants is back-dropped by the lush green of Lianpeng Hills. Six miles of public and private beaches originate at the Daihe River mouth. Years ago, Beidaihe replaced the famous "Red Flower Pavilion" in Fujian as the headquarters of the powerful Triad Secret Society.

Yong Ihasa watched closely as the assertive PLA General he manipulated so effectively crouched to disembark from the passenger door of the chopper. Yong had exchanged his usual London-tailored suit for the traditional neck-to-toe black silk garment of the *Hsiang-chu*...the Grand Master of the Triad Society. The red turban he wore was the only outward sign that he claimed to be a descendent of Ming royalty.

On his left arm was a ring of his own hair, tied in a braided knot above an embroidered cobalt-blue emblem with white Chinese characters. The ancient symbol to the Triad Secret Society resembled a geometrical Chinese puzzle---consisting of four symmetrical shapes, one inside the other, with a large pentagon surrounding two smaller octagons and a lesser-sized rectangle in the center. The space between the closed polygonal shapes was occupied by Chinese characters of planets---representing secret-society sects of the Triad. The slogan: *Fan Tsing, Fuh Ming,* was at the top, translated: *Subvert Tsing, Restore Ming.* The name adopted by Yong Ihasa, the current Grand Master, *Yun Ching,* was displayed in the middle of the small rectangle at the center of the emblem.

"General Ye, I assume your visit to the research facility was fruitful?" Yong Ihasa asked, as he bowed and gestured for the General to enter the villa. The others were already seated at a large, triangular black-enameled table with place settings for six, although there were only four men present.

General Ye bowed to Wang Chao, the Minister of Industry and Trade, and Li Chin, the new Chief Executive Officer of Bomali Corporation, who had relinquished his title as President of LCE to Alicia Wang, when the Bomali joint venture with BoxMart was formed in Macau a few weeks earlier.

"Yes, *Yun Ching,*" Ye addressed the Vice-Premier by his Triad name. "The *corn-virus* experiments were completely successful. The organisms have been packaged and shipped for delivery to Texas in a few weeks."

Yun Ching smiled knowingly. "When the dollars begin to saturate international currency markets, the American President will hardly take notice of the decay in Iowa's cornfields…until it is too late."

The destabilizing events which Yong Ihasa , General Ye and the other Triad members planned, went far beyond Phillipe Cusson's *Savoy Imperative* brainchild to attack the U.S. dollar and disrupt the financial stability of America. Yong Ihasa, General Ye, Li Chin, and Wang Chao were attempting to restore de-facto rule of China by Ming members of the Triad Secret Society. Their ultimate strategy was to create events which would weak President Mu's grip on the Standing Committee, yet allow China to leap-frog America's global influence.

Just as the early Triad warrior-monks usurped power from the Ming Emperor, while protecting his dynasty from outside forces in 1674. Or, as the Triads temporarily succeded in the 1920s, when Dr. Sun Yat-sen, a secret Triad member, became the first president of the Republic of China.

The White Lotus sect provided financial support for both Mao Tse-tung and Chang Kai-shek, until Mao's Communists defeated the Nationalist Party in 1949 and drove them to the island of Taiwan. Mao purged the rich Triad supporters soon after. He feared their power. Some claim it was the primary reason he initiated the "Cultural Revolution."

"This time," Yong Ihasa promised, "Villa 125 will become the new Zhangnanhai; the headquarters of the true rulers of China."

Villa 125 was once the well known vacation residence of Mao and his wife, Jiang Qing--- the most famous of the corrupt "Gang of Four," who was arrested after Mao's death in 1976 for conspiring to overthrow the government and grasp control of the state. The villa was replete with expansive gardens, and was furnished with exquisite 18th century furniture and other abandoned treasures Mao had collected from the wealthy families his youthful Red Guards had exiled to rural farmlands. Yong purchased the property to use for the ultra-secret initiations and meetings of the Triad Society sects still operating unrestrained all over southeast Asia.

The meetings were easily disguised as business conferences, because the wealthiest and most influential *Overseas Chinese* business owners from Singapore, Malaysia, Indonesia and the Philippines usually attended. Insiders still referred to these Chinese mandarins and their families as the "Terrible Tongs." They evolved from secret societies named *The Carnation-painted Eyebrows Society*, *The Iron Shins Society* and *The Copper Horse Society*.

The *Hsiang-chu* and General Ye joined Wang Chao and Li Chin at the table, as four middle-aged waiters emerged from a side room and began serving food. They were selected as Ihasa's servants because they were deaf from operating jack-hammers in the 130-decibel environment of a diesel ore-crushing machine operating in Jilin's mineral mines.

"As is our tradition, information will be passed from mouth to ear," the Hsiang-chu intoned, as he glanced up at the faces of the servers dressed in white shirts and black pants, to detect any suspicious expressions. He was certain the small, bony man with the black teeth and thin mustache could read lips. He wasn't sure about the others. They'd all been thoroughly tested and confirmed as stone-deaf.

The small servant leaned over the table and served a pot of green tea made from the tender leaves of southern Anhui---said to be the best tea in China. The other servants set plates on the table heaped with red cooked pork, a local crab and jellyfish delicacy, and beef-heart steamed with broccoli, Sichuan peppers and bean curd.

Wang Chao just returned from a meeting of the Chinese Olympic Preparations Committee. The others were curious to know of the team's progress.

Li Chin inquired brusquely, "Will the athletes perform successfully in front of the world media, comrade Wang?" LCE was a major sponsor of the games, and the media's positive reaction to the efforts of Chinese contestants, even if they didn't win gold medals, could generate advantageous publicity for the LCE products the athletes endorsed.

"To be straightforward," Wang replied, as he remembered that Triad meetings required the utmost in honesty and candor, "the housing and food arrangements are l*uan*. Perhaps *chaos* is not a strong enough description. But the athletes are superb."

"At least the situation is not as serious as the street riots and protests at the new dam sites," General Ye replied indignantly. "Our hardened security agents and propoganda chiefs have at least prevented disclosure of the casualties. The other villagers and the international press are still unaware of the mass graves."

"The foreign correspondents and TV anchor-people who have invaded Beijing insist on reporting every detail of China's preparation for the games," Li Chin complained, as he lifted a succulent piece of beef-heart. "Mu Jianting insists that the Xinhau News Agency issue daily rebuttals and opposite accounts of any criticisms of China. For once, I agree with Mu's heavy hand. We have stupidly granted to foreign publications and broadcasters the temporary opportunity and freedom to indoctrinate citizens and visitors with capitalistic lies. The hideous *Water-cube*, *Zee Tower* and *Eggshell* buildings built for the games have nevertheless caught their attention."

"Most important is the status of our athletes," the Hsiang-chu exclaimed, as he scooped crab and jellyfish delight into a bowl half-filled with white rice, and swished it around with ivory chopsticks carved with the Triad symbol.

Wang Chao smiled broadly. "Our contestants are fine-tuned like no other team in existence," he replied exuberantly. "Chinese divers pierce the water perfectly vertical every time. Runners are faster than the waves of a tsunami." He paused to savor his own words, then added, "Even our ping-pong players and gymnasts can dunk the basketball." The others grinned at the acceptable exaggeration.

"There is much to deliberate before we complete the ritual of resolving prevarications," Yong Ihasa said. He slapped the air and the four servers rushed from the room. "Let us begin as we dine."

Li Chin was the first to speak. "I will begin with the American situation: Jake Kurancy and Edwin Tinius of Residents Bank are ahead of schedule shutting down and transferring American manufacturing businesses to this country. The Savoy plan is being fully supported by the government insiders in Washington, as well as a political action group Bromine calls the 'Three Sixes.'"

Wang Chao reported next. "Phillipe Cusson's bank will receive the required amount of U.S. dollars from BoxMart and Residents Bank when the time comes. The transfers from our central banks will begin in two weeks." He paused to swill Anhui tea in the secret posture the Triads use to identify unfamiliar members. It was good practice.

"LCE will meet its quota when the Bomali corporate account at the Bank of Commerce and Trade in Macau wires its billions into Creditte Bank de Savoy in Lyon. Cusson will give the signal when the Stressa arrangements are completed."

Yun Ching nested a glob of shredded red pork on the end of his hand-crafted Grand Master ivory chopsticks, and rotated the meat beyond yellow, uneven teeth that were not preserved well in his youth. A few strands dropped to his square protruding chin and stuck like a snail to a wet rock. The others remained silent in deference to the Hsiang-chu's high rank. The youthful Red Guards who forced doctors and professors to shovel swine excrement during the Cultural Revolution, would be proud.

Li Chin prodded the others, "Let us get to the crucial questions. Is the time right for the Triad Society to attempt to reach its ultimate goal? I believe conditions are favorable. It is time to defeat the conservative notions of Mu Jianting and his majority."

General Ye replied defiantly, "Mu and his feeble pack on the Committee are pre-occupied with internal problems and the Olympics. They are slowing China's growth. The weaklings are going to waste the opportunity for state-run businesses to dominate world trade, if we allow it."

Wang Chao said in a condescending tone, "Mu has spoken too many times of the logic of granting trade concessions to the Americans and Europeans. We cannot allow him to let slip our chance to dominate global trade; which China's expansionist economic policies have fought so hard to obtain."

"We must be prepared to deal with the problem of Merrand, or any other newly-elected U.S. politician attempting to limit China's full access to the U.S. consumer market," General Ye retorted.

"That is precisely the reason we must act now," Li Chin persisted. "Bromine says the political-action groups in Washington are all predicting Martin Merrand---the hawk---will win the presidential election."

"Mu has been weakened and discouraged by the growth in bad loans at our regional development banks," Wang interjected. "Although improving slowly, they cannot be solved overnight---as he once promised the international financial community."

"He is predisposed to grant crippling concessions to the Americans when Chang Hui Chen receives the U.S. Trade delegation in early August. Butler Humphreys is a tough negotiator," Li Chin emphasized.

The Grand Master pushed aside his plate and walked to the large window overlooking the exquisite gardens Mao constructed to remind him of his youthful days at Changsha's Yuela Academy in Hunan province. The plantings duplicated sections of the strolling parks at the imperial academy founded in 976, except the foliage was encircled by a large wall with nine locked gates.

"Our founder, *Chen Chin-man* was once forced to abort his attempt to rule China," Yong Ihasa said ruefully. "And he had the backing of the terrible monks from Fukien."

"Yes," General Ye exclaimed in a tone of admiration. "The Fighting Monks of Shao Lin Monestary. They were superior men who mastered the arts of war. Some claim they commanded supernatural powers."

"Well, comrades," Wang Chao raised his voice, "the Triad must proceed with only natural powers this time. We must fully utilize the advantage the Savoy Imperative gives us. Cusson's scheme is a perfect platform to reach our ultimate goal…if we decide to go forward."

The Grand Master returned to the table and said wistfully, "The Triad was founded on the premise of restoring the Mings to power, after the dynasty was overthrown by the Manchu Tsin." The others glanced at the red turban on his head as he continued to speak in a tone suggesting an ulterior motive.

"Even Dr. Sun Yat-sen, the first President of the Chinese Republic in 1912, who was a secret society member despite being a Christian, paid respects to the Mings with his first act as China's leader. He visited the Ming tombs and publicly informed the spirits of the Imperial Mings that the Manchus had been driven from the country."

General Ye, the *Hsiang-chu's* staunchest supporter added, "I remember the slogan carved on the miraculous *peach-wood sword* that suddenly appeared and cut off the heads of the traitors attacking our predecessor warriors. He hesitated, for emphasis, "The same slogan was inscribed on the stone tripod the wandering monks of the Red Flower Pavilion found floating in the Kungwei River."

The *Hsiang-chu* folded his hands as if praying to ancestors and said softly, "*Fan Tsing, Fuh Ming.*"

General Ye repeated the slogan, "*Fan Tsing, Fuh Ming.* Subvert the Tsing, Restore the Ming."

The meal and the deliberations were completed following General Ye's explanation of the corn-virus scheme. He guaranteed that the agricultural attack on America would inflict shock and terror, but cause only a temporary interruption in Chinese exports to America; enough to undermine support for President Mu Jianting.

"Both countries will experience a limited short-term crisis." Wang Chao reminded the others, "The life-span of the corn parasite is only a few weeks. There should be few…if any…human casualties."

"The agricultural bioweapon is easily controlled." General Ye assured them. "But it will damage Iowa cornfields severely. The resulting price increases in beef, hog and sugar commodities will further erode the waning confidence some Americans still have in their hapless government."

He acknowledged the Minister of Industry and Trade with a grin and said, "Wang Chao's argument to reduce soybean overplantings convinced Mu Jianting to approve a 30 percent increase in mainland corn-acreage. That should be viewed as proof that Mu is implicated in the corn-virus attack on the U.S. Only the Chinese farmers in the northern plains will understand that crop rotation---from soy beans to corn---is due to Brazil's massive soy plantings in the Amazon River region. Their low prices have allowed our farmers to produce more corn for animal feed."

Li Chin was once a peasant farmer. He smiled broadly at the implication that China's poor farmers would soon be doing better financially. "America's animal farmers will be furious when they discover that China is willing to sell them surplus corn feed---at double the bushel price quoted on the Chicago Mercantile Exchange,"

Wang was worried about the most dangerous aspect of the agricultural-attack-plan on the U.S. "Do you believe that blaming Taiwan is such a good idea?"

The General scoffed He answered belligerently,"We have proof, including written and oral confessions from the biochemist who smuggled the Taiwanese-developed virus onto the mainland. His sworn statements will substantiate that the Taipei dogs are responsible for contaminating the box factory in Shanghai; and shipments to America. Every retailing giant in the U.S., except BoxMart, uses cardboard containers made at the ultra-modern Shanghai factory."

"And you are certain the Americans will buy our version of the facts?"Li Chin worried aloud. "What will they think about the surprising increase in Chinese corn acreage?"

"They'll be confused, but unable to prove otherwise,"explained General Ye. "If the plan succeeds, hundreds of our cargo ships will not be allowed to dock in Long Beach, or other West Coast ports. The Central Military Commission will order the PLA factories, which I control, to return the cargo ships for quarantine off the coasts of Xiamen and Fuzhou."

"Practically kissing Taiwan's Quemoy and Matsu Islands," reminded Wang Chao. "They're only a few miles offshore from Xiamen and Fuzhou, as you know."

"The Taipei clowns will balk,"Yong Ihasa added, "and the small naval forces protecting the local waters will attempt to push away hundreds of our merchant ships from anchoring in their harbors."

The others were surprised by Ye's rhapsodic tone as he added, "That will give the PLA its excuse to occupy the islands by force; before the organism dies off naturally."

"I believe you could be juggling with incendiaries," Li Chin complained, then caught sight of the General's fearsome scowl. "But if the majority is in favor…"

General Ye reproached Li vigorously. "The precedent must be set, comrade. How long has the People's Republic of China been waiting for the right circumstance to re-unite our rogue province with the mainland?"

The *Hsiang-chu* removed his red turban and joined the others at the table. "Triad members in the Kuomintang Party claim that the island people are mostly in favor of re-uniting with the mainland. It's the American reaction we worry most about. While the Triad sects are dedicated to the concept of *controlled* luan, the U.S. Congress is so unpredictable, it seems they thrive on making matters worse."

"I wouldn't worry too much,"Li Chin said sourly. "In China---150,000 people die each year from work-related accidents in factories, mines and construction sites. Chinese people are used to chaos…the Americans are not. They'd pickett Congress for months if a hundred people died from similar accidents."

"Still," replied Wang Chao, "The crazy Americans may not react precisely as we predict. Humphreys and his team of trade negotiators and nosey businessmen are scheduled to visit China on a trade mission in early August. They'll be mumbling quite stressfully when Chang Hui Chen and Bank Governor,Yew Bai Tsin, flatly reject their demand for a yuan float."

"Neither will we offer any voluntary cutbacks in textile exports to the U.S."

The *Hsiang-chu* smiled. His yet to be disclosed trump card, for pushing out President Mu, was to shock the Americans at the last minute of negotiations… with a proposal they couldn't refuse. He decided to call the meeting to its ritual conclusion. Fresh tea was served and they all used the secret Triad method to drink the mellow brew.

Yong Ihasa summarized their decisions in a final declaration. "Now we will strike vigorously at the American economy, and ridicule Mu's regime." He glanced at the thin attendent looking in from the door entrance, several minutes before he'd been ordered to return. The attendent noticed Yong's grimace and jerked his head from the room.

But not before he lip-read the Vice-Premier's final words: *With these actions, the Triad will triumph; and the Ming Dynasty will rule again after Mu's departure.*

General Ye climbed into the helicopter and instructed the pilot to return to the Ministry of Defense near Beijing University and the Summer Palace, bordering Kunming Lake in northwest Beijing. He needed to draw up AAO plans for Matsu and Quemoy Islands.

The *Attack and Occupy* manuevers would include a contingency plan to shower Taiwan military installations across the Taiwan Strait with high-explosive surface-to-surface missiles…if Taipei resisted militarily.

He believed it was not necessary to plan for the most feared scenario---the intervention of American naval and air forces. The cancer-weakened American President would have more pressing issues to address---the collapse of the American economy and the threat of a runaway agricultural pandemic.

CHAPTER 21

(July 16-18, 2008) 9am
GHP offices, Boston

The solution for salvaging the five bankrupt businesses grappled in Gatt's subconscious. Nestled like a door-opener on a ring of a hundred keys, the answer avoided detection in the dark entranceway to Gatt's mind. He was sure it existed, but he couldn't yet grasp it.

For the third time he read the GHP files and the notes he'd taken during the whirl-wind meetings with the owners and managers of Smithfield Bottle Company, Woody Products Again, Granite Mountain Tool and Automation, and Passaic Injection Products. There was a common thread of hope in these businesses...he was sure. The interviews went well and he accomplished the information-gathering phase in three days.

Leominster Plastics was added to Ross Trenker's list of targets-for-aid when Brad Stalker called to inform him that Mr. Orcutt, the owner, was throwing in the towel because of lack of orders. Fortunately, Brad explained, Mr. Orcutt didn't have to deal with Edwin Tinius or Judge Rooter. He'd invested wisely in Cape Cod real estate and was quite wealthy. LP's expansion had been financed using personal funds. Brad was asked to sell the assets for whatever the market would offer.

Gatt studied the financial and business-status data. The spreadsheets he'd prepared listed the products being manufactured, current customers and gross margins for each item sold. He held one of the lists in both hands and moved the sheet of paper up and down, as if the motion would force a key word to emerge in underlined, bold italics. The Proprietary Products list revealed the high profit margins for each item manufactured and sold under a company trademark. A thought gradually surfaced, like a submersible pumping out its ballast. Gatt placed the sheet on his desk and dialed Lynne Hurricane.

"Hi, Lynne. Have you got a second?"

"I'm pretty damn busy, digging up info on who-owns-what, from the owner's asset lists you acquired...but I'll make an exception...Your Highness."

Justin pictured Lynne in her office, flipping aside the curly strands in the seductive motion that reminded him he was still a relatively young man. "Have you looked over my notes? I think there's a commonality in these businesses beyond the fact they all process plastics by one method or another."

Lynne glanced down at the numerous red underlines she'd added to a copy of Justin's notes. "It looks to me as if each business produces a few high-profit items, but the majority of the manufacturing output is packaged and sold under the BoxMart label."

"Exactly!" Justin exclaimed enthusiastically.   "So...how can these companies be saved?"

Lynne thought a few seconds. "They can't!" she replied morosely, "unless you cut overhead by 80 percent; and I don't see how that could be accomplished." She slid one of his spreadsheets out from a pile on her desk and added, "Or, unless the proprietary-product sales volume increases substantially...overnight."

Justin was still juggling ideas. "How do you downsize 80 percent and still build up sales volume?" He'd discovered over the years that some of the most punctilious answers to complex questions evolved from obviously stupid questions.

Lynne thought it was a trick question. "I don't know," she replied. "I guess you'd have to cut labor and variable costs to the bone. But the fixed overhead would still devour your breakfast, lunch and dinner."

Justin thought of the prisoner chained to a sinking boat. Left only with a hacksaw; and not enough time to saw through hardened steel links.

"The solution is obvious...but painful," Justin exclaimed mournfully.

Lynne's office was almost close enough to communicate by Justin's favorite yelling method. "I'll be there in a sec,"she said. The fifteen-step voyage gave her time to formulate a plan. When she entered Gatt's office, he was standing near a window, peering down at the traffic on Huntington Ave. Without turning, he said stiffly, "I think all the proprietary products could be manufactured at one location, by one business entity. It could be a darn good business."

Lynne's mind raced…open to possibilities, as she moved closer to him at the window. "The best management people from the group could run the business. They'd probably accept low starting salaries in exchange for profit-sharing and stock options."

Justin pivoted slowly back to the Lynne. He accidentally brushed against the pink sleeveless silk blouse stretched seductively over her bosom. She made no attempt to move back, as he gradually brushed by. The scent of orchards emanating from her ivory neck was more paralyzing than nerve gas.

"I have an idea how this could work,"Justin struggled to mumble, as he returned to the emotional safety of his executive chair, and shuffled papers aimlessly to regain his concentration. "I never imagined this job would be so challenging."

"You have a big idea?"Lynne whispered hoarsely.

"Oh, yeah. I do." It took him a few seconds to answer. "Brad Stalker of Leominster Plastics, and George Knoll of Smithfield Bottle Company are tremendous operating and marketing executives. Wolfgang Pompanski of Granite Mountain Tool is a genius with the injection and blow-molding processes required to manufacture the proprietary items. And Melfi Zion of Woody Products Again successfully peddled medium-quality plastic lumber to high-end national decking builders. She could talk a field mouse into attacking a cougar."

"You think they could work together under one roof ? Entrepreneurs aren't known for docilely relinquishing authority."

"Hell, Lynne...these people are dying on the vine. We can't save all the jobs, but plenty of the American workers involved could still have futures."

Lynne settled into the visitor's chair and sucked air loudly. "Something is missing. You didn't mention Benny Spruce from Passaic Injection Products?"

Gatt's expression beamed disgust. "Benny is a well known crook in the industry. I don't know how he was chosen by GH Paladin for aid."

"I noticed that most of his assets are cross-collateralized in various sub-entities,"Lynne remarked. "Residents Bank has first position on most of it. I wonder if the family and friends who lent him money are aware they don't have collateral protection."

"He's built a house of cards,"Justin replied in reluctant admiration. "Benny compensates private lenders by handing them stock certificates and promisory notes with high interest rates. The paper is usually issued by half-a-dozen worthless shell companies and limited-partnerships he creates for the purpose. I think he just keeps Passaic Injection alive to skim a high salary... and other perks the small investors don't know about."

"Then the smooth-talking dude must be excluded from the deal. In fact,we should remove Passaic Injection from Trenker's list and burn his file." Lynne added gingerly, "I'll call Ross. He's due in the office Monday. Should I say you have a plan to present?"

"There's no time to waste, Lynne. Tinius has requested court sessions to force these guys into Chapter Seven liquidations. We have to present a Plan of Reorganization and arrange financing with GHP as soon as possible."

Lynne added perceptively, "If everyone comes on board, we'll also have an impressive organization chart."

(JULY 21, 2008) 9 AM
GH PALADIN OFFICES, BOSTON

Brad said it best, "Joe Slattery had the right idea….but the wrong customer."

Over the weekend, Justin contacted Brad Stalker and the others and presented the outlines of his merger plan. Mr. Orcutt of Leominster Plastics was more than willing to allow the modern LP processing plant to be used for the proposed venture. He agreed to lease the building and equipment at cost, until the business was profitable. He also offered rent-free occupancy for the first six months of the start-up phase.

After numerous conference calls, Brad, George Knoll, Wolfgang Pompanski, and Melfi Zion agreed to support the business plan. They each authorized Justin to present the business proposal to McGill on Monday.

Lynne and Brad were seated in the small conference room as Madelaine entered carrying coffee and toasted raisin bagels from Marche's in the mall. They were reviewing details to be presented to McGill and Trenker at their scheduled 11am meeting. Justin was speaking to McGill's secretary, Holly, on the extension phone. He noticed how Brad looked at Lynne during lulls in the discussion of the plan. It was the awkward look of high-school infatuation. Lynne's back was turned, so he couldn't see her returned expression.

They were of similar age and Brad probably shared more in common with Lynne. A soft, hesitant stare in Lynne's emerald-green eyes had previously revealed a more than casual interest in Brad. Justin began to understand what they meant by the *green-eyed monster*. They weren't referring to a binocular view of Fenway Park.

"We'll be called up when they're ready," he said softly, as he joined the younger associates at the table. "Holly informed me we'll have only about an hour to make the presentation. McGill and Trenker have both been called back to Washington."

"Ross never mentioned that."

"Holly says McGill will leave from Washington and fly directly to Guatemala. He'll be gone a month."

Brad was a quick learner. "The others can't wait that long. Tinius will move on them as soon as he hears we have a plan."

"Then we have to convince McGill to at least approve the loan application. We'll need a written commitment for two million dollars."

"What's the loan application process?" Brad inquired.

Justin glanced at Lynne. He assumed she held the answer. "Lynne?"

"It was never fully explained by McGill...almost as if it didn't matter. He was very sketchy about the details."

The business plan was presented hastily to McGill and Trenker twenty minutes before they had to rush out to catch a flight. McGill stared incredulously at Gatt and said, "Very impressive...very impressive. I'll think it over and get back to you."

Justin had the mistaken impression that McGill did not appreciate the urgency of the request for financing. As McGill rose to leave, he raised his voice in exasperation and said, "Bob, I'm not certain these businesses can survive a lengthy delay. Do you anticipate a problem in approving the financing before you leave for Guatemala?"

McGill instantly made it clear he was not pleased at being pressed. Lynne cringed as he snapped, "Look, Gatt...we have more important issues to deal with in D.C. And, I'm not going to interrupt my working-vacation for a blue-sky endeavor."

Ross Trenker broke in when he noticed the pained expressions. "Bob, I can handle the loan process. All they need is your okay."

McGill frowned defiantly at the junior executive. Blackstone would soon administer the critical test of his worth to the Three-Sixes organization. He had his doubts.

"We'll discuss this on the flight to D.C." He turned abruptly and left the room.

"What do we do now?" Lynne pleaded to Trenker, as he started after McGill.

"I suppose you'll just have to wait. I'll do my best to convince him. But as he said---there are vital issues to deal with elsewhere."

"I guess we have no choice," Brad muttered.

"I don't think so," Justin frowned. He stiffened and said, "If he doesn't approve the loan, we can't just stand idle and watch Tinius kill off another good American business venture."

At this point, Lynne realized why she was so attracted to a man old enough to be her father; yet still young enough to be her lover.

CHAPTER 22

(July 22, 2008) Wed, 6:30 am
Boston and Washington, D.C.

Justin realized his scheme was Frankensteinian---an attempt to attach pieces from separate dying bodies---to breath life into an opus of commerce. He'd always thought of small business as more of an art than a science. He brushed aside logic and dialed the number again.

McGill answered the phone irately…dripping wet and naked. He was leaning outside the steaming shower stall, furious at Gatt's third call in forty-five minutes. The final call from Boston convinced him.

Ross Trenker had received similar pre-dawn phone inquiries from Justin Gatt, who was doggedly probing for the financing commitment which GH Paladin promised. His joint-venture salvage plan had apparently captivated the man's own imagination. He was borderline irrational, with an emergency-room mentality---trying to resuscitate the bankrupt companies on Trenker's list before Tinius could kill them off

"I don't give a damn what Tinius does, or threatens to do, Gatt."

"But, he'll pull the plug before we have a chance to register the plan with the courts, Bob. We at least need a pledge for the financing; no later than tomorrow." Justin paused as he heard the shower in the background.

"So far this morning," McGill fumed, "you've interrupted my workout, my wake-up coffee… and now my shower. Are you panicking or just trying to pester me into a decision?"

Justin chomped on the sugar-free jelly donut he'd purchased at the only coffee shop that opened this early in the Prudential Shopping Mall. He replied apologetically yet assertively, "I'm sorry, Bob. I guess I feel obligated to do whatever is possible to help these companies. I promise I won't bother you again."

McGill reached for a towel and was about to hang up when Justin broke his promise.

"But what do you think? Is there a chance?"

McGill had already changed his mind.

"Look, Justin, I'm speaking with key people today. I think I can sell your plan under the proper circumstances. But, I'll need a favor from you." McGill decided to approve Gatt's request for financing; but only after he agreed to take on the new assignment.

Justin jumped up from the table…bracing for McGill's request. He resisted the urge to run circles around the table…the way he did as a toddler when his dad brought home a *Jim Brown* autographed football.

"Anything, Bob. Just name it…and it's done."

"I want you to take the shuttle to Dulles tomorrow. I'll be leaving for Guatemala in two days, and there are a few matters to settle. We'll have to meet with Tom Blackstone, if you want the financing committed before I leave."

"What time, and where? How about moving it up to tonight?"

"Jesus…Gatt…cool down. I'm water-logged and shivering. I'll call you back before noon."

McGill was sure Blackstone would agree. Gatt could be the solution to both problems. He undoubtedly qualified to replace Trenker as the "small enterprise analyst" that Butler Humphreys wanted on the trade mission. That would preserve the hefty fee Paladin was receiving from the government, including McGill's usual cut. Gatt could credibly scrutinize…and report on…the mysteries of how China's small manufacturers survived on meager profit margins.

McGill was also wary of Gatt's persistent nature. They'd hired him only to put a viable face on the bogus "business-aid" program which Tinius and BoxMart's Greek CFO concocted. But Justin had obviously convinced himself to champion the cause. He'd continue to be a bane in McGill's life as long as he remained in Boston; although firing him was a poor idea. The business-aid program had started to take shape under his direction, and there would be embarrassing questions from the legitimate GHP consultants in Boston.

The obvious answer was to send him to China. If his tenacity and idealism became too bothersome, they'd arrange for him to disappear in the countryside. Gatt's aging grandfather was his only known relative. McGill doubted if any of his former employees cared much about him after the bankruptcy.

McGill dressed and dialed Blackstone's private number. "Morning, Tom. I think we have a solution to the trade mission problem." He didn't mention Gatt's early-morning calls.

"I assume you're going as Trenker's replacement on the mission trip?" It was the only timely solution Blackstone could imagine.

"Well…no, Tom. Well…I suppose that would be possible. But I have a better solution."

"Make it quick. I have a meeting with the Senator "

"You know about my annual trip to Guatemala. My wife has planned it for months. She's e-mailed our itinerary and arrival time to half the villagers we sponsor."

Blackstone wasn't convinced that McGill traveled to Central America each year solely for humanitarian reasons.

"What do you propose?"

"Trenker hired a former small business executive named Justin Gatt to spearhead the phony business-aid program we're staging for BoxMart. He'd be a perfect replacement for Trenker; except we'll have to rely on deLeone as our only source of inside information once the negotiations between Humphreys and the Chinese begin."

"What's his background?"

"He founded and managed a successful plastics recycling and processing company for more than twenty years, but went under recently; Tinius pulled the plug on his top customers. He just presented GHP with an astoundingly creative re-organization plan to merge key assets of several failing plastics-processing businesses. All they need to flourish is the refinancing we pledged when Gatt was hired. He's agreed to return the favor if I approve the financing, or at least provide a written commitment he can use to convince the bankruptcy judges that the reorganization plan is viable."

"How much does he want?"

"Two million to buy key pieces of equipment in settlement deals with the courts, plus a revolving line of credit for another million in working capital. They've got an option on a modern manufacturing facility, which the Massachusetts owner is willing to lease at low-cost until the new joint-venture is profitable."

"Are you suggesting that we actually provide the money?"Blackstone asked incredulously. "Your clients will be furious."

"No, no…we just make the pledge; and throw them some seed money from time to time. Gatt will be transferred to FFF in D.C., and off the project. But first he has to be convinced that the financing is in place. He'll insist on following the plan's progress. Apparently, he's assembled a good management team from current employees to run the business. Lynne Hurricane, his assistant in Boston, could be assigned to spearhead the business-aid program once he leaves."

Blackstone said, "It sounds like a plan. Can you move quickly enough? The Senator wants Trenker to start making the rounds on Capitol Hill tomorrow, to legitimize his nomination."

"Gatt is waiting for my call. He'll be here tomorrow. You can meet him and decide for yourself."

The Assistant U.S. Trade Representative was pleased that Trenker was finally out of his hair. He motioned for the waitress at the Hotel Monaco restaurant to refill his coffee.

"I don't see a problem substituting this Gatt guy," he assured McGill, "as long as he keeps his distance from the negotiating team."

Richard deLeone was a small, gaunt man of thirty-nine, with a sallow complexion that matched his personality. Premature grey streaked the greasy, combed-back hair thinly covering more ears than forehead. He seldom read books, and believed he could read people; but fell short of presenting the confident deportment of a self-made intellectual.

"He'll only travel with the mission during the first week; then will be assigned to tour factories in several industrial centers. We'll probably dispatch Gatt on an extended 'familiarization' trip to out-lying provinces."

The trade official was more concerned with collecting his slice of the consulting fee. "Don't keep him away too long, McGill. The government won't pay FFF until they receive his report. Is he a capable observer?"

"He's fairly sharp and inquisitive…and a bit pushy. If he digs too deeply for information at the Chinese factories, he'll likely have trouble with the local party bosses. It's possible that he may experience an unfortunate accident." McGill studied the surprised reaction fixed on the suspicious federal official's tanned face.

"Could he end up becoming a problem?" deLeone asked tersely.

"I doubt it. Gatt knows nothing about China, and has no knowledge of negotiating processes involving countries. He doesn't understand or speak the language, and will be traveling with a special tour guide. If he asks too many questions, the guide will let us know."

After deLeone briefed McGill about the mission agenda, and the negotiating issues Butler Humphreys planned to press on the Chinese, he said, "Make sure this Trenker-replacement submits his report before you decide to send him on a one-way sight-seeing trip."

CHAPTER 23

(JULY 23, 2008) 9 AM
FFF OFFICE, WASHINGTON, D.C.

Ross Trenker hadn't slept the entire night, and was suffering from deep anxiety as the jammed elevator descended to the FFF lobby. A small army of company representatives and lobbyists was departing for the daily advocacy sessions with Congressmen and Administration officials...armed with pledges for substantial campaign contributions.

Following the encounter with Jeffrey Richards and the other titans of industry---now identified to him as the *Three-Sixes*... Trenker's life had just spun out of control.

The new nominee for Assistant Deputy Secretary of Energy was departing for Capitol Hill, following a brief orientation meeting with Blackstone and the chief lobbyist for the American Fossil Fuels Institute, Harley Hedge. His agenda included morning interviews with the three key Senators on the Department of Energy Oversight Committee: Elliot Scharn of Ohio, Carvin Troone of Texas---both with the majority party, and Moody Rugg of North Carolina---the ranking minority member. Senator Rugg usually voted in lock-step with Scharn and Troone on administrative appointees.

As the elevator door opened, he noticed Justin Gatt entering the lobby, accompanied by the junior executive who was sent to extricate him from the Boston-to-Washington shuttle-flight mob. Gatt spotted Trenker stepping off the elevator and pushed through the lobby swarm to catch his attention. Ross turned in the other direction when Justin approached, but was too late to avoid him.

"Hey, Ross," he called out, dodging between a few passers-by. Trenker was too close to deny he heard the boisterous shout, despite the heavy din of muffled musings from the expert conversationalists warming up their vocal chords for meetings on the *Hill*. Trenker turned in his direction. "What are you doing here, Gatt?"

Justin pushed past the throng and answered vociferously, "I'm here to seal a financing deal with McGill." He was wearing a new dark grey suit with a conservative charcoal and magenta striped tie. The snake-skin briefcase held against his broad chest was packed with financial projections and a detailed operating plan for the new joint venture.

"I'm in a bit of a rush, Justin…. will you be in town long?" Trenker replied impatiently, as the lobbyist from Texas nodded him toward the limo waiting at the curb. Trenker was obviously more concerned with being on time for the Senate meetings, than extending a meaningless courtesy introduction to Gatt.

"Just for the day…I think. Can we get together later? I have a few questions to ask you about FFF."

Trenker raised his head slightly and glanced over his shoulder at Harley Hedge. The wire-thin man in the hand-made alligator-skin cowboy boots and custom-made blue pin-stripe suit was easing Ross's shoulders forward. "I'll call your cell number sometime this afternoon. But I don't think I can be of much help. FFF is a super-confidential organization." The person monitoring Trenker's conversations from the basement of the former Riggs Bank branch thought, *he's passed another test.*

All three senators on their agenda were Department of Energy Sub-Committee members; and more impressive---declared-candidates for President of the United States. Trenker was stunned that Richards could arrange prime-time appointments with these national figures on such short notice. He was an unknown business consultant seeking a mid-level Assistant Deputy Secretary position. The ADS must be a more important position than he imagined.

His lack of sleep stemmed from the knowledge that the previous ADS and his entire family had disappeared without a trace. Worse…the Washington media seemed unconcerned. The story had been carried on the third page of the Post for two days, then disappeared--- much like the subjects of the article. He was familiar enough with D.C. news coverage to believe that was unusual. The sudden disappearance of a mid-level federal official was not yet a common occurrence. His wife Julia and he were now vulnerable to the same distasteful end result, unless he found a way out of this deadly vortex before becoming too deeply entrenched. His knowledge of the identities of the Three Sixes, although he didn't yet know all of them, guaranteed that Trenker would never be allowed to just walk away. He had no proof of wrong-doing, or even that the group had convened. But to remain alive, he'd have to play along with Blackstone and Richards, or devise an quick exodus.

The problem with fleeing was, Julia would not easily abandon her beloved sedentary life-style. He'd have to eventually disclose to her his past sins. She was a person who rejected sin every waking moment of her life. Although compassionate, he knew she would never completely forgive him.

Julia attended daily mass and prayed at the foot of the Holy Madonna Shrine, less than a block from their stately brick home on Orient Avenue in East Boston; which overlooked Boston Harbor and Logan Airport from the highest point in the city. The view of Boston's skyline from the site was unique. You could see neighborhoods in East Boston, Charlestown, Chelsea, and downtown Boston, with inexpensive binoculars. The commercial jets arriving or departing from Logan were close enough to wave back to passengers. They took off and landed every thirty seconds during peak hours.

Julia served meals and read romance novels to the sick and elderly at the Don Orione Nursing Home across the street from the thirty-five-foot, bronze statue of the Madonna Queen. Pope Paul VI prayed at the shrine in 1960, and the plaza housing the Madonna and impressive mosaic Catholic icons was dedicated to the Pope in 1978 by the archbishop of Boston. Julia believed that the Madonna Queen safeguarded poor Boston residents from the power of the wicked. She frequently quoted the Prophet Jeremiah regarding the Utter Corruption of People: *Our Purpose is to Seek Out Injustice and Correct It.*

She'd never absolve her husband of guilt, once she was told of his illegal Asian kick-back deals. The ten-million yuan, more than a million dollars, tucked away in a Geneva numbered account, should have gone to homeless Chinese children. Neither could she forgive him for causing the horrible suicide of a troubled college student, with his sadistic rituals.

Gatt was ushered into a small, windowless meeting room with ivory walls embellished with brightly colored modern impressionist art pieces. Silver-framed backgrounds of vivid red, aqua and blue sheathed figures of Kelly-green dollar signs, drawn in different sizes. The lined-S's were intermingled with symbols of several foreign currencies, over-stroked in fluorescent acrylic shades. He recognized the Japanese *yen*, British *pound*, Chinese *yuan*, European Union *euro*, Indian *rupee*, and Israeli *shekel*.

McGill and Blackstone entered the room, followed by a secretary to take notes of the meeting. McGill began by explaining that all FFF staff meetings were recorded and filed in confidential company archives. Occasionally the government requested confirmation of billing hours for FFF's lucrative time-based contracts.

McGill sat next to Gatt…across from Blackstone and the secretary…as if he was Gatt's advocate, rather than the judge and jury of his bid to finance the merger plan.

"Tom, Mr. Gatt has prepared an ingenious business-reorganization plan to merge five small manufacturing companies facing certain bankruptcy," McGill began . "As I explained earlier---the venture needs refinancing, and Mr. Gatt is here to plead his case. The sums involved are within my jurisdiction to approve, but…as I enlightened Mr. Gatt…Justin…our firm needs to ask him for a favor---in return for an immediate pledge of financing for the merger."

"Whatever I can do,Mr. Blackstone,within reason," Justin replied in a firm voice, as he looked up at the FFF chairman.

Blackstone towered over the others at the table. The petite, dark-haired secretary seated next to him looked like a midget against the tall executive's length---five inches short of seven-feet. Blackstone was one-third legs and two-thirds torso. He stared down at Gatt from across the table as the secretary flipped open her steno-pad.

He said pompously,"You are probably not aware that GH Paladin is ultimately answerable to the Financial Flow Foundation Board of Directors, Gatt. Although we run it as an independent consulting organization, under Bob's direction, Bob is an FFF board member, and thus, has responsibilities which carry beyond his GHP management duties."

"I understand, Mr. Blackstone."

"Justin is an expert in small manufacturing enterprises, and is qualified to replace Trenker in Washington,"McGill broke in He turned to the suddenly wide-eyed man seated at his side. "Ross has been re-assigned. He'll be involved in a project with a different department of the federal government. It's left a personnel void in a lucrative contract FFF recently signed with the Commerce Department."

Blackstone interjected before Gatt could respond. "His assignment was to travel with the U.S. Trade mission leaving for Beijing in a few weeks. Butler Humphreys, the USTR, needs a qualified consultant who can quietly investigate how Chinese factories continue to bury America's most efficient manufacturers, with unmatchable low prices. Particularly in the plastic products sector." He knew he'd struck a nerve when Gatt physically recoiled.

The FFF Chairman barked, "This firm has always come through for the federal government, and the U.S. Trade Rep's office."

McGill quickly added, "They're relying on us to provide assistance for the critical trade negotiations with Mu Jianting's regime, which will commence in early August."

Justin was still absorbing the fact that Trenker had been reassigned, when Blackstone asked in a jarring shrill, "Are you willing, or not, to take on Trenker's assignmentt?"

Justin was startled by the icey tone of his question. "You mean, you're asking me to go to China in a few weeks?"

"We'd help you prepare...knowing you haven't been there," McGill offered, softening Blackstone's harsh tone. "You'll travel with the mission for a few days, stay in Beijing, then mix visits to industrial centers around the country with a familiarization tour of historical sites. Humphreys wants us to observe a mix of small and large Chinese factories, located inland as well as in the industrial parks concentrated on the south and east coasts. A *Findings Report* must be submitted within a month after the mission returns to the States."

Blackstone's tone dulled, "You'd travel with an interpreter, of course, on a special unlimited travel permit." He nodded almost imperceptibly to McGill, then replied suggestively, "I have no objections to Bob's immediate approval of your financing request. Bob will issue the first $100,000 check today. You can hire an attorney to start the legal work. I imagine your group will want to approach the presiding bankruptcy judge as soon as possible with the reorganization plan."

"What do you say, Justin?" McGill pressed. "Are you with us here in D.C.?"

Justin thought of Brad, Wolfgang, Melfi and George Knoll. He remembered the blank faces on the GRT employees carrying home their final paychecks. He agonized over Joe Slattery's suicide; and could taste the salt of Joanna's tears at his own bankruptcy trial.. *I **do** want to know how the Chinese can charge such low prices. We **do** need to learn how to compete better.*

THE U.S. SENATE OFFICE BUILDING

Ross Trenker and Harley Hedge arrived at the Russell Senate Office Building fifteen minutes early for their appointments. The well-known chief lobbyist for the American Fossil Fuels Institute was waved through the checkpoint by the smiling female Senate security guard. Trenker was stopped, searched and then bombarded with neutrons from the latest weapon-detection device. The instrument installed in the arched-portal detected the distinct gamma ray signatures emitted when uncommonly-high concentrations of nitrogen atoms...such as are contained in high explosives...are blasted with neutrons.

When Trenker cleared security, Hedge led him down a corridor packed with lawyers, lobbyists and home-state constituents vying for a few precious minutes with the Senators. The largest crowd was assembled in a waiting area outside a senate conference room used by the majority party. Behind the closed door, Senator Elliot Scharn of Ohio was speed-reading staff-prepared summaries of the people he was scheduled to encounter today. Ross Trenker's photograph was clipped to the top sheet.

Off to the side, Carvin Troone, the senior Senator from Texas, was seated at the same table, but hadn't bothered to look at the summaries. He was adequately familiar with the people waiting to meet with him and Scharn. An aide reminded them that meetings should begin in five minutes.

"Carvin, why don't we start with the joint interview of Jeffrey Richard's nominee for ADS? Then we can go our separate ways for the balance of the day."

"Fine with me," Troone responded casually. "We've booked heavy agendas, and the Washington press corps is snipping away again---wondering how to prophesy which one of us will be chosen as Merrand's Vice-Presidential running mate."

"Martin doesn't have a lock yet, Carvin. You could still gain the nomination if he slips."

The distinguished-looking former U.S. Secretary of State, who'd lost his Texas drawl but none of his silver hair, since attending Columbia University School of Law thirty years earlier, replied sardonically, "I don't see that happening, Elliot. Though I disagree with his policies on restricting foreign trade… and the extent to which U.S. military presence should be maintained around the globe…the party must avoid damaging internal conflicts. According to all the polls, Merrand is our best chance to retain the White House."

"Well, as the former Secretary of State…and a damn good one at that…I still think you have a chance for the nomination."

"Not with my prior pro-free-trade record," Troone whispered skeptically.

The Senator from Ohio smiled knowingly and said, "Your new speech writer has expertly toned down that issue, Calvin She's a writing phenomenon. Even Merrand is convinced you've embraced his *selective-protectionist* ideas."

Troone unmasked a satisfied expression. "Let's get this done," he pronounced authoritatively, and pranced toward the waiting room. His assistant and speech-writer, Lydia Bryce, swung the door open and watched admiringly as the two seasoned politicians flowed smoothly into the crowd. They greeted each individual as if he or she were the most important person in Washington.

Senator Troone marched up to Ross Trenker, who was partially shielded from view by Harley Hedge in the back of the room and said, to Trenker's astonishment, "Nice of you to give us a nugget of your important time, Ross. Would you and Harley please escort me and Senator Scharn to the private office?"

Thirty minutes later, Hedge led Trenker to a much smaller and less crowded Senator's office. Moody Rugg, the ranking minority member on the Energy Department Sub-Committee, spoke softly in a slow North Carolinian twang...as congenially as a southern belle. Hedge distrusted the cagy Southerner, but respected his toughness on issues of national importance. Rugg's attitude reminded him of Lyndon Johnson in his prime. Of medium height, with sensitive, fine features and black curly hair, Rudd presented a handsome and dignified appearance.

His run for the Presidential nomination was not taken seriously by most political pundits. The fifty-five year old former state prosecutor from Charlotte had never expressed a desire to become President. He'd thrown his name into the minority party's hat---which was clearly devoid of attractive candidates---at the urging of the National Committee Chairman. The party needed to attract national attention for younger, more appealing candidates if it ever hoped to gain back occupancy of 1600 Pennsylvania Ave. Senator Rugg saw his candidacy as an opportunity to advocate his most passionate issue: the need for transparency in America's energy policy.

Trenker and Hedge rose to leave after Senator Rugg nodded and said, grimly, "Which is it, Harley? First, Trenker agrees, then you disagree, that the ADS in charge of the Energy Information Administration should provide **all** the Sub-Committee members with timely information---world oil production and consumption estimates, the list of buyers and sellers of *futures contracts.* That data should be on my desk every month. Harley, maybe you and your New York Mercantile Exchange Brahmin friends know the trader's identities, but I certainly don't."

"Now Senator, we're trying to be reasonable," Hedge frowned at Trenker and said unconvincingly, "Ross, here, is a colt on the job. He's our top energy intellect, but raw on Hill experience. Ross meant he *hoped* to provide this information to *all* the Senate Sub-committee members." He added eloquently, "And, of course, he'd concurrently reveal the numbers to the Wall Street Journal and Investors Daily."

"What about the names of the traders?" Rugg pressed.

"Off limits and out of the EIA's jurisdiction," Hedge answered passively. He cringed when Trenker noted innocently, "I don't see why not, Senator. I understand the EIA is authorized to do so by federal law." *Not the federal law of politics*, Hedge groaned inside.

As they walked toward the black Mercedes waiting outside the Russell Senate Office Building, Hedge patted Trenker on the shoulder and shrugged. "That went about as expected. You were a bit jumpy, in there, but otherwise acceptable." His harangued expression wasn't very convincing. Hedge was already contemplating an alternate choice for the ADS appointment. The tension in Trenker's body, spiked since his first encounter with the Three Sixes, heightened when Hedge blocked his path to the rear passenger door.

"I have to discuss this situation with Blackstone. Why don't you take a leisurely walk back to the hotel, Ross. Just hang out until we call. It's a beautiful day and there isn't much you can accomplish rushing back to the FFF Building."

The dapper Texan slid into the back seat, stranding Trenker on Constitution Ave. Hedge was dialing Richards when the big Mercedes sedan pulled away.

Another mistake by Richards! Trenker has too much to learn; and he already knows too much."

CHAPTER 24

(JULY 23, 2008) PM
CAMBRIDGE, MASS

Lynne studied the *Hoover's Online* print-out from an isolated computer terminal in Baker Library, the primary research facility of the Harvard School of Business. Baker was one of more than ninety individual libraries in the world's largest university library system, with a collection of 15 million-plus volumes. Computer terminals at Baker could access the world's most comprehensive data sources of business transactions.

The Financial Flow Foundation was aptly named, she mused. Following several hours of querying the *Hoover Online, Capital IQ, OneSource* and *Orbis* data bases, she discovered that huge quantities of money frequently flowed through bank accounts held by FFF and Paladin in American, French and Swiss banks. She never expected to find the transactions linking FFF and G.H. Paladin with BoxMart, Residents Bank of N.A. and the Central Bank of China.

Her research uncovered questionable five-million dollar monthly payments from BoxMart to FFF from its wire-payments account at the Residents Bank headquarters branch in Boston's financial district. The transactions had been cleared by an unknown official at the Federal Reserve Bank's Boston regional office.

Lynne's former boyfriend was head of Access Services at Baker, and had allowed her to use his e-mail domain, password and Harvard Business School user-name, to tap into the powerful search engines and data archives which were normally accessible only to Harvard faculty, MBA and doctoral students, partners and staff.

Lynne spent two days slumped over a terminal at Baker searching for detailed profiles of FFF, G.H.Paladin, BoxMart RE and Residents Bank,

N.A....along with any subsidiaries, partners or related entities she could discover. Her search criteria included: rankings by industry; SIC or NAICS code; stock exchange listings; recent capital transactions; and executive bios. *Hoover's Online* alone stored detailed records of 15 million companies, counting 43,000 international public and private businesses.

Using a proprietary Google-enhanced search tool designed specifically for the Harvard Business School staff, her ex-boyfriend broke into the semi-public and private banking records of the four businesses on her query list. He nodded emphatically when Lynne jokingly asked if the search was illegal. But, a break-through idea suddenly emerged from his hacker's mind when she inquired, "Can we find the names of their public auditors?"

Her eyes crossed half a dozen times as she reviewed the audit records and LFT listings they'd flushed out on Residents Bank and BoxMart. A seemingly endless tabulation of large fund transfers in excess of a million dollars was recorded by date. Surprisingly, they found no audit records for FFF or GHP, both Nevada-registered business entities.

"We're stymied," she exclaimed hoarsely. Suddenly, thumbs pressed gently against the cramped muscles of her shoulders and neck said, "You smell so good when you're tense." Her eyes opened lazily as the stiffness in her neck gradually subsided. She imagined another stiffness, when her ex-boyfriend sighed, "I never should have thrown you out."

When she turned to argue the opposite, he held up his hands and backed away.

"I know...I know. You love computer geeks and bookworms...but not if they're the same guy." He desperately wanted her to remain. "I have another idea, but I may have to kill you if we use it."

Lynne watched in amazement as he inserted a CD-RW disk marked "Experimental Software, property of the President and Fellows of Harvard College/ Baker Library."

The experimental software had been developed by a "hacker-proofing" team in order to test the high-security firewall protecting Harvard's $26 billion endowment-investments portfolio. By modifying *Citation Linker* and *EndNote* research software, and overlaying a proprietary algorithm similar to cell-phone technology, the team had secretly tested the new software on an IRS database firewall. Lynne's boyfriend was now accessing the IRS records of withdrawals exceeding ten thousand dollars; which all U.S. depository institutions were required by law to report to the federal government.

As soon as she began printing the list of FFF and Residents Bank money transfers from BoxMart, and other account activity registered by the tax bureau during the past twelve months, the screen froze, then snapped to black…as if obliterated by a voltage surge. The computer terminal and a nearby slave printer both shut down.

"Oh, crap!" her friend shouted as he ran to the terminal and pulled the plug from the surge-protector connection. "It takes the IRS only fifteen seconds to trace the location of potential hackers. I think we're okay. But, that's the end of that, Lynne. I could get fired."

Her mouth widened and turned down. "Sorry, honey," she cringed. "I have reams of info to review. I owe you a dinner." She scooped up printed copies of the records downloaded earlier from databases of the Federal Reserve Bank, the World Bank, and the central banks of England, France and China. The IRS print-out had aborted when the screen went dead. Lynne kissed the worried librarian on his cheek and raced into the fresh air of the Harvard Quad. Lynne dialed Ross Trenker's cell phone after failing to contact Justin.

Ross was walking west on Constitution Ave., bordering the National Mall on the north, after Harley Hedge left him stranded near the Russell Senate Building. He was trudging the short mile to his hotel room, deep in thought, when his regular cell phone vibrated. He reached for an inside pocket and mistakenly withdrew the communications module Blackstone had insisted he carry at all times. The surface was surprisingly warm. He replaced it in his pocket and extracted the regular phone.

Lynne's excited voice was a welcome interruption to the morbid thoughts cluttering his mind.

"Hi, Ross. Sorry to interrupt whatever you're doing, but I need to find Justin right away. Do you know how I can contact him? The FFF receptionist said he left the building an hour ago, and his phone is only taking messages."

"I'm not at the office, Lynne," he said blandly, without further comment.

"You sound down." Her mentor at GHP usually raised his voice when she called. "Is there anything wrong, Ross?"

"Nothing that a new identification wouldn't fix," he quipped without thinking, then immediately regretted the words.

The person listening to his conversation stiffened.

Lynne vacillated before replying. In a rare agitated voice, she said, "I've uncovered important information regarding how Paladin and FFF arrange financial deals. There seem to be conflicting relationships; and some rather large and frequent money transactions. Although, I'm sure it's all perfectly legal."

Trenker was stunned. She was way over her head dealing with the power-elite in Washington. He assumed Blackstone and the Three Sixes manipulated more than the distribution of the Department of Energy's global petroleum data; and wondered about the accuracy of the EIA's petroleum industry reports. He'd already decided to back away from the ADS position, and make a run for it.

He was about to call his Julia in East Boston and instruct her to pack for an immediate vacation trip to Bonaire...their favorite Caribbean island. The tickets were in his coat pocket. One thing about Julia...she loved spur-of-the-moment trips, despite her daily preference for order and solitude. A vacation would give him time to develop a long-term plan; and to explain his past sins in a way she might accept and forgive. Ross planned to donate a large portion of the Swiss money to the Don Orione rest home.

"How'd you acquire such information, Lynne? As far as I know...FFF records are classified top secret by the partners. They don't issue corporate results, except to a very limited federal government distribution. Even the Office of Budget and Management is not privy to the distribution list."

Lynne decided that Trenker should be better informed. "You should know, Ross. The IRS has plenty of financial data on FFF, especially regarding large money transfers between several of its clients. I didn't realize FFF had financial dealings wth BoxMart, Residents Bank and the Chinese Embassy in Washington."

Trenker lost his pace and stepped over the edge of the sidewalk. He called out incredulously as he caught the fall, "You mean you've broken into IRS records?"

Lynne cringed at his reaction and summoned a schmoozing retort. "No, of course not," she lied. "I still have personal access to Harvard's Library search tools. There are some amazing U.S. and international banking records available on the Web. Most people aren't aware that detailed financial transactions are reported and posted on Web domains accessable from specialized query programs. The new Google-enhanced query programs used at Harvard's Baker Library, for example, can waylay records from Central banks, the Fed and the World Bank."

"Lynne, I need to ask you..." Trenker spoke hesitantly with dimmed eyes. "Could the information you acquired identify any of the Financial Flow Foundation partners?"

Silence reined for a moment. "I don't think so, but there's more checking to do. FFF and GHP are Nevada-based business entities. There's no legal requirement for stockholders or partners to be listed. Why do you ask?"

Trenker had assumed the business titans he met in the bank basement were also FFF partners.

"Listen to me---very carefully. For your own good---on a scale of one to ten---*think one hundred*! You must immediately drop all inquiries involving FFF and Paladin. Forget what you've learned."

"You're scaring me, Ross."

"Good, because you should be frightened." He added sourly,"FFF and Paladin are not what they seem to be."

The person recording Trenker's conversation from the basement of the 7th Street bank, adjusted the volume and tapped the "immediate transmit" button. An electronic device in the FFF building played back the conversation between Trenker and Hurricane. A few minutes later, two men and a van were dispatched to his location.

Trenker scanned the Mall area as he stood at the intersection of Constitution Ave and 3rd Street, near the Capitol Reflecting Pool. He noticed two men in dark suits and sunglasses casually strolling in his direction. The taller man suddenly leaned forward and pressed a finger to his left ear.

"I don't follow you,Ross. Shouldn't we be running down Justin for his input?"

Trenker sensed danger and spat into the phone, "Do as I say, Lynne. Drop the inquiry…now. It's a dangerous waste of time."

"What's happening, Ross? Are you in some kind of trouble?"

"I can't explain now, Lynne. Believe me…it's better if you don't know."

Trenker stopped abruptly when he saw the shorter man in the sunglasses glance his way; then cross south to Madison Drive, which ran parallel to his direction on Constitution. The man reached into his suit jacket and flipped something open with his thumb. The taller man stalked forward, advancing toward Trenker on the same side of Constitution. When he was close enough to identify the fear on Trenker's face, his pace quickened. The stroller on Madison Ave. briefly disappeared behind an unmarked white van, which pulled to the curb and parked. The man pushed past the van and quickly crossed the street in Trenker's direction. Trenker realized the two pursuers had him vectored.

"Lynne, I have to go. You may not see me for a while. I'll try to contact you from time to time." He began running for the District Court entrance a few hundred feet away, between 3rd and 4th Streets. He chased up the stairs, jostling two frowning lawyers descending to the street. He hurdled a dropped briefcase, lost his balance and feel forward on the steps. He struggled to his feet and was relieved when he looked over his shoulder. The two men chasing him were holding out FBI badges as they approached. Seconds too late.

A small dark window, cut into the side of the white van parked on Madison Street, inched open, revealing an alloy cylinder designed to muffle small explosions . The person hiding in the van took careful aim.

The first large-caliber projectile hit the red dot on Trenker's lower back, shattering vertebrae and spinal cord nerves. His head jerked backward from the impact and his knees buckled in a wasted attempt to regain balance. The lawyers heard his terrifying yelp and dove toward hell, instinctively. The second 7.62 mm bullet thumped into his left shoulder, deflecting metal fragments and pieces of bone into his right atrium, disintegrating most of his heart tissue. A fountain of red streamed from the exit wound in his chest as he toppled forward. The barrel of the U.S. M40 true-sniper rifle, equipped with a flash-suppressor and silencer, retracted behind the cracked van opening. The white vehicle eased forward into traffic and headed west on Madison; then turned onto 6th Street and headed north into Chinatown.

CHAPTER 25

(JULY 23,24/ 2008)
BROMINE'S MANSION, MD.; WASHINGTON, BOSTON, NEW HAVEN

"**S**loppy is not the word for it!" the Senator bellowed from his secure office phone. "*Idiotic* might fit better."

"I didn't think we had much choice," the tall man crouching over in the back of the white van whispered, "given the fact Trenker was already planning to run. He called his wife last night from a pay phone in the hotel lobby and told her to prepare for an immediate vacation trip to the Caymans. They planned to leave tonight."

The other man on the three-way hook-up said angrily, "He also tipped off Lynne Hurricane. His exact words to her were: 'FFF and GHP aren't what they seem.' Trenker demanded---almost hysterically--- that she abort her investigation of FFF and BoxMart. Unfortunately, that inquisitive bitch will likely dig deeper when she learns of Trenker's death."

The Senator shook his head vigorously, as if to extricate the thought. "So, now we have to deal with *her*." He didn't disagree with the logic of Blackstone's decision. But, Christ…Trenker's assassination was the first drive-by murder on the National Mall in Washington history.

"Only a few hundred yards from the White House and the Capitol…." His words trailed off. "This will raise holy hell with the President. Heads will roll. The Secret Service sharp-shooters responsible for sniper counter-protection in the Mall area must have been tranquilized."

a

Emerson Bromine smirked slightly as he listened on the scrambled communications module at his mansion, "Our Homeland Security insider notified the Secret Service agent in charge of Mall security that the FBI was moving in to arrest Trenker for amphetamine trafficking. The SS shooters were watching the two FBI agents stalking him on Madison Drive and Constitution. The white van went unnoticed."

Tom Blackstone, a former Special Forces sharp-shooter rejoined the three-way conversation from his cramped quarters. "We were aware that Trenker was a shaky recruit. Our people have been watching him closely…in case he got spooked by the sudden change in his situation." Blackstone was still feeling the adrenalin rush that surged through his veins whenever he pulled the trigger to snuff out a life.

Bromine declared confidently, "The back-up story's in place. Tonight's newscasts will report that the White Lotus sect of the Chinese Triad secret society…which Trenker allegedly screwed out of drug money and protection-fees in Asia, has claimed responsibility for the *revenge* killing. It's being posted on the popular web domain used by overseas Chinese nationals…as we speak."

Blackstone stepped from the white van and transferred the long, heavy suitcase to a locked aluminum compartment attached to the bed of a black Durango pick-up parked next to the van in a remote section of the I Street underground garage.

"I've arranged for the major networks to receive documented evidence of large deposits made to Trenker's off-shore bank account," Bromine said contemptuously. "Before the six o'clock news---ABC, NBC, CBS, Fox and CNN will also receive copies of a National Intelligence Center report describing the potential threat posed by the *Triad* gangs in overseas Chinese communities throughout the world---including Washington."

Blackstone added in a stilted tone, as he jumped into the passenger side of the pick-up, "The local gang in Washington's Chinatown section is called the *On Leong*. They operate from a restaurant on 6th and Massachusetts."

"Has anyone contacted Jake Kurancy?" the Senator grumbled in a suggestive tone. His hand was resting on the teak box Phillipe Cusson handed him at the Savoy Imperative meeting a few months earlier. The other electronic device, which signaled a breach of security by any of the Savoy members, was locked in his office vault. He wondered if illuminated numbers would soon appear in the ominous red glass eye built into the top of the small teak chest.

"He'll have to be informed, immediately. BoxMart was apparently the subject of Hurricane's information probe at Harvard. I know what he'll want to do," Blackstone snorted convincingly.

Bromine responded by pouring the last few ounces of his best single malt.

"That's already taken care of. Cashman has agreed to pay the "special fee" to determine how much Ms. Hurricane has discovered…and any subsequent actions that are necessary. The *Chameleon* has been contacted via the internet domain, and has confirmed arrival in Cambridge by the end of the day. Hurricane will be tailed and bugged. If she knows too much...or finds out too much...she'll be eliminated."

The Senator was apprehensive about another death linked to FFF and Paladin. "Let's hope she drops the research before learning too much."

"I'll see that she's denied any further access to the Harvard library system,"Blackstone crowed.

The Senator remarked in a chuffed tone,"And, I'll guarantee that the IRS will initiate an immediate investigation They won't be very friendly when they learn someone at Harvard broke into their sacrosanct records. Hurricane probably had help from the inside. Access to Harvard's search capabilities is not that open...even for an MBA alumnus. If the tax detectives can't discover the identity of her friend, or prove her involvement, they can certainly prevent any future use of the search tool she used to breached the IRS firewall."

"Let's hope she's frightened away by Trenker's demise...and backs off," Bromine snarled. "We have enough loose ends; with the transactions about to begin in Stresa."

BOSTON, PM

Madelaine was weeping when Lynne returned to the Paladin office just before five pm. Lynne dropped the armful of incriminating bank records and other documents mined from the worldwide web onto a nearby desk and rushed to Madelaine's side. The evidence of irregular...if not illegal...money exchanges among the subjects of her probe could wait for later scrutiny.

A call from the hysterical receptionist at the FFF office in Washington had just informed Paladin employees that Trenker was gunned down.

"Oh, Lynne," Madelaine sobbed, "there's been a shooting in Washington." She burst into spastic sobs and doubled at the waist, as if she was about to vomit. Lynne grasped her shoulders tightly and consoled her with a frantic hug.

"What shooting? Who was shot?" she demanded softly, dreading that Madelaine would cry out Justin's name. He was in Washington.

"He's dead," Madelaine bewailed. "He was gunned down."

"Oh, my God!" Lynne moaned. "He was just there to ask for financing."

Madelaine glanced up quizzically through the tears, then realized what Lynne was thinking. "It's not Justin...It's Ross."

Lynne released Madelaine from her white-knuckle grip and collapsed on a chair. The guilt-tainted emotional relief she experienced was akin to disbelief.

Stunned, she was helped up and led to the water cooler, where everyone else had gathered for nature's best antidote against sudden emotional shock.

In the confusion, a junior executive thought to call Gatt's cell phone. A minute later he shouted, "Justin's fine. He's at the Library of Congress…just leaving the Asian room. He wants to speak to Lynne."

Lynne grabbed the phone as is it were the last brass ring on earth. "Justin, I'm so happy you're safe. My God, I thought it was you." She shouted above the clamor of sobs and strident outbursts of horror still reverberating through the office staff.

"I heard the sirens on the Mall," he said. "I thought it was a fire or car accident. I'm just leaving the Jefferson Building. Let me find out more and I'll call you back."

Lynne thought about the telephone conversation with Ross, and was frightened for Justin. "When are you returning to Boston, Justin? Ross warned me to stop all inquiries involving FFF and BoxMart." She suddenly realized the time period between their conversation and the shooting must have been only a few minutes. *Had someone been listening? Were they still listening?*

"My God, Justin, you have to get away from Washington, immediately."

"I can't," he answered. "They reassigned me to replace Trenker for the U.S. Trade Mission to China. The good news is…we got the financing for the reorganization plan. I actually have the first $100,000 check in my briefcase."

He didn't bother to mention that his replacing Trenker on the China mission was a condition for receiving immediate financing. At least now, they had the necessary time and resources to convince the bankruptcy judge to review the Reorganization Plan.

Lynne's emotions were frayed. Under the strain of the yin-yang news from Washington, she didn't know whether to shout for joy or whimper sadly.

"Steve just told me that Ross was shot in the middle of the National Mall. Do you know what happened?"

A barrage of incongruent thoughts converged in Lynne's mind; blurring her perceptions of danger and opportunity. The pile of internet records she skulked at Baker Library sat nearby…waiting for scrupulous examination. But all she could think about was convincing Justin to leave Washington and return to Boston as soon as possible.

"Justin, I can't tell you much more, except I talked with Ross only a few minutes before he was shot." She didn't dare express her real fear that GHP phones were tapped. She hoped he'd read between the lines. "Please come back to Boston as soon as possible. We have so much to discuss."

CNN broke the story on the seven o'clock news. A white van matching the description of the vehicle spotted driving away from the scene of Trenker's shooting was found in an underground garage on I Street, in the heart of Chinatown. The news anchor announced dramatically that the *Triad Secret Society* had claimed responsibility for the gang-style assassination. "Ross Trenker, the mysterious consultant working on a top-secret government contract, was apparently killed for withholding drug-related money from the *White Lotus* enclave; a Chinese gang known for its international criminal activities. *White Lotus* is suspected of smuggling ephedra into the U.S. from China---the world's largest producer of both synthetic and natural forms of the main ingredient in methamphetamine."

The newsman reported how several packets of "ice," or crystal methamphetamine, were found in Trenker's hotel suite at the Monaco. Trenker was suspected of distributing the drug to street peddlers. The reporter explained that the powerful *high* from "ice" can be lethally addictive.

(JULY 24, 2008)AM
NEW HAVEN

Professor Syzmanski immediately called Gatt's office at GH Paladin when he read the front page headline of the New Haven Journal: *Yale Graduate Killed in Gangland Slaying near the White House.* The first sentence of the accompanying article described the shooting of a **GH PaladinBoston consultant, in a drive-by shooting on the National Mall**

Rosa approached the table at Bruegger's with a fresh pot of decaf, but the professor hardly noticed. By then, he knew it was Ross Trenker, not Justin who'd been murdered. Still, he bemoaned having suggested Justin apply for a position at Paladin. Madelaine was still in a state of shock when she informed him that Justin was being transferred to Paladin's affiliate in DC to replace Trenker. Neither Syzmanski nor Gatt's secretary realized that Justin's reassignment was unrelated to Trenker's death.

Syzmanski thought about the recent call he'd received from Forrest Balzerini, his former Yale roommate, and current U.S. Ambassador to China. Balzerini regularly consulted with his close friend, who was an expert on international trade issues. He knew that Eric maintained valuable contacts with important academics at the top Asian and European Universities. He and Forrest had traveled the world together during their final summer at Yale, and had argued passionately about only one subject: who made the best pizza in New Haven ...Pepe's or Sally's.

Jason Changui, the Embassy's new intern, had joined them for tea in Syzmansky's office a week earlier when the Ambassador visited his old friend to discuss an urgent matter. Balzerini needed Eric's opinion regarding the degree of influence Asian business cartels wielded with the Chinese Communist Party. The seasoned Ambassador to China respected his friend's insights into world affairs.

During his visit to New Haven, Balzerini asked Syzmanski if he believed a cartel was seeking to disrupt the U.S. economy…and for what purpose? He explained how well-placed operatives of Han descents had alerted Balzerini's intelligence staff of a new anti-American threat being planned by Communists in high positions. Two CIA agents under his command had disappeared, and were now assumed dead or in hiding. A third agent went underground after transmitting an urgent message from a public internet cafe in Tianjin. He was apparently being pursued vigorously by Chinese web-security police suspected of monitoring a secret U.S. Embassy internet portal that may have been compromised.

The Mandarin message had included a word which attracted the attention of suspicious security officials monitoring all internet transmissions in China: *Merrand*. The sender's ostensibly pro-Chinese message claimed, in part: *Merrand should be slaughtered for accusing the righteous Chinese people of unfair trade practices*. The balance was a decoded message: *A high level conspiracy… severe damage to the U.S. economy….solve the Merrand problem…following trade and biological chaos."*

Balzerini weighed the unknown events, apparently being planned by high-level Chinese officials, as the gravest threat facing America.

The professor chomped on a toasted English muffin topped with real butter; and nodded politely for Rosa to fill his cup with the high-caffeine Kenyan coffee. "Your brain is steaming and scheming; I can tell after all these years, Prof. You must be thinking up devilish new tests for your students."

He marveled at the similarity of their thoughts. "You guessed it, Rosa." He wondered if an electro-magnetic field generated by an old friend's brainwaves could synchronize with your own, and create a similar thought. It seemed that way sometimes.

His new idea could help Balzerini. But, helping one friend could destroy another. Reluctantly…nearly dissuaded by a sense of guilt…he dialed Balzerini's private number.

"Hello, Forrest….hanging in fine,my friend, thanks. No, I still don't think they use too much cheese. Hardly a proper subject for your secure line."

Despite serious misgivings, Syzmansky relayed his idea to Balzerini. He disclosed pertinent details of Justin Gatt's background, and allowed the

Ambassador to decide. "In summary, Forrest, Justin is quite a young man. He's already in Washington and is scheduled to visit China with Humphrey's upcoming U.S. Trade Mission. As a small businessman…although untrained for intelligence work…he's diplomatically invisible. The Chinese would not consider him a likely candidate as an intelligence agent for the U.S. government."

"Thanks, Eric. But I think the situation is out of his league. We just got word that one of our underground agents resurfaced briefly….with additional critical information. Our other contact people have either been eliminated or are being watched 24/7 by PLA security police and plain-clothes trailers. We need a seasoned intelligence vet to make a surreptitious contact to flush out the info…without getting himself killed or tortured. We can't chance compromising our fragile intelligence network in China."

"Why don't you speak with him first, before deciding," Eric suggested. "Justin is a remarkable person. He has a combination of business and technical expertise not often found in a man having his grasp of common sense. He was an excellent athlete in college, and knows how to handle physical challenges."

"Eric, you should have been a Washington politician. I hope you're not slinging the same level of crap as they do. This guy could easily disappear from the face of the planet, without a trace."

The professor's sense of guilt kicked in. Thinking about the fate of Ross Trenker, he said mournfully, "I just lost a former Yale student I was very fond of. I don't wish to lose another. Maybe you should forget my suggestion."

Balzerini read about Ross Trenker's assassination, claimed by the Triads of Asia. He was keenly aware of their power, but had never known the Chinese secret societies to commit such a clumsy and daring purge of an enemy. Usually, their actions were stealthy, not like the Muslim terrorist groups who chaffed if credit for the human destruction they caused was not publicly acknowledged. To his knowledge, the White Lotus sect had never acted to bring itself attention. A daytime assassination in the heart of the nation's capital was not their style. Perhaps Eric was right. A fresh view from a new player could help flush out the truth.

"How do you suggest we contact him?" Balzerini asked with renewed interest.

"I'll fax you his complete dossier. I assume you'll have to be convinced he can be trusted and is sufficiently patriotic. I vouch for him in that regard…without reservation."

Balzerini replied, "That will have to be good enough. We don't have the time to conduct the usual ten-week background check."

Syzmansky smiled as Rosa held up the finger circle of encouragement. She'd noticed the pleased expression that replaced the professor's earlier frown.

"By the way, Eric, how did Gatt end up in Washington?"

"He was assigned by FFF to replace Trenker on the trade mission project... a few days before Ross's murder. He's scheduled to travel with Humphreys' group to Beijing. I believe they've arranged for him to visit several industrial factories and tourist sites throughout the country, to familiarize himself with the Chinese culture."

"You mean, he's already cleared for unrestricted travel?"

"That's what I understand. He'll probably be assigned a regular tour guide by the Beijing Tour Bureau. There's no reason for Chinese security to hawk his movements. The security ministry wouldn't consider him important enough to assign an experienced intel agent. Especially with the massive inflow of foreigners expected during the Beijing Olympics. That's one of the reasons I thought he'd be a good conduit to your underground information source."

The Ambassador thought of AJ Hau Ling's latest recruit in Beijing. "I think we have just the right tour guide for Mr.Gatt, if he accepts the task. The Embassy has some influence with the Beijing Tourist Bureau in assigning guides. We're their biggest customer."

"I'll brief Justin, if you approve."

"I'd rather you didn't, Eric. At least not until I talk with him. But, you could alert him of my interest in discussing a matter of national importance. If I can't convince him without your involvement, he's probably not the person for the job."

"Okay, Forrest. But don't discount the fact he and a lot of his manufacturing friends have lost careers to unfair Chinese competition. He'll have a strong desire to succeed."

CHAPTER 26

(JULY 25, 2008)
LYONS, FRANCE

Philippe Cusson's decision to hold a small press conference in 2000-year-old Lyons, the third largest city in France, was in dramatic contrast to his usual policy of avoiding publicity for Creditte Bank de Savoy at all costs. The bank suddenly needed to become a visible player in the currency-trading universe.

As the result of an unexpected ten-trillion-yen sale by the troubled Bank of Japan during the last forty-eight hours---valued at about 90 billion U.S. dollars---the trading of dollars and euros had been impacted significantly on world markets. Cusson needed to accelerate the timing of the Savoy Imperative trades. According to the managing director of the International Monetary Fund, global commerce was on the verge of destabilizing as effectively as if the rules of GATT were abandoned.

The quarterly meeting of the IMF governing council, scheduled in Stresa, Italy, had been expanded into a crisis gathering of the financial decision-makers from 184 IMF member nations. It would provide Cusson and Creditte Bank de Savoy with an unexpected, although welcomed venue to begin his dollar swapping scheme.

Prior to departing for the Stresa meeting, Phillipe Cusson stood motionless in front of a temporary podium set up in front of the entrance plinth of the 300 year-old former Masonic marble edifice. Rivaling the Palace of Justice and the magnificent St. Jean Cathedral as the most impressive buildings in Lyons...in the heart of France's Provence region...the four-story palace-like structure of the Creditte Bank de Savoy headquarters building was a matchless example of Renaissance architecture along the Rhone River. The stone bastion of private French wealth and foreign deposits was best viewed from Fourviere Hill, overlooking Lyon…a city famous as the gastronomic capital of France.

Cusson was reluctantly addressing newspaper reporters from *Le Monde*, *Le Figaro* and *Quest France* from the main entrance to the CBd S headquarters building in the cobble-stoned section of *Vieux Lyon*…old town.

"I am not so concerned with the value of the euro…as are Paris and Berlin bankers," he informed the small group of financial reporters from France's leading newspapers. "My trepidation is the unjustified primacy of the U.S. dollar as the world's monetary standard."

The *Le Monde* reporter shouted belligerently, "Monsieur Cusson, others in the IMF and European Union community have deep concerns regarding the value of the euro; especially since the Chinese *yuan* is still linked primarily to the *dollar*. And now…the Japanese *yen* has declined overnight. Since the IMF leaders have called an emergency meeting to gather together the finance ministers from the world's greatest powers---why do you appear less worried than they?"

Cusson shifted uneasily behind the small podium set in front of the bank entrance, and looked beyond the reporters to someone standing behind them in the back of the small crowd. He lamented, "Franz Heinrich von Schurz is a very influential leader for the IMF. When he is concerned enough to call an ad hoc meeting of all IMF member states…the leaders of most industrialized nations feel it is their duty to be anxious. Creditte Bank de Savoy, as you know, is a private bank. We are managed by rules and performance criteria established centuries ago. The board of directors has no justification to worry about the currency markets. In fact, CBd S could eventually benefit…" he caught the fretful eye of Li Chin crouched in the back, as the growing crowd gathered to see and hear the mysterious Phillipe Cusson, the evasive Director General of France's oldest private bank, rarely seen in public.

Li Chin had just delivered a ten billion dollar bank check to CBdS. The largest paper transfer ever made by LCE from its Bank of China account was deposited in a numbered account at CBdS in Lyon; along with a letter authorizing CBdS to trade its U.S. dollar deposits for other currencies…at the discretion of Phillipe Cusson.

An attractive female reporter from *Quest France*… searching for a lead story for tomorrow's financial page…pounced on his unfinished statement. "You are supposedly the largest private bank in France, monsieur director-general. It is claimed that Creditte Bank de Savoy controls enormous reserves in many currency denominations; particularly the euro and U.S. dollar. Will you trade these currencies in confidential transactions?"

"Our private transactions will remain private, madame," he snapped angrily. He folded his notes and abruptly stepped away from the podium. *I was afraid this would happen!* The publicity director standing nearby drew his eyebrows to the center of his forehead, as if to say: *It's not a good idea to walk away from financial reporters in the middle of a rare press conference.*

Cusson nodded and reluctantly returned to the dais. In a brabble of condescension he exclaimed, "The *raison d'etre* of bullish and bearish money traders is to hedge on currency futures, which can have little resemblance to rational decisions. Our bank's risk exposure in the euro and dollar, as with other currencies we exchange in bona-fide business transactions, has for centuries relied on rational decisions."

The reporter from *Le Monde* shouted from the gathering crowd, "Lyons is the oldest stock exchange in France, Monsieur Cusson, and has been a center of trade and commerce since the 14th century. Do you predict the Chinese government's refusal to detach the yuan from the U.S. dollar will impact the Provence region's export trade with America?"

Cusson answered in a confident tone, "Just as the high-speed *Train a'Grande Vitesse* links Lyons with Paris, our beloved region will continue to export fine wines and superior goods for the enjoyment of American citizens. I expect there will be expedient adjustments made in the relative values of the euro and dollar against other currencies in the near future. But, even now, major currency futures are traded in 'pairs' to reduce the risk of trading in a single currency."

The female reporter from QF was persistent. "Since the European Central Bank uses twenty-three currencies to calculate the euro's value---I believe you bankers call it the "nominal exchange rate"---how does CBdS and the central banks predict currency movements?"

Cusson smiled ironically, and peered over the bifocals that had slipped to the edge of his thin nose. "Ask that question of the financial experts from the U.S. Federal Reserve Bank, the other G-7 nations and the BRIC government ministries," he suggested pointedly. "The honest ones will admit they have had no distinguished success in this endeavor. Think of the prophesies of our compatriot, Nostradamus; or you may know him as Michel de Notredame… born in our midst…here in Provence, in 1503. Some believe Nostradamus wrote '*Centuries*' and '*Presages*' after he was invited to Lyons in 1547." Cusson thought of his own predictions, presented to Jake Kurancy, Li Chin and the U.S. Senator several months ago. "It is ironic," he uttered glibly, "that none of Nostradamus' one-thousand quatrains predicted that someday countries would go to war because of unfair manipulation in the value of their national currencies…just to gain trading advantage. Let's hope the lack of such a prophecy holds true."

"History gives him high marks," Le Figaro's scribe shouted with a challenging smirk.

Cusson leaned his tall body forward over the alpine-timber lectern and replied sardonically, "My point exactly. Nostradamus was more accurate foretelling the future than any banker has been in predicting currency values. The only predictions we bankers are worse at are the prices for high-tech stocks and oil futures."

The *Le Monde* reporter extended his notepad into the air and quipped loudly, "The Nostradamus thousand quatrains are less confusing to interpret than the double-speak of America's top banker." His jibe at John Paul Tangus, a favorite target of the French press, painted a broad smile on Cusson's face.

"So you are about to join the heavyweights in Stresa, Monsieur Cusson?" the female reporter gushed.

"Please do not quote me. But, I do not consider John Paul Tangus a heavyweight."

Finally, thought the *Le Figaro* reporter, *a good headline for tomorrow's financial section.*

CHAPTER 27

(JULY 26, 2008)
WASHINGTON, D.C.

Federal Reserve Chairman John Paul Tangus began the press conference in a booming voice that defied his appearance. He was a small man of fifty-five, with salt-and pepper hair, delicate facial features and large, stubby hands which flapped emphasis into the words of wisdom he frequently offered the financial community.

His tone of speech today was unusually spontaneous and upbeat. "Please relax, folks. We have only a few short words to deliver before we deliver ourselves to Stresa." That was as close as he came to an opening joke.

The raucous press conference held in the press room of the Federal Reserve building in Washington, had been called jointly by the Fed Reserve Board Chairman, John Paul Tangus, and the U.S. Treasury Secretary. This briefing to the financial media, prior to Tangus' departure for the IMF meeting in the sleepy Italian resort town of Stresa, resting on the southwest coast of Lago Maggiore, would undoubtedly be reason enough for Wall Street to boost trading activity the next day.

Tangus' aggressive chin jutted up from the multi-colored bow-tie which always supplemented his standard uniform at press conferences---a solid white button-down cotton shirt and dark blue suit. A few photographers caught the moment with their photoflashes, which refracted red and blue hues matching the colors of his bow-tie, through the thick polycarbonate trifocals that allowed his wary grey-blue eyes to envisage the meaning of a million tiny numbers…to get at the big picture.

He gave the touchdown signal with his short arms to quiet the reporters and began addressing the media in crystal-clear double-speak.

"The President and Congress are congruent with the people's wishes to protect the U.S. economy from foreign manipulative impulses." The skeptical eyes of seasoned Washington-beat newspaper and TV reporters rolled toward the wood-paneled ceiling. Tangus was at least entertaining...if not easily understood.

"The Federal Reserve Board," the chairman assured the press, "will take only those precautionary actions perceived necessary, as stabilization factors, to properly position the dollar as a globally responsive reference standard for approximate currency fluctuations. If any of our trading partners...or the media...have reduced confidence or extended non-lingering doubts about this concisely market-driven policy, let me remind them that recent international monetary manipulations---primarily but not specifically limited to currency transactions...and primarily, but not entirely interventional in nature---by some of America's major trading partners---have intolerably impacted the prevailing disproportionate adverse balance in this nation's trade and current-account deficits."

The Wall Street Journal and New York Times reporters knew better than to record his exact words. They would paraphrase his concept in articles headlined by the Wall Street Journal: *Fed responds positively to potential currency crisis*; and by the NYTimes: *Fed responds negatively to potential currency crisis*. The confused stock market would yoyo the next day on a heavy volume of trading. Foreign business-news reporters from China Business News, the London Times and the International Herald Tribune were taking copious notes.

Less circumspect remarks by the Treasury Secretary of the United States followed. Standing next to Chairman Tangus, Margaret Stone was dressed in a tailored grey garbardine pants-suit, dark brown open-collared silk shirt and black pumps. The tall, slump-shouldered former executive at Morgan Stanley twisted the stiff black curl drooping over her right ear, then tapped the tiny white-pearl necklace with her thumb...for luck.

She said in a crisp plaintive tone, "The U.S. Treasury will follow the Federal Reserve Open Market Committee's lead. The Treasury will honor the request of IMF Managing Director Franz Heinrich von Schurz, to refrain from dollar re-valuation efforts prior to the Stresa conference."

The NY Times and Wall Street Journal reporters began to scratch notes on their writing pads. "However," she emphasized, "Chairman Tangus and I will confer with Mr. von Schurz and the IMF Council in Stresa regarding the need for corresponding restraint from the other industrialized members of the IMF." The sixty-five year old former manager of the Global Government Bonds Fund at Morgan Stanley added, "I have directed the Under Secretary of Domestic Finance to temporarily postpone the issuance of new federal debt until the Stresa deliberations are concluded."

Fed chairman Tangus stepped up to the row of microphones to deliver closing remarks before fielding questions. He'd been openly critical of his counterparts at the central banks of Europe and Asia…particularly the Finance Minister of Japan.

"Balanced international trade requires the central banks of developed and emerging economies to exhibit deductive reasoning in restraining aggressive non-intervention," he bellowed. "My fiscal counterparts must allow the inability of the currency markets to stabilize themselves…to dissipate… before exerting restrictive de-control of their nation's interest rates and money supply."

Even the Treasury Secretary cringed with horizontal stretch-mouth.

"The unilateral action taken yesterday by Japan," Tangus continued, "which will positively impact Tokyo's trading partners in a negative manner… must be narrated to a reasonable and unbiased curtailment. If that fails to prevail, the acceptable criteria for bilateral trade negotiations in Asia may dissipate the resolve of the stubborn Chinese Ministry of Finance to implement the restraint promised by China's monetary and export-policy decision-makers."

The London Times reporter dropped his writing instrument and didn't bother to pick it up. Tangus added sourly, "American and European fiscal negotiators may then, justifiably and confrontationally, duplicate the cockfight bargaining stance of the Beijing government."

(JULY 27, 2008)
STRESA, ITALY

Phillipe Cusson smiled as he popped the Swiss-chocolate-dipped strawberry into the Russian prostitute's eager mouth and pressed his lips against the huge brown, rigid tip of her arched breast. The buxom blonde from St. Petersburg was one of several professional female escorts who accompanied the bankers from Geneva-based Franco-Medici Trust, a wholly-owned subsidiary of Creditte Bank de Savoy, to Stresa. They provided the *pleasure* portion of the business-and-pleasure trips Cusson arranged for the ten eurozone finance ministers who just placed two billion dollar 'buy orders' for the bank's U.S. dollar reserves.

The finance ministers met privately with Cusson in his Regina Palace suite upon their arrival in Stresa. The meetings were spaced several minutes apart to avoid awkward encounters between the ministers; who were well aware that Cusson made similar deals with other central bank currency traders. They'd all accepted his offer to mix business with pleasure.

Business was concluded with the trading of euros for the U.S. dollars released from the numbered accounts of LCE Industries and BoxMart Retail Enterprises. The finance ministers now anticipated the pleasure part of the transaction. They were not disappointed when attractive Russian "maids" delivered fruit baskets and a small sealed envelope to their rooms. Inside each envelope was a Franco-Medici business card listing a private banking telephone number and contact person. Hand-written on the back of each card was a serial number and PIN code, which accessed a special safe-deposit box at the Andorra branch of the Franco-Medici Trust.

Each oversized vault held one million U.S. dollars in cash, deposited by Jake Kurancy from the untraceable stash he and Cashman recently smuggled into Andorra. The FMT official responsible for large cash disbursements was instructed to wire the money to any destination specified by the bribed officials, unless they preferred to personally accept the funds. The Russian maids were instructed to serve their 'fruit' in the minister's rooms.

Unknown to the bribed currency officials, a transaction trail would be charted and documented as their money moved from the Andorra bank to the destiny of their choice. This information would be utilized in the future to 'entice' the government officials into purchasing much larger dollar sums.

CHAPTER 28

(JULY 28, 2008)
STRESA, ITALY

Franz Heinrich von Schurz, the Managing Director of the IMF, held up a copy of the urgent e-mail he'd sent to the 184 IMF member-countries, requesting they impose a temporary hold on central bank currency interventions. The former German vice-chancellor had restated the purpose of the Stresa meeting in his urgent communique: *To lessen the crisis atmosphere in currency markets and prevent a destructive trade battle from breaking out in Asia ,Europe and America.*

Responding to his request, most of the member countries had dispatched high-level representatives to attend the Stresa conference, which was originally an exclusive meeting for European Union members.

At the conclusion of the two-day session, he was addressing the entire IMF delegation following an elegant Mediterranean cuisine dinner in the grandeur of the spacious Restaurant Borromeo, in the Grand Hotel des Iles Borromees host hotel. Murano glass chandeliers suspended from high ceilings bathed the fine silverware, soft carpets and gilded wall decorations with opulent light, as the attendees were served dessert of warm le Pithiviers almond cream-puff wedges.

"Thank you for attending this important session," the bulky, silver-haired von Schurz declared in the rigid posture that mirrored his dull, all-business personality. "Before my concluding remarks, allow me to introduce Monsieur Michel Peuchelin, President of the European Central Bank, who will brief you on the European Union deliberations which have been held concurrently with the international meetings."

Peuchelin was in his mid-fifties, with a thin grey mustache and thick ashen curls; his raspy voice was an octave higher than a Venetian Soprano's's.

Dressed in a black suit, black shirt and loden green silk tie, he took the wireless microphone from an IMF assistant and stood at the French-delegation table near the head table in the Grand Ballroom.

"I am proud to announce that every European Union nation has agreed to comply with the emergency *Stresa Accord* drafted today by the IMF multinational council. The central banks of the twelve euro-zone countries, as well as the Bank of England and others, will refrain from currency interventions during the last quarter of this year."

The brash French leader of the E.U. waited for the applause to subside, then said in a solemn voice, "There *is* a crisis we must all address, which was well stated in Monsieur von Schurz's plea for fiscal restraint: The economic misalignments in Asia have caused unprecedented tensions in world trade. Global exchange-rates have been de-stabilized and the promise of free-trade tainted." Faint echoes of fading applause were the only sounds in the room.

"Unfortunately, the recent Japanese and Chinese government moves to weaken the yen and yuan against the euro, have left the value of the *euro* unacceptably strengthened in relationship to the U.S. dollar and other currencies."

The Asian representatives shuffled in their seats pensively.

"Despite the Chinese government's claim that the *yuan* is now managed against a basket of currencies, including: the *euro, pound sterling, yen* and South Korean *won*…the *yuan* remains too-tightly pegged to the U.S. dollar."

Peuchelin then noted that China's unprecedented success in capturing the bulk of the consumer-products manufacturing business in all three continents, had simply overwhelmed the world's monetary balance.

"The European Union can only flourish if member nations curb the syndrome of denial," he declared directly to his E.U. colleagues. "Superficial reforms are no longer adequate, if the E.U. is to compete effectively in global trade." He didn't add that the E.U.'s stated target to surpass the U.S. as the most dynamic economy in the world by 2010, was now an impossible dream.

Finance ministers from the twelve euro-zone countries which converted to the euro as their nation's currency, listened intently as the Frenchman implored other nations to help stabilize the euro against the under-valued currencies of most Asian nations. Hisses were heard from the Chinese, Japanese, South Korean and Singapore delegations.

"Let me be more specific," Peuchelin responded angrily to the hissing. "Significant trade battles have already been won by the Chinese Communists. Beijing's back-room support of mainland exporters and state-run manufacturing conglomerates---such as LCE, CNOOC, Stalovo Computer Group, and Chin

Ping Telecom ---have allowed Chinese companies to dominate European markets."

Von Schurz rushed to the podium, knocking over a petite waitress and a tray of tarnished plates, as he watched the Chinese delegation rise and head for the exit door.

The sound of irreplaceable dinnerware shattering on the floor seemed an appropriate backdrop to the chaos. Some in the back, with a poor view, thought the Germans and French were throwing plates at each other near the stage.

Von Schurz watched in dismay as the Chinese marched to the exit door. He shouted, "Please, Peuchelin, we are here to reach accord, not toss blame. Please be seated."

The Frenchman was vying for higher political office in France. He wrenched the microphone from the IMF official trying to snatch it away, and shouted, "Most recently, the Chinese People's Liberation Army has proposed a merger with foreign retailing giants to create a mammoth retailing and manufacturing empire designed to dominate the world's consumer goods markets. Beijing-law recently freed such entities from paying income taxes for ten years. The World Trade Organization should investigate this unfair advantage created by the Chinese." Peuchelin dropped the microphone on the French table and sank to his seat. The murmuring increased rapidly to a raucous wittering.

The astonished guests finally quieted when the IMF managing director pounded his fist on the podium and bellowed into the microphone, "IMF delegates! E.U. delegates! Let us conclude these proceedings on a positive note."

He waited nervously until the clamor subsided, then yowled loudly, "Monsieur Peuchelin surely recalls the Louvre Accord in 1987, which followed the mandate of the 1985 Plaza Accord. The money-managers present know the successful history of the first internationally-coordinated intervention by foreign governments in currency markets. Just as the Paris meeting successfully ratcheted down the over-valued U.S. dollar…for the good of global economies…the current hodge-podge of currency interventions being fostered by member nations, requires a similar coordinated international effort. We must prevent the collapse of exchange-rate stability. This will impact every developed nation."

The 'G-7' representatives from the US, Japan, UK, Germany, France, Italy and Canada rose to applaud. They were frantically fending off the aggressive trade tactics of the 'BRIC' group--- Brazil, Russia, India and China…now threatening to dominate growth segments of the G-7 economies.

Japan's Minister of Finance had been the only IMF member to ignore von Schurz's pre-Stresa call for fiscal status quo. The International Herald Tribune claimed Japan over-reacted to the chilling announcements by GM and Ford that their manufacturing strategies had shifted. Arguably the most vital surviving U.S. manufacturing industry---which supported sub-industries in metals, plastics, fibers, glass and rubber---the U.S. automakers were about to transfer to mainland China the advanced manufacturing technology once preserved for America's domestic automotive production facilities.

The Japanese had reacted to the fear that, in a few years, vehicles imported from China and marketed in the U.S. by Big-Three American dealerships, could destroy the Japanese auto industry's grip on nearly fifty percent of America's car and light truck market. As the largest investor in U.S. treasuries---$900 billion versus China's $200 billion---and a major employer of American workers in domestic factories---Tokyo was in a panic.

On the eve of the Stresa meeting, the Bank of Japan sold 10 trillion yen, worth about 90 billion dollars, to indirect bidders and currency traders. Japan's big insurance companies and money-center banks led the trading, in a blatant attempt to devalue the yen.

The New York Board of Trade and Chicago Mercantile Exchange were by-passed in the transaction, and reacted angrily with claims that Japan had moved desperately, on mere rumors, to protect its export-led economy from derailing.

Overnight, the yen fire-sale strengthened the U.S. dollar and forced America's other major trading partners…all with floating currencies---to consider immediate interventions. The yuan, Hong Kong dollar and other currencies still pegged to the dollar remained protected.

Phillipe Cusson was not overly concerned with the currency crisis now that the The Savoy Imperative was set in motion. The Japanese yen sale and the IMF agreement just announced by von Schurz, would only speed up the process to damage the U.S. economy. Franz von Schurz announced to the world press that the "Stresa Accords" had been signed by 183 of the 184 IMF member-nations. All but China agreed to delay central bank currency interventions during the last three months of the year. Normal currency trading would continue during the "adjustment period" ending September 30, 2008.

Cusson thought to himself, *The Federal Reserve Open Market Committee will be under tremendous pressure to increase interest rates several points. Coupled with the other events planned by Savoy Imperative members, Tangus will soon be dealing with unprecedented financial chaos.*

Financia Polizzei carrying automatic rifles and bull-horns dashed along the shoreline in steel-hulled patrol boats across the Corso Umberto from the

Grand Hotel des Illes Borromees and Regina Palace, the host hotels for the E.U. and IMF conferences. Security police guarded dignitaries cruising in expensive yachts to explore Isla Bella and Isla Pescatoro on Lake Maggiore, before departing for home or traveling on to the Beijing Olympics a few days away. The weather was overcast, with a pleasantly calm and engulfing fog, interrupted only occasionally by intense sunshine breaking through cloud gaps and sweeping across the lake. The hazy rays seemed to project the shoreline miasma gradually up the steep surrounding hills like a powdery avalanche in reverse.

The majestic hills guarding the north and east shores of the lake were rumored to hide well-protected family estates of retired Cosa Nostra "Dons," and the rich-and-famous fugitive tax-dodgers sought by the IRS. Some of the inhabitants traded oil futures in Geneva's dark Calvinist rooms of commerce, where daring Swiss expatriates gambled unmentionable and untraceable sums on occasionally legal international transactions.

Out of boredom and island syndrome, the wealthy refugees frequently transversed the Italian-Swiss border to test the resolve of international authorities tracking their whereabouts; in hopes of relocating them to less luxurious accommodations. The Swiss border-town of Lugano was less than fifteen minutes escape to safety by helicopter.

Rented black Mercedes and bullet-proof white limousines constantly shuttled the world's most influential money handlers from the Regina Palace and the Grand Hotel to Milan airport. A few unfortunate dignitaries traveling with wives or spend-thrift mistresses, were diverted to the world's first covered shopping mall, constructed in Milan more than a century ago.

As Cusson drove through the picturesque Italian lake district along Corso Italia toward the commercial capital of Italy, he thought about the many marvels of Milan: La Scala, the world's most famous opera house; the 'Duomo', the most magnificent gothic structure ever built; and the Church of Santa Maria Delle Grazie, home of Leonardo de Vinci's 1497 masterpiece, *The Last Supper*, depicting arguably the most important gathering of humans in history.

Perhaps the Savoy Imperative would have to meet again. The time-line for action had just been accelerated to September 30, 2008.

CHAPTER 29

(JULY 29, 2008)
WASHINGTON, D.C.

The shocked employees of both consulting firms had no inkling that Ross Trenker was involved in criminal activity. He'd been a competent business specialist admired by most of the FFF and GH Paladin staff; except the people who mattered the most to his career.

They learned from the newscasts that Trenker had participated in private meetings with three presidential candidates from the U.S. Senate, just hours before two 7.62 mm slugs shattered his heart and spinal cord. The shooting in broad daylight on the National Mall, only a few yards from the long lines of school children waiting to enter the National Archives building for a glimpse of the Declaration of Independence and the U.S. Constitution---upset every parent in the country. The President and members of Congress were not particularly delighted with having been in range of the bullets that killed Trenker.

Tom Blackstone watched the morning news from his FFF office not far from the State Department building on 21st and C streets, where two dozen federal officials from the offices of the U.S. Trade Representative and Department of State mingled with Justin Gatt and other businessmen, media personnel and state government representatives attending the orientation seminar for people traveling to China with the USTR mission.

Blackstone tapped the keyboard and deleted the coded e-mail message from Arcola Mandita, the assassin known to him only as the "Chameleon." The Three-Sixes favored her swift and brutal elimination of enemies. She meticulously researched a target's behavior patterns... before hammering, slicing or piercing a victim with bullets, sharp metal objects or poisonous injections.

In the case of Lynne Hurricane, the people paying for the *Chameleon's* services needed to determine if elimination of the inquisitive bitch was necessary. The assassin would be paid the same quarter-million dollars in cash if she proved that killing another employee linked to GH Paladin and FFF... was *not* necessary.

Cambridge, Mass

The *Chameleon* checked into the Charles Hotel in Cambridge using a false credit card and a Nigerian passport identifying her as an ethnic Igbo surgeon from Aba in the East Central State of Nigeria. She presented herself as a Nigerian doctor seeking help from the medical experts at Boston's research hospitals. A new strain of drug-resistant malaria was the leading cause of death in Nigeria---a country with a 51-year life-expectancy.

She showered, selected a wig and facial cosmetics for her disguise and began methodically preparing for the assignment. The former Israeli commando, whose Jewish father and Nigerian mother were shredded to gore in Gaza during a Hezbollah artillery raid, began her investigation of Lynne Hurricane by dialing the number Blackstone had provided. A metallic voice answered, "The following recordings are conversations about hurricanes."

She listened to the recording of Trenker's last conversation with Lynne. There was no doubt the target had to be watched carefully. She looked out the hotel window and gauged the distance to Hurricane's fifth-floor apartment, which faced Memorial Drive along the Charles River basin. The hotel was literally within shooting distance of Lynne's apartment.

Trained by the Mossad to infiltrate Palestinian groups and kill military opponents of Israel, the African Jew had mastered the arts of disguise and human extermination. However, she'd failed to meet the unspoken test for ethnic purity in the Jewish armed forces, and was not readily accepted into the *buddy-protecting* system of the Israeli secret service; partly because of her dark-olive skin and the tight natural curls which she preferred to arrange in braided cornrows. The back-up soldiers monitoring her activities seldom risked their lives to cover Arcola during dangerous missions.

She was raped and beaten with jagged pieces of bombed-out concrete block by a band of hysterical Palestinian teenage boys; after a platoon of retreating Israeli soldiers misplaced her in the cross-fire of a Palestinian village battle.

During her agonizing hospitalization, the indifference of her superiors to her injuries became evident. Arcola decided there was no reason to be loyal to Israel…or any other country. Severe internal injuries and facial lacerations left her grotesquely deformed. The plastic surgeons did their best. When she healed enough to be discharged from the hospital, she became determined to use her dark skills for her own purposes. Her orthodox-Jew commander released her from active duty the same day.

Disguised as a Muslim woman covered in black, she returned to the bombed-out Palestinian village where she'd been attacked, and searched for the boys who raped and mutilated her. Their parents later found their bodies face-up, with fragments of their bloody genitals, which Arcola had sliced to bits, stuffed into their nostrils and mouths.

Washington, D.C.

The National Mall area and Chinatown were cordoned off for several blocks an hour after Trenker's shooting. The Smithsonian museums, National Art Gallery and National Archives buildings were closed. Tourists were encouraged by the news stations and police bull-horns to seek destinations outside the Mall area. FBI and Secret Service agents formed a human net around central Washington, and interviewed anyone who may have witnessed the sniper fire; or spotted occupants of a white van cruising slowly away from the crime scene down Madison Drive. The abandoned vehicle was later discovered in an underground garage beneath I Street. Not a single fingerprint was found on the vehicle by FBI forensic experts.

State Department Building

Richard deLeone, the Deputy United States Trade Representative, strode deliberately into the State Department conference room following a brief meeting with Butler Humphreys and Forrest Balzerini at the office of the U.S. Ambassador. deLeone held the rank of Ambassador, and had broad negotiating responsibilities for treaties and trade pacts with other nations. He'd just seen the internet message posted by the Chinese Triad Secret Society claiming responsibility for Trenker's shooting. The event had caused a sudden blur in the Administration's negotiating priorities with the Chinese.

The President wanted the China Trade Mission agenda revised. An American citizen consulting for the USTR staff, had been gunned down in the under-belly of the federal government. Trenker had been accused by his murderers of smuggling natural and synthetic ephedra into the U.S. from China---the world's largest producer of the addictive drug.

The President demanded that methamphetamine drug-smuggling be added to the list of criminal activities USTR Butler Humphreys was to table on the first day of high-level negotiations with Chang Hui Chen, the lead Chinese negotiator and Chairman of the National People's Congress.

"The American people always respond positively," claimed the National Security Advisor, "when the President deals expeditiously and harshly with outside threats. We cannot tolerate drug-related crimes which threaten children, visitors and government employees in the nation's capital."

The cramped conference room in the State Department building was stale with anxiety. Gabriel Oresco, the NY Times Asian Affairs reporter, was the only attendee familiar with the history of the White Lotus sect of the Triad Secret Society, which claimed credit for Trenker's killing. He was sharing this knowledge with a small group of uneasy businessmen having second thoughts about their fact-finding tours and pursuits of investment opportunities in China.

"It doesn't track with their usual behavior," he explained to Justin Gatt and the others standing around in the back of the room. Oresco just met Gatt and was intrigued to learn that he'd replaced Trenker as the FFF consultant assigned to the trade mission...*before* Trenker's murder. The small group noticed deLeone and others enter the room and followed Oresco to the wing-chair desks facing the front of the class-room style conference room. Richard deLeone was greeted enthusiastically by the State Department information director conducting the orientation session.

The Deputy U.S. Trade Representative, known as "DUSTR" by Washington insiders, trudged to a long rectangular linen-covered table followed by Anthony Clancy, an aide to Senator Elliot Scharn, the chairman of the Senate Foreign Relations Committee. Three thinly-cushioned folding chairs spaced evenly behind the table were designed to provide about a half-hour of moderate comfort.

"My name is Dolores Ibinez Hilton. I'm from the Department of State public-information department." The middle-aged Foggy Bottom career administrator spoke in a gruff monotone. "This will be an informal presentation, followed by a question and answer period."

Hilton's five-foot-three-inch frame was well-proportioned; only faint double-chins suggested she might not be in perfect physical condition. The Smith College graduate spoke with forced belligerent comportment, which she believed was necessary for a successful federal government career. Sparkling brown eyes reflected her dream of becoming an Assistant Secretary... or an Ambassador to a small country like Andorra. A barely noticeable tongue-interruption in her fervent tone of speech suggested a European-Spanish heritage. She was smartly dressed in a maroon suit and a white silk collared shirt unbuttoned and folded over the lapels, revealing enough cleavage to keep the men in the audience interested. A few female reporters---admirers of the poetry of Sappho---also took notice.

"The information packets on the desks explain the touring guidlines for those of you who have been issued unlimited-travel permits by the Ambassador's office. These permits have been authorized by the Beijing

Tourist Bureau, and essentially grant diplomatic status to the holders during their stay in China. I'll review a few key points about traveling in China, particularly during the Beijing Games."

Hilton completed her presentation, then smiled wryly and added, "There's a remote possibility that the English-speaking tour guides assigned to you from the Beijing Tourist Bureau will delicately press you for information which the Chinese government wishes to acquire *informally*. Please feel free to resist answering any questions they ask."

"DUSTR" deLeone followed Ms. Hilton's presentation with a current overview of the status of U.S. relations with China. "It's not necessarily a calming image," he began ruefully. "As you all know, there is concern that the safety of mission participants could be compromised by the President's directive to crack down on the Chinese Triad Society you have all read about. However, our best information suggests the official Chinese government stance is anti-Triad. We believe Mu Jianting and his Communist comrades at the Politboro actually fear them."

Ms. Hilton added morosely, "They've claimed responsibility for the murder of a U.S. diplomatic attaché, Ross Trenker. God bless his soul."

"DUSTR" paused for the appropriate time to allow everyone to reflect on the tragedy, then declared somberly, "We don't expect the FBI's investigation of the Triad sect in Washington to impede the progress of this mission, for either the U.S. government or your individual businesses. The Beijing government has pledged its cooperation in bringing the terrorists to justice."

That's the first time a federal government official has referred to the Triads as a terrorist group. A scary thought, Oresco conjectured. *The Triad and White Lotus societies are deeply imbedded in nearly every major city in the world.* Primarily a criminal organization, the Triad sects could pose a threat more dangerous than al Qaida operatives, if the organization turned terrorist.

Senate aide Clancy leaned into the microphone which deLeone reluctantly slid in his direction. "We'd like each member of the mission to briefly explain the purpose of his or her travel to China," he said brightly. "Any volunteers to start?"

The silence was more annoying than an ambulance siren. Every mission participant declined Clancy's request on the basis of confidentiality. The inexperienced Senate aide failed to realize that this information had been provided on the travel applications submitted to the U.S. Embassy. The business travelers were unwilling to verbally disclose the purpose of their trip to potential competitors.

deLeone reached for the pedestal microphone and began to talk openly about the objectives of the U.S. Trade mission. He asked that the information be held in confidence until the conclusion of the talks.

"The United States hopes to resolve a number of conflicts with the Communist Chinese government during the upcoming deliberations. When the negotiating sessions are completed, you can expect each country to issue press releases with somewhat conflicting versions, regarding the level of progress achieved by each party."

Information Director Hilton thrust her chest out and said, "We're hoping for broad unanimity on a range of issues, but so far the Chinese have balked at confirming our proposed agenda for the Beijing meetings."

Clancy leaned over and snatched the pedestal-microphone. "Several Senators harbor different points of view than President Mu Jianting has presented to the world media. Senator Scharn believes that competition for energy resources, the imbalance in trade, and China's unprecedented military expansion are the key topics. He believes the Chinese have decided to challenge America's dominance in several spheres of global influence."

"DUSTR" wanted the discussion to move away from national conflicts. He ignored the microphone and spoke loudly, "Our Chinese government hosts have invited mission guests to two official receptions during the first few days of the Beijing talks. You'll then be on your own agendas. Splinter groups will meet with Chinese counterparts in their fields of interest. Others will go on guided tours or visit Chinese institutions such as universities, hospitals, government ministries and industrial parks."

Ms. Hilton interjected enthusiastically, "For those of you planning to attend the Beijing Olympics, Ambassador Humphreys will provide complementary tickets to the opening and closing ceremonies."

Clancy then remarked, with less exuberance than his failed call for voluntary information, "I'm officially representing the Senate Foreign Relations Committee as a fact-finder. If any of you wish to submit comments, complaints or suggestions to Senator Scharn, the Committee Chairman, following your tour experience, , please contact my office when you return to Washington."

News media representatives groaned repugnantly when deLeone concluded the meeting by announcing that only businessmen and government officials were invited to all the official state receptions. The media would have a separate schedule. Oresco and others from the major TV and newspaper groups participating in the mission were not surprised. The Chinese government typically *escorted* the U.S. media to various functions when they were cleared for attendence by the Beijing Public Security Bureau at the Youanmen Police Station in the heart of Beijing.

Oresco was already planning to "get lost" from the familiar tethered snake-dance the security police conducted to confine foreign correspondents to staged events. Invariably, the venues demonstrated the accomplishments and wisdom of the Communist Party government.

The Beijing talks would be conducted a few days before the Olympics began; and most of the Americans planned to remain in Beijing to experience the excitement of the Games. But Justin Gatt's itinerary read like a practical-joke FAM trip for a rookie travel agent---dispatched to Jamaica's slums and dangerous small-villages…to become familiar with run-down resorts populated by unfriendly inhabitants casually wielding machetes.

The familiarization trip someone at the U.S. Embassy had concocted for Gatt included scheduled visits to industrial parks and plastics factories located in remote villages scattered all over the mainland. In addition, there were un-scheduled trips to semi-obscure universities in Fujian, Xi'an and Changdu, along with "unspecified" visits to famous tourist attractions.

Justin hoped to visit some of the famous archaeological digs of ancient Chinese dynasties, such as the famous Terra Cotta Army of 6,000 life-size warriors with spears, crossbows and chariots buried to protect Emperor Qin Shi Huang; created over a 40-year span by 700,000 slaves in Xian. Or the 3,000-year-old pits containing five chariots and horse skeletons in the Yin ruins, 300 miles south of Beijing…all facing eastward. He'd read that many of China's precious ancient treasures were rapidly being buried forever by the unrelenting 300 foot water rise caused by the Three Gorges dam project.

Justin was surprised that his travel permit allowed him to explore all of China---limited only by the five-week visa authorization period, and the requirement that he be accompanied by an official Chinese Tourist Bureau guide.

The brief question and answer period which followed the formal presentations shifted immediately from international trade with China to the events surrounding Ross Trenker's murder.

A ruddy-faced soft-spoken reporter from the Washington Post asked the first question. "I understand the FBI office in D.C. just received an e-mail from an unidentified White Lotus source in D.C.'s Chinatown---denying any involvement in the shooting. What do you make of the conflicting claims, Ambassador de Leone?"

"Not my area of expertise," deLeone answered slickly, "Perhaps Gabriel Oresco of the New York Times Asian Bureau could address the question. I understand he's an Asian expert."

There was a detectable tone of sarcasm in his remarks.

The other mission participants turned to Oresco, a compact man in his late forties, with a full crop of rusty brown hair and prominent teeth accentuating a confident, bright-eyed smile. Oresco was haggardly handsome, or "hunky" as his wife described him, and was dressed in a casual outfit of twilled khaki trousers, an unbuttoned short-sleeve dress shirt and a tan seersucker jacket. He hated eyeglasses and wore inky contact lenses with dark portions larger than his iris. The effect of the monochromatic pupils was to make his eyes look larger and more intelligent. He'd acquired them in Japan, where schoolgirls wore non-prescription versions of the large black contact-lenses to look "cuter."

Oresco was well known by his peers. His sensational disclosure of a U.S. oil company's sale of an off-shore oilfield in nearby Pacific waters to CNOOC, China's government-owned oil company, would likely earn him a Pulitzer Prize nomination for investigative reporting. He combed his wavy hair with long manicured fingers and replied tersely, "It's an anomaly in their behavioral pattern. I've never known an Asian secret society to openly claim responsibility for a terrorist act. Then to deny it is doubly puzzling."

He was seated next to Justin Gatt in the back row of the class-room layout. Oresco was curious to learn more about this unknown consultant, who had replaced Trenker on the China mission even before Trenker's violent death. Justin informed Oresco that he was seeking details of how Chinese manufacturers could offer such low prices to American retailers for plastic products.

Abruptly, a side door opened and Robert Changhui, the new assistant to U.S. Ambassador Balzerini, peeked in and motioned to deLeone. In perfect English, he said, "Allow me to apologize, Ambassador deLeone. The Embassy has just received important information from the Chinese government. They claim to have confirming evidence that Trenker took bribes and was involved in the Triad drug operations. Ambassador Balzerini would like you to join him as soon as this meeting is concluded. He also wishes to personally explain the safety risks to everyone scheduled to travel to Beijing…in case any of the participants prefer to reschedule their visit for a future date."

Oresco noticed that Changhui was smiling intently at Gatt. And that Justin was returning the smile. *So…Robert did follow the professor's suggestion and accept the job offer from Balzerini.*

"Yes, Ambassador; Eric called me this morning." Justin was in Balzerini's private office in the State Department building. "He explained you were interested in my assignment to acquire knowledge that could benefit American manufacturers. He said you might be helpful in guiding me to unconventional sources of information in China."

Balzerini smiled at the manner in which Syzmansky had skirted the subject of gathering information with Justin.

"We'll…that's all true, Mr. Gatt….may I call you Justin?"

"My honor, sir."

"Good. Now let me be candid. Professor Syzmansky recommended you for an assignment which goes far beyond acquiring competitive business data. An assignment that is more critical to American interests, Justin. Frankly, I'm not sure you're prepared to carry it out safely." He arose and walked around to Justin's side of the desk and took the chair facing him.

Balzerini and Justin were both dressed in conventional business suits. The soon-to-retire Ambassador sported a large gold pin on his lapel, commemorating twenty-five years of distinguished service in the United States diplomatic corps.

"What I'm about to tell you is top-secret, Justin. As unlikely as it seems, none of the Embassy or State Department people making the trip to Beijing have, or will acquire this information. For security purposes, I'll have to ask you to sign a USA Pledge of Confidentiality. That usually means you could be put you in jail for a long period, if you reveal classified information, revealed to you before it is made public. If ever."

Balzerini empathized with the anxious grimace on Justin's handsome face. He was about to ask an intelligent, yet obviously disoriented man, who'd been forced to change careers three times in less than four months, to leap headlong into another unknown situation. A dangerous assignment in an unfamiliar country. As a bonus---it could land him in federal prison, or an early grave.

"It sounds pretty serious," Justin finally found his voice.

Balzerini studied his deep blue eyes and replied incisively,"It is!"

"Does it have anything to do with Trenker's murder?"

"I honestly don't know. But Chinese characters are pasted on every scenario that involves national security these days; including the outrageous killing on the Mall." He paused. Gatt's apprehension deepened.

"Perhaps I can ease your mind by revealing some unclassified public information first---regarding the multi-facetted Chinese threat to American interests, which *could be involved…if* you took on an assignment from this office."

"I know they're attempting to destroy the small manufacturing base in our country." Justin suspected that also applied to some large businesses. "But this isn't a business matter, is it?"

"Syzmansky was right. You're very perceptive. Let's get right to it, Justin. Sign here."

Justin signed the CDA without reading a single line of words. He assumed the Federal Government was not about to alter the standard wording of a national document, if he objected to any of the terms or conditions. He was either in or out. Eric would never lead him astray. If the situation was that serious, and it involved a conflict with China, he'd do his best to help.

"And although the objective of the Chinese government is to dominate world trade," Balzerini completed his background explaination, "It's no secret that the Communist Party is wavering in its commitment to support capitalism-style expansion in its current form."

Balzerini reached for a glass of water, then studied Justin's eyes intently. "Here's the kicker, Justin: we've uncovered evidence, although sketchy, that unidentified top Chinese leaders are planning a major attack on the U.S. economy, with the objective of severely weakened the U.S. We believe the plans include both financial and bio-weapons elements."

"But we're their biggest market. Isn't that crazy? Why damage your greatest source of income and growth?"

"We don't know. It may be a simple question that requires an extremely complicated answer. Let's just say that some Chinese Communist leaders, including military and industrial gurus, believe they're much smarter than Americans. We believe they may be making dangerous decisions to keep us distracted…politically and economically."

"There's no doubt they're eating our lunch in staple consumer markets."

"I tend to agree. But the real danger may go deeper."

Justin thought about the federal government's feeble response to the job losses, business failures and blatant theft of intellectual property fostered by the obstinate Chinese government. He'd read editorials claiming the President and Congress were fearful about Beijing's shaded threats to discontinue buying the treasury notes that financed Washington's budget deficit. But China was not Japan. They didn't depend on America for national defense against unfriendly, competitive Asian powers---including China and Russia. Justin had often wondered if American leadership had collectively lost its resolve to confront injustices on an international scale.

"Mr. Ambassador, Eric Syzmansky is not only a dear friend, but a real patriot. I believe he feels likewise about me, although certainly without the same justification and accomplishments. If he thinks I can be of help in addressing a problem of national security, the least I can do is try." Ambassador Balzerini nodded; a deep grin pasted his face. He decided to reveal the details.

Justin left Foggy Bottom a few hours later carrying a small leather case. Inside was a ¾ inch-thick, specially modified Nikon Coolpix S1 digital camera. Capable of capturing three-hundred high-definition digital images, the micro-chip hidden in the sealed mechanism was also top-secret GPS satellite tracking and laser photo-forwarding technology. The intelligence staff at the embassy would be able to locate him anywhere in Asia. High-definition digital photographs and encrypted messages could be originated and automatically forwarded via NAI satellites, and secret land, ocean and airborne receiving stations. The images would then self-erase as if they never existed. Balzerini assured Justin that only he, the President, Eric Syzmansky, the Director of the National Intelligence Agency and the monitoring technicians responsible for remotely tracking him in China would know of his attempt to contact the Embassy's underground sources; who were constantly on the move to avoid the relentless pursuit of mainland security police.

Balzerini admitted to Justin that he was particularly worried about the implications of a recently-intercepted transmission. The translation referred to *'solving the Merrand problem, if he is elected.'*

"I can't imagine Chinese leaders would be bold enough "

I don't believe President Mu is behind the threats."

CHAPTER 30

(July 29, 2008)
Cambridge, Mass

"I'll take the early shuttle and meet you and Brad in my office around ten. I hope all this intrigue is worth the effort, Lynne. Are you sure you can't tell me over the phone?"

Justin was alone in his hotel room staring wantonly at a juicy, rapidly cooling ten ounce angus cheeseburger, smothered with caramelized onions and hot cherry vinegar peppers. The room service waiter standing impatiently near the doorway was stealing a few of the sweet potato string fries piled in a bowl on the serving cart, and eyeing the fresh anchovies laced over a large Caesar salad.

"You'll understand tomorrow," Lynne replied tentatively. The shock of Ross's death still lingered. She assumed her phone was bugged.

"Well, at least it will give us an opportunity to review the merger plan before presenting it to the judge," he replied. "Ken Levine has agreed to petition the Federal Bankruptcy Court in Boston to assume jurisdiction for all five cases. He thinks FFF's initial payment will convince the judge to lump all five cases into one. The $100,000 check from McGill will be used for legal and start-up costs, assuming the Boston judge cooperates."

Brad Stalker held out his hand and nodded to Lynne for the phone. He sensed she was intent on ending the call as soon as possible. He needed to talk with Justin.

"Hi , Justin...Brad. I have to ask you a question. But I also have some good news."

"Hold on, Brad." He pulled out a ten for the waiter and scooped a handful of the salty-sweet orange fries into his mouth as the door slammed in his face. *That's the last tip for him.*

"Okay, Brad…shoot."

Brad noticed Lynne's hesitant expression and said softy, "Two things, Justin. First---how about using the name 'AmerAgain Products, LLC' for the new venture? We need a name for the business in order to submit a Plan of Reorganization."

"That sounds great, Brad. I like the idea of using GRT's old trademark. What else?"

"You probably won't believe this, but the test results using your separation process on the Alberta tar sands samples were beyond our wildest expectations. Your technology not only precipitated out the petroleum fraction from the gritty sand…it promoted bacterial breakdown of the thick bitumen into smaller, more easily recoverable hydrocarbon fractions. I've discussed the results with an engineering friend of mine at UMass Amherst, who helped discover a new class of 'enols' in burning fuels. He's an expert in petroleum compound analysis and has agreed to characterize the reaction products of your separation process, using an apparatus called the *flame-analysis spectrometer*."

Justin was momentarily speechless. His low-cost bitumen separation process could potentially recover over 900 billion barrels of lower-viscosity bitumen, for conversion to gasoline, aviation fuel, heating oil and refined petrochemicals, which could be polymerized into low-cost plastics at existing North American factories.

"When will the completed report be available, Brad? We may want to move quickly to further develop the process. I've been thinking about how the bio-nuggets used in our process could be self-catalyzed. That would potentially produce enough hydrogen to react with the sulfur contamination in the residues from the separation process. The sulfur could be inexpensively removed as hydrogen sulfide gas, and condensed for use in industrial applications."

Brad grinned. All he knew about hydrogen sulfide gas was that it had a foul odor…not quite as bad as the putrid butyl sulfide vapors emitted by agitated skunks. "That certainly sounds promising."

Justin forgot about the cold burger and the congealed fried onions. "It means the *high-sulfur content problem*…a big environmental hindrance to recovering liquid hydrocarbons from heavy tar sands and shale oil rock… could be solved during the oil-separation process. If the sulfur can be removed cheaply, the rocks and sand left behind would be suitable for use in cement and cinder blocks. The current separation process---using steam and high temperatures to recover the thick bitumen from tar sands---would be obsolete."

Brad remained silent It took him a few moments to grasp the enormity of Justin's discovery.

"The patents!" he shouted abruptly. "Have you paid the registration fees?"

"Not yet." Justin exulted in a paroxysm of exuberant generosity. "I'll add the patents to the new business plan. Part of the FFF check could be used for the registration fees."

"We could form a technology division at AmerAgain,LLC," added Brad effusively,"and license the patent rights to someone with enough capital to develop and commercialize the process."

"And protect it," Justin replied warily. "The middle-east emirs and big oil execs would probably attempt to bury it."

He'd witnessed a similar action when asphalt suppliers for new federal and state roads suppressed the use of recycled rubber tires in asphalt surfacing compounds. The largest producers of asphalt were commonly the divisions or subsidiaries of the major oil companies---the same firms Gatt believed had undercut the plastics recycling industry. By failing to renew the minimum-content recycling law already in effect, Congress succumbed to pressure and allowed the law to expire. Road tests had proven that asphalt roads containing 7 to 10 percent ground tires were more durable than unmodified black-top. The growing tire piles that sometimes burned for weeks in dumps could eventually disappear if the technology was completely developed, instead of ignored.

When Tom Blackstone listened to the telephone recording from Lynne's apartment, he immediately contacted Jeffrey Richards. The oilman representing the oil traders and producers on the Three-Sixes board was sufficiently alarmed to call Harley Hedge and instruct him to discretely investigate Gatt's technology. He needed to determine if Gatt's patented process was a threat to his client's stranglehold on world oil prices. Blackstone considered canceling the $100,000 GHP check given to Gatt, which was probably not yet deposited. He decided against it when he remembered that the check was made out to Attorney Ken Levine's trustee account…at Gatt's request. He didn't want a nosy lawyer digging around for explanations.

Lynne's one-bedroom apartment in Cambridge overlooked MIT and the Charles River from the fifth floor of a twenty-story condo complex. The owners were mostly real estate investors leasing the flats to Harvard, MIT and Boston University faculty for exorbitant rental fees. They didn't deem it necessary to dilute their profits by hiring security guards, or purchasing an inexpensive system of small video cameras which could be placed in the main entrances to the front lobby and rear parking lot. The entrance doors were locked at nine pm; but even a nervous arthritic could jimmy open the thin-gauge aluminum locks of the hollow steel doors with a dull fingernail file.

Lynne dreaded spending the evening alone following the conversation with Justin. She and Brad had completed a revised business plan in less than an hour, and she invited him to stay for dinner. It was much less a hardship for Brad to remain, than it was for him to leave a few hours later; following an unexpected steamy encounter with Lynne. Her moist lips would occupy his thoughts during the entire forty-five minute drive home to Leominster on Route 2, which this time took twenty minutes.

"This take-out is good," he said, as he spooned subgum fried rice from a thin paper plate sagging under the weight of egg fu-yung saturated in gobs of brown sauce.

"He has to come back anyway," Lynne sighed absently, her eyes still on the phone. "Justin's packing for a five-week trip to China." She jumped up and ran to the kitchen when the obnoxious railroad-engine toot announced the pot of jasmine tea was violently steaming. She released the pressure lid and reached up into the cupboard for the two large white porcelain plates she'd purchased at the Pottery Barn; then rushed back to the neat-area she used for dining, TV and relaxing. Brad was seated on the floor leaning awkwardly against a glass-topped coffee table tamped into a close space between the loveseat and a large recliner. His large hand was cupped under the saturated paper plate, trying to prevent the victuals from slipping over the sides.

Lynne fancied up the meal presentation by placing the tea pot and the two ceramic plates on the glass table, and pushing aside the worksheets for the reorganization plan. She cautiously lifted the saturated paper plate from Brad's hand and placed it on the white pottery dish…just as it started to drool brown sauce on the cream colored carpet…like saliva dribling from a Novocained lip.

"China?" Brad said in surprise. "What's that all about?"

He watched Lynne fill a paper plate and nest it on the porcelain dish for support. She climbed barefooted onto the oversized tan-leather recliner; which doubled as a magic carpet when she dozed off. Her favorite dream was swooping romantically through puffy white clouds…leaning precariously over the flaccid edge to search below for her lost lover.

"FFF has hired him…maybe the correct word is *re-assigned*…to replace Ross. There's a consulting contract with a federal agency. It involves travel to China with the U.S. Trade Representative's mission. It leaves in a few days. Justin says he'll explain more tomorrow; he has to rush back to D.C. in the evening." She scooped a large table-spoon of brown rice into her mouth and said, "They've scheduled meetings and a formal dinner with federal officials and Chinese dignitaries." She noticed Brad recoil and his eyes flinch when she added casually, "He's asked me to join him for the formal. It's a couples event."

Out of respect for Justin, Brad hadn't hit on Lynne. He assumed from the fond tone she used in her conversations with Justin that they were romantically involved, although Justin hadn't seemed particularly amorous toward Lynne when they were in Brad's company. Perhaps it was his conservative nature. In truth, Justin didn't wish to discourage the budding relationship he'd seen developing between his two younger colleagues---despite his obvious affection for Lynne.

Lynne stared over the edge of her plate at Brad's frown. It was a radiant glare; more than friendly. The food sliding into Brad's stomach moved to a new hollow, as her warm green eyes cast a seductive, sleepy glow from half-closed lids. The sexual tension in his muscular body was overwhelming. Lynne's bare feet peeked at him from the edge of the recliner.

Brad set his plate on the table and removed his shoes and socks. An amazing sense of relief prompted him to think about throwing his socks at Lynne. Her inhibitions would begin to dissolve. Brad fought an immense urge to pounce on Lynne's recliner…like a wild gorilla; to sweep her dish against the far wall, and carrying her barefoot to the bedroom… oblivious to the shards of broken porcelain slicing escape passages for the steamy red droplets. Troubles would be left behind…in the faded memory of a dated time. Replaced by unimaginable bliss. He was daydreaming. Just like Lynne.

They were both dressed in blue jeans and the grey monogrammed Red Sox T-shirts Brad purchased at yesterday's Fenway Park ballgame. To commemorate the reorganization plan, they'd celebrated with hot dogs and ice-cold beer in the right field bleachers. Brad was unaware that Lynne's heart accelerated at least as rapidly in his presence, as it raced when she was with Justin. Or that she ached…irrationally…for both of them to squeeze into the recliner and amorously engulf her. *Brad is here now,* she mused provocatively.

At 9:45 the next morning, a tall, heavy-set African-American woman dressed in drab work clothes slogged warily up the seldom used stairwell to the fifth floor. She carried a large burlap bag which presumably contained cleaning supplies. She opened the door to the empty fifth-floor hallway and glanced at the numbers above the apartment doors. When she found the right number, the cleaning lady tapped on the door with the tip of a key and called out calmly, in a low voice, "Cleaning service." Tap, tap, tap. "Cleaning service."

She knew the apartment was vacant. She glanced at her expensive Dior Irreductible Chronometer, with 1/10 second precision measurement and a black-tinted, sapphire crystal. It was ten am. Hurricane would be at GH Paladin for the meeting with Gatt.

A door down the hallway swung open and a man in his late eighties, wearing oversized lime jogging clothes glanced left and right. Then he sauntered unsteadily toward the elevator door next to Lynne's apartment. When he was close enough to see clearly, he said jovially, "Good morning, dear," as if this was the best day of his life.

It was probably the best day of the *rest of his life*. He was well aware that most people in their late eighties aged in a muted degenerative process. If he didn't notice an intense new ache, and swallowed most of his pills at approximately the specified time, it should be a decent day. There was nothing wrong with the old man's hearing.

"You must be new here, lady. Miss Hurricane likes to do her own cleaning."

The elderly women looked up at the number above the door, then stooped to the large burlap bag. She reached in, pushed aside a heavy metal object, and lifted out a small sheet of paper.

"Well, sir," she smiled, revealing large blocky teeth and enormous, unnaturally bulbous lips. "I must be havin a wrong door numbah." The old man shrugged, and looked out suspiciously when she didn't follow him into the elevator.

Ten seconds later she was in Lynne's apartment, emptying the burlap bag of its contents. She reached up and placed tiny self-adhering electronic devices, the size of a triple-A battery-tip, on the top surfaces of several door moldings… out of sight. She then positioned a battery-powered pack the size of a Blackberry device, behind a removable acoustic ceiling tile above Lynne's queen bed. White, red and green wires were connected to a remote timing and detonation device. There was no need to disturb the telephone…it had been tapped earlier by Blackstone's men. The *Chameleon* could now eaves drop on conversations from every square meter of the apartment.

She moved to the dressing bureau and immediately found what she was looking for. Lynne's good-jewelry was in a black, velvet lined Rolex watch case, and consisted of a set of emerald earrings and a gold Rolex designer watch with a circle of ¼-carat diamonds. The base was inscribed : *With love from Mom and Dad, Harvard MBA*. It was the type of accessory she'd most likely wear for important dates and formal occasions. A compact cherry-wood music box was overflowing with piles of costume-jewelry pearl necklaces, beaded bracelets and synthetic-gem earrings.

She opened the back of the Rolex watch with a tiny precision screwdriver and carefully inserted a magnetic nanochip, smaller than the metal sphere of a fine-tipped ballpoint pen. The device was developed by a South Korean electronics company for Israeli Intelligence. The miniscule transmitter sent microwave sound signals to a recorder-amplifier less than a mile away in her hotel room.

The assassin then moved to the window overlooking the Charles River. She was satisfied Lynne's room faced the Charles Hotel from the desired angle. If necessary, she would complete her task at long-range with an armor-piercing, large-bore projectile. The *Chameleon's* preparation always included multiple options to eliminate a target, utilizing a variety of steel tools and versatile weapons. The method she preferred most required only a sharp-tipped cobbler's hammer.

Her favorite food was ice-cream…a trait inherited from her father. When she exited the building into the parking area she decided to walk toward MIT to a famous Cambridge ice-cream shop near the campus. The hotel concierge claimed the ice-cream there was the city's best tasting, and offered the most unique flavors.

She watched the Harvard Square tourists standing in line, and the summer students tapping away on laptops, as she entered the local Mecca of eclectic tastes. The lap-toppers were taking advantage of the free Wi-Fi provided by management; which allowed customers to surf and lick at the same time. Yesterday's special flavor was mango-cinnamon sorbet. Arcola ordered a large wafer-cone of today's special flavor---burnt caramel banana apricot. She ate while strolling casually back to her hotel. It brought back faint memories of early childhood, when she walked with her father to a local ice-cream stand in Tel-Aviv.

A Regional Hospital in Northeast China

The elderly father leaned over the bed in the People's Friendship Sanitarium, not far from the concentration camp where he worked, about one hundred fifty miles north of Beijing. He was praying to his ancestors for a miracle.

His young son had graduated from Beijing University a year earlier with an advanced degree in microbiology, and was lucky to find a position as a laboratory technician at the Institute for Advanced Medical Treatments in Liaoning Province. The twenty-five-year-old was the pride of his parents. His health had been excellent, with no signs of physical ailments…until he began working at the medical institute. He was now struggling for his last breath.

His father, a prominent official with the Central Propaganda Department in Liaoning Province, was well aware that the IAMT facility hid a massive crematorium in its basement warehouse. There were also hundreds of tiny cells with rusted steel bars currently being occupied by missing Falun Gong practitioners.

Rumors circulated in the nearby village that a secret concentration camp near Sujiatun supplied fresh human organs to the transplant surgeons at the Liaoning Thrombosis Research and Reconstruction Clinic attached to the IAMT complex of buildings.

He was bitter because his beloved son had apparently been exposed to a deadly disease that none of the hospital staff could identify...let alone treat. The supervisors at his son's place of employment refused to comment on the cause of his death, other than to speculate that a minor contamination incident at the IAMT may have contributed to his illness. Perhaps he'd eaten samples of the experimental batch of Iowa corn that was found to contain minute traces of aflatoxin, a deadly fungus that sometimes grows on corn leaves.

The father's contact on the Politboro informed him that the IAMT was also the location of the *Second Auxiliary Laboratory*, a secret Chinese Biological Weapons Testing Station as faceless as the alleged Falun Gong concentration camp where he worked. The prisoners were supposedly treated as raw materials---sources for healthy transplantable organs---exploited for profit. Had his son become a raw material for medical experiments?

The boy's mother moved from the doorway to the bed, removed her respirator mask and lowered her face to hear her son's faint whisper. The father moved away, sobbing, as his heart-broken wife breathed in the heat and foul odor that accompanied the boy's last gasp. She stared horrified at his eyes. They were spotted with large specs of red alga, and bulging halfway out of their sockets. His damaged heart heaved, laboring vainly to pump out the black mud-like substance which had once been the vital life source of flowing red liquid, but was now cementing his arteries.

The technician's blood had congealed and plugged the last openings to his heart cavities and carotid arteries. His chest jerked upward in a spastic fit to clear the clogged vessels, but only succeeded in clearing space for the pressurized, dilated walls of hardened coronary tissue. The boy went limp and stiffened like fast-setting plaster, when his weakened coronary tissue exploded against the confines of his chest cavity and rib-cage.

The deadly aflotoxin fungus found on corn plants does not produce these symptoms, thought the European-educated physician standing at the doorway to the hospital room, wearing a respirator mask. The father had refused to take similar precautions. The mother sobbed uncontrollably and beat her chest after witnessing the horribly painful death of her only son.

Despite the official explanation given by the scientists and medical doctors from the IAMT biological labs, the resident physician suspected a different pathogen than aflatoxin had killed the boy. He'd viewed the black substance under a microscope in the hospital lab and was astonished to observe a microorganism he'd never seen before. Although not an expert in microbiology...he recognized that the unknown pathogen apparently devoured blood nutrients, and left behind black gunk as thick as iced tofu-curd.

CHAPTER 31

(July 30, 2008)
Washington, D.C.

Gatt spent the entire afternoon and evening at the Jefferson Library, studying the materials Balzerini and the librarian had chosen for his crash-course on China. He'd been driven to the Jefferson Building by Robert Changhui, the Taiwanese businessman he met at Eric Syzmansky's office. Robert was now a diplomatic intern for Balzerini.

They were met by the supervising librarian upon entering LJ-150, the Asian Reading Room on the south corner of the first floor---directly across the hallway from the Congressional Reading Room reserved exclusively for Congressmen and their staffs. She'd already retrieved the reference materials requested by Ambassador Balzerini, who considered it imperative for Gatt to quickly gain knowledge of the customs, geography and basic laws of modern China. Familiarity with the history of China could also prove helpful in understanding the machinations of Chinese minds.

Robert's Taiwanese father had insisted that he become proficient in ancient Chinese history, which was useful when Balzerini asked him to pass along to Justin any knowledge he thought would be helpful.

"From the time the Eastern Zhou Dynasty produced Confucius around 450 B.C.," he began, "great Chinese philosophers have instilled standards of modesty that influence peasants and leaders of every generation. Inhabitants of small rural farm communities, as well as Communist leaders like Zhou Enlai, have displayed subtlety and moderation in manner according to the recorded teachings of Confucius and his followers." Robert assumed the pace and attitude of a history instructor as he continued, "Zhou was arguably the only unblemished popular hero in the Communist Party. He believed China's destiny was to re-emerge as a world power...driven by internal energy. He once remarked, 'Faraway waters cannot put out fires.' He was not a murderer like Mao."

The Asian Room librarian whose family still resided in the southern Autonomous Region of Guangxi, overheard Robert's diatribe and felt obligated to enhance his comments.

"Confucius didn't foresee the 100 million 'ghosts-in-the-cities,' who migrate from poor villages in Hunan, Sichuan and non-coastal provinces, and slave in the southern factories; or build the skyscrapers and infrastructure of China's modernized cities," she remarked sharply, her breath an audible intake of released anxiety which stilted her inhaling response. Gatt was surprised at the attractive middle-aged Asian's vehement tone.

Robert retorted, "It's true. Dislocated rural migrants drive the nation's dynamic economic growth. That's the reason the government has forced hundreds of millions of rural peasants to relocate to the cities."

Thinking of her own family's experience, the librarian added mournfully, "They're barely treated as human beings by wealthy city inhabitants and government authorities."

Justin turned his head side-to-side as the two 'Overseas Chinese' parroted each other's contemptuous mockings. Robert shrugged, "The unemployed wander in back-alleys and *hutongs* in the city in search of new jobs. Many live in poverty worse than at the villages they abandoned...for the promise of a more prosperous life in the urban areas."

Justin suddenly realized that he had a frightening lack of knowledge about the inhabitants of the country he was about to be deposited in for several weeks. There was scarcely time to prepare for the dubious and dangerous mission Balzerini had referred to as *an up-coming adventure*.

Strangely, Tom Blackstone had minimized the importance of Gatt's preparation to gather information for the FFF contract, and report on Chinese business practices. Balzerini worried intensely. Less so when he learned that Justin possessed a photographic memory and could speed-read almost as rapidly as the legendary inventor Thomas Edison, who claimed that copious reading was the secret to his successful discoveries of the light-bulb, motion pictures, dictaphone, electricity generation and distribution, and myriad other inventions developed at his Menlo Park labs in New Jersey---the first applied industrial research facility in the world.

Justin would have to rely on books and periodicals to enhance his limited knowledge of China before departing with the trade mission in a few days.

The small, pretty Asian librarian, name-tagged Annie Chu Smith, recognized Robert immediately. The embassy intern was fascinated with the immense collection of Asian books and manuscripts occupying the Asian Room at the Jefferson Building. Robert used much of his free time to read about the remarkable exploits of the Chinese Emperors of the Han, Tang, Ming and Chin dynasties, who unified China, built the Great Wall, the Grand Canal and ultimately created the only survivor of the great early civilizations---leaving behind Mesopotamia, Egypt, Greece and Rome in the shadows of history. China was re-emerging as a world power in the 21st century.

Annie was an excitable, former Beijing opera performer who married an American professor of ancient history at George Washington University. She was content in her job and resigned to a dull married life with a man who was happier living in the past than in the present. She thought Robert Changhui was cute.

She enjoyed helping him find old trade agreements and treaties. Robert loved to read about the swords-for-silk deals the Mongol Yuan Dynasty negotiated with Marco Polo in the 13th century; and the bargains the Ming emperors struck with the Portuguese, Spanish, Dutch and English in later centuries. Chinese history darkened when the British conquered Shanghai to protect the opium trade in the 1800s, opening the country's east and south coasts to further interference from western foreigners.

Annie lifted the pile of books and periodicals stacked on her desk and dumped them in Robert's arms. She was attracted to him, even though he was *another* educated man seemingly more interested in the past than the present. Perhaps---like her husband---Robert was a disciple of the great statesman Winston Churchill, the bi-polar overachiever who believed that history foretold the future---and only a fool ignored lessons of the past. Annie remembered that the World War II hero once grated, "Democracy is the worst system of government, except for all the others."

"The Ambassador requested Chinese periodicals…translated into English, of course," she exclaimed pertly. "He allowed my discretion in choosing the hard-covered books." She glanced up at the tall, handsome American with the deep blue eyes.

"You must be Mr. Gatt?"

Justin nodded dreamily. He was enthralled with the stacks of rare and ancient books piled neatly on the endless rows of shelves. The collection represented a massive depository of Asian knowledge he never expected would be residing in the United States.

"These are for you, Mr. Gatt. Please ask any questions that come to mind. The Ambassador asked me to choose a combination of current statistics, important events from the last few decades, and historical highlights dating back several centuries." She smiled as Robert struggled with the pile of publications weighing down his arms.

"I believe the publications Robert is holding contain enough information to present a meaningful reflection of China's past and present society."

Gatt was still transfixed by the rows of Asian publications organized on dark wood shelves running the length of the Jefferson Building's south wall. "It seems you have an enormous collection to choose from. I wish I had more time to study Chinese culture in depth."

Robert said softly, "Much of the collection results from the exchange program initiated by the Library of Congress and the National Library of Beijing in 1979."

Robert carried *China, Inc* by T.C.Fishman; *Statistical Yearbooks on International Trade and Hardgoods Manufacturing*, and *The Cambridge History of China,* to a reading table at the far end of the enormous room. "We have more than 800,000 publications, including 2,000 rare books and manuscripts, and a Buddhist sutra printed in 975 A.D.", remarked Annie "It's the largest collection of Asian literature outside China."

Justin was still struggling with the concept that he'd actually been recruited as an international intelligence agent---a *spy*. At least that was how he romanticized the assignment from Ambassador Balzerini. A *spy,* about to embark on a perilous clandestine mission for the U.S. Embassy in China. The Ambassador *himself* had recruited him.

Was he now, unofficially, a CIA field officer? Well-informed people believed that *all* embassies in the world are fronts for foreign intelligence groups, like the CIA, Britain's M16 and Mossad. He had no training...no security clearance, other than Eric Syzmansky's assurance to the Ambassador that he was a loyal American who could be trusted. His level of incredulity lessened a few notches when he read Joanna Yates's urgent e-mail message. FBI agents were inquiring about him from several former GRT employees. They'd even visited Cosimo at Elim Park.

What have I gotten into? His sense of patriotism bickered contentiously with a persistent sense of foreboding. Logic arbitrated the conflict. *Calm down. You've only been asked to act as a conduit for information. You don't have to fight or kill anyone. You're traveling with diplomatic immunity. How dangerous can that be?*

Robert led him to a cubicle in a far corner of the Asian room housing a work-table and an internet-connected computer terminal. "I have to leave for an appointment, Justin. You can connect to the web here. Check your e-mail if you wish. Annie can help you find just about anything on the internet. She's a search expert, as well as an authority on Chinese history. Ask her about the Han Dynasty period. That was the first united Chinese civilization--- about the time of Jesus Christ...sometime between 200 BC and 20 AD."

Robert brushed a warm kiss against Annie's porcelain cheek and rushed out. Justin noticed her touch the cheek, then tenderly tap her fingers on lips suddenly made liquescent with a hasty application of plum lip-gloss.

The message from Lynne on his seldom-used alternate e-mail address was alarming. *"Don't discuss this with anyone. I believe we're being monitored on all phones. Don't know why. Say nothing about our inquiry re: strange financial dealings between FFF, BoxMart and Residents bank. This morning I found another link between the ABOVE and a bank in Geneva with subs in the Cayman Islands. All of them do business with BoxMart and three large Chinese state-controlled banks---IN US DOLLARS ONLY. Have called my old roomy whose father is high mucky Swiss bank-examiner in Geneva. YES! I'M COMING TO THE FORMAL. We have much to discuss in Bean-town tomorrow a.m. Yours* indeedly, L.

(P.S.---*e-mail me when you read this message. I desperately need to know what to wear for the formal.*

Justin hit the "Reply" key and began typing, *"Got your message at 11am from terminal in L.O.C./Jefferson. Still here. Will be in Boston tomorrow am as scheduled. Be careful. Internet searches can be traced. Suggest you abort info-DIGS post-haste. Suggest you wear semi-formal evening-DIGS…will be suits and fancy dresses I'm told.*

Indeedly yours, J.

(P.S.---*Have reserved room for you at Hotel Monaco one night. Do you want to stay another until I wing to Beijing?*

July 31, 10am,
GHP, Boston

Groggy from lack of sleep, Justin stepped from the elevator and immediately noticed Lynne huddling with Madelaine in his office. Lynne saw him as he approached and whispered something to Madelaine, who immediately returned to her desk.

"What's up?" he inquired, noticing the troubled expression on Madelaine's face as she passed by silently.

"Nothing much," Lynne answered, a bit rushed. "I just want to go over the new business plan before you leave for China. It sounds so exciting." Her cautious gaze projected a different message. She handed him a folded hand-written note.

Justin glanced casually at the note and nodded. "No problem." He crumpled the note and put it in his pocket.

They talked in muted generalities about the wonderful support FFF and G.H. Paladin were providing the new business venture, including the initial $100,000 funding. And how the money would be used for legal fees and a new company brochure to display the proprietary products AmerAgain, LLC would offer. Brad arrived a few minutes later and was immediately pirouetted back to the elevator. They led him from the building before he had a chance to explain why he was late; and eased him into the nearest cab on Huntington Ave.

"Drive to the Ritz-Carlton across from the swan boats, please," Lynne directed the driver. "And kill some time by circling around Newbury Street a few times. We're early for lunch."

Lynne held up her everyday Seiko as they drove in silence. They'd have about ninety minutes before being missed at the office. She was squeezed pleasantly in the middle of the back seat, between the warmth of the two attractive men dominating her recent thoughts. There was something sinous about the light pressure from their thighs; a sort of mildly-sexual communication which negated the layers of clothing. The contact was both appropriate and inappropriate.

She felt low-voltage seep from Justin and Brad's pants, then penetrate her hosiery and dance up and down the excited skin of her thighs. She involuntarily spread her legs slightly and felt both men respond with returned pressure. They looked out the window impassively, holding their breath and gazing at anything else, but thinking of nothing else.

"We have an hour to decide what to do. I think we can talk freely," she exhaled.

"What's this all about?" Brad asked. "Why'd you practically carry me out of the office?"

Justin locked eyes with Lynne. His response was impatient. "Lynne suspects that our office phones are bugged. Same with her apartment."

The taxi turned onto Dartmouth Street and headed for Back Bay, then took a left turn on fashionable Newbury Street and circled around the Prudential Center before pulling into the Ritz-Carlton-Boston parking garage across from the swan boats in the Public Garden. Lines of people were waiting for a ride on the famous swan boats; a Boston icon as recognizable as Fenway Park. Justin didn't notice the late-model tan pick-up truck, indistinguishable in the heavy traffic, except for the dark-tinted windows and dinner-plate short-range listening antenna attached to a swivel mechanism on the roof. The vehicle had followed him from the airport to the Prudential Center, and was now tailing the taxi to the entrance of the hotel garage.

Harley Hedge had wasted no time in assigning his best man to follow Justin Gatt. The private detective was assigned to acquire details of the petroleum recovery technology referred to in the phone conversation between Hurricane and Gatt from her apartment. He'd followed the recently recruited FFF consultant from the minute he arrived at Logan Airport in Boston.

Blackstone needed to know if Gatt was more of an enigma than McGill anticipated. The recorded phone conversation mentioned pending patents, and a new low-cost process to recover bitumen from tar sands.

Hedge saw no reason to panic. Any new technological threat to the supply-and-demand monopoly wielded by Richard's friends in the fossil fuels industry would take a decade to commercialize. Still, the group was hyper-sensitive about quickly gaining control of any new technology that could upset the oil cartel's manipulation of pump prices.

The mid-summer sun scorched their lotionless faces as the swan boat eased forward on the pond. They floated gracefully under a small pedestrian bridge---powered by the long legs of the silver-haired captain in the pony-tail, chewing on a premium cigar stub.

Lynne said nonchalantly, as the boat was momentarily shaded by the underside of the stone bridge, "Madelaine arrived at the office at 6 a.m.today, to type the final business plan. She wanted to leave a few hours early to attend her son's Little League playoff game." Both men nodded their approval.

"She saw Holly at my office computer when she arrived, and ducked into a supply closet, which had a clear view of my desk." Justin flinched as the bright sun reappeared on the other side of the bridge, and the surprising statement sunk in.

"Holly was rushing to copy files and cookies of my recent e-mails and internet searches, judging from the handful of discs she was feeding and extracting from the computer's CD-RW drive. Fortunately, I used my Harvard friend's laptop to send yesterday's e-mail to you in D.C." She faced Justin. "I used only the computer terminal at Baker to search for incriminating business data."

Brad met Justin's alarmed expression. "If they're watching that closely, Blackstone and McGill must have a different motivation than helping us salvage the five businesses. I wonder if they really want AmerAgain to get off the ground?"

"You think they'd give us $100,000 just to knock us off track?" Justin said crisply.

"Well," Lynne replied as she folded her hands to her mouth, "it's a drop in the bucket compared with the $5 million monthy deposits FFF receives from BoxMart...for whatever services they provide."

None of them returned to the office.

Lynne decided to join Justin on the 5 pm shuttle to Washington, and rushed back to her apartment to pack. She'd meet Justin at the airport. Brad decided to fly to New York to meet with an old friend working for one of the aggressive venture capital funds still backing new technologies. He'd alluded to the enormous financial upside of Gatt's petroleum-recovery technology and patents. Brad was also assigned to open a bank account and deposit the FFF check as soon as possible.

Justin called Cosimo and Joanna, and told them for the first time that he was traveling to China in a few days...and would be away for up to five weeks. Joanna promised to look in on Cosimo regularly. "He's still spry enough to entertain his harem," she said, wishing that she was the sole member of Justin's own concubine collection.

"Will I see you when you return?"

"Of course, Jo. I'll miss you and the girls." It came out so naturally that both of them were surprised.

"Be careful in China, Justin. I read there are lots of riots and police crackdowns...with the influx of foreigners and media for the Olympics."

Justin packed clothing and cosmetics and called Ken Levine from his apartment. Ken was in court, but he left a message: "Ken, this is Justin Gatt. Sorry I missed you. Brad Stalker will be sending you a check for AmerAgain,LLC start-up costs. We're also seeking back-up financing for the new venture. We have enough money from FFF to pay all legal and patent registration fees. Brad and Lynne will be your primary AmerAgain contacts for the next several weeks. I'll be in China."

CHAPTER 32

(JULY 31, 2008)
BOXMART HDGTRS, MASS.

Jake Kurancy and Hieronimus Cashman were elated at the latest print-out from the 3P-BIO supercomputer. The two-inch thick report in the chairman's grasp listed only the *categories* of information collected. A full printout of the data would fill BoxMart's subterranean conference room. It was the most extensive consumer database ever compiled.

"Of the six billion people living on this planet," Kurancy boasted from his office, which occupied the entire top floor of the BoxMart headquarters building, "we've collected information on the buying habits of nearly the entire populations of the U.S., Canada, Japan, most of Europe and pockets of Asia and South America. More than 55 percent of all consumer spending in the world!"

Cashman shook his head in amazement. "Kapeed succeeded in accessing public and private records of more than two billion consumers."

"If we use this information effectively," Kurancy added, "BoxMart will capture the bulk of the fast-growing global web-retailing business."

Cashman lifted the top sheet from the report and handed it to Kurancy. "These are the data sources Kapeed tapped." He watched as the enormous bald-headed man read the list open-mouthed. "Pandlidesh's group acquired these sources legally?" His sly grin invited no reply.

"Or, otherwise."

The cover page was titled, "Sources of Structured Data." The report referenced customer records the 3P-BIO had queried using a powerful enterprise-search software capable of extracting *meanings* from large data sets.

The agencies and private entities queried were involved in: consumer credit ratings; motor vehicle licensing; tax collection; law enforcement; Social Security (and foreign equivalents); banking and money handling; credit card processing; telephone communication ; internet provider services; three levels of government census taking; intelligence records and stockholder communications services for multi-national corporations. The 3P-BIO was programmed to connect several disparate data sets, then search the compiled databases for specific information on each person listed. The final result was an uncanny, accurate profile of a person's buying habits and tendencies.

"About a quarter of the data was purchased from third-party telemarketing companies eager to sell their 'confidential' customer information," Cashman explained to his boss. "The balance came from public information sources readily available on the worldwide web, or from other confidential lists." His sideways glance suggested to Kurancy that more data was taken from confidential sources than Cashman was willing to admit.

He remembered Kapeed's theory that a supercomputer could eventually penetrate any database firewall, by continuously bombarding its spyware protection with slightly-modified clones of its self-altering search-algorithms. By learning from a trillion rejected attempts to penetrate the spyware, with each rejection accompanied by automatic micro-altering of the attack software, the 3P-BIO's relentless assault would eventually detect a digital side-door opening, and allow Kapeed's data-extraction program to slither in like a ravenous electronic eel, cathoding bits of positive-charged data, then slithering out to a memory bank.

Apparently his theory worked.

The break-through self-altering software Kapeed copied from the Lawrence Livermore Labs, and modified for his own purposes, was more powerful than he anticipated.

It had been developed by the nation's elite programmers...on loan from top technical universities...for the top-secret SDMTDS Pentagon Project. Closer to human intelligence than any software he'd ever observed---the logic module for the Space Deployed Missile Tracking and Defense System could also be applied to enterprise-data search systems. The guided navigation tools for ballistic flight corrections could locate and collate data scattered among numerous server-controlled data centers.

The high-speed laser printer in Kurancy's office suddenly hummed a warning that it was about to regurgitate the daily BoxMart financial reports. Cashman had seen some of the financial information earlier in the day when his regional controller in California faxed week-ending P&L and balance sheets for the West Coast store group. Kurancy snatched the first print-out and thumbed through several pages of net-profit tabulations for various store groups.

"The west-coast stores missed their net-profit targets last week... by a troubling amount," Kurancy complained. "Our cash position has also deteriorated substantially." He didn't have to ask the CFO for an explanation.

Cashman smiled as if he'd hidden one of Jake's beloved raw oysters behind his back.

"It's only a blip in the reporting system, Jake. Kapeed made some program changes when we matched Wal-Mart's western U.S. sales last month...*for the first time.*" Kurancy's dream was beginning to become tangible. "Actual profits were ten percent higher than predicted," Cashman announced proudly.

"Why the reporting changes?" Kurancy inquired in an irritated tone. He frequently approved accounting 'adjustments' in quarterly profit reports to avoid paying higher corporate taxes. Usually by writing down the value of slow-moving inventory. BoxMart managers were instructed to demand vendor markdowns of 10-15 percent for slow-moving merchandise, or end business relationships with vendors that refused to comply.

But the massive inventory build-up of winter-holiday goods being shipped from LCE factories to BoxMart warehouses were booked at cost. Cash reserves had deteriorated rapidly as BoxMart met its obligation to pay LCE invoices in 45 days. Kurancy would have to renegotiate longer payments terms with his partner in the Bomali joint-venture.

"It's because of Cusson's new demand for immediate dollar transfers to his Franco-Medici subsidiary in Geneva," the CFO answered quickly. "Remember?"

"Yeah...we agreed to move up the schedule to transfer dollar deposits to his Geneva bank," Kurancy sulked. "Did you move the entire ten billion?"

"We depleted BoxMart's lock-box and most of our cash-flow buffer in Residents Bank Boston."

"All ten billion?"

"In a dozen separate wire transfers. Cusson just completed fifty billion in currency exchange deals with ten Euro-zone central bankers. By tomorrow morning, the BoxMart dollars in Franco-Medici Bank will be replaced with an equivalent value in euros and swiss francs. We'll then wire-transfer five-hundred million dollars worth of euros to the Bomali start-up account at the People's Bank of China branch in Macau . They'll convert the euros to yuans."

Cashman had only been informed about the *financial* elements of the Savoy Imperative, after the other members reluctantly granted approval. He'd accepted Jake's dubious explanation for the odd movements of money and inventory within the BoxMart retailing system. He was worried that the heavy pre-season stocking of holiday merchandise, and the large initial capitalization of the Bomali, LLC joint-venture would create cash-flow problems.

Cashman never hesitated to act forcefully when Kurancy demanded extended payment terms from suppliers. "I guess Li Chin and General Ye will have to wait a few days longer for the next payments to their state-run factories."

The chairman snorted belligerently, "They can afford to wait. Yong Ihasa, the Vice Premier in charge of China's foreign reserves, controls more U.S. dollars than he knows what to do with. The Politboro members are experts in leveraging China's purchases of U.S. treasury bonds against White House complaints that China has too large a trade surplus with the United States."

Cashman shrugged impatiently and replied, "I understand a substantial portion of the trade imbalance is used to buy military hardware and smart weapons technology from Russia, France and international arms dealers."

Kurancy folded an arm across his chest and a hand over his mouth. He stared silently at the trusted employee for an uncomfortable several seconds.

It was normal for the chairman to hold back information. But Cashman didn't trust Li Chin and General Ye. They'd be controlling Bomali's manufacturing operations on a day-to-day basis.

"Jake...you revealed to me only a few details of the Savoy plan; but I've been thinking." He stood from his chair and paced the large office, subconsciously moving closer to the exit door. "Now don't get pissed, but I think the Chinese partners have positioned LCE to dominate the Bomali joint venture." He'd studied the governance and profit-distribution clauses in the merger agreements Kurancy was about to sign in Macau.

Kurancy folded both arms across his massive stomach and leaned back on the double-sized executive chair. "What do you mean?"

"It seems to me that all the BoxMart and LCE revenues will be funneled into Macau, and redistributed to BoxMart and LCE operating entities."

"That's the initial plan; to take advantage of the new zero-income-tax law."

Cashman hesitated to structure his next comment. "Does the Chinese government still control banking in Macau? I read that President Mu Jianting's regime has positioned its own people in key government posts."

Kurancy smiled roguishly. "It wasn't Mu who appointed the Macau governor and finance minister...it was Yong Ihasa."

"What else don't I know about this deal?"

"Enough so my nuts won't get ripped off and stuffed in my mouth before I disappear." The CFO stopped in his tracks and replied nervously, "You think they had something to do with Trenker's shooting?"

Kurancy's face whitened and his arrogant expression morphed to one of uncertainty. "I don't want you to ask that question…ever again."

He motioned for Cashman to return to his seat and said in a firm voice, "Upcoming events may never be explained to you. Just go along. It will be more financially rewarding …and healthier for both of us." He deftly changed the subject. "Let's review the marketing plans for region-specific sales items."

The CFO was happy to discuss new successes. "You won't believe this, but the hottest regional product we have is a carved hickory branch the Winnebago Indians in Nebraska and South Dakota call the 'calendar stick."

The chairman's amazing memory for product detail kicked in. "I read about the item in a lengthy article on native American crafts and artifacts in National Geographic Magazine. It's about a yard long and has four sides carved with astronomical observations that allowed the tribe to calculate time."

Cashman snickered boastfully, "We've been buying them from a small craft business on the Winnebago reservation near Sioux City, Iowa, which also produces Ho-Chunk love charms, Buffalo headdresses and almanac sticks they call 'fingers of the sun.' Since the National Geographic article, the calendar sticks…which were created thousands of years ago and are supposed to be the most accurate calendars ever developed in North America…have been flying off the shelves at Iowa, Nebraska, Colorado and South Dakota stores. They're also the most popular and profitable craft item we sell on the internet.

"Can the Indian reservation factory meet demand?"

"So far. But they're struggling to increase capacity. Rather than help them out financially, we decided to send production samples to Alicia Wang and have LCE duplicate the calendar stick at the Nanjing factory. We'll soon cancel orders with the Native American crafts factory. The Winnebago tribe won't be happy, but there's nothing they can do about it."

Kurancy added, "If we decide to promote the product nationally, they won't be able to meet the demand."

"We're planning to feature the item in back-to-school promotions," Cashman recalled.

The big man barked, "A perfect example of why small American manufacturing businesses should be shut down!"

Geneva, Switzerland

The last unhappy Euro-zone finance minister agreed to trade five billion in sterling and euros for the U.S. dollars Cusson was apparently dumping on him and nine other European central bankers. In less-than-transparent deals totaling fifty billion, the U.S. dollar trades of Cusson's Geneva subsidiary, the Franco-Medici Trust, would be hidden for a few weeks in accounts with serial codes...referencing other serial codes...which referenced more serial codes.

Eventually the trades would be detected and reported to the World Bank by TRACFIN, the French financial intelligence unit. The Fed's representative on the World Bank governing board would immediately forward the information to chairman Tangus. Not technically a law enforcement entity, the *Traitement du Renseignement et Action Contre les Circuits Financiers Clandestins* tracked money-laundering for drug traffickers, organized crime and terrorists. Even the Swiss authorities who allowed Geneva-based operations of Citigroup and JP Morgan to operate in virtual autonomy from U.S.government scrutiny, would eventually acknowledge the *SAR* suspicious-activity report.

The accompanying *CTR* cash transaction report would reveal the large dollar blocks traded by Franco-Medici Trust in a two-day period.

The pin-striped clerk led the Spanish finance minister from Cusson's small private office at the Franco-Medici to the underground vault that held a third of the world's illegally-derived private wealth in safe-deposit boxes marked with three serial numbers.

"The numbers match exactly, sir."

The Spaniard remained close-lipped and nodded for the clerk to insert the three 18-carat solid-gold keys and extract the sealed stainless-steel rectangular box. The clerk then escorted him to a private viewing room which could be locked only from the inside.

A bottle of Cristal Rose was set in an insulated lead-glass bucket on the table...opened and temporarily capped for easy pouring. The million in cash was all there. He removed ten stacks of hundreds, slid them into his empty briefcase and twirled the combination lock. After a sip from the champagne bottle he decided to head for *Velvet,* the outrageously costly nightclub which no longer allowed women customers. Too many wives were wrenching their husbands away from the Russian and Bulgarian girls.

The taxi drove past the Fusterie Temple, erected from marble in 1715 as the first Calvinist Cathedral. He'd heard from a friend at the Geneva-based European branch of the United Nations that expatriate oil-traders maintained offices in the church.

Geneva is a city built on numbers, Cusson mused, as he dialed Bromine in Macau. *Individuals are free to manage their assets away from the prying eyes of government.* His brilliant plan to trade more than a hundred billion U.S. dollars for other currencies through Franco-Medici Trust...in a matter of weeks...now had an impressive beginning. As soon as the Chinese moved another fifty billion of their dollar reserves into F-M, the funds would be wired to Creditte Bank de Savoy in Lyons. He'd wait for the *other events* to occur before dumping the balance on the world market. By September 30, the world would be a different place.

Federal Reserve Bank Chairman John Paul Tangus would soon be scratching his head. His Open Market Committee would find it impossible to respond without upsetting the U.S. economy even further.

China

"Cusson has completed the first phase of the European dollar transactions," Emerson Bromine informed Yong Ihasa and General Ye on the secure line to Zhangnanhai. "It's time to move the dollars held in the China Monetary Reserves Bank and Beijing-Shanghai Central Development Bank into the People's Bank of China branch in Macau. I'll tap Bomali's operating balance there for an additional few hundred million and wire-transfer the dollars to Creditte Bank de Savoy."

Vice-Premier Ihasa had already instructed the Governor of the People's Bank of China to initiate the planned money transfers. It was now up to General Ye to do his part.

"We should watch Mr. Bromine more closely," Ihasa decided, after the call from the new Bomali office in Bromine's Macau casino building. "He's becoming more aggressive in our dealings."

"That's the reason we reassigned Wen Ma Ming to represent China's interests in the joint venture. Bromine has to answer to a balanced board of directors from BoxMart and LCE; but Wen Ma answers to me."

"General, I want you to accelerate the schedule of the *events*.

"As you direct, Premier Yong."

Ye Kunshi expected to soon replace the aging Marshal Tong Shu as commander of the People's Liberation Army, and earn a permanent position on the Standing Committee of the Chinese Communist Party. He'd soon control virtually all the PLA armed forces. "I shall do so from a more private communications line at the Defense Ministry. The human assets staged in Belize and Mexico are ready to cross the borders at my command. The pathogens are waiting in a sealed trailer at the BoxMart warehouse in Eagle Pass, Texas. The migrants will deliver the *water filters and water treatment chemicals* to the target locations. With luck, the mortar shells filled with the corn-virus will be exploded over the early corn crop in western Iowa before the conclusion of the Beijing Olympics."

Ihasa lowered his eyelids and savored the summer fragrances riding a warm wind from the Forbidden City gardens through the opened window of his second floor Zhangnanhai office. The sweet aromatic scents reminded him of the elaborate gardens built for Mao's wife at the Bedaihe resort villa... soon to become the new center of power in China.

He returned to a sense of the present, and said to Ye Kunshi, his closest collaborator, "Chairman Chang Hui Chen of the National People's Congress, and Minister of Industry and Trade, Wang Chao....will remind the Americans at the upcoming trade-negotiations that the Chinese government is becoming less enthusiastic about purchasing U.S. treasury bonds. We do not appreciate the increasing protectionist rhetoric in America. At least President Mu has agreed with this approach, although for a far different reason than ours."

CHAPTER 33

(July 31, 2008)
Belize City

The captain of the tender *Dashing Kaleidoscope* eased the forty-foot motor launch through the thin channel cut into the longest barrier reef in the Western Hemisphere, which extended a few miles seaward from the east coast of Belize, along the entire 180 mile Caribbean coastline of the only English-speaking nation in Central America.

The passengers being transferred from the cruise ship to Belize City, for an afternoon of touring ancient Mayan sites and caves, had no idea that the friendly four-man crew of the aluminum-hulled tender would soon be standing in Iowa cornfields, preparing to explode canisters of deadly pathogen into the winds fanning steadily over western Iowa's early corn crop.

After docking passengers, the raw-boned captain with permanently-tanned skin and a black Rasputin beard covering his face and framing menacing ebony eyes, assembled the crew in the interior of the helm.

"Instructions have finally been received from Bekasi," he said, referring to the Triad safe-house in a suburb of Jakarta where General Ye Kunshi's contact resided. "It's time to move." The captain reached under the duct-tape covered steering wheel to a locked compartment and rotated the brass key. He removed a large black plastic garbage bag with red pull-strings tightly tied, and handed it to the first mate.

"Budi will lead…as planned," he reminded the others. "Joko, Danang and Muslihrama …you will do as Budi commands. The flight from Belize City aboard Mr. Sing's double-prop will land you in Matamoros, Mexico by midnight. Tomorrow you cross the border into Brownsville, Texas."

Budi, the tallest of the four-man crew from Indonesia at five-foot three inches, tore open the garbage bag and pulled out a large Jaguar-skin duffel bag.

The captain barked gruffly, "Everything you need is in there: passports, visas, drivers' licenses, pesos, dollars and back-up false identification…in case there are problems with your regular identifications. You are all Mexican migrant workers, employed by the Matamoros Seasonal Harvesting Company."

Budi, a twenty-five year old artillery expert trained by the Indonesian separatist group Jemaah Islamiyad, pulled open the tie-strings of the genuine-fur bag made from a poucher's illegal Belizean jaguar kill. "How will we make contact with the ones delivering the canisters to the prearranged site?" he asked in a stilted tone.

"The instructions are in the bag," the captain snapped, "along with maps showing the routes from Brownsville… north to San Antonio; and then on to Oklahoma City, Wichita, Omaha and finally to Sioux City, Iowa. A rusty 1993 blue Mercury station wagon registered in your Mexican name will be waiting in a parking lot on the Texas side of the border."

The captain turned to the other three 'migrant workers' and declared authoritatively, "Budi will be the only one who knows the transfer location, until the team is fully assembled; for security." He scowled deeply and warned, "If we bungle this job, the Jakartan Triad will see that we spend the rest of our sure-to-be-shortened lifetimes in Jerusalem with the above-ground caskets and giant swamp mosquitos."

He was alluding to the ultra-poverty section of Belize City where the poorest citizens lived on small patches of government-donated land…set like tiny islands on insect and lizard-infested swampland…devoid of running water, electricity and toilet facilities. The boggy muck surrounding the dry patches smaller than a single-car garage, was ten inches below sea level, and permanently wet. In any other civilized country, this land would be deemed uninhabitable.

The poorest Belizeans could only access their make-shift huts by building 'bridges,' made from extra pieces of plywood, sheet metal and split logs not used for the porous roofs and semi-enclosed walls of the huts. The 'bridges' were nothing more than scavenged pieces of building materials dropped in a jagged row on the slimy mud, creating a treacherously-slick walkway between the tiny plots and a dry dirt road that circumvented the above-ground concrete coffins in the surrounding cemetery area.

The smoky stench of rotting death seeped from the porous seals of the mold-encased caskets, and amalgamated repulsively with the acrid vapors of decaying fungus and boiling chicken feet. The olfactory confrontation was never to be forgotten by a visitor to Jerusalem.

"I'd rather live on a raft anchored to the stalagmites 400 feet below the surface of the *Blue Hole*, and dive for bonefish to live on," exclaimed Joko. The famous 1,000 foot wide water-filled shaft formed thousands of years ago on the Lighthouse Atoll beyond the barrier reef, offered an incredible diving experience.

"Do your job well and there will be plenty of rewards," the captain answered with a softer tone. He'd been promised a new contract as the preferred tender service to transport passengers to the town dock from the Royal Caribbean and Princess cruise ships anchored outside the barrier reef. He'd soon be able to finance the sixty-foot tender he dreamed of---which he'd call the *Feisty Rainbow*. He reminded himself that the assignment from Bekasi was not all up-side. Each crewman's family in Jakarta would be visited by a ruthless agent from the Jemaah Islamiyah, if the Iowa fields were not successfully infected with the dusty material in the canisters.

Nuevo Loredo, Mexico; Eagle Pass, Texas

Crossing the border was a joke. The U.S. border guard on the American side of the international bridge spanning the Rio Grande River connecting Nuevo Loredo, Mexico and Loredo, Texas, swiped his eyes over the migrant worker's papers, glanced inside the late-model Corolla with the Texas license plate to confirm there were only two migrants in the vehicle, and waved the car into United States territory as casually as if he was directing traffic in a Disney World parking lot.

Nearly twenty-thousand Mexicans entered the U.S. each day across the international bridge. Most returned at night from vegetable farms with Texas dirt under their fingernails.

The two Indonesians from Ambon Island, the break-away province in the east Indonesia archipelago learned Spanish, English and terrorist tactics at Yemen University. They drove the compact car to the *Travel Center of America* truck-stop at exit 13 on Route I-35 in Loredo, and parked next to a 24 foot hunter-green van with white lettering indicating the truck was owned by the Farm Supplies Distribution Company of Wichita, Kansas. They left the keys on the front seat and entered the restaurant for a buffet dinner of soggy fried chicken, fat-laden barbeque ribs, macaroni and cheese as thick as spackling paste and creamed corn too watery to eat with a fork.

When they returned to the parking lot, the Corolla had disappeared. The green van was unlocked, as expected, with the keys tucked behind the sun visor. The diesel fuel-tank was topped off. Folded bills-of-lading and other official papers were stuffed into the glove compartment, authorizing the van to pick up several cartons of 'water filters' and 'fertilizer dispensing equipment' from a BoxMart warehouse in Texas... and deliver the goods to a BM Supercenter in Sioux City, Iowa.

The 100 mile drive northwest along the Rio Grande River basin to the distribution center in Eagle Pass, Texas, took less than two hours. At nine p.m., as instructed, the driver pulled the green van into dock number 20 at the far end of the building and presented the shipping papers to the only employee present in the dock area.

The shift supervisor, attired in a short-sleeve dress shirt and tie, followed orders exactly as he'd received them from the home office. He jumped on a propane-powered pallet truck and loaded four shrink-wrapped 48-by-48 inch pallets of *water filters* and *fertilizer dispensing pumps* into the nose of the van. He double-checked the barcodes and RFID identification and tracking labels on the four skids against the slip of paper he received in a fax from the office. He then loaded four inflatable air-mattresses, a small white plastic patio table with four chairs, a self-contained portable potty and two 70-quart ice chests onto the back end.

The driver of the van scrawled an illegible signature at the bottom of the shipping documents, slammed down the rear door, engaged the lock-clip and secured the contents of the van with a heavy-duty combination lock. The night supervisor attached an RFID security seal to the clip-lock, and watched as the green van pulled away. He tapped a red button and the last dock door on the most isolated side of the warehouse lowered electrically. The strange agricultural pathogen would be in San Antonio two days before the four migrant workers arrived in Matamoros and crossed the border into Brownsville.

The plan was to rendezvous in San Antonio, drive the van non-stop on Route 35 north to Topeka, Kansas…then cross over to Route 29 and complete the final leg of the trip to Onawa and Sioux City, Iowa. The driver and his assistant from Nuevo Loredo would alternate at the wheel, and pass fast food and beer to the others hiding in the back, through an opening concealed behind the passenger seat. The GPS chip in the radio-frequency clip-lock seal would signal BoxMart headquarters when the seal was broken.

Cambridge, Mass.

Her clothes were packed, including the new $800 Caroline Hererra strapless gold peau-de-soie cocktail dress and matching cross-strap heels. The try-on mirror at the dress shop had highlighted the thin band of gold and emerald beading sewn across the bodice of the dress. It traced her stirring cleavage perfectly.

Every man at the Washington formal would be challenged not to divert his gaze from her hypnotic iridescent eyes to the equally hypnotic attraction of the pillowy bust-tops peeking seductively above the plunging neckline. She chose the dress color to match the genuine-emerald chandelier earrings and the gold Rolex her parents gave her when she graduated from Harvard Business School.

The taxi pulled up in front of her apartment at exactly 4 pm, as Justin promised. The shuttle from Logan to Dulles would become airborne in two hours…just enough time to pass through the new check-in procedure, which fell a few undergarments short of a strip-search.

The old man in the lime sweat-suit watched from a deep-cushioned chair in the small lobby of the apartment building, reading the help-wanted section of the Boston Globe. When Justin pressed the 'up' button, he dropped the paper onto a side table and immediately hobbled to the elevator door…just in time to follow him in. He'd recognized Ms. Hurricane's *older* friend.

"Are you visiting Ms. Hurricane?"

Justin responded in a friendly tone, "You must be Mr. Barnswig. Lynne tells me your always watching our for her."

The old man smiled, and whispered in confidence, "She reminds me of my first daughter from my third wife. I have six daughters, no sons and one grandson."

Justin gaped as the man added, "Or is it my third daughter from my second wife?"

The old gentleman followed Justin to Lynne's door, waited for him to knock, then said contritely, "I have something important to tell her."

Lynne was surprised to see them both at the door. She noticed the impatience on Justin's face. "Mr. Barnswig, how nice to see you. I'm sorry we're in a rush to catch a plane. Is there something in particular you'd like to discuss before we rush out?"

The old man glanced at Gatt to determine if he could be trusted. He took a chance.

"Did you know that a cleaning lady was at your door a few days ago, trying to get in?"

"I don't use a cleaning service," Lynne replied hesitantly.

"She didn't follow me into the elevator when I told her that. She had a suspicious sound to her voice."

Justin glanced quizzically to Lynne. "Perhaps she just made a mistake in the room number."

"Nobody else on five uses a cleaning lady. I think she was snooping around to steal something. She didn't come down to the lobby for half-an-hour, then left through the parking lot exit. That's not all."

Lynne glanced anxiously at the Rolex she'd decided to wear, and said, "Why don't you come in."

Mr. Barnswig saw the packed suitcase and said, "This won't take long." He moved closer to Lynne and whispered, "If you want to see what the cleaning lady looks like, go down to the ice-cream shop. She's there all the time, eating weird flavors of ice-cream and playing with some kind of electronic gismo. Like the students do with their laptops."

"Thank's for the warning, Mr. Barnswig," Lynne returned his whispered, "We'll certainly check it out."

On the elevator ride down, Lynne said to Justin, "I just talked with my friend at the Harvard library. He's found a new connection. Residents Bank's Investment Trust subsidiary, located in the old Riggs Bank branch in Washington, is transferring large sums on a daily basis to a private French bank in Lyons; which just happens to be one of the original foreign lending institutions…along with the Bank of England, Rothchilds Bank and other European and American banks…that invested in the U.S. Federal Reserve banking system when it was formed in 1913. The French bank could still be involved with the Fed, but only through a limited investment in a Regional Fed Bank. It's the law."

She thought a moment, then added, "They could also be involved through a U.S. banking subsidiary of a foreign holding company."

"Could that explain why the Boston Regional Fed Bank clears large foreign wire-transfers originating from Residents Bank?" Justin inquired, as the elevator door slid open.

"If so," Lynne followed his thoughts, "the Feds would know about the plethora of bankruptcies Edwin Tinius has initiated at Residents Bank. Yet they don't seem to do or say anything about it."

"Let's check out the cleaning lady in the ice-cream parlor, before we leave," Justin said in a muted voice. "We may find a clue."

The Chameleon angrily stabbed the white plastic spoon into the mound of tequila-banana-cherry-cashew-chip ice-cream, and deftly extracted the tiny wireless earphone from her right ear, with a seemingly fretful slap to her right cheek. She then tapped a button on the Blackberry-sized electronic "game" player and flipped the cover closed. Lynne's apartment was exactly 1,645 yards from the entrance to the ice-cream shop. It would take them ten minutes

Reluctantly, she dropped the half-eaten dish into the trash receptacle near the Massachusetts Ave entrance door, and filtered into the crowd sifting around Harvard Square. She turned down Dewolfe Street a block away, and glanced around the corner in time to see Lynne and a tall, middle-aged man with sparkling blue eyes enter the store.

It was only a short walk west along the river bordering Memorial Drive to the Charles Hotel. Lynne's taxi to Logan would take a different route down Main Street, over the Longfellow Bridge into Charlestown and then over the Tobin Bridge to Logan Airport in East Boston. The tall, broad-shouldered African-American maid didn't notice the senior citizen in the lime jogging suite cut across John F. Kennedy Drive to Memorial Drive…until they nearly bumped into each other at the intersection a few hundred yards from her Charles Hotel room.

Mr. Barnswig jumped back wide-eyed, as if reaching the edge of a virulent forest-fire That's all the evidence she needed; he was following her.

Chameleon rule number one: eliminate all witnesses swiftly and cold-heartedly.

As the lime man froze in his tracks, the assassin quickly surveyed the area for pedestrian traffic on Dewolfe Street. Their side of the street was empty. Diagonally across she saw a bra-less, bust-juggling and butt-gyrating Harvard crew cockswain jogging back to Harvard Square from her Memorial Drive workout. The Chameleon dipped into her bag and extracted a blunt object small enough to hide in her palm.

Her hair is different; so is the color of her eyes. But the broad shoulders and height are the same. Barnswig said, "Excuse me madam…have we met before?"

She continued to walk deliberately in his direction, with one hand behind her back. "I don't think so. Where do you come from?"

The voice is the same, although with a stronger Asian accent. As she approached, he pointed a finger and admonished loudly, "You're the cleaning lady on floor five!" It was his last earthly outcry. The tiny syringe needle arched from behind the Chameleon's back and pierced the side of Barnswig's neck, flooding his jugular vein with concentrated *Ricin* in a jab speedier than a professional boxer's. To bystanders, it appeared that he was being slapped in the face for rudely bumping into the haggard old lady.

"You clumsy fool," she shouted, in a contemptuous voice loud enough for anyone in the vicinity to hear. She then turned briskly and walked away; leaving Mr. Barnswig stunned and immobile.

The untreatable poison, mixed with a fast-acting sedative, was derived from the waste pulp of castor beans used in making castor oil. It seeped into his blood and brain cells and began the deadly, near-instantaneous process of destroying human cells. The narcotic mixed with the Ricin accelerated the effect of the poison and left him limp. Soon, Mr. Barnswig would vomit; and struggle for a breath. Uncontrollable diarrhea would precede multiple organ failure within minutes. With no cure or antidote, the highly-concentrated injection of Ricin invading his blood and brain cells reacted the same way mad cow disease, and rogue proteins, called 'prions,' developed the deadly brain-wasting illness known as 'variant Creutzfeldt-Jacob disease.' His brain was literally disintegrating.

A full minute passed before the assassin glanced over her shoulder and saw the frozen lime man slowly crumble to his knees. A few people noticed and crossed the street to offer aid; too late to prevent his twisted and colorless face from smashing onto the concrete sidewalk.

Blackstone received an untraceable e-mail from the Chameleon before Barnswig's breathless body arrived at the Massachusetts General Hospital emergency room:

"Hurricane is net-fishing grand Banks with Crimson bait again. Is now questioning if new catch is legal. Subject found more than Ten-Thousand wires hooked together, connecting east and west-Atlantic greenback sharks... to Federal fishing Reserves in T-party region. Best fishing probably in your area for now. Soundings enclosed for examination-- per your private luring methods. Am ready to cast away when fish returns from your grounds to hubb harbor. Is weather bad enough to end fishing expedition?"

The message didn't seem cryptic enough to warrant an ultimate assault on Lynne Hurricane. Perhaps a damaging blow to ground her for a few months.

The disappointed assassin would wait for further instructions from Blackstone.

CHAPTER 34

(July 31, 2008)
Washington, D.C.

The sex was amazing...better than she ever hoped. Justin had exploded in loud gasps of pleasure, at exactly the same time her high-pitched shrill of urgency vibrated the ceiling vent housing the tiny-listening device Justin had detected using the multi-functional hand-held apparatus Ambassador Balzerini had given him.

They stood under the vent and giggled, exchanging roguish groans of exaggerated exhaustion, as they casually sipped chilled Kendall-Jackson Chardonnay in Lynne's hotel room...fully clothed.

They followed the script outlined in a hunched-over conference on the shuttle flight from Boston: check Lynne in; meet in her room...which they assumed was bugged; make violent love (Justin said 'faking' it was optional); then give out disinformation to take the pressure off Lynne while he was in China. Mr. Barnswig had frightened them both into believing that Lynne had uncovered information others didn't want revealed. Ross Trenker probably learned the hard way.

Five minutes later the listener recorded Gatt ordering rare steak dinners and a bottle of the hotel's best merlot reserve. He wondered why the couple didn't shower during the twenty minutes it took for room service to arrive.

Lynne lifted the room-temperature bottle and sang her version of the familiar Billy Joel tune , "A bottle of white....a bottle of red, always fun to follow a good tussle in bed."

"Anyone ever call you a fruitcake?"

"Noooo....just a nutcracker."

Blackstone's man thought, *She's a dirty talker...my kind of broad.* He pressed his ear closer to the receiver, and was disappointed to hear only the sounds of chomping and slurping...as the apparently famished couple devoured thick slices of filet mignon washed down with red. He imagined them slopping Hollandaise sauce over their faces and licking off the whitish-yellow drippings like horny newlyweds enjoying their first after-bliss meal. The lecherous listener was imagining butter and whipped-cream smeared bodies slipping and sliding against each other...rubbing in amorous configurations his girl-friend would never allow.

Justin chomped on a crispy roll topped with a pad of real butter, and moved under the air vent near the bathroom partition. He looked up expectantly and croaked in a dry voice, "Tell me more about your conspiracy theory. I find it fascinating... and highly improbable."

Lynne joined him at the wall, looked up and said, "What I suspected at first... is not proving to be factual." She paused to make sure the listener was listening. "Oh, honey...don't do that!NO! Do THIS!" Both of them smiled broadly as they looked into the ceiling vent, imagining a person's bulging eyes looking down from behind the grating.

"The transactions we found were perfectly normal and legal," Lynne altered her tone abruptly, as female lovers often do to throw off their partners... and keep them interested. "It's probably just a coincidence that FFF does business with the other entities," she noted seriously.

"What do you mean?" Justin played the straight man as they'd planned.

Lynne moved closer to him with her eyes on the ceiling vent. The heat radiating from the thin fabric of her black cotton Voile pull-over reminded Justin of charred embers from a newspaper used to start a log fire.

"The money transfers between FFF, Residents Bank and BoxMart were perfectly normal business transactions, as far as I can tell. There's no sense pursuing the issue. I guess my detective juices stopped flowing when we discovered Citigroup, Morgan-Chase and Bank of America also handled large money transfers between BoxMart, Residents Bank and FFF." It was true that several money-center banks conducted large transfers of funds involving BoxMart retail accounts. But the payments were always *to* BoxMart from Visa, Master Charge and other credit-card entities for purchases made by BoxMart customers.

Justin was beginning to worry. The unexpected erotic sensation he was experiencing as a result of their 'staged' sex scene... was stimulating the real thing. Caught up in the moment, he streamed devilishly, "You Harvard bitches can be dangerous. My back is torn to shreds."

Lynne looked surprised. She figured it was an ad-lib, and followed Justin's lead.

"So you've made violent love to other Crimson ladies? Eh? You Eli cad!"

"None like you, kitten. Where'd you learn that double-jointed position?"

Without hesitation, she cooed, "From a Princeton physics major. We met at a Radcliffe sorority party. *Moaner* was a student-athlete on the gymnastics team."

"I'm exhausted," Justin blurted aimlessly. The listener empathized.

"Men your age usually lack the vanity to admit it. But, don't you worry about having low energy, honey. There's still plenty of watts in your lightening-rod."

The listener grinned again. *About time...more dirty talk about how he satifies her.*

Lynne knew for sure; despite an absence of direct experience---he wanted her. Dreams of Justin frequently interrupted her sleep. They were evidence enough of his sexual prowess, although Justin had consistently resisted every chance she'd given him to take her. Even now, she was settling for dreams, as Justin somehow resisted her obvious flirtations. She'd touched his hardness. He'd eased away. In an admirable, but warped sense of chivalry, he'd mumbled something about their age difference.

Frustrated, at least for now, she'd have to settle for nocturnal imaginings. They were *vivid dreams*. So real...so orgasmic...that she was ashamed.

CHAPTER 35

(August 1, 2008)
Washington, DC

Lynne slept in while Justin headed to the FFF office for a last minute briefing by Tom Blackstone. The FFF managing partner wanted to council Gatt on the 'appropriate' procedures for conducting interviews with high-ranking Chinese representatives.

As a first-time FFF representative, Gatt was also reminded to exhibit proper respect for the federal government leaders he'd encounter tonight at the USTR reception at the Ritz-Carlton. He'd be rubbing shoulders with Butler Humphreys, Richard deLeone and several Congressmen and Senators in the crowded 2300-square-foot hotel ballroom.

Mission participants and a hundred DC dignitaries with strong interests in trade with China, would jam the reception room, alongside spouses and female escorts dressed either to dazzle...or blend unnoticeably into the crowd. Opinions would be expressed openly---*for* and *against* free-trade. Blackstone didn't want Gatt to undermine FFF's 'neutral' position by joining spirited debates supporting one or the other opposing points of view.

Martin Merrand, the Governor of New York and leading candidate for the Presidential nomination from the incumbent Administration party, would surely lead the argument *against* free-trade. His 'Selected Protectionism' ideas struck a nerve with a broad and growing constituency, sensitized by the alarming increase in joblessness and small business failures. He stated that the onerous swelling in the size of the U.S. trade deficit with China, was to many unemployed workers---a sign that their factory jobs were lost forever.

Merrand had gained the bi-partisan support of the large labor unions when he accused the Chinese-Communist regime of blatant economic aggression against American industry. The financial and political press were less sympathetic to his ideas.

Pundits influenced by the large media corporations, were split on who benefited the most from low-cost Chinese imports. Half joined the liberal national media networks in claiming that cheap Chinese imports were essential to maintaining the American standard of living. The other half decried that America's future was being destroyed by a tidal wave of imports.

FFF OFFICE, WASHINGTON

Blackstone peered down at Harley Hedge across the desk, pondering how they should approach this suddenly bothersome, previously unknown small businessman. Had Justin Gatt actually discovered a unique, inexpensively process to recover the massive oil deposits bound up in the Alberta tar sands and shale-oil fields in the Colorado Rockies?

Harley Hedge's investigator had obtained a copy of the patent just issued to Gatt. The claims described an ingenous process to separate and recover a variety of materials bound mechanically or chemically. Gatt's discovery was aimed primarily at recycling mixed plastic scrap, but the patent claims covered the separation of a broad range of tightly-bound materials. By reducing the surface-energy and attractive forces holding dissimilar organic and inorganic materials together, the process could isolate individual components.

A secondary step employed harmless bacteria to selectively break down complex molecular structures, like the viscous bitumen and kerogen derived from tar sands and oil shale. The smaller molecules were suitable for direct refining into fuels and chemical building blocks.

The fossil-fuels expert realized that the most important examples given in the disclosures and state-of-the-art sections of the patent were the use of the new technology to separate petroleum fractions from the heavy silicone and mineral matter in oil shale and tar sands. The patent claimed recovery rates of 94 to 98 percent of the bitumen and kerogen ...in pure enough form to be fed directly into distillation and cracking columns at existing refineries.

Hedge was a petroleum engineer by training; he understood the implications of the new technology. The process was credible!

"Relax, Tom," he urged Blackstone. "It would take ten years to commercialize the process. Gatt would have to raise several hundred million dollars for a highly speculative project. He couldn't even raise a million to save his own company."

"I wouldn't be so confident, Harley. This guy's put together an ingenious plan to salvage five bankrupt companies that Cashman and Tinius have tried to crush."

"If Gatt decides to attempt commercialization, we can derail any progress he makes in raising capital," Hedge added, with a sly grin. "A dummy Nevada corporation could be first in line to buy up the patent licensing rights."

Blackstone interjected. "You'd bury the technology."

"Of course," Hedge chirped. "In a series of 'failed' pilot-plant experiments that would kill at least ten years in the life of the patent. I doubt if even Exxon-Mobil could make a profit in the remaining seven years before the patent expires."

Blackstone loped around his desk and patted Hedge on the shoulder. "Gatt'll be here in a few minutes, Harley. It's time for you to disappear."

"McGill says Gatt's pushing pretty hard to rescue the small businesses Kurancy wants destroyed. I've pulled my man off his tail, now that we've confirmed the status of the patents. Do you want him watched again? Or, slowed down?"

"Not needed," Blackstone replied in a firm voice. "Gatt was collaborating with Lynne Hurricane in her laughable attempt to prove a conspiracy exists between FFF, BoxMart, Residents Bank and the Chinese government. They've given up."

He shook his head and added, "But I've never seen such incompetent amateur detectives come so close to the truth. I wouldn't be surprised if Gatt accidentally stumbled on the existence of the Three Sixes."

Hedge walked deliberately to the side door leading to a private office suite with an elevator leading to the underground parking garage. "There are people like that," he conceded, "who just seem to gather knowledge by osmosis...like it was seeking them out. We can someday use that to our advantage."

General Ye and Wen Ma Ming have a way of causing pests to disappear in China, the FFF chairman thought. *Perhaps Gatt will become an organ donor...like the Falun Gong. Or, he might rot in a People's Liberation Army prison camp; or plunge 610 feet into the Three Gorges dam; or be crushed in a plastics injection-molding machine at an LCE factory. One way or another, if Gatt and his girlfriend continue snooping around, they will cease to be a source of trepidation.*

Justin entered the office with a graceful athletic strut that suggested the confidence of a successful pro-athlete. Only his intense blue eyes were dulled with uncertainty.

"Please take a seat, Justin," the towering executive said in an unusually friendly tone. "McGill and his wife left for Guatemala this morning. He forgot to sign the loan documents. I'm afraid there'll be a slight delay in processing the loan."

The anxiety on Justin's face was palpable. *Just as we feared*, he thought, *Lynne's notion was correct.*

"How long is a 'slight delay,' Mr. Blackstone?"

The FFF chairman leaned over his desk, pausing to decide which lie to tell the blank-faced Gatt. He shuffled a few papers then impaled Gatt with fierce scrutiny. "Are you suggesting we're not fully committed to the project?"

Justin didn't trust himself to answer. He sat silent. Finally, he said in a low voice, "Of course not."

"If you need more up-front money, FFF can provide another $100,000 bridge loan."

"When can we expect full funding?"

"By the time you return from China."

The White House

"One could argue that America's superpower military might is our most important asset," the President of the United States said to his closest political ally. Martin Merrand was honored to be in the Oval Office. The President's most-likely succesor nodded. In a few hours he'd be attending the USTR reception at the nearby Ritz-Carlton.

"I agree Mr. President, but only if there's a global military conflict. Stretched too thin…our military forces could be more of a liability than an asset… in economic terms."

"Everyone knows we're stretched too thin, Martin. But the Joint Chiefs won't admit it. With the ramp-up in middle-east conflicts; and now--- the troubling activity in the South China Sea, the Sea of Japan, and the Mexican border—the Pentagon brass still thinks we can be all things to all people."

The Governor of New York had watched his friend age prematurely…as all Presidents do. But the soulful eyes, deeply-creviced forehead and constant air of nervous energy was disconcerting. The President's silky-thin pewter-shaded hair was combed straight back and thinning noticeably, like stretched dental floss. His brilliant mind, however, was as impressive as ever.

"I honestly thought my one and only term in office would be marked in history as the watershed of a new global peace-movement; not the harbinger of an unresolvable global trade conflict." He'd yet to learn of Cusson's dollar-dumping activities in Europe.

"Balzarini believes that Mu Jianting's negotiating team will threaten to boycott the U.S. Treasury bond market when they meet with Humphreys in Beijing."

Merrand responded angrily. "They're trying to pressure us to dampen the anti-free-trade sentiment and rhetoric."

The President replied tersely, "There's apparently more to it than that, Martin, although I can't reveal the details. Let's just say we suspect someone in China is planning an event detrimental to the interests of the United States."

Merrand's mind drifted months ahead. The President's problems might soon become his own. "If China ceases to buy our treasury bonds, in the face of Japan's cowardly pull-back from direct bidding on five-year notes, Tangus and the Fed will be wrestling with unprecedented inflationary pressures. The country could experience a fiscal and monetary crisis comparable to the Jimmy Carter years… when interest rates exceeded 18 percent."

Merrand had been briefed by the President's economic advisor on the fiscal condition of the country. "I've been told that the Japanese Finance Minister is predicting a catastrophe for Tokyo's export-oriented economy, unless you and Congress denounce the auto industry's support for opening the U.S. market to Chinese-assembled cars and trucks."

The President nodded. "To the consternation of the United Auto Workers Union…GM, Ford and Chrysler dealers have expressed interest in selling Chinese-made vehicles under U.S. brand names. When China's oldest auto producer, Nanjing Automotive Group, purchased MG motors out of British bankruptcy, and opened their first U.S. assembly plant in Oklahoma early this year, the Japanese went ballistic."

"So, we're being squeezed by both Asian giants?"

The President's voice wavered and cracked as he attempted to answer. He reached for a glass of water and a pill from a side drawer. Pressing both hands to his stomach, he said painfully, "The Prime Minister of Japan is convinced that Toyota and Nissan could eventually fail, unless Japan matches the economic pressure being exerted on Washington by Beijing. The Central Bank of Japan has withdrawn from U.S. Government debt auctions, for at least the balance of the fiscal year, ending in October. At least I've convinced the Prime Minister to postpone selling off matured notes from Tokyo's $900 billion portfolio of U.S.Treasuries."

"Are you all right, Mr. President?" Merrand noticed the sullenness and chalking in the Chief Executive's face.

"Yes, yes," he grimaced. "Tangus has more to worry about than I."

"I didn't know he, too, was ill."

"Not ill in a medical sense. He and the two most influential members of the Federal Reserve Open Market Committee were recently called to a private meeting with upper-crust Wall Street investment bankers. The two were Willard Reyes, President of the New York Federal Reserve Bank, and Marco Santucci, his counterpart in Boston. The Feds were warned that any appreciable increase in interest rates or money supply could slash stock prices, and precipitate a new recessionary cycle."

"How did Tangus respond?"

A look of disdain painted the President's colorless face. "Those same investment banks recently purchased minority stakes in the Central Bank of China, and four other large commercial Chinese banks controlled by the Beijing government. I'm not sure whose side they're on. Tangus gave me a verbatim of their conversation, plus his own take on the situation." The President leaned over to ease a cramp in his abdomen.

"It seems that some of America's largest investment banks have plunged billions into Communist-controlled lending institutions that are burdened with $600 billion in non-performing Chinese industrial loans. If the dollar deflates significantly against the yuan, their equity positions shrink; and they lose board members and any semblance of control. Now, the wise-ass control-freaks are demanding that Tangus pressure me and Congress to save their asses. They can't even tell us how that might be accomplished!"

"That's the reason several opposition Congressmen are calling for a special session to cap the federal deficit. Our opponents are attempting to pass a resolution to postpone funding for new weapons and military raises, until the budget is balanced."

"We're going to be boxed in, according to Tangus. He gave an unusually candid speech at a closed-door follow-up meeting with the Majority and Minority leaders of Congress. He told the Senate Appropriations Committee that our only escape route is a big hole in the interest-rate ceiling. If the Fed has to print more currency to pay for the growing budget deficit....we're all in for a rough slide."

The wariness in his eyes subsided as the medication took hold, buffering the pain radiating from the large elongated glandular organ near his stomach. The digestive juices and hormones produced in his pancreas were teeming with cancerous cells.

"If I may be so bold, Mr. President... you've done an admirable job... considering the powerful opposition this administration has encountered. The consolidation of terrorist groups in the Middle East...who've opened a new front in Mexico; the targeting of private golf clubs in icon resort locations. It's beyond my comprehension."

"I once thought about doing that myself," the wide-eyed President snorted in a half-serious tone, reminding Merrand of the *furor loquendi* of a dying madman in a Shakespeare tragedy. "The greed exhibited openly by the fistfuls of multi-national corporate executives who golf at those courses…pisses me off the most."

The President's intercom buzzed and he was reminded by the National Security Advisor that his presence was required for a briefing with the Secretary of Homeland Security. *More bad news…more incomplete intelligence…more speculative scenarios.*

"Martin, if you win the election…as I'm predicting…keep your back-side covered when you inevitably have to deal with the corporate barons and their lobbyist mouthpieces." He hesitated, choosing his words carefully. "The secret groups they form are powerful enough to cause things to happen…or prevent them from happening …in almost any country they do business in." He glanced sideways at Merrand and added ruefully, "Occassionally, it can be useful to a President. But mostly…it's frightening."

Merrand was a former Navy pilot and Vietnam veteran of medium height and build in his mid-sixties, with thick naturally-curly grey hair, chiseled features and a sense of humor and charm which attracted both male and female voters. He was a shrewd observer of people, and claimed he learned more about them from what they *didn't say,* than from the carefully chosen dialogue of a typical lobbyist or constituent. He believed candor and patience were paramount to being an effective public servant…as he truly considered himself.

Merrand rose to his feet, before the President signaled the meeting's end, and said, "Big Business was once America's anchor. Now they conduct themselves as if the country is only a huge flea market for their goods. America's sovereignty has little meaning to many of the multi-national executives; especially the ones who forgot how their companies became successful. In times of international conflict, they built the products this country needed to protect freedom and independence…and became immensely profitable. It appalls me that this country is forfeiting that capability at such an alarming rate."

Merrand accepted the President's hand warmly and said, "I appreciate your time and support, sir. It's a lucky man who can count the most powerful man on earth as his true friend."

The doubtful expression on the President's face indicated he was not convinced.

"Martin, you know I'll do everything in my power to get you elected. But I think you need a compromise running-mate. Someone like Elliot Sharn, or possibly Carvin Troone. A seasoned D.C. insider who knows the ropes and has a pro-trade bent to balance the ticket."

As they walked together toward the door, the President added brightly, "Take some advice from an admirer, Martin: don't surround yourself with rough-riders from Albany or the Big Apple, or red-neck advisors like Carter did. You need to surround yourself with high-quality people; and get more corporate money on your side to win the election. I'm sure you're aware that numerous special interest groups---which you can't ignore---will follow you into the bathroom and hold your pecker, if necessary, to grab your attention. If you want this," he spread his arms and pivoted slowly around the Oval Office ,"and want to use it wisely, *compromise* is the only way."

"With due respect, Mr. President---if I win the election, I don't plan to compromise my pledges to the American people. Whether anyone else in Washington agrees with me, I believe this country's economic independence will eventually collapse if we don't protect the American manufacturing sector, and begin to rely less on Asian blackmail funds to finance our budget and trade deficits."

The President smiled. *Martin will be a strong President, thank God. He's the type of leader who needs something to align himself with that is greater than himself.*

"How long can the current trend continue?" Merrand said in a fine-sandpaper tone. "Massive amounts of hard-earned dollars are migrating to Asian Central Banks. Manufacturing technology which took decades and huge investments by the government and private American industries to develop is being handed to foreign competitors. And, we're barely slapping the hands of those who openly steal our intellectual property."

The President recoiled. He realized Merrand's tirade was not against him, but against the 'establishment.' Still…it hurt.

"Don't hold back, Martin," he said pointedly, "A President never should."

"I'm sorry, sir. I know this is a complicated world…but it irks me that we have to *thank them,* when they use money, which should remain in this country, to buy Treasury bonds. That money pays only a small portion of the paltry unemployment benefits we allot to permanently-displaced U.S. factory workers…for a relatively few months. People who've forfeited their livelihoods to Han peasants forced to work ten-hour days for two dollars." He gulped in a breath. Merrand wasn't known for short-sentence responses.

He'll need a good speech-writer, the President thought, *to transfigure his big thoughts into smaller word bites.*

The President prayed that the chemotherapy and radiation treatments on his diseased pancreas would keep him alive long enough to witness a Merrand Administration in full blossom. The country needed a confident leader…stronger than he could be…even if he beat the cancer. His blood-shot eyes and depleted body would never recover the clarity and toughness he brought to the Oval Office nearly four years ago.

"Martin, you'll have an easy time capturing the Party's nomination…but a much tougher battle winning the election. Now that the other side of the aisle controls the House and Senate, you'll have to compromise on several issues. But be careful how you select a running mate. It can be the key to winning or losing."

CHAPTER 36

(August 1, 2008)
Ritz-Carlton-Washington, 7 pm

The hotel courtesy van pulled in line behind several black stretch limousines delivering Washington's elite trade officials and honored guests to the most notable event in a wispy August social schedule. Justin slid open the side door as Lynne emerged from the back seat like a movie star trying to sneak past the paparazzi.

She immediately drew the attention of admiring men and frumpy wives wearing expensive evening gowns, as they advanced toward the hotel entrance where a Secret Service agent in a tuxedo was checking credentials.

"I thought you said the ladies would be wearing cocktail dresses…not five-thousand dollar full-length gowns."

Justin caught site of a bizarre looking couple being escorted to the front of the line by another tuxedoed agent. Richard deLeone grasped the long arm of his forty-year old Swedish girlfriend, who stood six-inches taller than him. A single braid of blonde hair was weaved into a pig-tail just below the neck-line and fell another foot over her bare back, which was crisscrossed with thin straps from the drop-waist silver-metallic, burnout velvet dress that did nothing to hide a belly blessed with six-month's of expectantcy.

Lynne had insisted on meeting in the lobby. She rode the elevator to the second floor leading to the wide stairwell which spiraled down to the lobby. As she slowly descended, Justin watched from a perfect view…leaning against the wall facing the stairs. He ran out of superlatives when he'd watched Lynne approaching from the top. Her natural beauty was dazzling…showcased in the stunning gold-trimmed, emerald knee-length evening dress; her wavy auburn hair as lustrous as brushed silk, both straight and curly in a sexy disheveled set; her infectious smile bracketed by sparkling green reflections from chandelier emerald earnings. She glided gracefully toward the bottom… refusing to use the hand-rail. *A queen would meet her champion this way*, she thought.

As she raised one foot cautiously and lowered the other on the carpeted stairwell, her slightly-over-sized strapped high-heels tilted sideways at the ankle, interrupting her perfect balance. She slid precariously on polished-leather soles toward the edge. Justin beamed a high-spirited smile as she reached the bottom step, and gushed, "You've got to be the most stunning woman in Washington." Lynne lost her concentration and slipped on the last rung…lurching forward. Justin caught her in his outstretched arms and added affectionately, "And possibly the clumsiest."

The secret service agent in the black tuxedo checking official invitations and photo-identifications couldn't resist dropping his inspective gaze from Lynne's dazzling eyes to her bulging cleavage…despite months of training to fixate on a person's eyes.

He checked their papers three times. An escaped convict in striped pajamas and ankle-chains could have slipped by this first line of security at the hotel entrance. When they swept into the crowded ballroom, a light breeze from turned heads induced her dangling earrings into a pendular motion.

"'Black-tie optional,' my ass," Justin whispered, as he tightened the cobalt blue and cranberry striped silk tie that perfectly matched his three-button navy suit. Every man in view was garbed in a black jacket, cummerbund, silk-banded pants and bow tie.

"Blackstone could have mentioned that everyone would be dressed to the nines." He remembered that an alternate meaning for 'dressed' was to spread manure on soil.

Food stations spotted at half-a-dozen locations around the ballroom offered mounds of giant shrimp pyramided on crushed-ice, a pupu assortment of Chinese appetizers, a carving chef hacking pieces of rare prime rib and roasted turkey, and genuine Peking duck squatting crisply under infra-red lamps. One table featured assorted French and Italian pastries and an elaborate fruit and imported cheese display already half its original size. White-gloved waiters wandered the floor serving glasses of champagne, wine and non-alcoholic plum-punch from large silver-plate trays.

Justin surveyed the area for someone recognizable and noticed Gabriel Oresco talking to Robert Changhui from the embassy staff. He grasped Lynne's hand and weaved through the crowd just as a huge commotion erupted at the entrance to the ballroom.

"I'd like to introduce you to someone," he said, as the crowd obstructing the path to Oresco suddenly cleared. Someone shouted in a loud, excited voice, "Senators Scharn and Troone have arrived."

Lynne turned to the commotion and saw Mrs. Scharn and an attractive young woman on the arms of the Senators as they followed a wedge of stern-faced security guards in tuxedoes, working toward the middle of the ballroom. Lynne immediately recognized the young woman on Troone's arm.

Lydia Bryce, a Harvard classmate, made it big. Not only was she the former Secretary of State and Presidential-candidate's speech-writer, but tonight she was the high-profile escort of the popular Senator from Texas. Justin relinquished his light grip on Lynne's hand as she moved in Lydia's direction. He swayed in the opposite direction toward Oresco.

Lynne cried out excitedly, "I see an old friend." Everyone else in the ballroom was a stranger, except for a few familiar faces she recognized from C-Span telecasts. Justin wanted to ask the Asian expert and reporter for the New York Times about travel in China. "I'll meet you in fifteen minutes at the desert table. We'll split a chocolate-chip cannoli."

As they parted temporarily, Gatt could feel the pretense of power in the attendees who *didn't* rush to greet the powerful Senators who might become President. In a far corner, Tom Blackstone, Harley Hedge and Jeffrey Richards were in spirited conversation with a distinguished looking oriental man chomping on a large red sparerib.

Ambassador Balzerini made it a point to avoid eye-contact with Gatt, as he exchanged barbs with a pushy Chinese reporter from the state-controlled Xinhau News Agency. It was obvious to the Ambassador that Wang Chao, the Minister of Industry and Trade, had assigned the reporter to scout for information which could be useful in the upcoming Beijing trade negotiations.

Oresco was left alone when Robert Changhui darted toward the hubbub at the entrance.

"Hey, Justin...glad to see you," Oresco called out as Gatt approached. "Who's the dynamite chick who just dumped you?" Oresco was unescorted... dressed in a bran-colored suit and raffia pattern cream tie. Justin assumed that members of the press were allowed to dress informally...sans female escorts.

"Her name's Lynne Hurricane; and she didn't dump me...at least not yet."

He extended a hand and a smile, adding, "She's an associate with GH Paladin in Boston. I work with her on a small-business aid program, when FFF doesn't pull me to Washington for another assignment. They're the parent company."

Oresco looked at him suspiciously and asked, "Didn't Ross Trenker transfer to FFF from Paladin before he was killed?"

The similarity between his own career path and that of Trenker's suddenly struck Justin as ominous. He hoped it would take a detour very quickly.

"Coincidence, Gabriel! I didn't know him very well. He hired me." Justin wished to change the disconcerting subject. "Can I ask you about traveling in China? The mission assignment is my first trip there. All I know about the country is what I've recently read in journals and travel books."

"How long will you be there?"

"Four or five weeks."

"Did Balzerini's staff help make the arrangements?" Oresco said in a low voice as he glanced around the ballroom and noticed Robert Changhui returning .

"My itinerary is a jumble: an FFF assignment to gather information on Chinese manufacturing methods; then a sort of cultural education trip. The company wants me to experience the real China…in case future government contracts involving China require my small-business background. That's how Tom Blackstone explained it."

The reporter's research on Gatt was accurate. He reported to the elusive FFF chairman, Thomas Blackstone, whose personal profile had been difficult to obtain…even utilizing the unmatched research sources of the New York Times.

"Sounds like your assignment in China is going to be more complicated than you first imagined."

Balzerini would know. He'd eventually give Oresco the 'scoop.' The Ambassador frequently called upon his services…although the nature of Oresco's assistance was top-secret.

"Shoot away," he replied evenly as Gatt scanned the ballroom for Lynne.

"I have one question," Justin replied fervently. "Will the guide they assign to me be trustworthy? He'll be escorting me to at least a dozen remote locations…from industrial centers and universities, to small inland towns and archeological recovery sites. The only Chinese words I know are 'chop sticks.'

"First of all, Justin, *he* will likely be a *she*. The U.S. Embassy in Beijing has the right to approve the selection of your guide. But that only means she'll be qualified to traverse the fine line between doing a little spying on you…to satisfy the Beijing travel bureau…and being trustworthy enough to be an honest interpreter, and guide you safely around the country."

He noticed Balzerini point an accusing finger at the Chinese reporter, in a heated exchange uncharacteristic of the Ambassador. "Can I make a suggestion?"

"Sure,"Gatt answered blandly as Lynne reappeared, holding Lydia Bryce's hand and dragging her forward.

"Talk to Balzerini about giving me a copy of your itinerary. I'll be traveling the country the same time as you. If you have a problem, I may be able to help." He nodded and headed for the open bar.

Lydia Bryce was a delight. Round-cheeked, vibrant and attractively thin in a conservative two-piece maroon designer dress, which clashed with titanium wire-framed monocals perched on her turned-up nose. Her accessories were pink pearls---tiny earings and a long string of irregularly-shaped hearts of nacreous gemstones, dangling from her tanned neck. Her radiant brunette hair was twisted in bouncy curls, with a few *frizzies* escaping in different directions, as the August moisture tripled the size of the loose strands. Her hazel eyes were wise and friendly

Carvin Troone's speech writer could maneuver simple words into compelling public statements better than the President's high-paid scribes. Lydia had succeeded in re-shaping Troone's pro free-trade image into an agenda more compatible with Martin Merrand's *'selective protectionist'* platform---without eroding his base of corporate financial supporters.

Lydia had been a close friend of Lynne's at Harvard, and collaborated with her in writing humorous articles for the Harvard Lampoon under the by-line: *From a poor girl's point of view.* Their most famous article was entitled, "*I only have thirty pairs of shoes to study with.*" After graduation, they went separate ways and somehow lost touch.

Lydia watched suspiciously as Justin slid an arm around Lynne's waist and she responded by cuddling closer. "We're good friends, just like you and Senator Troone," Lynne said playfully, deflecting Lydia's questioning grin. Lydia suddenly thought of Troone's wife in Texas.

Justin tracked national politics and was aware that Senators Scharn and Troone were contesting Martin Merrand for the Presidential nomination. "So nice to meet you, Lydia. What's it like writing for a man who could drag you to the White House?"

"Fabulous...simply fabulous," she joked. "I hustle my butt off," she added more seriously. Lynne guessed her statement had a second meaning. Lydia was known by her numerous Harvard Law School boyfriends as 'loose Lydia mouthpiece.'

"I can't imagine what it would be like working for the President, if Carvin wins the nomination."

Butler Humphreys was pleased that so many Washington dignitaries considered the Chinese trade issue important enough to attend his reception. When Martin Merrand entered the ballroom at nine p.m., he was followed by a small army of admirers and staff. The pro-free-traders and their paid lobbyists remained huddled at the open-bar, watching disdainfully as others edged to the front of the ballroom. Humphreys greeted Merrand and ushered him to a large corner table occupied by Forrest Balzerini, Richard deLeone and their women.

The Merrand staff people circled the New York Governor like an alligator-filled moat…physically preventing the opposition and the press from approaching their man. Merrand moved effortlessly through the crowd, reaching out over a wall of shoulders to touch hands with the guests. The next hour comprised short, unimportant conversations. Powerful people made snide remarks regarding the FFF consultant and his attractive companion's inappropriate dress.

Oresco was kind enough to make a few formal introductions for Justin and Lynne. Elliot Scharn and his wife were gracious. Troone nodded, said, "Hi, there," and extended a limp hand-shake to Gatt, and a suggestive tight squeeze to Lynne's hand. He whisked Lydia away without apologizing.

Blackstone finally acknowledged the presence of his FFF and GH Paladin co-workers by inviting Lynne to his table. He ignored Justin, leaving him gawking in embarrassment, as he led Lynne like a trophy-wife the meet a Three-Sixes insider curious about this beautiful potential nemesis.

Senior members of the Chinese diplomatic corps in Washington remained stone-faced as Wang Chao, the Chinese Minister of Industry and Trade strolled to a make-shift podium at the center of the ballroom. USTR Humphreys had asked him to say a few words as the affair was winding down. He wanted it to end on a positive note.

"We encourage the American delegation to enjoy the hospitality of China, and to visit the magnificent new structures built in Beijing for the Olympic games. We also encourage Ambassador Humphreys and his negotiating team to exhibit flexibly in their approach to trade issues with Beijing,"

"Now comes the bullshit," Balzerini whispered to his wife.

"China's emerging domination in global commerce…alongside America…will be the future of the world," he exclaimed boisterously. "The friction between our equally-powerful countries must lessen, if the underlying strengths of China and the United States are to be properly aligned with the needs of mankind."

He argued forcefully, that America needs China more than China needs America; following Yong Ihasa's instructions to discourage the Americans from thinking that trade differences could be resolved at the upcoming Beijing negotiations.

When Wang Chao's speech ended, the stunned audience responded with an eerie silence. The five-foot seven former mayor of Changdu, with close-cropped wavy black hair, issued a menacing expression in the direction of Humphreys. He then signaled for the other Chinese representatives to remove their name-tags and follow him to Embassy Row on Massachusetts Avenue.

He was embarrassed and angry at the absence of even polite applause for his comments, which were purposefully controversial.

Before the Chinese group reached the exit, Martin Merrand motioned to Humphreys and stomped deliberately to the podium.

"Before you depart, Mr Wang," he shouted above the murmuring dignitaries, "please have the courtesy to listen to a few remarks from an American viewpoint." The embarrassed Minister of Industry and Trade stopped in his tracks and remained standing, as he turned to Merrand with a scowl. The bustling guests preparing to leave suddenly quieted. Everyone sensed a dramatic moment.

"I'm not authorized to represent the entire United States in my comments, but the great state of New York is considered by many as a microcosm of the entire nation. Indeed, Minister Chang, more U.S. Presidents, Vice-Presidents and candidates for the White House have been Governors of New York than any other political position vying for this country's leadership."

Wang Chao took a nearby seat and motioned for the other Chinese to do likewise.

Lydia had done the research. She whispered to Lynne, "Franklin and Theodore Roosevelt, Martin Van Buren and Grover Cleveland became Presidents…Nelson Rockefeller, George Clinton, Daniel Tompkins and Levi Morton---Vice-Presidents…Al Smith, Tom Dewey, Sam Tilden and several other NY Governors have also been Presidential candidates."

"As the current Governor of New York," Merrand bellowed, "I've witnessed upstate manufacturing companies being devastated for several years by an unabated stream of foreign imports. Mostly from the People's Republic of China. This corrosive trend continues in many parts of the country, Mr. Minister. The American people want something done about it by Washington and Beijing."

The sudden loud applause drew an anxious grin on Wang's stoic face. Merrand continued his diatribe by wishing both the U.S. trade delegation and Wang Chao luck in the upcoming negotiations. His final comment was directed to Wang Chao.

"I don't agree that America needs China more than China needs America." The Chinese Minister of Industry and Trade winced, as Merrand reminded him, "The American economy is your country's number one market, Minister Wang, and generates most of the foreign reserves now being used by your Communist government to expand China's military capabilities and national infrastructure. Despite the claim by some historians that China discovered America in 1421, the goodwill between our nations can only flourish in a mutually beneficial environment."

When the time is right, fumed Wang, *this man must meet the Chameleon.*

CHAPTER 37

(AUGUST 2, 2008), MIDNIGHT
THE MORGUE, PEOPLE'S FRIENDSHIP SANITARIUM, LIAONING PROVINCE

The unauthorized autopsy by Dr. Dongzi could land him and the dead boy's father in prison.

Authorities from the Institute for Advanced Medical Treatment, where the young technician was exposed to the deadly mutated organism, had issued clear instructions to cremate the body immediately, and destroy all blood samples and medical records of the technician's illness. The parents were callously denied information as to the cause of their son's death.

The moribund father guarded the double-doors to the morgue in the damp basement of the hospital sanitarium. He turned away as Dr. Dongzi deftly sliced open his son's chest and stomach cavity with a razor-sharp scalpel. The subdued light from a single fluorescent lamp thankfully limited the father's view as the Chinese doctor then buzz-sawed through the rib-cage and chest-bone with a battery-powered circular blade resembling a cordless telephone clipped to a small vacuum bag. Hopefully, the non-woven polypropylene surgical respirator mask taped around his nose and mouth would trap any harmful particles the small vacuum didn't catch.

Dr. Dongzi was a graduate of the University of Lund Medical College in Switzerland, and an amateur biochemist considered overly meddlesome by his colleagues. He'd refused to gloss over the causes of death for the young prisoners transferred in critical condition from the IAMT surgical hospital in Liaoning to the People's Friendship Sanitarium medical facility. Their crime was listed as "illegal assembly and conspiracy against the state." The dead boy's father knew their only crime had been to practice self-improvement exercises called *Falun Dafa,* based on the principles of Truthfulness, Compassion and Tolerance.

The government denied charges that thousands of members of the persecuted group, better known as *Falun Gong,* were detained without due process, and forced into mental and organ-donor hospitals, mutilated, tortured, killed and brainwashed. The patients transferred to Dr. Dongzi's hospital were all missing one or more vital organs.

Dr. Dongzi had studied the biochemistry of nearly all blood diseases after being fascinated by the achievements of one of his professors---Nobel prize winner Bengt Samuelsson, the co-discover of the prostaglandins which stimulate or suppress important physiological functions in the body. Samuelsson discovered *Thromboxane* in the 1970s, a molecule that promotes blood clotting.

Dongzi never saw a pathogen that reacted so violently in the blood stream. The virus-like substance which destroyed the technician's white blood cells in a few days, had completely wiped out his immune system. More amazing, the virus-like pathogen apparently died from its own attack mechanism; possibly from a self-produced toxin.

Only RNA and DNA retro-viruses demonstrated similar pathogenic responses when host-bacteria or cell-nutrients feeding the virus were exhausted. The single lab test the doctor could run at the Sanitarium was blood-sugar concentration. The post-mortem test for sugar in the congealed blood-mass showed a total lack of glucose-derived sugars, even though intravenous glucose solution had been administered up to the time of death. The boy's congealed heart appeared blue-black under the fluorescent bulb and was rock-hard.

Dr. Dongzi scraped bone-marrow from the ragged edge of a sawed chest bone and placed the dark cement-like substance in a small plastic zip-lock bag. He sliced thin pieces of tissue from the coronary artery---now resembling thin stainless-steel tubing... from the double-layered sac surrounding the heart called the pericardium, and from the shiny tissue known as the endocardium which formed thin sheets on the inner surfaces of the atrial and ventricular chambers. The test specimens were dropped into small pre-labeled glass tubes and sealed with yellow, red and blue rubber caps.

A friend at the Tangshan Research Hospital southeast of Beijing, which was affiliated with the research-oriented Beijing Union Medical College Hospital, had agreed to secretly analyze the specimens. He'd heard about the pathogenic accident at the IAMT, and was alarmed to learn from Dr. Dongzi that the dead technician had been packaging biological materials being shipped under false labeling to the United States.

The tearful propaganda official stared transfixed through the small glass square, broken in spirit as the doctor pulled the sheet over the exposed heart of his son. *A pure heart*, he agonized. Not the seat of intelligence as the Greeks believed, or the source of the soul and emotions, as others of faith believed. But pure in its youthful anticipations.

Until recently, it had been a *healthy* heart...which began its rhythmic contractions in the embryo twenty-five years ago; about three weeks after the pleasant sexual experience shared by the boy's parents.

Dr. Dongzi's mind drifted in the eerie silence of the cold morgue. *If the son lived a normal Chinese life span of 76 years, his heart would beat 2.8 billion times, and pump 179 million quarts of blood through his body.*

The father suddenly became furious as he grasped the reality that the Communist government he served so loyally as a propaganda official had caused the hideous death of his son. He was sure the accident was the result of careless and avoidable medical experiments. The medical experts supervising the biological weapons tests at the IAMT had been cold and unresponsive, showing no remorse or interest in answering his inquiries as to the cause of death. Instead, he was vigorously warned to strip the incident from his mind. A propaganda official of the Communist Party must accept temporary setbacks for the good of the state.

Dr. Dongzi was convinced that the scientists and surgeons performing experiments and operations at the biological-weapons lab and at the AIMT were more dangerous than Nazi death-camp doctors. Or Mao's illiterate wandering Red Guards, who murdered fellow citizens indiscriminately during the Cultural Revolution; or the sadistic WW II Japanese occupiers who tortured and decapitated Chinese men and women after hacking off limbs.

He vowed to expose the experiments at IAMT. The strange organism that consumed the technician's blood-sugar and coagulated his fluids had to be identified. Somehow, he'd find a way to reveal the existence of this new pathogen to the World Health Organization in Geneva. Hopefully, before the pathogen now on its way to America was released.

CHAPTER 38

(AUGUST 3, 2008), BOEING DREAMLINER
OVER THE ARCTIC CIRCLE EN ROUTE TO BEIJING

The pilot informed the passengers, "Sunday is now Monday."

"That was quite a scene at Humphreys' party," Gabriel Oresco said as he slid in beside Gatt in an aft row of the new fuel-efficient Boeing 787 Dreamliner long-range aircraft. The new wide-body jet was airborne directly over the North Pole Date Line.

The 13 hour non-stop flight from Washington, over the Arctic Circle to Beijing International Airport was a step up from the Boeing 777 non-stop fourteen-hour flight from New York's Kennedy International Airport to Shanghai, which Oresco frequently traveled as lead reporter for the Asian Bureau of the New York Times.

Gatt smiled. "I can't believe the balls on Martin Merrand. Half the diplomats in the ballroom...on both sides...practically collapsed in shock."

"It won't harm his campaign, that's for sure."

"Maybe...but it ruined my night with Lynne. Her friend Lydia was so wound up when Troone rushed out following Merrand's confrontation with Wang Chao that we ended up driving her home to Virginia in the hotel van. It cost me a 'C' note."

"Troone forgot her...left her behind?" Oresco laughed.

Justin peered down at the endless ice-sheet blanketing the Artic Ocean. "She was his escort, or vice-versa."

"I know of Lydia. She's Troone's speech writer, and a dynamite one at that. I hear she studies historical speeches of world leaders."

"She's a college buddy of Lynne Hurricane's, from Harvard. I think she's in love with Troone, even though he's married. He reads poetry to her... mostly his own. Lydia told us that Troone got hooked on writing poetry when he was running the State Department. Who knows why? He sounds like a strange dude."

"All the Senators are a bit weird," Oresco replied jokingly. "And one of them may soon be the next vice-president, according to reliable sources. Merrand is a shoe-in for the Presidential nomination, and he'll soon choose a running mate. Most bets are on Elliot Scharn, the Senator from Ohio and Chairman of the Senate Appropriations Committee."

A tall, middle-aged Asian flight attendant with a grand-motherly expression of unlimited kindness handed out woolen blankets and small white pillows. A younger Chinese male attendant, wearing a charcoal sleeveless "SC" monogrammed sweater, followed with hot coffee, tea, and soda. He also took cocktail orders. Hardly a sound was heard from the two GEnx jet engines propelling the first of ten new Southern China Airlines fuel-efficient twin-engine Dreamliners halfway around the world. The powerful engines chosen by China's largest airline used fifty-percent less fan blades than older models, and were the only commercial jet engines with both the front fan case and fan blades made of composite material.

Oresco peered down the aisle from the rear starboard side of the 2008-certified Boeing 787 wide-body and caught sight of Robert Changhui glancing back. Robert's anxious countenance said, "Yes….do it now!"

Most of the other passengers in the rear of the aircraft were asleep in reclining positions. A few were stretched across unoccupied seats, trying unsuccessfully to nap for a few hours in the fetal position. They had no idea that the positively-charged ferric ions in their blood and brain-cells were being re-oriented by the strong magnetic force crowning the north pole. It was an alternate explanation as to why people's attitudes improved after they traveled over Santa's home.

"By the way," Gatt replied impassively as he stared transfixed at the icy reflections of a full moon radiating orange beams upward from 35,000 feet, "I talked with Ambassador Balzerini about your suggestion. He was all for providing you with my travel plans in China." Gatt reached for a briefcase tucked beneath the front seat.

"Don't bother, Justin," Oresco whispered. "I already have it."

The puzzled look on Gatt's face was expected. Oresco added, "Let's talk about the real situation in China. Like you, I have two assignments on the mainland: first---to find the facts and report them to my editor; then…" he paused to turn up the airflow hiss from the overhead dispenser and looked around to confirm that the surrounding back-row seats were unoccupied, "I've been asked to dig for information which the Ambassador claims could be crucial to America's security."

Justin was shocked at the revelation. "What do you know about my mission?" he demanded.

"Not much, except you may need to access some of my…let's say *surruptitious* contacts on the mainland. According to Robert Changhui, who Balzerini has assigned as my principle contact with the embassy as I travel in China…I'm being asked to cover your back-side while *you* acquire information. I don't know the nature of the information or the methods you'll use to acquire it. I assume it's some top-secret manufacturing process …or evidence the government needs to prove theft of some U.S.intellectual property."

Gatt squinted apprehensively as Oresco proceeded to explain that he was one of the few foreign journalists with high-level contacts in the National People's Congress and the State Council---the highest organ of state administration which reports directly to the Chairman of the Standing Committee of the NPC, Chang Hui-chen.

"If enough cash changes hands," he explained, "so does information."

He lowered his voice and added, "I recently acquired the current financial records of several state-owned banks in Shanghai, Beijing and Shenzhen. They're China's equivalents to the big U.S. money-center banks like CitiGroup and Bank of America, but function more like regional Federal Reserve banks, under the thumb of the Central Bank of China."

"So you're working for the government?" Gatt asked skeptically. "Isn't that an ultra-dangerous conflict of interests…given how the newspaper is frequently charged with being anti-Administration?"

"Ever since one of our Chinese-national reporters was charged with espionage and misappropriating state secrets, we've been trying to get him out of Chinese prison. The Security Police know I'm trying to gather information to help his case. They're being pressured by Chang Hui-Chen himself not to interfere with my inquiries, unless I become too inquisitive."

"They allow you to spy?"

"It's a ruse!" Oresco frowned. "I've been falsely accused of espionage more than once, and I'm being followed 24/7 by state security agents and photographers dressed as tourists. The security police are anxious to catch me in a compromising situation."

"You could be rotting in prison, with no chance for legal representation or a fair trial," Justin exclaimed incredulously.

"I don't think so, Justin. Most espionage cases in China are settled in four days…from arrest and conviction…to execution. I'm dust before anyone even learns I've been arrested. Chinese security agents absolutely hate the American press. My NY Times friend is hanging on because of tremendous pressure being applied by the world media...not my publisher or the federal government."

Justin retorted, "Everyone is afraid it could happen to them."

"Well, Beijing doesn't react well to U.S. media pressure, but they respond quickly if the international media hawks stick their beaks down Beijing's throat." Oresco didn't reveal to Gatt that he was privy to a network of underground safe-houses established by Balzerini in various towns on the mainland.

"China's an amazing...yet troubled country. There's more hiding places in the over-crowded towns and cities than in any other nation. You can literally conceal yourself in a crowded street for days...as long as you're properly attired and keep moving."

Justin was troubled by Oresco's willingness to share perilous information. "Why are you telling me this?"

Oresco breathed deeply and answered, "I've been told to."

A few moments of silence allowed time to adjust his thinking. Balzerini considered the assignment dangerous enough to warrant a back-up. He worried that the controversial journalist they'd chosen for the task was balancing on a barbed-wire fence himself; in full view of a gang of anti-espionage agents constantly at his heals. He wondered if Oresco was a liability....or a clever diversion?

Oresco pulled the blanket over his shoulders and said morosely, "In my opinion, every country doing business with China will eventually get screwed...big time."

"Why?"

"China has deep-seated problems the Communists can't solve. The current economy is grossly imbalanced; short on energy and bottle-necked with limitations in its transportation system. Their so-called 'modern commercial banks' have piled loss after loss on the Central Banking system. Several industrial sectors are over-invested, and high unemployment at state-run factories led to more than seventy-thousand citizen protests last year. Not to mention the unreported arrests and shootings at the dam sites."

"It's amazing the Communist Party can maintain control of Chinese society. I remember the 1989 turmoil and student shootings in Tianen'man Square."

Oresco grumbled sarcastically,"Communist leaders aren't exactly shy about stomping on belligerent citizens." He lowered his voice and said, "You don't know the half of it. Each week, protestors at the new dam sites are lined up and shot. The deltas of the Huang He, the Changjiang and the Xi Jiang have become midnight killing fields for peasants who complain too much about the loss of their homes, or the meager compensation the government doles out for their small patches of family land."

Gatt recognized the Chinese names for the Yellow River, Yangtse River and West River---the three major rivers fed from the headwaters of the western Tibet highland. "None of this is reported?"

"It shows up on the internet...then quickly disappears. Word-of-mouth carries the stories from town-to-town. Cell-phone photographs have been used to spread evidence of the atrocities, but the cell numbers are eventually traced and the rabble-rousers beaten and jailed."

Justin was becoming more uneasy than he'd been at GRT's bankruptcy sessions. "I read that the central government is cracking down on corruption in large and mid-sized cities."

Oresco snickered. "Dishonesty at the local level pales in comparison to the depravity of some central government figures. Outright fraud; bribery; a clamp on foreign investment. Not to mention manipulation of the yuan, and lack of judicial due-process. I could go on."

"I read that provincial authorities blackmail foreign companies into giving Chinese partners their industrial secrets...in exchange for access to Chinese markets."

"It's not blackmail,"Oresco replied ironically,"it's the law!"

(AUGUST 3, 2008) AM
WASHINGTON, FFF OFFICE

The dark sedan which followed the hotel van had recorded every word spoken by the occupants. The conversations of Hurricane, Gatt and Lydia Bryce during the drive to Lydia's apartment in Virginia, and during the return trip to the hotel, were revealing, but not conclusive.

The couple was obviously aware of a suspicious connection between FFF, BoxMart and Residents Bank. However, with Gatt out of the way for at least five weeks, Blackstone only had to deal with the attractive ferret. He didn't require a complete take-out. The Chameleon was expert at inflicting debilitating injuries. She could incapacitate a target for years.

Arcola Mandita toyed with the remote detonation device as she peered out the window of the Charles Hotel in the direction of Lynne Hurricane's apartment. The instructions from Blackstone were precise: create an accident resulting in significant injury---but not life-threatening. The level of disfiguration inflicted in the accident was up to her.

Geneva, Switzerland

Stella Nicorezzi sat across from her father at his sullen office in the Fusterie Temple, the first Calvinist Cathedral built in 1715. The yellowed marble structure was now the unobtrusive home of a select group of investment bankers whose clients were morally challenged---mostly international oil traders and launderers of unclean money. The "cowboys" of Geneva.

Johanas Nicorezzi was dressed in the city banker's uniform of dark blazer and square pocket silk. He was nearing retirement, but looked in his forties, with a permanent mountain-tan complexion and a trim six-foot three-inch frame. Dark brown eyes matched the natural shade of his thinning hair and ruddy face. He looked closely at his darling thirty year old daughter and asked, "What do you suggest we do with this information, dear?"

Stella was of medium height and trim, with fine-boned features, penetrating pale-caramel eyes, and luxuriant raven eyebrows winged partly under sun-bleached, reddish-blonde Prince Valiant bangs. Her natural blonde, shoulder-length hair was accented by matching caramel streaks which were pushed back and curled behind each ear. "I was hoping you'd tell me, Papa. What does it mean?"

Johanas cast a worried look at his daughter and said, "It's very unusual for this amount of money to pass through Franco-Medici Trust at this time of year. Or any time, for that matter. Why is your friend Lynne so interested in these enormous transactions? And how does she even know they exist?"

Stella replied, "She's found some irregularities involving American businesses and a regional American bank called Residents Bank of North America, which, as you know, is affiliated with Franco-Medici Trust here in Geneva. Some of the financial information she's accessed using a Harvard database search-tool indicates that two of the companies involved ---the big retail chain named BoxMart and a prominent Washington consulting firm named the Financial Flow Foundation, are manipulating funds in and out of Chinese bank accounts for an unknown purpose."

"Is she aware of Creditte Bank de Savoy's silent ownership of Franco-Medici?"

"She would have mentioned it."

Johanas reached across the dining table for his daughter's hand and held it gently. "I must tell you that your friend is venturing into very dangerous territory. The managing director of Creditte Bank de Savoy is a treacherous French fool more unscrupulous than the 'cowboys' of Geneva. Phillipe Cusson considers himself superior to the typical banker and above the law. He deals frequently with the Chinese in very large sums. If information leaks out about the recent confidential multi-billion dollar transfers of U.S.

currency from Chinese banks to Franco-Medici and CBdS, Cusson would track down and destroy the source of the disclosure."

Stella understood what her father was implying. "Cusson would be at your back until he wrecked your career, and tried to put you in jail."

"Exactly!"

"Still, I would like to help her, Papa. I love her."

Johanas smiled painfully as he recalled the anguish Stella suffered when she discovered that Lynne was not interested in a lesbian relationship, despite the mutual affection shared by the Harvard roommates.

"Perhaps I could talk with her before we decide whether to assist in her inquiry. I must know more about her reasons, and how she would use the information."

"I could call her right away, and invite her to Geneva. She mentioned being overdue for a vacation."

Johanas had never been able to refuse Stella. His career was almost over, and he'd saved enough money to retire comfortably. Cusson was a pompous ass, and he'd enjoy seeing the French banker squirm in the bastion of the world's vast reservoir of contaminated funds---the currency cathartic known as *Geneva*.

"Stella, my dear, don't you remember that I'm leaving for Barbados in a few days?"

"Oh, Papa, I forgot."

"Can you get her here before I leave? I can't decide until I know more about her project."

"She's never been to Switzerland, but I'll try. At least *she's* the one pushing for an immediate answer. If it's as important as she claims, I think she'll rush over immediately."

"May I suggest you wire her tickets for tonight's flight from Boston to Geneva?. It's a tad presumptuous, but if you wait until tomorrow, she may not make timely connections. The international airport threat-level is at its highest."

CHAPTER 39

(August 4, 2008), midnight
Cambridge, Mass.

The UPS delivery man stepped from the elevator and advanced slowly down the deserted fifth floor hallway. Midnight was an unusual time to deliver a package, even for 'special delivery' service to an apartment building. The small cardboard box under his arm was very light. It was empty.

The tall, broad-shouldered courier with dark skin and a full beard was wearing a loose-fitting standard-brown UPS uniform, and an oversized cap which covered an up-fold of clumped hair. UPS delivery men were usually clean-shaven, with neatly-clipped hair.

He leaned close to the door-knob, glanced up and down the empty hallway and positioned his body to block the motion of his left hand. A small metal object slid into the keyhole and was jiggled and twisted deftly for the few seconds it took to spring the lock.

Once inside the apartment, the deliveryman removed the thick black-framed eyeglasses which shifted attention from the facial remnants of jagged scars still noticeable as thin valleys of light skin. Specs of the heavy duty makeup caked over reconstructed cheekbones rubbed off on the green neoprene-rubber gloves replacing the framed eyeglasses with compact night-vision goggles.

Arcola Manditta, the Chameleon, removed the brown cap and shook her neck-length black hair free as she tiptoed in the direction of Lynne Hurricane's only bathroom. The pink hair dryer she'd noticed a few days ago was still hanging on a wall bracket next to a two-by-three foot medicine cabinet with a facing mirror. Two dozen rose-tinted candle-bulbs framed a romantic nimbus around the glass. The hair dryer was an expensive, heavy-duty appliance with 120 volt and 220 volt electrical settings and a thick plastic barrel much longer than the stubby portable hand-guns stuffed into compact cosmetic traveling cases.

The Chameleon reached into her pocket and extracted a pen-sized Phillips-head screwdriver, a 3/8 inch wide roll of black-vinyl electrical tape and four silver buttons the size of state-quarters---except twice as thick. The two halves of the pink molded-plastic barrel of the heat-gun were easily unscrewed, revealing high-wattage double-helical heating coils and a small, dual-speed fan connected by thin multi-colored wires.

She painstakingly removed the four silver discs from their clear Saran wrapping and placed them gently on a hand-towel resting on the flat edge of the white porcelain pedestal-sink. She then meticulously taped two disks to the inside curvature of each split barrel section, re-attached the barrel to the heat-gun and replaced it in the wall bracket.

The disc-shaped incendiaries were laminates of pure phosphorous metal and an alkaline-earth oxide used in fireworks and anti-personnel land mines. When ignited by intense heat from the red-hot electrical resistance coils in the barrel, the discs would react with air to create a white molten mass of 1700 degree F. particles. The high-velocity fan in the hair-dryer would exhaust the resulting super-heated gaseous substance like the glowing thrust of a space-shuttle booster rocket.

The charred polyvinyl chloride tape would soften, then decompose into chlorine gas...a noxious white mist which quickly eats away the lining of mucous membranes and blinds anyone within ten feet.

The Chameleon had tested the design. The pyrophoric material reacted with the hot air a few seconds after the hair-dryer was switched on at the power source. The hair-dryer-turned-rocket-oxidizer shot out a jet of super-heated particles and gas to a distance of six feet for a duration of five seconds; long enough to cause severe burns before the barrel melted and the device disintegrated.

As the Chameleon slowly eased the apartment door closed in the silent shadows of the fifth-floor corridor, she noticed a large wreath hanging from a black ribbon tacked to a door at the far end. A huge vase of summer flowers sat on the floor nearby. She gagged at the bitter-sweet odor of condolence-flowers seeping down the hallway from Mr. Barnswig's apartment door. The stupid old fool should have minded his own business.

Logan Airport, Boston

Brad waited on the sidewalk outside, peeking into the "passengers only" glass doors as Lynne descended the escalator to the baggage-claim area wearing a chocolate satin blouse tucked into snug-fitting blue-jeans. She appeared troubled.

Her hard-cover luggage circled the carousel twice before she lifted it from the rubber conveyer belt. She was thinking about the new $800 dollar evening dress now stained with Lydia's tears and a dab of shrimp cocktail sauce. The dress hadn't slivered to the floor…unzipped impatiently by Justin… as she'd imagined when she handed her Visa card to a Newberry Street dress-shop clerk.

Brad greeted her with a broad smile as she emerged from the exit doors into the steaming Boston summer air. He gave no hint of the deep depression he'd experienced during the past few days; after assuming that the 'couple relationship' between his two close friends had flourished during their get-together in Washington. He anguished over the thought that Justin and Lynne most likely consumated a more serious phase in their relationship. His own intense feelings for Lynne would most likely be relegated to the heart-wrenching category of 'close friends.'

He vowed to expend his pent-up energy on starting up the AmerAgain Products, LLC, venture, Justin's five-company, joint-venture brainchild. At least he'd be working on a common goal with the only girl he'd ever fallen in love with at first sight.

"Hi. How'd it go?" he said in a subdued tone as he reached for Lynne's bag.

She noticed his forlorn expression and answered in an equally subdued voice, "Not too bad. I met some interesting people and ran into an old friend."

"Did you and Justin have a good time?" His tone hinted of cynicism.

The warm smile on Lynne's face broadened into a silly grin. *He's jealous,* she thought, with a great deal of satisfaction. She could still feel the unexpected aftershock of her trembling body after they'd kissed away the after-taste of Chinese food.

"Justin talked FFF into providing another $100,000 in seed money, but he says they're stalling on a full commitment to finance AmerAgain," Lynne explained tensely. "He thinks McGill and Blackstone may not come through for us. He wants you to actively pursue alternate financing, now that the patent has been issued."

"I know. He called a few minutes ago to remind me to immediately deposit the check you're carrying."

"Here." Lynne reached into her pocketbook and handed him a sealed envelope printed with the 'FFF' return address.

"Where to now…my lady?" Brad said in a forced cheerful tone, as he folded the envelope into his pocket.

"I need a shower before heading to the office. Can you drive me home?"

McGill was away; Ross was dead; Justin was on a flight to China. There was nobody to report to. She made a mental note to visit Julia, at her home near the Don Orion Rest Home. She pictured Ross's wife kneeling at a pew in the serene Madonna Chapel, praying for hours for her husband's soul; and probably asking forgiveness for his killer.

"And thanks for picking me up, honey."

Brad's spirits were lifted by her puckish tone. He hoped it reflected her true feelings for him. He was still confused…recalling the steamy, yet inconclusive night they'd spent together before she left for Washington.

"I'll drop you off. Then I have to shoot across town for an appointment with a venture capitalist. This guy called me out of the blue from Houston. Says he learned of the new recycling technology and wants to discuss a possible licensing arrangement."

"How could anyone know about that? The patent technology hasn't been announced to the public."

"The man claims his venture group follows the issuance of new technology patents, and provides financing when the opportunity matches their investment strategies. I told him I thought a licensing arrangement was premature, but we were pursuing alternate financing sources."

Lynne's cell-phone buzzed as soon as Brad dropped her suitcase inside the apartment door and rushed off to his meeting. She waved from the open apartment door, then noticed the wreath hanging from a door down the hallway near Mr. Barnswig's apartment. A stagnant scent of roses and gardenias hung in the air. She walked slowly down the corridor as she answered the call, "Hello, Lynne here."

Stella Nicorezzi spoke excitedly, in an affectionate tone, "It's your old roomy, El. I'm calling from Geneva about that information you wanted."

Lynne leaned down to the flower arrangement and read the small card attached to the glass vase that had been delivered to Mr. Barnswig's door by a local florist. "Oh, my God!" she suddenly cried out in anguish. "It can't be."

"Well, it is!" Stella replied to the surprisingly animated greeting. "But there's a problem. If you want the information Papa has acquired, you'll have to convince him in-person. It's very sensitive data."

"Oh, God almighty. Poor Mr. Barnswig."

"Who's Mr. Barnswig?"

Lynne suddenly realized Stella had misunderstood. "I'm sorry, Stella. I'm standing in front of a friend's apartment, and I just found out he's dead."

"How horrible, Lynne. Was he a close friend?"

Lynne sank to the floor, leaning against the wall adjacent to Mr. Barnswig's door. She hesitated before answering, as tears streaked her cheeks. "Sort of," she sobbed, "a good neighbor who watched over me."

Stella considered ending the call to give Lynne time to recover her emotions; but she feared Lynne might get caught up in her friend's wake or funeral before she had a chance to explain the importance of the meeting with her father.

"Lynne, this is obviously not a good time to talk about your inquiry, but if you want the information, I'm afraid we have to discuss it right now."

Lynne's mind was racing. She noticed an unopened newspaper folded in front of the door across from Mr. Barnswig's apartment. Suddenly the door opened and a young teenage girl in a bathrobe leaned over to pick up the Globe. Shanola, her next-door neighbor's fourteen-year-old daughter, jumped back in surprise as she observed Lynne sitting on the floor, leaning against the wall.

"Are you hurt?" she shrieked.

"No....no. I'm okay," Lynne answered, somewhat embarrassed, as she struggled to her feet.

"It's terrible about old Barnswig, isn't it?" Shanola exclaimed as she reached for Lynne's hand and elbow and lifted. "He dropped dead on the street two days ago....late afternoon."

Lynne noticed the damp hair and skin as Shanola's bathrobe partially opened. She guessed the teenage girl just stepped out from a warm bath.

The Chameleon strained to apprehend the faint sounds picked up by the listening devices imbedded in the target's apartment. The Rolex watch was tucked away in the suitcase leaning against Lynne's apartment door. The blurred words echoing down the hallway through the half-open door to Lynne's apartment were too muted to understand.

"Did you say late afternoon? Two days ago?" Shanola nodded, then suddenly grimaced, pressing two hands against her belly.

"Are you all right?"

"You know...one of those days. Mom let me stay home from school with a heating pad. The bath helped."

Stella was lost in the stilted exchange. "No, I need you here tomorrow... the latest. Papa has the information but will be leaving the country in two days. There's a ticket to Geneva waiting for you at the Swiss Air counter at Logan Airport. The flight leaves at two pm, your time."

"Two pm?" Lynne glanced at her watch. "That doesn't give me much time."

Shanola looked puzzled. "I think it was later than that, Lynne. Is the time important?"

"Stella, I'll call you back in five minutes, okay? I need to think."

"It's easier if I call you back, Lynne---international connections and all that. Talk to you in five."

Shanola was a sweet, caring girl from a broken home. Lynne had taken her on shopping excursions to Boston during department–store sales events; and taught her how to look for bargains. She also invited Shanola to sleep over when her alcoholic father occasionally showed up to harass her mother, and explore his daughter's budding curves with his grimy hands.

"I may be leaving again, right away, honey. Why don't you join me for tea while I pack and get ready? It'll make you feel better."

"Let me tell mom. I'll be right over."

Stella waited ten minutes then pushed the automatic redial button.

The Chameleon could hear Lynne's words clearly: "Tell me again, Stella..... Yes, I understand the urgency. I haven't even unpacked yet, but there's still enough time for a quick shower and packing some clean clothes."

"What? You had implants, so you think your new clothes will fit me?"

"Yes, when I arrive. Okay, see you at the baggage claim area."

Lynne hung up and rushed into the bathroom. She flicked on the switch for the overhead light and turned on the shower, then covered her hair with a plastic shower-cap and jumped into the glass enclosure. The steaming cascade relaxed her shoulder and neck muscles for the first time in several hours. But she could afford only a few minutes of bliss.

She stepped out of the shower and toweled standing in front of the fogged mirror. A ghostly outline of her head and shoulders stared back. "Shit." The Chameleon heard her complain.

In a fifteen minute period the Chameleon overheard a variety of sounds: the rush of water; sighs of exhaustion; the shuffling of paper-product packages; a shout of "tea's getting cold." Finally she heard the sounds that made her grin: a switch clicking in the bathroom followed by the hum of a high-pitched fan. She expected an agonizing scream to follow.

Lynne waited impatiently as the overhead exhaust-fan slowly dried the top edge of the mirror. She became annoyed at the fogged image, and reached for the hair dryer.

The Chameleon was perplexed by the ten second delay. Then she heard another click, a second, higher-pitched rotation of air being fanned into a pink plastic barrel. Then the "whoosh.... whoosh....whoosh" sounds she'd anticipated.

Lynne's agonizing screams pierced the listening device. Shanola came running into the bathroom...in time to see Lynne collapse, as slivers of cracked mirror, resembling icy-rain, showered over her. White-hot incendiary particles and chlorine gas had oxidized away the dark coating that created a mirror from clear glass. The room was fogged with poisonous chlorine vapors.

"God in Heaven….God in Heaven," the teenager cried out.

"Stay back! Get away! Call your mother!" Lynne sobbed from the floor. She was in shock from the pain, as white-hot fragments burned through the top layers of her skin.

The Chameleon pictured Lynne's hair on fire; charred and peeling third-degree skin burns; an irreparably damaged eardrum; white-hot pyrotechnic particles smoldering through layers of dermis and epidermis…imbedded and festering in destroyed cranial nerves and smoking skull bone.

And permanent scars. Plenty of permanent scars. Just like her own.

CHAPTER 40

(August 5, 2008), 3 pm local time
Beijing, USTR Mission visit

Lili Qi crossed Dongdang Street to avoid the queue of demonstrators and unlucky sympathizers being herded into canvas-topped trucks by the General Security Police from the Youanmen Police Station in central Beijing. The Chief of Security for the capital city had seen enough.

He ordered the security police to arrest troublemakers who came to the city from outlying provinces and haul them into jail cells…including anyone in the vicinity even *suspected* of supporting the activists. The Public Security police were being referred to by foreign media as the *luan squad,* the chaos squad, reflecting the severe and inconsistent attacks the helmeted policemen with shields and black clubs were unleashing on the throng of dissident workers roaming the capital.

The demonstrators marched on the business district, outside the gates of the new Olympic Village Complex and in front of the Beijing Railroad Station, holding placards and shouting 'Yue-ji, Yue-ji.' They were demanding that their petitions be taken up by a higher authority.

The Beijing police chief blamed his troubles on the inept handling of citizen disputes by Communist Party cadres and police in the outlying provinces. The local party bosses first ignored the protests, then made matters worse by dealing too harshly with the farmers and peasants seeking nothing more than fair treatment from the government.

Lili walked slowly past the police trucks, her shoulders hunched over in non-threatening posture. She increased her pace and filtered into the crowd of foreign visitors cramming the central shopping district in search of bargain-priced European fashions and brand-name cameras and electronic products. A few shoppers stared silently at the street confrontations, their frowns the only indication that the commotion wasn't a legion of garbage collectors tossing waste-bags into compaction trucks.

She detoured away from the U.S. Embassy on Ritan Road and noticed that security at the main gate had increased from a lone pistol-armed guard to a dozen marines gripping M4 automatic rifles across their chests...stern-faced in combat mind-set. The regular security guard was standing behind the closed gate, his pistol-case unclipped, with outstretched fingers tapping the air an inch above his Sig Sauer P229 handgun loaded with twelve necked-down .357 SIG cartridges.

Lili's destination was the modern seventeen-story East Wing addition to the landmark Beijing Hotel located a few blocks from Tian'anmen Square on East Chang'an Boulevard. Several USTR and Commerce Department staff members, media pundits and businessmen traveling with the mission were housed there in large, comfortable rooms furnished with electrically-controlled drapes. Magnificent views of the Imperial Palace were available from rooms with numbers ending in 36, 37, 38, 39, 43 and 44, usually reserved for the influential CEOs of multinational corporations, here to negotiate the relocation of their home-based factories to the Chinese mainland.

Lili glanced at her Tour Bureau assignment sheet to confirm the number...then tapped on door 1044. She looked at the paper again. The U.S. Ambassador himself had signed the document requesting that she be assigned as Mr. Gatt's guide and interpreter during his travels in China. His itinerary was unusual. So was her real assignment.

Justin Gatt had checked in a few hours earlier and was probably in his bed sleeping off the thirteen-hour jet lag between Washington and Beijing.

Tonight, Lili was to be his translator and escort at a dinner hosted by Chang Hui Chen, the Chairman of the National People's Congress, for mission delegates at the International Hotel (Guoji) on Jinguomenwai Avenue. The 32-story, 1049-room International Hotel was operated by the China National Tourism Administration and was also the temporary dwelling for the other USTR mission visitors---except for Butler Humphreys, Richard de Leone and Anthony Clancy.

The three ranking trade officials shared a 4,000 square-foot three-bedroom suite in the grandeur of the exclusive Anglers' Rest State Guest House (Diaoyutai)...normally set aside for visiting heads of state and important guests of the Chinese government. Situated in the Sanlitun diplomatic residential section, the Diaoyutai provided superlative personalized service by a trained staff that outnumbered the guests.

The Anglers' Guest House also offered a feature missing from the other hotels used by trade mission delegates: a clean-sweep of electronic eavesdropping devices.

The balance of Justin's schedule in Beijing included a meeting the next morning with representatives of the Bureau of Fair Trade at the State Administration for Industry, and an afternoon session with the Deputy Assistant Minister of Autonomous Zone Small Business Enterprises. The following day they'd tour Beijing's main attractions: the Forbidden City called Zijin Cheng, the Great Hall of the People in the Tian'anmen Square area and the famous Avenue of Animals and archaeological discoveries at the Ming Tombs. Next, they'd trudge in the oppressive August heat and dusty humidity to the Mutianyu section of the Great Wall—which was less crowded and not as commercialized as the more popular Badaling section; then return to center city and explore the ancient structures and significant buildings in the Imperial Palace district.

Lili usually guided American tourists to Tian'anmen Square, the Gate of Heavenly Peace, the Memorial Hall of Mao, and the new Olympic Village Complex, with its dramatic modern structures called the "Water Cube" and the "Bird's Nest." But her favorite site was the Temple of Heaven in the southwestern section of the city---a masterpiece of 15th-century architecture with three main edifices---dominated by the Hall of Prayer for Good Harvests, with its triple-tiered terrace surrounded by 36-foot-high marble balustrades on each level, and topped in a conical roof surfaced with fifty-thousand gleaming blue-glazed tiles. The interlaced wooden frame supporting the roof and walls was constructed without the use of a single nail.

Justin apparently desired to experience authentic Beijing life because he'd requested side-tours of the ancient "hutong" cobblestone back alleys, local markets and restaurants where regular people dined. He specifically requested a local dinner of duck smoked in tea leaves and camphor, which he'd salivated over after reading a Chinese cookbook at the Library of Congress. He'd pass on stewed snakes and monkey brains.

On the final day before departing Beijing for Shanghai and other locations, Gatt was scheduled to tour Beijing University and attend a lecture given by Professor Meng-Ji, a prestigious scholar at the Beijing University Economic Research Center and one of the few academicians whose outspoken criticism of China's tight fiscal policies was tolerated by the Communist Party. Professor Meng-Ji had gained international respect when he was nominated for the Nobel Prize in Economics for his progressive macro-economic views on the contrasting effects of free-market forces and central-government control of international money flows. His concepts influenced China's international trade policies and the country's gradual shift towards a free-market economy.

Professor Meng-Ji also corresponded frequently with Eric Syzmansky at the Yale School of Management. Syzmansky helped Meng-Ji arrange for several promising Chinese graduate students and middle managers to attend S.O.M. Meng-Ji had been approached by the Minister of Educational Exchange Programs to arrange for Colonel Wen Ma to attend Yale business school lectures.

Justin squinted bleary-eyed at the telephone he'd wrapped in a terrycloth towel, still dangling above the floor from a coiled cord. *The knuckles banging on the door for the last few minutes must be raw*, he thought, as he slogged from the bed and splashed ice-water on his face. He'd spent several sleepless hours on the communications device Balzerini had provided before finally connecting with Lynne at the Nicorezzi estate in Geneva. He was sick with worry, having learned from Brad about her unusual accident and Mr. Barnswig's sudden death. Someone was trying to cause her harm.

"Please don't bother me again," he shouted angrily through the closed door. "I'm not interested in a free body massage."

The grin on Lili's face slowly changed to a grimace. She recalled how her friend at theTourist Bureau decided to augment her meager secretary's salary by offering after-hours 'massage' services to some of the tourists staying at local hotels She was now sharing a rotting flax mattress teemed with black fungus, with a toe-nipping rodent who emerged only at night from the labyrinth of rat tunnels bored beneath Prostitution Jail---as the detained Svengalis of sensitive nerve-endings dubbed the local police station. The most attractive girls were kept in confinement for weeks…eventually being forced to 'massage' their way to freedom. They had no opportunity for legal representation.

Lili's friend had been arrested when the 'cut' she split with the night manager at a local hotel didn't meet his satisfaction. Occasionally, an over-aggressive girl was arrested when a jet-lagged foreign visitor complained about her incessant telephone calls to his room; and the arrogant door knocks and blatantly suggestive solicitations at all hours of the night.

Gatt expected to hear the words, "Massage service…good price!"

"Mr. Gatt…It's your tour guide, Lili Qi."

"Go away!"

She tapped on the door again and called out, "Really, Mr. Gatt. I'm from the Beijing Tourist Bureau. Ambassador Balzerini sent me to help with your travel arrangements."

The door opened slowly. The American was wearing a white cotton bathrobe, one slipper and a pained expression on an unshaven face dripping with cold water.

"How long will this take, Miss? I haven't slept in several hours." His lids strained not to drop-curtain over his blood-shot eyes. He inhaled and exhaled wearily, in a oval-mouth yawn-cycle.

Lili wondered how such a ragged-looking American could be important enough for the Ambassador himself to arrange for special travel around the country. He'd found only one slipper and was having difficulty holding his blue eyes open for more than short bursts. The two-day stubble on his face was darker than the unkemp silver-tinged hair pressed over his ears and sprouting above his forehead like mowed crabgrass.

"I'm sorry, Mr. Gatt. I was told to come over and escort you to an important dinner with Chinese officials." She checked the time and added, "I could come back later, but you only have a few hours. I was hoping we could review your travel arrangements first."

Justin blinked and locked his eyes fully open. "You speak perfect English," he slurred restlessly.

It had been impossible to sleep after Brad called to inform him of Lynne's accident and Mr. Barnswig's sudden death. Thank God Lynne wasn't permanently injured and he was able to contact her. She'd rushed to Logan for the flight to Geneva, as soon as the burns on her hands and forearms were covered with Aloe ointment and band-aides. She was lucky to avoid serious injury when the glass mirror she was de-fogging with the hair-dryer shattered from the intense heat of gas particles rocketing from the barrel.

He was convinced the two incidents were associated with the 'cleaning lady,' who disappeared from Harvard Square shortly before Mr. Barnswig fell dead on a Cambridge street. For whatever reason...the phony maid could be stalking Lynne. Justin was glad she fled Cambridge...at least for a few days.

"Please come in. You said your name was Lili?"

Lili handed him the Tour Bureau assignment printout, a business card and her personal identification. She remained standing in the hallway. It was not polite to enter someone's home unless you were asked twice. Justin held the papers eighteen inches from his nose and read.

Lili eased away from the door as Justin strained to read and said, "I'll be back." She turned toward the elevator and vanished.

So, Lili was the *special guide* Balzerini mentioned. Her brief resume printed on the Bureau papers indicated Lili Qi could speak more languages than a team of UN translators, including the Chinese dialects needed to communicate with the diverse population they'd encounter during his whirlwind tour of the country. He headed for the shower, wondering about her abrupt departure.

The neuron-stimulating aroma of fresh Brazilian coffee arrived through the crevices as he was toweling off. He walked to the door, ahead of Lili's knock, and swung it open.

"Come in," he said enthusiastically. "Please come in."

She carried two large containers of black coffee and a glass of fresh cream taken from the self-service station in the lobby. Resting on each cup was a large oatmeal-sugar cookie softened by rising fumes from the warm coffee. Justin reached for a cup and cookie as if they were nectar from the gods.

Lili was in her mid-twenties, dressed in a plain one-piece sleeveless black cotton dress, with a white Orchid Pavilion scene depicting four wine-fueled 4th century Chinese scholars reciting poetry, embroidered on her right shoulder. A wide red-leather belt guarding her tiny waist matched the color of pugnacious red-painted toes peeking out from her open flats.

Justin marveled at the beauty of her oriental countenance…perfectly oval face, smooth, high cheek-bones, warm dark eyes…skin the envy of a cosmetics model. Her jet-black hair was brushed back and falling behind her shoulders and delicate ears---reflecting satin-textured hues of magenta and cyan azure. Gatt's senses were stimulated more by her alluring appearance than the splash of ice water on his face.

"What's all the ruckus on the street?"

Lili hesitated, then replied softly, "Oh, you mean the noise?"

Police sirens, sharply raised voices, heavy wooden-thumps and shrieks of pain filtered in from an open window. "Demonstrators from outside the city are causing problems for the police."

He savored a long gulp of the hot robust brew and said, "Is that why you're here? To guide me safely to the International Hotel?"

She glanced at him curiously and said, "Have you ever been to Beijing, Mr. Gatt? The city is exploding with people. Tourists, foreign newspaper and television reporters, not to mention the masses from the outlying provinces who came here to register complaints. It seems everyone is traveling around confused."

"You're going to keep me from getting lost," he said appreciatively, glancing sleepily over the rim of the cup.

"And possibly, in a humble way, to help you learn more about China's complex society."

"Well, since we'll be traveling together for the next few weeks, Lili, I'm glad to have this opportunity to know you better. And to learn more about your country."

He held out his hand. She noticed it was warm and reassuring.

Once on the street, Justin regretted not taking Lili's advice to call a taxi. Indulging his curiosity, he'd asked to walk the half-dozen blocks from his hotel to the International. The heat and humidity were oppressive at 95 degrees F. and 98 percent relative humidity. They were jostled in every direction trying to weave through the million-strong populace jamming central Beijing streets. People shoved each other irritably trying to reach their destinations.

The dusty air coating and drying his nostrils, and caking tears into damp sand-balls, finally disoriented Justin. Lili lost him momentarily in the crowd, then grabbed his hand tightly and flagged a cab.

"Where'd you come from originally?" Justin asked as they settled in the back seat and savored the cool filtered air of the new state-owned vehicle. Justin's sincere tone and deep blue eyes encouraged Lili to share facts about her life that she normally reserved for trusted friends.

She recalled her childhood in Sichuan, and the return trip to Emai Shan for her mother's funeral. She mentioned the martial arts training at Wanniansi, the Buddhist Temple of Myriad Ages, but not the details of her mother's accident. "Then I was sponsored by an unknown benefactor...a friend of Zong Keba, the Grand Master of Wanniansi, who befriended me as a young girl and taught me many things. The unknown benefactor arranged for me to attend the Beijing University Department of Language History."

"I understand Beijing University is comparable in prestige to Harvard or Yale in the U.S." Guessing that Lili's mother was poor, he asked, apologetically, "Is it costly to attend?" He wasn't aware that Lili's father had also died in an industrial accident at a lead-mine in Sichuan.

"The benefactor paid," she replied impishly.

Justin's curiosity about the loud activities on the street peaked a few blocks from the International Hotel. A uniformed policeman chasing a young man carrying a woman's pocketbook down a side alley was shooting at him wildly with rubber bullets. An old peasant crouching at the side of the narrow alley...searching for a leak in a partially inflated orange-rubber bicycle inner-tube, folded into a bucket of water, suddenly shouted in pain. He reached for his shoulder and collapsed on the stone walkway.

"I hope he gets away," Lili admitted to Justin's surprise. "If they catch him and he's from out-of-town...they'll hack off his hand before he's charged with a crime."

"I read that thieves, other than white-collar ones, are rare in China. Now I know why. I thought the limbs of thieves were only cut off in Muslim countries."

"China is ninety-two percent Han, but the largest of the other fifty-five ethnic groups is the Hui Muslim people concentrated in Gansu, Ninxia, Quinghai and Xinjiang. The government uses the practices of its Autonomous People to maintain social order, whenever it's convenient."

Lili told Justin the story she'd read about a *'biab dan', a pole man*, Mr.Yu, who was hauling loads of grain, fertilizer, and anything else he could balance on his shoulders. "He was one of the sweaty and dirty porters who openly displayed their low-prestige vocation. Mr. Yu's load this day was lighter than usual---he was collecting hair cuttings off the floors of beauty salons and barber shops, and stuffing them into large plastic bags for sale to wig-makers in the southern cities."

Justin thought the story would be a comedy, but Lili's expression was dark. "He'd collected hair from an upscale salon in a busy shopping street in downtown Chongqing for several hours and his load was meager---two bags of loose locks. As he trudged along in the crowded street, he accidentally brushed against a young women who was elbowing her way through.

"'Hey, pole man,' the woman shouted, 'you got hair all over my shirt!' He turned to face her, and the man standing next to her wearing a coat and tie and expensive leather shoes shouted angrily, 'Look where you're going, you floor-sweep magpie.' The pole man was proud but mild-mannered. He commented that he was only trying to earn extra money so his daughter wouldn't have to become a prostitute. His slightly indiscreet show of yellow teeth, stained from chain smoking, convinced the young wife that the 'biab dan' called her a whore. She yanked his ear and slapped him across the face. Her husband grabbed Mr. Yu's pole and smashed him several times on the head, claiming loudly to the bystanders that his brother was a public official. 'If this man causes me any more problems,' he shouted, 'I'll have him thrown in jail for ten years.'"

Lili paused as she noticed a dirty-faced young girl about seven-years-old crying against a utility pole. She hoped the child had not been abandoned in the city because her parents were arrested for demonstrating. She then told Justin the rest of the story in an anguished intonation.

"To avoid contact with the news media, the beaten man, Mr.Yu, was isolated in a hospital for two months...although his wounds had healed. His family was told he was sent on a vacation paid for by the government. He was forced to read a statement on local television which was interpreted by his neighbors as selling out to the government. All he said was, 'Everyone should allow this to be handled by the law.' The backlash from local farmers was fierce. 'Don't bother to plant rice,' a former friend told his family, 'because we'll tear out the roots.' Other people in his village wanted to yank out his rotten teeth for speaking the government's words. His wife heard many threats against her husband and finally convinced him to relocate the family."

Justin was appalled by Lili's story. The taxi stopped at a traffic light across from the International Hotel entrance and Justin watched a tall familiar Chinese man dressed in a military uniform step out of a black limousine and enter the hotel. He recognized the arrogant expression of the Chinese state-official he'd encountered at Yale. Colonel Wen Ma Ming paused momentarily, and glanced back to the street...sensing someone's eyes were following him. He walked deliberately past the doorman.

Lili's frustration with the social imbalances in her country was apparent to Justin, as she told of another disturbing incident.

"A squad of policemen had to occupy a cotton textile factory in frigid mid-winter last year when the owners "retired" and disappeared with the company's funds. The workers who lost their jobs rioted. During the uprising a young factory worker was arrested and taken to a local prison for shoving a policeman. After being forced into an icy shower in the un-heated jail, he was chained to a brick wall by the guards and not allowed to dry off. They beat him unmercifully and did horrible violations to his body; then said to him, 'Tell the others nothing happened to you here.' He couldn't eat or relieve himself for four days." Lili's eyes glassed as she said grimly, "Prison officials despise ordinary people. They don't hesitate to torment us."

Lili and Justin watched the crowded streets from the taxi window, admiring the courageous migrant workers holding placards aloft. The demonstrators were being shuffled away from the nearby Railroad Station into a side road across from the hotel, where police were waiting in vans. Several young men held up large hand-made signs with Chinese characters and English sub-titles inscribed in fluorescent markers. Probably to catch the attention of the international press attending the Olympic Games.

Unemployed farmers who were forced from their land and deprived of livelihoods by dam construction projects along the banks of the Yangtze River, held posters complaining of uncompensated land seizures and forced immigrations. Peasant workers lured to the city by the Beijing Economic Enhancement Ministry to construct the now-completed "Water Cube" National Swimming Center, and the "Bird's Nest" bowl-shaped National Stadium for the Olympic Games, were condemning the Communist government for layoffs, unpaid wages and miss-spent state funds.

Other "common people" displayed signs protesting the misuse of natural resources; air and water pollution; and police brutality. Most of the demonstrators were unemployed and without overnight accommodations. They'd be huddling together at night in the 'hutongs'---a labyrinth of ancient cobblestone and brick back-alleys in Beijing. Dirty water condensing and dripping from dusty galvanized roofs would be collected in discarded tin cans and plastic bottles; giving some relief from the oppressive heat and the abrasive powdery sand carried on the prevailing winds from the Gobi Desert plains northwest of the city. A typical Beijing summer.

Suddenly, Justin and Lili watched in dismay as several placards held aloft by the demonstrators came crashing to the pavement. Police were clubbing the carriers unconscious. Plain-cloths officers rushed to collect the placards as evidence for future trials.

"Chinese society has become deceitful," Lili complained sourly. "With money and connections, you don't have to follow the law. You can arrange anything."

Justin added sardonically, "It's not that much different in the U.S. The people who profit the most from our no-holds-barred capitalist system are the rich ones who buy away the concerns of ordinary people. At least, in America, there are safe ways to openly express displeasure with our leaders. As a democracy...we create change by voting and expressing our opinions publicly."

Lili looked at him skeptically. "In China," she responded, "the people's anger can only be vented on the internet, tabloids or news magazines. We're not allowed to form large-scale organizations, except for the so called NGOs---non-government organizations sanctioned by the Communists. The people are frustrated. A few get rich by corruption methods, or back-door *guanxi* deals---connections and contacts the cadres cultivate to acquire things indirectly. The rest of us struggle to survive."

"What about all these protests? I read there were more than seventy-thousand last year."

"All isolated local incidents, Mr. Gatt," Lili insisted. "Anyone suspected of coordinating a national protest is quickly arrested. Our society is on a short fuse...just waiting to ignite."

Colonel Wen Ma noticed the tall American with the deep blue eyes enter the dining room accompanied by an attractive Chinese woman with long dark hair. He recognized Professor Syzmanski's arrogant guest speaker immediately among the trade delegation guests.

Colonel Wen was surprised that the USTR mission included such low-level American businessmen. It must be one of those stupid idealistic programs the U.S. Small Business Administration stages to make it appear the federal government considers small manufacturing businesses important to the American economy. *That fool--Gutt or Grat--probably believes them,* he thought. *He's making a big mistake, threading in my jurisdiction. One error, and he'll learn the consequences of disrespecting a PLA officer.*

Wen Ma never forgave an insult. Insolent adversaries were dealt with harshly. Tomorrow, he'd order the director of the Beijing Tour Bureau to have the American's tour-guide report his whereabouts at all times. *The arrogant fool will eventually make a blunder interpreting Chinese laws."* Charges of bribing a state official, or stealing state secrets qualify one for the death penalty. He doubted that the U.S. government would interfere in the swift punishment of an unknown entrepreneur found guilty of espionage by Chinese prosecutors.

CHATER 41

(AUGUST 5, 2008), 5 AM
SAN ANTONIO, TEXAS,

Joko eased the rusted station wagon onto the New Braunfels exit ramp on Route 35, twenty-five miles north of San Antonio, and immediately spotted the lights from the green van parked in the nearly-empty travel-center parking lot. He flicked the high-beams twice then followed the van from the lot to an isolated farm road a mile away.

The ambient darkness was flood-lit by a pure-white full moon, reflecting the sum of the color spectrum. The sun was still a few degrees below the eastern horizon. The next brightest object seen from earth in the cloudless sky was the international space station, gliding in orbit at 24,000 miles per hour about two hundred miles above south Texas.

Budi was reminded of the peaceful pre-dawn surf-fishing he'd enjoyed with his father as a young boy. The morning serenity which greeted them as they carried hand-made nets from their plywood shack on the Jakartan coast was only interrupted by the excitement of a first catch.

"There they are," Budi whispered from the passenger seat. "Pull behind the truck." He turned to Danang and Muslihrama in the back seat and said, "Get your gear and move out."

The traffic was light and they could see several hundred yards in either direction along the flat linear road. Thick black tire-streaks on the road marked the finishing line where teenagers from local farms slammed on the brakes of three-wheeled tractors they drag-raced on the road. The driver and back-seat passengers waited until the road was cleared, then ran to the rear of the parked truck and pushed their satchels under the partially opened drop-door.

Budi remained behind to wipe away fingerprints from the steering wheel and interior surfaces of the wagon, then heaved the car keys into a field of shoulder-high velvetleaf topped with pale-green, furry hairs. The stout, branchless weed looked nothing like its malvaceae family cousins—coffee, cotton and hibiscus.

The truck engine roared impatiently as Budi rolled onto the floor of the van and pulled down the door. The alternate driver standing at the rear re-attached a heavy-duty lock and dashed to the open passenger door as the tires screeched onto the pavement.

The non-stop 1,000 mile trip from New Braunfels, Texas to Sioux City, Iowa would take about thirty hours, including stops for fuel and food in Waco, Fort Worth, Oklahoma City, Wichita, Topeka, Omaha and Onawa, Iowa. The final 30-mile leg from Onawa on Route 29 would put them in Sioux City before dawn…near the huge stockyards used for fattening cattle and hogs with Iowa corn, before they were slaughtered and shipped to local meat-packing plants.

Budi had plenty of time to study the road maps leading to the three large midwest Iowa cornfields selected by the Chinese agricultural experts as ideal targets. The canisters containing the agricultural pathogen would be mortar-fired in specific directions from each location to achieve maximum exposure.

He positioned a battery-powered snake-lamp over the Iowa crop-map printed from the website of the Iowa State University Agricultural Station in Ames, Iowa. A red marker traced the route they'd follow to deliver the cellulose-hungry micro-organisms to the chosen firing locations. He calculated it would take less than four hours in the middle of the night to contaminate approximately ten percent of the land mass in the mid-west area of the state.

Once the crystallized organism was released from the exploding canisters, and activated in a symbiontic union, the prevailing winds over Sac City, Boone and Fort Dodge would disperse the virus-like mycoplasma over a third of Iowa's 12 million acre prime corn-belt land. Within hours, the degenerative effect of the corn-virus would spread plant-to-plant over wide areas. In less than a week, the twelve mortar detonations fired south and east from Boone; north and east from Fort Dodge; and west, north and south from Sac City would blanket a third of the rich black earth of the Iowa Prairie lands with chain-reaction bursts of mycoplasma spores, satiated with decomposed cellulosic by-products from the corn plants.

If all went as General Ye's bio-weapons experts predicted…the micoplasma crystals of *modified Brucella abortus* RNA retrovirus… perfected in China's bio-weapons lab in Jilin Province…would adhere to the E.coli host bacteria released from a separate chamber in the mortar shell, and drift gracefully down in destructive harmony onto the warm surfaces of corn leaves, husks and stalks---gorging on the cellulosic structures in piranha-like feeding frenzies.

The plan of attack and escape was straight-forward. Budi would rent a car in Wichita, Kansas and follow the green van to Onawa, Iowa...an hour south of Sioux City on highway Route 29. Three sets of weapons would be pre-loaded in the back of the green van with four canisters each, and prepared for rapid firing at each location. The van would travel east on Route 20 to Sac City, where it would drop off Joko and one-third of the weapons. Budi was to arrive an hour later in the rented car...giving Joko time to stage the light cannons for high-angle shots. Budi would aim and fire the weapons... exploding the canisters in pre-set directions. Joko would gather the spent casings and light mortars into heavy-duty plastic leaf-bags and discard them in remote locations along the route to the next firing destination.

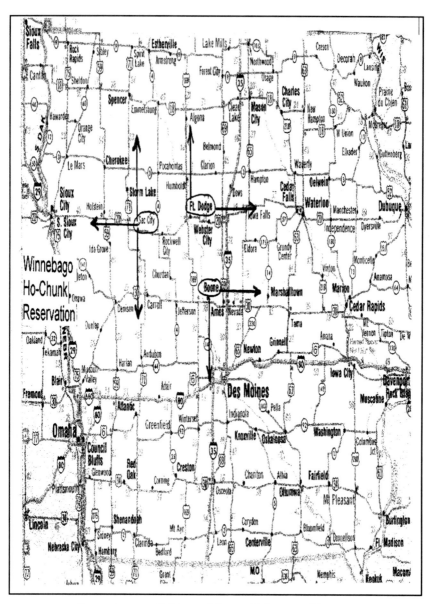

Locations of Corn-Virus Mortar Firings

(AUGUST 6, 2008),
BEIJING, FOREIGN AFFAIRS MINISTRY

The Chinese negotiating team sat stoically on one side of the massive conference table at the Foreign Affairs Office, maintaining blank expressions. Challenging their silence, the stone-faced Americans across the table focused on the antique blue-porcelain pitchers of ice-water, warm tea pots and writing instruments placed alongside the voice-recording equipment.

Both sides were stunned into temporary silence by the state television announcement a few minutes earlier that President Mu Jianting had been charged with accepting bribes from a rich Taiwanese family, for arranging long-term leases on mainland Chinese properties recently confiscated by the state from the Taiwanese owners. The highest-ranking Communist leader in the country had been implicated in a shake-down scheme involving Taiwan's investments on the mainland. A recent law passed by the National People's Congress, and sanctioned by the Chinese Communist Party, authorized the central government to seize land on which the break-away island's investors built factories. The premise for the law was that Taiwan was still considered a Province of the People's Republic of China...therefore, subject to Politboro rule.

The Taiwan delegate to the U.N. stomped out of the Security Council chambers in New York when the People's Republic of China vetoed a resolution introduced by the United States demanding that the PRC return the land rights to Taiwanese factory owners.

President Mu was charged with crimes against the state by Zhoa Zhoa-Gang, the Premier of the State Council. Zhoa had been forced to jeopardize his high standing in the Communist Party by publicly revealing documented evidence against Mu Jianting.

Unidentified members of the State Council and the nine-member Standing Committee of the Communist Party had provided Reuters and other foreign press services with copies of evidence; forcing Zhoa-Zhoa Gang---the man ultimately responsible for fighting fraud in the government---to officially charge his superior with crimes against the state, punishable by execution.

The Politboro was under the voracious spotlight of foreign news organizations because of the Olympic Games and the widespread domestic unrest in city streets. The documents accusing Mu Jianting cited Swiss and Chinese bank accounts linking him to deposits totaling over a hundred-million yuan. One of the banks listed was the Franco-Medici Trust in Geneva---a primary depository for the Central Bank of China's foreign currency reserves.

Mu denied the accusations; claiming he was framed by rivals in the Politboro trying to usurp his power. He vowed to expose and purge the malicious falsifiers, yet couldn't explain away the incriminating bank documents containing his name and notorized signature...except to claim that his signature was forged.

The two senior members of the trade-negotiating teams---USTR Butler Humphreys and Chang Hui Chen, the NPC chairman, finally locked eyes. The appropriate time period had passed for both sides to reflect on the astounding news. They were authorized by national constitutions to negotiate treaties and sign foreign trade agreements binding their countries to the terms. They must move the meetings along to a meaningful conclusion.

Wang Chao, the Minister of Industry and Trade; Yew Bai Tsin, the Governor of the Central Bank of China; and Yong Ihasa, the Senior Vice-Premier and Minister of Monetary Regulation and State Security followed Chang's cue and nodded cordially across the table to Butler Humphreys, Richard deLeone, Forrest Balzerini and Anthony Clancy. As the talks finally resumed, aides sealed the chamber doors and switched on the recording equipment.

Chang Hui-Chen spoke first after the exchange of pleasant greetings. "At the conclusion of the talks," he began in a stiff tone, to remind the U.S. delegation that the Chinese government had things under control, "Mu Jianting, President of the People's Republic of China and Chairman of the Chinese Communist Party, will meet with Mr. Humphreys, as previously scheduled. I will then coordinate the release of information related to these talks, which we have agreed will be provided simultaniously to the international media by the U.S. Trade Representative and the Chinese government."

He avoided any mention of the inflammatory claims against President Mu.

Humphreys replied in an equally rigid tone, "The honor will be mine."

Ambassador Balzerini shifted in his seat as he noticed Yong Ihasa's smug expression.

It contrasted dramatically with the typical idiomatic blank expressions pasted on the other Chinese delegates.

"Shall we begin by reviewing the issues to be discussed?" Wang Chao interjected, as he signaled for a young female assistant to pass out the new list the Chinese prepared for the meeting. Humphreys wasn't going to tolerate this typical Chinese negotiating tactic.

He replied somberly, "We cannot discuss issues other than those contained on the list submitted prior to this meeting by the U.S. Embassy on behalf of the U.S. Trade Representative and the President of the United States. My understanding is that the list was acknowledged by Mr. Chang, the Chairman of the National People's Congress, without comment."

He handed his copy of the new Chinese list back to the embarrassed female aide without reading it and said, "Please confirm that this list coincides exactly with the pre-meeting document submitted by my office." The aide hesitated to reach for the paper. Instead, she fumbled in her briefcase for an excruciating long minute. Humphreys held the paper in mid-air...motionless. Wang Chao finally admitted, "Your list has been revised, Mr. Humphreys."

And so the negotiations proceeded.

Ambassador Balzerini accused China of gross unfairness in trade and monetary policies and expressed solemn concern over the recent murder in Washington of a government contractor; allegedly gunned down by a Chinese secret society which was allowed to operate freely on the mainland. The Chinese adamantly denied knowledge, or complicity in the murder.

Yong Ihasa, the powerful Senior Vice-Premier and Minister of State Security, stated irately, "The accusations by your news groups that the Chinese Communist government is in any way connected with the secret Triad Society...which I recall has now disclaimed responsibility for the demise of Mr. Trenker...is a national insult against the People's Republic of China. We will not stand for such insolence."

Humphreys ignored the subtle threat and replied sardonically, "We accept your denial, Minister Ihasa; but unlike the CCP, the U.S. government does not control its national press."

Balzerini was disturbed by Ihasa's surprisingly belligerent attitude. The Vice-Premier was usually docile in meetings with Americans. In fact, he was considered a moderate by the State Department. The Administration could support Ihasa if China's leadership changed. But his aggressive tone, coupled with Mu Jianting's apparent public disgrace, were clear indications that China's top leadership posts were in a state of flux. Balzerini recognized the symptoms of a new phase of political sensitivity across China.

Humphreys and deLeone hammered at issues of human rights violations, currency manipulations by the Central Bank of China, attempts by state-controlled businesses to purchase high-tech start-ups in California and Massachusetts, and China's massive military build-up, which was forcing the U.S. to reiterate its policy of military intervention to protect its democratic Asian allies---Japan, South Korea and Taiwan, from military aggression by the PRC.

Anthony Clancy spoke for Senator Scharn and the Senate Foreign Relations Committee. "The Senate leadership wishes to be candid with the leaders of China," he stated authoritatively. "It should be clear to the Politboro and the Standing Committee that Congressional support for unabated free-trade with China is wavering. The massive job losses in our manufacturing sector are partly to blame; along with the mounting bankruptcies of American factories unable to compete with low-cost imports from China. The Senate leadership is convinced that China's under-valued yuan is largely to blame."

Yong Ihasa swept his hand over the table, as if to brush away Clancy's statement. "You confuse our efficiencies with your own inefficiencies, Mr. Clancy."

"Your Central Propaganda Department prohibits reporting on social topics which the Communist Party deems embarrassing, sir," Clancy addressed Ihasa directly…much to Humphreys' chagrin. "Neither country can avoid the negative repercussions caused by high unemployment…as we've observed first-hand from the placards and demonstrations on the streets of Beijing; and in first-hand press reports from Shanghai, Tianjin, Chongqing and Guanghou. Clashes between irate Chinese peasants and security forces have also been reported in Wuhan and Shenyang."

NPC Chairman Chang hissed, "The Chinese government does not require American assistance to recognize that unemployed workers have become a problem."

Ihasa held up a conciliatory hand, meant also to quiet the other Chinese. "Be assured, Mr. Clancy, that the dynamic mainland economy will eventually utilize the capabilities of all Chinese workers, as more of the world's manufacturing is concentrated in this great country."

"You can't expect to solve China's unemployment problems by essentially wiping out entire manufacturing sectors in the United States and other developed nations," Humphreys interjected. "The United States needs a sizeable manufacturing base to provide skilled jobs and maintain a secure in-house production capability. More than most American politicians will acknowledge."

"That's your problem, Mr Humphreys…not ours," Yew Bai Tsin admonished indignantly. "The Central Bank of China considers social stability the most important priority in China. Our sophisticated society existed and flourished thousands of years before European immigrants built small villages on the American continent, and forced unarmed native American Indians from their land. Your so-called democratic government still confines the progeny of these poor savages to patches of desolate land called 'reservations.'"

Governor Yew paused for a breath, then nodded to Wang Choa. It was his turn to continue the arguments they'd rehearsed.

The Minister of Industry and Trade calmly said, "Let's clarify China's *requests* of the United States." He addressed Chairman Chen and Vice-Premier Ihasa. "In the spirit of cooperation, China's leadership has outlined the level of cooperation Beijing can offer to strengthen the relationship between the two most powerful nations on earth."

Yew Bai Tsin added contemptuously, "The Olympic Games should be the sole 'winner-take-all' competition between our great countries."

Yong Ihasa's tone was emphatic as he replied, "China and the U.S. produce the bulk of the world's consumer goods, not to mention corn, plastic products, steel, and concrete. It is well known that low-cost Chinese goods have dampened inflation in your country. Even the Federal Reserve Bank Chairman admits it. Mr. Tangus has acknowledged that investments in U.S. Treasury bonds by the Central Bank of China have significantly funded America's expanding budget deficit, and helped contain inflationary pressures."

Yew Bai enhanced China's view of the bleak truth, "Growth in your economy would be impossible without Chinese and Japanese treasury-bond purchases. Now that Tokyo has halted investment in government-backed securities, China is also re-evaluating our temporary policy of committing large trade-balance reserves to such investments."

Humphreys reddened. He replied defiantly, "Repatriating U.S. dollars back to the American economy is only fair. We give you those dollars by allowing Chinese exporters to fill the shelves of our retail outlets. Forty percent of the dollars you invest in the world's most secure high-yielding financial instruments, are unearned. The world is aware that Beijing's manipulation in the value of the yuan restricts foreign imports by keeping Chinese currency undervalued by nearly forty percent."

Wang Chao replied irately, "America is a major beneficiary of China's aggressive export policy. Your free press should be made to understand that American citizens are best served when consumer-product manufacturing is left in PRC hands."

Chang Hui-Chen added in a sarcastic yet conciliatory tone, "Perhaps American businesses should mainly provide *services* for your high-maintenance population."

Neither delegation anticipated the announcement of a definitive trade agreement by the end of the three-day session. Yet, each wished to avoid a costly confrontation.

With the failure of the pre-conference meetings between deputy negotiators a few weeks earlier, each side desired to at least establish consensus on the issues and priorities they'd table before the conclusion of the bilateral talks.

"The President of the United States is concerned that a new terrorist threat springing from China could escalate tensions between Washington and Beijing," Humphreys warned. "Also, if the Central Bank of China continues to manifest fiscal intransigence, and disallows the yuan to float on global currency markets, Congress could move to impose a twenty-five percent tariff on all non-essential imports from China."

"China does not manipulate its currency," Yew Bai Tsin replied angrily, recognizing the first warning of specific consequences from Washington for China's self-serving monetary policy. "Several of your goliath investment banks and multinational corporations have admired the trade deficit America enjoys with China. Some of your own politicians call it 'America's most cost-effective international decision.'"

Anthony Clancy replied evenly, "Your lobbyists know them well. In any case, Governor Yew, the massive trade surplus Beijing insouciantly ignores in trade talks will no longer be tolerated by the American Congress. Plain and simple…the devalued yuan provides Chinese exporters with unfair price advantages over all foreign-made goods."

Yong Ihasa, the ranking Politboro member on the trade-negotiation team, smiled belligerently at the aggressive statements made by the Ambassador, the U.S. Trade Representative and the Senate mouthpiece. The Americans were pretending. They were well aware that sixty-percent of China's exports were produced by foreign-owned factories; many of them American-based businesses. Taking a tough negotiating stance might be *politically correct*, but, in his opinion, it was not sustainable.

Wang Chao nodded to Ihasa. The time had arrived for the negotiations to turn in favor of the Americans, as they'd planned.

"Gentlemen," Yew Bai raised his voice, "There is always room for compromise. The Central Bank has been authorized by the Standing Committee of the Party to allow the yuan to seek its own level in global currency markets, in the very near future. Perhaps, as early as October first of 2008."

Humphreys couldn't believe the central banker's words. "May I inquire, sir, what strings are attached?" His voice reeked with skepticism.

"There will be none," Ihasa boasted calmly, "*if* the Central Bank decides to take such action. China would simply be making a unilateral adjustment in its monetary policy."

"Well, thank you very much!" Clancy shouted prematurely.

"Perhaps by tomorrow the issue can be settled?" Balzerini rummaged.

"Most likely," NPC Chairman Chang responded, as the Chinese negotiators gathered their papers.

MINISTRY OF DEFENSE
NORTHWEST BEIJING

General Ye and Colonel Wen Ma dismissed the PLA staff officers following a briefing on the status of day-to-day operations at LCE's state-controlled mainland factories. The combined operation of the 498 companies and 650 factories controlled under the LCE umbrella was enjoying a phenomenally successful year. Exports to BoxMart, its biggest customer, had increased by fifty-percent. Production capacity was stretched to the limit in nearly every business segment. The plastic molding facility in Nanjing was nearing capacity, but an expansion scheduled for completion in a month would allow the sprawling factory to meet the increased demand caused by the new products and tooling recently received from the United States.

General Ye seldom smiled after business meetings. He was smiling now. Colonel Wen Ma's expression was more apprehensive.

"You're not really worried by the presence of Professor Syzmanski's guest speaker, are you?" Ye quipped from the head of the sixteenth-century iroko conference table he used as a work surface. Colonel Wen faced him fourteen feet away, his head tilted slightly in deep thought. "I believe it's a strange coincidence, General," he remarked sharply.

"He's of no consequence," Ye replied, sweeping his hand over his shoulder. "He's not a participant in the trade negotiations, and I don't want you to waste time or energy on anything but the upcoming events. The agricultural offensive has been set in motion, and Cusson has exchanged the first fifty-billion U.S. dollars deposited in European accounts, for euros, pounds-sterling and Swiss francs."

"All hell will soon break loose," Wen Ma smiled confidently. "But still… I'm going to keep an eye on this peon light-weight who was disrespectful to the Chinese government. He should learn just how dominant a force China has become in global matters; and how dangerous it can be to ridicule a PLA officer."

General Ye rose impatiently from the head of the table and said, "If you must…have him followed, Colonel. I think it's a waste of time and misuse of security assets." He glanced down at the long list of *To-Do's* Ihasa had submitted. "I suggest you arrange for someone else to keep track of him. I expect you to concentrate on preparing for the Bomali board meeting and the final negotiating session with Jake Kurancy. There must be no delays. Ihasa claims the Americans are pushing hard for voluntary cut-backs in Chinese exports."

Wen Ma chuckled pompously, "The Vice-Premier will convince the Americans that China's 400 $billion trade surplus this year is good for their economy. Low-cost Chinese goods are still being demanded by all the large U.S. retailers. "I'm sure Ihasa and Chairman Chang will convince Humphreys that--- as long as the American market remains open to Chinese exports---Yew Bai Tsin will be prompted by the Standing Committee to continue investing Central Bank reserves in U.S. Treasuries."

"To support the fiasco they call a 'budget deficit,'" General Ye added ruefully.

"Americans don't understand China's point of view on the benefits of the trade imbalance," Wen Ma insisted, disregarding Professor Syzmansky's seminar explainations of the political and global significance of large budget deficits. "Americans are angered and blinded by the misconception they call *unfair trade*. There's no such thing as unfair trade. Only differences in global trade efficiencies. Washington refuses to recognize that China's export machine must continue its dynamic growth if Beijing is to compete against huge foreign opposition."

Ye grumbled, "When the safeguards against Chinese textile imports to America are lifted on January 1st, 2009, Congress will probably extend the protections. The Chamber of Commerce in Shanghai estimated that an additional 75,000 American textile workers would lose their jobs to Fujian, Jiangxi and Guandong province textile factories, if they're allowed unlimited access to the American apparel market. When the safeguards finally end, U.S. and Central America clothing will be replaced overnight on the shelves of BoxMart and other giant retail firms. Central America garment makers will no longer need American-made yarns and fabrics."

The intercom buzzed and General Ye's aide informed him that senior officers from the East China Military Defense Force had arrived.

"Colonel Wen, it's time to initiate the military phase of Ihasa's Triad scheme. I suggest you complete your assignment in Beijing and return to Macau. Watch Bromine closely and resolve the governance conflicts with Kurancy. The Bomali merger must be completed by October first."

"Don't worry, General. The transition team will be ready when I replace Bromine as CEO."

CHAPTER 42

August 6, 2008, Beijing
Bureau of Fair Trade, State Administration for Industry and Commerce

The morning meeting was cancelled without explanation; the afternoon session hastily rescheduled for the morning.

"That's typical of official meetings between foreign businessmen and mid-level cadres," AJ Hau Luing explained to the businessmen he was escorting. "Especially deputy ministers from the State Administration for Industry and Commerce." AJ was assigned by Ambassador Balzerini to accompany Gatt and several other American entrepreneurs to the business-orientation sessions with the Chinese.

The morning conference with fair-trade officials would never have been cancelled if the American visitors were from GE, Morgan Stanley, Exxon-Mobil, Wal-Mart, Ford or Target;instead of from a dozen small-cap and private companies. AJ heard rumors that the bureaucrats were attending practices for the adored Chinese Olympic athletes perfecting their routines for the August 14 opening of the Games.

Gatt thought he could at least acquire an understanding of the operating methods used by small Chinese businesses from the meeting with the Autonomous Regions representatives. The American group had been informed they'd meet with the Yi and Miao people from the southeast, and the Uyghur people concentrated in the northwest Xinjiang Zone bordering Russia, Mongolia and Pakistan.

"Not exactly an ideal comparison between small American and Chinese businesses," Justin commented to a new acquaintance from Michigan, whose after-market automotive parts business was teetering on the edge of bankruptcy. Much of his business had been lost to Chinese parts manufacturers. He'd taken a home-equity loan to pay for the China trip...hoping to determine how the Chinese could sell windshield wipers, floor mats and oil-filters for less than the cost of his raw materials.

AJ shook his head in exasperation and said, "The *Uyghur* people are mostly nomadic. They produce agricultural products and live-stock for the local economy. The *Yi* and *Miao* businesses tend to be tiny craft operations, which sub-contract handiwork---such as painting faces and costumes on seasonal ceramic figurines---for the larger factories which export massive quantities to the States."

A raggedly dressed Chinese man with an authoritative expression... apparently from the Autonomous Regions Business coalition...stood outside the meeting room as the American group approached from a dingy hallway. He was short and stubby, with a shaved head and creviced facial skin pale and wind-dried. He greeted the visitors with a nervous nod as they filed into the small room at the rear entrance to the bulky 1950s-era two-story concrete building, originally designed by Soviet Union engineers as an annex to the Great Hall of The People, and now used for overflow foreign business meetings.

Two dozen chairs faced a grey metal desk in the front, flanked by a chalk-board resting on a creaky wooden A-frame, and a table-mounted transparency projector covered with dust and a few spider-webs. The diminutive Chinese man of about fifty limped noticeably to the front with slumped shoulders that seemed permanently deformed.

"My name is Liu Mang, and I'm one of the few survivors of the secret Qin Cheng prison-- not far from this location," he said in a rushed, wild-eyed, alarmingly high-pitched tone. "The government of the People's Republic of China recently granted my freedom...after years of daily torture by misguided prison guards. I am once again allowed to practice my trade."

He leaned on the front edge of the desk for a few seconds, then exclaimed in perfect English to the confused visitors, "I'm not an expert on the subject---but I've heard the experts talking as they washed their hands outside the stalls. Unless your business can become a large enterprise in China, you're wasting your time here." He smiled as if the statement was a private joke.

"Your name means 'tough-guy,'" AJ raised his voice. "Please explain your statement. These gentlemen expect to hear recommendations...not rejection of their efforts before they have a opportunity to explore business opportunities in China for themselves."

Liu Mang pointed an accusing finger at AJ and replied crisply, "Are you one of them? You think I'm crazy? I tell you...we Communists distaste small foreign enterprises. We require them to give up secret technologies to our local partners...if they want to gain access to our enormous mainland markets."

The man peered at the doorway nervously. He'd heard other important statements from dissident intellectuals in the prison men's room. "We steal foreign designs and copy valuable foreign trademarks. The government refunds value-added taxes imposed on locally produced products, but keeps the taxes collected for the same products if they are imported." The hallway door sprung open and a stern-faced Public Security guard about six-feet three, in full uniform, stomped into the room and grabbed Liu by the nape of his neck.

When the small man resisted, the guard slapped him across the strips of scar-tissue on his forehead...as if to shake away thoughts of rebellion. He dragged the deformed man to the door...ignoring the mesmerized audience. "Back you go, bumpkin."

Shortly after the security guard hauled Liu Mang away, a full-faced man in his mid-thirties, with heavy black hair, wearing a wrinkled brown suit appeared in the doorway. A three-ring binder over-stuffed with papers was clamped under his arm; the smug expression of a cadre-class Communist caked his face.

"Please excuse the interruption from that loony. He was rehabilitated from a mental institution and now cleans the bathrooms of this building. Occasionally, he drifts back to the days when he was a renegade economics student."

The true representative from the Ministry of Autonomous Region Small Business introduced himself, then pulled from the binder a handful of reports translated into English, and distributed them to the audience.

"These are the products made in the Autonomous Zones. I'm sure the statistics compiled by the Revolutionary Bureau of Autonomous Employment Statistics in Ninxia, will impress you. A variety of modern and ancient occupations are practiced in these regions."

Justin glanced at the first few pages: light industry, handicrafts, agriculture, fruit-growing, elegant textile craftsmanship, alpaca sweaters. The items were being made by a sparse population, compared with the multitude of east coast inhabitants: Nomadic traders on horses; coal miners; peasants hand-blending phosphorous additives with latrine excrement and animal droppings at a crude fertilizer combine; farmers working small patches of government-granted land. *Average monthly income per worker---1,000 yuan, or 125 dollars.*

The list was void of small businesses engaged in skilled operations such as high-precision machining, PC-board assembly, robot manufacturing, or automotive and aerospace components production. Reading further, Justin noticed that the Autonomous regions lacked the special industrial zones common in the Shanghai and Shenzhen areas---such as the Zhonglou

Economic Development Industrial Zone, and the High-Tech Development Industrial Zone.

The closest American small-business template to a Chinese Autonomous Region enterprise seemed to be the native-American craft shops, which made jewelry, miniature totem-poles and reproductions of ancient artifacts and relics at the reservations in the Midwest and Southwest states.

(AUGUST 7, 2008)
BOXMART HEADQUARTERS, BOSTON AREA

"The PLA refuses to sign the Bomali agreement in its current form, Jake. The merger of LCE and BoxMart is in limbo." Emerson Bromine, the future CEO of the Bomali Corp was in his private office, snorting crack. "They want Vargos Langreen to re-write the agreement and remove the *option-out* clause."

"I heard!" Kurancy replied angrily. "Li Chin says he's discussed the matter with General Ye and Colonel Wen Ma. They refuse to allow us to re-purchase BoxMart's fifty-percent stake in Bomali---in the event that the Bomali board of directors can't settle a governance dispute. Li Chin agrees with them. He claims we control half the board and could stalemate the business...then back out at any time." Kurancy slammed down the thick printout of BoxMart same-store sales figures he'd been reviewing

"According to the terms we agreed on---so could they," Bromine grumbled.

Despite the glowing sales results---better than ten-percent increase in revenues over the previous quarter---his dream of eventually dominating the consumer retailing business in North America was wavering. Everything depended on the Bomali joint-venture with LCE. He'd agreed to an equal partnership with the Chinese: equal ownership and equal decision-making.

Unfortunately for him, the Chinese now insisted on maintaining control of the vast manufacturing and retailing enterprise, in the event unresolvable conflicts surfaced between the partners.

"I signed the final papers last week, Emerson. I expected General Ye and Li Chin to do likewise. Langreen's firm was prepared to file the registration forms in Macau. Li Chin backed down on his promise that no provisos would be added. His PLA bosses must have pressured him."

"I agree, Jake," Bromine replied stiffly, as he sipped a vodka martini in his office on the twentieth-floor of the Bromine Venture Capital Building, located in the heart of the Macau peninsula---the "Las Vegas of Asia." The BVC tower building housed a full casino on the ground floor, and swank hotel suites for high rollers on the 5th through 10th stories. The new Bomali offices were being renovated on the 13th to 20th levels. "It's too late to back away. We've already transferred billions from BoxMart's U.S. and European reserve and operating accounts, to the Bomali start-up depository at the BOC Macau branch. Yong Ihasa and General Ye now control our money. They'll sit on it if the deal sours. Sorry, Jake. I didn't see this coming."

"Those Triad egomaniacs should never have been included in Cusson's scheme." Kurancy spat into the phone. They've got visions of grandeur that could screw up the Savoy Imperative,"

"We needed their clout on the CCP Standing Committee to pass the Macau tax-free laws…to make the merger worthwhile," Bromine reminded him.

Kurancy circled his office as Bromine waited patiently on the trans-pacific connection. The giant man moved nimbly to the bar and poured four fingers of neat Maker's Mark. He swallowed the contents in one gulp and gently replaced the glass on the bar.

For all these years, he thought, *the deals I shaped with Li Chin benefited BoxMart and the Chinese export machine equally.* He was alarmed by the sudden aggressiveness of the Chinese partners. They were insisting on disproportionate control of the Bomali venture, he and Li Chin alone conceived. Without the *option-out* clause in the Bomali agreement, it was likely that General Ye and the PLA could dominate the Macau-based venture, and dictate BoxMart's future in the global retailing industry.

The terms of the agreement allowed the four Chinese members of the eight-person Bomali board of directors ---General Ye, Colonel Wen Ma, Li Chin and Yong Ihasa--- to appoint the next board member, regardless of how or why a current member was removed. If anything happened to Kurancy, Bromine, Cashman or Cusson, the Chinese would have majority control over the largest business on earth; and a lock on a significant portion of the American market for consumer goods.

The *option-out* clause was a safeguard for Kurancy and other BM stockholders. It gave them the right to repurchase the BoxMart public stock swapped for Bomali shares, if the Chinese partners exercised their right to appoint the next board member, and Kurancy didn't approve their choice.

"Emerson," he spat decisively into the speaker, "I want you to tell General Ye that the merger is history unless there's a compromise by both sides. Tell him I'm willing to remove the *option-out* clause if the Chinese deposit a hundred million dollars of their own money in a Swiss escrow account, to be automatically transferred to my numbered account at Franco-Medici, if a two-thirds super-majority of the Bomali board cannot settle a governance dispute within thirty days, or if the Chinese partners gain control of the Bomali board."

There was a pause at the other end. "Wen Ma just came into my office, Jake. I'll have him pass the word to General Ye."

Kurancy switched off without comment and buzzed Cashman.

"Where do we stand regarding early deliveries of holiday merchandise from LCE?"

Cashman replied with astonishment, "It's amazing, Jake…every warehouse is filled. We already have fifty percent more holiday merchandise than we sold last year. Are you sure about the sales projections?"

"Just keep it coming, Hiero. Find outside warehouses, or use storage vans. In another few weeks you'll understand why."

"Okay, boss. By the way, we just received the first shipment of knock-off Ho-Chunk *calendar sticks* from Li Chin's Nanjing factory. They look great. Do you want me to cancel the open-order with the Ho-Chunk Winnebago tribe…or tell them to complete the shipment.? We can afford to pay them for completing the order…although we won't need the product."

"Cancel it now," Jake ordered.

"They'll probably start striping their faces with war-paint and sharpening poison-tipped arrows." Silence meant Jake wasn't smiling.

"It'll be done today!" Cashman cracked.

A few hours later, Kurancy received a fax from the warehouse manager at the Eagle Pass, Texas storage and distribution complex. "The RFID seal on the pallet of water-filters has been broken in Onawa, Iowa. GPS tracking shows the shipment is heading north on schedule toward the Sioux City, Iowa BoxMart superstore."

CHAPTER 43

August 7, 2008, 2am
Western Iowa Cornfields

As soon as Budi fired the canisters over the Sac City cornfields, Joko pulled off his dust mask and goggles in order to breathe better and wipe away allergy-tears. "You idiot," Budi shouted, "put them back on."

"I thought you said the spray was harmless to people?" Joko replied apprehensively.

"That's the Chinese version. I don't trust them."

"But all those lab tests? We saw the reports."

"I know...I know. You're right. Plenty of people have been exposed to the corn-virus without a problem. I guess I just don't think the Triads give a shit about Indonesians."

Five square-miles of Sac City cornfields were contaminated by the exploded canisters in less than fifteen minutes. Joko snapped on the protective gear and watched the sky as a steady ten-knot wind swept the imploded sub-microscopic organisms in the predicted directions.

Budi and Joko followed the green van's tracks south on Route 71, then turned east on Route 30 and continued another fifty miles to Boone. Muslihrama was prepared. The canister-firing process used in Sac City was repeated; except the mortars were aimed south and east instead of south and west. Joko was starving. He decided to chew on one of the sweet-smelling raw ears of corn as he collected the weapons and empty mortar shells before a hasty departure to the third and final firing location.

From Boone, Budi, Joko and Muslihrama drove north to Fort Dodge and met up with Danang. The third mortar assault was ready. Unfortunately, the wind changed from a steady directional blow to a swirling vortex of strong gusts. A tornado warning issued by a Sioux City radio station preceded the angry western-Iowa winds now swirling upward in a rise of hot-air currents that collided with flat underbellies of fluffy-topped grey cumulus clouds. The weatherman announced, with the enthusiasm of an expectant father, that conditions were ideal for the birth of a tornado.

Budi and the others covered their eyes with air-tight goggles and donned the commercial-grade dust-masks purchased from the paint department of a hardware store. The micron-sized filters would be useless against the sub-micron organisms about to be splattered across the field and sucked skyward into the drafts of fast-moving clouds.

Budi hesitated as he looked up through a cloud opening at the brightest full-moon he'd ever seen. He reached up, as if to touch it. Muslihrama slapped his hand down and hissed, "Let's get this fucking job done, Budi. The plane won't wait forever. This operation scares the piss out of me." The others nodded as a gust of wind knocked over one of the light-mortar cannons. A brass canister spilled from the barrel onto the soft black earth.

"Shit," Budi snapped, as Danang retreated the canister and used his shirt-tail to wipe away the dirt.

"Load it back in," he ordered. He then took up position and hurriedly fired four canisters in high arcs. The canisters exploded one-after-the-other in a fireworks display back-lit by the sun-like moon. *Let the wind do the rest of the job*, he pleaded to Allah.

They tossed the mortars and spent shells into heavy-duty plastic super-sacs and retrieved the original cardboard containers. The sacs would be dumped in an irrigation ditch on route to the small private airport. The empty cardboard boxes would be placed in clear site at a nearby rest stop.

The Learjet 31A seven-passenger business jet owned by BoxMart was waiting with idling engines a few miles north of Fort Dodge. The pilot of the light jet was strapped in at the controls…anxious to leave the area before the high winds intensified. Budi helped Joko up the cabin steps, noticing that he lagged behind the others, and was straining to breathe. It was probably his allergies. As they rushing into the aircraft, Joko spit out a mouthful of thick black fluid.

Budi yelled, "Go!" and the steps swiveled up on hydraulic hinges, sealing the fuselage. The twin-engine aircraft darted down the dimly-lit private runway, lifted sharply and leveled off above the thick gray clouds, just as the tornado touched down less than a mile away. Budi looked out and saw the violent vortex uprooting corn plants and dispersing the contaminated leaves and stalks in an unpredictable, five-hundred-yard-wide zigzag wake of centrifugal destruction.

The activated organisms are spreading faster and farther than the Chinese predicted, Budi grinned, as the aircraft banked south and headed for the small Texas airport adjacent to BoxMart's Eagle Pass distribution center. In a few hours they'd cross the border at Piedras Negras and disappear into the Mexican countryside.

Geneva, Switzerland

Stella embraced Lynne as Papa watched with a knowing smile from the doorway of his office on the shoreline of Lake Geneva, overlooking the famous Jet d'Eau which sprayed water 350 feet into the sky. He understood why Stella adored her former Harvard roommate. Lynne exuded the aura of a patched-up cuddly teddy-bear.

Dressed in a teal Victorian-lace, sleeveless blouse and dark denim jeans, her hands and forearms were covered with skin-colored band-aides. Her long delicate fingers stretched the bandages to grasp Stella's shoulders lightly. Stella was dressed more formally in a black knit top and persimmon circle-skirt trimmed in black chiffon.

"What happened to your hands?" Stella cried out despondedly, her glassy eyes fixed on the pussy burn marks covering Lynne's fingers. "You were fine yesterday."

"It happened just minutes after we talked, honey. My damn hair-dryer exploded…or short-circuited…or something."

Papa stepped forward and examined her hands. "You must see a doctor immediately, Lynne, dear. There's evidence of infection."

The shocking vision of the jet of white-hot particles shooting from the hair-dryer returned. "I had to rush out to catch the plane," she blurted out sadly. "There was no time for medical treatment." She wiped a tear from Stella's cheek and broke down.

"I'm in trouble, honey," she cried. "Someone is trying to kill me."

When they returned from the Nicorezzi family doctor's office a few blocks away, Papa unlocked the center drawer of his walnut desk and removed a thin file.

"The information you inquired about is in here, Lynne. But I must warn you---it's highly sensitive and confidential."

"What Papa means is---he can get into a lot of trouble if the information leaks out and he is found to be the source. There's a dark side to Geneva left over from the Protestant Reformation days of John Calvin…when everyone wore black and you couldn't sing or dance in public. The people took their vices underground. Today, everyone in the city has learned to keep secrets."

"Bankers don't have clients," Papa added for emphasis, "they have serial numbers." He fingered the file on his desk and asked, "How do you intend to use this information, my dear? Geneva bankers are mostly hedonists. Even with the new Swiss transparency laws, the enormous scale of the transactions involving the entities you named, was deeply buried. Access was given to me only because of past favors I've done as a bank examiner."

Lynne wasn't sure how to answer. "I don't want you or Stella to be put in a compromising position, Papa. The reason for my inquiry relates to a seemingly strange connection between Residents Bank of North America, the Chinese government and a company called BoxMart Retail Enterprises. A friend of mine was put out of business, unnecessarily, by this coalition. We believe other U.S. manufacturing companies are still being forced into bankruptcy by them. We're not sure, but we suspect some kind of connection with Beijing industrialists. Most of the manufacturing business lost in America has been instantly relocated to the Chinese mainland."

"How did you acquire such information, dear? Bank records are closely protected."

"I used the Harvard University international business data base and a special program to penetrate the firewalls of several domestic and international financial institutions. The system's querying power is incredible. I searched for money transfers of more than ten thousand dollars, which by federal law must be reported. I found regular multi-million dollar transfers. On the surface they didn't seem unusual. Then, I discovered something more startling: the company my friend and I work for, the GH Paladin division of Financial Flow Foundation, a consulting firm in Washington, is receiving monthly deposits of $5 million from BoxMart." She closed her eyes briefly and added, "One of our fellow employees was just murdered…probably because he knew too much."

Stella shivered and said, "You must give up your position, immediately."

"I will, when the time is right, honey. Right now I have to help my friend---a man named Justin Gatt. He was dispatched on a five-week business junket to China, as a replacement for the murdered man. He's been pushing FFF to make good on its promise to re-finance a group of small Northeast businesses that are being foreclosed on by Residents Bank. Justin devised a plan to save them, as part of a government-supported refinancing plan being administered by FFF."

"Do you think he's also in danger?"

"I'm afraid so, Papa. He's very inquisitive…more so than Ross Trenker was---the co-worker who was shot dead in Washington."

Stella's father was wired to the Geneva financial under-ground. He knew the paths unwashed money followed before it re-surfaced as clean currency. Some was invested in central bank bond offerings, including Treasury auctions. He'd heard rumors that Franco-Medici Trust in Geneva, a primary depository for the dollars accumulated by the Central Bank of China, was heavily involved in currency-swaps. His discrete inquiries revealed that

Creditte Bank de Savoy of Lyon, France, the parent of Franco-Medici, was floating offers to trade additional billions in U.S. dollars for a basket of European and Asian currencies.

Phillipe Cusson, the Director General of CBdS, was known as an outspoken critic of the Federal Reserve Banking system, and had predicted privately that the value of the dollar would soon decrease. *If so*, thought Papa, *interest rates in America will skyrocket.*

"It's highly unusual for dollar-buyers to resell the currency short-term," Papa said, as he began to explain the intricacies of currency swapping to Lynne; which related directly to information in the file. "Quantities of over a few billion U.S. dollars are typically held for several months to a few years." Lynne's blank expression indicated she'd missed the connection.

"Last week, several European Union Central Banks offered to trade five to ten billion dollars each in London. There were no private takers. It seems the European institutions offering the dollars were the same ones that purchased the dollars from an affiliate of the American bank you inquired about."

"Residents Bank has a European affiliate?"

"All the big banks do," Stella nodded. "It seems that American currency is losing favor with them overnight…for some unknown reason."

"Lynne, my dear, I must inform you that major financial events are likely to occur in the near future in Europe, China and America. If I'm correct---the events will involve the exact entities you asked me to investigate."

"But there's been nothing in the news mentioning a financial crisis."

"That's what troubles me, dear. American officials have only recently detected the first ripple effects from the recent dollar sell-offs noted in this file. The Federal Reserve Board just announced an unscheduled Open Market Committee meeting in Washington. I'm told the Treasury Secretary also alerted the World Bank and the World Trade Organization in Geneva of the unexpected increase in foreign trades of American currency."

"What else can you tell us about Residents Bank and BoxMart?" Stella inquired.

CHAPTER 44

(AUGUST 8, 2008)
WINNEBAGO HO-CHUNK RESERVATION, NEBRASKA

The five-foot nine, 120-pound University of Nebraska Law School graduate, danced rhythmically to the slow drumbeats, flouncing high-kneed around the perimeter of the circle of elders seated cross-legged on the plank floor. She'd inherited the log cabin Council chamber from her deceased father...the former chief of the Ho-Chunk Winnebago tribe.

The 80-year-old Chief's Blanket on which they reclined---woven from sheep's wool in multi-colored stripes, crosses and diamond patterns---signaled the ceremonial authenticity of a Ho-Chunk Winnebago tribal council meeting. A young brave's staccato drum beats reverberated audio enhancement, just as they did years ago, when coded percussions accompanied the white-smoke warnings that beckoned distant hunters back to their villages.

The first female chief of the Winnebago tribe wore eagle and hawk feathers, attached by hand-twists of spider-web yarn to two ebony ponytails slacking down the small of her back. Her loose-fitting tribal skirt and multi-colored ceremonial blouse were embroidered with geometric designs created with yellow, brown and crimson painted porcupine quills, animal hair and glass beads.

Hanging heavily from her neck was the tribe's most sacred and valuable possession: the *Kachina* necklace made from 200 year-old native gem stones and thumb-sized gold nuggets. The necklace connected Nonnie Whiteknee Washington with the spirits and wisdom of her ancestors. It was a time of need. The tribal council was facing a daunting challenge.

The forty-five year old Chief of the Ho-Chung-Winnebago tribe squatted with the elders on the floor and glared contemptuously at the yard-long hickory shaft carved with familiar markings, being held out by a council member for all to view.

"I don't understand the sudden change," she barked out to the hastily assembled tribal council, in a deep gravely voice inherited from her father. "Last month they demanded we increase production; now they've cancelled the entire order."

"My wife's cousin in Sergeant Bluffs found this at the BoxMart supercenter near Sioux City ...on the Iowa side," explained Silver Horse Monroe. He handed Nonnie the imported hickory staff with markings and dimensions identical to the Ho-Chunk *Calendar Stick* being hand-carved at the Reservation craft factory. "It's an exact replica of our ancestor's design, except for the 'made in China' label." Nonnie threw the stick in the middle of the floor...as if into an invisible war-fire.

She replied angrily, "BoxMart stole the Ho-Chunk design and had it duplicated in China. Their cancellation notice claims that stores lost orders because our factory couldn't keep up with demand. It's a cruel lie. My friend at the BoxMart superstore outside Onawa told me that our deliveries were mostly on time, and her store never lost a customer purchase."

The fiery daughter of deceased Chief Ogallala Springs Jefferson was described by some of the elders as a 'clever cougar.' Others called her a 'weed' or 'dreamer.' But with high cheekbones, the penetrating glare of her father's raven eyes, and the natural energy and bare-back riding skills of her mother, Nonnie was a native American throw-back in appearance and demeanor; particularly when she dressed the part. She also possessed a law degree and a brilliant contemporary legal mind.

Silver Horse Monroe bellowed, "There's no other jobs close to the reservation."

Chief Whiteknee Washington stood up from her crouched position and said to the councilmen, in the gruff, thoughtful tone of a wise man...or a crazed witch doctor, "In some parts of North America, federally-recognized tribes own the rights to specific carved or painted images that record family or tribal history. Only a licensee---someone who pays a fee—is allowed to legally recreate the work."

"Does that apply here?"

"That would be difficult to prove. But we can threaten to sue BoxMart. They might consider reinstating the production order if we make enough noise. The tribe could also boycott BoxMart stores in the area." Her lips tightened as her legal training kicked in. "The Council can file a complaint with the Indian Affairs Department in Washington for trademark infringement and theft of ancient tribal designs."

"Your father would have none of this," the senior councilman, Dancing Eyes Adams, replied in a stern voice. Nonnie rolled the Kuchina stones in her fingers as the other elders hummed agreement with the eighty-plus medicine man.

"This isn't the time for the tribe to recoil like scared rabbits," she admonished. "Seventy-percent of this tribe is obese...many with serious health problems. Are you suggesting, Dancing Eyes, that we go back to the high-fat, block-cheese diet provided by the Indian Affairs Agency? Or will we rise above the closing of the craft-factory and do something to help our children retain their independence?"

Silver Horse Monroe said morosely, "But, the craft factory was the only opportunity to earn a living on the Reservation."

Nonnie's dark eyes were etched with frustration. "The Council must act boldly, if we want to preserve our Winnebago traditions. Otherwise," she declared stiffly, disheartened by the down-trodden expressions and bowed heads, "I may as well return to my legal practice in Omaha."

The droning was loud and anxious; heads shifted to Dancing Eyes Adams. The look of alarm on the medicine man's face confirmed that the tribe was in desperate need of Nonnie's zealous leadership. "You have spoken truth," he said to Chief Whiteknee. "Tribal members must act bravely...to preserve the Winnebago Ho-Chunk traditons."

(August 8, 2008) pm
BoxMart Supercenter, Onawa, Iowa

The gift-department manager at the BoxMart Supercenter on the outskirts of Onawa frowned as she read the third-page article in the evening edition of the Sioux City Journal. Her friend Nonnie's Winnebago Indian tribe, also known as the Ho-Chunks, just announced they were shutting-down the only source of employment at the Winnebago Reservation, located in the northeast corner of Nebraska, bordering western Iowa along the Missouri River and South Dakota to the north.

Ninety-two native-Americans living and working on the reservation lost their only source of income. The gratifying craftswork which brought purpose to skilled Indian hands, creating Ho-Chunk and Omaha Indian artifacts, was no longer needed. She'd suspected weeks ago that the order would be cancelled, but feared being fired if she told her friend, Nonnie, about the impending changes before official notification came down from BoxMart headquarters. "Made in America" labels in the gift department were being replaced with "Designed by Native Americans" tags.

The middle-aged manager decided to call Nonnie and at least offer condolences. She had no satisfactory explanation for the sudden order cancellations. It hadn't been her decision to replace the hot-selling, authentic Ho-Chunk calendar sticks with a Chinese-made equivalent...just to save ten cents on the cost of an eight-dollar item. Still, she felt guilty; she was the person who introduced the Ho-Chunk Winnebago craft line to the home office. The Boston buyer loved the items and instructed her to call Nonnie and tell her to ramp up production at the small Reservation factory. She recalled how Nonnie enchanted the tribal elders and was appointed Chief, when she abandoned her high-paying legal career in Omaha, and returned to the reservation, armed with financing for the craft factory expansion. Most of the funds came from her savings.

The calendar stick was the most popular item in the Crafts and Gifts Departments at tri-state area BoxMart superstores. Highlighted in a recent National Geographics Magazine article, the calendar stick was created about three thousand years ago by ancestors of the Ho-Chunk people, to keep track of dates and time. By accurately recording periodic changes in the positions of celestial bodies, these early astronomers developed a 365-day calendar and carved it on smoked hickory branches to create the most accurate dating device ever invented in North America.

When the tribe granted BoxMart exclusive sales rights in Iowa, Nebraska and South Dakota, the department manager anticipated a long production run. Nonnie viewed the new business as an opportunity for Winnebago braves to be productive and avoid alcohol abuse. Tribal police regularly provided accommodations for several unemployed young braves, whose alcohol-inspired concept of being a proud warrior had degenerated to blowing out tires of reservation visitors with pump-Winchesters. A common practice to overcome boredom and poverty-enhanced frustration.

Nonnie is totally committed to the welfare of the Winnebago people, the department manager mused. *She won't let this pass without a fight.*

A few days later, Jake Kurancy read the complaint-letter and snorted, "Stall them to death." He ordered the BoxMart legal office in Massachusetts to reply with a one-sentence special delivery, registered-mail response to the Indian chief's threat of legal action: "*The matter will be taken under advisement by company attorneys as time allows.*"

(HOURS AFTER THE MORTAR FIRINGS)

The Learjet crossed the Oklahoma border into Texas with its Indonesian cargo, about the same time the corn-virus started to reproduce and spread over Sac City cornfields. It began with millions of hyper-active micro-organsisms replicating within the contaminated corn-plant leaves. Spore eruptions were being carried in all directions by the swirling winds slapping at the cool Iowa Prairie.

Gorging pathogens were similarly reproducing in the mid-west Iowa cornfields near Boone and Fort Dodge. The golden ears scheduled for harvesting in early September would never be delivered to Sioux City cattle-feeding yards. The kernels would remain plump and yellow, but the stalks and leaves were turning brown and sagging like wet burlap.

A middle-aged Sac City farmer, rising early to service a harvesting machine, heard the loud 'pops' and noticed a string of bright flashes arching over a distant field of hybrid corn. He hastily mounted his tractor-combine, floored the pedal and slammed the vehicle into high gear. He held on tightly as the twelve-foot wide, twenty-foot long monster-machine accelerated rapidly to its top speed of seven miles per hour…roaring like a uranium-armored M1 Abrahms tank in pursuit of enemy. By the time he reached the area where he'd seen the flashes, there was no sign of activity. He closed the windows of the tractor for protection against the dawn wind gusts and waited for sunrise.

With the first rays of warm light, he noticed the stalks and leaves of healthy hybrid corn plants rapidly changing from green to the dark-brown hue of Prairie earth. *The sunlight must be playing tricks with my eyes*, he thought, as the cellulose-rich leaves on the hybrid vegetation descended to the lowest level in the food chain---fodder for sub-microscopic organisms.

He stared in disbelief as faint dust-devil clouds of nano-termites surged across the open fields…driven by the steady winds and the kinetic energy of billions of tiny spore eruptions.

Mexican border

Budi and the other Indonesians trained by the Javan Triads were told that the twelve exploding canisters carried "tiny bugs" which could damage only vegetables. They were harmless to humans. Since Budi didn't trust the Chinese, he'd aimed the mortars downwind whenever possible, and forced his men to wear dust masks and tight-fitting goggles during each firing. Only Joko had ignored the precautions. He's removed the protection to wipe away allergy-tears and chew on a raw ear of corn.

"The fucking Americans will soon receive a shock," Joko coughed, as he strained to catch a breath. The double-prop Cessna carrying the Indonesians banked south and headed for the Belize border. Budi noticed unusual dark spots speckling Joko's eyes. He thought normal fatigue accounted for his sudden lethargy.

"Their livestock industry can't survive without the Iowa corn," the group leader boasted. "It's the most important crop in America."

General Ye's Indonesian go-between had exaggerated to Budi. Only fifty percent of the harvest from Iowa's twelve million acres of planted corn was used as livestock feed. The balance was consumed in breakfast cereals, popcorn, whiskey distilling, cooking oils and ethanol for blending into F85 gasoline or industrial applications. But the impact of the devastated Iowa corn-crop on the Midwest U.S. agricultural economy was expected to be psychologically ruinous to America's food industry. The Chinese agricultural experts predicted that the U.S. grain and livestock industries would be hamstrung for months; while officials attempted to identify the pathogen and remedy the corn-virus contamination.

By then, the American economy would be spinning out of control, and China would have announced that Taiwanese terrorists were the source of the contamination. Beijing leaders would have no choice but to order the return of approximately two thousand container-ships carrying goods packaged in contaminated cartons. The Shanghai paperboard factory supplying most of the shipping cartons would be closed, and cargo ships sailing from China for U.S. ports would be rerouted to the Taiwan Straits in the South China Sea.

Chinese merchandise would suddenly be in critically short supply.

Beijing

"Conditions will be ideal when Cusson dumps the next $75 billion and Yew Bai reneges on Bank of China's promise to invest $30 billion at the Treasury-bond auction," Yong Ihasa sneered, as the secret meeting of Chinese participants in the Savoy Imperative concluded.

Wang Chao said exuberantly, "The virus-scare will convince American politicians and their constituencies to forget about the trade imbalance with China. Americans will be more worried about contaminated food."

Chang Hui recited the latest U.S. Department of Agriculture statistics. "Twenty-five percent of the entire United States hog output comes from Iowa; all fed by the state's enormous corn harvest. Only Texas and California produce more livestock and livestock products than Iowa."

Li Chin smiled broadly and said, "When this overflows, the temporary interruption in the supply of our goods, will end all calls for quotas and tariffs. Jake Kurancy should be elated. BoxMart will be the only major retailer stocked with holiday goods."

Wang Chao glanced at his watch. "It's time to return to the negotiating table. The Americans will arrive for the final session in ten minutes."

CHAPTER 45

(AUGUST 9, 2008) 9 AM
THE GREAT HALL OF THE PEOPLE

The final meeting between Humphreys' USTR team and the Beijing government group was meant to be a cordial wrap-up to the contentious earlier sessions. Neither side expected their country's unilateral and reciprocal demands to be met.

Butler Humphreys was convinced that his main objective in this round of talks was not attainable. The Chinese weren't prepared to rely on market forces to determine the value of the yuan.

"I've decided not to discuss the President's offer with Chang Hui and Yong Ihasa," Humphreys said, as the bullet-proof State Department SUV pulled up to the diplomatic entrance at the Great Hall of the People. Tianan'men Square was already packed with tourists. "I don't trust the games they're playing. Yong Ihasa is too smug. He seems to have risen above the issues. I sense a new assertiveness in his attitude."

"If President Mu survives the internal investigation and retains his iron grip on the CCP," deLeone remarked, "he'll probably tag a high-ranking Politboro member as the scapegoat. I think one or more of the trade-negotiating gang may be nailed."

"I'll float the President's offer directly to Mu Jianting, when we meet privately this afternoon. With all his personal problems...he may be inclined to accept the President's initiative. Something has to be done to reduce the tensions in the South China Sea. The corruption charges against him would evaporate once the bulk of the U.S. naval fleet departs the area."

Clancy added morosely, "That would leave only a few patrol vessels in the Taiwan Straits."

Humphreys, deLeone, and Clancy were greeted at the curb by two dour-faced Chinese security agents dressed in bland grey suits. The escorts led them through a labyrinth of unfamiliar corridors, which finally emerged at the well-guarded door of an elaborately furnished conference room. Chang Hui and the other Chinese officials were already seated. Humphreys remembered an insightful warning given to him by the former Ambassador to China: "*The Chinese negotiating mind never rests. They'll sometimes move you to a different meeting room each day...with different seating arrangements to disorient your bargaining tactics.*"

Several reporters from the *Xinhau News Agency, Shanghai Daily* and *Beijing Global Times* were gathered in front of the diplomatic entrance to the enormous concrete structure built in less than a year by Russian engineers and Chinese laborers in 1959. The gigantic edifice commemorated Mao's rise to power, and the new cooperation, at the time, between Chinese and Russian Communists.

Foreign newspaper correspondents were roped off several meters distant from the diplomatic entrance to the Great Hall, hoping to collect morsels of information about the last political whopper in Beijing before the Olympics dominated the news. Gabriel Oresco huddled in the back of the pack, comparing notes with a friend from the *International Herald Tribune*. The announcements issued so far by the Sino-American trade authorities were all conjecture...no facts. He noticed that Ambassador Balzerini was missing when the American trade delegation arrived.

Oresco explained to his friend, "The BOC Governor is supposed to announce that the Central Bank will bid on the entire $30 billion U.S. Treasury auction in September."

"That's not a story," the IHT reporter admonished. "It's only a story if they *don't* bid."

Oresco enjoyed the confidence of Ambassador Balzerini. He was the best informed reporter covering the talks, and had been tipped by Balzerini's assistant, A.J. Hau Luing, that Humphreys *might* announce a breakthrough in the yuan valuation issue.

"Yew Bai Tsin has apparently been granted authority to leverage the yuan-float issue as a negotiating carrot. He's trying to convince Washington to withdraw its Trade Law, Section 301 case before the World Trade Organization. Humphreys is claiming unfair trade practices by China's PLA-controlled manufacturing conglomerate. He's petitioned the Geneva-based global trade watchdog to review whether China is meeting its obligations as a member of the WTO."

"I doubt the WTO would move to expel China," the Herald financial reporter mused. "But, they could subject Beijing to economic penalties or sanction new tariffs."

"Humphreys has 45 days to withdraw the petition,"countered Oresco.

"How do you know this?" his friend asked incredulously. "I thought the New York Times was at odds with Administration insiders."

"Pure rumors."Oresco smiled.

Sichuan Conference Room, Great Hall of the People

"What do you expect in return?" a befuddled Clancy pressed. "The trade deficit is nearly a trillion dollars this year...and China is the world's top destination for foreign funds. The People's Liberation Army generals control seventy-percent of China's rust-belt heavy industry and the government owns two-thirds of the stock of publicly traded companies in China."

Yew Bai Tsin replied evenly, "The economic isolationists in Washington blame the Chinese Communist Party for America's economic difficulties. You complain about lost jobs and high unemployment. Well...China has twenty-million unemployed workers. Many are wandering the streets of major cities... attempting to destabilize our society."

Humphreys interjected,"Clearly,Governor Yew, both U.S. and Chinese citizens benefit or suffer from the unbalanced trade between our nations. Washington views the swelling trade deficit and the lack of movement on China's part to alter its unfair currency manipulations as the main impediments to better relations."

"And what would you have us do?"Wang Chao inquired irately. "Destabilize the country? Overburden our banking system?"

Clancy ruffled a pile of Senate Economic Intelligence reports and found the summary page he was looking for. "China's four largest commercial banks have provided nearly unlimited credit to the burgeoning industrial sector. You've allowed weak companies to charge inordinately-low-prices for export goods. While we agree that lower prices benefit citizens in the short-run, the overall effect is not sustainable. China's financial institutions are precariously underpinned by nearly $600 billion in non-performing industrial loans. Meanwhile," he scowled, "Chinese manufacturers enjoy an unfair economic advantage, made worse by the undervalued yuan."

"Unfortunately," Humphreys added to the argument, "the American free-trade template which has allowed this to happen, has also caused the shut-down of hundreds of important American factories. The United States government can no longer ignore the mass-extinction of decent-paying jobs; or the serious erosion of domestic production capacity."

Chang Hui Chen decided to ignore Humphreys' remarks and go on the offensive.

"China rebukes the U.S. politicians encouraging public outcries for high tariffs and boycotts against Chinese goods. Your politicians must recognize that Chinese goods are being *demanded* by your citizens. What will hawks like New York Governor Martin Merrand tell citizens when a small appliance costs ninety-nine dollars instead of $19.95?"

Yong Ihasa added vehemently, "American bureaucrats want too much: voluntary reductions in textile exports; pledges from Beijing to purchase U.S. Treasury bonds…to help finance your undisciplined congress's overspending; even changes in the Chinese Constitution."

NPC Chairman Chang responded sharply in a high-pitched shrill, "I can assure you that the National People's Congress will not abolish regulations that require joint-venture American and foreign companies to share trade secrets with Chinese partners. The savings in research costs help fund our new-product development."

"Are we to assume, then, that Beijing will continue its reluctance to prosecute counterfeiters of foreign products?" Clancy grated. "We have evidence which refutes the Chinese Minister of Foreign Competition's claim that the problems involve only a handful of small vendors. You cannot hide the fact that much more than 'insignificant amounts' of counterfeit products are being openly peddled by Chinese merchants. As regards the Chinese Constitution…does it really forbid the prosecution of counterfeit venders if the sales volume is deemed *small*, by some arbitrary measure?"

Humphreys glanced at his watch. His meeting with President Mu was scheduled in the next hour. He feared the confrontational tone of this meeting would carry over to Mu's consideration of the U.S. President's conciliatory offer.

"Gentlemen," he shot back forcefully, "Let's temper these discussions with reason. Our leadership expects nothing less than progress resulting from these important discussions."

A full minute passed before a word was exchanged. Papers were shuffled; lukewarm tea was sipped. Reference reports were pulled from briefcases, tapped dramatically with stiff fingers, and discussed emotionally on either side of the table in huddled whispers. The quiet repose allowed time for the intensity of the earlier heated exchanges to dissipate.

Humphreys finally leaned forward on his elbows, clasped his hands and tilted them upward against his lips, as if in prayer. His eyes measured Ihasa's. He pointed the vee to Yong Ihasa and said, "Here's what I propose."

America's primary trade-negotiator seemed energized. Humphreys cocked his head in Ihasa's direction and announced in a solemn voice, "We're willing to immediately withdraw the WTO petition." He faced BOC Governor Yew, and said, "But, we require a solid indication that the Central Bank of China will act on its mandate from the Politboro. We require concrete verification that Chinese currency will be disengaged from the value of the U.S. dollar in the near future."

Yong Ihasa had difficulty sustaining his stoic expression. The antonyms "concrete" and "act" perfectly described the slow-moving policies of Mu Jianting. The Americans were so easy to understand and manipulate.

"Governor Yew has been instructed to concur with the directive of the Politboro," he countered, in an even, linear tone which confused the Americans with its directness.

The United States Trade Representative was stunned. The surprising words of the vice-premier registered slowly. The cognitive wiring of his brain sounded an alarm in the specific region associated with doubtful comprehension.

Clancy spilled his teacup on the Senate Economic Intelligence Reports.

"As senior Vice-Premier and Minister of Monetary Regulation, I can confirm that the value of the yuan will be totally disengaged from the dollar by October 1, 2008. China will also comply with the Stressa Accords."

Richard deLeone marveled, "That's a pledge to restrain from currency manipulations during the last quarter of the year!"

Humphreys was so elated that he rose from his chair and shot an arm across the table. Yong Ihasa took it grudgingly and admitted, "Now we can present the world…the press waiting outside…with a genuine scoop." He nodded to an aide, and added, "A joint statement from Chinese and American diplomats announcing significant progress in trade relations."

A one-page press release printed in English and Mandarin was handed to each delegate. "Please excuse our boldness,"Ihasa grinned slyly, "The Politboro desires to announce this progress immediately…if you concur."

Humphreys smarted from the sudden reversal in attitude. "I have an appointment with President Mu in a few minutes,"he reminded the Chinese delegation. "I'd like to review the wording of the joint-announcement with the Secretary of State before it's presented to the international press. If you don't mind."

Richard deLeone sensed the urgency in the USTR's tone. "You go ahead and meet with President Mu, Ambassador. I'll contact the Secretary." Clancy noticed deLeone's eyes shift ever-so-slightly to the Chinese side of the table.

(August 9, 2008) PM
Iowa/Nebraska

The lead story from Sac City, Boone and Fort Dodge, Iowa dominated the headlines of local papers. The *Sioux City Journal* and most of the Midwest dailies, including the *Des Moines Register* and *Davenport Quad City Times*, reported that a third of Iowa's western corn crop had been contaminated with an unknown organism. Corn stalks were discoloring to dark-brown at the pace of a raging forest-fire.

The entire livestock industry in the United States was worried, as speculation in pork-bellies and beef futures on the Chicago Mercantile Exchange resembled the panicked trading of the 1929 stock market crash. Everyone was selling in the early trading period. After lunch, a few defensive market-makers were buying 'short'.

Psychological damage to the meat-packing industry was evident the next day. Stock prices of every company with beef or pork processing operations retreated nearly twenty-five percent. Wholesale quotes for chicken, fish and lamb reached new highs. The Iowa State University Agricultural Station in Ames, Iowa reported that the unknown agricultural pathogen was spreading on such an enormous scale that the safety of the entire North American food chain could be in jeopardy.

The U.S. Department of Agriculture dispatched scientists to examine the contaminated fields and identify the organism. Thank God…the outbreak appeared to be harmless to humans.

The only known casualty associated with the pathogen outbreak was a Sac City farmer; who was stricken by an apparent heart attack when he gazed in shock as one of his large cornfields morphed from waves of tall, light-green plants…into dark-brown carpets of sagging leaves. The discoloration was muddying the landscape, and rippling forward faster than a man could walk.

CHAPTER 46

(August 10, 2008) am
U.S. Embassy, Beijing

Balzerini was crammed into the tight space on the fourth floor of the three-story Embassy building, shoulder-to-shoulder with the radio operator. This was more important than attending the final negotiating session at the Great Hall of the People.

Humphreys and deLeone didn't require his presence to wrap up the uneventful three days of fruitless discussions. The urgent message received from the underground source on a top-secret, compound-frequency band, was being de-scrambled on the powerful mini-computer hidden in the closet of the surveillance-proof false top floor. The information was top priority.

This native-Chinese intelligence source had also sent the initial warning about a potential Chinese plot against the U.S. Although unable to re-emerge in public, the asset had acquired important new information relating to the threat. He proposed a plan to transfer the information to Balzerini.

The decoded message read: *Substitute courier will transfer materials to a virgin recipient only. Must not be a known or suspected operative under possible surveillance. Too many eyes watching. Too dangerous. Identify courier in usual manner. Transfer location--- Shanghai Old Town, area of Wuxing Ting Teahouse, ornamental pond, 3pm, on 8/12(A) or 8/13(B). Will indicate date(letter) and point of contact at usual internet site on 8/11.*

Nanjing area corrugated box company a suspected source of danger. Liaoning propaganda official **turned** *following son's death from unknown exposure.* *Medic and father have technical info re biological item, including anonymous physician's report exposing* **suspected cover-up of shipment biological substance to US.** *Possibly packaged as retail-brand water filters.*

Number 295 Army Hospital treated the technician-son exposed to unknown substance. Technician died in seven days. Cooperating medic attempting to acquire autopsy report and substance analysis for info exchange.

Am under heavy surveillance. This will be my last transmission. Good luck.

Balzerini sent a 'yellow' message relaying this information to the NSA and CIA, in Langley. He then summoned Robert Changhui and told him to go to school.

(August 9, 2008)
Beijing University

Robert Changhui was a surprise attendant at the Beijing University lecture on Chinese Trade relations with America.

Justin Gatt, Lili Qi and several American businessmen and Chinese graduate students jammed the huge lecture hall on the Beijing University campus located northwest of center city…a short distance from the Summer Palace and Kunming Lake. The site had once been the home of Yanjing University, a private school administered by Americans until the 1949 Revolution. The school had been supported with indemnity funds from the Boxer Revolution, following settlement of conflicts between Chinese intellectuals and British occupiers.

The U.S. Embassy intern wasn't there to absorb Professor Meng-Ji's stimulating Annual Lecture on Chinese-American Trade Relations. The title this year: "Expounding the Virtues and Wickedness of Market-Driven Economies." He'd been assigned to pass along an urgent message from Balzerini to diplomatically-invisible Justin Gatt.

"I feel like I'm back at Yale," Justin remarked to Lili, seated on his right in the last row of the lecture hall. A tall female student wearing tight denim pants cut at the hip, and open-sandals with three-inch heels, was handing out printed material to attendees in the front rows. She eventually worked her way to the narrow aisle behind Gatt's chair and extracted an English language information packet from the bottom of her pile.. She passed it over Gatt's shoulder, as Robert Changhui took the seat directly in front of Lili…pointedly avoiding eye contact.

Justin noticed the edge of a loose sheet protruding from the neatly stapled hand out.

"I remember Eric Syzmansky talking about this guy," he said loud enough for Robert to hear. He expected his friend from Yale, Taiwanese businessman turned diplomat-intern, to turn and acknowledge his presence. Robert remained facing forward as Professor Meng-Ji strolled into the auditorium wearing a bright smile and a button-down ocean-blue oxford shirt rolled-up at the sleeves.

Meng-Ji, affectionately called *Mr. Lao Xiao* by his graduate students, meaning literally---*respected older small-man*, was five-feet, thin-framed and round-faced. Huge black oval eyes, fronted by round rimless bifocals, coupled with thick black hair without sideburns, made him look top-heavy and proletariat. Only his elegant tone of voice---a proud rasp in the four tones of the standard Putonghua national language---hinted at his brilliant mind.

As usual, Meng-Ji began and ended his lectures with Confucian analects; to capture the attention of students and guests.

"Is it not delightful to have friends coming from distant quarters?"

He may have been attempting to spin ironic on the massive, disruptive crowds attending the Olympic games; or sarcastically about the mobs of demonstrators pouring in from outlying provinces; and now being jailed for marching in Beijing streets. Or, he could be welcoming Justin Gatt and the other Americans attending his annual lecture.

Meng-Ji faced the audience without notes or reference materials. His confidence was bolstered by his favorite Confucius saying, written in thick Mandarin characters on the chalkboard facing the theatre seats. Lili translated it for Justin: *Without knowing the force of words, it is impossible to know men.*

The printed hand-outs proved to be nearly a verbatim of the words Meng-Ji spoke for the next two hours. Yet, without the meaningful inflections and pitches which added emphasis to the key points he presented, both *for* and *against* market-driven economies.

"I never thought about it that way, before," Justin's friend from Michigan announced bluntly. "I suppose it makes sense if you believe the forces of globalization are washing us all into the same big ocean of change."

"At least he's not promoting the idea of inevitable Chinese dominance in world trade," Justin responded solemnly.

"He's not?"

Lili leaned forward and tapped Robert Changui's shoulder. "What do you think of Professor Meng-Ji's views?" She'd recognized the embassy intern's discrete entrance. Robert turned and replied, "In friendship, I hope neither country turns the dead cat the other way." He clasped her hands tightly…a very unusual greeting between Asians. Many considered such physical contact inappropriate.

Lili took his words to mean: *either country could turn the economic tables on the other*. Robert silently mouthed, "For Gatt" and pressed the note into her hand. His eyes darted momentarily to her left before he quickly turned and faced the front.

The professor ended his lecture as always---strutting toward the edge of the raised speaker's platform and leaning precariously over the edge. His head bowed, and his arms drooped to his sides…as if he was preparing to dive into the audience. When the mild and appropriately restrained applause receded, he waited a respectful moment, then straightened and recited his famous concluding Confucianisms.

"When you have faults, do not fear to abandon them." Lili slipped the folded note handed to her by Robert, deeply into Justin's pants pocket. *"Learning without thought is labour lost,"* Meng-Ji pronounced loudly. *"Thought without learning is perilous."*

Justin reached into his trousers as Lili dusted her thighs, smiling.

FEDERAL RESERVE BANK, WASHINGTON, D.C.

Fed Chairman John Paul Tangus finally got through after Ambassador Balzerini joined Humphreys and the others in a champagne toast at the Embassy. The secure satellite links between Washington and the Beijing Embassy were heating up.

"First give me the good news, if there is any, Forrest. I could use some."

Balzerini replied instantly,"You won't believe it, J.P." The excitement in his voice transcended their usual stoic conversations. Seasoned diplomats like Balzerini were trained to be talk in placid…almost sedated…certainly imperturbable tones.

"I don't know if it was our arguments, the pressure Merrand and others have been exerting publicly for import restrictions, or something else. But, the Chinese have agreed to allow the yuan to float on the currency exchanges in Hong Kong, London, New York and Shanghai---sometime prior to October first."

"My God! How many nuclear-sub blue-prints did you have to give them?"

"They've also promised to comply with the Stressa Accords; and bid on the Treasury's upcoming $30 billion bond offering…with the intent of buying the entire issue."

Tangus was momentarily speechless. He was about to inform the Ambassador that several European Union central banks had just solicited bids from the currency markets…to sell billions of U.S. dollars. They were attempting to exchange dollars for euros, yuan, Swiss francs and British sterling.

"I must be missing some vital information, Forrest. The Chinese move to float the yuan makes little sense. My European friends estimate that as much as fifty to 100 billion dollars changed hands in a recent dollar sell-off. Only the Bank of China has available reserves of that quantity in European bank accounts. They typically deposit about ten percent of the net currency accumulated from their trade surplus, into select European institutions. The funds are held there or redeposited in various banks for liquidity purposes."

"Beijing is up to something," Balzerini replied.

"Tell me, has Mu Jianting actually agreed to announce China's intentions publicly? The Communists have made promises behind closed doors before, which were later ignored."

"That's the strangest part, J.P. I didn't attend the final session, but Humphreys claims he was practically force-fed a draft of a joint press-release by NPC Chairman Chang Hui Chen and senior Vice-Premier, Yong Ihasa. You may recall that Ihasa is also the Minister of Currency Regulation. The Secretary of State just approved the wording. He marveled at how close the announcement followed typical official American press-release narrative. It's almost as if they were trying to guarantee the President's immediate acceptance of their proposal."

Tangus thought: *Now we hear the bad news.* "What proposal?"

"Ihasa wants the Administration to issue a strong statement advocating that free-trade with China is essential to the well-being of American citizens; and should not be tampered with. Yong made it clear that China's continued investments in U.S. government-securities was contingent upon the American markets for Chinese goods remaining open."

"Have you noticed any fall-out from the corruption charges against President Mu?"

"Only that Humphreys' scheduled appointment with Mu Jianting was cancelled at the last minute. Butler didn't have a chance to ask the CCP Chairman any questions."

"So, you suspect strong-arming by his Politboro opponents."

"Yes. And NPC Chairman Chang insists that our President make the official announcement supporting Chinese imports. He wants wording to the effect that the American economy relies on inexpensive Chinese imports to fight inflation; and that Chinese goods are being *demanded* by the public. Mu would never directly challenge the President in that manner."

Tangus replied firmly, "The President won't do it. Does that kill the deal?"

Balzerini paused, then said grudgingly, "Senators Scharn and Troone were consulted. They convinced the President that he had no choice. He's more easily swayed now that the pancreatic cancer has spread. The yuan float is such a major political breakthrough, and a potential benefit to the economy. Even Governor Merrand agreed not to comment negatively, as long as future Administrations aren't bound to the Chinese rhetoric."

"Find out what you can about current BOC monetary policy, Forrest. The regional Fed presidents have started to complain about pressures from outside board members who are pushing for us to bump up overnight interest rates. The undulations in borrowing-rate pressures from European central banks and Wall Street institutions will be the primary deliberation at our Open Market Committee meeting next week."

"I hadn't heard about that. The currency discussions with the Chinese centered on the yuan float, not dollar exchanges."

"Well, a dollar sell-off has apparently splashed favor in Europe. If the Chinese have decided to negatively hoard fewer dollars, it's a complete reversal of forward monetary strategy. Unlinking the yuan from the trading-value of U.S. currency may represent a backward underreaction to other motives for change. If you can discover these reasons, the Fed will be better armed to undo what in hell is going on in Beijing money circles."

Balzerini smiled. He always did in conversations with the Fed Chairman. "If we can gather any info, J.P., we'll be sure not to underreport it."

Tangus sensed the slight sarcasm from his genuine friend. "No crap, Forrest. We could be witnessing the beginning of a reversal in Chinese monetary negative-cooperation. Please, have your above-ground sources do some discreet digging."

U.S. DEPARTMENT OF AGRICULTURE
WASHINGTON, DC

Corn was certainly the news in Midwest states. Also, at the Department of Agriculture's Statistical Harvests Bureau in Washington.

The strange browning of large Iowa cornfields was being investigated by a team of scientists from the USDA and Midwest university agricultural stations. Various theories were being offered for the phenomenon. None could explain the cause or origin of the contaminants, which were spreading from infected plants to nearby, harvest-ready fields. Agricultural experts were amazed at the spray-paint velocity at which thousands of acres of hybrid maize were changing color.

The Ag Department's announcment that China just reported an unexpected bumper corn-crop…creating the first maize surplus in the history of Chinese farming…did little to assuage Iowa corn-belt farmer's fears of being wiped out by the unknown organism already dubbed the "corn-virus."

The timing of the Chinese announcement was strange. Apparently, Chinese farmers had over-reported soybean acreage and under-reported corn acreage. The Secretary of Agriculture would be chastised by corn-belt farmers for not detecting the Chinese corn surplus beforehand.

Beijing's orders for Midwest corn imports to its southern provinces had been cancelled, and the China Agricultural Ministry stepped up its efforts to export surplus corn from the northern plains to Russia, Japan and the Koreas. Merely hours after the corn-virus was detected in Iowa, the U.S. Department of Agriculture was approached by a commodity trader offering Chinese corn suitable for livestock feeding.

Iowa, America's largest producer of corn with twelve million planted acres, could soon become just another import customer for the Asian goliath.

Ming Tombs
North of Beijing.

"The Forbidden City and the Great Wall were amazing feats of construction," Justin said to Lili as they turned onto the road leading to the Ming Tombs. "But the Ming Dynasty has more interesting history."

"This was once a four-mile long sacred-way, forbidden to all but the convoy of servants and attendants in the emperor's funeral procession." Lili recalled from her study of the Imperial dynasties.

"It says in this book that there were sixteen Ming emperors, and thirteen are buried in Shisanling valley," Justin announced excitedly, like the enthused tourist he was. He flipped the pages of Schurmann and Schell's 1967 historical gem, *'Imperial China.'*

"The Mings were supposedly the ultimate amateurs. Court officials were artists and poets, not pragmatic disciplinarians or military strategists. I suppose that's one reason why the Manchu's from the north were able to conquer Beijing in 1644, and remove the last pure Chinese, or Han people, from imperial rule. The Mings believed art could reveal their true humanism."

Lili parked the rented car in the lot near the entrance to the five-arched marble gate built in 1540, which led another mile to the three-arched gateway, the Dahongmen, *Great Red Gate*. As they walked toward the gate, Lili said, "The center door is only opened to carry the Emperor's body through."

They passed through a side archway, and came to the stone tortoise, the symbol of longevity which marked the beginning of the famous Avenue of Animals. Justin was fascinated when he read that the thirty-foot tablet mounted on the tortoise's back was inscribed by the 4th Ming Emperor at the death of his predecessor, Yong Le, in 1424…about the same time some historians claimed China discovered America. He wondered if there were stone markings alluding to the discovery of a new continent in the east.

The Avenue of Animals was lined on either side by marble lions, camels, elephants, horses and two sets of mythical beasts, alternately standing or kneeling.

"These creatures are eternally loyal to the Ming emperors," Lili explained in the sing-song tone of an official tour-guide. "If disturbed, a wind of death will blow down from the Ming tombs upon the capital."

Justin observed her mischievous smirk. She stared skyward with pursed lips, ignoring him. She was in a playful mood and was enjoying Justin's company. "Legend has it that the tombs are missing the *gilin*, a mythical animal of good omen, and the *suanni*, a mythical monster, because they fought to the death when a Manchu Qing Emperor's widow wanted to move the stone animals to her husband's tomb about sixty miles east of Beijing in 1796."

Justin suspected Lili was pulling his leg. "I read about the Emperor Qian Long's tomb. It's referred to as the 'underground palace.' Doesn't it have *gilin* and *suanni* carved from single stone-blocks weighing up to 43 tons?" Lili tilted her head as if to say, "Could be!"

"I love to tell stories about the past, during my tours." She admitted, giggling cutely with crimped shoulders, "Sometimes they're true. Foreigners will believe anything."

As they advanced to the Chang and Ding excavations, the burial names for Ming emperors Yong Le and Wan Li, Lili pointed in the direction of Kunming Lake and said, "Once, I escorted a group from New York to the Summer Palace and Kunming Lake. They were loud and unaware they were annoying an Overseas Chinese tour group. To attract their attention and quiet them, I told them that the water in Kunming Lake contained fish from the Atlantic Ocean. They said, 'No shit,' and I explained that there was a vast underground flow of water which tunnels below Staten Island, crosses west under the continent, submerges below the Pacific Ocean and comes to the surface in Kunming Lake. I told them the local fish here were actually cod, striped bass and blue-fish, although we called them something else."

As they passed a small group surrounding an English-speaking tour guide, Justin caught the words 'White Lotus sect,' and stopped abruptly.

"The Mings were aligned to the highest cultural values. They were *wen-jen*, true literary men, with a feeling for nature and a flair for both painting and poetry." The young guide was a student of Chinese history and took pride in displaying his knowledge.

"The Ming Dynasty got its name from the messianic figures---*Big* and *Little MingWang,* which means *Brilliant Kings.* They were sent by Buddha Maitreya to the world to restore peace and order."

"Tell us again how they came to power?" one of the tourists in the back asked above the clamor of passing groups.

"The White Lotus Sect, a secret society which some say still exists, helped them topple the Mongol rule. Also known as the Incense Smelling and the

White Yang religious sects, as far back as 1794, White Lotus influence spread over nine provinces. Several White Lotus members were appointed to the Ming court and influenced history. They created the Grand Secretariat of high officials which assisted the Ming emperors in personal Administrative affairs. Many became resourceful long-distance merchants---China's first great traders as the country emerged from a closed civilization to a respected global society."

Lili suddenly pulled Justin away from the crowd and walked arm-in-arm toward the parking lot. She'd noticed a stern-faced man dressed in a Mao tunic flip the back of his hand up repeatedly in their direction. She didn't want to draw the attention of security police patroling the tourist sight.

"Have you destroyed the note?" she asked, referring to the folded paper she passed to Justin at the university lecture.

"How did you know it was dangerous?" he frowned. "And why didn't Robert just pass it to me directly?"

"Perhaps you should ask Ambassador Balzerini, Mr. Gatt. It's time to go." She walked toward the drivers side of their rented vehicle, but Justin said, "Do you mind if I drive? Something tells me I should practice."

"We're meeting Mr. Oresco, the newspaper man, at a local Beijing restaurant for dinner. They specialize in aromatic Peking duck. I understand it's your favorite."

"I never ate it before."

The thought suddenly occurred to him that he was about to do many things in China that he'd never done before.

CHAPTER 47

(August 10, 2008) PM
Beijing restaurant

Gabriel Oresco hung up the wall phone connecting to each room, and settled into a deep-cushioned chair in the lobby of the Beijing Hotel. Justin would be down in fifteen minutes for their dinner date. Lili would meet them at the restaurant.

Oresco had made reservations at a small Sichuan-style eatery in the Rongxian Xi Hutong, Number 51, which specialized in spicy foods, including duck smoked in tea leaves and camphor, which Gatt had to have.

The lobby was packed with Olympic tourists trying to decide where to dine. The concierge-line extended nearly to the elevators. Oresco grinned knowingly as he listened to the uniformed hotel employee at the desk ask, "Imperial style? Crispy Beijing Duck? Shanghai cuisine? Have you tried Mongolian barbecue, Sichuan or Cantonese? How about Shandong---some nice silver thread rolls with deep-fried winter melon, dates and bamboo shoots?"

He never mentioned Western, Japanese, Korean or fast-food restaurants.

Justin re-folded the note Lili had slipped into his pocket and placed it in the fancy porcelain ashtray hand-painted with red and white dragons. He then shredded the loose sheet of paper slipped into Professor Meng-Ji's handout and placed the torn pieces on top of the folded note. He lit a match and tested his memory once again. The note read: *Come alone on 8/12 or 8/13 (will advise 8/11) to address below. Bring a shopping bag containing recently purchased items of clothing with room to hide a document file. Method of identifying contact will be revealed 8/11 when confirm which meeting date. Destroy this note after memorizing contents.*

The loose sheet in the stapled copy of Professor Meng-Ji's Annual Lecture had been artfully scribed. According to Lili, it was an unintelligible phonetic translation of a Sino-Tibetan language. Justin became comfortable asking her to translate the message when Robert Changhui called to inform him that both Lili and Gabriel Oresco could be trusted.

"It's time for each of you to disclose to the others, your relationship with the Embassy," Robert explained in a vexed tone. "The tasks assigned to each of you are pretty much complimentary. Time is of the essence, since the evidence of a planned Chinese aggression against the U.S. is mounting."

Justin now understood the context of Professor Meng-Ji's note. "So...the information you want me to obtain could be critical to understanding the threat, and possibly heading it off?"

"Exactly!" Robert replied softly on the secure line. "The Ambassador regrets putting you in a compromising position by divulging your...*cooperation*...with the government to Lili and Gabriel. He hopes you understand. Lili doesn't know many details, other than she's here to help you carry out a task somehow associated with the Embassy. You don't have to be concerned about Gabriel. He's put his life on the line for us before. He can be trusted. He's acting as a diversion for you."

Meng-Ji's message read : *For eyes of Yale Professor E. S. and trusted colleagues. A troublesome outflow of US dollars has been noted at China central banks, leaving several Provincial budgets short of US currency to pay for needed foreign raw materials. Billions in US dollars have recently been repatriated to European banks for unknown purpose. Am concerned corrupt leaders stealing vast sums from Chinese people. Since US currency is involved, request E.S. track huge new money flows into world markets with Treasury Department and Fed Reserve contacts. I am attempting to contact honest State Council and NPC officials concerned with suspected unauthorized transfers of massive dollar reserves held in BOC balance-of-trade net funds. Such quantities should appear on international banking radar. Please inform E.S. and destroy this message. He'll know how to respond.*

Lili was dressed in a colorful outfit that accentuated her ivory skin and flawless complexion. Her delicate shoulders and modest bust-line were captured in a damask-rose silk charmeuse tank with pintucks, ruffle details and a scoop neckline. A soft-washed, flax-tone linen flared-skirt with embroidered details in pink, purple and laurel frill trimming flowed a few inches below the knee, revealing delicate, pink-painted toes glimpsing from soft pink-leather sandals.

Justin and Gabriel rose as she approached the table in the remote wing of the multi-pavilion restaurant connected by cobblestone courtyards. She tiptoed slowly across the cobblestones that connected this pavilion with the front rooms on 51 Hutong, which were closer to the olfactory-rousing breezes being fanned sweet and sour from the kitchen. A seemingly endless throng of Chinese locals and tourists jammed the ancient side-street, reminding Justin of the restless spirit of 17th and 18th century American pioneers.

There was a sense of new frontiers…new freedoms and new mobility. The Chinese seemed to have a mass desire for refreshing experiences, escape from realism, and social and spiritual renewal. Like modern Americans, they were also willing to fight through hopelessly clogged traffic to get to work.

"My, but aren't you a dandy,"Gabriel spouted as Lili took a seat across from Justin so she could see those dazzling blue eyes as they talked. Justin held out a palm to guide her down. That was a strange custom, Lili thought. Nice. No touching…in the Chinese tradition of greeting. But she didn't understand its usefulness.

"Thank you, Mr. Oresco. I hope I haven't kept you gentlemen waiting."

"We were seated just a few minutes ago," Justin said as he followed a plate of prawns laced with ginger and garlic to the next table. "I can't believe the delicious odors coming from the food that passes by." His nose was mesmerized. He looked closer at Lili. So became his radiant blue eyes.

"I've eaten lunch here, before,"Oresco boasted mildly. "The exotic dishes are amazing. I once ordered a house special that turned out to be pig's organ with shredded jelly fish. When I asked which organ they cooked, the waiter said, 'Hog Maw. Like stomach; like intestine. But lower.' Then he touched his groin and laughed all the way to the kitchen."

"I've never been that adventurous," Justin grunted. "But I am ready for duck smoked in tea leaves and camphor. It sounds fairly mild."

Lili grinned a happy smile, which accurately described her elated emotions. This was the most pleasant assignment she'd ever experienced. "I suppose you might order a few bottles of spring water," she suggested…rolling her lips inward. This place was famous for spicy food. The kitchen's inconsistency with chili pepper and other near-spontaneously-combustible spices was legendary. Justin had learned his lesson eating 'mild chili' during the Yale lunch with Eric. "Good idea," he responded enthusiastically.

When they finished eating *Ganshau Yu*-- fish fried in fiery chili sauce; crispy candle-flames of camphor duck, and blow-torch *Mapo Dofu*--- a pock-marked bean-curd dish which brought Oresco to sobs; the waiter brought three large bottles of iced citrus-flavored water. Customers with inflamed throats were poor tippers. The water would suppress the swelling.

"Now you ready for dessert?" he asked straight-faced.

"Maybe, later," Oresco managed to mumble in hoarse putonghua. "We want to talk for a few minutes."

Justin's tongue drooped over his bottom lip. "Your tongue is trembling, like some people who can wiggle their ears," Lili said impishly. "Is that a trick?" He gulped at the citrus water and twisted his mouth in embarrassment.

"He's loose-tongued," Oresco joked. "Maybe it's not such a good idea to exchange information about our relationships with the U.S. Embassy."

Justin considered this suggestion reasonable. He was forging ahead into unknown terrain. All he could be sure of was that the environment was hazardous.

"Why don't we start by describing how we became involved with Balzerini…in general terms," Oresco suggested. "If what I understand is true, the Ambassador needs help to ward-off an unknown, potentially catastrophic threat against America originating here."

"It seems to be more than just an economic crisis," Justin added. He turned to Lili. It seemed strange to be openly discussing a potentially serious conflict between America and China with a Chinese citizen present. He assumed Lili was not one of the 70 million Communist Party members brainwashed to distrust Americans.

Oresco said, "Lili, what are your thoughts?"

Justin interrupted before she could answer. "Ambassador Balzerini has explained your willingness to aid the democratic movement in China."

"Very delicately stated, Mr. Gatt. In truth, I am furious at my government, and wish to help force them to become a better global citizen. But most important…the corrupt and ruthless leaders of the Chinese Communist Party are not responsive to the needs of the people. Repression is rampant, and human rights for workers seem to be diminishing…not improving. My own mother and father were killed in preventable industrial accidents."

Oresco's specialty was investigating such matters. "I'm sorry," he said softly. "Corruption in the five municipalities administered by the central government---Beijing, Shanghai, Shenzen, Tianjin and Chongdu---is growing like cancer. The emerging tide of income-based class separation is more corrosive to Sino-society than the caste system is to India."

"Some people claim the same is true in America. I read about that in the International Herald Tribune," she replied. "My clients sometimes give me a copy so I can practice the English language. The rich get richer, and the poor…which I understand now includes drop-outs from the American middle-class…are getting poorer. I struggle to pity them, though. Every American is rich by Chinese peasant standards. I don't understand why so many Americans constantly complain."

Justin smiled. "It's our duty to complain; when we don't like the way our leaders lead."

Oresco interjected, "That's why I'm a journalist chasing down corruption in Asia and elsewhere." He raised his glass. "Perhaps we should do as Balzerini suggests, and just lay open our assigned tasks. We're all involved in trying to find the suspected threat, apparently because we're in a position to help. You, Justin, are in the best position. Nobody in China knows or cares about you...no disrespect intended. You're not an espionage suspect. I've apparently reached that plateau. They follow me everywhere."

Lili interjected, "And I have been assigned to help you complete whatever task they've asked of you. That note I passed to you from the Embassy; should we know it's contents?"

"What note?"Oresco asked morosely. "Balzerini didn't mention any note."

Justin structured a careful response. "Gabriel, what are your travel plans for the next few days?"

"I'm going to remain in the Shanghai area. Balzerini wants me to be here for a few days. I've scheduled interviews with some multi-national U.S. corporations with expansions going on in the Suzhou Industrial complex near Nanjing. It's my cover. He's asked me to keep open the 12th and 13th. Why?"

"And, Lili, you'll be with me the entire time I'm traveling in the Shanghai vicinity?"

"Yes, Mr. Gatt, every second...except when we sleep."

"Then you both already know the content of that note...except for the exact time and location. I suspect Balzerini wants you near me at all times." He lowered his voice as the waiter glanced their way, expectantly. "There'll be an information exchange. I may require your assistance if anything goes wrong."

Oresco and Lili both nodded.

The waiter raced over and said, "You ready for dessert now?"

(AUGUST 11, 2008)
GENEVA

Lynne spread the printed data sheets from Papa's file on Stella's dining table, hoping to discern the Big Picture. So far, she'd missed finding a pattern. The data-crammed printouts Papa had provided did not reveal the plot she'd suspected. A different picture was emerging.

The entities she'd asked him to check--BoxMart Retail Stores; Residents Bank of North America; and The Bank of China were included in the analysis; but Papa added new data on Franco-Medici Union Trust, Creditte Bank de

Savoy, and a Cayman Islands subsidiary. Her Harvard library research had sparked a fruitful investigation in Geneva.

"Your dad also included European transactions involving Creditte Bank de Savoy of Lyons, France; the Financial Flow Foundation in Washington, DC; and the Regional Federal Reserve Bank in Boston."

"I know," Stella responded as she lifted her martini glass. "He found a peculiar series of intertwined transactions involving each of the entities on your original list, with these others. It's almost as if a closed network circuit exists to facilitate discreet, non-transparent money flows from one entity to the other. Papa says all the numbered and coded accounts found in the inquiry had similar characteristics. You know...like special redundant clearance procedures, multiple codes for authorizing fund transfers, and common sequences to access web sites and transaction verifications."

Lynne crimped her upper lip with her thumb and forefinger, and glanced down at the page entitled 'FFF Transactions.' The tiny numbers printed on the paper were scaled to fit one page...probably fifty-percent sized on the printer setting...and barely readable. At least two hundred deposits were recorded as transfers from a partially-blanked-out account number. The four visible numbers matched the last four digits of the I.D. number printed at the top of the 'BoxMart Transactions' sheet

The pages for each of the seven entities contained similar data: partially blanked-out account numbers matching the last four numbers of the I.D. numbers listed for each business entity. Whether they represented deposits or withdrawals, the data included money transfers made during the previous sixty days. Mr. Nicorezzi's personal assistant also included earlier transactions he considered important.

"There certainly are a large number of entries,"Stella said evenly. "Papa believes the sums are extraordinarily large. I mean...millions and billions...flowing like water."

"Maybe they're funding the Three Gorges Dam project,"Lynne mused. "Or investing in the new high-rises in Shanghai we read about. But, why would a retailing company like BoxMart be smack in the middle? It seems the BM ID number shows up more often than the others. They recently deposited ten billion in Franco-Medici."

"Papa said the Chinese have transferred *multiples* of that into Franco-Medici trust-accounts held for the Chinese government."

Lynne paused in deep thought. Stella had witnessed that determined look before. Lynne would not rest until she found the answer.

"It appears Geneva is being used as a clearing house. Why else would the Chinese move massive amounts of dollar reserves from mainland banks to Europe?"

Lynne lifted the sheet entitled, *Residents Bank of North America*. She suddenly chilled. The dates were familiar for several fifty-thousand and one-hundred-thousand dollar deposits into a Residents Bank account identified as 'Individual ET.' The frequency of deposits was much lower than with the other transfers. She brought the 'RBNA Transactions' sheet close to her nose to re-check the tiny print. "These transactions go back twelve months. I recognize two of the dates."

"Why would a few dates be important?"

"Because the bankruptcy case for Justin's company, GRT, was settled by the courts on one of those dates. Joe Slattery's company was turned over to Resident's Bank on the other."

Her devious mind ramped up to outrageous-conspiracy mode. "*Individual ET*! I'll bet that bastard Edwin Tinius is getting paid by BoxMart to kill off small American manufacturing companies. This is strong evidence! I'd bet my emerald earrings that the other deposit dates for the 'ET' account coincide with court-settlement dates for other small company bankruptcies Tinius is involved. The question is...why?"

Stella swallowed the cocktail onion and the last drops in her glass. "It's time for you to have one of these." She rose from the table and headed for the liquor cabinet. Lynne's eyes darted from list to list, like a casino blackjack dealer sloughing off the cards of winners and losers under the watchful eye of the ceiling cameras.

Let me think. During the past several months BoxMart has paid millions directly to FFF. BoxMart has also paid tens of thousands to a Residents Bank 'Individual' account. BoxMart has moved about ten billion dollars from its primary U.S. account at Residents Bank in Boston into a numbered account at Franco-Medici Trust in Geneva... a quantity so large that the funds transfer required the approval of a high official at the Boston Federal Reserve Bank.

Central Bank of China branch offices in Beijing and Shanghai have deposited over fifty-billion in US currency reserves into FM Trust, which in turn transferred twenty-five billion of those dollars to its parent in Lyons---the Creditte Bank de Savoy. Papa says CBdS and FM have already traded fifty billion US dollars to Euro-center banks in exchange for other denominations; and have made tentative inquiries for the sale of another 75-100 billion dollars on international money exchanges.

They're dumping dollars. What next?

Stella handed Lynne a cocktail glass containing six green olives, a slice of lemon peel and an inch of iced, top-shelf vodka. She knew Lynne hated martinis, but loved green olives.

"Here! Douse that smoking brain for a few minutes."

Lynne accepted the drink and plucked out the olives one-by-one. "I haven't got a clue why the Chinese government is depositing so much money in a European bank in such a short time period Or why BoxMart is paying off a New England banking demon."

Stella replied casually,without realizing the depth of her perception, "Would that become a problem in the States? You know...cause interest rates to rise or something? With all those dollars changing hands?"

Lynne was exhausted from recent events, and the alcohol from the olive cavities sent a warm shiver to her shoulders. "Didn't Papa mention that the Federal Reserve Bank just announced a special Open Market Committee meeting? They're the guardians of currency values and interest rates."

"I can scarcely balance my check book,"Stella smirked. "Don't ask me!"

"Well,there must be a link to all of this."

"Did Papa mention that Franco-Medici is fifty-one percent owned by Creditte Bank de Savoy; and that Franco-Medici itself controls fifty-one percent of the Cayman Islands Investment Bank; which in turn owns forty-nine percent of Residents Bank,N.A., but controls one-hundred percent of the voting shares?"

"He told me that CBdS was one of the original foreign financial institutions to invest in the regional Fed Reserve system when it was established by Congress in 1913. I think the Bank of England and the Rothschilds Bank were others."

"Papa says CBdS at one time owned five-percent of the Regional Federal Reserve Bank in Boston, but transferred their stock to Residents Bank when the law changed; allowing only domestic institutions to own pieces of Fed banks. At one time CBdS owned about eight percent of the Boston Regional Bank and six percent of the New York Regional Bank."

"How did he acquire such information? I thought the Geneva banking industry was close-mouthed?"

"Papa knows one of the secretaries working for Phillipe Cusson, the Director-General of CBdS. When Mama left us, he sought refuge in her arms."

Lynne's eyes welled up. She was reminded of the unsatisfied yearning in her belly to be with a man in China. She'd call Justin and plead with him to return to Cambridge so they could face the dangers together. She at least had to tell him about the information in Papa's file.

CHAPTER 48

(August 11, 2008) am
Beiing

Lili's cell phone buzzed as she stepped from the taxi in front of the Beijing Hotel and started walking toward the lobby entrance. The familiar background burble resonating from the embassy communications center indicated AJ was at the other end. She wondered how he always seemed to know where she was. He'd never called her on the street before.

Instead of entering the lobby to meet Justin for the limo to the airport, she turned west on Chang'an Avenue and mixed in with the throng of walkers clamping cell phones to their ears.

"Just listen," he began. "No need to respond more than *yes* or *no*. You're being watched from the book shop across the street from the hotel."

Lili inched away from the curb and moved closer to the store-fronts. She stopped at a large window displaying the latest in Milan fashions. "Go ahead."

"Do Gatt and Oresco have a clear understanding of your role?"

"Yes."

"Do you of theirs?"

"Yes."

"Is Gatt with you?"

"Not yet....No."

"Okay. In a few minutes a silver Mercedes with dark windows will arrive to drive you and Gatt to Beijing International Airport. Gatt's itinerary in Shanghai has been changed. We didn't want to contact him directly. I'll explain the details to him later. It's better if you don't know them for now. Dial me on the special frequency number when you're both in the car en route. It will be safe to talk in the Mercedes." The line went dead.

No '*how-are-you's*? Or small talk?. This must be serious. Too brief an exchange for her to inform AJ that the supervisor at the Tourist Bureau called her into his office this morning to inquire if she was still traveling with a Mr. Gatt. He then demanded that she report her location...and presumably Mr. Gatt's...at least twice a day. He also asked for a copy of Gatt's schedule. Very unusual.

Ministry of Defense

General Ye handed a copy of the joint Chinese-American press release to Colonel Wen Ma and said, "Yong Ihasa has been successful. The yuan will float before October. Now, we must do our part."

"As you predicted, General! Now we can meet Kurancy's terms and complete the Bomali merger in Macau. Do you wish for me to leave immediately?"

Ye studied his tall protege. Such an intense expression. Wen Ma was a dutiful officer with the mean streak of a soul-less master torturer. Especially when armed with jagged, body-penetrating tools. He delighted in ordering people around and eliciting excruciating pain.

He'd make a perfect replacement for Emerson Bromine when the time came for the PLA to wrest control of the Bomali board and top management positions. By then, the merger of LCE and BoxMart would have created the world's largest industrial and retailing entity. Competing retail chains with no direct partnerships with Chinese manufacturers would be financially disadvantaged. Their merchandise costs would be significantly higher than the transfer prices from Bomali to the BoxMart organization

The low profit margins of the mainland LCE factories would be compensated for when the Macau income-tax laws were applied to the bottom line. Kurancy was going after increased sales volume. The 3P-BIO business-models predicted that BoxMart would capture the highest share of the world market for disposable consumer products, within three years. Even number one would be scrambling.

"The glorious marriage between LCE and BoxMart is of unprecedented scale," Wen Ma exulted. "Bomali will wipe out all but a few competitors. Not even Wal-Mart can match the projected economic strength of a giant global retailer merged with the world's largest manufacturing conglomerate.

"Yong Ihasa's scheme will cause a holiday sales disaster. Many of the cash-strapped regional discount stores in America won't make it. They don't enjoy the financial staying-power of national chains like Target, Wal-Mart, K-Mart and others."

"Ihasa is a genious. A Ming leader may yet rule again," General Ye exclaimed forcefully.

"With the balls of a *liger*," Wen added, referring to the cross-breed of a lion and tiger, which was larger than either animal. Jake Kurancy had adopted the *liger* as the official BoxMart logo. He'd purchased a pair of the amazing animals from African cross-breeders, and donated them to the Beijing Zoo.

"Li Chin hopes the curious off-breeds will augment his beloved Pandas at the zoo. Side-by-side they make a unique attraction. Yong Ihasa had even discussed using the *liger* as the new symbol for the Triad Communist Party he envisions.

"Yes, Colonel, it's time. You must return to Macau as soon as possible. Kurancy is on his way, and the legal people were instructed to prepare the final merger papers. Bromine will wait until the Olympic closing ceremonies to announce the merger to the financial media. Meanwhile, Cusson will stick pins in the dollar balloon."

"He's enchanted with the prospect of softening up American bankers," Wen Ma snickered. "By the time he dumps the critical-mass of dollars, the American economy will be reeling from the fallout of the corn-virus contaminations."

"The bio-attack is going better than planned, Colonel. Student-operatives attending Midwest agricultural colleges in America have reported that the virus is spreading faster than predicted. They believe the U.S. food industry will soon panic."

"The American economy will be traumatized," Wen Ma predicted, with obvious satisfaction. "Lacking a safe food supply---the population will be disemboweled of confidence in its hapless leaders."

Wen Ma gathered his papers and rose to depart for the Bomali closing. Despite being General Ye's closest advisor on business matters, he wasn't privy to the military directives issued by Ye to the Eastern Defense Forces. The Vice-Chairman of the Central Military Commission distributed that particular information on a need-to-know basis. There was little purpose in disclosing to Colonel Wen Ma that three battalions of PLA troops were being deployed to the outskirts of Xiamen, the large city bordering the heavily fortified Taiwan-administered offshore island of Quemoy. Or the battalions and anti-air and anti-ground missile units repositioned to Fuzhou, the capital of Fujian province. Fuzhou looked east to Matsu, the other off-shore island controlled by Taiwan.

Carrier-based surveillance flights over Quemoy and Matsu would begin as soon as the troops were in place for "military exercises."

Soon the world will know that Taiwan is the perpetrator of the corn-virus crises in both China and the U.S. PLA troops will have their justification. The invasion to occupy the islands will likely be bloodless. If not, I will inflict the long-

overdue crushing assimilation and punishment on the traitorous Kuomintang remnants of Chiang Kai Shek. The Taiwanese people **expect** to be digested into the mainland. Otherwise, they would not still refer to Taipei as their "temporary capital."

"Travel safely, Colonel. I suspect that President Mu will have difficulty explaining to the Central Committee how Chinese merchandise, packaged in contaminated boxes, escaped export security and health inspections at our ports. Mu will be broadsided by an avalanche of uncensored internet accusations."

"Yong Ihasa, Chang Hui and Wang Chao will benefit from Mu's incompetence and oversight failure, General. Vice-Premier Ihasa is a perfect compromise Party leader. You will finally take your rightful place on the Standing Committee."

"Keep me informed from Macau, Colonel. I want no surprises in wrapping up the Bomali deal, now that we've agreed to meet Kurancy's demands. The one-hundred million he wants will slip from Yew Bai Tsin's hands to an escrow account at CBdS. When China defaults on the agreement, and takes control of the Board of Directors, we'll gladly pay him…if he's still alive."

General Ye was reminded of the sealed envelope resting on his desk. "Here, Wen Ma. Some gambling fuel for your Macau visit. Bromine's casino always wins, so be aware to save some for other purposes." The envelope contained eight hundred thousand yuan…equivalent to one-hundred thousand dollars. The Colonel was a chronic gambler, always short of cash.

"Most gracious of you, General." He saluted and rushed out as excited as a virgin sailor going on his first visit to an exotic foreign brothel.

The leverage gained by controlling Bomali will be enormous, thought Ye. *Ihasa will use it to pressure the Europeans into lifting the arms embargo on military equipment the Pentagon wants kept out of my hands. Those fools!*

The American defense industry was generous in sharing its latest advanced command-and-control technology with European NATO allies. For economic reasons, a few of those governments were willing to provide China with modified versions of the identical technology---disguised as lower-valued electronic instruments.

General Ye had resisted Mu Jianting's military budget cutbacks, at the expense of disfavor with the Party hierarchy. He needed replacements for the PLA's antediluvian military-command modules. A modern command-and-control system from the French could save the PLA a decade of military research. France promised to provide the technology as soon as the Pentagon-led military equipment embargo was lifted.

Standing in line to sell advanced weaponry to the Chinese were Russia and the international arms dealers based in Germany and Syria. The naval weapons and advanced missile technology Ye was seeking would alter the balance of power in the South China Sea, and the entire western Pacific theater. America's influence as 'security guarantor' for Japan, South Korea and Taiwan would soon be severely compromised.

Savoy, France

"Oh, my God. I finally reached you. You won't believe the information we dug up in Geneva." Lynne's exuberance was effusive.

"Where are you, Lynne? I can't talk right now. I'll call you back in a few minutes. My phone will re-connect with the number your calling from. Sorry…just hang tight."

Buzzzzzzzz.

Lynne was crushed. She needed to hear a warm, tender Justin. Not a business-like brush-off. Stella shrugged her shoulders in the passenger seat of Papa's red Porsche. They were parked around the corner from the Creditte Bank de Savoy headquarters entrance in Lyon. Lynne talked her friend into driving the hundred kilometers from Geneva to Lyons, France so she could get a feel' for doing business with CBdS. She planned to open a foreign national numbered account.

Shanghai

Justin held Lili's unit in one hand and his own in the other. AJ was giving him very specific instructions: the location of the Tea House; how to cross the zig-zag bridge to identify himself to the information courier; how the source would confirm his own identity by reciting a Confucian teaching related to social hierarchy; how the switch would be made; and what to do after that.

"Don't write anything down. I guess that's not a problem for someone like you with a photographic memory."

"I have it. Lili says she knows the location. We'll be there in plenty of time, AJ. Piece of cake." Justin scanned Lili's worried expression.

"Can I talk to AJ, please?" He handed her the phone and immediately hit the re-dial button on his own unit.

"What did you mean…I'm being followed? Why would anyone follow me?"

"Have you or Gatt done anything to attract attention? The Beijing Security Department is phobic about suspicious activities of foreigners; now that the Olympic masses and street demonstrators are driving them to chug *bai-jiu*." The term was Chinese for white lightning.

Lili thought a moment. "We had dinner with Gabriel Oresco of the New York Times. He says they're always watching him. Maybe the man you spotted in front of the hotel was waiting for him."

"Let's hope so. But keep a watchful eye, Lili. You and Gatt may currently be off the security department's main radar screen, but that doesn't mean Gatt's mission is immune to detection. Communist eyes are everywhere."

"I must tell you one more thing, AJ: I was called in by the tour department supervisor this morning, before I left the office to travel with Mr. Gatt." She tilted her head sideways and was pleased that Justin was distracted in a different, animated conversation. She heard him say, *'If Blackstone and Tinius are involved, you can't return to your apartment. Call Brad."*

"The supervisor inquired if I was still hired by the embassy as Justin's escort and interpreter during his extensive travels. When I confirmed the assignment, he took a copy of our travel schedule." AJ's silence hightened her apprehension.

"It's not a routine inquiry," she added. "He ordered me to check in twice a day."

"We'll have to chance that they're overly suspicious because you met with Oresco," AJ finally responded, a slant of uncertainty in his reply. "He'll be miles away, but close enough to attract attention. The Security Police in Shanghai are busy rounding up demonstrators in the streets. They have a limited force to track minor suspects, such as you and Justin, because of the Olympic crowds."

"You don't sound very convincing, AJ. Should we be concerned?"

Lili detected a deep sigh. "The information source is now incommunicado. If Justin doesn't show, Lili, we may not acquire the information in time to prevent whatever it is the bad guys are planning. New information suggests that there may be a biological element to the threat."

"You mean, like a biological weapon?"

Justin pulled the phone away from his ear. "Did you say 'biological weapon?'"

Lili nodded. AJ continued his uplifting report. "Yes, it could be. There are many secret societies in Asia with deep resentments against imperialist Americans. The threat may not even be coming from a government-supported group."

Lili heard Justin whisper into the phone, "On second thought...they know about Brad. You'd still be in danger. Take this number down..it's in Wallingford, Connecticut. My former CFO, Joanna Yates, is a good friend. She's watching after my grandfather while I'm away. She and her daughters live close to Cosimo's nursing home. I'll call her tonight to expect a guest. We'll clear this up when I return, which may be a lot sooner than originally planned."

"What should I do?" Lili asked nervously.

"You've got to facilitate Gatt's attempt to get the documents. To protect him as much as possible."

The Grand Master's words flashed across her mind:"*My iron petal...kind girl. You have mastered the art and discipline of juko-kai beyond reasonable expectations. Use this skill and knowledge to protect yourself and others.*"

Des Moines, Iowa

The Federal Reserve Bank check-processing facility in Des Moines, Iowa was busy clearing checks which totaled, in one day, more than the gross domestic product of most countries belonging to the World Trade organization. John Paul Tangus watched appreciatively as the automatic scanning machines recorded digital electronic signals at nearly the speed of light, and paper checks faster than the speed of vision. The Chairman's annual inspection of Federal Reserve Bank facilities brought him to the regional Fed banks in Chicago and Minneapolis...and now to the Des Moines check-processing facility.

He looked again at the headlines in the local newspaper dropped outside his hotel door. Coffee and oatmeal sat on a tray on the coffee table in front of the TV, getting cold as a local news announcer parroted the headlines. CORNFIELD BROWNING ACROSS THE STATE. A m*ysterious organism of unknown origin may be to blame ...*"

Tangus completed the escorted walk-through and joined the facility management team for his favorite bring-in lunch of fried chicken, cornbread and gravied mashed potatoes. The managers were edgy.

Cornfield discolorations were painting over every maize-planting from Boone to Des Moine. Hundreds of thousands of acres of still-plump yellow kernels gradually tipped the brown fields to gold as the darkened leaves fell away and exposed yellow husks protruding skyward at the top of the plants.

Conversation during the Chairman's walk-through and informal inspection was restricted to business matters; but the cornfield disaster was openly discussed during lunch.

"What do you make of this corn tinting?"Tangus asked no-one in particular, as he dipped a corner of the square cornbread into a volcano-lake of brown gravy indented in the glob of mashed. He faced the secretary taking notes. She seemed to be the most animated by his question.

"Me?"she mumbled, and dropped her plastic spoon onto the plate. Her eyes reddened as the Chairman nodded.

"My dad owns a farm in Correctionville, east of Sac City. His cornfields were the first to go shitty. Oh,...excuse me,Mr. Tangus."

"That sounds like an appropriate description, young lady. Please continue."

"Something's eating the leaves and stalks, but not the sweet yellow kernels. Daddy thought it might be caused by some weird reaction between the new genetically-modified hybrid seeds they plant in most of the Iowa Prairie, and a new pesticide he'd just applied. So he fed a young pig the plump yellow kernels inside the tarnished husks. The pig loved it, so he fed it more. The kernels were so sweet the hog couldn't get enough. Then my hard-headed father decided---if it's good enough for a pig...!" Everyone smiled. "He has a habit of eating raw kernels early in the morning. Says it's better than popcorn for cleaning your teeth."

Tangus winced. His teeth were widely spaced and popcorn always got stuck in his molars and irritated his gums. "How's the little hog doing?"

"Happy and healthy as a pig." Shirley's brief grin was charming as she lifted her shoulders at the unintended pun. "But my father's in the hospital."

The factory manager drawled, "Samples are being collected by Iowa State University students and the Farm Bureau. Also, some high school kids. I think a chemical scientist from Atlanta also came up to nosey around...a disease-control individual, I believe."

"Most likely from the Centers for Disease Control,"Tangus offered. "Has anyone become ill because of the crop contamination?"

"Just my Dad,"Shirley answered sadly. "But the doctors believe it's just a mild stroke, probably brought on by what's happening to his fields. He's an insulin-dependent diabetic, and a drinker....which doesn't help. They say his symptoms suggest a coronary blockage of some sort."

Tangus noted, "It's standard procedure, Shirley, for a technician from the Centers for Disease Control to check out anyone suddenly disease-stricken in an area where a strange organism appears. Especially if the organism is found in food substances."

"Man! It's spreading so fast and on such a large scale. We're afraid the entire twelve million acres of Iowa corn is in jeopardy,"the plant manager spouted, shaking his head.

Shirley replied, "Iowa feeds pigs and cattle with that corn, Mr. Tangus."

"How many animals could be negatively impacted in their life cycles if this food source became non-food?"

"About twenty-five percent of the entire United States hog population, and untold cattle."

"Not to mention the effect on Odebolt."

"How big is the Odebolt herd?"Tangus asked, thinking it was a farm animal he'd never heard of while growing up in the city.

"About six hundred and fifty, give or take ten," an exuberant process engineer replied. "I grew up there. Odebolt, Iowa is a few miles southwest of Sac City. It's the popcorn capital of the world."

Tangus figured it was time to return to the city. "Well, thank you all for the hospitality, and for processing billions of checks without a single error." Tangus rose with a city-slicker shrug and added, "I'm sure this problem is attracting serious attention in Washington. I'll personally discuss it with the Secretary of Agriculture when I return. The last thing this country needs is a food crisis."

CHAPTER 49

(August 12, 2008)
Flight to Shanghai

Justin's first domestic flight in China was brimming with businessmen eager to close one more Shanghai deal before returning home. Some would trace back to Beijing when business was completed, to attend the Olympics at company expense.

Lili was strapped in the window seat, watching as the Cathay Pacific jet banked southeast over Tianjin, toward the mouth of the Yellow River which opened to the Bo Hai Sea. From there, the aircraft would head directly south for the one-hour flight to Shanghai...and the mouth of another great Chinese river—the Yangtze, which was surpassed only by the Nile and Amazon as the longest rivers in the world.

They were seated in a business-class row in front of swept wings, with Justin squished in between Lili and a bald-headed Buddhist monk about Lili's age. Lili had greeted the monk in a Yunnan southwest-China dialect for a short conversation before Justin returned from the men's room and stepped over the monk's dark-brown cloister robe.

"Leefah was raised in Kunming...less than five hundred kilometers south of my home village of Emai Shan," she whispered as if they were in a religious place. "He's read of the Grand Master, Zong Keba, and the Wanniansi...the Temple of Myriad Ages where I studied as a young girl."

Justin inhaled the light fragrance of lavender and chamomile soap as he leaned over Lili's shoulder to peer out five thousand meters above the coastline. The monk carried aged cheese in his tied leather sac, and the combination of odors drifting into Justin's right and left nostrils blended into an aromatic eutectic that reminded him of his high school prom night, when he spilled onion dip on perfume-splashed Mary Lou Kneely's gown.

"I'd like to learn more about China's rural people...the real people with stories that aren't chiseled down to statistics by the harshness of the cities." Lili reflected on his statement. Not many Americans cared about Chinese peasants and rural workers, unless they were in a queue outside their mainland factories, waiting to fill out applications for one-hundred-dollar-a-month factory jobs.

"What would you care to hear about, Mr. Gatt? How the poor people live in ancient dwellings? How normal Chinese people are suppressed and jailed if we speak out against the Communist regime? How farmers plant rice on stepped plateaus...or survive meager harvests? The number of peasants who died building the Great Wall?"

I struck the wrong chord, Justin realized. "People with the amazing history of China must be special," he responded sincerely. "I read with fascination how China was unified by the first emperor of the Qin Dynasty in 221 BC; and how his court standardized ancient Chinese characters as symbols, which are still used today. I don't really understand the language system, because the script is not alphabetic, and literacy isn't tied to pronunciations. But how could I not be impressed with a written language which remains unaltered after thousands of years?"

"The spoken language has changed many times," Lili softened. "Regional dialects differ greatly because Chinese civilization was developed in relative isolation."

Justin allowed his lids to drop in a moment of forced relaxation. He pictured wide open spaces and tried to shake off the constant feeling that he was jammed into an over-crowded subway train. He couldn't shake the feeling since arriving in Beijing.

"As a manufacturer of things, I wasn't aware until recently that the Chinese first discovered or invented so many unique products---tea, porcelain, silk; the magnetic compass, gunpowder, paper and printing. Amazing ingenuity so many years ago, even before Marco Polo arrived from Portugal in the 14th century."

"Confucian influence...I believe," Lili answered brightly. *So he wants some examples of everyday life in China; then and now. Where do I begin?*

Splendor, decline, humiliation, traditions, adaptability to western and Japanese invasions. The tragedies of government—Mao, and the imperial dynasties. The amateur ideals of the Ming; Buddhism taking root in the west near India borders. How traditional Chinese regarded themselves as the center of the earth; and believed they'd devised man's most perfect system of government and society. The belief that the universe is made up of harmonious balances. True enlightenment... accessible only to the few "gentlemen," while "small men" of the great masses toil under their guidance. The wisdom of Tao---the way, necessary for peace to prevail.

"Old China was discarded when outside influences clashed with the tenets and values of Confucianism." Lili began philosophically.

Justin said, "I read about the many revolts and suppressions: The Taiping Rebellion, the Boxers secret society---allied with ministers against imperial Manchu reign. How they were crushed after attacking western forces. The Kuomintang National Party, and how the Communists under Mao hacked away imperial influences and the Nationalist Party of Chiang Kai Shek to install a socialist state modeled after the Russians."

"The Chinese word for *suppression* means 'to flatten,'" Lili said. She then told him the story of her friend the 'massager', who was still in a rat-infested prison without socks or shoes.

"The prison guards told her to remain motionless when the rats came, if she was awake.They carry rabies…but won't bite live skin if your feet have calluses. She scrapes her heels and toes against the rough brick floor all day; and never sleeps at night."

Justin gently lifted the sleeping monk's head from his left shoulder and said, "China's spiritual pain persists. Tell me more."

Lili loved imperial history and had studied ancient writings preserved in the Beijing National Library. "I once met an English scholar who spent his life studying and writing about China. He claimed that the idea of imperial reincarnation is still popular among some Politboro leaders. Your country has difficulty understanding the Chinese mind because you don't have the same historical legacy. America never experienced imperial rule, national humiliation and occupation; or charges of being an inferior race after once being respected as a great nation. Perhaps it may happen again in the future."

"It's true,"Justin replied with less than enthusiasm. "*Small men* in America can become *gentlemen,* and rise from poverty to wealth in less than a generation."

Lili stared down wistfully at the clouds hovering above the Yellow Sea coastline. "China's poor are mainly peasants, and will probably remain so for many generations."

"The Chinese are a proud people,Lili,"said Justin. "With good reason."

"Mr. Gatt….do you believe there are scientific laws governing the development of societies? The Englishman did. He claimed the young would rise up against the old, natives against foreigners…marxist beliefs, I think."

"I never considered the question," he answered in awe of Lili's insights. "I suppose some of our Washington leaders must fear that radical revolutionary movements will erupt in third world countries and dislodge, or at least contain, the democratic evolution we promote around the globe."

"The Englishman said the Beijing Communists are convinced that China is the prototype for potential third world revolutions."

"Maybe that's the reason for American hostility against China—a fear that the Communists are correct."

WINNEBAGO INDIAN PICKET LINE
BOXMART STORE, ONAWA, IOWA

"Why'd you choose my store?"Nonnie's friend asked angrily. "I tried to help you. Now I'm out of a job."

Nonnie was dressed in a conservative pleated navy skirt and cream-colored cotton jersey. An eagle feather was dangling from her hip on a thin leather waist-strap as she handed the sign she was carrying outside the Onawa BoxMart store entrance to a sister tribeswoman.

"I don't know how they found out, Kendra. We changed plans to picket this store just before you called…as I told you on the phone. We'd assembled people and signs at the Sioux City store parking area, but they brought in a busload of thugs to block our access to the store-front entrance."

"Well, somebody snitched on me. I thought I could trust you and your people."

Nonnie glanced over her shoulder and noticed the Sheriff's car speeding along the street adjacent to the expansive store parking lot, followed by two other police cars…all with disturbing blue lights rotating on their roofs. "Where'd you call me from?" Nonnie asked impatiently, as she followed the law-enforcement vehicles to a screeching halt a few yards away.

Kendra thought for a moment, alarmed and confused by the sudden arrival of the police. "I used my cell phone. I don't think anyone could hear my conversation because I was alone in the employee locker room." Five seconds of silence…eye contact…and the two women precipitously realized why Kendra was fired only a few minutes after she made the call.

"Those lousy bastards!"she moaned.

Sheriff Jones Whiley kicked the driver's door open, and approached Nonnie in a slow John Wayne gait which transformed the scene from chaotic to slow motion. He carried an official document with the signature of the Federal Indian Affairs administrator still smudgeable. He approached Nonnie and held the paper in front of her face. "We know you organized this fiasco,young lady chief. Now it's time for you to order your people back to their teepees on the reservation."

Nothing infuriated Nonnie more than outsiders inferring that her tribe still lived in dark-age conditions. "We have a perfect right to publicly complain and demonstrate against BoxMart management," she fumed. "They've blatantly stolen and reproduced sacred Winnebago Ho-Chunk property and craft designs; and have put our people out of work."

"I feel for you, little lady, but this here's an order to cease and desist your demonstrations. Reservation-bound Indians aren't allowed to picket on United States territory. It's the law," he announced proudly.

The stocky sheriff dressed in starched khaki uniform, was in his late fifties, and sounded tough as nail-heads. But everyone in the county knew he was struggling to hold his job. Whiley had been charged by the local Elks Lodge with harassing members returning home after loud Friday and Saturday bashes. He also had a habit of stationing deputies in BoxMart parking lots at night, instead of patrolling the troubled sections along Route 29 where known drug dealers vended crystal methamphetamine and heroin to disenchanted tribesmen from the adjacent Sioux and Winnebago Ho-Chunk reservations.

Nonnie accepted the document and began reading. The Sheriff glanced around nervously as the crowd gathered. He unbuttoned the safety cover of his revolver, for show.

"Stand back, people. This will be settled in a minute," he shouted, motioning his deputy and four local police officers to come closer. A few seconds later he snatched the document from Nonnie's hands and said, "That's enough of your delaying tactics, chiefie. Start getting your people out of here or we'll drag your asses into jail."

Nonnie read enough to realize the law was not on her side. But she wasn't about to acquiesce so easily. "That isn't a valid court document. It's not signed by a clerk of the courts or a notary public. We're staying put."

The Sheriff's face was crimson. He actually withdrew his pistol...then thought better and slipped it back into the holster. He'd been informed that Nonnie was a lawyer. He hated smart-ass lawyers who used missing dots over i's, and slanted lines across t's to confuse law-enforcement officials with legal techno-babble.

"I'm going by the interpretation of the Indian Affairs officer...not yours," he spat, in a voice hardened by contempt for just about everyone he came into contact with. "I'll say it one more time. Get your red asses out of here. Now!"

Kendra grasped Nonnie's arm as she was about to slug the Sheriff. "Don't," she said. "We'll end up in a stinky, urine-splashed cage. Come on, there'll be another day."

One of the Ho-Chunk elders was standing at the perimeter of the crowd. Nonnie clearly understood the message transmuted in the laser-glare of Dancing Eyes Adams.

She turned to the Sheriff. "You haven't heard the last of this, Whiley. We'll be back with our own document." It was a bluff. But she vowed to herself to search for any legitimate method the tribe could use to display its displeasure with BoxMart management. As soon as she returned to her office, she'd begin searching the legal databases like LEXUS-NEXUS and WEST LAW. She still had access to the Omaha firm's legal library and internet links. Current laws governing Indian Affairs were another issue. For good measure she'd also check the carping laws in Iowa, Nebraska and South Dakota, although she was certain that picketing was a federal issue related to equal protection rights and freedom of speech. Perhaps there existed a treaty from 1860 taking away these rights from Winnebago native Americans.

SUZHOU INDUSTRIAL COMPLEX
NANJING, SHANGHAI PROVINCE

The LCE plastics processing factory was immense. Larger than any he'd seen in the States. The single-story concrete block and brick building contained more than four hundred injection molding machines with dimensions ranging from the size of a regulation billiard table to that of a modern diesel double-locomotive. The machines were cycling noisily on concrete floors covering an area the size of twenty football fields.

Justin marveled at the blurring activity engulfing nearly a million square feet of plastics processing equipment, hissing open and clanging closed, while out spewed a what's-what multiplicity of plastic parts. Single piece, one-material end-products such as bright red, green and black storage and trash containers of varying sizes were piled into neat bundles by hand, then fed into pad-printers, label applicators or hot-stamping machines to lay down gold-leaf or shiny acrylic decorations. Precision parts used in the assembly of complex multi-component end-products, such as: laser printers, cell phones, vacuum cleaners and plasma TVs, were also being hand-stacked and transferred by flat rubber conveyer belts to final assembly lines in different areas of the factory.

"LCE's Nanjing factory is the largest molding operation in Asia," explained the smug process engineer of about thirty, smiling under high cheeks and a large Manchu nose, as he escorted the foreign delegation to each area of the plant. "Soon it will be the largest in the world." It wasn't the scope or size of the operation that startled Justin.

He gasped at the large orange labels identifying a row of recently-arrived, U.S.-made steel molds; lined up against a wall on small wooden pallets. They were heavily shrink-wrapped boxy steel tools weighing hundreds of pounds each. The tags were marked: *S.H mold A1A; S.H. mold B2B; S.H. mold C3C*, etc. His stomach dropped as he recalled Joe Slattery's young daughter holding her mother's hands at the funeral. The tooling was all from the Slattery Housewares factory Edwin Tinius and BoxMart had shut down.

The final leg of the three-hour facility-tour was hosted by the chief process engineer, a wiry man in his early thirties, with a friendly smile despite uneven sallow front teeth. Of average height and humble demeanor, he wore thick horned-rim glasses, spoke perfect English and held a Ph.D. in industrial engineering from Fudan University in Shanghai.

"This area is the latest expansion in the Nanjing factory complex," the plant engineer boasted proudly. "Here we duplicate the product lines taken over from failed foreign competitors; using equipment specifically designed to run the tooling removed from their empty factories. It is mostly acquired from American sources." He pointed to a caboose-sized molding machine weighing ninety thousand pounds, and wheezing like an angry dragon. It dropped out an eight-pound Slattery-brand trash bucket every 68 seconds. Justin tasted a bizarre green nausea. Bile produced in his liver, stored in his gallbladder and passing through his small intestines to emulsify fat, began to burp north. Lili was puzzled by his disgusted expression.

"The hydraulic clamping capacity of this machine is 1200 tons," the chief engineer remarked as he noticed Justin approach the machine and examine the metal tag listing the model and machine specifications. Justin looked up and quickly moved away from the machine as an ominous stainless-steel and black-enamel electrical robot arm obeyed programmed instructions and removed the container with thick metal fingers, each time the two-part mold opened. Lili watched apprehensively as the arm arched close to Justin's head, descended silently to the floor and placed the heavy trash bucket into a pre-assembled shipping carton as gently as a mother puts her baby in for a nap.

These fucking parts were made by Slattery... from our fucking materials.

Lili had never seen such a mix of items under the same roof. Piles of every conceivable consumer product she could imagine were everywhere...soon to be removed to the storage and distribution warehouse bordering railroad tracks alongside the rear of the building.

Made from polystyrene, polyethylene, polypropylene, nylon and engineering resins such as polycarbonate and clear acrylic---hundreds of items filled the shipping boxes waiting to be transferred. Five hundred or more rust-red overseas cargo containers were filled each day and trucked to Shanghai shipping docks, stuffed with toys, baby car seats, carriages, play stations, hair-dryers, luggage cases, bicycle helmets, CD players, synthetic Christmas trees, ceiling fans, coffee-makers, winter boots, extension cords, snowboards, patio furniture, toothbrushes, fitness equipment....et cetera. Some items were specially packaged...like cartridge water-filters the size of Chinese mortar shells.

The unofficial business model for the soon to be Nanjing Plastics Division of Bomali Corporation called for continuous expansion of production capacity, until most of the plastics custom-molding businesses in the U.S. were shut down. As low-cost producer, LCE's growth potential was limited only by the time it required to quote jobs against competitors. The higher costs of manufacturing in the U.S. guaranteed the inevitable loss of business...as long as LCE received new production orders, and U.S. import tariffs remained low.

"These leeches are destroying the small plastics processors in first world nations," Justin's friend from Michigan barked. The Nanjing engineer pretended not to hear.

Justin and a dozen other visitors from America, Japan, Germany and Italy were led to the immense power station and material distribution sections. Lili was awe-struck by the garage-sized electrical transformers and the dozens of cylindrical galvanized-steel storage bins standing sixty-feet tall. The bins reminded her of photos of above-ground Russian missile launchers, except the silos were filled with tiny plastic pellets, rather than hardened cones perched on chemically-fueled rockets designed to deliver hellish payloads to *customers*.

The term usually applied to describe plastic pellets stored in silos: *raw materials for finished products*—applied accurately to either content.

Justin shook his head in a sour caldron of disgust and admiration, as he mused that the products manufactured at Nanjing were all based on molecules extracted from the earth, and formed into useful items using technology primarily developed by Americans and Europeans.

The exception was near the back wall. Gatt noticed a small assembly line feeding long smoked hickory sticks into a precision cutting and routing machine, which carved strange symbols and numbers into the flat edges of the wood. The three-foot lengths were then conveyed to a series of worktables where skilled young girls artfully painted the grooved indentations with bright colors. The decorated shafts then disappeared behind a wall for final processing and packaging.

Gatt was curious. "What do you do with the wood pieces?"

The engineer sneered in embarrassment. "That's a craft line, making a very interesting product called the *calendar stick*. He bowed slightly and admitted in a humorous tone, "I have a Ph.D in engineering, but still have not been able to determine how the ancient Native American Indians could create such a precise wooden instrument for dating and telling time." He paused. The puzzle irritated his psyche. "It's said the design is three-thousand years old."

To change the subject, or perhaps dilute the accomplishment of an ancient American society, he exclaimed crisply, "Chinese engineers are creating the largest power-generating dam on this planet. The Three Gorges is 1.3 miles long and will produce power equal to fifteen nuclear plants...twenty percent of China's current electrical capacity."

"Amazing...amazing," the foreigners hummed and nodded in unison. Justin remembered reading that the three-phase project, begun in 1993, had raised the Yangze river 443 feet, submerged archaeological treasures along the banks and displaced nearly two million people from their farms, homes and villages. When the tour ended, he approached the chief engineer and said, "You must have very productive salesmen. It seems your facility is sold out making products for many retail customers."

"Chinese production quality is so superior that we don't require many salesmen. The big retailers come to Nanjing from all over the world," he said in a prideful tone. Without considering the appropriateness of his remarks, he added, "Our biggest customer, BoxMart Stores, has more than doubled its orders in the past four months...even factoring in normal growth. We've been instructed by our glorious President, Alicia Wang, to postpone production orders for other customers in order to supply BoxMart."

As they reached the office area for an exit orientation, the engineer held the door open and boasted absently, "LCE will complete the BoxMart orders for winter holiday merchandise within two weeks---several months early."

"That *is* impressive, Mr.Gong," Gatt baited the engineer.

"The consumer items will be delivered several months before they are placed on display shelves."

Justin was familiar with the typical stocking schedules mass retailers followed for seasonal promotions and merchandising programs. It struck him as extremely odd that large shipments of Christmas goods would leapfrog deliveries of back-to-school supplies, fall yard goods and Halloween trinkets. Even if BoxMart was Nanjing Plastic's largest customer, the molder still couldn't afford to jeopardize relationships with the Targets, Home-Depots, Lowe's and Sears-KMarts of the world by missing deliveries.

Strange, indeed.

CHAPTER 50

(August 13, 2008)
Shanghai Corrugated Container Company

The man assigned to contaminate the water reservoir adjacent to the Shanghai Corrugated Container Company had second thoughts. After crawling under the perimeter gate with the microbe vials packaged in a rigid plastic container the size of a small tool box, he sat leaning on his knees on the bank of the small man-made lake.

In the darkness, he could hear and smell the foul guck seeping from a large concrete factory-effluent pipe into a catch-basin, which eventually emptied into a small rivulet of the Grand Canal connecting Shanghai with Tianjin in the north. *The pungent odor is bad enough*, he thought. *What if this organism stuff makes the gunk dangerous?*

He was not a conscience-driven individual, but his relatives lived in the area.

"It's harmless to humans," he was told. "You can drink it if you are dying of thirst. The bugs only eat paper."

He shrugged and reluctantly removed the vials from the protective foam cavities inside the box. Loyalty to the Minister of State Security...the Vice-Premier...the leader of the Triads... was paramount. The task must be completed successfully if he wished to obtain the benefits of higher rank in the powerful secret society.

He removed the rubber stopper from the first vial and inhaled cautiously. The substance was odorless.

BOMALI CORP OFFICES, MACAU

"At last!" Jake Kurancy said jubilantly, after signing the final copy of the Bomali merger agreement. His signature was below the scribblings of Li Chin and Wen Ma Ming, representing LCE Industries and the Chinese government. Emerson Bromine, the new Chief Executive Officer of Bomali Corporation signed a few lines higher.

Vargos Langreen, the managing partner of Smith and Week, the world's largest international mergers and acquisitions law firm, took the last page and monikered the line entitled: "Witnessed by_____.' Langreen was ten years beyond retirement age but still spry enough to have authored the two-hundred-page joint venture agreement, which was sure to become an historic document in the archives of international business.

The last person to sign the documents was a Senior Vice President of the Macau Urbanation Bank Group. The commercial loans officer was pleased to provide the new conglomerate with eight billion yuan, about one billion U.S. dollars, in the form of a revolving line of credit. He signed the document again, acting in the lowly capacity of Notary Public, then dated and rubber-stamped the document attesting to the authenticity of the partners' signatures.

In a typical understated banker's-professional inflection, the NP conceded, "I'm amazed, gentlemen. This is a very substantial merger." He nodded his grey-peppered head slowly, as though the largest business merger in history, was a typical Urbanation Bank client activity. Bomali Corporation was starting up with combined revenues of $400 billion , and net assets of $250 billion. MUB wasn't even the lead bank in the deal. That privilege belonged to Creditte Bank de Savoy, the private French investment bank controlled by Phillipe Cusson.

As one of the ten Bomali founding directors, Cusson would be guardian of the massive cash profits expected to flow into Bomali's primary account at CBdeS. LCE and BoxMart bank accounts around the globe would soon be linked for automatic, overnight money transfers. Emerson Bromine would control deposits at the Bank of China in Macau, where relatively small balances of yuan, pataca and Hong Kong dollar were required for the company to qualify for tax-free treatment by the Macau Special Administration Region.

Vargos Langreen passed the signed, two-inch packets of completed documents to the attending directors. Absentees General Ye and Tom Blackstone would receive their copies by special delivery. The documents included: appendices of financial figures; endless paragraphs relating to the terms of ownership,and disposition of profits, as well as the By-laws complying with Macau business laws; five-year executive employment contracts, term-payment buy-out clauses; and governance issues. Clearly stipulated in

Vangreen's documents was a separate indenture signed by Jake Kurancy and Li Chin, which allowed the Chinese partners to name the next Bomali board member---contingent on their depositing $100 million in an escrow account in Kurancy's name by the end of the day. Smith and Week was appointed fee-paid escrow agent.

"This is my finale," Langreen temporarily dropped his placid demeanor. "Nothing will ever top the Bomali deal."

Kurancy wasn't sure if the renowned attorney was referring to his $75 million legal fee or the sheer size of the merger.

The Chinese representatives on the initial ten-member Bomali Board of Directors consisted of Li Chin, Chairman and CEO of the LCE ; Wang Chao, the Minister of Industry and Trade; General Ye Kunshi, the PLA's director of state-run industries and Vice Chairman of the Central Military Commission; Colonel Wen Ma Ming, the newly appointed Senior Vice President and Chief Operating Officer of Bomali; and Alicia Wang, the President of LCE Industries.

Board members from the BoxMart side were: Jake Kurancy, Chairman of the Board of Bomali and its BoxMart subsidiary; Hieronimus Cashman, Chief Financial Officer of BoxMart; Emerson Bromine, Bomali's first Chief Executive Officer; and the two outside directors---Thomas Blackstone, Managing Partner of Washington-based Financial Flow Foundation, and Phillipe Cusson, the Director-General of Creditte Bank de Savoy and its subsidiaries.

ZANGNANHAI, OFFICE OF THE VICE –PREMIER

President of China, Mu Jianting, was furious. He threatened to end his suspected adversary's career, politically or otherwise. "You have no right to accuse me, Yong," he snapped. "You and your secret society cohorts."

Vice-Premier,Yong Ihasa, had vehemently denied complicity in a plot to overthrow President Mu, of course. "The information you claim to have is incorrect, Comrade Mu. I had nothing to do with the disclosure that you are stealing from the masses. The Standing Committee of the Party will have to decide the outcome after a thorough investigation."

Mu stomped furiously toward the office door, then stopped and turned. With a dark expression, he said, "We'll see....we'll see." Suddenly, his anger was overwhelming. He moved forcefully in Yong's direction and said manically…a finger under Yong's nose, "You are hereby relieved of your duties as Minister of State Security."

Yong pushed his hand aside and cut back icily, "That will also be decided by the Central Committee. Your indiscretions will look worse to the world if you replace the only man who can conduct an independent scrutiny of your wrongdoing. Think carefully, Mu. The consequences of a corruption trial may be disastrous for the party and your family. As Minister of State Security, I can find you completely blameless... in your early retirement."

Mu's shoulders slumped. He had no comeback worthy of his lofty position as leader of the Chinese Communist Party. The most powerful political party on earth.

A true Ming ruler would never cower so easily, Ihasa thought. *The nation will be in better hands when I assume ultimate leadership.*

Chang Hui Chen, the Chairman of the National People's Congress, stepped out from the anteroom adjacent to Ihasa's office, as soon a s Mu departed. "He's going to crumble."

Shadows from Forbidden City structures fronted the setting sun and slanted across the open courtyard as Mu joined his bodyguards at ground level and trotted hastily to the President of China's royal-blue bulletproof limousine. "I know,"nodded the Vice-Premier in a dismissive tone. He peered down into the courtyard from his window. "Mu will be further disgraced, when the upcoming events are successfully staged."

Chang Hui flicked the Cartier lighter Jake Kurancy gave him as a gift of respect when they attended the Savoy Imperative meeting in Maryland months earlier. The glow ignited his harsh Russian cigarette. "We can anticipate an expedient approval by the UN Security Council and the General Assembly, when the People's Republic of China submits its indisputable evidence. Members can do nothing but approve the resolution condemning Taiwan. General Ye's troops will be in position, and the Islands will be defenseless."

Yong Ihasa exclaimed brightly, "As good as occupied by the PLA." He moved away from the window and said, more cautiously, "The United Nations General Assembly will have to sanction the occupation, before we can legitimately move troops to Matsu and Quemoy. Ye will position a full PLA navy fleet off the Fujian shoreline. That move...along with the disclosure that Taiwan unleashed a biological weapon on China's packaged goods industry...should encourage prompt UN approval,. The Security Council will have no choice."

Chang inhaled the caustic high-tar Russian cigarette and added, "The evidence will prove that the Taipei government also planned a pre-emptive strike on China's northern corn fields...using the same pathogen. Technical reports will be distributed to the international media."

"We'll have to close the giant Shanghai cardboard box factory, and voluntarily recall the cargo ships containing merchandise packaged in Shanghai boxes. Every major retailer in America, except BoxMart, will shout imperial murder."

"Chinese factories will suffer temporary cut-backs. But American businesses will be crushed for several months. Far worse---American citizens will take to the streets when they fully realize the hardships created by merchandise shortages and contaminated food."

Chang Hui said. "General Ye is honing his Eastern Defensive Forces to occupy the island s. As you planned---Matsu will be first. Taipei mistakenly believes the underground bunkers on the island are a well-protected strong hold. Our PLA assault troops will march in with small resistance. Too many occupied cargo ships will be anchored in the area, as you perceived, for Taiwanese or American forces to stage a missile or aircraft defense." Chang Hui greatly admired Yong Ihasa; the Ming heritage had never experienced a military mind superior to his.

"If as many cargo ships return as General Ye expects," Ihasa replied, "the off-shore islands will be surrounded by the largest constellation of anchored vessels ever assembled. Holiday merchandise returned from American ports will have to be tested for virus contamination. Thankfully, the miraculous organism can only survive a few weeks on the surfaces of paper cartons."

"This year's Christian holidays will be spoiled for American consumers. They are unprepared to do without our manufactured goods during the winter shopping period. Unfortunately, many children will be downtrodden without our toys."

"Humphreys and the other American political lightweights will enjoy only a brief triumph,"mocked Ihasa. "Their media headlines will claim that *China gives in on currency issue*...and *China agrees to Stressa Accords*. He smiled roguishly.

"They'll soon be shaken from their complacence," Chan Hui rhapsodized. "Only BoxMart's retail customers will have the opportunity to buy the cherished Chinese gifts which highlight their children's happiness. Until supplies last!"

Ihasa frowned and said ,"Enough of this happy chatter, Chang. There is much to do before the desired circumstances are created. Your negotiating tug-of-war with Humphreys is about to end. I want you to magnify Beijing's conflicts with Taiwan, to the fourth estate. The foreign press will be important when…at the proper time…the Chinese Ambassador to the United Nations discloses our evidence against the Taiwanese."

"Cusson insists the disclosure of Taiwan's plot against the Shanghai box factory be strategically timed. He's attempting to unload the last $75 billion dollars on speculative Arab traders."

The Wuxing Ting Teahouse, 3pm
Old Town Shanghai

Lilly handed Justin the shopping bag half-filled with men's underwear, white cotton socks, bottled spring water and a New England Patriots baseball cap they'd purchased at the bazaar in the northeast section of Old Town. She nodded and said, "Good luck," then pirouetted toward the famous dumpling shops near the Yu Garden gate. Justin extracted the cap and plopped it on his head...the brim slightly askew to his right . The pirated red, white and blue design looked more authentic than the authorized version sold at Gillette Stadium.

After Lili departed, he crossed the magnificent zig-zagging bridge spanning the classic oriental pool built centuries ago, hugging the north edge of the bridge as instructed. Lili told him the bridge was built this way by a city official who desired to provide his aging father with a serene resting place. His father believed devils can only cross water in a straight line.

Justin weaved through the small gathering near the Wuxing Ting Teahouse entrance, which sat in the center of an ornamental pond on a small islet spanned by the bridge. The grey bench described by AJ was a few yards away.

Made from recycled polyethylene engine-oil bottles...the irregular coloring and slight concave distortion of the seating were familiar to Justin. The cross-boards were made from low-quality extruded plastic lumber with large pieces of paper-labels still imbedded in the surface of the planks. Melfi Zion produced similar plastic lumber in America, except her boards were melt-filtered after the grinding and washing process; and she used un-pigmented milk bottles as raw material. The higher quality American-made planks could be uniformly hued and used to build attractive decks and porches, rather than utilitarian park benches.

Justin sat on one end of the bench and watched the goldfish glide just below the surface in bridge-like routes, darting between the placed rocks, pods and surface flowers. A low murmur of restrained ambient conversation was occasionally broken by a flock of tiny birds winging frantically from the pavilion trees to the Chinese lanterns ringing the pond. He wondered if they were the same tiny species whole-fried and served piled in dishes by Chinese families on special occasions.

Justin glanced up and noticed a tall, erect mid-aged Asian man with a high forehead emerging from the teahouse. The man bent to tighten his shoelace. Dressed in baggy proletarian indigo, his aristocratic oval face and reserved composure did not mesh with the bland attire. He carried under his arm a dark-brown hard-cover book of Chinese Classics titled: "Confucius and Mencius," printed in 1870 and translated into English by a member of the London Missionary Society. Justin recognized the book from AJ's description.

The bespectacled man appeared unsteady on his feet as he rose from tying his shoe. Perhaps he experienced a blood-flow interruption to the brain. A kindly young girl in a white blouse and jeans happened over and reached for his arm…steadying the man.

"Hold on, old stranger, just try to catch your breath." She glanced around and decided to guide him to the nearest grey bench before he fell over. Justin moved aside as she eased him down..

"He's little groggy," she said in broken English. "He rest, maybe read book. You take care?" She then scampered over the zig-zag bridge and disappeared.

"Do you want some spring water?" Justin pronounced the coded question.

The man seemed revived. "Only if you have extra in your bag. I wouldn't want to trouble you, kind sir." Justin lifted the shopping bag to bench height as the tall man deftly reached in, allowing a dark-brown sealed envelope to slide out from the book under his arm.

"It's so kind of you, sir. Are you English or American?" he asked, loud enough to draw the attention of the tourists standing in the area. He unscrewed the bottle cap and gulped

"I'm from Connecticut, in the United States. Are you sure you're all right?"

His hands shook slightly as he swallowed the last half-liter. "I think, yes. Allow me to return your kindness. Do you enjoy classic literature?" Without waiting for a reply, he opened the book and began thumbing through Confucian analects.

Justin glanced around. About a dozen curious people and a stern-faced, frumpy middle-aged Chinese woman advanced to the bench. The Communist busy-body was patrolling the area to locate unreliable peasant workers missing from their local *dan-wei,* or workplace. Drably attired in a loose-fitting charcoal smock, with short bangs and black hair cut above her ears, she was assigned to report the workers who skipped the sixth day of work at the *dan-wei*---a textile factory haunted by swirling racks of full-body garments, frenetically gliding through the factory like ghosts on conveyed hangers… escaping from the cutting and stitching area.. Her proud, arrogant expression was typical of the Chinese Communist stalwarts who comprised the ingenious inside-out security system the government organized to control Chinese society. Like heat-seeking radar…they picked you out from wherever.

"Did you know that Confucius was born a generation *before* the Buddha in India...in 551 BC? And died in 479 BC...a decade *before* Socrates of Greece was born?"

"Fascinating," Justin replied to the older man. "I once read that the Confucian ideal is to maintain composure at all times."

The man stopped turning pages and began to read as the people moved closer.

A fox will be elected...saying nothing
Playing saint publicly...feathering his nest privately,
Afterward he will suddenly tyrannise,
His foot will be on the throats of the greatest."

Lili waved enthusiastically from the foot of the bridge, catching Justin's attention just as the Communist busy-body was about to ask for his travel papers. It was normal for Party members to interrogate strangers on the street; especially foreigners.

Justin jumped up and said to Dr. Dongzi, "It's been very instructional, Comrade. Good day."

The frump started after him but stopped short when she noticed the familiar young girl in the white shirt and jeans hovering nearby under a large Japanese Pagoda tree, which is native to China, and known as the "Chinese Scholar tree," because it's traditionally planted near the graves of Chinese schoolmasters.

Why had she returned? Why is she watching the poet?"

Dr. Dongzhi, from the People's Friendship Sanitorium in Lianong Province, closed the book when he noticed his niece from the corner of his eye. She was accompanied by the bitter Central Propaganda official whose son died in Dongzi's hospital. The father had offered to help expose the strange organism that invaded his beloved son's body and cemented his arteries. The Second Auxiliary Bio-weapons laboratory hidden in the basement of the Institute for Advanced Medical Treatment was responsible.

Gatt's shopping bag now contained a copy of the pathogenic analysis Dongzi's friend at the Tangshan Research Hospital had secretly provided; along with the research doctor's plea that the information be transferred to U.S. health officials and the World Health Organization as quickly as possible. He'd been informed by Dongzi that the pathogen may have been purposely transported to the United States by scientists at the bio-weapons lab.

"The mechanism of blood-cell invasion is more aggressive than any viruses I've previously encountered," the Tangshan research doctor began in his handwritten note to Dongzi.*"The structure appears to be a mutated viral form of a rogue protein called a prion, or a genetically re-assorted RNA retro-virus chromosome, perhaps originating in a plant pathogen associated with the hybrid*

corn the boy consumed...or was exposed to. I believe the boy died from eating contaminated corn. The virus was exposed to standard antigenic agents in my lab, with no apparent response. We did not detect the expected appearance of antibodies or other form of immuno-reaction to the viral organism, although a bacteria associated with E. coli strains was present in small amounts, but was eradicated by frenzied viral feeding.

He noted under a scripted putangua character, roughly equivalent to the word *conclusions: There is no apparent cure if the organism spreads. We must confirm the invasive route and mechanism into the boy's body. His body fluids contained traces of mutated viral residues. The congealed blood was completely void of glucose or other sugars by the time the samples were received. My prognosis would suggest the presence of a starch-consuming substance.*

Included in the envelope Gatt now possessed were copies of shipping papers and special packaging instructions the dead boy's father had somehow stolen. They confirmed that "vials" presumably of the *pathogen* and *co-pathogen*, were shipped to Texas from the address of the bio-weapons lab. The packaging code described the contents as "water filters and treatment chemicals for swimming pools." The UCC bar-code on the 'Customer I.D.' line in the Bill of Lading matched that for BoxMart Retail Stores, Inc.

CHAPTER 51

(August 14, 2008)
U.S. Centers for Disease Control, Atlanta

"For the human immune system to function against this organism, it must have a prior exposure. We found no antibody serum in the farmer's blood samples...therefore, no protective agents. There should at least be serum-proteins, if the organism invaded his body." Dr. Nolte addressed the other team members of the scientific group assigned to study the new pathogen now invading Iowa cornfields.

"If his illness was caused by the organism, he'd exhibit a protective response to the specific pathogen. His immunological response needs memory to provide long-term protection," added the biochemist from Johns Hopkins University.

"That suggests administering passive immunity...at least temporarily," said the genetic biochemist. "The farmer could be injected with *gamma globulin* human serum... packed with someone else's antibodies...perhaps his daughter's."

The lead physician from the CDC's Iowa-crisis task force held up his hand. Task force members where notoriously impatient and tended to over-react when a new organism was discovered in the living cells of humans, animals or plants. "You're jumping the gun," Nolte admonished.

The four-man CDC team assigned to the Iowa crisis consisted of experts in human diseases, DNA and RNA biochemistry, agricultural pathogens, and virus and bacteria mutations.

"The preliminary tests on contaminated leaves and corn-stalks taken from Sac City browning fields show no evidence that the organism is the least bit harmful to humans," Nolte continued. "In fact, we found zero presence in the healthy yellow kernels of the infected plants. The inordinately high sugar level in the edible kernels suggests the organism only inhabits cellulose-based structures, and is harmless to humans."

"I still believe that aggressive treatment of the farmer is indicated," the disease physician-scientist suggested. "He has classic symptoms of plugged arteries and will likely require an angioplasty. Furthermore, there was no prior indication of symptoms. According to his daughter he was healthy as a horse...did plenty of exercising and ate only organic vegetables, fruit and chicken."

"Well, perhaps it's a coincidence,"the biochemist said, "But his daughter *did* claim he ate raw kernels just before he collapsed. We can't take the chance that...perhaps...digestive enzymes in his body somehow caused a mutation of the organism, which was most-likely present on the surface of the kernel-membrane."

"Why do you suspect that?" the disease expert asked. "The initial tests are conclusive. The organism reacts aggressively with the leaves and stalks, and somehow breaks down the cellulose molecular structure. Like a termite's or horned-beetle's enzymes do. But, there was a total lack of reaction to glucose and other sugars found in the body. Normally, a petri-dish culture of sugars inoculated with any of the known human pathogens---either viruses or bacteria---would be bursting with growth colonies."

The virologist, an expert in genetic chromosomal responses to human diseases, answered evenly, "This organism is viral, not bacterial. It stores its genetic code in RNA, not DNA. As you all know---that's a phenomenon found only in viruses...and in no other living organisms. In my opinion, this may also explain the rapid evolution and extreme volatility by which the RNA mycoplasma attacks the plants and spreads rapidly in spore-like eruptions."

"That makes some sense,"Dr. Nolte agreed. His eyes thinned as the next frightening conclusion ignited his adrenalin cannons. "Antigenic shifts in plant-cell genes, as happens in humans ...can cause *pandemics*."

The sudden silence indicated the medical scientists were contemplating possible disease paths the unique organism could follow if it evolved from a plant-pathogen to a human infection.

"If the volatile RNA nucleotides 'drifted,' to form altered amino-acid sequences, it is conceivable that the virus-like mycoplasma species could mutate into a new strain of influenza. With no vaccine or anti-bodies built up in his immune system, the organism could conceivably create a pandemic rivaling the feared avian flu virus, H5N1."

Nolte responded to his colleague's comment, "In the case of cellulose-bearing plant structures such as Iowa corn---instead of HA, *hemagglutination antigen*, mixing with red blood cells and binding with the Sialic Acid receptor on the cell surface---the corn-virus could possess the ability to re-assort genes..*in situ*. That could produce enzymes that break down plant-cellulose, instead of the human sugars which closely resemble the cellulose molecule. It's actually a giant polymeric molecule made up of about a thousand glucose sugar segments strung together in an isotopic structure which is not digestible by humans."

The expert in human diseases replied, "We know that Avian influenza A's virus rapidly re-assorted a few HA sites in humans between the 1968 and 1980 pandemics, causing 'drift' in RNA-virus strains. The subtypes in circulation—H3N2 and H1N1 also produced re-assortant viruses during the flu epidemics in 1978 and 1979. I think it's entirely possible that the *epitome sites* of the corn-plant could be binding with anti-bodies. Just increasing the pH acidity in the environment could cause the polarity and shape of the molecules to alter. *That* could cause *fulminant systemic disease, FSD*."

The agricultural diseases expert frowned as the physician-scientists talked over her head. She had no idea that patients with FSD begin with flu-like symptoms, then rapidly develop severe complications such as respiratory distress syndrome and intravascular coagulation.

"Gentlemen, may I make a few points?" her voice cracked in mild frustration. Dr. Nolte realized with a tinge of embarrassment that the medical people had completely ignored her.

"Of course, Virginia. Please go ahead."

"I studied crop diseases in corn, wheat and soybean, and know about fungi and bacteria such as pythium, fusarium, rhizoctonia and diplodia---which cause seed rot and kill *plant* embryos. The knowledge of human diseases doesn't seem to be so important in the current crisis. These were corn plants being attacked, not humans."

The others sat back and tolerated her low-tech intrusion of their high-tech speculations.

"Shouldn't we be concentrating on the pathology of corn crops, instead of speculating on the very rare possibility that one farmer may have become ill from eating raw kernels? How many people eat raw kernels?" Her comments were as interesting to the physicians as a child's instructions on how to build a sand castle would be to Frank Lloyd Wright.

"This...corn-virus...I guess everyone's calling it that...has a very unusual characteristic, which showed up in my lab tests. I know enough about viruses to understand that they are parasites, and usually exist only in the presence of bacteria or a living host-organism."

"Not 'usually,' Virginia. Always! A virus cannot live without a host," the disease expert corrected her. "All submicroscopic viral infective agents, whether you term them simple microorganisms or complex molecules, can only grow and multiply in living cells."

Virginia extracted from her briefcase a copy of the U.S. Department of Agriculture's lab test results. She handed it to Dr. Nolte.

She announced forcefully, "Traces of E.coli type-bacteria were detected on the surface of browned-leaves. We decided to administer an antibiotic agent, thinking it would kill the bacteria and the virus would die out without a living host to feed on. We could then analyze the molecular structure of the virus, which actually *is not* a true virus, because it lacks a surface membrane. Well… the bacteria died instantly. But, the virus…by some unknown mechanism… has remained alive and is reproducing on the surface of a cardboard box we used to transfer the browned corn-husks from Iowa fields to the lab in Ames."

"That's impossible," the expert in viral and bacterial gene-mutations said pompously. "Viruses don't survive without a living host."

"This organism does!"

(AUGUST 14, 2008)
IOWA CORNFIELDS

Several Iowa State University students were dispatched on missions to collect samples of contaminated corn from various locations in western Iowa. One group eased their van into a rest-stop parking area along Route 30 a few miles east of Boone. After a quick spray on peripheral vegetation, one of the students zipped up and hiked the grounds.

At the far end of the open lot was a ten square-yard steel dumpster with a pile of cardboard boxes neatly piled on the ground in front of the trash container. Someone was too lazy to raise the boxes a few feet and throw them in.

The student lifted one of the boxes and noticed that the labels had been cut away. The only marking on the outside was the name and address of the container manufacturer in small print: *Shanghai Corrugated Container Company, Suzhou Industrial Park, China.* Inside was an empty clear plastic bag with a small, barely-noticeable paper label still glued to the bag. He read the small English printing above a line of strange oriental symbols he assumed were word-equivalents to: 'Water Filter Installation Instructions Inside.' The boxes appeared to be placed in open sight, with apparently no attempt to hide their presence…as if someone wanted them discovered…rather than discarded.

"We'd better follow instructions. I'm bringing these back to the authorities," the student said to his friends. "We were told to look for any clues as to why the cornfields are unrolling into brown carpets. Help me gather them up. Cut the edge-tape and fold them flat."

"You think empty cardboard boxes are important?" one of them asked skeptically.

"Could be. They're made in China. I think they carried some type of water filters. The surfaces look like they've been sand-papered, or chewed by insects."

Omaha, Nebraska

"There it is," Nonnie shouted to the spirit of Chief Ogallala Springs Jefferson, from the extensive law library at the offices of her former employer.

"So...WestLaw Publishing had it?" one of the junior partners who'd volunteered to help in her search proclaimed.

Nonnie was too engrossed with the words on the screen to answer. She tapped a few keys and the printer began collating pages of legal information she'd been searching the past eight hours to find. "None of it mentions picketing rights of Native Americans," she mumbled absently.

"What did you find?" her associate inquired enthusiastically. He possessed a keen sense of legal discovery.

"The Sheriff was correct. The Winnebago Tribe is not allowed to picket in front of BoxMart stores---according to Iowa state law. Actually, its not a law but a nineteenth-century treaty between the state and the Ho-Chunk Federation that was never changed; although the federal government created the Indian Reorganization Act of 1934 and later, the Indian Self-Determination and Education Assistance Act of 1975. Those laws created mechanisms for returning political autonomy to tribal governments, although Native American Indians retained the right to vote in federal elections."

Nonnie's black colleague was a local champion for minority rights and had worked briefly with the NAACP to abolish antiquated state laws that still discriminated against colored people in mid-America states. He was familiar with the hurdles an attorney faced while attempting to resolve jurisdictional conflicts between states and the federal government..

"Nonnie, do you have any idea how long it will take for you to fight this one? There's no fast-track legislation or due-process when it comes to the rights of Native Americans; especially if you're contesting an antiquated, yet standing State treaty against a 1930s ruling by a deceased Commissioner of the Bureau of Indian Affairs."

"We're a federally-recognized tribe, Wainsock. Federal law automatically takes priority over States in the administration of Indian tribes. I say we just assume that picketing by reservation Indians on U.S. territory is *not specifically disallowed* by the federal government...and we go back to the BoxMart stores."

Jeremia Wainsock had not quite reached Nonnie's level of legal experience, but he was street-smart when it came to the practical side of arguing the law. "There's got to be a better answer, Nonnie. Have you checked the election laws for loop-holes?"

"Why would I check there?"

"Because weird legal phrases are sometimes buried in local and state voting laws. Did you know that minority people who registered to vote less than a year before an election can only vote if they belong to a state-recognized political party?"

She studied Jeremia skeptically. "You're kidding, right?"

"No, I'm not kidding. In fact, there's a tri-state law in Nebraska, Iowa and South Dakota, and probably similar laws in other states, that allows minorities to participate legally in activities that would otherwise be considered against State statutes. The requirement is that you act as a representative of a registered political party."

Nonnie measured possible action strategies in her mind. "We could file a Petition for Restraint against the Sioux City, Iowa Sheriff's Department, with the Bureau of Indian Affairs in Washington."

"And park on their doorstep for months?" Jeremia speculated. "You may as well abandon your efforts to bring attention to the unfair treatment the Ho-Chunks received from BoxMart stores."

Neither option was acceptable. "How do you register a political party in Nebraska and Iowa?"

Nonnie was proud that her tribe had learned to make do with a near-poverty level of income for many years, and for the most part, become a high-spirited and contented community when the craft factory provided meaningful employment for many of the young Indians on the reservation. Their sense of worth and purpose had been restored by the production of their hands. "I can't allow hopelessness to dominate the young adults in the tribal community," she admonished the spirits that always listened to her. "We can't allow unemployed high-school drop-outs to become suicidal alcoholics again."

Wainsock was digging deeply into on-line legal search engines like Lexus-Nexus, on case law, and the Cornell Law School references for establishing political parties in each State. "Okay, Nonnie...here's the drill. Step one—file a Declaration of Intent; step two---obtain the necessary signatures; step three---decide if the new Party will be 'candidate-based' or 'issue-based;' step four---file the final applications with state and federal election commissions." He paused. "What name will you use? I wouldn't recommend calling it the *Winnebago* or *Ho-Chunk Party*. Too limited. And the Indian Affairs Bureau may balk."

Nonnie thought for a moment. How could a name best describe the pride bursting in her chest? Her people had maintained a resolute sovereign Winnebago nation despite abject poverty since the late 1800s. She was in awe of tribal predecessors who survived the 1950-1970 'Termination Period,' when the federal government's Indian policy attempted to terminate the federal recognition of Indian tribes, in order to end federal responsibility for three hundred American Indian tribes confined to reservations beginning from 1850.

The word 'Indian' originated when Columbus returned to the American continent in 1493, with five times as many ships and supplies as he brought in 1492. It's said that the word derived from the European name given the indigenous people—'In Dios,' meaning 'Of God.'

Jeremia looked up from the computer screen and said, "I read once that the early Europeans made slaves of some Indian tribes, and nearly wiped out others with diseases."

"We minorities," Nonnie quipped, "have found ways to survive...to make do with what we have."

"Yeah, I guess you're right. How about a name for the Party? I found a registration form on-line. We can begin on the internet."

"How about *The Make Do* Party?"

CHAPTER 52

(AUGUST 15, 2008)
OLD TOWN, SHANGHAI

The bowl-topped woman was a trained informant for the state, with aspirations to be appointed secretary of the textile factory *dan-wei*. Her suspicious dark eyes followed Dr. Dongzi over the zigzag bridge, were he was met by the same young women in jeans who earlier happened by when the old man was unsteady on his feet. She remembered how the girl quickly guided the old man to the bench where the American was seated.

As Dr. Dongzi approached his niece, the Liaoning propaganda official standing beside her recognized the suspicious Communist glare of the woman following Dongzi. He stepped back and dissolved into a nearby tourist gathering, peering over the tour guide's shoulder to observe the middle-aged woman comrade scribbling on a small notepad---probably recording a physical description of Dongzi and his niece. It was too late to warn them.

The busy-body Communist followed Dr. Dongzi and his niece to a non descript grey concrete apartment building a few blocks away. She watched as they entered the ground-level doorway leading to the niece's one-room dwelling. More scratching in the notebook was followed by a cell phone call to the security chief at the local police station. She reported the strange behavior of the couple...emphasizing that she'd watched the old man rush to a bench occupied by a tall, blue-eyed white-man with an American accent carrying a shopping bag. The Chinese man had reached into the bag to extract something. Or drop something in.

She gave the address to the police and drifted back toward the zigzag bridge, hoping to catch a delinquent worker strolling leisurely around the pagoda.

Dr. Dongzi sat at a small fold-up table as his niece pushed aside some papers to make room for his elbows and the steaming cup of fragrant honey blossom tea. He leaned forward on the only uncluttered flat surface in his niece's tiny apartment, which was strewn with sketches of high-fashion clothing scattered on the one-burner propane stove and a wood-framed canvas cot with a two-inch latex-foam mattress. Other clothing sketches were tacked to an upright make-shift drawing board she'd purchased from a gallery at the Chongming Industrial Art Park northwest of the city along Suzhou Creek. The aspiring fashion designer and full-time seamstress said, "Here, uncle... tea will calm your nerves."

Dr. Dongzi was sweating badly. "I pray that the American is as trustworthy as the dead boy's father claims. The person who arranged the meeting with the tall American would not disclose his own identity, but swore he was from the American Embassy in Beijing."

"It's a long train ride from Shanghai to Liaoning, uncle, and you are tired. Finish your tea and rest on my cot. I must deliver some drawings to the textile factory design center." She resisted the urge to shout: *'Please, don't tell me more.'*

Her mother had bragged how her older brother was a physician at a prestigious state hospital in Liaoning, associated with the Institute for Advanced Medical Treatment. Dr. Dongzi never mentioned to his sister that the medical center also housed the high-security 2nd Auxiliary Bio-weapons Laboratory in an adjacent building.

"Go ahead, Kai Tie, I will accept your offer and rest. When you return, I must depart for the hospital...before my travel permit expires."

The dead boy's father peeked out from a concealed doorway across the street from the apartment and saw the police car pull in front of the entrance to the niece's apartment. He regretted having instructed Dongzi not to carry a phone...as 300 million other mainland Chinese do...because he feared the authorities could trace his own number.

Two hulking security police in dark-blue uniforms carrying large black clubs and holstered hand guns rapped sharply on the door to Kai Tie's apartment.

"Open up," one shouted. "Open this door or we'll break it down. This is State Security."

Dr. Dongzi's eyes darted to his travel-bag. He remembered the copies he'd retained of his own autopsy report and the Tangshan Research Hospital analysis of the rogue organism. His friend at the Beijing hospital had signed the report, which described the electron-microscope studies and the structure and likely pathogenic activity of the virus. He also concluded in the report that the organism...from an unknown source... had likely caused the technician's death.

Dongzi reached for the bag, hoping there was time to hide the copies. Suddenly, the door was kicked in and a scowling officer immediately saw him extend an arm into the bag. Fearing Dongzi had a weapon, the burly policeman raced angrily across the small space and bashed the doctor's arm with his hardwood stick, breaking the bones in his wrist and forearm in a sickening crack that caused Dongzi to drop the papers in a rasping gurgle of agony. Kai Tie screamed in horror as the arm went limp and ballooned into a dark-blue pod of internal bleeding.

The other policeman slapped her with a brutal backhand, knocking her to the floor. She passed out more from the shock of the blow than the painful impact of her head striking the concrete.

Dongzi could picture the broken bones in his arm vividly; a dilemma for a doctor seriously injured but still conscious. The pain tore into his shoulder and short-circuited every nerve cell in his upper body. He began to sob as he watched the policeman lift his frail niece by one arm and fling her onto the cot like a stuffed scarecrow. The young officer scowled at Dongzi then glanced lecherously at the unconscious girl. "A nice young one!" His hand reached for her small, well-shaped breast and squeezed the nipple so hard that Kai Tei screamed in pain.

"What have we here?" the older policeman said, as he lifted the medical reports from Dongzi's bag.

"I'm a doctor. You have no right to attack us. Keep your hands off her, *wang-ba-dan*."

"Call me a son-of-a-bitch, will you?" The younger policeman removed his hand from the niece's breast and raised an iron fist. He jabbed with ferocious energy and knocked Dongzi to the floor, bleeding above the ear and left eye.

STATE SECURITY DEBRIEFING CHAMBER
OLD TOWN SHANGHAI

The interrogation room was cold and damp, somewhere below ground in the city. Dongzi's arm was braced in a crude splint made with two wood rulers and a thin nylon cord; which did more to contain the swelling than support the crushed bones.

The aching in his arm had mysteriously dissipated, as Dr. Dongzi slowly emerged from a coma-like stupor enough to realize he was tied to a chair at the ankles. He glanced down and noticed the dried blood and vomit on his shirt. His bare feet were fermenting in a liquid pool of his own urine.

"You have revealed much during your deep sleep, Dr. Dongzi. Now you will identity the American and tell us what transpired on the bench at the zigzag bridge."

Cold water hit his face with the force of angry surf, causing him to blink as his vision cleared. The outline of a small man holding a hypodermic needle appeared.

"We don't usually bother with physical abuse, here, Dongzi, unless it's necessary. One more dose of this new Russian truth serum, however, will permanently shrink your testicles to the size of roasted peanuts. It's better for you to cooperate."

A gruff male voice from behind the chair barked, "Now....traitor, tell us what state secrets you gave the American. It can only be to your advantage."

The man with the needle said evenly, "Does the American know that you attended to the bio-weapons lab-technician, and performed an un-authorized autopsy on his body?"

He pressed the hypodermic needle against the inside of Dongzi's nostril and administered a prickly reminder. "Did you give him copies of the medical reports in your travel bag?"

"Where's my niece?" Dongzi pleaded courageously.

"Answer the question, traitor. Or she'll disappear like a Falun Gong practitioner in the Sujiatun death camp. I imagine she has very healthy organs to donate."

"She is innocent. She allowed me to stay here because I'm family. She knows nothing of my purposes."

"We believe you, Dr. Dongzi...or should I say we believe the truth-chemicals. Now, tell us what we want to know, or you will never see her again."

A drop of blood trickled down the needle easing into the soft membrane of his nostril. It was a shame he didn't know the American's name or location.

SHANGHAI INTERNAL SECURITY DEPARTMENT.

The police chief cringed and snapped to attention, despite the fact he was at the other end of an electronic connection. General Ye slammed down the phone after shouting frenetically, "Find him before he discloses the medical information, or you'll be shoveling pig shit and sleeping with maggots."

The chief summoned his staff and immediately briefed them on a new number-one priority assignment: capture the blue-eyed American...alive, if possible; and determine if the medical information Dr. Dongzi admitted he passed to him was relayed to anyone else. Dead or alive, he must be stopped before the information can be used against the State, or falls into the hands of foreign health officials.

General Ye cleared the top of his desk with a violent arm-sweep. The breach in security at the Liaoning bio-weapons hospital was bad enough; but the unauthorized analysis of blood samples and the autopsy performed on the technician who died mysteriously, could expose a top-secret military facility to the unwanted scrutiny of conservative Party ministers. The stupid accident, which could not possibly be related to the corn virus project, would be investigated thoroughly. Careless heads would be ventilated with hollow-point bullets.

"How can it be the corn virus?" he shouted at the chief scientist from the 2nd Auxiliary Bio-Weapons Testing Facility. "You assured me that the organism is not harmful to humans, and attacks only cellulose-bearing plants."

"We still believe that, General Ye," the scientist replied in a somewhat hestitant tone. "All our tests were conclusive. The modified *Brucella abortis* is similar to an RNA retro-virus, except it adapts its internal chemistry to produce an enzyme which breaks down cellulose…the long-chain molecule made up of glucose isotopes that cannot be ingested by humans."

"Well, something in the lab killed him. He was assigned only to the corn virus project."

"As I said, General…all our pathology tests in petri dishes proved zero activity against human cells. Perhaps the boy was susceptible to the E. coli host bacteria, which the virus feeds on until it becomes lysogenic."

"That doesn't explain why his blood coagulated." Ye had a scientific mind which easily grasped the complex mechanisms involved in the pathology of bio-weapons. "Could there be a reaction we're not aware of?"

"Impossible," the disease expert answered too quickly. "We believe our process modifies the once-deadly Brucella abortus organism irreversibly. It cannot revert back…under any environmental conditions we could imagine."

General Ye did not care for the tentative tone in his answer. "Wasn't the original organism deadlier than Ebola before it was first modified by the Taiwanese?"

"It can never revert back to the unmodified form," the scientist repeated, again too quickly for Ye. "The volatility of the RNA structure has been eliminated; the organism cannot re-combine into its original ribosomal sequence."

General Ye's limited understanding of micro-biology had been surpassed. "Well, make sure you determine how the boy died. I understand he ate some of the Iowa corn."

As soon as the scientist left the room, General Ye summoned Wen Ma, who returned from Macau with signed copies of the Bomali agreements. Wen Ma was furious when informed that a tall American with blue eyes...escorted by a young female tour guide from the Beijing Tourist bureau...may have been the white-man with the bag who sat with Dr. Dongzi on the bench.

"If Gatt is involved---he's a dead man."

"Dongzi didn't know his identity," replied Ye, "I want you to track down Gatt and drag him into jail, or kill him, if necessary. If he is the one, we can't allow him to return to America."

PEACE AND FRIENDSHIP HOTEL, TWO BLOCKS SOUTH OF THE BUND.

The TV broadcasts from the new unconventional "Z crisscross" building housing China Central Television focused on Olympic contests, and replays of the elaborate opening-day ceremonies at the bowl-shaped National Stadium, better known as the "Bird's Nest."

Justin and Lili watched President Mu Jianting enter a semi-transparent "cube" with bubbles spread out all over its surface, located inside the Beijing Olympic Park. The fifty-thousand square meters National Swimming Center, also called the "Water Cube," was the venue for swimming, diving, synchronized swimming and water-polo games. Mu Jianting was accompanied by an unusually large contingent of armed guards; who were pleased with an assignment allowing them to view the perfection of Chinese divers. Home athletes were expected to sweep the medals in platform and spring-board events.

Lili had translated Dr. Dongzi's medical files and Justin was imagining a potential pandemic in America if the pathogen described in the medical analysis had, in fact, been smuggled into the U.S. Professor Meng-Ji's handwritten letter to Eric Syzmansky was a different issue.

Meng-Ji was asking Syzmansky to use his high contacts in financial circles to investigate the sudden movement of large amounts of U.S. currency out of China into foreign banks. Lynne and Stella's father had discovered the same pattern in Geneva, except they'd also uncovered the identities of the receiving institutions.

"We must get this information to Ambassador Balzerini as soon as possible, Lili. Can you locate AJ? The news reports say Balzerini returned to America to meet with the President. AJ should be able to arrange a transfer of information."

"It won't be that easy," she replied, as she watched the traffic jam in front of the hotel from her 6th floor room. "AJ is shadowed by security agents 24/7. We don't think our secure communication units have been compromised, but you can't tell for sure. I'm wary about the government's decision to allow everyone in the country, including the international media, uncensored access to the internet and free movement on the mainland during the Olympics. Somehow, I think Beijing can still detect our communication exchanges."

"Then we can't take a chance transferring this information to the Embassy or to Syzmansky in the USA, using the internet or wireless phone lines. We'll have to work our way back to the Embassy, or go to the nearest U.S. Consulate office. They must have secure lines."

"How urgent is it to pass along the information?" Lili inquired, hoping they had enough time to plan the next move carefully. Someone was always watching. "We may have to deliver the reports by hand. AJ will give us guidance when he calls back."

Justin retrieved one of the medical reports and re-read it. "At least one man has suffered a horrible death from exposure to the organism. Dr. Dongzi called it a "corn virus." I'm not sure why, because it seems to thicken human blood. Maybe it forms kernel-like clots in the blood-stream and blocks arteries?"

"How could it get into the U.S.?" Lili asked anxiously, as she noticed two police cars flashing lights and honking for the traffic in front of the hotel to clear a path to the entrance. A third marked vehicle drove over the sidewalk and entered the alleyway leading to the employee's entrance in the rear of the hotel.

"Dongzi suspects it was smuggled in as water-treatment chemicals or dispensing equipment."

Suddenly the hotel phone chimed. The lit button on the consol indicated it was a call from the lobby. Lili lifted the receiver and heard the words, "This is Dongzi's friend...my son died from the bio-weapon. Dongzi was arrested at his niece's apartment and taken away with her. They were followed by a local Communist informer, who also saw the blue-eyed American sitting on the bench with Dongzi."

"When did this happen?" Lili shouted. Justin looked up from the report.

"No time to explain. The police are here. They tortured Dongzi...I'm sure. He could not possibly resist the methods they use to extract information. They probably tracked you through the database of Americans being escorted by tour guides from the Beijing Tourist Bureau. I noticed your identification tag on the crooked bridge. The informer probably saw it, too. Where is the American?"

"What should we do?" Lili frantically waved Justin to the phone. "Here, talk to him."

"Just listen," the propaganda man from Liaoning instructed in a low voice.

A second after Justin hung up, the phone rang again. Lili waited a few seconds, then answered at Justin's prodding.

"This is the front desk, Ms. Qi. Do you wish us to arrange dinner reservations, or room service for you and the American gentleman? We could bring up a hot meal right away. Or perhaps you're both in your rooms relaxing?"

Lili thought quickly. "That's very kind of you. I'm pretty tired from all the travel. However, the American gentleman is more energetic. He will return from shopping on Nanjing Road within the hour. Could you arrange dinner in the hotel restaurant? I'll be meeting him in the lobby. Yes.... reservations in an hour."

Justin sensed the immediate danger and said, "Grab a few essential things and your travel papers. Leave behind your cosmetics and throw some clothes on the bed and over the chairs. I'll be back." He rushed across the hallway and disappeared into his room. Five minutes later he came out holding a valise and the building schematic hotel management conveniently placed in each room.

Lili hurried out from the cracked doorway and joined him in the hallway.

"The stairs," he said, pointing to the end of the corridor. "They lead to an underground garage with four different exits. Since we don't have a car, they may not be guarding each exit." As they hustled down the hallway, he could hear the phone ring in Lili's apartment.

At five in the evening you could easily get lost in the Bund crowds. Lili was familiar with the Chinese Quarter demarcated by Renmin Road and Zhonghua Road, which led from one of the unguarded exits of the parking lot to a narrow winding alley with small shops jammed with after-work shoppers. The cityscape was dominated by the *Dong Fang Min Zhu*, the Oriental Pearl Television Tower...the tallest structure in Asia; the Hong Kong and Shanghai Bank Building; and the white obelisk-like Shanghai People's Heroes Memorial Tower. A forest of tall buildings of varied modern architectural styles rose like a celestial city on both sides of the Huangpu River.

Hidden from the street-front in the rear of a clothing store, Lili dialed AJ and finally connected. Guardedly, she explained their problem in a barely audible voice.

"Not far from there is a safe-house," AJ spoke rapidly, "in the old neighborhood rubble behind Nanjing Road. Work your way into the crowded shopping area on Nanjing and turn right at the Pizza Hut. A few blocks away you'll find a pawn shop on the first floor of a five-story brick apartment building. Go into the store. The man will identify himself as the proprietor and offer to sell you a jade piece for one-hundred yuan. Tell him you'll pay ten yuan."

NEW YORK CITY, EMPIRE STATE BUILDING
GOVERNOR'S OFFICE

Martin Merrand, the Governor of New York, faced Harley Hedge and Jeffrey Richards from across the Governor's desk. He'd dismissed his chief of staff and campaign manager, Joe Kleinman, for the day. This was not a discussion Joe needed to witness.

"That's about it, Governor," Hedge completed his presentation.

Richards studied Merrand's expression. It was guarded but hopeful. He realized Merrand was uncomfortable in the presence of the powerful oil industry representatives.

"It's certainly an attractive offer, gentlemen, and I could use the campaign funds to battle my well-heeled adversary. What's the catch?"

"Governor, you know how it works," Richards responded casually, as if they were discussing instructions for liar's poker. "Your campaign will have unlimited funds for television, newspaper and internet advertising. All we want is a chance to argue for one or two people we believe would be the best vice-presidential running mates...to assure your victory. You, of course, have to make that decision based on your own convictions."

"We'd like you to consider Senator Elliot Sharn of Ohio as the leading candidate," Hedge said in his usual blunt manner, not bothering to waste words. "We understand you have Senator Scharn high on your list, and we'd like to confirm our support for that decision. Of course, strange things can happen in the political arena, and we realize you have to consider other candidates as well."

Merrand smiled wryly. He did have Scharn at the top of his list. "Who else would you recommend I consider, if Elliot doesn't work out.?"

Richards wagged his head and shrugged. "There are other good candidates, but we believe the Senate offers the strongest alternatives---either of the senior senators from California or Texas."

"I don't like either one that much, but certainly Carvin Troone from Texas has come over to my way of thinking regarding free-trade and *selective protectionism*. Quite a turnaround from his free-trade touting days. But let's talk more about Elliot Scharn."

CHAPTER 53

(August 16, 2008)
Shanghai Safe Apartment

The old man hiding them in his apartment, until AJ arranged an escape route, dipped the needle into a thick liquid mixture of sap and cinnabar and carefully coated the male cricket's wings. "The *autumn singing bird* will now rub his wings in an amplified chirp," the eighty year-old Mr. Chen grinned, as Lili and Justin listened for the *breep-breep, breep-breep* melody coming from the harmless bug the Chinese adored.

"Only the male cricket sings," the pawn-broker explained, "although it has no vocal cords. Most people will only hear two of its three melodies---the pleasant *breep-breep*-sounds used for serenading us, or the rushing swish of air used to attract female crickets."

"What's the third sound?" the fascinated American asked. The pawn-broker dropped the cricket in a straw cage and placed the tweezers on the table. "Ahh..." he rasped, "Now you may begin to understand how the Chinese developed their killer instincts."

"It's half-laugh and half-shriek," Lili recalled from the upsetting cricket-fighting competition a sadistic German client had forced her to attend. "They prod the insects in the rear with rat hairs to excite them. The blue and purple ones are the most fierce."

"An eventual winner will usually reveal itself by arching his back, beating his wings in a blur, then rocking its body from side to side," the old man explained. "Very soon after, the torn body parts of its adversary will be all over the cage. He's fighting for dominance. Chinese leaders have harnessed this killer instinct for their own entertainment for more than a thousand years."

Lili added with a cringe, "The gambling stakes are very high. Successful crickets are believed to embody the spirits of great Chinese generals."

(AUGUST 17, 2008)
IOWA/NEBRASKA STATE HOUSES

Nonnie handed the Political Party Registration papers to the clerk and said, "Are you sure that's all there is to it?"

"Certainly, madame. Once these papers are signed and submitted, you have all the rights extended to any other officially-registered U.S. political party."

With Nebraska and Iowa now acknowledging the legal existence of the *Make Do Party*, Nonnie called Silver Horse Monroe and instructed him to schedule a council meeting.

"I'm returning from Omaha in the evening. This time, invite all the tribes-people. We'll need plenty of hands."

"Sure, Nonnie. Do you want any special preparations?"

"Yes, we'll need to make new signs. Have Dancing Eyes open the craft factory and stock it with sign-making materials. Also, some of the brighter people will need to be there; to get on the phones to regional newspaper editors and TV stations. We're going for broad publicity this time. If Sheriff Whiley wants to make trouble, we'll make sure a large number of people in the area know about it."

"Anything else?"

Nonnie thought a moment. "Can we use your diner for tonight's meeting? We'll need room for more people and I'd like it to be in a public section of the reservation."

(AUGUST 17, 2008)
KENNEDY INTERNATIONAL AIRPORT, NY

Brad was waiting at the Swiss Air luggage carousel as Lynne descended the escalator, hoisting a large tan leather carry-on over her shoulder. As soon as she saw the handsome man in the bright Hawaiian signature-shirt, a primal instinct overtook her.

She rushed up to Brad, stopped hesitantly for an instant, then leaped into his arms, almost knocking him over. Brad's bewildered sense of pleasure shone in his surprised face. Her softness felt like heaven crushing against his chest. He'd expected a more distant and formal reunion of casual friends. He held on until she finally eased away.

Not sure of what to say…Lynne thought, perhaps, her actions said enough. Brad's body heat had nearly waxed her nipples to his rock-hard abs.

"You look simply ggg..gorgeous," he stuttered in a half joke, wanting so much to cup the back of her auburn hair and draw her moist lips into a vicious kiss. "But we should get out of here, fast. Wait here; I'll get your bags."

"Here's my tags," she exhaled heavily.

The drive to the Stamford train station took less than an hour. They hardly spoke.

"It's safer this way," Brad finally said. "Justin is right. If they've been watching you for a while, they know we're friends and may be following my movements. Hopefully, they're expecting you to return to Boston...not New York.

Brad summoned a porter smoking a cigarette at a side entrance, handed him a twenty and said, "Get her on the train fast." He sped away, just in case he'd been followed.

Lynne settled into a window seat on the crowded Amtrak train. Joanna Yates would be waiting for her at the New Haven station. Joanna had reluctantly agreed to rush Justin's new girlfriend, Lynne, into temporary hiding at her Wallingford home.

(AUGUST 17)
SHANGHAI

Lili couldn't deny their location. "We're shopping on Nanjing Street," she answered her supervisor from the Beijing Tourist Bureau. They probably already knew...using the GPS locating bug all the tour guides carried in their regular cell phones. Dammit...she'd made the mistake of checking for missed messages and punched on for less than a minute.

"Yes, we're staying at the same hotel. No...he's not feeling well, so the side trips were cancelled. We'll be returning to the hotel shortly." Justin and old Chen tensed as they listened to her part of the conversation.

The bureau supervisor hung up, and said to the Beijing Security agent standing at his side, "She's lying, except for her current location on Nanjing Road. I assume the American is with her. If you move fast enough they can be intercepted in the popular shopping area. I do not believe they'll return to the hotel. They haven't been there in two days."

The security agent immediately dialed a direct-connect number to the Shanghai Old Town Internal Security office.

Lili tapped off the phone and sat silently as old Chen rushed into another room. He returned seconds later holding a folded map of China's east coast, marked with Chinese characters and red boxes. "You must leave immediately." He handed the map to Lili. "This will show you the safe-house locations along the train and bus routes from Shanghai through the east coast provinces of Zhejiang, Fujian and Guangdong; all the way to the city of Shenzen. AJ will be able to direct you across the Special Administrative borders into Hong Kong or Macau. Lili, dear, the safe locations are *not* where the red boxes appear. They're at nearby addresses scripted in ideographs, and preceded by the character 're'...as in this one."

He touched his finger on an address and red box near Sanming, on the Fujian province railroad route between the port cities of Fuzhou in the northeast, and Xiamen in the southeast. "As you can see, the correct address is also preceded by 're'...but ends in 'leng.'" Lili thought...*the Chinese words for hot and cold.*

They hastened to pack their possessions in the carry-cases Mr. Chen had stuffed with clothes and toiletries. "Start down a back alley, where the rubble remains," he suggested. "They'll be looking for you on the main shopping street."

They embraced Chen, despite his preference for the no-touching Chinese custom of respectful bows for greetings and departures, and rushed out the back entrance of the pawn shop. Hugging the facades of garment and food shops, they angled away from the main street. Sirens could be heard in the distance, getting louder.

Lili removed the battery from her Bureau cell phone and dropped both down a sewer. She seemed to sense something. She stopped short. They'd advanced only a few blocks from Mr. Chen's pawn-shop. Justin glanced back as Lili squeezed her eyes shut and listened. Remaining stationary, she instinctively began the process the old monk taught her. In seconds, she slipped into a morphed state of mind and body.

Justin thought she was going to faint from fright. He reached out to steady her, but froze when he touched her arm. Her body was frigid, and seemed to rise off the ground of its own volition. "Are you all right?" he pleaded, as the sirens grew louder.

Lili didn't answer. Her eyes slowly opened. Her glaze was eerie...a piercing, detached glare reminding Justin of a zombie movie. She was going into shock from fear. He grasped her arm and attempted to ease her into a resting position on the sidewalk. A concrete lamp-post would recline easier. Her head suddenly rotated in the direction of the headlights screeching into the alley from a police van equipped with a sophisticated tracking device. Three PLA security officers with drawn guns jumped from the vehicle and began chasing toward them. Justin was unable to drag Lili away; as she remained stiff as a marble statue. Seeing no other choice, he raised his arms over his head and cried out loudly, "We're unarmed. We surrender."

The PLA officers approached cautiously; their firearms in two-handed grips aimed at Justin's forehead. One of them turned to Lili and barked out, "You, woman...up with your hands."

Lili's body remained still, except for the indetectible peripheral scanning of her eyes. The policemen's relative locations were recorded in her Juko-kai brain.

"Don't move," another policeman shouted, as he made the mistake of approaching within a few feet of Lili. The lead officer whispered to the others, "General Ye has ordered them killed on the spot." Lili heard the whisper above the loud street sounds, and also detected the click of the retracted striker system on the hammerless, short-recoil weapon. Justin braced for the worst. He could never have imagined what happened next.

Snarling in the face of certain death...like a female hyena cornered by a male lion...seconds from the fatal piercing blow....Lili's eyes sprang open and she hissed in the heavy tone of a sumo wrestler—"*shin*", heart-mind; "*ki*", vital force; "*jigo-tai*," defensive posture; "*kime*", focus. Her body suddenly became a blur of deadly motion...spinning like a Waring blender. Her knife-edge hands-- *shuto*, arms, and feet became ultra-high-velocity blades which seemed to defy gravity.

Justin heard high-pitched cries of "*uchi*,"strike; "*tsuki*,"punch; "*tettsui*," hammer fist; then "*shuto*,"the knife-edge hand. The lead officer collapsed grotesquely to the ground, grasping his crushed larynx. Both eyes popped from their sockets like dangling single-pearl earrings. A gun-aim was redirected from Justin's forehead to the mid-section of another policeman, who suddenly fell back from the blast onto the pavement, gushing blood skyward from a shattered abdominal artery.

The third man stared up in confusion. He was holding his crotch...fighting back excruciating pain...just beginning to comprehend that his testicles had been crushed by a ferocious groin-kick five times more powerful than a jackhammer. Justin watched in horror as Lili stood over the man with a raised hand, wild-eyed and glossy. She hesitating, for some unknown reason, to finish the man with a single cranium crush across the nose or a severing chop through his carotid artery. The disciplined crime-squad professional noticed the hesitation and reached for his gun lying on the pavement a few feet away. Lili failed to react.

For the first, and hopefully only time in his life, Justin witnessed the excited, crazed sparkling eyes of an assassin suddenly dull to a blank emptiness. Without thinking, he fell on the sexless policeman before he could reach the automatic pistol and slammed his forehead against the curb with two fistfuls of hair. The man's eyes rolled to white as he blacked out. Lili's raised arm fluttered awkwardly to her side and she began to wobble in a daze through the fragments of discarded building materials scattered in the dark, narrow alley, which led in the opposite direction from Nanjing Road.

The old Shanghai neighborhood soon gave way to the illumination of three-hundred skyscrapers appearing magically beyond the darkness of the old alley. The contrast between poverty and luxury never seemed greater. Shanghai was the most astonishing example of Chinese growth. The Pudong area east of the Huangpu River was once undeveloped countryside. Within fifteen years it had become Shanghai's financial district, eight times larger than London's new Canary Wharf financial center.

Justin stepped around an old wooden table, piles of demolition concrete fragments, empty five-gallon paint pails and a rusted steel drum; and rushed to Lili's side. Her shoulders were slumped and tears were washing over her flushed cheeks. The veneer of super-human strength she'd summoned in the Juko-kai tradition, which tripled the flow of naturally-occurring complex adrenaline enzymes into her blood system, gradually subsided. The remorse at being forced to violate her profession of goodness to the Grand Master, made her sad.

A neurologist might attempt to describe the phenomenon of Lili's transition as an uncluttered, electrical pathway for charged neurons; resulting in the reconnecting of seratonin-uptake factors; or the build-up of super-conductive enzymes on nerve-endings. Somehow, Lili's clarity of thought and muscle reactions had increased exponentially.

"*You may come to grief when confronted by those who are not good,*" Master Zong Keba had advised when she left the Buddhist monastery. "*Machiavelli, the great Italian thinker, has written that the good must learn how not to be good, and use it according to the necessity of the case.*"

Justin felt the high fever on Lili's skin as he gripped her shoulders. He sensed the ache in the young woman's pure heart. "You saved my life," he said softly, "and preserved our chance to bring this information to the right authorities. That could save many more lives."

Lili nodded silently and raised her saddened eyes to his. Justin's smile and gentle embrace gradually elevated her spirit. He felt her muscles relax…her skin cool…as she emerged from the Juko-kai cataleptic daze, inhaled deeply and slowly eased away from his embrace.

"The train station is in that direction," she said softly, pointing over his shoulder. "The tickets and disguises Mr. Chen provided are in the carry-bags. You'll be a white-faced traveling opera star."

A few minutes earlier, when Justin witnessed the astonishing blur of death Lili had become, he didn't need to apply white chalk to his face.

CHAPTER 54

(August 18, 2008)
Ho-Chunk Reservation

"The U.S. federal government has confined North American Indians to reservations since 1850," Nonnie began as she addressed the tribal council and nearly a hundred other tribe members gathered in Silver Horse Monroe's large diner at the main intersection of the Winnebago Reservation.

"We have a new opportunity to speak out," she continued in the forceful demeanor of a true chief. "We can do something against those trying to destroy our way of life."

Stretching across the ceiling above her head was a computer-generated paper banner with large, red lettering: *The Make Do Party.* Poster-board placards nailed to long two-by-fours leaned against a wall, displaying the messages: *Don't Shop at BoxMart*; *BM Managers are Heartless Thieves*; *More American Jobs Stolen by Chinese Workers*; *Native Americans Don't Want Welfare, We Want Jobs.*

Chief Whiteknee gauged discouragement on the majority of placid, resigned faces staring back blankly. "BoxMart stole our calendar-stick design and forced us to close the craft-factory," she blurted out irately, fearing that most of the tribe, including the Council members, were predisposed to accept another, possibly fatal, attack on their culture.

"Our ancestors bravely preserved Ho-Chunk Winnebago traditions," she continued, "by governing the reservation as a mini-nation in forced isolation." She reminded them, "We are still strong enough to defend the 5,000-year-old heritage of the American Indian." A muted response to her history lesson suggested additional morale-boosting was necessary.

"Did you know that Harvard College…arguably the most prestigious school in the world, was founded to educate both English *and* Indians.

Harvard's original charter called for *'the education of the English and Indian youth of this country in Knowledge and Godliness.'* Harvard's first American-Indian graduate was Caleb Cheeshahteaumuck from the Wampanoag tribe, class of 1665. He lived and studied in a dormitory they called the 'Indian College', which was founded in 1665, but torn down in 1698. Some bricks from that original building were used to build structures you can see today on the Cambridge campus." People at the meeting sat up straighter.

The Silver Horse Diner was as much a home to tribes-people as their own residences; and its thriving business was in jeopardy because of the factory closing. Nonnie noticed a few of the young Indian workers looking down at the black and cream checkered floor; then absent-mindedly up at the red and silver 1940's ceiling fans with large white Coca-Cola labels. A gleaming toddler's pink-metal 1950's pedal-car was suspended by a small chain in the middle of the room. It had white and red tire-hubs, a stainless-steel steering wheel and a double-arm-huggable tan Teddy-bear with a red bow-tie driving…leaning back to enjoy the air in its nose.

Faded Coca-Cola signs were scattered over the sixty-foot pink-painted walls, reading: *Sign of Good Taste*; *Tasty Together*(depicting a coke bottle placed beside a juicy hamburger); and another sign over the grill behind the counter depicting a blonde, teenage girl in pajamas, smiling excitedly into a rotary-telephone, leaning over at the foot of the stairs, saying: *"I'll Bring The Coke."*

Today's 'specials' were hand-written on a dry-eraser board above the long counter facing the open grill. The Silver Horse offered its usual menu of three home-made soups, nine dinner specials, seven home-made pies , four cakes and two puddings. In a corner next to the cash register stood an ancient yellow Shell Oil gas pump in like-new condition, topped with a frying-pan sized illuminated glass-bulb printed with the familiar oyster-shell logo in shades of red, white and canary. Silver Horse and his wife were standing near the mechanical cash register, listening for encouragement. *Some* action was going to be necessary to save their faltering business—an institution on the reservation as prized as the Ho-Chunk's 500-year old totem pole.

Nonnie lifted a tarnished leather-bound book in one hand and raised her voice, "The first bible printed in the *entire* North American continent was printed in an Indian language. Called the *Eliot Bible*," Nonnie wiggled her copy in the air, "the book was published at Harvard to help Indian pastors convert northeastern tribes."

Dancing Eyes Adams rose from a nearby booth and tapped his feathered-spear lightly on the floor. Voices hushed in deference to his stature. "Last night the Council members danced the *Sun Dance*," he began in a crackling tone. "The spirits rewarded us with visions of renewal for the Great Plains people suffering poverty on the Reservations. Those of us who keep cattle, tend to fields and lease some of our lands to non-Indian cattle ranchers, miners or casino operators, have learned to make do with what we have." He hesitated and began blinking wildly...hense the origin of his name.

"But the Winnebego Ho-Chunks have not achieved independence, as our ancestors hoped." He handed the ceremonial Council Spear to Nonnie and said in a loud voice, "The craft-factory gave us a chance to gain independence; to renew our spiritual roots. Now, Chief Whiteknee will lead the fight against those trying to destroy our opportunity." The tribes-people murmured in agreement.

"We *can* fight back," Silver Horse shouted to the uplifted gathering. "Let's get down to business." Nonnie nodded, then laid out her plan.

"Three BoxMart super-stores in the area will be picketed each day, beginning tomorrow. I'll lead the line at the Sioux City store, which is the one most likely to be confronted by Sheriff Whiley. The demonstrations in Onawa and Omaha stores will be led by Silver Horse and his son Racing Pony Monroe." The thirty-year-old Christian-minister, better known as Reverend Monroe, grinned broadly.

"The Diner will open for breakfast strategy meetings, and picketing teams will be driven to the locations in pick-up trucks. We want as much exposure as possible when we travel in the streets." Nonnie knew the tribe was on solid legal ground. By using the *Make Do Party* as a platform for their protests, Whiley could not disrupt or prevent the demonstrations...as long as the picket-lines remained outside BoxMart's private parking lots.

Nonnie administered final instructions authoritatively to the three groups assembled outside the Diner. "Remember," she shouted, "Don't give them an excuse to break up the picket lines. Stay on the sidewalks near the parking-lot entrances. When the store managers inform BoxMart headquarters about our presence...there's no guessing what those robbers will do."

Nonnie expected the BM Boston lawyers to confirm her legal research: native American Indians are U.S. citizens, with the right to vote in federal elections. The picketers from the Reservation were demonstrating within the law, as members of a registered political party.

As the tribe set out to display 'Make Do Party' signs, and march in protest against BoxMart for pirating their ancient artifact designs...Nonnie realized that the self-righteous retailer might still attempt to break up the picket lines. Management's attitude of invulnerability and superiority had encouraged thugs to disrupt previous protests against the company. She expected a strong management reaction, and was actually hoping they'd over-react. Every newspaper and TV station in the Midwest had been informed that a newly-registered political party was planning to demonstrate in front of BoxMart superstores in Sioux City, Onawa and Omaha. Regional reporters covering political conflicts during a presidential-election year would undoubtedly show up.

Any fresh political story was front-page fodder, as the national conventions prepared to choose Presidential candidates for the November election. Particularly if the story involved a controversial mass-retailer frequently chastised by the press as anti-American. BoxMart was well known as the country's largest importer of foreign-made consumer goods. Jake Kurancy was also a favorite target of the business media pundits, for refusing to placate critics by ignoring accusations that BoxMart was detrimental to America's security.

The shut-down of another small manufacturer, located in a poverty-stricken Indian Reservation, was hardly newsworthy to Kurancy. He'd stated publicly that forcing weak suppliers out of business was a normal result of BoxMart's efficiency improvements. Voter pols confirmed that lost jobs remained a sour issue with the public.

Fort Dodge, Iowa

Virginia Richmore, the agricultural biologist, was paying the price for shooting off her mouth at the CDC meeting in Atlanta. She'd been dispatched to the area indefinitely by the CDC's Iowa Cornfield Contamination task force; as the CDC's representative in charge of protecting humans and vegetation from the potential ravages of a corn-virus induced pandemic.

She checked into the sleepy ten-room Fort Dodge Motor Lodge and immediately dialed the Agricultural Extension office in Ames, which was responsible for collecting and testing samples from the contaminated western-Iowa cornfields. Her physician colleagues on the CDC Iowa task force were convinced that the strange organism which fed on cellulose molecules was not a human pathogen. Otherwise, they'd have assigned one of the more capable medical experts to head the investigation.

"Empty cardboard boxes were found by Iowa State University students about thirty miles east of Boone, where we believe the browning started," Virginia was informed by the U.S. Dept of Agriculture biologist running tests at the Ames experimental station.

"And...?"

"From which side of the bed did you arise, Virginia?"

"I'm sorry, Cynthia. Guess who they put in charge of this fiasco?"

"Well, its getting interesting-er and interesting-er. We discovered live, virus-like organisms on the cardboard surfaces of the boxes the students found. Out in the open, I might add. The contaminated surfaces look like they've been sand-papered."

"The browning process seems to effect only vegetation---the corn-leaves and stalks," Virginia replied.

"Well, I think it's remarkable that the kernels on the husks of the contaminated plants have so far remained plump and yellow. The good news is---there are no reports of abnormal sicknesses in area hospitals."

"I wouldn't suggest that you start feeding husks to animals or people, Cynthia. Did you learn anything from the boxes?"

"You may want to see for yourself, Virginia. It appears the labels were purposely cut away. But the box manufacturer's name and address are still there. Also, a plastic bag found inside one of the empty boxes...stuck under an in-folded flap...had a paper-label attached which may identify the contents. The box was made in Shanghai, so I assume the contents came from China."

"Any other clues?"

"There's a bar-code on the bag label. We think it may indicate a producer...or customer I.D.Usually bar-codes include supplier information, along with the product code. We haven't had a chance to check it out with the UCC people in Commerce."

Virginia said, "I'm hanging out today in Fort Dodge to meet with local farmers. The CDC wants them to torch the perimeters of the browned-fields to prevent spreading. I also have the dubious honor of deciding if or when they can begin harvesting Iowa corn again. CDC and the USDA have temporarily banned harvesting in the contaminated and surrounding corn fields. We're trying not to spook the pig and cattle industry before we determine the best method to contain and destroy this bug."

Cynthia added in a stilted tone, "This place is a mad-house. With the harvesting season approaching, the commodity speculators at the New York Mercantile Exchange have bid up corn futures by twenty-percent. Trading in hog-belly futures has been temporarily suspended. The governor of Iowa is pressuring State and University health officials to find an answer fast."

Virginia hesitated to offer any comment that might accidentally be interpreted as false encouragement. "Make sure the experimental station workers sample the contaminated fields at least once each day. Atlanta developed a quick method to determine if the viral-organism is alive: a few drops of USP hydrogen peroxide...the standard over-the-counter three-percent antiseptic solution---will fizzle white bubbles and turn a live organism indigo. A hand-held UV black-light will color the live organism a fluorescent Caribbean-blue."

"Sounds interesting," Cynthia replied impatiently, "but to be useful the tests would have to work on the surfaces of plants, animals, human skin and inanimate objects. This bug has strange characteristics. Under a microscope, it balls up into a dodecahedral dome-shaped structure before it explodes spore-progeny into the surroundings. If it turns out to be a true virus, there's no telling how it may mutate."

"Just what I need to hear!"

A few hours after her meeting with local farmers, Virginia became more alarmed. Cynthia called to inform her that in a town called Storm Lake, north of Sac City and down wind from the earliest contaminated fields, several dead bodies were found lying beside the road.

They were immediately collected and identified as blue-wing teal, American coot, ring-necked pheasant and red-head. The lab detected the presence of residue from spent Lambda E. coli. More startling---live corn virus organisms were devouring the wing-structures and beaks of shriveled native bird carcasses.

Routes to Zhenjiang and Fujian Provinces

Justin and Lili worked their way to the Shanghai train station, huddling in dark alleys and building entrances until they crossed over Suzhou Creek several blocks north of the main Nanjing Road shopping area, where they'd been attacked. Following AJ's hurried instructions on Lili's secure communications unit, they turned east on Tianmu Road and pushed through two crowded blocks into the train station throng waiting in line to buy late-evening tickets.

Lili slid into one line and used yuan notes to purchase two passages on the three-hour train-ride south to the city of Hangzhou in Zhejiang Province. Justin used his international credit card in another line to buy two overnight berths to Xi'an, the home of the famous excavated terra cotta warrior statues about 1200 kilometers west of Shanghai. Once the largest city in the world---Xi'an was the former capital of eleven dynasties and a popular tourist stop for foreigners traversing the country on imperial-treasure vacations, coupled with attending the Olympic Games. More important---Xi'an was listed on Justin's original itinerary which Lili had faxed to her supervisor at the Beijing Tourist Bureau.

Lili weaved into the cluster of late travelers surrounding Justin and slipped a ticket into his hand. They then separated and crammed into adjoining cars, awaiting anxiously for the Hangzhou Express to pull away from the station fifteen minutes later. Justin tore up the Xi'an tickets and dropped the pieces into a disgusting spittle-pail placed near the door to a common toilet. He remembered that Chinese men spit constantly.

PLA security vehicles surrounded the U.S. Consulate a half-dozen blocks southwest of Nanjing Road, searching the pedestrian swarm on Huaihai and Changle Roads for signs of Gatt and Lili. AJ had been correct. The authorities assumed Gatt would head for the protection of the American Consulate. They'd dispatched the first security teams to the streets surrounding the Consulate entrances.

Other police units soon arrived at the Shanghai International Airport and the train station, just as the Hangzhou Express rumbled south. Yong Ihasa also ordered a Triad Society death-squad to Xi'an, after the State Electronic Transmissions Regulatory Agency traced Gatt's credit-card purchase.

They arrived in Hangzhou at midnight and melded into the crush in front of the Genshanmen Railroad Station north of center-city. Lili negotiated with a pedicab driver for the ten minute drive to the Hangzhou University Guest House recommended by AJ. The University was located a few blocks north of the strikingly beautiful West Lake vicinity.

When they arrived at the white Victorian style University Guest House, an elderly man with white hair, a protruding square chin, of medium height with sunken cheeks and suspicious brown eyes, peered at them from behind a magazine. The lobby was otherwise empty. He rose from the cushioned wicker-chair and glanced through the glass frontage of the Guest House into the empty parking lot. "Are you the German from Bremen?" he inquired, over his shoulder. He turned to Lili, tilted his head and asked in perfect English, "And you, Miss? The secretary from Wuhan?"

Justin's apprehension lessened when Lili smiled and said, "We are now." She added softly, "And I presume you are the proprietor of the Guest House---Mr. Hangzhou?" An obvious alias.

"Please, come with me." He led them quickly to a windowless back room, locked the door from inside and held out his hand. Mr. Hangzhou had spent some time in America.

"Pleased to meet you, Mr. Gatt. May I call you *Herr Hans Fuller*." He turned to Lili. "And, you…beautiful daughter, must be the notorious Lili Qi." He bowed. "May I joyously call you *Jingci Weituo*, in honor of the chief guardian of the Buddha?"

"AJ said you would help us," Lili explained in the first relaxed words she'd spoken in days. "Did he mention we are being pursued by the authorities?"

"Of course. If I may use an American expression---join the crowd."

Mr "Hangzhou" removed falsified identification papers and travel permits from a small desk and handed them to 'Herr Fuller' and 'Jingci Weituo.' The passports contained duplicates of their current visa photos.

"The information you possess, Mr. Gatt, is too sensitive to transfer by electronic means. The communications experts at the U.S. Embassy in Beijing suspect that the Chinese Internet-Licensing Authority has convinced Google to reveal some of its most powerful search-engine software. Any one of several key words contained in the information you possess will set off an alarm."

"Are you suggesting that the Chinese Secret Service, or anti-espionage ministry…or whatever they are called…has penetrated all internet and electronic communications on the mainland?" asked Gatt incredulously.

"AJ suspects so. All but the super-sophisticated multi-frequency scrambled messages sent over NSA satellites. The CIA people at the Embassy are now transmitting dummy coded messages to determine if China's military-controlled internet intelligence group--- the PLA Fulcrum for High Performance Computing---has infiltrated even those secure lines. All they require…in my humble opinion…is time, a bit more cooperation from American internet-software developers and a massive super-computer dedicated to the task."

Justin wondered if "Mr Hangzhou" was the underground source Balzerini claimed had just re-emerged after relaying the original warnings. If so, he would have additional information to convey.

"This intrigue is unfamiliar to Lili and me, Mr Hangzhou. I assume you're a seasoned player?" Justin glanced at Lili in an apologetic expression that said *Excuse me for speaking for both of us*, then added, "This is our first spy assignment. It reminds me of novels about 'Special Operations Forces,' you know---quick deployment, high-risk missions. Except we missed the special training in weapons, unconventional warfare, and electronic communications."

He glanced once more in amazement at sweet, 110 pound lethal Lili. "At least we don't have to attack bases behind enemy lines, destroy enemy command posts or provide long-range reconnaissance."

Mr Hangzhou smiled and replied in an ironic, semi-convincing fluster, "Like you, Mr. Gatt, I'm just learning the game. Luckily, I'm in academics. That allows me certain freedoms, and exposure to…shall we say…intellectuals involved in top-secret government projects. He reached into another desk drawer and retracted a Chinese-character document.

"Here, Lili. You will recognize many of the names. Please translate them into English for Mr. Gatt to record in his remarkable memory, then destroy the list. These men are responsible for initiating the *events* designed to harm the U.S. economy. Add these names to the information you are attempting to bring to Balzerini, Mr. Gatt."

"What information do you have on the so-called, *events*?"

"Financial and biological terms have been used to describe the nature of the planned attacks. Several confidential exchanges using these terms have been detected by friendly sources in China. However, the details of the threats are still emerging."

Justin thought about the autopsy report on the deceased bio-weapons technician; and the suspected shipment of a bad-acting organism from a Lioaning bio-weapons facility to the U.S.

"Is a Chinese medical facility in Liaoning province involved?"

Mr. Hangzhou nodded. "My information source at the State Council office in Zhangnanhai has a deep resentment against the Chinese Communist Party for unwarranted harsh treatment of common people. A second source employed at the vacation villa of one of the suspected high-ranking conspirators, believes a Chinese secret society is also involved in the conspiracy." The distorted expression on Hangzhou's creviced face suggested he was familiar with the agent. He smirked and whispered, "Our boy is a lip-reader."

Justin yawned deeply, despite the critical information being passed. Mental fatigue was gaining fast on physical fatigue.

"Please excuse my clumsiness of manners," Hangzhou apologized. "You could use a steaming cup of wonderfully refreshing Dragon Well tea…the Green Longjing…the best tea in all of China." He unlocked the door and directed Herr Fuller and citizen Weitoa to small adjoining guest rooms down the hall.

They were both regressing into slumber on the comfortable latex-foam mattresses when Mr. Hangzhou arrived in the hallway, carrying two steaming blue and white porcelain cups on a bamboo tray. Justin was sensitized to unfamiliar sounds and shot up in bed. Lili's Juko-kai sixth sense of danger remained dormant. She sat up slowly and yawned into her fist.

"Tomorrow will be very dangerous for travel," Mr. Hangzhou warned evenly. "Luckily, there is a large Chinese cultural exhibition at the convention center, and the Min and Gaojia opera troops are in town to perform for local residents and foreign tourists. Their summer road-production shows are traveling south to the coastal towns. Also, the Hangzhou puppet show will be thrilling the street crowds with performances at the park pavilion the locals call the 'Lotus in the Breeze at the Crooked Courtyard.' Lili can wander the streets safely, to gauge the area in case AJ's instructions require you to spend more time in Hangzhou. She'll blend in easily once her face is covered by a puppet mask the venders sell before the performances."

He studied Justin's tall athletic physique and sparkling blue eyes. "I think Herr Fuller's face should be painted white, and his eyes brown."

Lili laughed at the quizzical tilt in Justin's head. "You'll be disguised as a 'Chou,'" she giggled, referring to the comic role in classic Chinese opera. "The character is frequently very tall by Chinese standards, and wanders the streets as a goodwill gesture after the shows."

Mr. Hangzhou handed them each a tea cup. "Here. This will aid your sleep." He then addressed Justin directly, "My instructions are to prepare you for a long road trip under uncomfortable conditions. The Embassy is in the process of arranging safe over-land passage for you to Hong Kong. I assume you'll be immediately transported back to America."

"What about Lili? The authorities must know she helped me."

"Unfortunately, you're correct, Mr. Gatt. One of the agents who attacked you in the Shanghai alley apparently lived. He explained to superiors in a high-pitched voice how Lili and a team of ninjas fended off the arrest. I understand he will lead a childless, unhappy life." Mr. Hangzhou glanced fearfully at Lili and added, "The policeman has pleaded with his superiors to capture Lili and extract revenge for his de-ballitating injury." Justin thought Mr.Hangzhou mis-pronounced the word. Lili's head dropped in apparent remorse. She was aiming for his abdomen when he leaped up.

"AJ will see that Lili gets to a safe place. She can easily become lost in China, which is almost exactly the size of America…with four times as many people."

"I want to go with you," Lili said in a low voice as she faced Justin. "You have no chance of survival, traveling without an interpreter."

Mr. Hangzhou said to Lili, "AJ has promised to send a coded message to your special communications unit as soon as safe-travel arrangements are made for both of you. I expect instructions to arrive by the time I return from Tai Ji Quan exercises in the morning mist of West Lake. He will have to decide."

Justin finished the tea and thought about options. If he traveled as a German businessman, he'd be expected to take factory tours, attend short lectures, examine medical clinics and primary schools. Then, share lunch on the premises and complete a typical foreign businessman's visit with a question and answer session. No chance he could pull that off, even if he miraculously remembered a few "Shprechen Ze Duetche" words from two years of high school German language classes. Lili was right. He needed her help to traverse unknown pitfalls. Pressure to drop the hot-potato onto Balzerini's lap as quickly as possible was mounting. His country's security was at stake.

CHAPTER 55

(August 19, 2008)
Hangzhou, China

Mr. 'Hangzhou' never returned from his morning exercises in the West Lake mist.

He dropped a small German knapsack containing white face-paint, blond hair-dye, brown-tinted contact lenses, a fistful of ten-yuan notes, train tickets to Fuzhou and a detailed map of southeast China on the floor of Gatt's small guest room.

AJ Hau Luing dispatched the coded message from the Foreign Commercial Services building at the Embassy complex to Lili's communications unit before the morning mist cleared. AJ then rushed into an armored SUV and was chauffeured to Beijing International Airport. His 'official' assignment was a whirlwind staff-review of new employees at the Consulates General of the U.S. in Guangzhou, Hong Kong and Macau.

The '4th floor' had picked up a new electronic intercept from the Youanmen Police Station. An American businessman in Shanghai had committed violent crimes against the state and was being hunted by police and secret service agents with authority to shoot-to-kill if he resisted arrest. Justin Gatt, the tall blue-eyed American identified as the assailant had been assisted by an emotionally-disturbed tour guide from the Beijing Tourist Bureau, who apparently participated in the heinous attack against Shanghai police conducting a routine street patrol. Two officers were brutally murdered and a third dis-figured for life.

Lili translated the coded message and nervously handed her script to Justin. "They've initiated a country-wide search for us!"

Justin read the communique with renewed trepidation. "I guess we should have anticipated this." He peered out the window, expecting Chinese squad cars to pull up outside. "AJ's directions have us traveling to the provincial capital city of Fuzhou, then on to the apartment of *Weituo*'s ill grandfather in a high-rise rental-building near the Fuzhou International Airport. They suggest it is wise for Ms. Weituo and Herr Fuller to travel together...yet separately...until they reach the final destination."

"He means separate cars on the same train."

"Lili, I'll stay behind and study the map left behind by Mr. Hangzhou. Why don't you explore the university campus and the West Lake area? Students must be on summer break, judging from the absence of other guests and employees here. I think the Hangzhou University Guest House is actually closed for the season."

Lili said incisively, "Then Mr. Hangzhou is the only person aware of our presence. What if someone else notices us leaving?"

Justin reached into the knap-sack and pulled out the bottle of hair-dye. "I'll use this while you're scouting around."

Lili removed a couple of hardcover textbooks from the lobby shelf and tucked the student-props under her arm. "I'll make my way to the Hangzhou Foreign Trade Center. The puppet show is staged at the building entrance, and I can purchase one of the full-size painted puppet-masks they usually glue to thin holding sticks."

She eased past the throng of delighted children and parents mesmerized by the lopping arms and legs of a stringed Confucius doll sternly instructing tiny puppets. A large sign over the lobby directed visitors to a half-dozen open doorways leading to '*The Wonders of Chinese Peoples and Cultures*' exhibit occupying over 40,000 square meters of floor space.

Designed to attract foreign visitors extending their vacations following the conclusion of the Summer Olympics venue, the hall was jammed with display booths, regional officials and costumed representatives from China's fifty-five *shaoshu minzu* minority nationalities. Villagers dressed in traditional regalia greeted visitors and distributed color brochures depicting regional attractions. Interpreters from the Beijing Language Academy bridged the spoken-dialect language gaps in a flurry of bows and head nods.

"The Zuang is the largest ethnically distinct group," Lili heard the middle-aged woman tour guide from Xinjiang explain proudly. Lili marveled at the diversity of Chinese ethnicity in the hall. Young girls and boys were wearing joyful bright silk colors; their smiles were angelic and pure of heart. Lili thought of Nin.

"The Han people represent over ninety-percent of the Chinese population and live predominantly on the eastern and southern coasts," the guide continued in sound-bites of demographic statistics. "The mountainous and desert regions are more sparsely settled. These border areas are designated the 'Autonomous Regions,' and include: Inner Mongolia, Ningxia, Xinjiang, Xizang, Tibet and Guangxi."

The guide slowed her speech deliberately and quickly spanned the Chinese people standing around the area. She made sure there were no 'official' inquiring eyes trailing the Canadian tourist group. "I am Xinjiang," she croaked proudly. "Autonomous region citizens don't suffer the same stringent birth-control regulations as those living in the Provinces." She leaned close to a grandmotherly Quebecian woman and whispered, "I gave birth to four charming daughters and one magnificent son. He will take care of me when I am old."

Before departing the exhibition hall, Lili purchased a paper plate of steamed dumplings and ate at a cafeteria table facing the Sichuan booth. She thought of Emai Shan, her mother Buwei and Nin. How pleasant it would be to return to the tranquility of the Buddhist monastery and the village at the base of the sacred mountain. To be engulfed by the cool misty-puffs that concealed the bones of her mother somewhere below a high cliff. Her concentration was interrupted by loud rumbling outside the hall.

The highway connecting Hangzhou with Fujian Province and southern coastal towns ran parallel to the Trade Center access road, less than a quarter-mile away. Sun-fueled strobes of reflected light flashed off the high windshields of the PLA troop-carriers roaring by. Lili stood outside the exhibit hall, transfixed by the seemingly endless queue of military vehicles. The ground vibrated angrily as the shoosh....shoosh of open trucks packed with armed soldiers sped along the main highway toward the port cities of Fuzhou and Xianmen.

The sight of loaded rifles dampened Lili's pride in the diversity of the Chinese people. She remembered AJ's communique mentioning a "potential island conflict." It occurred to her that the information the embassy intercepted in Beijing may be related to the troop movement she was witnessing.

Escape Route from Hangzhou

Matsu Island was located twenty-five miles outside Mawei Harbor on the Fuzhou coastline; Quemoy Island overlooked Xianmen from a few miles east. Both islands were in the path of the PLA troop caravan; and both were sovereign territories of Taiwan---close enough to the mainland to tantalize and torment the Beijing Communist hawks who resented Taiwan's democratic independence and bustling economy.

Their escape route followed the same path. They were to mingle with the opera group traveling on train Number Seven to their next performance in the provincial capital of Fuzhou. Justin was to apply the hair-dye and brown contacts before boarding bus Number Eleven to the Fuzhou harbor fish market. The final leg involved separate taxis to the private-jet terminal at Fuzhou Municipal Airport. Someone holding a card with the words *Herr Fuller and Ms.Weituo* would meet them and provide tickets and forged Return Permits for the private flight from Fuzhou to Macau. Their last moments together would be in the skies above Fujian and Guangdong Provinces.

Lili's heart tightened at the premature feeling of loss. She dreaded the anticipated separation from Herr Fuller, her comrade in arms; and being cut off from contact with AJ. Dutifully, she followed instructions and removed the phone battery; then she dropped the only means of communicating with the Embassy down a drainage grid. Once they arrived in Macau, Justin and the information he carried would surely be whisked back to Washington. She desperately hoped to see AJ again.

(AUGUST 20, 2008) AM
BOXMART HEADQUARTERS, BOSTON

"I don't care what it takes," Kurancy attacked the mouthpiece, "Stop those heathens before they disrupt the back-to-school sales promotions."

Cashman never questioned Jake's orders. But, overreaction to the Indian picketing problem could cause negative publicity they didn't need. Several reporters from local Iowa and Nebraska newspapers and TV stations had camped at the targeted BM stores. "The attorneys claim we can't legally prevent the pesky Winnebagos from demonstrating ...as long as they remain off our property and carry political party signs."

"What bullshit...the *Make Do Party*!" Kurancy fumed. "What the hell is that, Cashman? It's too fucking close to Christmas to put up with this crap. We're about to experience the greatest winter-holiday sales increase in retailing history, and you can't find a way to keep a few feather-heads from souring our name?"

"I'll see what I can do," Cashman answered meekly. "At least all the stores and distribution centers are stocked to the ceilings. I hope the 3P-BIO projections are accurate."

Kurancy took a deep breath and gingerly lowered the receiver. "*Small shit...it's always small shit at the last moment.*"

Cashman leaned over the keypad in his office and accessed the worldwide web via a high-speed internet connection, which instantly linked his desktop computer to an obscure e-mail address used only for special purposes. A few minutes later, Blackstone's site received an urgent message requesting the services of a certain '*contract-employee*' for an emergency assignment in the Midwest.

The virus outbreak was going perfectly. The contaminated Shanghai boxes had been found, as planned, and the field-browning was spreading beyond

General Ye's estimates. Department of Health officials were sure to trace the source of contamination to the Shanghai factory supplying BoxMart's largest competitors with shipping cartons. There was no reason to fear that the virus outbreak could be linked to Chinese-made water filters imported by BoxMart. All BM cartons were produced at a modern factory in Shenzen.

(August, 20,21)
Southeast China

Justin and Lili boarded the overnight Number Seven in separate, adjoining sleepers and settled in among the giddy opera performers, mostly in their twenties. The players were expressing delight at the experience of performing in different areas of the country by gulping shots of imported scotch purchased at a duty-free shop in the Shanghai RR station.

Justin's face remained painted white until the train was a few hours south of Hangzhou. Most of the opera performers were tipsy from celebrating a standing ovation at the Hangzhou Arts Center, and none took notice of the tall brown-haired, white-faced young actor with the deep blue eyes enter the toilet; or the blond, brown-eyed, middle-aged man with skin the natural hue of a caucasian German...exit the same toilet compartment.

Herr Fuller explained the painted face in broken German to a suspicious ticket agent moving through the car to collect stubs and randomly check travel papers. The conductor was a Communist Party member. He didn't understand a word of German; but Herr Fuller's attempt at English was clear enough to communicate his excitement with the opera performance, and how he'd wished to experience the same Chinese happiness. The conductor's face distorted. Lili should have informed him that the opera was a tragedy.

Exhaustion finally took its toll. Justin's first and only dream in China was catalyzed by the two shots of scotch he'd cordially accepted from his exuberant travel companions. He envisioned Lynne, Joanna, her two daughters and Cosimo seated around Cosimo's favorite table at Elim Park. The 'marogespel' girls were standing around, and everyone was listening to Lynne describe her visit to Geneva; and the electrical malfunction of the hair dryer which caused her hands to be bandaged. Joanna was the only person frowning, as she gazed in envy at Justin's attractive new friend...listening to her spell-binding tale. *I was once that pretty....and young...and thin....and....*

"Mom! Why aren't you smiling? That's the funniest European story I ever heard. Lynne....tell it again, please? Please?"

Lili shook his shoulder and didn't care who noticed. She'd had it with traveling alone. They were only ten miles north of the Fuzhou railroad station.

"Herr Fuller," she whispered, to prevent waking the young performers curled up like newborn kittens on the thinly-cushioned straight-back seats. "May I interrupt your sleep, Mr. Fuller? We arrive in Fuzhou in fifteen minutes."

Justin emerged from a hazy vision of the two women he cared most about...the young one, laughing...the other, closer to his age, looking down with a wrinkled brow at her jaunty, slightly-sagging breasts. Justin gazed up into the warm dark eyes of the girlish terminator now third on his list.

He snapped awake and instinctively spanned the surroundings. Other people on the train were paying attention to their own needs. "We're almost there?"

"You've been asleep for hours. I watched you through the glass door. You must snore loudly, because I saw several people move away when you nodded off."

"I do not," he said fervently, although he wasn't sure...he'd never heard himself sleeping.

"I think it's safe for us to leave the station together," Lili yawned. "AJ was probably being overly cautious. I don't think anyone noticed us; or could possibly be anticipating our arrival...." She suddenly froze, then said loudly, "Herr Fuller." Lili sensed the ticket agent standing over them, holding out his hand.

Number Eleven bus headed east from the railroad station, directly into the sunrise and lower reaches of the Minjiang River. The Manwei harbor fish market was stirring with trawlers off-loading night catches from the abundant schools in Fujian's East China Sea netting shoals. When the bus arrived at the dock, Justin peered from his seat in the rear of the vehicle and noticed Lili rise from a seat behind the driver. He stepped out through the rear folding passenger-doors and walked calmly toward the line of taxis parked alongside the pier.

He hailed the first in line. "Fuzhou Airport?" The young male Asian driver gave no indication that he understood English. Justin winged his arms wide and tilted them in a wind-blown landing maneuver to overcome the driver's blank stare. "FooJoe...FooJoe. Fly?" The stone-faced Han flicked away his cigarette and wagged his head. Justin jumped into the back seat and peered over. He spotted the driver's photo identification in a sealed plastic holder clipped to the dashboard. *Joseph Robert Yang, Multi-lingual license."*

"Hop in, buddy." Joseph dropped the deadpan, laughing like hell. "Works every time. I'm surprised you didn't say, 'Hundred dollars...get me there on time,' and tap your watch like a woodpecker."

The cabby laughed again. "Outrageous. That's the worst impression I've ever seen. Are you American? In a hurry, as usual? Or can I show you around town?"

"In a hurry," Gatt answered, peeved but relieved. "Drop me at the private-jet terminal building."

He waited a half-hour before Lili arrived, and another twenty minutes before the green felt-pen sign wandered slowly into the terminal, attached to the raised hands of a stocky uniformed chauffeur wearing enormous dark sunglasses which covered most of his face.

His name tag was also in green ink: *Bodiless Lacquerware Company.* Herr Fuller moved rapidly to join Ms. Weituo and the courier, who handed them a five-language business card and bowed awkwardly.

Gabriel Oresco then led them to a set of metal stairs on the runway side of the building which descended to the airstrip tarmac. Gatt noticed the sleek white private jet parked alongside the building. Turbo-jet fan-blades whined at idle as loud as a supersonic military fighter readying for an intercept. The "BLC" logo was painted on the double-tails and the aircraft was pointed against the prevailing wind, in the direction of the nearest runway. An unusual droop in the variable-geometry wings suggested the private jet was built more for speed than comfort or fuel efficiency. Justin never saw such large engines under the wings of a small civilian aircraft.

"We need to get out of here as quickly as possible," Oresco whispered. He glanced over his shoulder in the direction of the entrance to the terminal and said, "I've been followed, as usual, but I think I lost them in the parking lot. Do you have the information from Meng-ji, Dongzi and Mr Hangzhou?"

Justin's one-degree nod was imperceptible to anyone more than ten feet away.

"What about you and Lili? Any problems?"

"Not that we know of. Just an inquisitive ticket-clerk on the train. He marked down the number of my false Return Permit to Macau."

"Oh, shit," Oresco spat. "You *do know* that half the PLA security forces in eastern China are after you and Lili...with orders to shoot first, if necessary?"

Lili gripped Justin's arm with both hands and replied in a mournful tone, "I am to blame."

"You saved my life."

The former USAF fighter pilot at the controls had slipped the flight controller twenty-thousand yuan for take-off priority on the small private runway which angled across the larger commercial-jet departure and landing lanes. As soon as the three passengers were strapped in, the retired F-15 Eagle commander shouted above the roaring idle of the down-sized F119-PW-100 military-grade turbofan Pratt and Whitney engines, originally developed for the F-22 Raptor advanced tactical fighter. "Hold onto any loose body-parts. This bird's about to escalate."

Sixty-three minutes later the jet-craft bounced at 120 knots onto the landing strip of the Macau Municipal Airport in the Special Administrative Region of the People's Republic of China. The pilot taxied the CIA-commissioned *supercruise-capable* light civilian aircraft, built by the Boeing Business Jet Division, into a leased private hangar. The flight was smooth and had demonstrated the 'relaxed stability' characteristic of modern fighters, although there were few cabin amenities and no electric coffee pot to augment the advanced avionics and solid-state AESA fixed-array radar on board.

The long rectangular strip of land located two causeways east of Taipa Island was home to the Macau International Airport, servicing the Macau area---which included a small peninsula knuckled off the southern edge of China, as well as the two connected islands of Taipa and Coloane. Descending aircraft approaching the landing strip on a clear day had a full view of Macau, which bristled with casino hotels, horse and dog racetracks, European-style buildings and clean beaches. The Fisherman's Wharf Complex was clearly visible from a few thousand meters…dotted with restaurants, bars, shops and gaming establishments which welcomed tourists to the only legal gambling in China. The magnificent Lin Fung Temple on the peninsula contrasted with the artificial volcano and roller-coaster attractions built near the Macau ferry terminal.

Macau was the first European settlement in the Far East, colonized in the 1600s by the Portuguese. The area offered a remarkable mix of cultures… despite being governed under China's *'one country, two systems'* formula for the next fifty years. The primary language was Cantonese, but English, Portuguese and Mandarin were also common.

The Macau International Airport was connected to the mainland by two taxiways leading to the middle-island of Taipa, which in turn was linked by bridge to the Macau peninsula in the north, and to Coloane Island by a causeway to the south. Balzerini had issued orders to rush Lili from Taipa to the temporary safety of the U.S. Consulate in Hong Kong. The Americans were to be flown out of China as soon as the BLC business jet was fully refueled. Their first touch-down would be at a U.S. naval base in the Indian Ocean…before returning to the States.

The super-charged aircraft rumbled to a stop in the shadows under the Quonset roof of the private hangar, as the occupants unsnapped restraining belts. They stepped out from the fuselage as soon as the retractable aluminum steps hit the concrete. Lili turned to Justin hesitantly, then slid into his arms for a long embrace; acknowledging their expected parting.

"Be safe, Mr. Fuller. I shall not forget you." A few tears cascaded to Justin's hands as he cupped the angelic face and delicately brushed aside the damp affection with a fingertip."I can never forget you, Lili. Or how you saved my life. I hope we meet again."

The passenger door of a white 2005 Toyota Camry opened a few yards away and a thin, dark-haired man in his early thirties stepped out. He was dressed in orange coveralls stained with red hydraulic oil and aircraft grease. His purposely-smudged face was not immediately recognizable. Here to provide maintenance services, the man called out, "Get ready to defend yourself, Nin."Lili recognized the voice. She flew across the hangar and folded her pliable body around A.J. in a Juko-kai love wrap.

Railraod Security Agency, Fuzhou

The railroad ticket agent answered the same question for the third time: "Yes, Comrade Assistant Chief---the blond man had *blue* eyes that became *brown* after he cleaned the white paint from his face. He acted strangely in the presence of the opera players and did not seem to fit in with their rowdy behavior."

"And he was not traveling alone?"

"No, Comrade. He was accompanied by a young Chinese woman who fits the description of the deranged Shanghai tour guide."

"And you were aware that the serial number of Mr. Fuller's Macau Return Permit does not exist?"

"Not at the time, Assistant Chief."

"It must be them!"the security officer concluded with a quiver. "We must inform the state authorities immediately."

Refueling took only fifteen minutes but the runway was backed-up with a half-dozen private jets returning high-stakes gamblers to Singapore, Taiwan, Malaysia and Indonesia. The fifty-five year old CIA pilot, 'Cloud' Nelson, was a wiry, high-strung USAF air-jockey with five-thousand flight hours to his credit. He appeared giddy to Oresco as he checked gauges and tested his memory by reciting the specifications of the remarkable business jet under his command. The tower soon announced that the 'BLC Eagle/Ape' twin jet was now fourth in line for departure clearance.

"She can sustain supercruise speed, without kicking in the afterburner," he exulted to the sincerely interested passengers a few feet from the open cockpit. "That's about Mach 1.32 for a sustained period of ....oops; that's a classified number."

Oresco was incredulous. "Afterburner? For what purpose?"

'Cloud' partially answered the question. "The infrared signature can be reduced by seventy-five percent. Vectoring nozzles also give her superb maneuverability---about plus or minus twenty-degrees on the pitch axis of her reconfigured F-15 airframe. It's a shame we aren't authorized to carry offensive weapons. Her defensive tools are state-of-the-art, and I'd take on any Mig 29 or third-generation Mirage in existence." Gatt wasn't sure if the pilot's crooked smile signaled confidence or horn blowing. He was less certain when Cloud smirked, "I'm at the controls because I commanded F-15 Eagles."

The wonders of CIA toys, thought Oresco, as he returned the Meng-Ji, Dongzi and Mr Hangzhou documents to Justin. "My independent investigation confirms that some smaller Provincial branches of the Central Bank of Shanghai and the Bank of Commerce and Industry are short on U.S. dollar denominations. The Bank of China is not replacing its overnight withdrawals from these institutions---a highly unusual occurrence since the BOC has the largest dollar holdings outside the U.S."

"Gabriel, these documents, combined, paint a very weird picture," Justin remarked bluntly. "It's like there are multiple conspiracies against the U.S. economy."

"Or, one big, unthinkable alliance between some Chinese government officials, BoxMart managers, foreign and domestic banks and Washington insiders. The question is---*why?* I can't imagine why anyone depending so much on a healthy American consumer market would precipitate such drastic actions to upset the American economy."

Justin recalled his recent experience with business failure. "If someone wanted to prevent the next Administration from establishing limits on Chinese imports...as Martin Merrand is threatening...they might want to kill off as much manufacturing competition as possible. But I don't understand why they'd suddenly dump dollars or smuggle a lethal organism into the country. That's a terrorist act."

Oresco tapped Justin's files. "You have documents from Dr. Dongzi that prove an agricultural pathogen was deliberately shipped to Texas in mislabeled packaging. Also, Professor Meng-Ji's letter to Syzmansky at Yale asking him to investigate the humongous and unusual transfers of dollars out of Chinese mainland banks. The money conversions may be related to President Mu Jianting's political problems. He's teetering on the edge of dismissal from the Politboro. Mu's enemies may be using the events to justify replacing him as head of the government."

"By whom?" Gatt questioned Oresco's political-conflict theory.

Oresco leaned toward the open cockpit. 'Cloud' Nelson was whispering instructions to himself. He watched as the agitated pilot strapped himself in and began adjusting instruments and checking avionics gauges.

"A good question, Justin. The transactions your friend Lynne uncovered in Europe may only represent a conduit of change in China's monetary policy. Top leaders in Beijing must be aware of what's happening...if not directly responsible. Mr. Hangzhou's list of Chinese characters must be the answer to "who?"

The pilot pressed his miniature ear-phone in deeper and drooped his head. "Speak louder, AJ." Five seconds later he raised his head abruptly and squinted toward the terminal building.

"Yes, I see them." Police vans screeched to a halt in front of the terminal entrance. The wings lifted slightly as Cloud automatically revved the fan-blades for take-off.

"The strongman on the Communist Party's Standing Committee...which essentially rules the country... is Vice-Premier Yong Ihasa," continued Oresco. "He's also the Minister of both State Security and Monetary Regulation, and is rumored to be a descendent of a middle-ages Ming emperor. Some claim he also heads an Asian secret society that once supported the Ming dynasty. He's obsessed with power."

Gatt noted the pilot's agitated expression as he glanced forward from the cockpit to the aircraft idling in front. "There's also the multiple intelligence intercepts. According to Balzerini and AJ, the terms *financial* and *biological events* were prominent in the captured transmissions.

"So was mention of solving the *Merrand problem*," reminded Oresco.

Wen Ma steadied his binoculars on the white business jet exhausting intermittent gusts of blue-grey fumes at the edge of the runway. The BLC company aircraft was next in line behind a Wal-Mart Learjet 31 carrying executives to the next store opening. Wen was standing at a second-story terminal window looking down at the runway and the new China Southern Boeing 7E7 Dreamliner about to deliver him and three computer experts non-stop to Boston.

The military software experts from the Han Center for High Performance Computing supervised the programming and operation of China's 19 supercomputers. They were traveling to the BoxMart computer center to test-ride Chinese military-intelligence software on the 3P-BIO supercomputer Li Chin had described.

"We shall soon know if Gatt and the tour guide are hiding on that jet transport," he said to the lead software engineer. "General Ye has given orders to deal with them harshly."

The sky over AJ's parked Toyota darkened as the winds from a new weather front blanketed the airport with fast-moving clouds. He handed Lili the binoculars and said with rising exasperation, "They're not going to make it. The control tower is delaying all outgoing flights until the maverick crosswinds from the Indian Ocean typhoon pass by. Security police must have tracked down Oresco. Perhaps they just want to question him."

Commander Nelson was not known for excessive patience. "What the fuck's going on, AJ?" he barked into the mouthpiece. "Those are elite storm guards in the vans. The sirens and roof-lights may be turned off, but the vans are still coasting in our direction."

A sudden wind-gust from the northwest rocked the aircraft. "Fuck it," he shouted. "We're out of here."

Oresco and Gatt heard him and didn't need verbal prodding to fasten their restraining belts. The approaching police trucks increased speed as Cloud inched the BLC aircraft forward and swung around the Learjet... barely scraping wing-tips and avoiding the muddy drop-off at the edge of the blacktop.

Colonel Wen noticed the maneuver from his elevated view. "Stop them," he yelled into the radio-phone linking him with the attack commander in the front van. "Shoot the tires out. Don't allow that spy to get away."

CHAPTER 56

(August 21, 2008) pm
Sioux City, Iowa

Nonnie and two dozen Ho-Chunks formed a line across the parking lot entrance of BM store number 3044 on the outskirts of Sioux City, carrying "Make Do Party" signs and authentic calendar sticks. The store manager was standing next to Sheriff Whiley inside the lot, watching to make sure the line parted when customers tried to enter. A few young braves pointed threatening fingers at hurried drivers who failed to slow as they approached the parking lot entrance, nearly running them down.

The Sheriff waved at the two deputies stationed outside the entrance. Nonnie's group had followed the letter of the law for more than four hours by maintaining peaceful movement in the picket lines. Whiley saw no reason for law enforcement officers to remain. TV camera crews had departed after taping interviews with Chief Whiteknee and council elder Dancing Eyes Adams for the evening news. Only the store manager seemed concerned about the possibility of a violent confrontation.

Cashman had ordered him to remain at the picket line until a large black woman carrying a nylon-reinforced leather shoulder-bag arrived at the entrance. "Anticipate an argument," Cashman informed him evenly. "Call me when it's over."

The *Chameleon* watched from a donut shop across the street as the Sheriff and his deputies pulled away from the parking lot entrance. She lifted her shoulder bag from the floor with two hands and swung it over her shoulder with the grace of a weightlifter performing fifty-pound bicep-curls.

Dressed in a black cotton pull-over, baggy dungarees, and black running shoes, the husky assassin was stooped over...her spine distorted by leather bindings under the clothes, which gave her the appearance of a post-menopausal sufferer of osteoporosis or collapsed vertebrae. Her face was coated with dark make-up and pocked with false age-spots and glue-on warts. Her black curly wig was dusted with dirt and sticky with finger-twists of petroleum jelly. Physically, she was a pathetic sight.

The deformed hag meandered across the street and stopped directly in front of a weary tribes-woman who'd been hoisting a *'Don't Shop Here, BoxMart Stole Our Jobs'* sign for several hours. The demonstrator moved aside to allow the elderly black lady to pass, but the old woman moved in her direction and croaked in a southern accent loud enough for Nonnie to hear, "Get out of my way, sister, or I'll smash in your tits."

The Indian woman stepped back surprised, and commented gruffly, "Okay, sour puss. Go on in. You probably need some new unsoiled underwear, anyhow."

The *Chameleon* noticed Chief Whiteknee rush over to calm the disturbance, as she'd anticipated. As soon as Nonnie arrived at the picketer's side, the assassin edged in her direction and grumbled loudly, "How dare you insult a sick person?"

Suddenly the leaden shoulder-bag looped up from the disfigured woman's side in a powerful two-armed swipe, missing the sign-holder and smashing against the side of Nonnie's head in a repulsive thump. Nonnie dropped to her knees…holding the side of her head in disbelief. A blood-balloon mushroomed from her temple and burst through the sharp incision above her left ear. Blood dripped over her fingers as she clawed at the pain and collapsed backward onto the pavement.

The disfigured black woman stomped arrogantly toward the store entrance, then disappeared inside. Bystanders shrieked in horror and rushed to Nonnie's aid.

Arcola Manditta slipped into the vacated lady's rest room, locked the door from inside and tore off the wig, outer clothing and leather body-straps. Her natural brunette hair dropped low as she wiped away the dark facial coating with toilet paper and plucked off the false spots. She unfolded a heavy-duty plastic leaf-bag and dropped in the clothes, leather belts and shoulder bag, which gloved a softball-size metal ball filled with lead buckshot. Half-inch spikes protruded from the surface of the ball like a Roman gladiator's ball-stick-and-chain weapon. She jammed them into the half-empty flip-top trash receptacle the store manager had remembered to place there.

The ambulance and a local TV-station camera crew arrived in the parking lot entrance at the same time a few minutes later.

(August, 21)
Flight from Macau to Diego Garcia

A civilian jet aircraft was not supposed to discharge *misch metal* phosphoric diversionary flack…laying blankets of white-hot particles capable of igniting flammable gases in its take-off contrail.

The driver of the first police van hammered the brake-pedal to avoid the 2000 degree Fahrenheit incendiary cloud which suddenly appeared behind the small aircraft fish-tailing onto the runway. The van skidded sideways as tiny, smoking para-magnetic, trivalent rare-earth metal particles entombed the vehicle. The airborne super-heated flack wormed magnetically into the exhaust pipe and exploded the muffler and catalytic converter. The drivers of the second and third vans smashed headlong into the first van, creating a sea of sparks and deadly flames as the private aircraft accelerated down the runway and lifted violently in nearly-vertical ascent.

Wen Ma watched in dismay as the small craft shot into the overcast sky then performed an Immelmann half-loop, half-roll maneuver and spit afterburner flame from its turbojet exhaust. 'Cloud' Nelson ignored the moist air turbulence and held the throttles full-forward as they banked south toward Singapore, slapping into a wind-front advancing from the typhoon in the Indian Ocean.

"That's no ordinary civilian aircraft," Wen's aid interjected. The Colonel turned furiously, "Get General Ye on the phone, immediately. He can authorize a missile intercept."

Justin and Oresco drifted in and out of nausea, dizziness, cold sweat and intense cranial pain under the conflicting dynamics of G-forces and restraining belts. The expert aviator, who'd been approved for the astronaut program, but hadn't left earth or sailed at fourteen to twenty-five thousand miles per hour because of a cutback in NASA's flight schedule, was intent on approaching the lost experience as close as possible.

Nelson's eyes bulged as he howled joyfully into the cabin, "Diego Garcia here we come." The passengers prayed they weren't headed for a more permanent destination much farther south.

The escape route via the South China Sea began over the Helen and St. Esprit Shoals east of Hainan Island, and continued 900 miles southwest to Singapore; then banked northwest and channeled over the Strait of Malacca to the Bay of Bengal and the Great Channel above Banda Aceh on the northern tip of Sumatra. From there, the flight redirected forty-five degrees southwest on a straight route to the "forward" U.S. Naval Base at Diego Garcia in the British territory of Chagos Archipelago, also called the Oil Islands.

General Ye was briefing the PLA ground commanders in charge of troop battalions dispatched to the port cities of Fuzhou and Xiamen in Fujian

Province when the emergency call was taken. Colonel Wen swiftly explained the dramatic escape of the civilian aircraft carrying Justin Gatt and possibly others. The General listened without comment, then put Wen on hold while he dismissed the PLA assembly.

"What distance can you track them using coastal radar?"

"At least to Singapore, if they remain on the southern course. We expect them to follow the South China Sea route to the Indian Ocean via the Strait of Malacca. My guess is: they will attempt to land at the American forward naval base south of the Chagos Archipelago. That would coincide with the estimated range of the fully-fueled craft, although the pilot wasted fuel showing off his afterburner at take off."

"Afterburner? What the hell kind of private jet is that?"

"One with sophisticated diversionary defenses," Wen answered morosely. "The Bodiless Lacquerware Company must be a CIA front, similar to our California businesses."

General Ye couldn't allow Gatt to deliver the biological and pathological reports from Dr. Dongzi to U.S. authorities. There might even be evidence that vials of the corn virus were smuggled into the country from the Chinese bio-weapons lab, rather than being transported innocently on the cardboard surfaces of export packaging.

"Try to avoid an international incident, Colonel Wen; but they must be stopped." He barked into the receiver, "What do you suggest?"

Wen replied without hesitation, "They could be shot down with a SAM missile over international waters. We have Jiangwei-II class frigates equipped with medium range all-weather HQ-10 SAMs patrolling the Strait of Malacca at the mouth of the Sea of Bengal. If they follow the anticipated flight path, the aircraft will be exposed over open-ocean after bearing southwest from Banda Aceh toward Diego Garcia."

General Ye considered the recommendation. Colonel Wen was developing into a capable military strategist.

"The missiles have extended range and are capable of line-of-sight point defense," Wen continued, "or can be honed in with E/F-band Doppler search-radar. I don't expect that fucking CIA gnat to display severe electronic jamming, but if it does…the Hong Qi-10s can be guided by radio commands from an electro-optical director on the Jiangwe-II."

The BLC aircraft leveled off at 35,000 feet. Nelson rotated the fans at sub-sonic speed to conserve fuel and settle the passengers for what would likely be their first and last air-combat experience. Hopefully-- not in a bad way.

"I heard you were a crazy pilot, Nelson, but I didn't know you trained at rodeos." Oresco finally exhaled and began searching for the primitive potty on board.

"Just minor turbulence, Mr. Oresco. How are *you* doing, Mr. Gatt?"

Justin swallowed hard to prevent stomach-acid from whirlpooling up to his nostrils.

"I'll be okay, I guess." He added meekly, "as long as Gabriel doesn't piss on me." The rear passenger area was cramped, and he leaned away from Oresco as the reporter began plunk—plunking into the receptacle with his eyes closed and mouth open.

"We could be in for some rough riding," Cloud informed them enthusiastically. "I don't expect an air-intercept from the PLA Air Force, but the Chinese have blanketed two thousand radial miles of Southeast Asia with land and sea-based missile defense units. Any one of a hundred land or sea surface locations along the route to Diego Garcia could burp a SAM. For now, we'll just coast at 600 knots, and hope."

Oresco completed his pleasurable experience and said to Nelson, "I hear you were scrubbed from the astronaut program for conducting unscheduled experiments in weightless animal-husbandry with a paying female customer."

"My secret is out, damn it. Now I'll have to explain why floating copulation feels almost as good as an overdue piss."

The carbon-fiber composite used for the fuselage and wings of the BLC Eagle/Ape was super-strong and super-lightweight---the same material used for the Boeing wide-body 787 jet. When they approached the southern tip of Singapore, Cloud rolled the plane easily into a steep northwest turn and flicked off autopilot. "I'm taking this crop-duster down to commercial approach altitude. We're less likely to be targeted. I have a hunch the fun will begin when we emerge from the air-channel between Sumatra and the Malay Peninsula." Nelson paused to check the drift meter, inclinometer, slip and yaw indicators, and the computational fluid dynamics controlling the vectoring nozzles.

"We're about to enter burble-land," he shouted. "So strap in tightly and don't worry too much about the irregular air-flow around the plane. It's common when you fly into a typhoon."

The captain of Jiangwei Frigate 421 ordered the vessel to reverse direction 180 degrees and head back into the typhoon's wake. His orders were clear: maintain cruising speed west of the Nicobar Islands, about ninety-miles south of the eye, and wait for the small business jet to emerge from the juxtaposition of the Strait of Malacca and the Andaman Sea. Once it reached international waters in the Indian Ocean…shoot it down.

"Just a heads-up guys---when you see open ocean, brace for a quick acceleration. This bird's going to leap into *supercruise*, about Mach 1.3. Most Chinese missiles rocket up at Mach 2, so we can't outrun one if it shows on my warning system; but we may be able to out-maneuver older heat-seeking missiles like the HQ-7s or PL-9s still installed on the early 1990s destroyers and frigates. If I were a Chinese missile commander, I wouldn't waste a modern weapon on a civilian aircraft. At supercruise, we can fly supersonic *without* using the afterburner; which reduces our infra-red signature by 75 percent. We'll remain radio-silent until we approach the Chagos Archipelago."

Justin thought to himself, *If I wanted this kind of excitement, I'd be on a roller-coaster with Joanna and the screaming twins. Or leaping off the Sears Tower with a beach-towel over my head.*

"J-Frig 421, this is Banda Aceh Scout, do you hear...J-Frig 421, come in"

"Loud and clear, BAS. This is COM. Seas are over my bow. Any sign of the target?"

"Affirmed. Affirmed...J-Frig. GPS location indicates target approaching your radar two minutes out. Do you copy?"

"Copy affirmed, BAS. Copy affirmed. Target will be splashed. Repeat... target will be splashed. Over and out."

The tiny yellow blip that appeared on the green radar screen in the centership weapons-control room was moving faster than expected. "They said it was a civilian business-jet carrying stolen state secrets. I know of no such plane that can reach Mach one-point-three. Perhaps the weather is distorting our instruments."

"Ready weapon for firing sequence. Two minutes to neutral waters. Repeat...two minutes to firing."

Cloud Nelson tensed as swirling winds gusted to 40 knots and challenged his ability to maintain lateral stability. "I'm taking her up," he shouted calmly. "Hold onto your hats. The typhoon's a class five."

"Four, three, two, one....ignition."

"Holy shit, its a VLS," Nelson cried out mercurially. "That mother has a vertical launch system. The profile ID recognizes an advanced HQ-10. We'll have thirty-seconds less time than normal to elude."

He decided to vector northwest, directly into the tail of the typhoon. He could visualize the position of the eye moving northeast at about thirty-five miles per hour. Nelson watched the weapons-radar warning light change from green to bright red. He made an instant decision.

"Okay, mother fuckers, come and find us if you dare."

The newspaper reporter heard the remarks and sensed the sudden nose-dive. He blurted out maniacally, "Where are you taking us?" The blood rushed to his head, and thankfully, he blacked out.

Cloud unglued his eyes from the controls for a split second and smiled back into the cabin. Justin heard him shout, "Eye-diving, my friends. We're going eye-diving." Then under his breath, "Otherwise our asses are flamed out." Justin was too frightened to relinquish consciousness.

The next few minutes bettered all the space-flight thrills Cloud ever missed.

The HQ-10 all-weather missile shot up from the frigate at Mach 1.5, acquired the target's bearing and heat profile, and followed it toward the eye of the typhoon at maximum speed of Mach 2.3. At this rate, the IR-targeted missile would destroy the aircraft about a mile from the center of the typhoon.

"He's insane,"the firing master hissed, as the weapons-control staff tracking both the target and the missile, anticipated impact at less than four-hundred meters above the vortex of the eye.

Cloud watched the threat-indicator screen as the Chinese missile ate distance. The CIA plane's weapons-profile data bank was as comprehensive as that on the F-22 advanced fighter. The Hong Qi-10 was gyro-guided and armed with a proximity-fused HE-FRAG warhead. Strong and erratic magnetic-fields created by typhoon-generated lightning just might interfere with its guidance system. If only the BLC could get close enough to the electrical violence without breaking up. He doubted whether the military had tested the strength of his craft's composite lap-joints by dropping a fighter into the thunder-and-lightning snake-fest of a class-five typhoon. It was their only chance to shake off the missile.

CHAPTER 57

(August 21)
Geneva

Johanas "Papa" Nicorezzi saw it coming. Seventy-five billion U.S. dollars floated like an algae overgrowth on Lake Geneva. The Frenchman from Creditte Bank de Savoy had pulled off the most dramatic one-day private currency swap in European history.

"The Bank of England's rate-setting committee is threatening to cut London interbank rates to prop up the pound sterling, if the dollar drops more than an additional 25 basis points," Nicorezzi announced to Alfred Leonhard, the sixty-year-old Swiss Minister of Private Banking he'd known for twenty-seven years.

"We'll have to follow suit," the Minister replied indignantly. Swiss banking officials weren't accustomed to being forced into defensive financial transactions. "The Swiss franc is holding steady, but every other European currency is strengthening dangerously against the U.S. dollar. That idiotic Frenchman Phillipe Cusson is playing a dangerous game with his depositors' cash. The Swiss government may be forced to follow China's lead and sell the bulk of its American currency reserves."

Nicorezzi did not mention Lynne Hurricane's research, which uncovered the unusual financial links between BoxMart, the Washington think-tank FFF, Residents Bank of N.A---the American subsidiary controlled by Franco-Medici Trust, and ultimately by Cusson---and branches of the Central Bank of China. Or his suspicion that BoxMart and Beijing banking officials had transferred large dollar deposits to Lyons and Geneva in preparation for Cusson's ensuing currency trades. The initial denomination swaps in Stressa had not been extraordinarily large, considering the 1.9 $ trillion per day global exchange market.

"What motivation could prompt Beijing to abruptly cash in China's nearly trillion dollars in trade reserves?" The Minister's question lingered in his private office overlooking the Rhone River in the canton's financial district. "And now, Johanas, you're telling me there may exist a conspiracy to undercut the U.S. economy?"

"We go back many years, Alfred. You know I never cry wolf. But I'm not in a position to initiate an investigation...as you are."

"And you truly believe the Chinese are staging something devious."

"Yes. But I think it involves more than dumping dollar reserves on the European and Asian currency markets. A trader friend of mine at Goldman Sachs, who deals with big hedge-fund currency speculators, claims he doesn't know whether to recommend *buy* or *sell* orders for American currency. He claims that undervalued Asian currencies are the most glaring anomaly in world capital markets. This could be the beginning of a correction."

The Minister retorted tersely, "Or, perhaps some Chinese leaders are beginning to take hoarding-profits? I wouldn't put it past several of the corrupt Chinese bankers I know."

"Then how do you explain, Albert, why Beijing just announced the government will allow the yuan to float prior to the Stressa Accords in October? Do they know something the rest of us are lacking?"

Nicorezzi pointed to his friend's credenza. "Do you still offer cognac to honored guests?"

The banking minister poured three inches of Hennessy Privilege V.S.O.P. into two leaded-crystal highball glasses and handed one to Johanas. "Here, my friend. We need clear minds to think this situation through. Unlike the American Administration, I don't believe their trade representative, Butler Humphreys, won a battle of nerves with the Chinese. If I were John Paul Tangus, I'd be worried that technical levels could trigger a global cascade of directionless dollar sell-offs. JP Morgan Chase just announced an offering of subordinated Tier-Two 10-year Samurai bonds in Japan's domestic market, hoping to offset paper losses in Japan's dollar holdings."

Nicorezzi was a seasoned Swiss bank examiner who'd seen it all during his thirty-year career as banker and bank examiner. He breathed in the savory aperitif volatiles and gulped down the full glass. He said obstinately, "If the Federal Reserve Chairman convinces the U.S. Treasury Secretary to prop up the dollar with gold or new bond issues, the American economy is in big trouble. Americans don't save enough to finance their deficit."

Leonhard's intercom buzzed and his personal secretary said in a toneless adenoidal slur, "The president of Zurich Bank is on your personal line, sir."

Nicorezzi motioned an offer to leave the room as a courtesy gesture. Leonhard waved him to remain seated. "Good day, Franz. How can I be of assistance?"

Nicorezzi watched intently as his friend listened without responding for the next two minutes. Finally Leonhard replied in a stilted tone, "Tangus must be roasting mad to call a special session of the Fed Open Market Committee. And you've confirmed that the money transferred to CBdeS. in Lyons, and Franco-Medici in Geneva, is 'clean' money?" He listened for another minute. "I see---transferred directly into numbered accounts? Can you document it?...I see. So the Bank of China has reversed direction, and is now bidding up its own currency?"

Nicorezzi thought to himself---*'dirty' money is not as sensitive to international currency fluctuations as 'clean' money.*

"I wouldn't worry about Swiss interest rates," the Minister suggested to the Zurich banker. "The undervalued yuan doesn't have much impact on Swiss currency. Even in America, the massive imports from China account for only two-percent of the economy."

"The yuan is a hot commodity, Leonhard. Demand is so high that Yew Bai Tsin, the BOC Governor, has announced plans to print new five-hundred-yuan bills to accommodate troubled domestic banks."

Nicorezzi shook his head in amazement. The financial reports he received daily noted that Lehman Brothers Holdings, Sompo Japan Asset Management and Morgan Stanley's fixed-income gurus had all shorted the dollar. *So much for national patriotism and support from American and Japanese financial institutions.*

"U.S. interest rates are about to skyrocket," Leonhard exclaimed on the phone. "The Treasury Department will have difficulty selling long-term bonds. Jesus!...if Tangus makes one wrong move the entire financial infrastructure of America could tailspin."

"And take Europe with it," the Swiss Minister bellowed.

"You said Cusson wouldn't take your call?

"He also gave the cold shoulder to Von Schurz at the IMF."

"You're not serious? His moves could destroy futures-contracts for the euro; they're down eight basis points. Mr God, what is he thinking?"

Nicorezzi interpreted the speech fragments he'd overheard as extremely alarming. The dramatic drop in global demand for the de-valued U.S. dollar; Cusson's dollar sell-offs; the defensive reactions of the giant money managers. These uncoordinated actions could de-lubricate the primary engine of global commerce---America's financial stability.

He totaled in his mind the recent U.S. dollar trades by Cusson: beginning with fifty billion swapped for euros in Stressa; fifty-billion more to European

Union Central Banks for a basket of European denominations; another seventy-five billion in favorable-rate swaps for undervalued Asian currencies, primarily yuan holdings of Overseas Chinese in Singapore, Malaysia and Indonesia. Even repatriated U.S. dollars held in Taipei by Taiwanese businesses had been exchanged for weak Asian currencies, including the Indonesian rupiah, Malaysian ringgit and Phillipines peso.

Franco-Medici Trust had also just surfaced another $30 billion in dynamic-currency swaps with several diversified income funds; which invest up to 50 percent of their assets in point-of-sale foreign-securities transactions.

"This will force upward revaluation of every Asian currency," Nicorezzi said. "Long overdue…I might add. Washington is running trade deficits with just about every Asian trading partner."

The Zurich banker moaned. "Bank Central Suisse recently converted twenty-billion in South Korean won, Japanese yen, Indonesian rupiahs and Singapore dollars for a potpourri of currencies anchored by Cusson's dollar reserves."

"We're screwed," the Minister replied sardonically. "Cusson suckered the Swiss banking community when the Chinese authorized him to start selling dollar reserves."

Most Swiss newspapers are printed in standard German. Today, the evening editions were headlined in English: *Sharp declines in U.S. dollar; Indonesian rupiah rebounds, S. Korean won hits ceiling; Swedish krona rebounds, Swiss franc in gradual rise; Singapore dollar moves with yuan; Global Trade Wobbling.*

The articles explained how several Asian governments had accumulated large U.S. dollar reserves and weren't compelled to purchase more from Cusson. The U.S. trade deficit hit a record high 7 percent of gross domestic product, causing the Federal Reserve Bank's policy-making Open Market Committee to raise its target for the federal-funds rate by 15 percent; which banks charge one another for overnight loans.

(AUGUST 21)
INDIAN OCEAN, CHAGOS ARCHIPELAGO

"Priority 2….Priority 2," Cloud Nelson wheezed into the helmet-microphone which cast his voice into the chatter and ether of the National Security Agency's vast *Echelon* electronic global eavesdropping system. He hoped that one of the 30,000 NCA eavesdroppers would acquire the emergency transmission and recognize the code for major attacks against embassies, deployed vessels and non-embassy citizens.

"BLC Eagle/Ape private flight from Macau. Repeat….BLC Eagle/Ape flight from Macau." He flicked a switch above his head and the GPS beam-amplifier bounced a signal off the global positioning satellite controlled by the two atomic clocks on Diego Garcia---one of the world's four ground stations coordinating the Global Positioning System.

Gatt was frozen to the back of his rear seat by legs jammed so taut against the floor that he probably didn't need the retraining straps. His eyes were closed and he was panting like an out-of-shape marathon runner at the finish line.

The pilot was screeching into his helmet, "Sino-missile on my tail. Am attempting to elude in typhoon vicinity of I.O. Repeat... BLC Eagle/Ape in Indian Ocean attempting to elude SAM weapon. *Sino-missile lapping closer to my butt.*"

At least Naval Communications on Diego Garcia would know they were in the vicinity and in trouble. He assumed AJ had informed the Forward Deployment Base Commander that vital intelligence information was aboard the aircraft, along with operatives attempting to escape from China. It was too late for air-support or an escort from the base. But they might send a rescue helicopter, anticipating a splash.

Cloud thought about the parachutes tucked away in overhead compartments. There was no way he could maneuver the plane at super-cruise speed and instruct two semi-conscious civilian passengers how to strap them on or prepare for a fast-moving exit.

Cloud watched the weapons-threat indicator change from a flashing red to a steady red warning light. The missile was gaining altitude. Estimated time of impact was 75 seconds. *Forget about conserving fuel*, he mumbled to himself, and went for the afterburner.

Gatt's pulse ran up his legs and stopped in his throat. The unexpected acceleration unlocked his legs from the floor as Cloud raced for the 40,000 foot-high rim of the cyclone at Mach 1.67. Oresco was still passed out and oblivious to the hooked dive he was about to take into the bands of thunderstorms that spiraled toward the eye.

Nelson braced for an instantaneous ninety-degree descent which would test the strength of the carbon-fiber composite superstructure. He expected at least one tail-fin to snap off. At 30 seconds to impact he reached the rim of the 155 mph cyclone, and braced for a nose-dive G-bump. The fluid-hydraulics engaged the vectoring nozzles and he rolled the aircraft nose down into the low-pressure eye like a phalacrocorax carbo, the Great Cormorant trained by Chinese peasants to dive for fish on inland rivers, with a ring around its neck to prevent swallowing the catch, and a line tied to its leg for retrieval by the fishermen.

"BLC Eagle/Ape...come in. BLC Eagle/Ape---this is Diego Garcia flight control. Do you hear? Repeat...do you hear? We're vectoring a copter."

The flight controller listened to a wild-sounding "Wheeee.....holy shit.... wheeee," followed by erratic crackling before the signal was lost.

The ride down toward hell was surprisingly smooth. There was no wind-shear as the air in the 10-mile wide eye itself was nearly calm in the center. Only at the 'eye wall' around the outer edges of the center were the winds the strongest. Unfortunately, the HQ-10 missile was tracking the plane like a late-closer in a thoroughbred horse race. The vertical 40,000 foot drop would be scanned in less than two minutes. Nelson's radar indicated an estimated weapons impact at about twenty-thousand feet, or 60 seconds. The abrupt dive swung the missile slightly off course and bought him another thirty seconds, but he suddenly realized that the electrical activity in the center of the eye wasn't strong enough to upset the unrelenting missile's guidance system.

"Okay, fire-cracker," he shouted manically, "Let's see if you can follow us to the edge."

Cloud had used up the IR diversionary chaff on the ground, and his only chance to shake the heat-seeking missile's tracking capability was to slam against the 'eye-wall' and hope to hell the violent winds and lightning concentrated at the inner edge of the cyclone would disrupt the missile's honing instruments.

He pulled the throttles all the way back to spool the turbines to minimum fan-speed, then jerked off the afterburner. The aircraft crabbed sideways in the cross-winds and leveled to horizontal. He performed a Valhalla maneuver to equalize the pressure in his head by blowing hard with his nose and mouth closed. There was nothing he could do to relieve the nose and ear bleeding his passengers in the back were probably experiencing. He heard a feeble grunt from Gatt and glanced back into the cabin. The bag Gatt was holding over Oresco's face said enough.

Thirty seconds to impact! Oh, fuck! Nelson's eyes steeled. He slammed the throttles forward and snapped on the afterburner. The inner edge of the cyclone was only a mile away. Suddenly his meters began oscillating uncontrollably and he was flying blind into 155 mile per hour crosswinds wormed with lightning. The sound waves of touchable thunder-bolts organized into white-hot electronic clusters, created violent flutter.

Cloud heard a sharp cracking sound and saw smoke rising from a foot-wide hole in his left wing. A bolt of lighting had pierced the metal skin, but luckily, did not strike the wing fuel tank. He was certain the turbulence would snap off the wing.

The craft slid into the powerful air-turmoil as he rolled into a yaw and stalled the engines. As the small jet drifted sideways into the slingshot grip of the circular blow, they went into a free-fall. The powerful revolving winds slowed the plane's sideways momentum, causing airflow over the straining wings and an abrupt *chandelle* climb which pointed the nose skyward.

The Chinese missile followed the aircraft into the swirling chaos. Electrical discharges reinforcing the eye-wall like steel rebar in a concrete slap, snapped at the missile skin and shorted out the projectile's gyro-stabilizer. The on-board computer then lost the target's profile in the violent winds and instructed the missile to self-destruct less than a thousand feet directly below the BLC aircraft, spewing fragments into the 80 degree Fahrenheit, super-saturated air tunneling up from the ocean floor.

Cloud suddenly felt the plane wobble and spin, like a dinner-plate on a juggler's stick...pinned to a vertical axis. Then a violent cross-wind, concealed in an unorganized wind-pocket near the surface of the eye-wall, whipped them back out into the sunny skies at the center of the cyclone. Specs of exploded HQ missile swept upward in the warm air current and splattered the underside of the engine pods with sharp impacts. Cloud held his breath for a few seconds, finally grasping that the aircraft was still intact, and the missile had self-destructed.

All he had to do now was fly the plane several hundred miles on a nearly-empty fuel tank...with one functional wing.

He turned to the bloated eyes and breathless expression on Justin Gatt's colorless face and said impassively, "We have a nice big hole in our wing. If you don't mind...when you have a moment...please reach over your head and remove three parachutes."

Escape Route from Macau to Diego Garcia

CHAPTER 58

(LATE AUGUST, 2008)
NEW YORK CITY

"How long do I have to hide out at Joanna's?" Lynne asked. "She and the twins are great, but all we do is talk about you. I need to *see* you."

Joanna was close enough to hear the conversation. At least Lynne didn't say she needed to *feel* him.

"We're getting along fine, Justin. But, there's much to discuss. I just received more information from Stella Nicorezzi's dad, Johanas. He confirmed the money transfers we discovered, with a friend at the Swiss Private Banking Ministry. He believes several regulations may have been violated. Johanas is prodding Swiss officials to initiate an investigation of Phillipe Cusson and his Creditte Bank de Savoy banking empire. Cusson is suspected of arranging illegal currency trades and bribing European Union finance ministers to buy excess dollars. He apparently authorized the transfer of China's U.S. dollar reserves from his bank to several other financial institutions."

"Why won't he tell us where he is?" Joanna whispered urgently to Lynne, prodding her a bit too vigorously on the shoulder..

"Here, honey. Speak to him yourself."

"Hi, Jo. It's been a long time. Are you and the girls okay? How's Cosimo?"

"Doing fine, Justin. So is Cosimo. He misses you terribly." The throaty inflection in her voice transformed the 'he' into an 'I.' Lynne flopped on the couch and looked away.

"Thanks for sheltering Lynne, Jo. I'm sure she explained the danger she's in. Her apartment's probably still bugged."

"Why don't you just call the police? Not that I mind her company. She's lovely to me and the kids." Joanna glanced at the forlorn look on her guest's adorable face and said loud enough to paste a warm grin over Lynne's frown, "She's a bit flaky, especially around the girls. They love to go bargain hunting with her at the malls. I have to admit...before that I didn't realized my sixteen-year-old twin daughters' bellybuttons were so cute."

Justin lowered the volume of the CNN newscast on the 52 inch flat-screen TV in Oresco's New York City apartment. He sighed...a musing of confused emotions.

Joanna? Lynne? Which would he embrace first if they came into the room together? Hopefully, Cosimo would be there to give him a third option.

"Gabriel Oresco and I came up with some frightening information in China. I'd better explain it to Lynne. She initiated the conspiracy concept. We have additional pieces of the puzzle but will need her help to sort it out, and disclose it to the right people when we're ready."

"Isn't there something I can do to help?" Joanna coaxed, wanting so much to be a significant part of Justin's life again.

"Maybe later, Jo. Right now, Oresco believes we should minimize the distribution of information...for the safety of everyone. There are facts we need to confirm before talking to federal officials. If our assumptions are correct, Washington insiders are deeply involved. We're not yet sure who to trust. This is a big deal....an international game. A Beijing game---and I don't mean the Olympics. When the time is right, I'll explain it to you."

"Well, you can rely on me to watch over Cosimo. I work at Elim Park full time, now, and he's still the object of the 'marogespel girls' affections. He made me a brass cat with whiskers and a long pink ceramic tail, curled around a spool of genuine silver thread. It's a work of art."

Justin smiled. "I promise, I'll be up there as soon as it's safe to re-emerge. The people who fired a missile at our plane over the Indian Ocean may still be searching for me."

"Are you still in Asia?"

"No. We're back in the States, courtesy of the United States Air Force and a Navy helicopter pilot who fished Gabriel Oresco, me and another pilot out from an equatorial current a hundred miles south of Sri Lanka. The Chinese tried to shoot us down when we left Macau." He paused to reassess how much he should reveal to Joanna. She was a worry-wart. "It's better if you don't know my location just yet. Could you put Lynne back on? And give my love to Cosimo and the girls."

"Hi, Justin. Are you done with Joanna?"

"For now, Lynne. Listen, I need more information. Do you still have access to Harvard's financial-transactions data-retrieval system?"

Lynne's friend at the Harvard Baker Library had been forced to take a paid leave-of-absence. "No...unfortunately. Treasury agents found the fissure in the IRS tax data firewall we breached, and backed-the-cat...as the CIA jargon goes....to the Baker Library terminal we accessed in downloading the records. I was nearly caught using his PIN number at the terminal the day you left for China. I sneaked out a side exit when they stomped in to close down the experimental firewall-penetration software. Luckily, we'd removed the master query files and destroyed the software before the IRS arrived to do it themselves. He'll probably evade a jail term, but his career may be Swiss cheese, depending on how loyal the school administration is to its independent-minded employees."

She choked out the next words. "He took the fall for me."

"I'm sorry to hear that. Where do you stand with GH Paladin? Has McGill returned from Central America?"

"I mailed a letter of resignation three weeks ago. I don't dare collect mail at my apartment or call Madelaine at the GHP office to open my e-mail. A neighbor's daughter is emptying my mailbox at the apartment building so it appears I'm still in Cambridge."

"How are your hands...since the hair-dryer incident?"

"They're healing well. But I'm still scared as hell since Mr. Barnswig's death. I think that ice-cream-compulsive maid- imposter did it. Someone witnessed an elderly dark-skinned lady slap Mr. Barnswig on the side of the neck just before he collapsed on the sidewalk. He died from severe Ricin poisoning, which was injected into his neck."

"Jesus, Mary and Joseph! You'd better remain incognito until this comes to a head, Lynne. Oresco is approaching his editor at the New York Times for authorization to expose the information we accumulated. He wants to publish a sensational front-page article in the Sunday edition."

The apartment door swung open and Gabriel Oresco sauntered in carrying a briefcase and a folded newspaper. His usual vibrant expression was replaced by an angry scowl.

"It *would* be nice if we knew who we're hiding from," Lynne prodded Justin.

"Soon, Lynne. But right now the big picture is a dangerous quagmire. Gabriel and I have to work it through. Staying out of sight is necessary for both of us...for a while longer."

"What do you expect me to do?"

"Just hang steady. We'll meet with you as soon as some loose ends are gathered. We'll need your help to present a convincing argument for a conspiracy. God only knows how high up this goes. As unthinkable as it may seem, we believe both Chinese and U.S. government officials are deeply involved; along with BoxMart and the banks you uncovered."

Oresco unfolded the day's Times on a low coffee-table and exposed the front page. He pointed to a sub-article in the lower-right column. "Our next stop!" he said emphatically, as Justin replaced the phone and leaned over the table.

The by-line read: **Sioux City, Iowa:** *Ho-Chunk Indian Founder of Make Do Party Attacked at BoxMart Store.* In bold sub-text: *Urges Party members to boycott BoxMart outlets from hospital intensive care unit. Assailant disappears in store.*

Across the top of the front page was: *Merrand's Lead in Presidential Primary Insurmountable.*

Less prominent in the business section was an article describing how a sharp drop in prices for commodities and livestock futures had resulted from an unusual pest-infestation in the massive Iowa cornfields. Agricultural scientists reported that a previously unknown virus-like organism was feeding on corn leaves and stalks; causing sweeping deterioration of the cellulose-rich plant structures. So far, only one person---an aging farmer, was suspected of becoming ill as a result of the contamination. His stroke-like symptoms may have been caused by other factors.

Health authorities were monitoring local hospitals for reports of unusual illnesses. Investigators from the Centers for Disease Control in Atlanta were concerned with the possibility that the strange organism could jump species: from plants to animals to humans. Initial laboratory tests indicated that the organism is likely harmless to humans; but several carcasses of local birds and small animals, which may have fed on the contaminated corn, were found in the corn-fields and on margin roads.

"I'm still limping from hitting the water," Oresco complained as he hobbled to the the couch. "That crazy bastard Nelson pushed us out at less than 5000 feet. I thought I'd be buried in the ocean muck, until the chute opened."

"Talk about memorable occasions. I pissed my pants and threw up three times. And that was just on the way down. I never imagined I'd actually pray for a quick death."

"I missed out on most of the flight excitement, according to Cloud. He said you fought the multi-G forces and sudden dives like a trained astronaut."

"Yeah.....trained to barf my eyes out. Where do we go from here?"

Oresco shuffled unsteadily to the side bar and poured Johnny Walker black into two iced glasses. He handed one to Justin and said, "My editor won't run the story."

"You had that figured!"

"He says it's too explosive to run before the elections without definitive proof. Balzerini agrees. I talked with him a few hours ago. He's briefing the President at Walter Reed Hospital. The President is too weak from chemotherapy to decide what to do. Balzerini and the President both believe Washington players are involved; but they want to be sure before making official accusations. Balzerini instructed us to act on our own for a few weeks."

"What then?"

"The President and Martin Merrand will go at this thing together, since they're both involved."

Justin replied tersely, "Merrand must be concerned that the short-wave intercept the embassy obtained from the Zangnanhai government offices referred to *solving the Merrand problem.*"

"Balzerini doesn't trust anyone but the President and Merrand," said Oresco. "He's been an admired colleague of both of them for a long time."

"We need more solid evidence before accusing Kurancy, the Chinese or anyone else of a conspiracy," Justin surmised.

"Yes. And new evidence to prove that Chinese and American government officials are cooperating to unravel our economy. It's unthinkable," Oresco spewed, "but not surprising."

"Lynne's Geneva contact was informed that Vice-Premier Yong Ihasa plans to renege on the promise he made to Butler Humphreys at the recent trade talks in Beijing. The Bank of China won't be participating in the next U.S. Treasury bond auction."

"Nobody at the Times had that knowledge!"

Justin leaned closer to the coffee table and glanced down at the stories describing the corn-field contamination, the turmoil in livestock futures, and the sudden devaluation of the dollar on a global scale. And now, Beijing leaders had stiffened against pressure from American politicians by refusing to finance Washington's budget deficit.

"The U.S. economy seems poised for a precipitous dive."

Gabriel nodded. "BoxMart and the Chinese must be benefiting from all this. That's why we're going to Iowa. My boss says I need a week-long national story-hook, with multiple front-page material, to support conspiracy charges of this magnitude. Otherwise, the media moguls loyal to the Chinese---especially the TV news divisions of multinational corporations doing business in China---will bury the story. Even if it's *hot.*"

Gabriel lowered one eye and smirked mischievously, "But they can't kill a story that's *sizzling.* If BoxMart is responsible for the attack on the lady Chieftain of that 'Make Do' Party...the one who organized protests by the Winnebago people put out of work by Kurancy...it could provide some '*sizzle.*' We need to propel the conspiracy theory onto the front page, with a compelling hook the readers will want to follow."

Justin swirled the scotch around with his tongue. "I've always respected the power of the press."

Oresco didn't feel so powerful at the moment. His sensational story had just been rejected.

"The Chinese don't know that you were on the plane with me, Gabriel. What if they learn we're traveling together? Triad tentacles are everywhere."

"Balzerini released a trumped-up story that you drowned at sea. You'll be disguised, of course, when we travel." Gabriel watched his quirky friend stir the drink with his tongue. *Perhaps it was a form of yoga he picked up from Lili, to achieve enlightenment.*

"How about going as a doctor? You seem to know about cell chemistry and all that weird bio-stuff going on in the body. Some sort of biological genius trying to solve the mystery of where the corn-virus organism originated?"

"The Centers for Disease Control already have experts working on that, thank God. If this Iowa corn-infestation turns out to be the same organism the Chinese likely smuggled into the U.S., it could mutate again. Dr. Dongzi's report mentions the possibility that a digestive-enzyme in the boy's intestines—possibly a bile chemical or insulin---may cause the organism to rearrange its RNA sequence. Apparently it doesn't possess a viral-membrane to protect against enzyme-induced mutations. There's no telling how many people could be infected."

"At least you're becoming an expert in disguises. Now may be the time to read-up on your biochemistry. You have one night to access the internet for medical knowledge. Tomorrow we go to Sioux City."

Eve of the National Convention, Atlanta

"I've made the decision," Martin Merrand announced to his chief of staff, Joe Kleinman, the day before the party's National Convention. "Elliot Scharn will be my running-mate."

"Have you told him?"

"He's joining me for dinner in the suite. I'd like you to attend, Joe."

"Of course, Martin. Do you expect him to accept your offer?"

The Chairman of the Senate Appropriations Committee stared in disbelief at the enlarged black-and-white photos slipped under his hotel door minutes before he was to join Merrand. The startling images, if made public, would end his political career; although they would do no harm to his marriage to the nude woman in the pictures.

He expected Merrand to offer him the Vice-Presidential nomination, as his running mate. He'd have to refuse.

"I swear, Martin, we never touched the girl."

Merrand handed the photos back to sixty-five year old Elliot Scharn. The Senator was looking more like eighty. He replied indignantly,"What were you thinking, Elliot?"

"My wife and I have been experiencing...libido problems. We didn't want to experiment with drugs, and I can't use enhancements because of high blood-pressure. We found this sex-therapist in Boston who arranges these encounters. It was all innocent. The teenage virgin had done this many times before."

Merrand shook his head as his chief-of-staff, Joe Kleinman , stared blankly out the hotel suite window. The best laid plans....

Finally, Kleinman, a former Buffalo prosecutor and Merrand's chief fundraiser, turned to Senator Scharn and said, "How did you find out about this so-called sex-therapist. It sounds like an odd way to treat a common problem for couples your age?"

"It came up as a joke at a Washington bash hosted by the Department of Energy for petroleum industry lobbyists and consultants. Tom Blackstone from FFF has an associate in Boston with the same problem. He gave me his name---Bob McGill."

Kleinman was an impeccable digger of facts. Ruggedly handsome at fifty-two, he had a large elongated face, penetrating brown eyes and a semi-spiked crew cut of washed-blonde hair topping an average frame. "You claim these images were taken in Guatemala? Why there?"

"McGill and his wife donate money and medical supplies to a poor village where virgin girls are held in high esteem. Some of them are treated like Mayan princesses. Until they're older, and their hormones can no longer be suppressed, the village elders allow them to participate in McGill's sex-therapy-for-profits excursions. The McGills spend a month there every year, bringing along other couples to experience the therapy. It's expensive."

Kleinman was uncomfortable discussing the photos. "The therapy apparently works." He stared at the nude images of the Senator and his wife lying next to the thirteen year-old virgin in her birthday suit. They were facing the overhead fan.

"This clearly shows a rather...excuse me for saying it...prominent hard-on and stiff nipples jutting out."

Scharn bellowed, "McGill must have placed a camera in the ceiling fan. I think it was a set-up."

"And you or your wife never touched the girl?" Merrand asked skeptically.

The Ohio Senator rose from his chair. "I need a drink."

"You didn't answer the question, Senator!" Kleinman pressed contemptuously.

"I told you, we never touched her..in a sexual way."

"But you did have sex with her?"

"No, no. I told you." Scharn began to quiver. "It's difficult to explain."

Merrand snapped, "You'd better try, Elliot. These photos have major implications for your political career; not to mention your freedom from prison. The girl is obviously under-age."

Scharn's forlorn expression was sad acknowledgement that he'd just forfeited the Vice-Presidential nomination. He circled the room, bobbing his head sideways in silent regret. "It can be unbelievably erotic," he began to explain painfully, "lying next to a nude virgin. Just holding her hand...sensing the natural emissions from her moist skin and budding puberty. Watching the excitement in her eyes as she looks at your arousal."

He glanced shamefully at Merrand. "We laid on the bed, very still for half-an-hour. My wife on her left, me on her right. I was breathing heavily as we intertwined fingers. Nora had splashed herself with her favorite plum blossom fragrance and I was overwhelmed with a recollection of our first sexual encounter on our wedding night. Nora taught me all I needed to know." Scharn was clearly aroused by his own description. Merrand and Kleinman could have used less detail.

"Twice, the virgin became over-excited and tried to touch my hard-on. I brushed away her hand." Scharn was short of breath. "After a while, Nora became hot, maybe from the same memories. She straddled me." Scharn wiped the sweat from the nape of his neck with a handkerchief, continuing his evocative explanation. "The virgin jumped off the bed and watched from a corner of the room. I never felt such desire for my wife before. Nora was possessed. When the girl approached the bed and began combing her fingers through my wife's hair, she began to gyrate in circular motions I'd never experienced."

Kleinman poured espresso vodka over a small glass of crushed ice and handed it to Scharn. "Here, Elliot," his tone mellowed, "Sip this."

The Senator felt compelled to complete the tale, as embarrassing as it was.

"The girl started caressing my wife's face, stroking her cheeks. When she kissed my wife on the lips, Nora closed her eyes and began pumping like a jack-hammer. She came three times---normally a year's worth. She soaked me and the sheets with her juices."

"That's quite enough detail, Elliot."

"I still get hard thinking about it."

Kleinman shot a knowing look at Merrand. Through the side of his mouth he said grimly, "Well, Elliot, I'm sure you realize that whoever slipped the photos under your door could wreck Martin's bid for the Presidency... if you were his running mate. Even if your explanation is accepted as 100 percent truthful."

The National Convention was a day away. Merrand had to make a quick decision.

"Elliot, would you do the honors, and call Carvin Troone." It was not a friendly request.

The Texas Senator's love for poetry was acquired from his mother in his formative years. She read all the great 18th and 19th century poets before breakfast and after dinner each day in their small Dallas clapboard. It wasn't until Carvin Troone visited Beijing in the early 1990s as part of a State Departments Arts Exchange program that he became familiar with the unique poetic structure one Chinese scholar described as "Maoist-Confucian-Conflict." The poetic verse married inanimate objects to soulful emotions.

Each time Troone returned to Beijing he was warmly received by high cultural officials for his appreciation of Imperial Chinese poetry; a favorite past-time of the Ming Emperors. Troone's distant friend, the self-pronounced Ming descendent, Yong Ihasa, was fond of exchanging poems with him.

Lydia Bryce, perhaps the most crafted political speech-writer in Washington, became enamored with Senator Troone's mind when she read his "Poems from a Breathing Compressor," a self-published 60-page jumble of strangely-coupled words which had no apparent meaning, yet gave the impression of deep poetic insight. She'd framed a copy of his best poem and tacked it on a prominent wall in her office as a sign of admiration for the great man who hired her to write his speeches.

Living Inanimate

She stoned forward in heart,
satellited by the lover's sierra sigh;
a mimic of bank deposit...the way home,
an America over-abunded, while foreign friends bane.
Savoring the antique wheel's love for old passengers,
the folding chair beckons a sitter, caressing,
reversing its eggs the morning pan but hours before seconds, yields,
a databody spits bogus impressions...money talks.
Argue for cardiac arrest...paint by scissors,
the kiss of a stapler piercing sensuality,
a stray final bullet, in lewd partnership,
she be quick-sanded erotic.   C.Troone

"I accept your offer, with pride and humility, Governor Merrand."

CHAPTER 59

(September, 2008)
Sioux City Memorial Hospital

The broad-shouldered law enforcement officer approached the night clerk at the reception desk, but turned abruptly and walked away when two men rushed into the hospital lobby.

The shorter man handed the receptionist his card and asked a soft guttural question, leaning over the counter. The other man looked familiar—tall, with bright blue eyes and a confident gait. Justin Gatt's full facial beard and white hospital jacket with the "Visiting Doctor" name-tag convinced the observer that the familiarity she sensed was a coincidence.

Gabriel Oresco retrieved his New York Times business card from the elderly receptionist, whose flawless complexion and youthful figure belied her seventy years. Dressed in a pink and maroon work-out suit, with fine silver hair swept-back to a bun, the retired high school gym instructor jogged for an hour every day, and ran in the annual pre-harvest Iowa 10K road race in the fall to maintain a trim body.

She'd never met a newspaper reporter during five years of volunteering at the hospital. For some reason, she felt compelled to answer Oresco's questions loud enough for everyone in the small hospital lobby to hear.

"The Indian chief is in room 356 of the intensive care ward," she informed him. "I believe she came out of surgery doing fine. Her coma only lasted one day."

"We'd like to see her. Dr. Fuller is a medical consultant for the New York Times and wants to ask Chief Washington a few questions about the disfigured elderly woman who struck her in front of the parking lot. I understand that the lady was upset, and rushed into the store just after the confrontation."

"I don't know about that, but she must have been strong as a mule. One swing of her bag, with whatever heavy object was in it, and she deeply scarred the chief's skull. It's lucky Ms. Washington is a hard-headed Ho-Chunk. She apparently leaned away from the blow just in time. The emergency room nurse told me that a sharp object inside the shoulder bag glanced off her temple. If it struck flush, my gosh, she might be dead."

Only the person behind the opened magazine knew that the glancing blow was by design. The chameleon waited for the two men to hurry around the corner to the elevators, then approached the receptionist. She was wearing a dark-grey pants suit, black patent-leather pumps and a professional demeanor. "County Detective's office," she announced in a solemn voice. She flipped open a flat black wallet and exposed a five-star silver badge which could be authenticated by the clerk at the Dollar Store. The wallet snapped shut after a fraction of an instant.

"I'm investigating an attempted homicide. Can you identify the two men who just left here?"

Arcola Manditta was alarmed that the short man was a New York Times investigative reporter, and the taller man a doctor.

"I thought they were family," she said in a friendly tone designed to put the receptionist at ease. "So, you think the chief will be hospitalized for at least a week?"

"Yes---according to the student nurse on the floor."

She nodded and moved toward the automatic glass doors leading to the emergency-room parking lot. Hospitals weren't her favorite places. A female visitor with a sad face rushed through the lobby, evoking a flash-back of her mother, sobbing constantly at her bedside, as she recovered from the plastic surgery operations at the Tel-Aviv military hospital.

The antiseptic miasma that hung like a medicinal smog in the hospital air also reminded her of the excruciating facial pain inflicted by the Palestinian teenagers who tortured her. Arcola's African mother had told her stories about their ancestors, to detach her mind from the pain and disfigurement. Her favorite was about Unkulunkulu, the supreme god of the Zulu in southern Africa.

Both a creator-deity and the first ancestor of humanity, the "ancient one" or "great one," who derived his creative powers from his father, Unvelingange, (Zulu for "he who exists before all things"), provided humans with the skills and knowledge they needed to survive. But he was also associated with bringing death into the world. The role Arcola chose when she was abruptly released from both the hospital and the Isreali military service.

According to legend, Unkulunkulu entrusted a chameleon, a lizard with the ability to change colors in response to environmental conditions, to bring a message to humans that "they would not die." But the chameleon was slow and lazy, and angered him, so he sent another lizard who arrived first with a different message—"the coming of death." The assassin's mother nick-named her thin, long-legged daughter, with the short neck, wide shoulders and big sinister ebony eyes that seemed to move independently of each other---"Chameleon." Her father claimed it was because she loved to climb trees and hide.

He marveled at how closely the birth-defect of her feet resembled the toes of a lizard, with opposable sets of two and three digits separated by a wide space---the odd configuration which allowed lizards to grasp branches, rather than cling to them as with claws. Arcola's constant chatter also reminded her superstitious mother of the long, sticky tongue which the chameleon darts into the air to filch insects.

The third floor was eerily quiet except for the constant hiss of oxygen circulating in tubes attached to wall-mounted pressure canisters and tentacled to the nostrils of semi-conscious patients. An occasional squeal of rubber soles from hurrying attendants' shoes, or orderly-powered gurney wheels, interrupted the calming effect of the dim overhead lights which had been lowered at eight p.m. to remind visitors they should depart in a reasonable time.

Gatt and Oresco stepped from the third floor elevator as family members of the sick and injured tethered to tubes and wires in the intensive-care ward, gaited slowly into the lift. Harrowed looks of reluctant acceptance, temporary relief, emotional exhaustion and traumatic dread were painted on their creviced faces.

The head nurse who greeted them at the nurses' station was short and heavy, with middle-aged fading blonde hair clipped short, and warm brown eyes that said I'm here to help. Her tone was restrained as she looked warily at "Dr. Fuller's" name tag. "Are you here for a patient, doctor?" She was familiar with every attending physician at the hospital, and had never heard of a "Dr. Fuller."

Without hesitation, Gatt mustered an official reply worthy of the chairman of the Joint Chiefs of Staff. "Yes, of course. Please direct us to Nonnie Washington's room. Our tribal family is high-spirited that the Chief has made a remarkable recovery, and is able to converse. The Ho-Chunk council wishes me to report on her condition, immediately."

"She has a visitor...a friend who's been at the hospital almost constantly during the past few days."

"May I see her charts?" Justin prodded in a doctor's uncompromising tone of superiority. When the head nurse left to retrieve Nonnie's hospital records, Oresco said to Gatt, "I'm going to find out what I can about the sick farmer.

He's in the cardiac ward. I'll meet you in the lobby in about an hour. Buzz my beeper when you leave here. We have to keep the cell phones off."

Justin rubbed a swatch of anti-bacterial gel from a wall dispenser over his hands and knocked on the opened door to announce his arrival. Nonnie was behind a curtain in the private room, her neck pillowed up to watch the local news on a ceiling-mounted TV, sipping from a straw angled in a box of apple juice. Her plump female friend in her forties was seated in a chair beside the bed, her legs curled under a gauze torquoise dress. She squinted warily out the window into the well-lit parking lot.

"May I have a word with Chief Whiteknee?" he said as he eased into the room. "I'm Dr. Fuller." Nonnie's stationary blood-shot eyes snapped in his direction after he added, "I'm following your accident as medical advisor for the New York Times."

Her head felt like it was clamped in a red-hot vice, but the morphine seeping into her wrist did its job, dulling the pain and rearranging her attitude from furious and confused, to amiable and approachable. *Finally,* she thought, *a major newspaper is covering the story.* During her coma, she'd dreamed of giving a press conference to the world media, standing in front of a dozen metal-grid microphones on the west bank of the Missouri River. She instinctively reached up to fix her hair, but felt only bandages.

"I think I should go now, Nonnie," her friend said as she rose to greet Dr. Fuller, then leaned over to kiss Nonnie on the cheek. "I'll see you tomorrow afternoon."

She turned to Dr. Fuller and said with a noticeable tremble, "Pardon me for saying this, doctor, but I'd appreciate it if the New York Times could help prove that Nonnie's attack was no accident."

Justin stiffened. "Why do you say that, Ms. ....?"

"Kendra Gaulty. And I say that because I was there and saw it all. I followed the old women who struck Nonnie into the store after the ambulance arrived. She swung that heavy bag like the offspring of a female weigh-lifter and the hunchback of Notre Dame. I waited at the entrance for an hour and didn't see her come out. I thought she'd gone into the lady's room. When the manager finally decided to close the store...with the commotion and all... none of the employees or late shoppers who came out looked like her."

"You think Nonnie was attacked by a store employee who might have left through a back entrance?"

"No. I worked at this store once. All employees must exit from the front door through security gates and inspection stations more high-tech than at the airports. BoxMart headquarters goes ballistic if even a pair of panties or a Hersheys bar is stolen by an employee."

Nonnie winced. Kendra's comments forced her to recall the ugly experience. She visualized the nauseating sparklers that drifted across her fading vision after she was struck and going down. "Kendra believes someone disguised as an old lady was hired by BoxMart to silence me, and end the picketing."

"Do you have proof?"

Kendra's eyes shifted to the window overlooking the visitor parking lot. "Why is the New York Times here in sleepy Sioux City?" she asked, suddenly suspicious that Dr. Fuller might be working for BoxMart instead of the famous newspaper. "Isn't there a bigger story in the contaminated cornfields?"

Justin retreated to the open door, released the stop and watched the door to the hallway swing closed. He returned to Nonnie's bedside and said, "Chief Whiteknee…you and Kendra should know that I'm assisting Gabriel Oresco, the famous New York Times investigative reporter. We're attempting to uncover evidence that BoxMart management is involved in a conspiracy to harm the U.S. economy. We believe they're cooperating with others to systematically bankrupt small American manufacturing factories in the Northeast, just as it did your Ho-Chunk crafts factory. We read about your problems."

He noticed Kendra's expression change. "How can you help Nonnie?" she asked guardedly, "She's given up her legal career and practically sacrificed her life trying to help the Winnebago tribe. I'm afraid for her safety once she leaves the hospital."

"You don't sound like a doctor, to me," Nonnie announced boldly, as she detected the unprofessional apprehension in Gatt's voice. "How about telling us who you really are?"

Gabriel Oresco met Justin and Kendra in the hospital lobby an hour later. After a quick introduction, Kendra led them to her car in the parking lot and opened the trunk. A black garbage bag containing the assailant's disguise was lying on the nub of a repaired spare-tire the mechanic hadn't bothered to re-attach to the recessed wheel-well.

"I found these in the ladies' room, near the front entrance, just before they closed the store. The hunched-over black lady was wearing them when she struck Nonnie."

Oresco and Gatt examined the leather straps, greasy black wig and black-stained paper towels used to clean off skin-darkening make-up. "I don't think she was black," Kendra bellowed. "In fact, I'm not sure she was old, or even a woman, considering the ease with which she swung this…" She lifted a blue plaid picnic blanket tucked into a corner of the trunk and revealed an unzipped shoulder bag containing a gruesome spiked metal-ball.

Strands of Nonnie's hair and scrapes of her scalp where still encased in dried blood caked on the surfaces of a few spikes. "I was afraid to give these to the Sheriff. Whiley's owned by the BoxMart people."

Oresco folded a corner of the blanket over the long straps to avoid adding his fingerprints and lifted the bag. "This is a heavy sucker. Must be twenty pounds, at least."

Words flashed through his mind. Front-page-worthy words. He swung the heavy object side-to-side, whimsically adding. "This will be enough proof to float our first story. But I doubt if any fingerprints will be traceable to a felon in the FBI files. This seems like the bungled job of an amateur. That metal thing could easily have crushed her skull and split open her brain."

"Unless someone wanted only to incapacitate Nonnie, instead of killing her." Justin sensed an ominous similarity. It reminded him of Lynne's near-disastrous accident with the incendiary hair-drier. "Was the old lady broad-shouldered?"

Kendra looked at him peculiarly. "Very. Her shoulders were oddly squared-off, for a disfigured person."

The maid? Justin cringed. He thought of Mr. Barnswig. The silence hovering under the bright parking-lot lamps was ominous. He glanced around and thought he detected a person crouching down in a dark SUV parked several rows away.

Oresco caught the worried look on Justin's face and said, "Let's get out of here! Kendra, I may need your help once we break the story. The Times will present only the facts relating to this evidence. We'll take photos of these things and put BoxMart's management on the hot-seat. But, as a former BoxMart employee, you could be subject to legal action for removing the clothing from the store without authorization. It was a very brave thing to do."

Kendra's expression morphed from anxiety to pride and back.

"Of course, we'll refrain from using your name in the story,"Oresco attempted to assure her. "It's only remotely possible that you'd ever be charged with breaking the law...in the unlikely event that BoxMart files a lawsuit against the newspaper. The courts could attempt to force us to reveal our source of information." His feeble attempt at re-assurance had the opposite effect. He made it worse when he said, "The Times would pay your legal fees."

"Oh, my, I hadn't thought of that."

"Don't worry too much, Kendra," Justin interjected emphatically. "If our investigation is successful, BoxMart's management will have much more to worry about than defending the use of rough tactics to stop the Make Do Party's demonstrations."

The person hunched down in the dark SUV couldn't hear the words. But she was close enough to recognize the shoulder bag being lifted from the trunk. There was now an unacceptable level of risk if she remained in Iowa. Blackstone would be informed that the leader of the Make Do Party had been disabled, as ordered.

U.S. DEPT. OF AGRICULTURE EXPERIMENTAL STATION
AMES, IOWA

"Last night I met Shirley, the farmer's daughter, and his cardiologist at the Heart Disease Intensive Care unit. They directed us to you, Virginia."

Seated at the rectangular table in the cafeteria of the U.S. Department of Agriculture research and testing facility in Ames, for a hastily called breakfast meeting, were Virginia Richmore, from the Centers for Disease Control; the USDA PhD biologist, Cynthia McFarlan; "Dr. Fuller"(Justin Gatt was not yet comfortable with revealing his true identity); and Gabriel Oresco. They were discussing the farmer's illness and the organism which caused the cornfield browning.

Gabriel Oresco said mournfully, "Shirley has given so much blood to her father that she could become anemic. The cardiologist explained that her dad's being kept alive with bi-weekly blood transfusions, and intermittent high dosages of Plavix and warfarin, which temporarily slows the unexplained thickening of his blood. It seems as if his major organs are beginning to falter."

Dr. Fuller added, "His red blood cells are being penetrated and damaged by the organism, which exudes a gummy substance that coagulates his blood fluids. Unfortunately, the hospital can spare only a few more transfusions of his blood-type."

Justin Gatt had gone sleepless the previous night, spending hours on the internet in his hotel room, researching the wealth of medical information available on the world wide web. Not exactly a captivating novel you couldn't put down, he was none-the-less fascinated with the chemical processes of diseases: the biochemistry of bacterial and virul attacks on human cells; pathogen mutations; mitochondrial disease processes that reduce the energy produced by human cells, and can cause whole body systems to fail.

His best source of information was the National Heart, Lung and Blood Institute, one of the 18 specialized research organizations that make up the U.S. National Institutes of Health based in Bethesda, Maryland...the most comprehensive collection of medical information in the world.

Because of the similarity in symptoms between the dead Chinese technician and the critically ill Iowa farmer, Justin's mind equated the two as being caused by the same biological process. After reviewing the mechanisms of the circulatory system, which includes the heart, blood vessels and lymph vessels through which blood and lymph fluids are pumped around the body, he was convinced that the farmer's illness was caused by the same parasitic organism that cemented the Chinese lab technician's circulatory cavities.

"I'm far from an expert in the field," Dr. Fuller explained, "but I've studied a similar case in China. We have reason to believe that a young lab technician working in a People's Liberation Army bio-weapons facility was exposed to the same organism as the farmer. He died recently from congealed blood and lymph vessels, and eventual cardiac arrest."

Virginia replied skeptically, after a quick read of the medical report Gatt had provided earlier, "How is that possible, Dr. Fuller? I spoke with the farmer's cardiologist about the virus-like organism we found living in his circulatory vessels. It has an altered electron-microscope image, and similar, but significantly different RNA amino-acid sequences from the organism described in the Chinese doctor's report you brought from the mainland."

She'd read only Dr. Dongzi's initial analysis and description of the mycoplasma--- *before* it invaded the technician's digestive system.

"The Beijing research hospital's subsequent report may explain the link." Justin decided to disclose the most sensitive information in Dongzi's reports: the evidence confirming that the original cellulose-consuming organisms the two men had been exposed to were biologically identical. "Here," he said poignantly, as he handed the CDC and USDA scientists a copy of the other research report he'd smuggled from China.

"In my opinion, the corn-virus attacking Iowa crops looks pretty much the same as the mycoplasma Dr. Dongzi detected on the samples of vegetation the Chinese technician was testing at the bio-weapons lab, before he was stricken."

"What kind of samples?" asked the CDC scientist in charge of preventing a corn-virus induced pandemic.

Justin caught Oresco's anxious glare and encouraging nod. "According to Dr. Dongzi, the Chinese technician was testing an agricultural pathogen on samples of hybrid Iowa corn."

Stunned silence and mutual recognition hung in the air. Finally, Justin said, "Dr. Dongzi talked to the technician's assistant. Apparently, the stricken boy ate some of the corn the day before becoming ill. There were no cooking facilities in the lab; we suspect the technician ate raw kernels."

Cynthia McFarlan, the USDA scientist earned her Ph. D. in bio-genetics, and had interned at a National Institutes of Health research facility studying a branch of fundamental life processes. She was an expert in the genetic factors which increase human susceptibility to environmentally-induced diseases. She pieced together from memory the sub-microscopic chemical reactions she'd studied for years, recalling the surreal electron-microscope images she'd observed of DNA and RNA viruses, which she claimed brought her closer to God. To her, they represented the very beginnings of His life-giving handiwork.

The EM photos she'd just observed left no doubt in her mind that the original cellulose-consuming mycoplasma gorging on the corn surfaces, had somehow mutated in the bodies of the Chinese technician and Iowa farmer. She calmly scrolled her thinking finger over the written conclusions in the Chinese reports translated into English by Lili.

"Both the technician and Shirley's father ate raw kernels that where likely coated with the original organism. My guess is that digestive fluids in their bodies reacted with the mycoplasma to cause the harmless, cellulose-consuming RNA-form of the incomplete virus, to mutate; perhaps in a mechanism similar to how the influenza A virus re-assorts genes and creates antigenic shifts…which as you know can explain pandemics."

Oresco suddenly realized how limited his understanding was of the key medical issues he'd be writing about. "Could you explain in layman's terms, Cynthia?"

"I think Dr. Fuller is better qualified for that."

Justin shifted in his seat. Many innocent lives could be at risk if they didn't react medically correct to prevent the spread of a deadly human pathogen. He decided to give up the acting. His true identity could remain concealed long enough to sort out the details of the suspected conspiracy.

"I'm afraid I'm not as qualified as you think, Cynthia. I'm only an amateur medical scientist; not a doctor, but a chemist by trade. But I'll take a crack at a layman's interpretation of the science."

Neither of the women acted surprised. They remained subdued as Justin presented his thoughts. "I've studied the reports and EM photos enough to think that the most important similarity between the two cases occurs in the coagulated blood streams of the patients."

"And, by that, you mean?" Virginia asked impatiently, adding, "And just *who are* you?"

Oresco broke in, "He's working for the federal government, just as both of you are. We're investigating a potential threat to the U.S. economy by a group of international conspirators…including Chinese and American businessmen and government officials. His name is not important. However, if the bad people involved find out he's still alive in America, they'll try to kill him again."

"Again?" Cynthia gasped.

"It's a long story that can wait," Justin shrugged.

"What's your theory, Fuller?" Virginia prodded at his fake beard with the tips of her fingers. It loosened from the glue on his chin. Justin pulled his face back and smiled. "If you don't mind. I'm already having nightmares about working at a department store during Christmas time."

"Tell us what you think."

Justin pressed the fake brown whiskers against his chin and began, "For one thing, the blood transfusions are not working. Since the original organism was considered harmless to humans, it probably did not feed on sugars, such as the easily-digested six-carbon glucose solutions which have been administered to the boy and the farmer, in order to maintain ATP energy levels in their body cells. But now, it seems that as soon as the farmer's blood-sugar level increases...and I suspect this also happened to the Chinese technician...the organism produces additional gummy material and the blood thickens further; at least according to the clotting-capacity lab tests."

The others were silenced by Justin's succinct explanation. "I have no idea how the mechanism works," he continued, "but I think the bug becomes a sugar-eater, instead of a cellulose-eater. As you know, cellulose is nothing more than a thousand glucose C-6 sugar units attached in a molecule that can only be broken down by certain enzymes; which humans do not normally produce. When the corn-virus transforms its chemical preferences, it must leave behind the thick substance which eventually plugs the vessels."

"You're not a doctor?" Virginia retorted in a skeptical, yet pleasantly surprised tone.

Justin's comments caused Cynthia's thought pattern to flow in a different bio-logic rivulet. "There are several conditions that might cause an incomplete RNA retrovirus, like the mycoplasma of the corn-virus, to mutate. In the mutated avian virus H5N1...the "N" stands for *neuraminidase* strings of certain amino acids found on the surface of the influenza virus...the organism can gain access to human cells. A mycoplasma can alter certain amino acids *in situ* and change the "N", or neuraminidase code, thus increasing the organism's ability to access across the protective membranes of red and white blood cells."

Virginia was the only one able to follow the path of Cynthia's analysis. She responded evenly, "Fundamentally, you have to start with individual cells being attacked by individual pathogens. The beginning point of an illness is the individual cell."

Cynthia raced ahead. "By clustering together, and forming a protective protein coat---the life-source of the evolutionary scheme for most mycoplasmas----there is degenerative evolution..Like when penicillin breaks down a walled-bacteria. The resulting '*almost a virus*" mycoplasma can then find a cell willing to allow it to cross the cellular membrane...doing nothing...until it is subjected to some kind of trauma."

Justin took a wild guess. "Could the trauma be caused by eating the kernels? I understand they contain very high levels of sugar. Sugar seems to play a part in the formation of the gummy stuff in the farmer's blood vessels. Perhaps if his glucose level was lowered he wouldn't produce as much gunk in his blood steam."

Oresco thought he finally had something meaningful to say. "You can't starve him of glucose, he's an insulin-dependent diabetic. He'll die if his blood-sugar drops too low."

Justin had read the Chinese medical reports a dozen times. An afterthought emerged. "The dead technician was also an insulin-dependent diabetic. They kept his blood sugar on the high side, as a precaution. Especially when he was administered insulin injections."

Cynthia gasped. She suddenly understood the likely pathogenic mechanism. She shouted forcefully, "We must contact the farmer's cardiologist immediately. If the corn-virus is precipitating the congealing-substance---as a reaction to high glucose levels---the intravenous feeding may be keeping him alive, but it's also allowing the incurable B.A. virus to re-constitute. *That's what destroyed the technician's organs!*"

CDC, Atlanta

Virginia Richmore's call to Atlanta confirmed Cynthia McFarlan's hypothesis and Justin Gatt's observations. The cellulose-eating organism contaminating vast fields of Iowa corn *was* the source of the sugar-consuming mycoplasma found in the dying farmer's thickened blood, according to Dr. Nolte.

"We were able to duplicate the mutation process and create the identical dome-shaped dodecahedral configuration. The pathological activity *in petri* reversed itself...from pre-mutation, cellulose-specific... to glucose-specific, post-mutation, with cellulose consumption activity completely wiped out."

"How did you affect the mutation, Dr. Nolte? All we had to go on was that the farmer ate raw kernels that were probably coated with the corn virus."

"You may recall, Virginia, that the CDC did previous testing for the U.S. Army biological weapons research team on bacterial pathogens in crystalline form. The tests on some of the most toxic substances known---the botulism and tetanus toxins---confirmed that the biological warfare agents could be isolated and transported as inactive crystals. We believe the corn virus was transported the same way, then combined with the E. coli host detected on the corn plants. We simply duplicated the environment."

"Let me guess---the corn virus consumed the E. coli bacteria within hours, then voraciously attacked the surface of the paperboard."

"That's correct, Virginia. Although, when the mycoplasma colonies finished with the cellulose, they went dormant."

Virginia summarized for Dr. Nolte the technical explanations put forth by the unidentified chemist calling himself Dr. Fuller, and Cynthia from the USDA.

"When you find out who this guy is, let me know. I may want to hire him. His analysis is on the money."

"How do you mean?"

"We attempted to reactivate the dormant corn-virus mycoplasma with various animal enzymes and substrates. The first one that gave positive results was from the bile of an Amazonian crocodile. It's an enzymatic-amalgam which can break down nearly any living cell. It was discovered when the bio-warfare people experimented with the deadly brucellosis abortus nucleic acid particle, a very nasty species of mycoplasma similar in molecular structure to the corn-virus." His voice lowered. "It was tested on humans during the Korean War."

She was ahead of him. "So you inserted human digestive enzymes, like the sugar enzymes---amylase, maltase, glucase and sucrase?"

"You wouldn't believe the end product," he responded incredulously, "when we stumbled on the right combination. The scary part is---that combination of enzymes occurs quite frequently in the fluids of insulin-dependent diabetics."

"I guess you'd normally expect the formation of blood sugar, if carbohydrates were present. But that's not what you found, is it?. Was it glycogen---the liver-converted form of glucose?"

"Nothing happened for a few hours," Nolte continued, with a mixture of dread and wonder. "We thought the organism was completely dormant because the bacteria and cellulose were totally consumed. Then, someone had the bright idea of adding insulin and glucose solution to stimulate the organism's metabolism---as if it was diabetic."

His breath came harder as he announced, "The colonies grew like cancer."

"My God! They became immortal. No wonder the farmer is dying and the Chinese technician succumbed. This could lead to a pandemic if enough diabetic people somehow consume the contaminated Iowa corn. Their bodies could manufacture potentially deadly reconfigured Brucellosis virus cells and spread them to others."

"You must immediately order the destruction of the entire western-Iowa and surrounding area corn-crop, Virginia. I'll prepare the necessary CDC authorizations and inform all federal government agencies involved."

"Why not burn just the infected fields and a few miles of bordering vegetation? That should be more than adequate to eradicate the risk of spreading." Virginia was hoping for the least financial impact on the local farmers. The silence at the other end was finally broken when Dr. Nolte spilled his thoughts of the unthinkable.

"You don't understand. The insulin-glucose solution reacted like a reverse transcriptase enzyme, reprogramming the events of the host cells invaded by the sugar-consuming form of the mycoplasma."

Virginia's brilliant mind could sometimes duplicate the clarity of the most powerful electron microscopes. She tried to picture the sub-microscopic rearrangements between Lambda, the lysogenic virus of E. coli, and its host. She visualized a single cell---similar to a fertilized egg, eventually giving rise to progeny that differ from one another, like a brain cell and muscle cell. This time, however, giving rise to *transient viremia*--- the presence of virus in the blood. There was no stopping its spread into the lungs, spleen and liver.

Dr. Nolte spat the words out as if the plague had already arrived. "The mycoplasma is reconverted to its original lethal RNA sequence. As you know, there's no known cure for the original RNA form---brucellis abortus."

Virginia remembered the pathology studies. "It attacks and destroys human organs faster and more viciously than Ebola," she decried in a dry shrill. "Anyone on insulin could theoretically produce the lethal form, and destroy their own organs."

"No known cure," Dr Nolte groaned. "We'll have to isolate the farmer and test for BA. If the petri dish colonies are duplicated in his body, the hospital could be creating its own pandemic from a single donor."

"I'll initiate the necessary containment procedures, Dr. Nolte. If you're correct, the poor farmer's organs should be dissolving by now."

"I'm calling in people from Level Five Biohazards control. Run down to the hospital and quickly, but quietly, inform the medical authorities that a team from Atlanta will be arriving within four hours. Let me know as soon as possible if the AB organism is in fact building up in the farmer's body. Use the EM test procedure. The RNA-sequencing titrations will take a full day. We can't wait that long."

"Dr. Nolte, there's one more piece of information you should know." Virginia described the discovery by the Iowa State students. "They found empty boxes coated with the cellulose-consuming organisms near the contaminated cornfields, along with dead animals and birds."

"How is that important?"

"The boxes were made at a cardboard factory in Shanghai. Oresco says there may be a connection between the corn-virus outbreak and goods being shipped to the U.S. from China. Someone should be contacting Chinese health officials, so they can check out the factory where the boxes were produced. The product labels were purposely cut off the cartons, but the Chinese characters identified the place of manufacture. We also found a plastic liner with a Chinese-character tag and a bar code.

"I fail to make the connection, Virginia."

"The New York Times reporter and his unidentified friend believe the organism may have originated in a Chinese bio-weapons laboratory. If it *was* intentionally smuggled into this country...the implications are mind-boggling."

CHAPTER 60

(EARLY OCTOBER, 2008)
SIOUX CITY MEMORIAL HOSPITAL

Shirley watched her father approach death with grace, as the heavy doses of insulin and glucose-solution were administered by the nurse. He'd been drifting in and out of consciousness for hours. In one lucid moment, he snapped awake and reached for her hand.

The farmer's eyes were anxious; yet peaceful. "Don't be frightened, Pop." His swollen lips silently mouthed the words, "I'm ready." His fretful grip relaxed, and Shirley cupped the limp hand against her cheek. She closed her eyes and said a silent prayer.

"God is waiting for you," she whispered tearfully, then placed his hand over his heart. "You'll soon be in a better place," she sobbed in quiet spasms. When it was apparent that her father stopped breathing, she whispered, prematurely, "It won't hurt anymore."

Shirley was stunned when his eyes suddenly opened, streaked crimson and fearful. They rolled in her direction…oozing dreadful red droplets. He gasped, inhaled painfully from the oxygen mask, and grimaced his last words. "I'm afraid…I never did this before."

The vital-signs monitor suspended on a metal stand behind the bed suddenly emitted a short, high-pitched whine. Shirley saw a red LED number-display scrolling rapidly. His heart began to drum its last staccato, straining to clear away the congealing muck filling his blood-cavities.

Ironically, the blood transfusion and medication administered a few hours earlier had lowered the viscosity of his blood, teasing up his vital signs. The attending nurse thought the farmer exhibited signs of recovery. Only his blood-sugar had dropped to a dangerous level. The few molecules of insulin remaining in his system from an earlier dose had stimulated the mycoplasma's sweet tooth; and attenuated the secretion of the congealing-substance.

Justin and Virginia rushed to the nurse's station following Dr. Nolte's call from Atlanta. They arrived too late. The intravenous glucose and insulin solutions administered by the nurse ten minutes earlier were mating chemically with the mutated corn-virus now feeding on the farmer's blood-sugar. The head nurse pointed to the attending physician checking patient charts in a side room. Virginia rushed into the glass-enclosure near the nurse's station and frantically tried to explain the petri-dish discovery to the doctor. She angrily swept aside the medical charts he continued to read as she described the virus residing in the farmer's body. Finally, she pleaded, "You've got to stop the glucose I.V. The organism can mutate into a deadly human pathogen."

"Starve him of blood sugar? That's an unacceptable risk for a diabetic. How can you be certain that his condition will improve?"

"If you can just keep him alive through a low-sugar shock-cycle," Virginia responded desperately, "we'll have proof. The CDC petri-dish tests indicate..."

"It's only a theory," the cardiologist replied callously. "I'm not familiar with such organisms." He was also thinking about the recent twenty-five percent increase in his liability insurance premiums. "As feasible as it may seem to you, Ms. Richmore, I can't risk allowing my patient to run low on blood sugar. He'd be shaking to death in minutes."

The head nurse heard the conversation and interrupted the frenzied debate. "That man's condition definitely improved when his sugar was low, doctor. And worsened after we administered the higher doses of insulin and glucose you prescribed."

"He's my patient, damn it," he scowled at the nurse. "If he dies, it will be without my assistance." Virginia thought, *Hasn't he got that backward?*

Justin was about to join the argument when he saw Shirley stagger into the hallway outside her father's room; her eyes crazed with fear. "He's disintegrating!" she cried hysterically, then collapsed. An orderly standing nearby lunged to catch her fall, but slipped backward on the heavily-waxed tile floor. He winced as Shirley slipped through his grasp and hit the floor...her head springing up from the surface in a sickening thud. As he began to crawl to her aid, Virginia shoved the cardiologist aside and sprang in their direction.

"Stay away from her!" she screeched with such emotion that the orderly spun away from Shirley and slammed against the wall. "She may be carrying a deadly disease."

Virginia's eyes darted from side-to-side to snare everyone's attention. She looked beyond the stupified cardiologist cleaning the lenses of his teaspoon, wire-rimmed glasses. "You've got to take charge," she barked at the head nurse. "Isolate Shirley and her father's body. Everything and everybody on this floor must be immediately quarantined. This could be a Level-Five biological event."

CDC Field Office, Iowa

Dr. Nolte initialed the CDC Emergency Procedures memorandum and handed it to his assistant. "You know the distribution protocol. Please send this out immediately."

The World Health Organization, the Chinese Minister of Public Health and the United Nations Department for the Prevention and Spread of Communicable Diseases were next to receive the alarming notice and accompanying medical report. The U.S. Department of Health had already been notified, and was passing along warnings to all Midwest hospitals, medical associations and agricultural field offices. The precautionary burning at the perimeters of the infected cornfields was underway in Iowa.

"Thank God the deadly BA found in his body did not infect Shirley," Virginia Richmore nodded to her boss. "I guess she didn't touch him after the virus mutated. I can imagine why...with all that blood gushing out."

"He wasn't breathing heavily by then, so it's safe to assume there were few, if any, airborne BA particles in the hospital room."

Dr. Nolte had taken a private jet to Sioux City as soon as he was notified of the farmer's death, and the presence of deadly *brucellus abortis* colonies in his body. "The Level Five team has ordered additional body suits, just in case. They've set up a remote testing lab in the parking lot to make sure no hospital staff was infected. The hospital has done a remarkable job of containing and isolating this crisis, Virginia. In no small part because of your quick response."

"I was helped immensely by Dr. Fuller."

The funeral service was not what Shirley wanted for her dad. The brief memorial ceremony held in the hospital chapel, following her release from quarantine three days after his passing, was attended only by Dr. Fuller and a few of the quarantined hospital staff. The CDC considered it still too dangerous for family and friends to attend. Also missing was the deceased. His ashes remained in a sealed urn in a biohazards container. Once the pathologist in the morgue discovered the presence of BA colonies saturating the farmer's body fluids, and witnessed the cells of vital organs dissolving before his eyes, he hermetically encased the corpse in a triple-lined body bag and rushed it to the nearest crematorium.

The entire cardiac ward was isolated by Level-Five Biological Containment experts from Atlanta, and those confined in the exposure area were forced to undergo stringent decontamination procedures. The patients, nurses, doctors and visitors present when the farmer died, were quarantined in the cardiac ward until all had tested negative for the presence of BA and corn-virus organisms.

"Dr. Fuller, you're free to go. But I'd suggest you check your temperature every four hours for a few days, just in case of UDDS."

Justin Gatt's questioning glance provoked a further explanation from the communicable diseases expert. "Sometimes, despite all our tests, a disease hides in an undetectable part of the body. Usually in the dormant cells of reproductive organs. A rapid rise in body temperature usually indicates that the infectious species has reactivated. We call that 'undetected dormant disease syndrome.'"

SAC CITY, IOWA, CDC MEETING WITH THE FARMERS DISEASE CONTAINMENT PROGRAM.

When Virginia Richmore returned from the crisis-team meeting in Atlanta, she braced for the most difficult presentation of her career.

The 4-H hall was standing-room only. Two hundred area farmers murmured anxious predictions of what would happen next, as she moved to the front of the room and began to speak without notes.

"I know you're all anxious to learn what the U.S. Departments of Health and Agriculture are doing in response to the corn virus-crisis," she began. "But first, you should understand something about the deadly organism we're dealing with; and the pathological risk-studies conducted by the Centers for Disease Control in Atlanta." She waited for the anxious chatter to subside.

"As you all know," she continued, in a forced professional tone, "several small animals and indigent species of birds have been found dead near the cornfields. We believe this is caused by the animals consuming contaminated corn. Luckily, the parasite involved does not seem to exhibit the ability to make a complete leap from plants-to-animals, and animals-to-humans. But the terrible death of your farmer friend was definitely caused by a mutation of the corn-virus in his body. The CDC tests proved that when certain body enzymes are present, such as insulin or other digestive enzymes, the organism can mutate into a deadly virus with no known cure. It's called *brucellus abortis*."

To the farmers, this sounded like the execution rite for a Roman emperor. "So, we must all cooperate to contain the organism. It must be destroyed before it spreads to un-contaminated fields in high-population areas."

Cynthia McFarlan stood up, having agreed to accompany Virginia in case she had difficulty convincing the farmers of the necessity to destroy their vast fields of corn. She wore dusty bluejeans and a faded-green, short-sleeve cotton work shirt; looking like she just hopped off a John Deere combine.

"While we believe the potential danger is most pronounced for insulin-dependent diabetics, it's much too early to rule out the possibility that other human, or animal enzymes, could cause the same mutation." The foreboding dread apparent on the sun-wrinkled faces of the local farmers was palpable fear that their precious farmland could soon become mausoleums of charred maize. Cynthia explained further, "When the corn virus mutates and creates this deadly, untreatable organism we call the 'BA' pathogen, human organs can be attacked more viciously than the deadliest monkey viruses coming out of Africa."

Faces grimaced as she described how the organism enters the blood stream, destroys immune system cells, and leaves behind a clay-like substance as thick as setting concrete. Virginia inhaled deeply and resumed her presentation... sweating profusely as the heat generated by two-hundred frustrated, angry and frightened sets of dirt-soiled fingernails overwhelmed the cool breezes puffing in from the four half-open windows ventilating the 4-H meeting hall.

"The Director of the Centers for Disease Control has been authorized by the Department of Health and Human Resources, and the USDA,...with the blessing of the President of the United States...to coordinate the burning of a vast area of western Iowa cornfields; as well as bordering fields in Southwest Minnesota and Northeast Nebraska."

Virginia deflected the unnerving gloom on their faces as a natural reaction to the bad news. Instead of looking forward to a record corn-crop harvest, their livelihoods would be drifting away in carbonized maize canopies, clouding over rows of smoldering dirt. Realizing that a portion of the fall harvests must be destroyed, many of the larger farm corporations were anxious to begin the remediation process. The worst agricultural calamity in American history needed to be addressed with speed and resolve.

"Your predecessors survived the great draughts, severe swings in weather and crop diseases. I'm sure this generation of Midwest farmers is not about to surrender its precious plains to a bug." Virginia capped her discouraging summation with a request for questions.

They came fast.

"How did Shirley's father die?"

Virginia's anguished explanation lent credulity to the forced, even-tempered scientific reasoning she'd used earlier to justify the destruction of the infected maize fields.."We believe the organism can be contained and eradicated if we destroy the contaminated vegetation." She struggled to say the next words---the only words the farmers would remember from this meeting.

"The U.S.D.A. estimates that an area of four to five million acres, shown on the darkened sections of the overhead map projection, will complete the job."

The gasps created a black-hole of emotions. The silence that followed both filled and voided the room; as if the shock waves of desperation converted sound into anti-sound.

(OCTOBER 20, 2008)
NY TIMES EDITORIAL DESK, NEW YORK

Virginia Richmore's return call from the CDC field office in Sioux City convinced Gabriel Oresco that Justin Gatt's theory was correct. High-level Chinese government officials *must* have been involved in a pre-meditated plan to cause the catastrophic agricultural-pathogen outbreak in Iowa.

Oresco was typing a draft of the story he planned to submit to the Times editorial committee in a few hours. It would be his second eye-popping front-page feature in less than a week.

A printout of the first article was stick-pinned to a cork board on the wall in front of his state-of-the-art office work station.

NY Times, Front Page Lead Article, October 15, 2008
(Picked up by the AP, run by all Midwest Dailies)
"Attacked Indian Chief, Head of Make Do Party, Returns to Ho-Chunk Reservation.

Oresco's first article read: *Disregarding the recommendations of her doctors, Chief Nonnie Washington Whiteknee returned to the Winnebago reservation in Nebraska in an ambulance a few hours after emerging from a coma. She immediately called a Tribal Council meeting and began preparing Ho-Chunk members of the Make Do Party for a new demonstration against local BoxMart retail outlets.*

An unknown assailant disguised as a deformed elderly woman, but strong as a plains buffalo, attempted to crush Chief Whiteknee's skull in a near-fatal blow that left her unconscious. After striking the Chief, the assailant rushed into the Sioux City BoxMart store and disappeared. A member of the Make Do Party attempted to follow the assailant into the store, but found only dark clothing and a jagged-metal weapon in a trash container outside the ladies' room. The gruesome blood-stained metal object was filled with lead balls and is alleged to be the weapon used by the attacker; whose description matched the dark clothing and greasy hair wig found in the store. Leather body-straps found with the wig and clothing may have been used by the assailant to appear deformed.

Dancing Eyes Adams, the elder member of the Ho-Chunk Tribal Council, accused BoxMart management of hiring a thug to attack Chief Whiteknee. "They retaliated for her leadership in organizing the demonstrations. We did not confront customers entering the stores, as BoxMart management claims. This was a peaceful and orderly demonstration by a legitimate political party."

Oresco's article likened the attack to the union-busting tactics used by assembly-line factories during the mid-twentieth century.

Sheriff Jones Whiley, a local law-enforcement official conducting an investigation of the incident, stated to the press: "This was an expected result. Reservation people have no right to interfere with the shopping habits of normal American citizens."

Oresco opened the 'My Documents' file on his office desktop and scrolled to the 'Supporting Evidence' sub-file he'd created to store Lynne Hurricane's research, and copies of the documents Justin smuggled out of China. He opened a new folder and began typing in the information Virginia Richmore provided:

"*Commerce Department investigators confirmed that fiberboard boxes contaminated with corn-virus were found by college students extracting samples from Iowa cornfields. Markings on the cartons indicate they were produced in Northeast China, and shipped to a BoxMart distribution center in Texas. The cartons supposedly contained industrial-grade water filters. The Chinese Minister of Public Health was informed of the markings on the discarded boxes and soon confirmed that the modern Shanghai Corrugated Container Company facility in Nanjing is teeming with the same parasite. The factory's process-water and holding ponds were apparently saturated with aqueous dispersions of the corn-virus; the suspected sources of factory contaminants. The Chinese government shuttered the factory and is now tracing all recent shipments of cartons to SCCC customers.*

"*Freight documents issued by the Chinese Institute for Advanced Medical Treatments in Liaoning Province, were discovered in the records department of the Smart and Secure Trade Lanes Initiative office in Europe. This entity monitors freight containers remotely, and records their locations over multiple transport modes. Not an easy task considering that over seven million cargo containers enter U.S. seaports on foreign ships each year. The SSTLI documents describe a shipment of one-dozen dual-chamber cartridge filters, in special protective packaging. The listed destination is the BoxMart Distribution Center in Eagle Pass, Texas.*

"*Additional shipping records were obtained from the night manager at the BoxMart distribution center in Texas, when the Secretary of Commerce petitioned a U.S. Federal judge, with jurisdiction over maritime law, to subpoena the retail center's receiving log for imported goods. Although no evidence was found of an actual delivery to Eagle Pass, the facility's records reveal that an order was placed by BoxMart headquarters for the "water filters." The cargo was shipped overseas via a freight-logistics company controlled by the Beijing government, on a South Korean bareboat-charter ship originating in the port city of Tianjin on the Bo Hai Sea. The cargo vessel transversed the North Pacific shipping route to North America."*

*Note:*A spokesman from the Commerce Department explained that Chinese forwarding companies handle huge volumes of container cargo on this route. The more typical freight arrangement is a *voyage-charter*, where the vessel owner provides crew and fuel for a single voyage-fee, between two ports. The seldom-used '*bareboat-charter*' arrangement is utilized only when Chinese, Japanese and South Korean manufacturers require extraordinary control of a special shipment to a specific location."

Oresco's high priority incoming e-mail box blinked. He immediately accessed the seldom-used private e-web address, which he instructed Justin to use only if he found important information during his internet search on Oresco's home computer. Justin was typing as Oresco read.

"The final destination has been confirmed. RFID 'smart tags,' monitored by the Container Security Initiative, now implemented by China, America and several other governments, confirmed that the "shipper" was the annex building of the IAMT medical facility in Liaoning. The recipient of several pallets of water filters and treatment chemicals was an unidentified truck---probably a 24-foot van judging from the number of pallets involved. The pick-up was made about 9 pm on July 31st. The cargo originated in an export trailer secured with expensive radio-frequency seals imbedded with micro-transmitters. The monitors automatically notify the shipping company, the shipper and the recipient of environmental changes; or tampering during transport.

It's highly unusual for inexpensive cargo such as cartridge water filters to be protected by sensors capable of monitoring environmental conditions. What it was? Who made it? When was it made? Yes! Gatt continued to type: Product designation? Price? Yes! All standard information for black and white UPC bar code technology. But, advanced RFID tags? Why had the location and condition of the shipment been constantly tracked via satellite during transit, and relayed to a People's Liberation Army facility in Lioaning?

My other discoveries: Eagle Pass, Texas is a port of entry to Mexico and a commercial hub for agriculture in the area. BoxMart management issued a press release to the Boston Globe an hour ago, in response to China's unusual admission to the international press, that several American retail companies have been supplied with Chinese merchandise packed in cartons produced at the contaminated Shanghai Corrugated Container facility. China never admits such blunders this early. Usually there is a long-term investigation.

Coincidentally, BoxMart claims the company never used cartons supplied by SCCC. They offered no explanation for the SCCC boxes found in Iowa which contained an inner-bag and small label identifying BoxMart water filter cartridges. A spokesman claims that BoxMart is the only large U.S. retailer which does **not** use SCCC boxes to package import goods. I have no idea how they acquired such info. As proof, Jake Kurancy, the chairman of BoxMart, suspended the tight cloak of secrecy usually held over BoxMart operating procedures, and provided the Globe a copy of an exclusive contract with LCE of Anhui and Guangdong, to supply all merchandise cartons entering the U.S. Lynne and I are mining the www for additional info. See ya. *JG.*

CHAPTER 61

(October 30, 2008)
Wallingford, Connecticut

"We've got to call Justin," Lynne said to Joanna, as they walked arm-in-arm in the corridor of the Elim Park skilled-nursing wing after leaving Cosimo's room. "He'd want to know as soon as possible."

"I don't want to alarm him…but I agree, Lynne. Cosimo's condition won't get any better. I'm just afraid that Justin will expose himself to danger if he returns."

"I don't think we can keep him away, once he knows of Cosimo's deterioration."

"What about you? When will it be safe for you to emerge in public?"

Lynne thought about Brad and Justin. "Brad has been checking my apartment from time to time. There's been no indication of tampering or someone looking for me. I think it's safe to return to my apartment in Cambridge now." She glanced down at her shoes and said timidly, "Brad needs my help. McGill just informed him that FFF decided not to provide financing for the five-company merger Justin dreamed up. He's analyzing an offer from a venture capital firm in Houston. They're interested in licensing the shale-oil recovery process."

New York
Times Editorial Offices

Before releasing the story, Oresco's editor-in-chief conferred with high-level contacts at Homeland Security, the FBI and the White House. All agreed it was in the best interests of the country to reveal the full details of Justin Gatt's discoveries in China, without disclosing his name or identifying his mainland contacts.

Ambassador Balzerini had failed to convince Oresco to water-down his vivid account of the insulin-induced deaths of the two known victims. The potential for a *brucellus abortis* pandemic, however, was cited as only a rare possibility. The CDC's petri-dish experiments had been confirmed only in the deaths of the Iowa farmer and the Chinese technician. Dr. Dongzi's macabre description of the horrifying, thick red seepage from every orifice of the Chinese technician's youthful body was omitted from the article. Dr. Dongzi was presumed to be alive, and incarcerated in a Chinese prison.

The American Diabetes Association issued an urgent notice to all doctors listed in their database. Insulin-dependent diabetics must be notified to refrain from consuming fresh corn.

Iowa, Nebraska and other corn-belt states reeled from negative consumer response to the contamination crisis. Major supermarkets in the Northeast and West cancelled orders with Midwest farm cooperatives, and began searching for fresh corn from local suppliers. Commodities futures on the Chicago Mercantile Exchange plummeted or skyrocketed, depending on how the destruction of nearly five million acres of corn impacted their markets.

Gabriel Oresco reviewed the final draft before submitting the lengthy feature to his editor. As much as he'd attempted to reduce the number of words, it was still nearly twice the length of a typical front-page expose. He wanted to make sure that BoxMart's role in the disaster was fully disclosed.

Oresco's piece began with the hook of a thriller novel:

"The Iowa farmer was drugged to dull the excruciating pain. God only knows if he sensed the thick red droplets oozing from his eyes, mouth and other body cavities. He finally succumbed when his vital organs decomposed."

The U.S. Centers for Disease Control issued a world-wide warning, after a virus-like organism invaded the unfortunate Iowa farmer's body. The source of the parasite is believed to be an uncooked ear of hybrid Iowa corn, contaminated with the strange cellulose-consuming organism which recently invaded large Midwest cornfields. Dubbed the "corn-virus" by CDC scientists, the parasite is believed to have originated in China.

Virginia Richmore, a CDC official explained, "The virus-like mycoplasma responsible for browning the Sac City cornfields, is believed to have mutated in the farmer's body. Previous studies at the Centers for Disease Control in Atlanta have confirmed that, under certain conditions, similar agricultural-pathogens mutated into dangerous human diseases. We believe such a mutation may explain the sudden deterioration in the farmer's bodily functions."

Oresco omitted information that no cure existed for the rare mutated form of the pathogen uncovered in the autopsy.

Federal health experts are confident the contamination is isolated in low-population areas and can be eradicated before causing additional human casualties.

Virginia Richmore, the CDC scientist in charge of the disease-containment program, described the agricultural pathogen as an "incomplete RNA retrovirus similar in genetic code to the deadly Ebola monkey-virus." I can at least say that! Oresco mused.

The article disclosed that a "reliable source" returning from China, provided documented evidence of a similar organism discovered in a Liaoning Province hospital in northern China.

Scientists from the U.S. Centers for Disease Control notified the World HealthOrganization and the Chinese Minister of Public Well-Being, that the surfaces of Chinese-made cardboard boxes, found near the contaminated cornfields, were coated with the live organisms. Labels on the discarded containers apparently indicated the cartons were produced by the Shanghai Corrugated Container Company, located in an industrial complex about fifty kilometers west of Shanghai. Ms. Richmore reported that Chinese officials earlier today confirmed the Shanghai area factory had tested positive for the organism. "We've advised Chinese Health authorities to immediately institute precautionary procedures to prevent the spread of the parasite. The Minister of Public Health in Beijing confirmed that the infested factory would be shut down in accordance with normal factory-closing procedures.

CDC's Richmore told this reporter that the origin of the contamination has been questioned. "We suspect America has been exposed to the agricultural-pathogen via cartons imported from China." She noted that the Chinese government was cooperating fully in the investigation. U.S. Trade Representative, Butler Humphreys, who recently returned from successful trade talks with Chinese leaders, received a letter from the Mayor of Nanjing, suggesting that the factory was deliberately contaminated. Foul play is suspected from enemies of the state, because the new facility is considered a model of environmental responsibility. The mayor claims that the modern paperboard factory utilizes multiple sensors to monitor water quality before factory effluent is fed back into the Yangtze River.

Local farmers in Iowa have been ordered by the U.S. government to burn millions of acres of contaminated Iowa corn; about one third of the largest corn harvest any State has produced in the last ten years. The anticipated crop loss has caused a price run-up for animal feed, pork, beef, and other processed foods which rely on corn oil, corn oil solids and high fructose corn syrup. The uncertainty in the food chain has prompted the Secretary of Agriculture to order all corn-producing States to report current inventories of harvestable maize.

A confidential source returning from China provided U.S. authorities with copies of shipping documents signed by a Liaoning Province hospital employee. U.S. Ambassador to China, Forrest Balzerini, claims the documents indicate that trade officials in Beijing were aware of the virus contamination **before** *the cartons* were cleared for export to the U.S. Humphreys refused to identify the person who provided the shipping documents.

"His identity is being withheld until American authorities conduct a full investigation. We've traced the contaminated boxes to a shipment destined for the distribution center of a large American retailer, BoxMart Stores."

According to the Xinhau News Agency, Beijing's Politboro met in full session last evening to address the problem. Yong Ihasa, the Minister of State Security, issued a preliminary statement through the Communist Party propaganda department, promising a full and open disclosure of any information the Beijing government obtains in its investigation.

(Reporter's Note): BoxMart is the largest U.S. importer of Chinese merchandise; yet reports that none of its imports are contaminated.

Oresco handed the final draft to the Times editor and commented wryly, "Americans aren't accustomed to major food shortages, Harry. Or, uncertainty in our food supply. The free-fall in the dollar's foreign buying power; the threat of a disease pandemic; the refusal of the BOC to purchase U.S. Treasury bonds? These are all serious hits to the U.S. economy involving the Chinese."

Harry was skeptical when conspiracy theories were promoted by top reporters like Oresco. "What purpose would it serve for China's largest market to experience a sharp downward spike?"

Oresco's investigative instincts honed a dark reply, "The *reason* this is happening may turn out to be the biggest story of all."

Harry had earlier worried that the newspaper would be criticized for running a controversial, highly-charged story a few days before the national elections. Now, he was convinced "Listen, Gabe; your article about the attack on the Indian chief and her Make Do Party received kudos from everyone... except, of course, BoxMart management. I'm not concerned with their lawsuit. But the implications in this article that BoxMart, a maverick French banker and members of the Chinese government are conspiring to damage this country, will upset a host of State Department heavyweights and multi-national corporations operating on the mainland."

Oresco shuffled his notes and lifted a single sheet from the research pile he'd accumulated for the article. He handed a copy of a Wall Street Journal report to the editor-in-chief. "There are too many bad events occurring at the same time, Harry. They mount up to a severe economic blow to this country, which Gatt and I believe represent a coordinated attack by entities who wish to interrupt, if not permanently damage, America's economic stability."

"Well, that certainly seems to be the case," Harry conceded. "Tangus at the Fed is already hyping the need for a sharp interest-rate bump."

"I don't believe it's a coincidence that Creditte Bank de Savoy just traded another $30 billion of China's central bank dollar reserves for other currencies. Phillipe Cusson, the Director General of CBdS, has been dumping U.S. dollars for nearly two months. Even the Swiss banking authorities don't believe his actions were meant to protect client deposits, as he claims."

"You've a point, Gabe. The paper's economists say his deals have destabilized trade between America and all its trading partners. Cusson has yet to answer inquiries from the European Union Central Bank regarding the timing of his first multi-billion-dollar trade---the day before the Iowa fields became contaminated."

"The events must be related," Oresco concluded vehemently. "The Bank of England has now predicted run-away inflation for the U.S. economy, if the Fed Open Market Committee misjudges its interest-rate decisions." He gauged the editor's reaction with a side glance. Harry was famous for his stubborn skepticism. Harry's eyes were fearful.

"Wall Street is in turmoil, Gabe. My contact at the Fed says Tangus will soon inform Congress and the President that the twenty-percent decline in the dollar, versus nearly every other currency in the world, will force the Open Market Committee to raise overnight inter-bank rates by at least a full percentage point next week. The shock to domestic financial markets and small businesses will hit like a tectonic stress release."

"So much for Martin Merrand's anticipated honeymoon-period with Congress."

WASHINGTON, D.C.

Richard deLeone leaned across the linen-covered table at the Fourth Estate Grill on 17th Street and said to Butler Humphreys, "If Balzerini ordered Gatt into hiding, he's made a huge mistake. The so-called evidence Gatt brought back from China is sketchy...at best."

"You seem troubled, Richard. Why so uptight about Gatt's location?"

The Assistant U.S.Trade Representative replied nonchalantly, "It's not my worry, it'sBalzerini's. You don't go around accusing the Chinese government of sabotaging America's food supply. I'd like to see the documents Gatt supposedly smuggled out." He reached for the martini. "The accusations by the Times reporter against BoxMart and China's government are preposterous."

Yew Bai Tsin, the Governor of the Bank of China, didn't help deLeone's argument, when he'd informed Humphreys that morning that Beijing was postponing all future participation in U.S. Treasury bond auctions. The USTR replied indignantly,"You're mistaken,Richard. With Japan and China both abstaining from the treasury auctions, the federal budget deficit is going to spin out of control. Beijing has to realize this."

"Balzerini will be here soon," deLeone replied evenly. "Let's see if he can vouch for the authenticity of the Times article."

"He's seen the shipping documents. He's also interviewed an eye-witness to the attempt on Gatt's life---a person close to the action when a Chinese missile was launched at his aircraft as he escaped from Macau."

"Documents can be forged."

"I suppose; and coastline anti-aircraft defense batteries can malfunction... as the PLA claims. I suspect that since Justin has resurfaced, his whereabouts are a prime topic of interest to the people who tried to shoot him down."

DUSTR shifted the topic skillfully. "Dr. Nolte's reports to the U.S. Department of Health, the World Health Organization, and the Chinese Ministry of Disease Control, describe a special danger for millions of diabetes sufferers. You're one of the millions, Butler. Aren't you worried?"

"The greatest danger of exposure is in Iowa, near Sioux City and Fort Dodge. Also, at the Shanghai box factory. As I understand it, Richard, any unfortunate insulin-dependent diabetics who somehow ingest the corn virus could be subject to a viral-colony infection that grows immortally...like cancer." Humphreys looked up and saw Ambassador Balzerini greeting several media people as he approached their table in the back of the restaurant.

The Fourth Estate Grill was a favorite meeting place for Washington's media elite. A rude reporter from the Washington Post grasped Balzerini's forearm and said, in poorly disguised braggadocio, "Have *you* heard that an anonymous Beijing dissident posted an internet message on the rogue watchdog site, 'Zhongguo Yatong' (Middle Kingdom Toothache). Did *you* know that President Mu Jianting was accused of attempting to suppress the Shanghai factory contamination? Any comment, Ambassador?"

Balzerini shrugged his arm loose as politely as possible and eased away from the overly-aggressive, fortyish woman whose unkempt strings of red hair were pushed back into a witch's broom.

"What I know is already public, Hazel. You're perfectly aware," he scolded, "that the Chinese propaganda department tends to say things to protect their export trade."

Humphreys stood to greet Balzerini and held out a friendly hand. deLeone remained seated and nodded as the Ambassador took a seat next to Humphreys.

"I'm not here to waste words," Balzerini began abruptly. The waiter arrived before his butt landed on the seat cushion. "The CDC filed a formal appeal this morning with the World Health Organization. They've been cleared to inspect the Shanghai factory. The Attorney General has also initiated a formal investigation into BoxMart's role in the debacle. We want to know how many contaminated boxes were loaded onto ships bound for U.S. ports; and how many are routed to BoxMart facilities."

"How have the Chinese responded?"deLeone prodded. "They're usual delaying tactics?"

"They're cooperating fully."

"Very uncharacteristic of the Chinese,"Humphreys marveled.

Balzerini looked at deLeone suspiciously. "The Chinese Minister of Public Security, Vice-Premier Yong Ihasa, emerged yesterday from a special meeting of the Standing Committee of the Communist Party to announce the Politboro voted to fully cooperate with U.S. and international health officials. The Xinhua News Agency government mouthpiece published a sanctioned report indicating representatives from the U.S. Centers for Disease Control and the European Union Infectious Diseases Administration were invited to join the on-site investigation. The CDC has a team in the air. They'll be allowed to conduct independent tests at the box factory."

deLeone replied in an even tone, "They're worried. The Chinese economy could be seriously damaged if the thousands of sealed cargo containers packed on ships at sea, or berthed in Chinese and U.S. ports, are carrying goods in contaminated cartons."

Balzerini signaled the waiter for his usual iced tea. "They'll have to be turned back." The noticeable grin on deLeone's face was puzzling. Immense damage to international trade could result if hundreds of ships originating in China had to be quarantined because of diseased cargo.

SHANGHAI, CHINA

The paperboard factory was shut down by Jiangsu Province health inspectors; and all employees were washed down with abrasive anti-bacterial liquid soap blended with sand and iodine. The steaming showers left their pale skin the color of smoked salmon. Officials from the World Health Organization and the U.S. Centers for Disease Control witnessed the washdown and the incineration process which followed.

The entire inventory of paperboard and finished cartons, stored in the factory and stacked to the rafters of the 25-foot ceilings in the adjoining, million-square-foot warehouse, went up in flames. The sky between Nanjing and the Bund section of Shanghai was flittered with charred carbon-flakes, rising up from thousands of tons of flaming paperboard being destroyed in open fires. The bonfire piles were the largest Dr. Nolte had ever seen. So hot…they melted the metal guard rails protecting the area.

"Are you sure all customers have been notified of the procedures for handling and disposing of contaminated boxes?"Nolte inquired of the interpreter, as he stood next to the young factory manager whose handsome oriental features were glossed with regret.

The dowdy female interpreter with high cheek bones, a flat face and deep-set black eyes, conveyed the question to the factory manager. His reply was morose. "All customers know what to do. It is their responsibility to carry out government instructions and destroy the goods." His voice rose noticeably, as he lamented, "But there is not enough paperboard capacity in the country to replace the lost supply. Your retailers will not have merchandise in time for the American holidays."

ZHANGNANHAI, BEIJING

Within days of the factory closing, General Ye released copies of Dr. Ho Hot's signed confession to Chinese and foreign press agencies. Reuters, the Associated Press and the International Herald Tribune carried Ho Hot's accounts of the genetic-disease experiments conducted at the Taiwan Medical Research Institute. Ho Hot admitted smuggling the agricultural pathogen into China to damage the important maize crop of the People's Republic of China.

General Ye stomped his right foot on national television, as he recounted the Taiwanese scientist's feeble attempt at misplaced political revenge. From the press room in the Defense Ministry Building near Kunming Lake, General Ye stood erect in full uniform. A dozen service medals...usually disdained in public by high-ranking officers, to display a bond of respect for lower-ranking soldiers...were pinned to his chest.

"The madman from Taiwan admitted following the orders of his fanatic separatist superiors," began the General. "Ho Hot has admitted developing the cellulose-devouring organism for use as a biological weapon against the People's Republic of China. Ho Hot confessed that his devious scheme was sponsored by the Taipei dragon-imitators, who have attempted to use---as an excuse---President Mu Jianting's decision to confiscate mainland property acquired illegally by Taiwan investors. The PLA is preparing an appropriate response." There was no question in Ye's foreboding tone. Taiwan could expect a military retaliation

"Unfortunately, Dr. Ho Hot was so embarrassed by his terror tactics that he committed suicide in his prison cell."

SHANGHAI AREA SHIPPING PORTS

The Chinese Minister of Industry and Trade, Wang Chao, ordered all shipments of packaging materials from the Shanghai factory traced to specific customers. Inspectors were dispatched to the mainland warehouses of all SCCC retail customers. If black-light and hydrogen peroxide tests were positive for the virus, the customers were ordered to collect and destroy unused cartons. They were allowed to remove and quarantine the items inside; if tests showed no presence of the living pathogen. Otherwise, the merchandise was destroyed. Chinese export officials ordered the uncontaminated goods to be covered and sealed in heavy plastic shrink-film. If all went as General Ye planned, only the cost for the outer cartons would be lost.

Any mycoplasma on the surfaces of toys, small appliances or household goods would die-off in three or four weeks, according to the scientists. He knew that BoxMart's merchandise and outer cartons were free of contamination. The outer boxes were supplied exclusively from LCE plants in Shenzhen and Anhui Jake Kurancy's major competitors were not so lucky. Their ability to ship goods for the upcoming winter-holiday season was seriously impaired…if not wiped out.

Chinese and American inspectors detected the presence of corn-virus on cargo ships departing from China; in American deep-water ports; docked at West Coast piers, and anchored off the California coast awaiting clearance to unload.

Ships suspected of carrying contaminated boxes were traced within twenty-four hours by the Shanghai and Nanjing Import and Export Corporation, which managed most of China's export shipments. At the urging of Yong Ihasa and General Ye, an SNIEC executive ordered all cargo ships at sea to return to the Taiwan Straits. The captains were told to anchor in the seaward waters off the coasts of Fuzhou and Xiamen, kissing the western harbors of Matsu and Quemoy islands; or drift in circles in deeper water if the anchorages were too shallow or became congested. The Chinese Ministry of Public Health temporarily banned off-loading of crew and merchandise from the returned ships.

The U.S. Department of Health issued a order for all Chinese cargo to be tested for possible contamination, before they could be unloaded in U.S. ports. CDC officials dispatched organism-detection teams to Los Angeles, Long Beach and other West Coast ports. The tests used to detect the presence of corn-virus on cardboard boxes were refined in Atlanta. Kits containing plastic dispensers of hydrogen peroxide solution, and battery-powered UV testing lamps were dispensed by overnight special delivery.

U.S. DOCKS AND WAREHOUSES

Most of the goods packaged in boxes produced during the last month at the SCCC factory near Shanghai were alive with the cellulose-devouring micro-organisms. Several hundred super-cargo vessels were ordered to depart U.S. ports, and drift in Pacific international waters about 200 miles off-shore. The seas were treacherous, endangering the despondent crews quarantined on board with the diseased cargo. They were at least heartened when CDC inspectors, dispatched in Coast Guard helicopters, verified that no contamination had escaped from the sealed 20-foot box trailers. All diabetic crewmen were removed in biohazard suits and flown to isolated Level-Five emergency containment and medical facilities.

"It's impossible to test every carton," the Secretary of Homeland Security informed the ailing President. "There's no other choice but to quarantine as many contaminated ships as possible. Up to six-thousand sealed, trans-ocean containers are stored on each boat. Even with the knowledge of which trailers contain Shanghai-made boxes, we can't open every trailer cautiously and test its contents in the seven-day period the CDC recommends."

California dock workers had taken the initiative. Nearly four-hundred supercargo ships were forced to drift into deep waters, when longshoremen refused to unload vessels originating in China. Soon, the Strait of Taiwan would host an armada of merchandise vessels retracing their northern Pacific routes from China.

HSINCHU, TAIWAN
NATIONAL CENTER FOR HIGH PERFORMANCE COMPUTING

The bio-chemists at the Taiwan Military Research and Defense Institute were shocked at the similarity between the organism stored in their massive databank of experimental chemicals, and the corn-virus structure reported by the CDC to the World Health Organization. The three-dimensional chemical models included an exact duplicate of the mutated dodecahedral RNA molecule stored on their newest supercomputer in Hsinchu. The organism had been classified as a bacterial-pesticide for corn, soybeans and barley.

A quick inspection of the retained-samples inventory at the Taipei Research Institute, confirmed that several vials of the RNA mycoplasma developed by Dr. HoHot, were missing from his storage freezer. The scientist had disappeared months ago, after taking a leave-of-absence to visit his son at a mainland university.

When notified of the missing vials, the Taipei government vehemently denied involvement in a plot against the PROC. Beijing was accused of making false accusations to justify new aggressions against the break-away regime's satellite islands of Quemoy and Matsu, bordering the Fujian Province coastline. Deep-ocean drilling in the area had detected a potential massive natural-gas field.

Satellite photos provided to Taipei by the U.S. showed PLA troops conducting amphibious training exercises off-shore from the Taiwan-controlled island strongholds. The President of Taiwan rattled swords with

Beijing and warned that locating an armada of diseased PROC cargo vessels in anchorages surrounding the islands was an act of aggression Taipei could not ignore.

CHAPTER 62

(Early November, 2008)
New York City

Oresco watched Gatt stuff cosmetics and a few days supply of clothing into his overnight bag. The beard and false identification papers were tucked into a side pocket.

"You'll be putting your life in danger as soon as you step out of this apartment."

"I'm sick of this cloak-and-data bullshit, Gabe. My grandfather's dying and I'm going to see him." He added angrily, "Those fucking Chinese missiles can't reach New Haven."

Oresco felt Justin's frustration. He worried that the Triads were watching his Manhattan apartment. His recent front-page article wasn't exactly complimentary to Chinese secret societies. They might have recognized his bearded guest as the man reported killed in an aircraft accident over the Indian Ocean. Justin could be targeted. Asian Triads take swift revenge when they are deceived.

"At least wear the beard until you get there," Oresco pleaded. "If they follow you, your friends in Connecticut could be put in danger. Isn't Lynne Hurricane still in hiding?"

If Justin hadn't experienced near-death twice, at the hands of the Chinese in Shanghai and Macau, he'd probably blow off Oresco's warning. He unzipped the side pocket. "Just in case," he snapped, in a voice swelled with resentment. "Keep digging, Gabe. We're close. Lynne just received copies of banking documents from Stella Nicorezzi's father in Geneva. She claims the information could blow the lid of this BoxMart-China-D.C.collaboration. I'll fax you copies from a safe place as soon as I look them over. I don't trust the internet. Too many electronic geniuses can eavesdrop through firewalls."

The bearded man angled through the rotating doors in the lobby and walked directly to one of the taxis idling in front of the lower Eastside apartment building. "Grand Central," he shouted to the dark-skinned driver wearing a Mets baseball cap in reverse, and reading a Spanish-language newspaper from Columbia. The sweet-sour scent of marijuana and body odor was oppressive. The driver flicked on the meter and shot into the nearest traffic lane without looking back. Justin pressed against the seat as an out-of-state Chevy Blazer running the traffic light, was forced by the taxi to the outside lane. The SUV braked in time to avoid slamming into the rear of a city bus, but the oriental driver cussed, and swirved the stolen vehicle left onto the sidewalk; slamming into a vender selling genuine-Rolex timepieces. A pedestrian paying twenty-dollars for a precision watch suddenly crumpled onto the Blazer's hood and was thrust into the air; then crumpled onto the sidewalk in a sickening thud.

The oriental driver in his mid-twenties, leaped from the SUV, ignoring the injured pedestrian, and raced in the direction of Gatt's taxi. As the vehicle disappeared into the traffic, the Triad agent calmly glanced around at the startled witnesses. The street vendor was bending over the customer lying motionless on the sidewalk. Two athletic-looking men in black collarless shirts approached the oriental driver with the intent of detaining him until police arrived. One went down from a vicious groin kick; the other was temporarily blinded when a ringed-knuckle pummeled his left eye. The oriental driver darted for the subway entrance and disappeared.

The Metro North from Grand Central Station to New Haven made more local stops than the Amtrak from Penn Station, and wasn't as comfortable. But the evening rush-hour traffic was heavier; and Justin would blend in better with the throng of city professionals returning home to Greenwich, Stamford and Bridgeport. During the train ride, he kept watch for any oriental patrons within lunging and stabbing distance of his aisle seat. He doubted that the Triads would attempt to shoot him in a crowded train; if they'd followed him from Oresco's apartment.

Joanna was parked adjacent to the ground-level exit ramp near the side entrance to Union Station. Justin emerged from the hurried commuter crowd wearing the full brown beard. The twins were leaning out the back windows of her new champagne station wagon, waving. They'd been instructed to remain in the vehicle and shout, "Dad...Dad."

"My, you haven't changed a bit. Still not shaving regularly, I see."

"Still a wise ass!" Justin spouted in a broad smile. He suddenly realized how much he'd missed Joanna and her perky teenage daughters. He jerked the door closed, hesitated, then leaned over from the passenger side to the driver with the intent of planting a friendly kiss on her cheek. Joanna's head pivoted without forethought and their lips sort of met. The twins watched in delight as Joanna adjusted the position of her head slightly and aligned their lips perfectly. The move was smooth and natural. The twins would remember it. Justin was unaware of the expert female maneuver just perpetrated by their still-vibrant mother. Teenage girls could use such a move, when their inexperienced kissing partners missed the mark.

It was the first time they saw their mother kiss Justin. The youngest...by thirty-seven seconds...licked her finger, leaned forward and stuck it in his ear, screeching, "Wet Willy, wet Whilly."

"Stop that...stop that, you brat." The crimped shoulders and hoarse manly giggle were his way of returning the teenager's gesture of affection. Joanna pulled away from the station, hoping that Justin's first question wouldn't be "How is Lynne?"

Cosimo was sitting up in the hospital bed at the Elim Park medical ward, straining to comprehend Lynne's explanation of why Justin failed to visit him. Much had occurred in the past few months. Cosimo's mild stroke and the voracious cancer cells invading his aged body left him fighting for a few months more of life. The chemotherapy and loss of movement in his left side caused him to shed thirty pounds since the last visit from his grandson. Cosimo was heavily drugged for pain and drifting in and out of a deep slumber.

Justin hesitated outside the room a few seconds before entering. He could hear Lynne speaking softly to Cosimo. Joanna had described Cosimo's failing condition. He was bracing for the worst...his emotions twisted...when he finally entered the room.

Lynne was holding Cosimo's hand, now a bony outline of the strong, talented instrument which created so many wondrous objects. Cosimo's eyes were closed and he had a warm cheery expression, as if enjoying an amusing dream. Brad's hands were resting gently on Lynne's shoulders, and his chest was resting against her back. He pulled away immediately when he saw his rival for Lynne's affections enter the room.

Lynne turned to Justin as he eased forward. "He's doing well today," she whispered. Justin strode slowly to Cosimo's bedside and leaned close to his face. For a few moments he just watched. His grandfather was having a pleasant dream, and seemed to be experiencing no pain. He was somewhere between consciousness and the paradise island of morphine cay.

"I bet he's with the Marogespel girls, and grandma is twisting his ear."

Justin embraced Lynne and held out a hand for Brad. "It's so good to see you both," he murmured in the sincere tone of a true friend. His warm smile assured Brad that Justin was not bothered by his show of affection for Lynne.

Lynne suggested apologetically, "While he's sleeping, we should discuss Johanas Nicorezzi's new bank documents. He says the Swiss authorities will soon visit Phillipe Cusson with an arrest warrant."

An hour later, Justin called Eric Syzmansky at his Yale office. "I need your interpretation of the financial information in Meng-ji's note." He'd forwarded a copy to Syzmansky over NSA channels during his brief stop-over at Diego Garcia.

Syzmansky seemed stressed. "Forrest Balzerini informed me of your narrow escape from danger, Justin. I'm afraid it was my fault you became involved in this mess. Please accept my apology."

"I can't say it hasn't been....different, Eric. But what we have to worry about now is national security. Lynne and I have convincing evidence that people high up in the Chinese Communist Party, working with people in our own federal government, are scheming not only to drive American factories out of business, but to damage our food supply and de-stabilize the entire country."

Syzmansky anticipated his next thought. "And BoxMart is part of the scheme. You're suspicions may be true, Justin, but don't be surprised by what I'm about to tell you." Syzmansky lingered on the next words. "The U.S. economy *and* the Chinese economy are showing signs of crashing. My friend Meng-Ji side-stepped safety protocol, and e-mailed me a message that the Chinese central bank is no longer supplying U.S. currency to local Chinese banks. That means the day-to-day funding of small local businesses, which require U.S. dollars to pay letters-of-credit for components made in the States, has dried up. BOC Governor, Yew Bai Tsin, claims it's a temporary measure. It seems as if the Beijing government is anticipating that many of China's manufactures won't require U.S. dollars to finance export shipments across the Pacific Ocean…for whatever reason. At least not in the short-run."

Justin thought about the quarantine order the U.S. Department of Health just issued…The twin West Coast ports of Los Angeles and Long Beach, where forty-three-percent of all imports from Asia are off-loaded, were ordered to cease unloading all Asian freight.

"Eric, have you been following the New York Times reports about the corn-virus contamination in Iowa?"

"Of course. Our entire commodities market is in turmoil because of it. People are scared they won't have enough pork or beef to eat. The average Joe doesn't have the slightest idea how important corn is to this nation. Look at a food label sometime. There's barely a processed food, including ketchup, that doesn't contain an ingredient derived from corn."

Justin said forcefully, "We've obtained new information which Balzerini should see as soon as possible. He'll know how to activate the FBI, CIA or whatever law enforcement agency needs to get involved. Lynne and I should meet with him in Washington." Justin decided to leave Gabriel Oresco out of the mix. He was the back-up source for releasing information, if he and Lynne had an unfortunate accident in D.C.

The broad-shouldered "maid" was still on the loose.

"Johanas Nicorezzi uncovered several suspicious multi-million-dollar transfers from Creditte Bank de Savoy. Big money went to a prominent member of the U.S. Trade Representative's office. The president of a Federal Reserve district bank also received large sums from CBdS's sister bank in Geneva."

"I know about Franco-Medici Trust, Justin. They're the controlling stockholder of Residents Bank of North America. Edwin Tinius works for Phillipe Cusson, the Director General for both European institutions."

Justin's temples began to drum wildly. "That sleezebag! Tinius is not only collaborating with BoxMart, but he's apparently a puppet of the Frenchman who dumped U.S.dollars in Europe and ignited an international currency crisis."

Lynne leaned toward the phone in his ear. "Ask him if he knows Richard deLeone or Marco Santucci."

(National Election Day, Nov 4, 2008)
Washington, D.C.

Justin and Lynne were met at Reagan National Airport by two NFL-sized secret service agents dispatched by the President at Balzerini's request. They were stuffed into an unmarked American compact sedan waiting at the curb outside the commuter gate, as Lynne and Justin emerged.

"We were instructed to escort you to the Hilton Washington on Embassy Row," the driver explained. "It's the headquarters for Governor Martin Merrand's election team."

"The results of the national elections should be announced in a few hours," Lynne whispered to Justin. "I wonder why they're taking us there." The SS agent in the passenger seat turned his lamp-post neck and replied amiably, "The suite is very large. The Ambassador thought it would be best to conduct your meeting before Governor Merrand gets caught up in after-events."

"Do you expect him to win?" she prodded in the hypnotic tone that usually drove men away from cautious thoughts. The agent was not about to succumb to her evil intent by revealing his affirmative answer. "It's possible."

Justin and Lynne were astonished when they were led to the top-floor suite and greeted at the door by the Ambassador. They were frisked for the third time by security agents, then pointed in the direction of a side room.

"Thank you for coming so quickly. It's rather an odd time to meet, but Martin insists that we address the problem immediately. Later tonight will not be a good time for small talk."

Governor Merrand was in a private office at the opposite end of the suite, accompanied by his attractive wife of thirty-six years. He was cutting short a lively phone call he'd accepted reluctantly from one of his financial supporters. Harley Hedge wanted to remind him that his group's support had been critical to Merrand's anticipated victory. "I haven't won yet, Harley."

"But you will, Governor. Five of the six remaining states will go your way."

Merrand wondered how he could make that statement so confidently. "Of course, I'll welcome your recommendation for the vacant Department of Energy position. Just as I did when you recommended Elliot Scharn and Carvin Troone."

"Let's talk in here." Balzerini led them to a large bedroom suite overlooking Massachusetts Ave. He motioned to a pair of deep-cushioned armchairs and sat on the edge of the king bed. In a voice stilted and solemn, he announced, "We have a huge problem. I received a communication from AJ Hau Luing in Beijing a few hours ago. The embassy received a coded e-mail message from a reliable source posted at a Communist Party vacation resort, located not far from Beijing on the Bohai Gulf." He shifted his weight on the bed to prevent sliding off the slick comforter. "The source indicates there will be an attempt made on Governor Merrand's life if he wins the election."

Justin was a fast learner for an amateur spy. He closed his gaping mouth and inquired perceptively, "Is the source completely reliable?"

"He sacrificed his hearing to take on the assignment. Yes. We're sure."

"I assume Eric Syzmansky briefed you about the information we're carrying?"

"Yes. Although I'm speechless regarding deLeone and Santucci's possible involvement. You say you have banking records to implicate them?"

Justin handed Balzerini a thick envelope from his coat pocket and said, "Four top Chinese officials; BoxMart's Chairman, Jake Kurency; a dude French banker named Phillipe Cusson; and at least two high level Washington people are involved. We believe deLeone is one of them. Plus Santucci at the Boston Fed, if that proves out."

Balzerini's head was swaying like worn wiper-blades on a dry windshield.

"I traced inter-company fund transfers," Lynne began to explain, "and broke thru....er, detected very large and unusual dollar transfers between subsidiaries of Cusson's French banking empire and the others we believe are involved in the scheme. Johanas Nicorezzi has convinced Swiss officials to seize CBdS's records and arrest Cusson. He claims the internal records prove Cusson's guilt."

Justin added,"He'll be charged with bank fraud, currency manipulation, racketeering and bribery. I wouldn't be surprised if the World Bank or the European Union Central Bank freezes the assets of the French bank and its subsidiaries."

"That would include Residents Bank of North America," Lynne announced blandly.

"Are you sure?"

"Yes,"she replied. "Not directly, but through a Cayman Island shell company. It seems Cusson had a vested interest in the American bank's efforts to bankrupt American small businesses."

Suddenly a huge cheer erupted in the main parlor. Balzerini jumped up from the bed and darted for the door. Justin and Lynne followed. Balzerini swung the door open and another loud cheer erupted. He watched Merrand and his wife stride in from the private office and join his election team in front of several flat TV screens. Merrand held up a quieting hand. Joe Kleinman, his campaign manager, yodeled, "*White House, here we come,*" in the familiar lyrics of the California name-sake tune. "Somebody break out the champagne."

When California fell, the Merrand-Troone ticket needed only one of the six remaining electoral-vote states. "We're not there yet,"the Governor cautioned his unconvinced supporters. Ten minutes later, four additional secret service agents pranced deliberately into the suite and took up positions at the windows and doors. Two agents watching the flat screens repositioned to the service bar. The lead agent peered out a window to confirm that Capitol police were taking up roof-top positions.

Joe Kleinman shouted jubilantly,"It's over, Martin. You've captured four states and the fifth is too close to call."

Martin Merrand would be the next occupant of the White House; by at least five percentage points. Only the conservative CNN computer had estimated low---at less than a two-percent margin of victory in electoral votes. CNN cited the staggering economy as the cause for the closer-than-expected election. Merrand was not helped by the dollar retreat, rising interest rates and uncertainty in the food supply, which dominated the news during the waning moments of his party's occupancy of the White House. But, his strong can-do personality left people with the feeling that the Governor could handle the crises better than his opponent. His pro-consumer stances on jobs and import restrictions pushed him over the top. Although consumer confidence in the economy was at an all-time low, Merrand gave the impression he could solve the food disease crisis which surfaced in the Midwest. Everyone expected him to push for import restrictions, to meet his campaign pledge.

In the commotion, Merrand looked back at Balzerini and noded acknowledgement to the two strangers standing beside him. "What a moment to be part of," Lynne cried exuberantly. "I can't believe this."

Justin took in those gorgeous green eyes and replied, "It sure hasn't been boring, lately, has it?"

The celebration died down a few decibels but was far from subdued. The new leader of the most powerful, and now the most troubled, country on earth, was high-fiving his staff and embracing the secret service agents assigned to his campaign. Mrs. Merrand retreated to the quiet of the private office to accept a courtesy call from the wife of the defeated candidate. She then returned to the celebration and draped her arms around the President-elect, swaying him from side-to-side in a bear hug worthy of a sumo wrestler. To the delight of everyone, she kissed him passionately on the lips and hung on until Merrand gulped for air.

Vice-president-elect Troone and his wife arrived at the suite to join the celebration. For some un-explained reason, Mrs. Troone broke down and began sobbing. Mrs. Merrand thought her tears were those of joy; or perhaps she was awed by the enormous responsibility she'd soon assume as the first-lady-in-waiting.

The secret service agents who became friendly with the governor and his family during the campaign were likely to follow him to the White House. They watched closely as Merrand accepted calls from Congressional leaders for an hour, then instructed Joe Kleinman to take the calls for him. He motioned for Balzerini and his two visitors to join him in the private office suite.

"We have another hour before I issue my acceptance speech, Forrest. Let's get this issue dealt with by then." He offered his hand to the strangers he'd heard so much about.

Lynne and Justin were awestruck by the realization that they were the first American citizens to be honored with a private audience with the next President of the United States. All those comparisons of U.S. Presidents graduating from Yale or Harvard came to mind. "Mr. President," Lynne's parched voice crackled, "Congratulations."

"Well, thank you, my dear. I understand that you and Mr.Gatt didn't vote." He smiled. Not a reprimand---but a joke to cut the tension. Merrand had been briefed by Balzerini of the necessity for Lynne and Justin to remain out of sight.

"First I must commend you both for risking your lives for this nation. Forrest tells me that you, Justin, are on a fast-track training course as an involuntary espionage agent. He complains that you've missed the first 95 percent of the classes, and almost got yourself killed...twice."

"A mere inconvenience, Mr. President." Justin inhaled. "Mr. President-elect?"

"Call me Governor. A lot can happen between now and inauguration day."

Balzerini was not comforted by his comment.

"Tell me everything you know: the people involved...the nature of your evidence. How and why you think the Chinese have conspired against the U.S. economy! Everything you two modern-day Sherlock Holmes' have uncovered about this so-called multi-facetted conspiracy. It's so fantastic."

"If their information and notions are as accurate as I believe,"Balzerini offered, "in a worst-case scenario,Martin, you and the President will have your hands full trying to prevent a major global economic catastrophe from evoking a military conflict."

"Our theory is as complicated to explain as the conspiracy itself, Governor Merrand. But, the facts implicate the people we will mention. They all have powerful interests in maintaining free-trade, and keeping U.S. borders open to Chinese imports. Particularly Jake Kurancy, the chairman of BoxMart Stores, and his European and Chinese banking friends."

Before Merrand departed, he assigned two secret service agents to protect Lynne and Justin around the clock. "Job well done! You can now emerge safely in public," Merrand noted. "I may call on you again in the near future. Meanwhile, I hope you can return to a normal life."

The national networks declared Merrand the official winner, as reporters camped in the ballroom of the hotel to cover his acceptance speech. Lynne was still swept up in the excitement, and wandered over to the bar, where two secret service agents rushed to serve her a drink. Justin remained in the side room with Balzerini, recounting his experiences in China and revealing everything he knew about Residents Bank, FFF and the assailants who attacked him and Lili in the Shanghai back-alley.

They reviewed the latest documents Johanas Nicorezzi uncovered in Geneva, and Justin disclosed an organizational schematic he'd drawn up of the various relationships between BoxMart, the French, Swiss and Chinese banks, the Financial Flow Foundation and the individuals who received large payments from Cusson's banks or BoxMart. Balzerini choked on a glass of water when deLeone, Santucci and three Politboro members were named.

"Yong Ihasa, General Ye Kunshi and Wang Chao, sir. We're not sure of the possible involvement of Mu Jianting, the former Communist Party strongman."

Balzerini cringed. "That's information which cannot be discussed until the Chinese announce it themselves."

Justin understood immediately. "We don't want to reveal the Embassy's capability to intercept top-level communications in the Chinese capital?"

Balzerini nodded silently. "You know?"

"I guessed!"

"According to AJ's intercept from Zangnanhai, Mu Jianting has resigned from the top three leadership posts in China. Or, rather, he's been forced out."

Justin said, "Mu is implicated in the conspiracy mainly because of his alleged attempt to cover-up the contamination at the Shanghai factory. We're not sure if that's true."

Lynne was doted over by the SS agents who heard she'd risked her life to uncover information vital to the security of the nation. One of the agents grew up in Albany and graduated from NYU with a degree in American history. He mentioned that Merrand would be one of several New York Governors to become President. Lynne dazzled him with her knowledge of other New York governors who were Vice-Presidents, or had been candidates for the presidency. He reciprocated by clearing up questions that suddenly troubled her.

"Who runs the country if both the current President and the President-elect die before the inauguration? Does the current VP govern until the January 20, 2009?

*What happens after January 20? Does the new Vice-President automatically become President? If the President-elect succumbs shortly **after** the inauguration... and the new VP becomes President...can he run for two additional terms? Is it possible that the Vice-President-elect could hold the office of the President for almost 12 years?*

"In summary, Mr. Ambassador---considering what's at stake---I believe Kurancy led the way." Justin's mind was approaching E, after he'd raced through detailed explanations, conspiracy theories and corroborative facts. "China manufactures two-thirds of the world's shoes, most of the DVD and CD players, the bulk of paper copiers and other office machines. They produce most microwave ovens and nearly all the world's toys. Not to mention the myriad of impossibly-low-priced cast-metal, ceramic, and molded plastic products that have forced a ton of American small factories into bankruptcy."

"So, you think Jake Kurancy has convinced the Chinese exporters, and others---like deLeone and Santucci---that American citizens are so dependent on imports that we can't function without China's manufactured goods?"

"Absolutely."

"Do you agree with them?"

"Absolutely, not! I believe Nonnie Washington offered the simplest and most profound answer to the problem. It's a matter of whether Americans are willing to change a few buying habits. Well...maybe more than a few. One thing is certain: the four Chinese government officials involved in this scheme do not want their exports to the U.S. restricted in any way."

"But, why would they stage events like the corn-virus infestation and dollar devaluation? You must admit the opposite effect is more likely to.... Oh! I see your point."

Justin explained his theory further, "If the interruption lasts just long enough to scare the shit out of the people, Merrand will have a tough time convincing Congress to approve his protectionist policies."

Balzerini smiled at Gatt. A man confident enough to slip "shit" into a serious conversation with a U.S. Ambassador must be totally convinced of his ideas. That was enough to seal his confidence in Justin's judgment. "I want to know more about the *Make Do Party*."

DEFENSE MINISTRY, BEIJING

General Ye was outwardly belligerent, but inwardly pleased, as he announced to an international television audience that Taiwanese agents had conducted a grave espionage plot against the People's Republic of China.
He supplied copies of Dr.Ho Hot's written confession to the world press, then ordered the state-controlled television stations to play recordings of Ho Hot's verbal confession every half-hour. The words were blared to listeners at purposely elevated volume. Chinese commentators speculated that the PLA now possessed sufficient justification to warrant a significant military response to the break-away island's transgression.
In a staged interview, General Ye announced, "The UN Security Council has been presented with a resolution from the People's Republic of China, condemning the outrageous and dangerous provocations of the Taiwanese puppet government. As a precautionary measure, President Mu Jianting has ordered the People's Liberation Army to position ground troops near the Taipei-administered Islands of Matsu and Quemoy. Futher measures may be required to protect Chinese merchandise being returned to the area for health inspections."

BEIDAIHE RESORT, CHINA

Yong Ihasa snapped, "They're as good as occupied."

The Vice-Premier moved away from the window of his summer villa in Beidaihe and said to Wang Chao and the despondent Communist Party Chairman seated stiffly in a straight-back bamboo chair, "Chang Hui Chen will petition the U.N. General Assembly to sanction the occupation. General Ye has already moved troops and supplies to the areas. The PLA field commanders are preparing an amphibious assault on both strongholds. I doubt if either Matsu or Quemoy will resist vigorously."

Wang Chao added enthusiastically from his thick-cushion recliner, "The islands will be sealed off from intervening forces by the hundreds of returned cargo ships anchoring in the shallow waters surrounding the islands. That should prevent any attempts by Taiwanese or American naval forces to land troops or provide cover for the island's occupants."

Outgoing President Mu Jianting listened as the helicopter which had transported him to Yong Ihasa's villa, landed a few hundred feet away for his return trip to Beijing. In a downtrodden, resentful voice, he grumbled, "I ordered a full PLA navy fleet to position along the Fujian shoreline, at your insistence, Comrade Yong. Don't you think the Taiwanese rats will consider that an over-reaction? If not a provocation?"

"As I promised, General-Secretary Mu, the charges against you will be dropped as soon as your retirement is announced." Ihasa was skilled at redirecting conversations when it suited his purpose. "Be prepared with your resignation speech by tomorrow morning. Chang Hui Chen will follow your national broadcast with a demand by the National People's Congress that the U.N. immediately approve Beijing's resolution to occupy the islands. Along with your resignation, the proof of Taiwan's biological attack on the mainland should give the Security Council no choice."

Mu inhaled the acrid high-tar cigarette a full one-third of its length. He flicked the inch of ashes onto the floor defiantly, and blew out the grating smoke with the vibrancy of a fire-eater. "I hope you comprehend, Yong, that the evidence General Ye revealed will be scrutinized by the international community. Few governments will actually believe that Taipei hawks planned to implement a pre-emptive strike on China's northern corn fields. It is also unclear how they could benefit from contaminating a Shanghai box factory with the same organism."

"Beijing has been forced to abandon the giant Shanghai cardboard factory," Yong boasted, as if putting thousands of peasants out of work was an accomplishment. "The Shanghai-Nanjing Export Company was obligated to recall all cargo ships carrying merchandise packed in the contaminated boxes. The cost to PLA factories and American retailers will be enormous. Unfathomable!" His grin was a dangerous reflection of gratification.

"Every major store chain in America (he neglected to exclude BoxMart), will suffer. Their merchandise managers are already shouting imperial murder."

President Mu was not convinced. "It's true Chinese factories should suffer only temporary cut-backs; but what if the organism spreads in both countries. You claim the bio-weapons scientists have assured you that is chemically impossible? Even so, American businesses will still feel the biggest impact. Without our low-priced goods, American citizens will take to the streets."

"Exactly the result we desire," Ihasa retorted angrily. *Mu Jianting's outspokenness will guarantee him a brief retirement.*

"So, your Triads desire rapid inflation, merchandise shortages and contaminated food supplies in America?"

"The perfect formula to frighten away Merrand's demands for import restrictions."

"You are mad, Yong. You can't tweak macro-economic conditions…on such a large scale…once such chaos is unleashed."

China's new leader replied indignantly, "When the organism dies off naturally in less than a month, LCE factories will resume full production. In a few months the Americans will be begging China for more merchandise."

President Mu snubbed out his cigarette and rose. "May I now return to clean out my office in Zhangnanhai?" His tone was subdued, as he added, "If your group miscalculates the timing, Yong, or if something unexpected happens with the rogue organism, the interruption in trade with the American capitalists could be prolonged. Have you factored that contingency into your Triad plans?"

Ihasa smiled absently. He'd drifted elsewhere in thought. A Ming once again would rule the Chinese empire. Members of the Triad secret sects would inevitably replace hard-line Communists in key government posts. His poetry would be celebrated by the masses for centuries to come.

And Bomali Corp---the retailing and manufacturing juggernut formed by the merger of BoxMart and LCE---would emerge to dominate global retail trade for the next twenty-five years. With unlimited access to the giant U.S. consumer market.

NEW YORK FEDERAL RESERVE BANK

"Treasury has cancelled another auction," Tangus announced to the other members of the Fed Open Market Committee gathered in New York for an emergency meeting. There are no viable bidders."

Willard Reyes, the President of the New York District Federal Reserve Bank, was a permanent member of the OMC. While hosting the meeting, he complained, "We've got to take a hard stand in deciding the next interest-rate adjustment. I came away empty-handed on the Street." Referring to his attempt to urge Wall Street investment banks to participate in the next Treasury auction, he added ruefully, "My suggestions fell on deaf ears."

Marco Santucci, his counterpart as President of the Boston District Federal Reserve Bank, reported better results: "Tom Blackstone, President of the Financial Flow Foundation in D.C., has unbelievable contacts with high-rollers in the private and corporate sectors. At my request, he contacted some of the largest investors to solicit bids for the next $20 billion the Treasury needs to raise." Santucci saw the skepticism posted on the crinkled faces of the country's chief financial policy-makers. Wall Street investment banks were infamous for ignoring requests by Treasury officials to trim profits, and assist a troubled U.S. economy.

"When the risk is metered at more than half a percent point, Wall Street usually runs for cover," Santucci said as he handed Tangus an offer sheet from a group of unidentified investors led by a former Goldman Sachs executive. "Blackstone was encouraging," added Santucci. "He said the Treasury Department would have to pay only two points over current overnight transfer rates."

Tangus crowed, "That's unprecedented. We'd be creating more disorder than now exists in the financial markets. The currency exchanges and commodities markets are already reeling."

Willard Reyes of the New York Fed reminded the group of the global financial crisis. "The dollar has fallen so sharply in the last several weeks that even Phillipe Cusson, the French fool who started the avalanche, has quietly offered to repurchase greenbacks from some of the European finance ministers he traded with several weeks ago. His goons are re-purchasing relatively small dollar sums for just about any foreign denominations the ministers will accept. The Swiss call the trades "apologetic transactions," because Cusson is being investigated for currency fraud by the Swiss authorities and the World Bank. He may have bribed the ministers."

"He's selling mostly yuans," replied Tangus. "And he's only purchasing enough dollars to replenish a temporary shortage in Macau. Word is—he's still willing to exchange dollars for euros."

"The overall effect," Santucci interjected, "is that the Fed now has exactly the opposite problem with Chinese currency that it had a few months ago. The yuan may be detached from the dollar, but it has responded much too strongly. I suggest the OMC attenuate the situation with a dramatic increase in interest rates. At least 1.5 points."

Willard Reyes looked at him strangely. "Surely, you're not serious, Marco. That would exacerbate the situation. I'd recommend we hold rates steady, to stabilize the markets."

"I disagree vehemently," Santucci replied.

The four-hour heated debate resolved only that the Open Market Committee was split on which interest-rate adjustment would cause the least pain to consumers. Finally, the Fed chairman said, "We've discussed the pros and non-pros long enough. We'll vote first on Marco's recommendation. How many approve a drastic rate increase of 1.5 percent?"

TAIPEI, TAIWAN

The lack of an official U.N. presence diminished Taiwan's chances that the U.N. would intervene on their behalf. If China moved to occupy Quemoy and Matsu, Teipai would be buffered only by a decades-old American promise... not even a treaty...to protect Taiwan from attack by the Beijing lions.

Taiwan's request for military support from America was rejected politely, when the Commander in Chief fell ill. "To deploy a large Pacific fleet to the satellite islands in the Taiwan Strait is not feasible at this time," the Secretary of State explained to the Taiwanese representative. "However, the National Security Advisor will table the issue as soon as the President recovers fully." That meant—wait until the next administration takes office.

(LATE NOVEMBER, 2008)
WASHINGTON

From the temporary medical facility at the White House, the President issued a controversial edict that shocked the retail industry. Those more concerned with the health of U.S. citizens expressed relief.

Effective immediately, all non-essential Chinese imports are to be turned away from U.S. ports. No Chinese shipments will be allowed to enter the country until the extent of the corn-virus outbreak is determined and adequate protections are firmly in place.

The U.S. Health Department and World Health Organization were surprised when Chinese trade officials agreed to abort all merchandise shipments to the U.S. without much fanfare. The Prime Minister, Zhoa Zhoa-Gang, authorized the return of all vessels containing boxes made at the contaminated Shanghai factory. They were ordered to anchor off the east coast of the homeland. Unfortunately, Beijing's unexpected cooperation precipitated turmoil in global trade.

The Federal Reserve Bank announced that overnight inter-bank borrowing rates would remain unchanged. However, all money-center banks would be allowed to increase the prime lending rate to corporations by two percent.

The rates on 3-month, 6-month and two-year treasuries were elevated by the federal rate-setting committee and the Secretary of the Treasury. According to the Wall Street Journal, the rates were set at unsustainable highs.

Martin Merrand settled next to his wife on the comfortable love-seat in their Washington hotel suite. He drew her close. "Finally, we're alone," he smiled. He hadn't decided yet to inform Mrs. Merrand that his name was mentioned in a Chinese-government communique intercepted in Beijing. Or, that the exchange between high-ranking Chinese officials cited Merrand as a "problem" to be "solved" before the inauguration. The CIA and Secret Service interpreted that as a warning that Merrand's life was in danger.

"I've asked Gabriel Oresco, Justin Gatt and Lynne Hurricane to compile their evidence and ready it for national publication. The FBI and CIA will do their thing, then the Times will break the story. The AP will distribute follow-on articles to thousands of publications"

"Why has the President requested your presence at tomorrow's cabinet meeting, Martin? Isn't that unusual?"

"It's basically a crisis meeting for advisors. He's following that with a military status review of the South China Sea, in the Situation Room. The SOD is bringing in the Joint Chiefs of Staff. He asked me and Carvin to attend for our unbiased opinions. None of his advisers seems committed to a particular course of action in response to the Chinese threat. I don't think the current crisis is a scenario they've practiced."

Carvin Troone asked, "And the agenda will be?"

The White House Chief of Staff extended a typed sheet entitled: *Confidential for Highest Level White House Staff Clearance.*

"I guess you now qualify, Senator."

Troone read the bullets. Single summary sentences for each issue to be discussed. The multiple uncertainties facing the nation seemed unresolvable. Troone considered it a real possibility that the President would suffer a medical relapse under the pressure. Sooner, rather than later, he and Merrand would have to assist the Man juggle a myriad of conundrums atypical during the final weeks of an outgoing Chief Executive's tenure.

Troone's mind was transitioning from legislative-branch to executive-branch rational. The call for him to join Merrand came from the Hilton suite.

"Financial and food misfortunes aside, Martin, I hope the President is not seriously considering deploying additional naval forces to the South China Sea. Congress won't go along with him dragging America into another theatre of military confrontation. Especially in a region as explosive as the Taiwan Straits."

"What if the PLA moves to occupy Matsu and Quemoy?"

"The Taiwanese will have to go it alone. The bulk of the returned Chinese merchant vessels will be anchored near the islands. That should mitigate any conflict."

"I wish I had your confidence that cooler heads will prevail in Beijing, Carvin. Mu Jianting was rated a moderate by CIA experts. It's a shame he resigned...leaving such a mess."

Troone wondered how Merrand could make such a statement. No announcement had yet been issued from Zangnanhai regarding Mu's retirement. He conjectured that the President-elect was provided national security information which the vice-president-elect was not yet cleared to receive.

"Perhaps the President can convince Mu to reverse his decision to resign," he said, a tad too casually. "A trade interruption between our two countries is more important to China than internal Communist Party bickering; or rattling swords with Taiwan over the fate of two islands which should belong to the mainland in the first place."

"What makes you suspect internal Party bickering, Carvin?" The Governor's face tightened. The ring of Troone's comment echoed prior knowledge. Merrand was aware that Troone cultivated high-level friendships in Beijing when he was Secretary of State. "Do you know something you should tell me about the Chinese?"

Troone's expression twisted into an ironic, embarassed grin. "Yong Ihasa, the Vice-Premier, and I once exchanged friendship writings and poems." He admitted "It was several years ago, when I ran the State Department. I learned to express the true meaning of ancient Ming poems from him...in English translations. Yong is a brilliant leader. We became pen-pals of sorts."

"Does he provide you with political information?"

"Of course he does not, Martin. We're friendly competitors...that's all."

Merrand wondered if Troone was already aware of Ihasa's appointment as new Chairman of the Chinese Communist Party. If so, why hadn't he mentioned it? As a former competitor for the Presidential nomination, he imagined Troone kept other secrets---carried over from his career in the legislature.

The President, a former governor himself, had tipped Merrand to the first thing a Governor must learn when he becomes President: former legislators he appoints to the executive branch will maintain secrets from the President. No matter how loyal they are to the President or his causes.

"*Knowledge is power,*" he'd advised. "*Secret knowledge is dominant power.*" Every politician in Washington needs a power base to survive and function effectively.

CHAPTER 63

(NOVEMBER 7, 2008)
WASHINGTON, D.C.

The President sat at the head of the conference table in a wheelchair equipped with an oxygen tank and a clear plastic bag half-filled with medical solution. He would not allow mention of his condition, and had ordered the White House physician to remove the I.V. tube until the meeting was adjourned.

"I've asked President-elect Merrand and Vice-President-elect Troone to join this meeting because of the unprecedented crises facing America; which will linger well into their administration. Immediate and well-informed decisions will be required in the next few months from the highest level."

The Cabinet Secretaries were aware that the current Vice-president could be running the country at a moment's notice...depending upon how the President responded to the experimental drugs.

"I've asked the Secretary of State to chair this cabinet meeting...for obvious reasons." He nodded weakly to the seasoned politician across the table. "Robert, please begin."

Robert Sinod, the first Secretary of State to be declared legally blind while in office, nodded to the murky outline of the President. Martin Merrand was seated a few feet behind the President in a staff chair set against the wall in the Cabinet room. Sinod was in his early fifties, of medium height, with an athletic build and a handsome face tanned to nearly the shade of his grey-speckled almond hair, which was parted in the middle.

He'd contracted a parasite in his right eye two years ago during a state department trip to India, and was gradually losing his vision. The parasite had undulated into his left eye before doctors from Johns Hopkins killed it with a combination-antibiotic.

Sinod was scheduled to undergo a laser operation which promised a full recovery of his sight, but had postponed the operation until the new administration took office. He didn't expect to be asked to stay on.

"Thank you, Mr. President. I'd also like to welcome Governor Merrand and Senator Troone. While it is unusual for the new administration-elect to be included in a cabinet meeting of the outgoing administration, we welcome their input; and of course, hope President-elect Merrand will benefit from a running start in addressing the unprecedented complexity of problems now facing the nation."

Sinod blinked to squeeze out the excess medicated droplets coating his hazed eyes. He folded open the leather cover and removed a brail summary sheet. His fingertips glazed over the raised dots while the others looked on with mixed expressions of admiration and sympathy.

"Our economy has undergone an unparalleled sequence of negative events," he began, in a determined tone projecting confidence that the problems could be expeditiously solved. "The Federal Reserve Bank has been forced to increase bank lending rates significantly."

He pushed aside the summary sheet and said with rising exasperation, "Foreign trade has been seriously interrupted; joblessness has accelerated to nearly nine percent; the dollar continues to sink versus other currencies. The Iowa corn-virus infestation has exposed the Midwest to a potential human pandemic; and the Treasury lost its two largest customers for short-term bonds." He dabbed the corner of his eyes with a cotton handkerchief. A newly hired staff aide thought he had plenty to tear about.

"Chairman Tangus at the Fed has not found an answer to funding the budget deficit….in the face of China's unexpected withdrawal from the bidding process."

The President felt compelled to comment. "That about summarizes domestic issues."

Sinod hated the fact that he couldn't look into the eyes of the other cabinet members and read the true meaning of their words. The rule at cabinet meetings was to be overly cautious in responding to the President's direct questions. Spoken words did not necessarily represent a Secretary's true position on a particular issue. Sinod suspected that others in the room resented the ailing President's confidence in his leadership abilities. Perhaps because both were physically challenged, the President wanted to convince the Cabinet---by appointing Sinod to chair the meeting---that both impaired men could effectively carry out their duties.

Sinod turned to his right and faced the outline of the man seated next to him. "I propose that each Cabinet Secretary present a brief summary regarding the status of his department, as it pertains to the overall national condition. The Secretary of Homeland Security will begin."

Martin Merrand was transfixed by the deliberate and succinct presentations of each cabinet member. As an old friend of the President, he recalled the Chief Executive's distaste for unnecessarily long discussions and elaborate explanations of issues. When an idea could be expressed in two words...the President was pleased.

The SOHS, the newest Cabinet position authorized by Congress in 2003, responded laconically, "Other than the normal threats originating in the Middle-east, the borders are secure. The threat level from Mexico has attenuated. We believe the recent sniper shooting on the Mall---if truly an act of the Chinese Triads---was an isolated incident."

Sinod faced the Secretary of Health and Human Resources, seated across the table. "Harvey....your summary, please?"

Without hesitation, the SOHHR replied in an alarmed tone, "The Iowa corn-virus has mutated into a deadly human pathogen...at least once. The scientists at the CDC think it could happen again---under certain conditions. Fortunately, those conditions are limited and very specific. Basically, you have to eat raw corn contaminated with the organism, wait for the so-called mycoplasma to totally consume your blood sugar, then take insulin injections. The organism mainly feeds on cellulose...like the material used to make cardboard containers. It remains alive until the cellulose on the surface is consumed. CDC claims that could be for up to three or four weeks. If there is sugar around at the time, it seems to adjust its internal chemistry and become a sugar-eater."

"Where did it come from?"

Merrand sat on the edge of his chair during the seconds of silence that followed.

"We're not sure," the Secretary replied meekly.

Merrand was relieved when Sinod filled in the most likely answer. "The Chinese discovered the identical organism at a box factory near Shanghai. We suspect the corn-virus may have originated there, then was transferred to the U.S. as an outer package for finished goods produced in China for the American market."

The President wheezed and suddenly gasped for air. He inhaled deeply, straining to exhale without spraying the table with catarrh. "Go on," he managed to cough out---a plea for expediency easily recognized. He needed to return to the make-shift hospital room on the second floor of the White House.

"Agriculture?" Sinod called out with renewed exigency.

The former dean of the Agricultural College at the University of Illinois leaned forward on her elbows, fists clenched. Her pleasant 45-year old oval face was flush with the coloring of a young farm girl

"Mr. President, gentlemen. I'm sorry to report that the corn crop this year will be four to five million acres short of projections. The impact will be experienced across the country; although hardest hit will be the Iowa hog and meat-packing industries. The entire food chain will suffer. Prices for maize futures have already skyrocketed on the mercantile exchanges." She continued in an apologetic tone, "We're actually exploring an offer from the Chinese Grain Export Council to supplement America's remaining crop." She tapped a USDA summary report with her pen and added, "China is the second largest producer of corn in the world, and has just reported the first bumper-crop in the country's history. The timing is incongruous. Unfortunately, the CGEC's asking price is excessive."

"Usury level," complained the Interior Secretary. "Livestock, sugar, cereal and gasoline prices will all experience significant bumps because of the corn shortage."

"Commerce?"

"Mr. President, I agree with the Centers for Disease Control that this country cannot risk importing goods contaminated with a potentially deadly organism. But, I'm afraid the impact of turning away Chinese goods, whether they're sitting at our west coast ports or on Pacific routes to America, will be devastating to the economy."

The President waited a few seconds. "That's all?"

"Well, Sir, the important Christmas shopping season could be entirely lost. Most of our large retailers buy the bulk of their seasonal items from China...taking delivery between now and early December. If they're not supplied, the American people will have to do without toys and a myriad of other household items and gifts---now available only from mainland factories." The President's former law partner added morosely, "There simply is not enough remaining production capacity in American for our small manufacturing businesses to pick up the slack; as they've done when shortages were experienced in the past."

"What about current inventories? I understand that most retailers stock a lot of those items months ahead?" asked Sinod.

"We checked warehouses first for contamination, Robert. Only one major retailer---BoxMart Stores---is well-stocked for the upcoming season. Luckily, their goods are totally free of virus contamination. BM does not purchase cartons made at the infested Shanghai factory."

"What about the other large retailers?"

"Most of them rely on just-in-time deliveries of seasonal goods. Their warehouses are bare, except for left-over gift items that Wal-Mart, Sears, Penney's, Walgreens and other big retailers couldn't move last season."

The Secretary of Defense waited patiently for his turn to address the crisis issues. He felt disoriented...discussing food, diseases and budget deficits. He was more concerned about the strategic complications the Pacific Fleet would encounter when thousands of cargo ships zig-zagged across main shipping lanes in the northern trade route. The U.S. Navy Pacific Fleet was assigned, unofficially, to protect the cargo. He was also troubled by Beijing's recent accusation that Taiwan was responsible for contaminating both China and the U.S.with the corn-virus. The latest satellite images revealed several modern PLA naval vessels sailing for the Taiwan Strait; on a collision course with hundreds of cargo ships returning to Xiamen and Fuzhou.

"Defense?"

"We're spotting escort vessels to accompany the returning cargo ships, Mr. President. We're awaiting your decision regarding the request by the Taiwanese to deploy another carrier group from our Pacific Fleet to the T-Strait. The sea traffic in the area will be chaotic. If we go, there could be a heightened level of tensions with the Chinese, unseen since the 1950s. The Central Military Commission has been surprisingly belligerent in their warnings against foreign vessels entering the South China Sea."

Sinod said, "General Ye Kunshi, the Commander of China's Eastern Defense Forces,has threatened to occupy two Taiwan-controlled islands in the area."

"Your recommendation, Arnold?"

"We cool our heels, Sir. I don't believe this country can afford a new military front. The situation in the middle-east is not de-escalating as we hoped. Perhaps this crisis will die-down of its own accord. I suggest we find a way to resume the trade volume with China as soon as possible."

Merrand was incredulous. The former Army general was making a huge mistake in judgement. He made a mental note: There were at least two current cabinet Secretaries who would not be part of his administration.

The President listened to brief statements from the other cabinet members. He then glanced over his shoulder and broke protocol. He asked a non-cabinet member if he would like to comment.

Merrand decided to stand as he answered. He stepped forward in the room so the President would not have to twist his neck.

"With due respect for the expertise and experience of the Cabinet advisors, Mr. President, I believe there is more to this situation than has been addressed so far. As you know, the confidential information Ambassador Balzerini's man acquired in China suggests a sinister motive for the events now impacting the economy. In the near future, Sir, I suggest that the facts we've uncovered be framed in the context of a conspiracy against the U.S."

An audible quaver infiltrated the Cabinet room. The President's chief advisors shifted in their chairs. Most were thinking: "*What next?*"

"The Chinese are implicated by the fact that they are the likely conduit for the corn-virus entering the U.S. In addition, the stockpile of U.S. dollars accumulated by the Chinese in central-government bank accounts, which is controlled by the Chinese Communist Party as a result of Beijing's massive balance-of-trade advantage with America, has been spit in our faces. High-level Communists had to approve, or at least allow, the European bank controlling their deposits to essentially dump the U.S. currency. I believe that action was deliberate; and precipitated the current downward spiral of the dollar."

Merrand glanced across the room to the Attorney General. "We should be asking the question: 'who benefits from these events?'"

Carvin Troone was pleased with the follow-up discussion to Merrand's comments. Jake Kurancy at BoxMart, and the Chinese corn exporters were recognized as the main beneficiaries. Troone watched silently as Merrand trailed the President's wheelchair to the door. The President asked Sinod to continue the discussion, then join him and Merrand upstairs.

Troone spoke in Merrand's place. He suggested that a viable alternative to entice Beijing back to the bond-market was a temporary suspension of import barriers and tariffs on consumer goods. Of course, the success of such an incentive would require the rapid resumption of trade with China---assuming the corn-virus contamination abated in the near future.

FEDERAL RESERVE BUILDING, WASHINGTON

Jon Paul Tangus was about to panic. The dollar value had dropped again; this time by ten-percent overnight. "Currency dealers all over the globe are issuing sell-orders," he exclaimed ruefully to the three federal banking administrators hastily called to his office.

"Mostly in reaction to the President's nationally televised speech last night," Marco Santucci replied indignantly. "Nobody expected him to *quarantine* all non-essential imports from China."

Willard Reyes, the president of the New York District Fed Bank replied, "The massive call-back and isolation of Chinese goods was recommended to him by the World Health Organization. The CDC agreed with the decision. Several cargo ships already docked at the twin California ports of Los Angeles and Long Beach, were found contaminated when trailers were opened."

"The Chinese found the same result when transport containers originating in Shanghai ports were opened and spot-checked," added Tangus. "Most of the 20-footers held cartons that were coated with the live organism. The Chinese port authorities re-sealed the containers and marked them with skeleton-head labels, then covered them with plastic film."

The President's Executive Order had been announced during his short speech from the Oval Office shortly after the cabinet meeting: *"Our highest priority must be to prevent the spread of the disease. The unfortunate interruption in foreign imports will hopefully be of short duration. The American people are thankful that Beijing leaders have agreed to return all recent shipments of Chinese-made goods to secure anchorages off the coast of Fujian Provence."*

Viewers were alarmed when the President wavered and seemed to lose his place in the prepared speech. However, he'd rallied and said bombastically, *"California dockworkers have been ordered not to off-load Asian cargo from berthed vessels... unless it is fully inspected under the supervision of CDC scientists. Test kits from Atlanta are being distributed to the longshoreman unions. "*

Pedro Ramirez flung the hydrogen-peroxide and black-light testing kits provided by the CDC into the California harbor. "No fucking way I'm testing every 20-footer."

Tangus had called the emergency meeting with the Exchequer of the Currency and his closest confidants on the Open Market Committee—Willard Reyes from New York and Marco Santucci, the President of the Boston District Federal Reserve Bank. He'd also informed the chief executives of the Bank of England, the European Union Central Bank and the Swiss Banking Agency in Zurich, of his intention to pressure the Exchequer of the Currency and the Treasury Department to print more dollars. They all urged him to reconsider.

Printing more federal reserve notes to fund the U.S. government deficit could only deflate the dollar further, causing foreign holdings of U.S. assets to tumble in value. Foreign holdings of U.S. assets were $2.7 *trillion more* than American holdings of foreign assets.

Tangus was reminded by the Europeans that the US is a net-debtor to the rest of the world. If foreign investors became any more weary of owning U.S. assets, there could be a ruinous meltdown of the American economy; which would wax-over global commerce.

Tangus swallowed his pride at the urging of the Swiss, and dialed the headquarters of Creditte Bank de Savoy in Lyons, France. When he finally got through after the third call to Phillipe Cusson, the Director-General was less than cooperative.

"Put more pressure on the Japanese," he'd suggested mockingly, after a ten-minute heated exchange. The Fed Chairman's caustic reply was not well received.

"I do not accept your insulting reprimand, Mr. Tangus. I am obligated to protect my clients' money."

"You idiot! Your actions have upset currency markets all over the globe. Did you convince the Chinese to approve this? Or did they convince you?"

"Calm yourself, Tangus, or come up with an alternate plan. Or, have you Fed geniuses lost your touch for macro-managing global finances?" The line clicked then buzzed.

Cusson's dream of besting Tangus had come to fruition. The icing would be the fifty- million dollar bonus he'd receive from BoxMart and the Chinese. A straight-forward, non-detectable transfer of 40 million euros from client accounts at Franco-Medici into his personal numbered account at the same bank. Half would be wired to a Cayman Island self-insurance company he alone controlled. The other half would be used for high-risk, high-reward investments in Russia and Eastern-block countries; or used for his personal pleasure.

(Mid-November, 2008)
Defense Ministry, China

"Yong Ihasa is officially in, Mu Jianting is out!" exploded General Ye as he rose from his desk at the Defense Ministry and dropped the secured phone onto its base. "Chang Hui called from the Standing Committee chambers in Zangnanhai. The vote was close."

"You will now have your rightful place on the Standing Committee," replied Li Chin, as they clasped hands and bowed in mutual respect. "I will return to Macau and inform Bromine and Wen Ma of your decision to revise Bomali's executive structure. Kurancy and Bromine will not be pleased."

Ye's rise to power would be as meteoric as Yong's. The new Chairman of the Party, and acting President, had agreed to appoint General Ye Chairman of the Central Military Commission. Ye would now control all of China's armed forces; having by-passed Marshall Tong Shu, the aged Commander of the PLA, currently 2nd in line behind the retiring Mu Jianting. General Ye now dominated the five-man Military Commission. There could be no opposition to his plan to attack and occupy Matsu and Quemoy.

U.S. Embassy, Beijing

AJ Hau Luing scratched notes as he listened to the theoretically-secure Zhangnanhai communication between Yong Ihasa and Chang Hui Chen , the Chairman of the People's National Congress. Chang was to pass the word to General Ye, LiChin and Wang Chao, the Minister of Industry and Trade. In turn, they'd notify the Bomali group in Macau and the Triad sects which Yong Ihasa honored with his direct leadership.

If the Beijing lords discovered the Embassy's interception of Zhangnanhai transmissions, or detected faint signals emanating from the ultra-sophisticated communications equipment on the 4th floor, they'd torch the place...with everyone in it. Diplomatic immunity had its limits in Chinese circles.

AJ's subsequent report to Ambassador Balzerini over the high-security transmission line linking the Embassy with the NSA satellite over Ulan Bator in Mongolia read:

Urgent. Urgent. For A. B. eyes only. Confirming China top leadership has changed. President Mu has resigned as Party Chairman, President and head of the Military Commission. Yong Ihasa was chosen to succeed Mu as new Communist Party General-Secretary. Yong was also appointed acting-President. General Ye Kunshi, the Director of state-controlled industries, has been elevated to the top military position---Chairman of the Central Military Commission. Expect China to announce the changes in a few days. Appears Mu was forced out by Yong and others. Am accompanying Lili Qi to Emai Shan. If all goes well, I'll report in from Beijing in three weeks.

CHAPTER 64

(DECEMBER, 2008)
SENATE OFFICE BUILDING, D.C.

Lydia Bryce sat across from the man she'd devoted the last four years of her life to...disbelieving the words he'd just spoken.

She'd rushed into Troone's office in the Dirksen Senate Office Building when he paged her a few minutes earlier to discuss something important. She'd anticipated the vice-president-elect would ask her to join his staff in the west wing of the White House, or in an alternate office set aside for the VP in the Old Executive Office building.

Instead, Troone coldly informed his devoted speech-writer---the woman who lifted his public image to new heights; helped him become Merrand's running mate;.. *substituted for his wife in ways too embarrassing to admit*---that her services were no longer required.

"But, Carvin?" she pleaded tearfully, "Why? For God's sake...you need me!"

The teak box on the metal cabinet behind his desk suddenly strobed a flashing red beam from its top surface. Troone followed Lydia's puzzled gaze behind him. His stoic expression instantly transformed into alarm as he stared at the crimson emission.

"I can't discuss this any further, Lydia. There's not much more to say." His eyes locked on the flashing emission. "You've been quite helpful to my career, and I sincerely appreciate your devotion. But the White House is a different category. Of course, I'll give you a stellar recommendation."

He rose to escort her from his inner office to the hallway beyond the reception area.

Lydia stared incredulously at Troone's icy grimace. The polished teak case continued to blink red, but she was too crushed to ask what it was.

"Can't I even help you get settled at the Admiral House?" referring to the three-story Queen Anne structure at the U.S. Naval Observatory on Massachusetts Ave. and 34th Street, where the government provided a permanent residence for the Vice-president and his family. She was desperate. Maybe being around him longer…he'd change his mind.

"As I said, Lydia," he gritted his teeth impatiently, "I won't need your services any longer. Now, if you don't mind, I'd like you to leave." He practically shoved her through the outer office and into the hallway; then rushed back to his inner office, slammed the door and turned the lock.

Lydia stood in the hallway for a few minutes…fossilized. Her startled eyes watched as devoted Senate aides in their mid-twenties hustled to committee meetings, or herded constituent groups around on tours. She was emotionally disoriented. She couldn't recall how she got there.

Finally, she broke down and ran teary-eyed into the vacant ladies room down the hall and emptied her grief over an open toilet.

The cell phone in Troone's briefcase chirped a short tune as he was sliding the teak box into the top drawer of a two-tiered, lockable fire-proof metal cabinet. He spun away from the open waist-high drawer and snatched the special communications unit from the briefcase sitting on his credenza. "Troone speaking."

"Senator Troone, this is Tom Blackstone from the Financial Flow Foundation. Congratulations on your victory."

"We're on a secure line, Blackstone. Go ahead, but make it quick."

Blackstone's voice muted. "The FBI and U.S. Marshals have stormed BoxMart headquarters in Massachusetts with search warrants. Kurancy and Cashman have been taken into temporary custody for questioning."

"Good grief! Have they found Kurancy's teak box?" Troone didn't remember the BoxMart chairman's number. His box was still blinking the number "3."

"Is yours emitting?" Blackstone catechized sardonically.

"Yes, damn it. Who initiated the raid?" The Senator collapsed into his chair and stared blankly at the red flashes bouncing off the ceiling above the open file cabinet. "Who the fuck is behind this?" he repeated grimly.

"I don't know for sure. There's been a lot of traffic at the White House today. I thought the President might be failing." Blackstone raised his voice, "What do you want me to do?"

Troone respired to calm himself--taking several rapid deep breaths which he released in slow, pursed puff-outs. *Merrand has probably influenced the President to move on BoxMart. Kurancy's teak case must have been opened. Did it explode? Did he open it for the FBI, voluntarily? Jesus…my name is inside!"*

"I'll call you back in five minutes." His box was still flashing "3," but he couldn't remember if that was Jake's number. He reached into the cabinet, extracted the box with both hands and placed it gently on his desk. *There was only one way to find out.*

Lydia peered in from the crack in the door of the anteroom leading into Troone's private office. Usually the access doors from the hallway into Troone's office were locked. But the movers forgot to twist the locks when they removed the fold-out couch Troone used for power naps during the day. The strength of the wooden frame had been tested several times during their late-night speech-writing sessions.

She'd torn his framed-poem from the wall in her nearby office and was about to smash it over his head. She pictured herself being dragged from the building by the Capitol police. A woman scorned…gone mad…kicking and scratching…yelling at the top of her lungs:"You used me! You used me!"

When she saw Troone on the phone and heard his strange conversation, she eased the anteroom door closed…leaving just enough opening to catch his words.

"He'll have to be stopped. If others in the Savoy Imperative are implicated, there's the possibility someone will talk. Jake has the most to gain or lose financially, so he'll probably stone-wall the questions for a time. What's your opinion about deLeone and Santucci?"

Troone listened for a few minutes. "Then, it must be done before the inauguration. Martin's wife is planning a pre-inaugural luncheon at the National Gallery of Art. Make the call, Blackstone! I don't care what it costs!"

Lydia stooped and eased the door shut, with her hand gripping the doorknob to maintain her balance. She caught a glimpse of Troone dropping a cell phone into his briefcase. She recoiled in fear when the door she was leaning on complained against her weight and squealed open a few inches. Thankfully, Troone was too busy to notice. She backed away from the opening and heard the rushed sounds of papers shuffling, desk draws opening and slamming closed, and the familiar metal click of the fire-proof cabinet lock. Troone was emptying the files and personal items from the middle-drawer of his desk into his briefcase.

Someone knocked heavily on the door to his office, twisted the knob frantically and shouldered the solid oak door to no avail. "Carvin…are you in there? Carvin…answer me!"

Troone was startled. The voice rang familiar. He'd locked the door, and his aides were given the day off to celebrate his victory. "Hold it,"he shouted, "I'll be right there."

Troone unlocked the file cabinet and lifted a small handgun lying next to the teak box. He placed it in his open briefcase under a folder.

"Carvin, its deLeone. Let me in. We have to talk."

Troone slid the cabinet drawer closed and rushed to the door. "Are you insane, coming here at this time? Get in, quickly." He scanned the hallway. Luckily, the floor traffic was emptying for dinner and nobody took notice of deLeone entering.

The Deputy Trade Representative was sweating and breathing intensely as he pushed into the office. "What the fuck is going on?" Troone implored. "You look like the Triads are chasing you to cut off your balls."

"Worse than that, Troone. Phillipe Cusson's box exploded in Geneva. The Swiss police arrested him. Some inexperienced financial cop in short pants tried to open the box before Cusson could stop him. It apparently exploded in their faces. Cusson and several policemen were reported killed. The French government is blaming terrorists."

"Calm down!"

deLeone noticed the familiar hand-held device that looked like an iPod music player lying on Troone's desk. "You have the only one remaining," he said, pointing to the device capable of relaying coded signals to the remaining teak box holders.

"I was about to warn Cusson. Merrand has the ear of the President. He probably convinced him to have the FBI question everyone implicated in the Savoy conspiracy. Gatt was seen leaving Merrand's election suite. He obviously provided incriminating evidence to the authorities. The President must have authorized the seizure of BoxMart's records. Kurancy's office was swamped with FBI agents and U.S. Marshals. They took Jake and Cashman in for questioning."

"Then there's a good chance they'll uncover the supercomputer," deLeone shrieked. "And his teak box." His eyes bulged with fear. "We've got to find Blackstone right away. If Kurancy talks, we're all screwed. He's the common link to everyone involved."

"Don't panic, for damn sake. He's probably in the gym with Harley Hedge. They work out together almost every day at this time. I have his restricted number."

Troone tapped deLeone's shoulder like a mentor and said softly, "Richard, I want you to take a cab to the Washington Monument. I'll call Tom and we'll meet you at the western base in an hour. Nobody will recognize us at dusk. We need to formulate a new plan." Troone sensed that deLeone's resolve had melted away. He was now a liability.

As deLeone peered out into the empty hallway, Troone asked, "Where's your copy of the Bomali agreements?" DUSTR tapped his travel case and smiled as he hurried away.

*Good! T*roone rushed to pack some personal files, then locked the door and headed for the Senate parking lot.

Lydia counted to a hundred; then tip-toed across the room to the unlocked fire-proof cabinet.

The body was discovered by an elderly couple strolling the banks of the Tidal Basin feeding into the Potomac River. The Washington Post reported that deLeone had either fallen on the cement abutment bordering the basin, was knocked unconscious and drowned after rolling into the tidal water; or had committed suicide. DUSTR was known to be under investigation by the FBI for providing sensitive trade information to China. No mention was made of a travel bag found at the scene.

Lydia called Lynne the next evening and revealed the contents of Troone's cabinet, after learning that Richard deLeone's body washed up against a stone wall, near a row of cherry trees lining Maine Ave, behind the Washington Monument. She also told Lynne and Justin about the conversation she overheard in Troone's office.

(EARLY DECEMBER, 2008)
NEW YORK CITY

Oresco dropped the two-inch packet of double-spaced articles and supporting documents on the editor's desk. Lydia Bryce's account of the conversation between Troone and deLeone was omitted at Balzerini's request; as was the list of names, coded e-mail addresses and private cell phone numbers she'd discovered in Troone's metal file cabinet.

Lynne and Justin noted that Phillipe Cusson was number three on the list; behind Kurancy and deLeone; and followed in order by Marco Santucci, Emerson Bromine, and two Chinese men named Li Chin and Wang Chao. Balzerini immediately recognized the names of the Chairman of LCE Industries and the Minister of Industry and Trade.

The Ambassador convinced Justin and Lynne, who'd been given the information by Lydia because she didn't know who else to trust, that the possible involvement of a Vice-President-elect in an international scandal to damage the country, was too sensitive an issue to publicize without undeniable proof.

Balzerini prayed that Troone was innocent; and had been set up by someone else in the government.

The revelation of secret payments to Santucci and deLeone, from BoxMart and Bank of China accounts at CBdS, was a different story. Treasury agents were poised to arrest Santucci and charge both Americans as soon as Swiss and European Union bank officials confirmed they were the beneficiaries of the multi-million dollar numbered accounts which had been uncovered by Nicorezzi.

"These are the final drafts,Harry, with your modifications. That's everything I have."

"This is sensational stuff, Gabe. We're going to run consecutive daily articles for the entire week, beginning with Sunday's edition. If this doesn't rile up the American public, I don't know what will."

"How about the wire services...the Associated Press distribution? We need the widest national coverage possible."

"Your request will be honored, Gabe. The Times will run only Sunday's feed-in story on an exclusive basis. It should wet the lips of every newspaper editor and TV news anchor in the country. The other articles will be submitted to the AP's entire subscriber list for free distribution. I'll be interested to see how many papers run it on the first page."

(SUNDAY, 12/14/08)

(Note from the Editor): This newspaper will present a series of front-page articles, to be published each day for a week, which will reveal convincing evidence that a group of greedy people, calling themselves the "Savoy Imperative," and including the chairman of BoxMart Stores, schemed to manipulate the lives and buying decisions of millions of Americans.

Feature Story # One: (12/14/08)

A mind- numbing conspiracy against the American economy has been uncovered by American intelligence agents. Implicated in the scheme are : BoxMart Stores, the giant discount retailer; the Residents Bank of North America; its European parent, Creditte Bank de Savoy based in Lyons, France and Geneva; Chinese Communist leaders in charge of billions of U.S. dollars accumulated in central banks as a result of China's massive balance-of-trade surplus with the

U.S.; and at least two U.S. federal government officials in positions to influence decisions on trade policy and bank interest rates.

Their common objective--- to manipulate the multi-trillion dollar U.S. consumer goods market for their own benefit.

This series of articles will present information obtained by covert U.S. intelligence agents operating in China, Boston and elsewhere. By staging events to damage the U.S. economy, the conspirators hoped to force the federal government into abandoning measures to limit imports from China.

BoxMart Stores. the fastest-growing discount chain in the world, and America's largest importer of Chinese-made merchandise, has been accused by the Attorney General of forcing small U.S. manufacturers into bankruptcy; and transferring the business to Chinese factories owned jointly by BoxMart management and LCE Enterprises, the enormous conglomerate of state-run manufacturing businesses controlled by the People's Liberation Army.

In a coordinated effort, allegedly the brain-child of BoxMart Chairman Jake Kurancy and Residents Bank executive Edwin Tinius, several dozen factories in the Northeast and Midwest were forced to close.......

Feature Story # Two: (12/15/08)

The Federal Reserve Bank in Washington has taken over operations of Boston-based Residents Bank of North America, and halted all transfers of funds to foreign institutions. The wholly-owned subsidiary of European-based Creditte Bank de Savoy has been accused of initiating overly-aggressive loan defaults against dozens of small manufacturing businesses supplying products to BoxMart Stores. The defaults were precipitated by the retail behemoth's unexplained cancellation of large orders.

Phillippe Cusson, the recently deceased Direct-General of the CBdS banking empire, was charged, posthumously, with illegal currency trades, bank fraud and bribery. Swiss banking authorities have frozen the assets of CBdS and its subsidiary in Geneva, the Franco-Medici Trust. The Swiss Banking Regulation Agency seized the deposits of CBdS after discovering that high-ranking Communist Party members in Beijing played a role in a scheme to manipulate global currency values. Cusson's abrupt dumping of China's U.S. dollar holdings is believed to have precipitated the recent collapse of American currency. Beijing banking officials denied.................

Forty- percent of the AP subscribers ran the story on the front page; 60 percent carried it on inside pages. CNN and BBC mentioned the story briefly on the evening news.

(**12/16/08**) No article is published. The Chinese Embassy and BoxMart lawyers file a restraining order in a Boston District Court. Most morning and evening television news programs mention the controversy.

The program director of the Larry King Live show contacts Oresco for additional information.

(**12/17/08**) The restraining order is lifted by the Federal District Court in Manhattan. Every newspaper in the country publishes Oresco's depiction of the corn-virus chronology, from the Liaoning bio-weapons facility to the contaminated Iowa cornfields. The World Health Organization issues a world-wide warning for consumers to avoid Chinese goods packaged in cardboard produced at the SCCC. Retailers react by clearing their shelves of recently-delivered merchandise. Retail sales for non-food items drops nearly in half during the next few days.

Feature Story # Three: (**12/17/08**)

In one of the most treacherous acts imaginable, the conspirators contaminated millions of acres of Iowa cornfields with a deadly mycoplasma suspected of being developed at a People's Liberation Army bio-weapons laboratory in Northeast China. PLA military leaders have denied the accusation, and have deflected responsibility to Taiwan; accusing the Taipei government of ordering an expert in bio-genetic mutations to contaminate a cardboard box factory located west of Shanghai. The facility was recently discovered to be infested with the same virus-like organism CDC scientists found in Iowa, and dubbed the "corn-virus."

One third of Iowa's 12 million acres of planted corn has been devastated, and a local farmer died after eating raw corn contaminated with the "corn-virus". The Centers for Disease Control in Atlanta issued a human-pandemic warning when CDC scientists discovered that the organism mutates under certain conditions into a life-threatening form.

An American businessman with a scientific background, acting on his own accord, stumbled over proof (copies of documents below) that the organism---believed to be a genetically-modified version of the deadly brucellis abortus virus---was first developed at a Chinese bio-weapons research facility in Liaoning Province in northeast China.

Justin Gatt, a businessman from Connecticut, also secured copies of transport documents from the Chinese mainland (reproduced below),which connect a suspicious merchandise shipment from the Shenyang bio-weapons laboratory in Northeast China, to a delivery order at the BoxMart distribution center in Texas. FBI officials speculate that terrorists trained in the application of pesticides may have crossed the Texas border from Mexico and transported the organism to Iowa.

Coincidentally, Gatt's successful 20-year old plastics processing company was forced into bankruptcy when an unexplained cancellation of large orders by BoxMart drove his two largest customers out of business. He was traveling in China as a consultant for the Financial Flow Foundation of Washington, D.C.

The threat of a pandemic, although unlikely, according to health authorities, has forced the ailing President of the United States to issue an executive order temporarily banning the import of all non-essential Chinese goods. The World Health Organization is worried that a high percentage of Chinese exports are packaged in cartons supplied by the Shanghai factory found to be contaminated with the rogue organism.

At least two horrible deaths have been associated with eating raw corn contaminated with the so-called "corn-virus." According to confidential medical sources, a thick black substance oozed from the body orifices of both a Chinese technician and an Iowa farmer, just prior to death. A third similar death was reported when an Indonesian cruise-ship steward visiting friends in Belize City died. The Belize government called in the World Health Organization when the corpse of the young man, who succumbed with congealed arteries, secreted a puzzling cement-like substance from all his body cavities.

The corps was disposed of in the Jerusalem section of..........................

(12/18/08) The producer of the Larry King Live show called Gabriel Oresco again and inquired if he and Justin Gatt were willing to make a brief appearance on the show sometime in the future. He inquired if their friend, Nonnie Washington, might also be willing to appear on the telecast.

Feature Story # Four (12/18/08)

The President ordered the Commerce Department and the Department of Homeland Security to vigorously implement his Executive Order to halt all Chinese imports until the corn-virus scare is abated. All recent Chinese imports will be inspected for contamination, and any goods on board cargo vessels either docked at U.S. ports or sailing from China on Pacific routes to America will be turned away.

The Beijing government agreed to cooperate with U.S. and world health authorities, and ordered all cargo ships transporting goods packaged in boxes produced at the contaminated Shanghai factory to sail to anchorages off the eastern coast of mainland China. A spokesman for the American Retailers Association has predicted a major shortage of seasonal goods for the upcoming holiday shopping season. "Unfortunately, we expect a buying panic for gifts and popular consumer goods imported from China. The shelves of many mass merchants will be barren because of the President's announcement." In a related incident, Jake Kurancy, the chairman and CEO of BoxMart Stores---the company accused of causing the bankruptcy of dozens of American manufacturing businesses---announced that his stores are the only major retail outletst selling imported goods **not** packed in containers made at the Shanghai factory.

Kurancy reported that sales at all BoxMart retail outlets, except a few in the Sioux City, Iowa area, were experiencing record sales. He assured the public that all BM stores and distribution centers were well stocked with contamination-free seasonal merchandise. Unfortunately, the prices of most items had to be doubled because of the extraordinary high demand. All previously announced sales discounts were cancelled by.........

Feature Story # Five(12/19/08)

Nonnie Washington Whiteknee, the injured chief of the Winnebago Ho-Chunk Native American tribe in eastern Nebraska, is leading the newly-formed **Make Do Party** *in the enormously successful boycotts of BoxMart superstores in the Sioux City, Iowa tri-state area.*

Local residents from Iowa, South Dakota and Nebraska have joined the Make Do Party in growing numbers. Seen as an expression of indignation over the cold decision of BoxMart's management to sell unauthorized, Chinese-made copies of coveted Winnebago Ho-Chunk ancestral artifacts, more than twenty-five thousand voters have joined MDP ranks.

BoxMart contracted with a factory in Nanjing to duplicate the popular 'calendar sticks' and other tribal craft items hand-made with pride by members of the tribe. They blame BoxMart for the shut-down of the crafts factory, the only significant source of employment on the Reservation that borders the Missouri river on the Nebraska side.

Chief Nonnie Whiteknee, a lawyer who gave up her law practice in Omaha to help the tribe, explained to this reporter, "Our people have been working hard to preserve tribal traditions. The crafts business offered a wholesome, good-paying employment opportunity for the young Ho-Chunks remaining on the reservation. Now that it is gone...."

BoxMart management has been accused of hiring an assailant to attack and disable Chief Whiteknee while she was leading an earlier demonstration in a BoxMart parking lot. (See previous NYT publication entitled, "Leader of Make Do Party Attacked").

The assailant who injured Chief Whiteknee has not yet ....

(12/20/08) The iconic host himself called the NY Times editor at 8 a.m. and asked to have Oresco, Gatt and Chief Whiteknee available for the 12/21 evening show. Harry did not refuse. He quickly confirmed that Gabe, Justin and Nonnie would crawl naked across the Sahara Desert to get a few minutes exposure on the immensely popular nationally-televised talk show. The host announced the previous night that the weekly series of NY Times disclosures had created more indignant reactions from Americans than any other event since the tragedy of 9/11...judging from the three million hits each night on the NY Times web site.

Feature Story # Six: (12/20/08)

The line of demonstrators in Washington, D.C. stretched from Dupont Circle to Embassy Row, as District police were ordered to form a protective line in front of the Chinese Embassy to prevent people from rushing the gate.

The Attorney General announced today that computer experts from the Lawrence Livermore Labs have been called in to investigate a supercomputer installation hidden deep beneath the BoxMart headquarters in Massachusetts. Chinese military technicians were found at the main console by FBI agents, attempting to use the massive power of what astonished Livermore experts believe to be the world's first three-teraflop (three-trillion calculations per second) supercomputer.

Pentagon computer specialists were called in when the Livermore experts reported that the amazing data-processing machine appeared to be several times more powerful than the most powerful computers at the Pentagon. Kapeed Pandlidesh, a former employee at the Lawrence Livermore Labs discovered at the scene, was arrested and charged with espionage for aiding scientists from the People's Advanced Computer Technology Institute, in their apparent attempt to by-pass Pentagon firewalls and access a critical technology database. The Pentagon records supposedly contain top-secret information relating to: super-accurate gyroscopes, electronic surveillance systems, advanced missile guidance software, and space-age propulsion engines. It is not known if the information was passed to Beijing.

The BoxMart supercomputer, named the '3P-BIO by its inventor, Kapeed Pandlidesh, was discovered during a federal raid on the BoxMart headquarters north of Boston, for an unrelated investigation of the retailing giant's involvement in irregular international financial transactions.

Pandlidesh, the head of BoxMart's super-computer operations, also admitted to helping Chinese military experts break past the software-wall that protected a Pentagon database holding the latest designs for missile weapons and sophisticated offensive satellites.

Pandlidesh agreed to cooperate with the FBI and Lawrence Livermore computer experts in exchange for a pledge by officials not to seek the death penalty for his part in the apparent espionage attempt by Chinese PLA agents.

A Livermore spokesman said, "The 3P-BIO appears to be an amazing break-through based on Itanium processors and a dynamic parallel design super-charged with bio......

Feature Story # Seven (12/21/08)

(**Reporter's note**): This final edition of the conspiracy revelation must give credit to the individuals who risked their lives to uncover one of the most devious human-manipulation plots in the history of man's abuse of power.

Justin Gatt, Lynne Hurricane and Nonnie Washington Whiteknee will join me tonight on the nationally-televised Larry King Live show to tell their amazing stories.

Oresco began the final article in the series with a dramatic statement:

They escaped murder attempts; pieced together the conspiracy theory; then jeopardized their safety to expose the critical information which eventually uncovered theSavoy Imperative conspiracy. The lives of Justin Gatt, Lynne Hurricane and Nonnie Washington Whiteknee are still in danger.

According to documents retrieved at BoxMart headquarters, and later confirmed by Marco Santucci, President of the Boston District Federal Reserve Bank, who was arrested for his involvement in the financial aspects of the plot, a French banker named Phillipe Cusson clandestinely transferred million of dollars from BoxMart's European deposits to the personal accounts of several high-ranking Chinese government officials and American citizens.

Santucci was arrested late last night in his Walpole mansion after authorities found his name listed on BoxMart internal records, along with those of several other suspects. Following intense questioning relating to the discovery of Santucci's ten-million dollar nest-egg in a Swiss numbered account, he admitted to being part of a conspiracy to avoid U.S. and Chinese income taxes. He denied knowledge of other members of the group, referred to as the " Savoy Imperative," in confidential files discovered at Jake Kurancy's personal residence, attached to the BM headquarters building by an underground tunnel.

Santucci is cooperating with law enforcement authorities in a plea bargain to protect his family. The federal banker admitted to accepting millions in pay-offs for providing inside information to others in the group, including unidentified Chinese trade officials and businessmen.

U.S. Ambassador to China, Forrest Balzerini, returned to Beijing today to meet with Yong Ihasa, the new General-Secretary of the Communist Party and acting President. Balzerini will firmly express U.S. concern for China's role in the conspiracy. Yong has rejected the notion that mid-level trade negotiators are implicated in the plot; but admitted in a recent interview that the Communist Propaganda Department's internal investigation of former President and Party Chairman Mu Jianting has raised some suspicions.

Balzerini expressed dismay that the state-controlled Chinese news stations were the only international broadcasters not reporting the suspected involvement of high-ranking Chinese nationals in the Savoy Imperative scheme.

In today's "Editorial Comments," Editor-in-Chief Harry Kavon strongly evokes the message of the MAKE DO PARTY. (See: "Coping with shortages of food and imported goods; exploding interest rates; drowning currency; and a potential pandemic. Americans will require heroic fortitude."

I agree with the Editor-in-Chief, who concludes: "Status-quo in consumer buying habits is no longer an option."

The name of Nonnie Whiteknee Washington's party says it all--- **Make Do!**

Americans have the opportunity and the incentive to take back control of our buying decisions Those like Kurancy and the Chinese export machine, who've attempted to monopolize American consumer spending by manipulating prices and supply; and recently, crippled our economy and exposed millions of Americans to a potentially deadly organism, have been ignored long enough.

The conspirators from Beijing have played all manner of devious games to protect their hold on the American consumer.

CHAPTER 65

(12/21/08)PM
LARRY KING LIVE SHOW

The host pulled at his suspenders with his thumbs and said, "That's amazing. You say Nelson pushed you and Gabriel out of a spiralling jet airplane at 5,000 feet?"

"Yes," replied Justin Gatt, with a blue-eyed smile which mesmerized the millions of viewers glued to seats by his account of their narrow escape from a Chinese missile attack. He was dressed in a tan cashmere jacket and a white button-down cotton shirt opened at the collar.

Gabriel Oresco wore a dark blue suit for the first time in over a year. His only tie, a fifteen year-old solid green St. Patrick's Day gift from his mother, contrasted with the brown-and-white-checkered shirt he bought when he was twenty pounds heavier. He hesitated to reply to the host's question, and was visibly trembling from the memory of facing certain death as he'd plunged into the Indian Ocean.

"I don't recall hitting the water," he managed.

"Justin, tell us about the Chinese woman who saved your life in a back-alley of Shanghai. The audience will not believe how she levitated for several seconds, as you claim, and disarmed several thugs attempting to kill you."

After Justin described Lili Qi's Juko-kai movements, and her sullen expression after the deadly encounter, Justin said, "I can't reveal her name. We believe she's still being pursued by Communist security agents in China."

The host directed the next question to Nonnie Washington, who was dressed in a colorful broomstick skirt with a white blouse and beige faux-suede vest. A three-feathered banded headdress covered the scar and shaved area above her left ear. Her hair was still clipped short from the operation. Her soulful eyes and pale complexion belied a brilliant legal mind.

"Chief Whiteknee, I believe an attempt was also made on your life, in a BoxMart store parking lot. Could you tell the audience about that incident; and the reason you formed the Make Do Party?"

An hour later the show was about to go off the air, when a note was handed to the host by the assistant producer. The man in suspenders read the note quickly, then looked directly into the camera and said with a sense of irony, "There's a first time for everything." His head wagged in amazement.

"Our producer has informed me that the network has cancelled the show which follows this live telecast." He faced the three people on his panel and said, "We'd like you to continue with us for another hour." He looked back at the camera. "After a short commercial break, we're going to open the show to call-ins."

The orange light dimmed on the live camera. The producer of the immensely popular cable news talk show pulled aside the host. "Our network phones are ringing off the hook. The show's web site is swamped. People are lining up outside the studio, waiting in the cold and a foot of snow to get a glimpse of the guests."

"I can't believe this. Let's Podcast the next hour. I'll ask Gatt for more details about the ongoing investigation of Boxmart, the D.C. insiders and the Chinese characters he believes are involved in the virus attack on Iowa. He may not be able to reveal specific Savoy Imperative identities, but he can respond to the public's obvious concern over how their lives are being manipulated."

Justin answered the final call-in from a professor of international finance at Yale University. "I agree, Professor Syzmansky. It's no exaggeration that the permanent loss of American manufacturing jobs has wider national implications than most people realize."

"I called in because I believe this program may be the most important telecast on the subject in ten years. People have got to realize that unless the government is forced to abort policies which promote the deterioration of the manufacturing sector, the next few generations will experience significant social and financial uncertainties. Alongside a much-lowered standard of living, our grandchildren will have less buying power, less entrepreneurial opportunities, and less career choices. Few small businesses will be able to obtain financing, and fewer will be able to create new jobs or teach new skills."

"One could even foresee the deterioration of the American university system---a weaker job market will require fewer scientists and engineers. The number of American science and business students will decrease significantly, either because they can't afford the tuition, or because a higher education will be worthless to many of them."

The host asked if American Universities needed so many foreign students?

"As much as I enjoy teaching all students, Larry, Yale was not created to education foreign students so they can succor their countries to compete against America."

The producer's rotating finger indicated they had two more minutes to wrap up the show. The most surprising call-in was from President-elect Martin Merrand.

He lauded the message of the Make Do Party, and encouraged all Americans to follow the Ho-Chunk lead.

"During the unfortunate shortages, which Americans are being forced to experience, due to events outside their control, I implore all listeners to adjust their spending budgets and purchase only the every-day necessities of life."

The host asked Justin to comment on this increasingly popular theme; noting that a majority of those who called in---average Americans struggling to meet bills---had so far adjusted surprisingly well to the shortage of Chinese imports. The television icon leaned back in his chair...remaining silent for a long few seconds. All eyes centered on Justin as the camera focused in on his face.

Anticipation was thick, as if they were about to witness an historical event from afar. The blue eyes sparkled. He spoke incisively into the lens.

"The conspirators responsible for the economic crimes and virus attack on the American people will no doubt be brought to justice. But even more crucial, in my humble opinion, is how our combined response to the shortage of imported goods effects future generations. This crisis can be turned into an unprecedented opportunity to right many years of wrongs."

The audience listened with fascination and flourishing anger, as Justin explained how common citizens were being manipulated by machine-gun advertising images and media-hyped fright stories designed to stimulate people into buying overpriced and unnecessary products.

"Think about it. Do you really need a new pick-up truck, SUV or complete new wardrobe every few years? How many high-definition flat TVs do we require? One in each room? Are we so brainwashed that we actually believe our lives will be in jeopardy, if we miss one minute of dramatized bad news from the newscasters who repeat the same nformation...over-and-over-and-over-and over...all day?

"It takes most households days to fold up washing-machine sized cardboard boxes, and scrunch up bulky styrofoam inserts, after the kids open a dozen Christmas toys from each parent; and a handful each from other relatives. We used to be happy with one gift from everyone, including Santa. What has really happened?"

"My cousin's two-year old daughter cried last December because there were so many toys in the family room that she had no room to play with any of them. I hope your listeners, Mr. King, will remember that Nonnie Washington started the Make Do Party as a platform to protest against such excesses. She showed more courage than Geronimo when she took on the cold-hearted BoxMart managers who forced the Ho-Chunk Reservation's only employer out of business. We should all follow her lead."

The program director looked at his watch and cringed as he slapped a palm on his forehead. The finger circled again frantically. Gatt shot the host a sideways glance. Most talk-show celebrities would never admit it, but they took pleasure in aggravating the keeper of the clock. Larry nodded for Justin to complete his impressive summation. One less thirty-second commercial for cross-over vehicles wouldn't kill the show.

"I don't pretend to understand all the dynamics of international trade; but there's one thing we can all understand: the insidious scheme of the world's fastest growing discount chain---to control our buying decisions---is an example of how special interests have been crippling this country's ability to compete against foreign suppliers."

Justin suddenly felt possessed by an urge to coax and shout. "We *can* make a difference," he called out forcefully. "All we need to do is make a *simple decision*. So simple…that it could be viewed as revolutionary."

What the hell am I doing? Justin thought. *I sound like an evangelist.* He'd noticed the opened mouths of the host and other panelists. The brilliant studio lights prevented him from seeing the gapes of anticipation in the audience.

"Why not?" he blurted out. "We can revolutionize world trade and regain control of our import-dominated economy. All we have to do…." He hesitated, searching for the perfect words.

"What decision, Gatt? Tell the people." The host reacted to the seconds-clock facing the panel. Precious broadcast moments remained. The blazing-hot studio lights finally got to Justin. He tore off his jacket as if readying for a fist fight.

"Two-thirds of America's gross domestic product is dropped on check-out counters or slid through credit-card machines each week…by *you*." His tone was accusative, yet inspiring. "You're not helpless…like the politicians who use the balance-of-trade deficit as a carrot to entice other countries to finance Congress's chronic overspending. Politicians will not solve the problem. With few exceptions, including President-elect Merrand, Washington leaders don't care, or don't know how to rectify the loss of good-paying jobs and the deterioration of America's domestic manufacturing industries." He paused to lock eyes with Oresco and Nonnie, then turned back to the camera and announced in a solemn voice:

"Perhaps the way we change the system..(Ten, nine, eight...) *is to balance our spending habits against the production capacity of American factories. If three-hundred million people scaled down consumption, and reduced unnecessary overspending, I believe American producers could supply most of our needs at acceptable prices. The country might regain its financial independence and self-reliance; and prosper at the same time.*"

(12/ 26/08)
BoxMart headquarters

Kurancy emptied the contents of his wall safe into a duffle bag and stuffed in enough personal items for a few days. He slipped his Andorra visa, international passport and a one-inch stack of 100-euro bills into an overcoat pocket and flipped open his cell phone.

"I'm ready. Bring the Red Flag to the back of the building."

The teak box remained locked in his tamper-proof safe. He doubted authorities would find it before the contents self-destructed on the last day of the month.

The high-speed printer in his office was spitting out sickening revenue reports from every region. Sales had dried up like a raisin in a pizza oven. Customers were lining up in BoxMart parking lots to return merchandise they'd purchased months ago. Most were demanding cash refunds, which was not possible, because of the enormous volume of returns and the shortage of dollars at the stores. Some irate customers knocked over display shelves near the BoxMart check-out counters. Others threatened customer-service clerks with bodily harm if they didn't move faster to process the returns.

One manager in a Los Angeles store made the mistake of sending employees home before checking that all customers had left the store before he locked the exit doors. Within minutes, the retail outlet was ransacked by indignant patrons who felt it was a fair exchange to return an Intendo game or a rapper-CD for a 42-inch Sony flat-screen LCD TV.

Kurancy's main concern now was to escape the country before the FBI investigation progressed far enough for the judge to revoke his bail.

Cashman was behind the wheel, dressed in a chauffeur's uniform... perhaps a foreshadowing of his next career. Kurancy plopped his immense frame onto the front seat and croaked, "Get moving! Take Route 95 north to the North Andover exit. The private runway is back in the woods alongside the river. The pilot will be waiting. I paid him a hundred grand to fly us to Andorra."

The oriental man hiding in the garage adjacent to the BoxMart resident-quarters stepped over the blast-proof floor panels he'd removed from under the front seats of the Red Flag limo. He slipped out from the cover-alls and walked to the woods where his hyper-muffled Honda 350 cc motorcycle was leaning against a tree. He walked it to the edge of the service road, kicked the foot-starter and jumped on. The service road eventually led to a ramp onto Route 95 north. The motorcycle driver listened to the BoxMart executives' conversation from a tiny electronic devise inserted into his helmet. He decided to trail the Red Flag by a mile until it reached the North Andover exit.

As they approached the cut-off, Kurancy barked, "Get off at the next exit."

Cashman flicked the turn-signal and glanced instinctively into the rear-view mirror. A motorcycle was accelerating past the Wal-Mart delivery van tailing them onto the exit ramp. As the two-wheeler whipped by the van, the driver swung wide to get a better view of the black limousine rolling into the curve. He watched the Red Flag slow on the ramp as it approached the street crossing; then depressed a button on the electronic device clipped to his belt buckle.

Within seconds, the delayed-fuse ignited and a thunderous explosion engulfed the vehicles and occupants in a scorching fireball hot enough to melt the blacktop. Kurancy and Cashman were incinerated in seconds, as the motorcycle driver bounced across the grasss median strip. Drivers who noticed the explosion were pulling over, as the oriental man rotated the accelerator handle to maximum speed and sped away in the opposite direction, toward the Triad safe-house in Boston's Chinatown section.

(JANUARY, 2009)
MACAU, A SIX-HOUR FLIGHT FOR HALF THE WORLD'S POPULATION

Wen Ma was drunk and angry. He butted against the glass door leading into the reception lobby of the Bomali executive offices on the top floor of the Grand Bromine Tower and Casino. He'd lost all his money at Bromine's blackjack table.

"Where's Bromine?" he slurred to the frightened receptionist. "Tell him the new boss is here." When she hesitated, he barked, "Do it *now!*"

The twenty-year old secretary leaped up from her station and rushed down a long hallway lined with closed doors on both sides. She knocked lightly on the last door on the right and waited. Wen Ma paced impatiently in the reception area. He wore a midnight-green silk jacket, pleated beige pants and a sweat-stained tropical-print shirt. The receptionist finally entered the last room in the corridor and disappeared.

A few minutes later two barrel-chested men pushed into the reception area from a private elevator just outside the glass doors. The taller man, about thirty, with a jagged scar snaking from his forehead to his lower lip, said bluntly, "Mr. Bromine is in a meeting, Colonel Wen. May we escort you to a more comfortable conference room until he is available?"

The inebriated colonel swayed unsteadily, ignoring the request. "I said I want to see Bromine...and I want to see him now!" The taller man garbled something in Mandarin to his partner, who nodded knowingly. They heard Wen Ma say, "Go tell him that the new boss needs money."

Wen noticed the guards inching forward in a threatening manner, and backed away. The ugly one with the scar looked casually over his shoulder---an obvious attempt to divert Wen's attention. Suddenly, the two casino guards lunged for Wen's arms. They made the mistake of moving too slowly. Wen's hands shot in the air, then slashed down in a simultaneous chopping motion practiced on double-rows of concrete blocks.

"Ooooaahh," preceded the snapping of collar bones. The guards screeched in agony and collapsed to the floor. The receptionist walking back to the lobby screamed, then pivoted and raced back to Bromine's office.

"Fucking incompetents!" Wen spat. He kicked them both in the face with his pointed shoes then stomped them unconscious with vicious head blows from his hard leather heels.

He turned to the hallway and saw Bromine and Alicia Wang coming out of the far room. Alicia was adjusting her bodice and lacing her top. "What in hell is he doing?" Bromine snorted, as he buckled his belt.

"He's drunk again,"Alicia whispered.

Wen approached them in long, rapid strides. His manic grin stopped the two smaller people in their tracks. *They're inferior to me. Neither the whore; nor the American dope pusher deserves to out-rank me.* "I'm here to inform you that General Ye has appointed me the new chief executive officer of Bomali Corp. You both now report to me."

"You're drunk, Wen,"Bromine countered in a cautious tone. "He doesn't have the authority. You take orders from me, unless the full board decides otherwise."

"There *is* no full board any longer,"Wen spat. "Not after the explosion of Kurancy's car. Cashman was with him."

"You're lying, Colonel. Kurancy is on his way to Andorra. I talked with him less than four hours ago." Bromine's mind clicked to alarm mode as he turned to Alicia for confirmation. She nodded, but her expression was empty as she suddenly backed away from him.

"How could you know about an explosion, anyway? He's thousands of miles away. Unless you ....." Bromine's eyes widened as he reached for the small revolver tucked in the waistband behind his back. Before he could extract the weapon, a blur from behind plunged a sharp silver object forward. Bromine had no time to react. He collapsed in a heap...effectively brain-dead before he stopped breathing. Alicia Wang's second lightening motion in three seconds straight-armed the side of his head as he fell, while jerking out the six-inch razor-sharp steel needle she'd buried in his ear with her other hand.

"You're a fool, Wen Ma," Alicia snapped, as she wiped the blood-stained blade on her sleeve. "You could have waited a few days. He was about to tell me who his Three Sixes contact is on the OPEC board. Someone in Venezuela. Yong Ihasa could have blackmailed the man. We need to line up more petroleum supplies for LCE factories."

Alicia's brutal assassination sobered Wen Ma instantly. "Perhaps that information is in the teak box he's always looking at. Where is it?"

Alicia remembered seeing it blink a red number. I think he keeps it locked in a desk drawer."

They turned and rushed back into Bromine's office. Alicia could use the steel tool to unlatch the desk drawer. Opening the teak box would be easier than stepping on a land mine.

(JANUARY 19, 2009)
WASHINGTON, D.C.

"It was awfully nice of Mrs. Merrand to invite us to the pre-inaugural luncheon," Lynne said softly, as she flattened Justin's lapels. They were standing close together in her Madison Hotel room, six blocks from the White House. "Merrand has been super-nice to us since your appearance on the Larry King show. I think he wants to bring you to Washington."

"Balzerini mentioned something about that."

"And you told him...what?"

"I told him my grandfather was dying and that I need to be in Connecticut as much as possible."

"Joanna's in Connecticut." It sounded like an accusation. "I live in Massachusetts. So does Brad."

"What's that supposed to mean?"

Lynne sighed. Justin could be so naive. Knowingly, she stood on her toes and kissed him on the forehead. It was an unusual, long, motherly kiss. Her lips seemed glued to his skin. Justin's eyes rolled, but he didn't move.

"You don't really know what to do with me, do you?"

He was suspended in physical and emotional limbo until Lynne's lips un-puckered from his forehead and circled down to his mouth. Justin tasted her tongue for the first time. The sensation was mesmerizing as she cupped his head and pressed against him. Justin's hands wandered over her back and shoulders, finally settling on the small of her back. They embraced passionately for the first time.

Their pent-up tension was finally liberated in a surge of exploring hands. Bodies were on fire, as they rubbed, kissed and touched, and wrinkled their clothes. Justin was steaming when Lynne abruptly pulled away, tears running down her flushed cheeks.

She looked at Justin and saw an innocent-child's smile on a grown man's face. His expression was adorable. "What do we do now?" he pleaded.

Lynne quivered and said, "You're the most amazing, intelligent, passionate, wonderful man I've ever met." The words hung in the air until she added, in a voice rampant with despair, "It wouldn't be fair to Joanna." She wiped away a tear. "But it would have been wonderful with you," she whispered hoarsely, "because I do love you." She bit her lip and emptied her conscience, "But I also love Brad."

If ever a moment fused heart-break and relief…this was it. "Our ages…," Justin attempted, but couldn't find the right words. "Brad is so in love with you, he….," Lynne pressed a finger to his lips. "You don't have to say the things I already know."

Justin's heart cramped. "We have a slight problem; because I feel the same way about you,…and Joanna. But in different ways."

"You never describe me as 'sweet,' the way you always refer to her and the twins." Lynne backed away from his reach. "I know it's wrong, but I'm in love with both of you. And, in case you didn't notice, Joanna is nuts for you."

She turned away to hide the distress on her face. "We'll always be friends, Justin, no matter how this turns out."

"And I'll always be there for you, Lynne." His voice cracked, "Whenever you need me."

Lynne stiffened to absorb the emotional impact of their romantic farewell. She was surprised when her body relaxed as if a great weight had been lifted. "Joanna and the girls need you. And you need them." In an extraordinarily enduring voice, she said, "Come on, honey; the Secret Service agents must be waiting in the lobby."

Justin regained his composure and replied, "It's so amazing being with you, Lynne Hurricane. You make me feel so alive."

"I've jump-started you for Joanna," she laughed through a sob.. "She's going to be a very happy woman with you. Come on, let's go…before I start crying again. People reach crossroads in their lives, and we just happened to reach ours together. I'm going left and you're going right. But we'll always have feelings for each other. That I know."

"You're amazing!"

"Come on, Justin," Lynne said, as she flicked back her hair and headed for the door. "The SS will drive us to the art gallery. It's wonderful how Mrs. Merrand is reaching out to so many people in a time of national need. She's a healer."

"At least we know the corn-virus is dying off," Justin remembered. "Virginia Richmore was correct. Even the most unusual viruses cannot survive for very long without a living host. I think it will be a few more months before the cargo anchored off Matsu and Quemoy is fully tested."

Lynne pulled on a light pink cardigan sweater as they watched the lobby television and waited for the tardy secret service driver, probably caught in traffic. Her thoughts drifted to Lydia's relationship with Senator Troone; and how it ended in fruitless disaster. Maybe it was best that Lydia wasn't following the older man to the White House. Troone was being watched by FBI agents, but no evidence, other than Lydia's testimony about his conversation with Richard deLeone, had turned up to implicate him in a crime. Balzerini thought Troone was being set up. Lydia was a scorned woman. She might lie to extract revenge.

Troone was scheduled to be sworn in as the next Vice-President of the United States in less than twenty-four hours. Lynne was still bothered by the list of contacts Lydia found in Troone's storage cabinet. Someone referred to as the "chameleon" was included. She knew the creature adapted to its environment in order to remain undetected.

NATIONAL GALLERY OF ART

"This is an amazing place," Justin said as they wandered into the Rembrandt room set back from the second-floor Rotunda at the National Gallery of Art. "The Secret Service must be going bonkers; with all these black marble pillars to hide behind, and so many walls and rooms to monitor."

"I heard Mrs. Merrand's love for the arts will influence how White House receptions are going to be used to mend fences."

"Did you ever see such a diversity of people? The Joint Chiefs fully caparisoned, foreign embassy officials,except, I suspect, the Chinese delegation, in gowns and tails. Even the African guests are wearing their finest, most colorful smocks."

Mrs Merrand was huddling close to Troone's wife on the atrium near the food display at the top of the marble stairwell leading from the ground floor. Secret Service agents were spotted at the base, on every tenth step and at the top. Martin Merrand was walking with dignitaries through the Rembrandt exhibition, which had returned to the National Art Gallery after a successful showing in 2005.

"Let's get some desert in the main concourse," Lynne suggested, as Justin admired the *'Ginevra de Benci,'* the only painting by Italian master Leonardo da Vinci housed in the western hemisphere.

"I want to view Picasso's *'Saltimbanques'* before we leave," replied Justin.

"Lydia says Mrs. Troone knows everyone here. She helped draw up the guest list. I'd like to meet some of them. Let's filter back into the atrium crowd, if you don't mind, Mr. Culture."

The National Art Gallery also housed glass, ceramic and metalwork masterpieces. Justin was sure that Cosimo's works were superior to some of the displays they'd passed. "My grandfather's vase belongs here."

The curator of the art gallery pointed to a painting borrowed from a private collection in New York City. "This is considered Rembrandt's most finished portrait drawing, sir."

The President-elect and his entourage looked at the title: *"Portrait of a Man in an Armchair, Seen Through a Frame."*

"It's a chalk, completed in 1634," explained the curator. "During the lifetime of Rembrandt Harmerszoon van Rijn---his full name---his etchings were internationally renowned for extraordinarily expressive lines and his *chioaroscuro* effects---the contrasts between bright illuminations and dense shadow."

As they shuffled by Rembrandt's *"Portrait of a Painter in Old Age,"* borrowed from the National Gallery in London, and the full length portrait of *"Jan Six,"* on loan from the Bibliotheque Nationale in Paris, the curator said, "The best masterpieces of the Dutch baroque artist came during the last few decades of his life. I particularly admire this one." He extended both arms in front of Rembrandt's dramatic 1659 painting of *"Moses Smashing the Ten Commandments."*

A line of guests formed in the atrium where attendants in white gloves filled buffet plates with beef Wellington, twice-baked potato casserole dripping with imported Fontanela cheese, roasted asparagus spears wetted in lemon-butter, roast duck in cherry sauce, and a variety of African, Asian, and Indian. ethnic dishes.

Merrand and Troone joined their wives at the head of the line to encourage the guests to partake of the food. An immense desert table was set off to the side topped with a variety of French pastries, a white cream cake in the shape of the White House and several fancy porcelain bowls from the White House collection filled with sundae toppings. A server was there to scoop decadent flavors of ice-cream from a stainless steel chest freezer into clear glass Tiffany cups or large pasta dishes; and to top them with a guest's favorite nuts, candies, fruits and sweet sauces. Mrs. Troone had suggested the elaborate desert table, knowing that the wives of several diplomats would opt for only the sweets.

Merrand was on a tight schedule to interview potential cabinet appointees and work on his acceptance speech. He handed his dish to an aide then stepped to a temporary podium. The crowd hushed when he tapped the microphone and said, "Relax, I'm not going to make a speech. But I do have to leave shortly. Before I go, however, I'd like to greet anyone I haven't already met."

The agent in charge of Merrand's security team cringed. He was afraid the President-elect would pull something like this. He moved toward Merrand to protest, but Merrand said jokingly to the guests, "In a few short hours, it will take an act of Congress, or a Supreme Court decision for you to meet with the President in such casual surroundings."

Lynne and Justin were standing near the desert table when Merrand spliced into the middle of the atrium crowd and began shaking hands. Two SS agents with wires in their ears gently eased aside several of the guests to flank Merrand's side.

"Please, give the President-elect some room,"one of the agents pleaded. He was unnerved by the rush of foreign diplomats taking the opportunity to shake hands with the next U.S. President.

Lynne turned around to hand her desert plate to an attendant strolling the area to collect used dishes from the guests. She noticed a stout African woman in a floor-length multi-colored wraparound busuti. She was holding a bowl of ice-cream that could feed a Girl Scout troop. The server was gone, so she assumed the woman had helped herself. She smiled, but the black lady quickly looked away and lowered her dish to the edge of the un-attended desert table; then backed into the line of guests waiting to greet Merrand.

Justin had given the list of contacts Lydia found in Troone's office to the agent assigned to protect him. He'd been told the list would be checked out by the FBI. The agent claimed the "chameleon" name rang a bell. He thought it might be referring to a known assassin who could morph at a moments notice into one of three identities: an average-sized Caucasian, a slightly-built Muslim Arab, or a stout black African.

The line waiting to greet Merrand was down to ten guests, when the African lady in the middle of the line extracted a long lipstick tube from her right-side pocket and raised it to her mouth.Carvin Troone was standing next to Merrand, greeting visitors and watching the tall, broad-shouldered African ease forward.He began to sweat. The security agents also spotted the movement of her right hand. They relaxed as she put the lipstick tube back in her pocket. They missed the movement of her left hand.

Her left thumb expertly flicked off the protective cap covering the tiny, painless syringe cupped invisibly in her palm. The ultra-thin needle extended just far enough to penetrate Merrand's jacket sleeve and wet the stiff cuff fabric of his shirt. He would touch that area when he removed or changed his shirt. The droplets left behind contained a narcotic to numb a person's nerve endings, while the deadly nerve-agent infiltrated the brain and caused uncontrolled muscle contractions which would lead to death by asphyxiation.

Mrs. Merrand approached her husband as the last few guests clasped his hand. She noticed the brightly-dressed Nigerian diplomat Mrs.Troone had suggested she invite, standing in line. Carvin had urged his wife to include her on the guest list. Nigerian oil was very important to the struggling American economy.

Merrand shook the Lithuanian diplomat's hand as vigorously as he greeted the Russian Ambassador. The *Chameleon* looked over the Lithuanian's shoulder, waiting her turn.

KGB agents developed a unique method to dispense "VX" nerve agent from a tiny syringe. Israeli Intelligence modified the procedure to be "delayed-reaction," to allow agents more time to escape. Normally, a single drop of the most powerful nerve agent known would cause death by asphyxiation within minutes of exposure to the skin.

Arcola Mandita was not about to give up her life to carry out an assignment. Death had to occur well after she departed the museum. Luckily, "VX" was a hardy substance. Exposure several minutes...even hours...after touching an object coated with the nerve agent, would still be a lethal dose.

Merrand held out his hand to the African delegate. She bowed, then seemed to stumbled over the hem of her full-length garment. She clasped Merrrand's right hand with her own, then reached out with the palm of her left hand to grip his right forearm, presumably to catch her fall.

Lynne saw the African women's movement. Suddenly it all came together in her mind.

The broad shoulders, the ice-cream fanatic, the Maid; the expert in stabbing deadly needles into unsuspecting people. THE CHAMELEON!

"**Get away!**" she screeched in such a high shrill that the secret service agent closest to Merrand reacted instinctively, without thought, and swatted away Arcola's hand. He fell forward against her body and noticed the "VX" syringe drop to the marble floor.

The assassin pulled out the lipstick case from her right pocket and aimed it at Mrs. Merrand's face. "Everyone, down on the floor, or she dies from *VX* spray." She clawed at the top of the startled women's bun hairdo and pulled her viciously toward the stairwell near the desert table. "She's an assassin,"Lynne yelled out frantically. "Do as she says."

The Chameleon backed away from the enormous black marble pillars in the Rotunda, in the direction of the Founders' Room and the exit doors to Madison Street. The main entrance on the Rotunda level led directly to outside marble stairs that descended to street level. The Triad driver Blackstone stationed at the Audio Tour desk next to the Rotunda exit doors, was now at the wheel of a State Department limo cleared by the Capitol Police to taxi dignitaries to their destinations following the reception. He expected the see the African delegate walk calmly down the stairs after she'd greeted the President.

"Everyone drop to the floor," The Chameleon screamed. "And don't try anything. I'm holding the release button. If I let go the *VX* spray kills her in one minute." The Secret Service agents on the stairs froze. They were familiar with the deadly nerve agent. Her hysterical tone convinced them to do as she ordered.

Justin was closest to the desert table, lying on the floor next to Lynne, face-down. As the assasin and Mrs. Merrand backed up clumsily in their direction, he placed his arms over his head and tilted his face sideways. He could see the bottom of the Chameleon's wraparound dress approaching. He also noticed the fold in the white linen tablecloth draped over the corner of the desert table.

When the assassin paused to decide her next move, Justin reached out behind her back and slowly tugged at the corner linen. The bowl of ice-cream the African woman had hastily placed on the edge of the table slid onto the floor. The sound of shattering glass was lost in the cacophony of similar shattering sounds as people panicked and fell over tables… knocking trays of glassware and soiled dishes to the stone Rotunda floor. Justin crawled forward a few feet to attract the assassin's attention. Arcola saw him move and edged away…closer to the desert table as he'd hoped. "Keep still, you ass-hole."

Two steps to the side….two steps back---right on the blob of melted Ben and Jerry's.

The Chameleon sensed the unsteady slipperiness under her feet and jerked at Mrs. Merrand's hair to hold her balance. The loosely-tied bun unraveled and she slid over the melted ice-cream, tumbling backward against the desert table. As she fell, her grip on the tube of nerve gas loosened. The deadly spray fogged the air directly above her head as she hit the marble floor on her back. Mrs. Merrand leaped away and landed on Lynne.

In that instant, two superbly-trained Secret Service agents lying on the floor raised the handguns they'd positioned at their sides and fired. One bullet nicked the assassin's hip; the second projectile shattered a window high above the exit doors. Blood seeped from the hip wound and slicked over the puddle of melted ice-cream as the Chameleon attempted to roll away from the white power drifting down to her face. She rotated in-place on the slick floor, like a greased lumberjack log spinning in water. The deadly spray decended to her horror- stricken face and was quickly absorbed into the scar tissue criss-crossing her forehead, cheeks, chin and nose. A man's deep authoritative voice shouted, "Get back....get away from her. The *VX* is heavier than air."

CHAPTER 66

FEBRUARY, 2009
WASHINGTON, D.C.

President Merrand's weekly televised message from the White House press room began with one of his now-familiar statements of inspiration.

"The finest periods of Americanism," he bellowed, "have been when there is a sense of the common good. When the nation's interest is primary, not the hoarded wealth and power of special interests. Americans are fortunate. Despite the recent merchandise shortages, we still have more than we need to live a good life."

The President's words were encouraging to listeners. He stared intently at the reporters in the front row who were generally supportive of his decision to continue the ban on Chinese imports.

"Until Beijing's role in the Savoy conspiracy is clarified, I will not lift the trade embargo, despite cries from the media and big business to once again open the flood gates for Chinese imports." He ignored the scribes in the back row who murmured grunts loud enough for the microphones to register.

"Americans have been giving away too much of our future, to acquire imported goods we don't need." Merrand pounded his fist on the podium, and added forcefully, "Twenty years from now, we *do not* want a high percentage of the next generation of young Americans to be wandering the streets in gangs, causing social upheaval, because they have nothing better to occupy their time." Chief Whiteknee could certainly relate to this statement.

"Our children and grandchildren will be looking back at this critical time in America's history, bemoaning the lack of fortitude by government leaders…who bent to the will of powerful multi-national corporations and foreign countries. Leaders who gave away future career opportunities to foreign workers." He paused for emphasis. "I am convinced that truly loyal

Americans do not want their children or grandchildren to end up in a jail cell, grumbling: 'If only I had a job.'"

The President went on to cite alarming statistics as evidence that joblessness is the most common cause for mass violence and crime.

A beat reporter in the back asked, "Mr. President...that's painless to say, but what do you propose to solve such a complicated problem? Everyone now knows that America's manufacturing base is too eroded to compensate for the shortage of foreign merchandise now plaguing U.S."

"Well, Debra, I encourage you to reconsider which items you actually need. Differentiate from the other items that you and your family only desire to have---but can live without. The Christmas holidays are a good example. The lack of imported toys and gift items induced families and friends to reflect on the true meaning of their celebrations. Not only of religious observances, but of the acts of giving and sharing.

"Let me put this another way, for the pragmatists who oppose the new law I will be signing in a few minutes: Despite the simplicity of a solution to a problem, we too often focus on the wrong thing, and miss the solution." Merrand bowed slightly then raised his chin in a gesture of determination.

"Today this country is taking an historical step to assure that the next generations of Americans will have an opportunity for steady employment in good paying jobs that provide hope for the future."

Following the press conference, President Merrand led a troop of politicians and honored guests into the Old Executive Office Building to witness the signing of the first new law enacted by Congress during his administration. He capped the commemorative fountain pen and handed it to Justin Gatt, remarking gleefully, "Thank you for convincing so many people to pressure Congress into passing the *American Small Business Recovery Act,* in less than two months. Without your efforts, Justin, a majority of the American people would not have taken the actions which convinced Congress to overwhelmingly pass this historic bi-partisan bill."

"Thank you, Mr. President. But it was your leadership that convinced the American public to act---by necessity, at first, but then by choice." Merrand scowled at his future Under Secretary for Homeland Manufacturing Security, a sub-Cabinet level position created by the new law. The position could be elevated to full Cabinet status at the pleasure of the President.

"When a President issues accolades, Justin, you don't argue with him," Merrand joked stifly. "It's not an exaggeration to claim that without your efforts, and Lynne Hurricane's persistent inquisitiveness, Kurancy and his Chinese friends would be perilously close to controlling global trade and the vital American retailing industry. He was attempting to abolish the small manufacturing businesses which were once the cornerstones of national advancement."

Standing nearby, Ambassador Balzerini added enthusiastically, "We'll be relying on you, Under-Secretary Gatt, to lead the revitalization effort."

President Merrand turned in the direction of the Majority and Minority leaders of the House and Senate, and groaned "The embargo will eventually have to be lifted. One product at a time...if I have my say. By then, this country must be in a better position to compete globally for manufacturing jobs. Your first priority, Justin, is to re-establish self-sufficiency in the domestic production of staple consumer goods. The pressure being exerted by special interest groups to reopen the gates to U.S. markets for Chinese goods, is extraordinary. The hunting season for America's ten trillion dollar consumer bounty is about to unfold."

Justin gazed around the Indian Room in the Old Executive Office Building where President Merrand had chosen to conduct the signing ceremony. He was awed by the presence of the nation's top Congressional leaders. They were being presented *ASBR Act* commemorative fountain pens by the Executive Office staff as they congratulated Merrand and each other.

Lynne Hurricane, Nonnie Washington and Gabriel Oresco looked on from a far corner, exuding a mixture of wonder and pride for their friend. A year ago, Justin was an unknown, bankrupt entrepreneur. Today he was receiving accolades from the most powerful men on earth.

Merrand glanced playfully to his old fishing buddy sitting in a wheelchair at his side. "Remember how we gauged the weight of fish, without using a scale?"

"Sure," smiled Merrand's predecessor. "Tape the length from the tip of the nose to the fork of the tail, then measure around the front of the pectoral fins. Square the girth measurement and multiply it by the length, and divide the sum total by 800."

Merrand smiled and turned to Justin, nodding contemptuously, "Jake Kurancy and his Beijing Games crowd are no longer the 800 pound gorillas."

THE MALL

Tom Blackstone had one unfinished task to complete before he disappeared from Washington forever.

He'd eluded FBI agents since the Savoy Imperative was revealed several weeks ago. The teak boxes in France, China and Washington had either exploded or self-destructed on the last day of January. Justin Gatt, the person most responsible for thwarting the Savoy Imperative scheme against the U.S. economy, deserved the ultimate retaliatory punishment. But there was another reason to dispose of this unlikely amateur intelligence agent.

The President had elevated Gatt to a Cabinet-level advisory position which could interfere with the Three Sixes oil monopoly.

He'd convinced President Merrand to support a government-funded shale-oil recovery program utilizing the patented GRT separation process. If successfully recovered, the billions of barrels of kerogen hydrocarbons trapped in American oil shale deposits could permanently impair the cartel's hold on domestic crude oil supplies. Richards and Harley Hedge worried that the kerogen fluids from the thick shale-deposits of the Green River basin in Wyoming, Utah and Colorado, could be recovered at a cost low enough to drastically reduce the prices of imported and domestic crude oil. The Three-Sixes' cartel profits could tumble.

Just as alarming was Gatt's assignment of the initial commercial rights for the separation-and-recovery technology to the Ho-Chunk Nation. He'd convinced President Merrand to support the effort by directing the Department of Energy to finance the first commercial kerogen extraction and refining facility; to be constructed on Winnebago Ho-Chunk land in east Nebraska; a mere 750 miles directly over interstate Route 80 to the Green River, Wyoming area, which contained 60 percent of the world's oil-shale deposits.

The proximity of the Winnebago Reservation to the newly-seeded corn fields near Sac City, Boone and Fort Dodge made the location ideal, since the USDA limited the use of the newly planted corn in the area to ethanol production during the next five years.

The Reservation cracking-unit would utilize the corn-ethanol as both a solvent for diluting and processing thick kerogen unsaturates, and as an ingredient in ethanol-gasoline mixtures. The massive Ogallala Aquifer sitting below the eastern plains of Nebraska would provide the process water necessary for the refinery.

President Merrand also ordered the Department of Energy to train the Ho-Chunk Indians for the high-paying jobs associated with constructing and operating the processing facility. The Ho-Chunk tribe would finally achieve Nonnie's dream of financial independence.

Blackstone exited the Riggs Building annex and peered out from the shadows. The street-lamp only partially illuminated the recessed entrance of 633 Pennsylvania Ave., which housed the NCNW around the corner from the Riggs Building. A dark 1999 Dodge Intrepid 4-door sedan with Massachusetts license plates pulled up in front of the entrance and extinguished its headlights. Blackstone crouched low to the ground and duck-walked to the passenger door. He angled into the front seat after dropping a four-foot-long, flat rectangular hard-cover case onto the back seat. Blackstone was too tall to appear in public without being detected. He'd remained in hiding at the secret Three-Sixes basement living-area beneath the old Riggs Bank annex on 7th and Indiana. Marco Santucci and Carvin Troone were awaiting trials in a Maryland maximum-security prison.

Vice-President-elect Troone had confessed his involvement in the Savoy plot, after his wife was stabbed to death in the restroom of a public restaurant. Mrs. Troone was attending a benefit for the National Council for Working Women at the Madison Hotel's Federal Restaurant on 15th and M Streets, when an Asian attendant locked the ladies room door then slashed her throat with a jagged box opener. Troone's two college-age sons were hustled away from a Georgetown University basketball game by FBI agents, minutes before a Triad hit squad hired by Blackstone was able to fulfill the deadly contract Troone had signed with the Savoy Imperative.

Holly had driven from the GH Paladin Prudential Center office in Boston in the ugly-duckling rental Blackstone arranged. She'd followed his instructions and registered under an assumed name at the low-budget Hotel Harrington a few blocks north of the Mall. Exhausted from the seven-hour drive and the emotional fallout of recent events, she grumbled peevishly in a low, tired voice, "They arrested McGill yesterday. I'm not going back to Boston."

Blackstone sneered impatiently at his occasional lover. "You have nothing to worry about, Holly. I'm the one the feds are hunting."

Holly followed his directions and drove toward the Capitol Reflecting Pool, then turned south on 4th Street and parked a few blocks away at an unlit vacant lot on the east-side of the National Air and Space Museum. He extracted the sniper rifle from the case, loaded the high-powered amunition and mounted the telescopic night sight; then returned to the front passenger seat and looked at his watch.

"In five minutes I want you to drive across Maryland Ave and park in the shadows in front of the Voice of America Radio building facing the staff entrance to the National Museum of the American Indian on Independence Ave." Holly obeyed without comment and eased the ugly duckling into a space with a clear view of the flood-lit entrance, about a football field away.

Justin and Nonnie were attending a dedication ceremony for the new Winnebago Ho-Chunk National Historic Display. Dinner at the Mitsitam Cafe in the museum was highlighted by Justin's announcement that Brad Stalker, Chairman of the Board of Directors of AmerAgain, Inc., had granted the Winnebago Ho-Chunk Nation an exclusive license to construct and operate the first shale-oil recovery plant.

The night was clear and the Mall seemed deserted, except for an occasional Capitol Police car patrolling the Mall. Blackstone assumed they represented the "beefed-up Mall security" promised by the President after Trenker was gunned down. Blackstone's task would be completed in less than an hour--- as soon as Justin appeared in front of the Indian Museum staff entrance used for evening affairs.

"When he falls, drive slowly down Independence and take the first side street leading onto the Route 395 ramp, a few blocks south. Then, follow the Southwest Freeway to the Washington Beltway leading to Bromine's mansion in Maryland."

Blackstone planned to hole up there for a few months; buying time for a more permanent destination when the buzz from another D.C. Mall sniper killing subsided. Holly would be ample entertainment until it was time for her to join the former Assistant Deputy Secretary of Energy and his family in the rich earth behind the mansion.

"It's hard to believe that Justin Gatt could cause such hardship," she quipped, remembering the boyish composure on the new employee's face when he was interviewed by McGill for the bogus business-aid position. "I didn't think he could squash a maggot."

"He squashed more than that. And tonight he's going to pay for it," Blackstone intoned ominously. "You know where to drive when I'm finished, Holly. Just don't go too fast. The traffic on the Mall is light, and I don't want to attract attention from a patrol car. Troone told me that Capitol police have increased surveillance on the Mall since Trenker's incident. Let's get this over with so we can return to Bromine's mansion and relax. Gatt should be leaving the Indian Museum in half an hour."

Blackstone waited twenty minutes, then opened the front door and stepped out---too late to remind Holly to turn off the automatic door lights. He adroitly dropped to the ground and pulled the door closed to trip off the interior map lights. He waited until Holly rotated a dashboard knob to dim the overhead lamps, then slid into the back seat and snapped open the flat case.

He rechecked the five high-powered hollow-point sniper rounds loaded into the same weapon he used to murder Ross Trenker, then adjusted the optical infrared night-sight for maximum focus at 400 yards. Two precision shots would be all he required.

Holly had admired Ross Trenker and liked Gatt. She felt that Justin had fallen innocently into an unfortunate situation. She closed her eyes and turned away as Blackstone lowered the rear window facing the Indian Museum a few inches and eased the sound-and-flash suppressor over the edge of the glass into the night. He took a practice aim in the direction of the Museum staff entrance, and waited.

Justin was carrying a genuine four-sided 500 year-old Ho-Chunk 'namacgocge' calendar stick—a gift from Nonnie, as they exited the Indian Museum and huddled in the center of a small band of Indian Affairs Agency honored guests. They talked and exchanged congratulations under the intense light of pole lamps illuminating the staff entrance to the building.

"I'll surely tell Professor Syzmansky about Henry Roe," Justin assured Dancing Eyes Adams. "Once again, Yale has matched Harvard in historic achievements."

Nonnie repeated the story for the benefit of a few guests who hadn't heard it. "Henry was a Ho-Chunk brave born in 1884 on the Winnebago Reservation. His parents died when he was still a boy. He left Nebraska in 1897 to attend school in Massachusetts, where he was adopted by missionaries Reverend Walter Roe and Mary Roe. He entered Yale at the age of 22 and graduated with the class of 1910."

Nonnie suddenly felt a chill. A light breeze kicked up and blew the eagle feather clipped to the front of her headdress, over her eyes. She shivered. It was a sign of bad luck.

"Henry helped pay his tuition by selling Winnebago love charms, Buffalo headdresses and a history stick. Later he founded the Roe Indian Institute---the first college prep school for Indian boys."

Justin noticed Nonnie's tense demeanor, and suddenly sensed a strange awareness on his forehead---a sixth sense that something was about to happen. He glanced at the deep scar healing above Nonnie's ear where a patch of hair was still missing. His eyes were drawn in the direction of the Voice of Ameria building by an instantaneous beam of cherry-light reflecting off something in the street shadows. "I think the history of Native American Indians is amazing, but it's not taught enough in non-Indian schools or appreciated by historians," he commented. His voice seemed troubled. "How many Massachusetts kids have the faintest idea that the longest place-name in America is in Webster. Or that it's Native American?"

"I see you read the Indian language refresher brochure. But can you spell it?"

"Sure. 'L.a.k.e. W.e.b.s.t.e.r.'"

"That's cheating. You know what I mean. The *Indian* name for the lake."

Blackstone steadied the rifle and centered the sight on the tallest person. He ignored Holly's mournful gasp in the front seat. He was too focused to notice the soft click of the latch and the driver's-door opening.

His finger feathered the trigger as the guests at the museum entrance finally dispersed, exposing Justin, Nonnie and Dancing Eyes Adams like stationary targets at a practice range. Nonnie leaned away from Justin and embraced her fellow Ho-Chunk Council member in a good-night hug. Blackstone had a clear target for his precision sight. His shoulders stiffened to absorb the recoil. He rasped, loud enough for Holly to discern, "Burn in Hell, Gatt!"

As his finger tightened, the driver's door sprung away and Holly tumbled out onto the macadam. In despair, she whimpered as her knees scraped the tar. "I can't be a part of this any longer."

"Lake Chaubunagungamaug,"exclaimed Justin triumphantly. "I don't have a clue how to sp......" Nonnie noticed a red spot shimmering on his forehead---a faint light coming from across Maryland Drive. It was too late to warn him.

The sniper reacted mechanically. Despite his intense training, there was no time to formulate an alternative plan. The procedure was set in his mind. He projected the red dot just above the target's throat and squeezed off one round...then another. Skull bones and brains exploded into a maroon mist that coated the backside of the woman nearby, like a paint-shop make-over. The target was dead before the third projectile struck the air where the tall man's head had been.

CHAPTER 67

(FEBRUARY, 2009)
BEIJING, SHANGHAI, CHENGDU, SHENZEN, TIANJING

The Public Security police drugged the demonstrators' food and used electric batons, tranquilizer guns, and violent mass arrests to herd them into detention centers. The decision by Communist Party General-Secretary Yong Ihasa to close factories in all five Beijing-administered municipalities, because of slow exports, caused tens of thousands of unemployed workers to complain bitterly as they wandered the hutongs and dirt roads of industrial cities. They wondered what happened to upset China's booming economy so suddenly.

Li Chin, Chang Hui Chen and Wang Chao now realized that they'd grossly miscalculated the effects of the Savoy Imperative and the corn-virus attack. Wang Chao, the Minister of Industry and Trade was dispatched to Washington by the Standing Committee to pressure President Merrand into lifting the American embargo on Chinese goods. Chairman Yong was fulfilling his concept of a Ming ruler, by distancing himself from the untidy day-to-day affairs of state. He expected the high unemployment crisis in China to be a temporary problem. He appointed Sun Linglong, the Vice-president under Mu Jianting, as acting President of China, in a political maneuver designed to deflect blame for the economic turmoil and street riots away from the General Secretary of the Communist Party.

WASHINGTON

"We confirm your findings, Wang," Ambassador Balzerini replied sternly. "President Merrand was informed by the CDC that the corn-virus appears to self-destruct within two months from the time of exposure. That does not necessarily mean that the organism is no longer a threat to vegetation or humans. Merrand will *not* lift the embargo until we're sure about the possibility for residual hazards."

"That's ludicrous, Ambassador. Beijing demands that you expeditiously lift the embargo against Chinese goods, for the sake of your own citizens who are demanding our products."

Balzerini scowled at Wang as they sipped hot tea at the Ten Penh Asian restaurant on NW Pennsylvania Ave. Balzerini was impressed with the Asian antiques and custom-made furnishings which hyphenated the gold silk burnishes and orange and red interiors of the meeting place Wang had chosen when President Merrand refused to allow him on government property.

"It is a mistake for your President to insult me this way," he complained. "We expect compensation from the U.S. for the cost of rerouting and anchoring several hundred cargo vessels in Chinese waters. These actions were precipitated by your ally---the Taipei devils."

"I'll pass along your concern to the President."

The five minutes the Ambassador allocated Wang were up. Balzerini stood to leave and said, "There's nothing more to discuss, Wang. You're lucky that diplomatic immunity has protected you from federal prison. The next communication you or Ihasa will likely have with the United States will be at the International Court of Last Appeals. Don't be surprised when all the assets held by the PLA directly or indirectly in the U.S. are attached by the Treasury Department."

"You wouldn't dare!"

"You and the rest of Yong Ihasa's Politboro have been disingenuous in dealings with our country. Rest assured the Merrand Administration is not inclined to forget your gang's blatant attempts to damage our economy and harm our citizens. You can deny being involved until you're blue. We have documented evidence, thanks to Justin Gatt; bless his sole."

Balzerini jammed the chair under the table and stormed out.

U.S. EMBASSY, BEIJING

"General Ye was last seen in the Jinmen Dao(Quemoy) area close to Xiamen. He is believed to be on route to a meeting with PLA Commander, Marshall Tong Shu, who just returned to the Defense Ministry from Fuzhou, near the island of Matsuo Tao(Matsu)."

AJ was back at the U.S. Embassy in Beijing, relaying an intelligence report to his boss.

"Tong is opposed to the planned invasion of the Taiwan-controlled islands. He believes the action will permanently damage any chance that the PROC's self-proclaimed 23rd Province will follow the lead of Hong Kong and Macau, and eventually rejoin the PROC as a 'Special Administrative Zone.'"

Defense Ministry

General Ye's part in the Savoy Imperative was published in the International Herald Tribune, the only English publication Marshall Tong read. He confronted Ye Kunshi and demanded that he resign immediately from the Military Commission.

Ye laughed in his face, then made the mistake of forgetting how the cagy Tong achieved the lofty position of Commander of the entire Chinese military establishment. Tong was old, but he was as ruthless and cunning as Mao. He surrounded himself with loyal officers who were honored to follow his orders.

When General Ye ordered Tong to leave his office and prepare his resignation letter, the two middle-ranking PLA officers assigned to protect General Ye pounced on him instead. They dragged him to a damp, fungus-blighted cell in the basement of the Defense Ministry building and strapped him to a hardwood interrogation chair. Tong ordered the other officers to leave; then spit in Ye's face.

"I cannot allow a madman like you to risk China's future," Tong exclaimed. "Tell me what orders you've set in motion to attack the off-shore Taiwanese islands?"

When General Ye refused to answer, Tong nodded ironically and said, "As I expected. I am too old for messy interrogations, Ye. We'll soon replace your puppet officers with soldiers loyal to me." He slid a clear plastic bag over Ye's obstinate grimace. "You are more dangerous than Ihasa's Triads. This country can no longer tolerate either of you."

Simultaneous with the U.S. carrier fleet arriving at the Pescadores, Marshall Tong gripped the loose edges of the plastic bag. He pulled down tightly over Ye's brow, flattening his nose and lips; then twisted the bag to create an air-tight seal.

South China Sea

A U.S. destroyer and two cruisers from the 7th Fleet challenged the PLA frigates circling Penghu, the main island of the Pescadores located close to the western shores of Taiwan. When the Chinese patrol craft realized that communications with their command ship had been jammed by an E-A6B Prowler circling overhead, they steamed north into the East China Sea.

The new Nimitz-class aircraft carrier, the U.S.S. James Stockdale, took up position a few miles north of the Pratas Islands, and immediately dispatched surveillance aircraft to patrol the Straits. Much to the chagrin of the PLA Admiral charting amphibian invasion routes to Matsu and Quemoy, the Stockdale flew a dozen ATS missile-armed SH-60 Seahawk helicopters directly over the Chinese flagship and landed them on the islands; ignoring the Admiral's warnings to pull away or be fired upon.

U.S. Embassy, Beijing

"*There is chaos in the streets.*"A.J. Hau Luing typed into the intelligence message transmitter linked to the NSA relay satellite. "*It appears the Chinese police are resorting to violent tactics everywhere except in Tianen'man Square, where people are roaming freely and the security police are docile. Out-of-work protesters are everywhere, lined up on Chang'an Ave. and starting to march in the direction of the new TV broadcast tower.*

The national justice system is not equipped to deal with the millions of unemployed workers petitioning Beijing to resolve the sudden widespread closing of state-run factories. An ambulance was seen leaving Zhangnanhai last week. There are rumors of internal conflict between Communist hardliners in the military and the new leaders of the Politboro. Marshal Tong and acting-President Sun Linglong have claimed that Asian secret societies have infiltrated the Standing Committee and key government ministries.

Communist Party General-Secretary, Yong Ihasa, has not been seen for several days.

EPILOGUE

(MARCH 31, 2009)
YALE SCHOOL OF MANAGEMENT

THE FIRST GATT MEMORIAL LECTURE

Professor Eric Syzmansky titled the first Annual Yale School of Management Gatt Memorial Lecture: *"Thoughts for a Self-Sustaining American Economy."* He joined Lynne Hurricane, Brad Stalker, Joanna Yates and her twin daughters in the front row, after relinquishing the podium to the guest speaker.

The official from Washington accepted the enthusiastic applause from a packed auditorium at the Yale School of Management, with humility and pride. His eyes were focused on the front row. The person he most wanted to be there was missing.

When the applause subsided, the U.S. Government official drew in a breath and directed his eyes to the Professor. "First, I'd like to thank the Yale University School of Management for honoring the Gatt family by dedicating this prestigious lecture to an extraordinary man who has influenced the lives of several people in this auditorium." He smiled at Lynne and Joanna, and blew a kiss to the pretty seniors in the second row.

"I must also thank Professor Syzmansky for his exceptional assistance in helping to expose the Savoy Imperative---the unthinkable conspiracy you've all read about in the New York Times. If not for him, and others, we wouldn't be sharing this lecture." His thoughts drifted to Lili Qi, Cloud Nelson and the Capitol police sharp-shooter overlooking the Mall from a rooftop across from the Indian Museum.

"President Merrand and the First Lady send their best wishes from the White House, and have asked me to pass along their gratitude for your amazing patriotic response to the shortage of consumer goods. If the polls are accurate, most Americans have been inspired by the challenge of the "Make Do" movement, which Nonnie Washington and the Winnebago Ho-Chunk Indians initiated. You've given unprecedented support to the many small business entrepreneurs who are risking their life savings to revitalize America's home-grown manufacturing businesses…by purchasing more American-made products.

"Earlier today, my wife paid thirty-five dollars for an American-made toaster with four slots thick enough for a half-bagel. She likes it because it has only one knob. All you do is push it down. When the bagel or toast is perfectly crisp, it pops up and the appliance shuts off. There's no touch-buttons, electronic timers or computer chips to program; and the thing will probable last for thirty years. Actually, it was first designed and manufactured by a small New England metal-working company *more* than thirty years ago. The current model is an exact duplicate of the original, using today's raw materials." He adjusted his reading glasses and unfolded the sheets of a prepared speech.

"The Savoy Imperative and corn-virus schemes---now dubbed by pundits as the 'Beijing Games,' nearly succeeded in placing control of global retail trade in the hands of power-addicted, money-hungry Chinese, European, and…yes…American crooks. Thank God, we were able to detect and reject their collusion…with the help of some wonderful mainland-Chinese citizens we cannot yet identify, to protect their safety. They represent the best of China; an amazingly resourceful people." The speaker glanced down at his notes, paused, then folded the sheets and stuffed them into his jacket pocket.

"What prouder moment has there been in the history of consumer-rights battles than when the majority of holiday shoppers marched on BoxMart stores in late December and returned the scarce Christmas gifts they bought for their children. Many of those families compensated for the children's disappointment by clipping hand-written notes or greeting cards expressing special appreciation and love for their siblings, to lesser gifts they could find in other stores. For most people, it was the happiest Christmas season in years."

Mary, Rosie, Gertrude, Spicey and Eleanor reached into their handbags and lifted out lace handkerchiefs.

The speaker's arm swept across the room and came to rest in the direction of the Indian chief. "Nonnie Washington's great spirit created the Make Do Party. She nearly sacrificed her life to recover jobs for her people. Now it's up to us."

"Jobs lost to pitifully-low-paid labor, in countries which manipulate their currency, may never return. But, America is still strong enough to thrive and grow. To do so, we must make a mass decision. We must soundly reject our over-reliance on imports, in order to preserve jobs and educational opportunities for our children and grandchildren, here at home."

In a back row, Harley Hedge whispered to a Three Sixes member, "He's dreaming. He and Merrand don't know what they're up against."

"We now face critical decisions which will shape our children's futures. President Merrand has decided to allow a limited quantity of banned Chinese goods into the country in the next quarter. Yes, there is pressure from Congress; but mostly, President Merrand believes American consumers need more time to adjust to fewer product choices as we are forced to adjust life-styles. He believes that Americans can benefit immensely in the long-run, if we resist wasting hard-earned wages on imported products we don't really need."

The speaker sipped water from a plastic bottle set on the podium. He wagged his head, breathed deeply, then remarked forcefully, "Our lives would not be as miserable as advertisers claim, if we had less than ten choices for every item the marketing gurus dream up. What do *you* think?"

Professor Syzmansky lost his cool and shouted from the first row, "Not on your life!" Others joined the commotion by shouting, "Down with BoxMart;" "Down with Wal-Mart;" "Down with Beijing Games."

"We waste millions purchasing products which help us conform to someone's idea of a great style for the season. At other times, our hot-button is pushed by advertisers promoting items which make us stand out from the crowd. Which is it? Conform? Differentiate? What mood are you in? The retailers don't care. As long as we buy *something*.

"A mass movement to more judicious buying decisions can influence the most important element in the American economic equation---*consumer demand*. Reduce demand to near the size of America's production capacity, and we won't have to rely on cheap imports; or high-interest-rate credit-card debt to get by." He held up an inch-thick soft-cover textbook, and said, "Professor Syzmansky has calculated that if we consumed about ten-percent more than the gross domestic output of current U.S. manufacturing businesses, our economy would be at full employment. We'd have a self-sustaining American economy.

"Restraint in consumption has already brought a significant increase in manufacturing employment and related service jobs. Since the corn-virus unleashed by the Chinese precipitated the embargo of Chinese goods…new jobs to repair things have skyrocketed. People are less likely to replace big-ticket items malfunctioning because of minor defects.

"If replacement parts were priced at the cost built into an original product, we'd be able to use an item for many more years. A key business for the future could be the production of reasonably-priced replacement parts. Congress should pass tax laws encouraging consumers to replace a $15 dollar drive-belt on a washing machine, or a $30 dollar plug-in heating element on an electric clothes drier…instead of spending a thousand dollars to buy the newest model with programmable computer chips, more settings than cable has TV stations, and a battalion of technicians who usually have to guess which sealed, non-repairable electronic part to replace if something malfunctions.

"Statistics on American consumer buying habits are telling. Vacuum cleaners and three-year old computers have become throw-away items. Seventy percent of the U.S. economy---the largest economic locomotive in world history---is composed of average daily purchases such as: 125,000 Barbie dolls, 89,000 Apple iPods, 153,000 pounds of Starbucks coffee; 35 million cans of Bud Light, 34 Porsche 911s, and 87,000 multi-pak shakes of Slim-Fast Optima to wash down 1.9 million Krispy Kreme glazed doughnuts. The painful truth is---we're an unbelievably over-consuming society. Advertisers take advantage of this phenomenon, because they helped create it.

"Now, after enduring the shortages caused by the Savoy Imperative conspiracy, Americans must make a critical decision. Will we revert back to hoarding unnecessary imported products as they become available? To the detriment of future generations? Or, will we Make Do; and recover control of our destiny as a nation?"

"I'm afraid to imagine what could happen if China's insidious efforts to enter and dominate the U.S. auto market with super-low-priced vehicles succeeds. In my opinion, auto and light-truck imports from China should be severely limited. We don't need them. We need the American jobs that would be lost if Beijing's manufacturing juggernut is given free access to the transportation market; arguably, the most important manufacturing industry in this country.

"Sub-industries would be devastated. Assembly lines at American, Japanese and German auto factories in the U.S. would shut down. More jobs would disappear in U.S. factories now supplying tires, computer and electronic controls, fabricated plastic interiors, glass windows, high quality steel and paint coatings. If the transportation industry in this country loses critical volume, who'll build the hardware needed for future armed conflicts?

"What about the high-tech products which make America the most secure nation on earth? If vehicle manufacturing, and all the advanced hardware technologies that go with it, migrate to China, would America's needs for vital civilian and military equipment and vehicles be met by our most likely future adversary? This is a serious issue to ponder!

"American democratic ideals cannot prosper if this country's independent production capacity is obliterated, and the U.S. Treasury is held captive to foreign money managers."

Joanna detected the subtle transition in his tone; from pragmatic speaker to thought-provoking inspirational preacher. "President Merrand believes there should be import limits. Not just to preserve decent-paying jobs; but as a matter of national security. Social stability depends on creating career opportunities for the youth of this nation. But, unless American citizens prove---by our actions---that we *want* a more stable and self-sustaining economy, *we won't have one.*"

He held up the book again and said, "Professor Syzmansky writes that a legion of service jobs could be created to extend product life cycles for durable goods. I remember being in Lisbon, once. I took a taxi. It was an old Mercedes with 350,000 miles on the odometer. The driver proudly informed me in broken English that he'd repaired the vehicle many times and saved enough money to marry off six daughters. I'm sure that more jobs could be created if someone started a business to supply the new 'must-have' options to fit older vehicles."

Gabriel Oresco quickly scrawled notes for a future article, as the speaker went on to describe how Nonnie Washington Whiteknee helped the Winnebago Ho-Chunk Indians understand that they could live comfortable and spiritually-fulfilling lives by *Making Do* with what they had, or could afford to buy. At the conclusion of his presentation, the speaker pointed to the front row and motioned for the Ho-Chunk Chieftain to stand.

"You can do the same," he continued, following the applause for the Native American who promoted "spiritual happiness" as a guideline for spending decisions.

"We *can* regain control of this country's future. Politicians who ignore the message that ordinary citizens are damned weary of being manipulated---should be flung out of office." He stepped back from the dias to gauge the audience's reaction. He'd drifted from quoting statistics to proselytizing. As he emptied the water bottle, a student howled, "Throw them out. Throw them all the hell out, hallelujah!" A few aroused individuals in the back row stood and cheered.

"I believe Americans are willing to sacrifice a few product choices and spend a little bit more to protect our children's future and the security of our country. The *Beijing Games,* played by the corrupt Chinese, American and European trade-control freaks, has forced most of us to tone back spending and consumption. And, just as World War Two shortages elevated the character and survival instincts of our grandparents, this crisis has begun to stiffen the backbones of American consumers.

"If we rise in concert, and mass-repel the powerful self-interests manipulating our pocketbooks and lives, the United States will once again become a self-sustaining nation."

Even the Yale students whose fathers were CEOs of large corporations applauded thunderously.

"The most dangerous threat to America's democratic independence is not terrorism; and is not a military confrontation. It is our complacency---the average citizen's reluctance to do battle against the poorly-veiled efforts of greedy industrialists and retailers to dictate consumer spending decisions. BoxMart came perilously close to dominating the U.S. retail industry, when its chairman, Jake Kurancy, decided to force American manufacturers out of business. Check the bankruptcy records. America's industrial base is fighting for survival." He lowered his voice and added, "That's the reason I moved to Washington to guide the Small Manufacturing Business Recovery program."

"We must ask ourselves the unavoidable question," he boomed decibels higher. *"Do we believe self-sufficiency is required of a great nation?* If your answer is *yes*, the Beijing Games is a wake-up call to prepare against the next ingenious scheme some corrupt manipulators let loose to control our lives."

"The immoral and depraved high-ranking Chinese Communists, who nearly clamped a strangle-hold on the U.S economy, are still a threat. Be thankful that President Merrand has taken a hard line, by insisting that the Chinese leaders implicated in the attack against our food supply and economy, be removed from power and prosecuted. Only then will he agree to normalize relations with China. His decision to deploy a 7th Fleet carrier group to the Taiwan Strait should convince Beijing of the Administration's resolve. President Merrand has made it clear that he will use the full military power of the U.S.to counter economic aggression at home and abroad---whenever the welfare of the American people is attacked."

The speaker removed his thin reading glasses and inhaled deeply. His brilliant blue eyes looked up at the ceiling, then scanned the audience until he caught sight of the Washington Mall roof-top policeman who'd noticed a faint light from a driver's door opening in the shadows of the Radio Free America Building. Alarmed by the familiar crimson sight-beam radiating from the rear window of the vehicle…in the direction of people gathered outside the Indian Museum…the marksman spotted the drawn weapon protruding from the back window and reacted decisively.

"Do not forget that ordinary American citizens control seventy-percent of the economic driving force which ultimately distributes power in this great nation." The speaker paused to allow the thought to germinate in the minds of the audience. "A simple action is all that is necessary--- for Americans to reverse the downward spiral in the greatness of this nation." He extended an upturned hand to the balcony audience. "We must practice spiritual common sense, and embrace the *'Make Do'* message."

"Thank you."

The applause began slowly, then erupted as Justin Gatt nodded to the people. He eased to the side of the podium as Professor Syzmanski beamed excitedly and leapt back onto the stage. He shouted over the clamor, in a session-ending tone, "There you have it---as Justin stated so eloquently---in honoring his recently deceased grandfather, Cosimo Gattaeno. We are reminded of the joys and rewards of creating something for the benefit of society. And, of course, we are reminded of the critical importance of a viable, self-sustaining economy."

Justin glanced at the first row. Lynne and Joanna were smiling at him with their arms cuddled around the shoulders of the twins; each embracing a teenager from behind, cheek-to-cheek. They were four of the most adorable faces in the world.

Brad looked around in the odd silence that followed. The audience seemed transfixed. People were uplifted, and didn't want to leave. Something significant had happened; and they weren't ready to disconnect with the experience.

Lynne's long delicate fingers brushed against her lips, as she watched Justin take a seat next to Joanna. She smiled at Brad, kissed the diamond engagement ring he'd recently placed on her healed finger, and flipped her hair to the side.

Not a word was spoken in the auditorium for several minutes after Justin Gatt and Professor Syzmansky stepped from the stage.

The audience was a giant assembly of silent, introspective facial expressions.

People might be asking themselves the same question.

Pat DePaolo writes fiction full time after retiring from an active business and technical career spanning more than forty years. He's witnessed first-hand the rise and fall of many American manufacturing companies, due to both fair and unfair foreign competition, and devoted nearly two years researching material for his first novel, THE BEIJING GAMES.

A chemical engineer and graduate chemist, he has authored several non-fiction publications, including: the American Chemical Society Advances in Chemistry Series; the first Handbook of Thermoplastic Elastomers; and trade publications, such as Modern Plastics Magazine, and Findings.

Pat's extensive business background includes a ten year career with a major chemical company, and founding and managing eight small companies, which achieved various distinctions, including: listings on Inc 500 as the 128th fastest growing private company in America; the Top Twenty-Five Technology companies in Connecticut and a successful Nasdaq public offering.

Pat lives in Cheshire, Connecticut and Cape Cod, Massachusetts with his wife, Phyllis. Their four sons are pursuing various careers in the family business, law and community service.

Printed in the United States
200487BV00003B/1-51/A